SILENCER

BLACKOUT

SILENCER

———

BLACKOUT

LONDON NEW YORK SYDNEY TORONTO

CONTENTS

SILENCER

This novel went through the careful
editorial hands of the following people:
Marianne Velmans, Alison Tulett,
Leda DeForge and my wife Rebecca. I'm
deeply grateful for their counsel and advice.

1

AT AN INTERSECTION IN THE MIDDLE OF NOWHERE A STOP
sign appears in the headlights, and Reuben Galindez
thinks, OK, this is heebie-jeebies time, I had enough, and
he opens the passenger door and steps out onto the
narrow blacktop.

'What the fuck?' the bearded guy at the wheel says.

'I changed my mind,' Galindez says.

'You *what*?'

'I been thinking. I ain't stacking groceries in some
supermarket in Scranton or whatever you got in mind. I
don't need that shit.'

The guy on the back seat, the guy with silver-yellow
sideburns, leans forward and says, 'Let me remind you,
Reuben. You signed on the dotted line. This ain't something where you got the option of changing your mind
and strolling the hell away.'

'Watch me,' Galindez says and he slams the door and
begins to walk down the blacktop, thinking he'll hitch a
ride as soon as a vehicle comes along this lonely road,
which may take some time out here, granted, but no way

is he going back inside the van with the tinted windows. No way is he stacking shelves or installing cable TV in Queens or *anything* like that. Four weeks he's been locked up in the safe house in Phoenix, climbing walls. Closing his eyes nights and seeing the flowery pattern of wallpaper behind his lids. Trapping cockroaches in beer bottles and suffocating the fuckers just for the sport. Watching TV, spinning through the channels until you're brain-dead. Four draggy weeks waiting for 'arrangements' to be made, and that's enough. Imagine living the rest of your life restricted. It ain't for me, thanks all the same.

'Reuben!'

Galindez looks back. The guy with the beard is outside the van now. 'You made a deal, Reuben. You can't just *walk.*'

Galindez calls back. 'Whatcha gonna do? Sue me?' He laughs, eh-eh-eh, turns and keeps on walking, the darkness of trees pressing in on him from either side of the road. This is the sticks, he thinks, but he couldn't hack sitting in that van a second longer, had to get out. His patience was stretched to breaking point and a voice he associates with the willies was rising inside his head.

'Reuben! Get your fat ass back here!'

Galindez glances round again. 'Yeah, yeah, yeah.'

'This ain't smart, Reuben.'

Galindez pays no attention. It's a free country. You're at liberty to change your mind. OK, he signed some documents, so what? You scribble your john hancock on a few papers, that means chickenshit to him.

He's 50 yards from the van and the bearded guy is still calling. 'Hey! Reuben! This is a real dumb fuck thing you're doing!'

Just keep walking, Galindez thinks. Keep cruising. Sooner or later they're gonna get tired shouting and they'll drive away, and then somebody's gonna come along and you'll hitch back to civilization. Happy days.

'*Reuben!*'

Galindez hears a faint breeze whisper in the trees. He doesn't look round. Screw them. Screw their documents and their promises, you got a life all your own to live.

The sound of gunfire freezes him. A single crack gouges the blacktop near his feet, and suddenly the night's filled with birds panicked out of trees and some scared furry four-legged thing dashes in front of him. He turns his face and there's a second shot that whizzes somewhere to his right and it's like the darkness is punctured and leaking air, and his heart is hot and thudding. This is some kinda joke, he thinks. But he's stunned and confused by the *fact* of gunfire because by rights – *by rights* – he ought to be able to stroll away, if that's what he wants to do, and fuck the agreement, which was only paper anyhow. And these guys – they shouldn't be *shooting* at him.

'*Just walk back, Reuben,*' the bearded guy shouts.

Galindez doesn't move. Walk back, he thinks. Yeah, right. Walk back to what exactly?

Another shot and the air around him fractures, and this time Galindez blinks at the flash of light and thinks, I've been hit. Dreamtime. Except it's no dream, it's no little carnival of the mind, because there's a pain in his arm and he feels blood against his skin. Jesus fucking Christ, he thinks. I'm shot. It ain't supposed to be this way. The world's all upside down and I'm bleeding.

'*The next one goes in the brainbox, Reuben!*'

They're going to *kill* you, Galindez thinks, and it's like a light going on inside the open refrigerator of his head. They're going to murder you just because you don't want to be a member of their goddam club. You did them a good turn, you paid your dues, but now you want out – only they won't let you. You're in, the door's bolted, and that's that.

Fuck them! Fuck Scranton, Queens, wherever!

Under a moon fogged by cloud, he suddenly runs down among the trees, crashing between trunks and overhanging branches, and there's blood streaming down his arm but this is no time to think Band Aid. This is a time for running and running and if you bleed, you bleed, and so what.

He's overweight and his flabby pecs bounce and his lungs don't know what to do with all this clean, upcountry air. He's a city guy and a chain-smoker, but these are minor inconveniences, because the only goddam thing that matters is getting away. He hears a small voice inside his head urgently repeating the phrase, Chug, chug, keep going. Down through the trees and don't stop.

Branches whip at his body and exposed roots curl raggedly underfoot and a few more spooked birds flap blackly on huge wings out of nowhere. But chug chug, you keep going.

Thinking, It ain't supposed to be like this.

His head's like an overheated radiator. Gotta stop a moment. Gasping for air, sweating, he leans against a tree, face down. He's wheezing like a busted accordion. Gotta move. Gotta keep moving.

'*Hey, Galindez!*'

The voice is what, 20, 30 yards away? Too close.

Then there's the second guy's voice. 'This is plain stupid, *asshole*!'

Thirty yards. You can't gauge distances in these woods, not after a lifetime spent measuring everything in terms of city blocks. Go three blocks west, two blocks north. But here it's different, no stars and the moon shrouded in the sky.

Galindez pushes himself away from the tree. Chug chug. Running. Arm going numb. For all he knows he could be chasing round in circles, clattering through fern and undergrowth and getting nowhere. And there's a funny taste in his mouth – which is fear. Bone-dry, metallic, like powdered rust in his throat.

And then next thing there's a flashlight scanning the trees and he ducks his head low, but his yellow silk shirt might as well be a beacon out here in the woods. He hears a gunshot and it echoes – *boomoomoom* – and he drops down on all fours and crawls through fern and fallen branches.

Another sound reaches him. Water. Fast-flowing. So, there's a river nearby and he thinks, If I can reach it I can float away. Downstream and outta sight.

The beam of the flashlight illuminates branches all around him. He hears the two guys clumping towards him, twigs snapping.

Galindez crawls towards the sound of the water. Sharp things snag his shirt and lacerate his body.

The flashlight is 10 yards from where he's crawling. He tries to make himself smaller, hunches his body, hauls in the band of blubber and just concentrates on believing he's a whippet of a guy who's in a hurry to reach the water. He also tries to divert himself with pleasing thoughts: playing the slots at the casino on the Gila Reservation, screwing some plump, nut-brown Indian chick in a trailer smelling of joss-sticks and maybe a little reefer.

Who's he kidding? This is life and death. This is all about survival.

Gunfire again. It blasts through the trees with a noise like a nuclear weapon, and there's a sizzle of red-hot light on the edge of his vision. The water. Get to the goddam *water*. Submerge yourself and hold your breath and let the currents sweep you away from these armed maniacs behind you.

Suddenly *holy shit!* – no more trees.

Suddenly a smooth pebbled shore and a suggestion of

15

white water frothing through the darkness.

Big Problem. He's exposed now and the yellow shirt's like a goddam distress rocket. He pads over the slick pebbles, grunting, scrambling. Get to the water, the goddam water.

He crawls to the edge of the river and eases himself into the chill current, but the water's only 18 inches deep and he finds himself half in, half out of the river, and oh Jesus the flashlight is right on his face like a malevolent eye, and he's blinded and electric pings of panic vibrate through him.

'I spy with my little eye,' one of the guys says in a sing-song voice. 'Somebody beginning with R.'

Galindez takes a few jittery steps back, the bank dips abruptly about 2 feet, and just as he's about to draw himself under the surface a gun goes off again with the sound of a thunderclap.

And Reuben – who thinks he sees the cylinder of a slot-machine revolve in front of his eyes and all the jackpot cherries appear simultaneously in the magic window – cries out, falls and slips away, turning over and over in relentless currents, leaving a spiralling trail of blood in the white wake of the river.

2

AMANDA HAD BEEN FISHING SINCE DAYBREAK WITH NO LUCK, trying to keep in mind what Rhees had told her about patience. You learn how to wait, he'd said. Remember, you're under no pressure.

Rhees lay on the bank with his eyes shut, raising a lazy hand now and again to brush aside a fly. A man in repose. A man on first-name terms with patience. Amanda studied her line in the water, concentrating on the little red plastic float that shivered on the surface. She was coming to the conclusion that either there were no fish in this river or else they were cunning little jokers who knew a trick or two about survival.

She looked up at the cloudless blue sky. Heat was beginning to build, the sun climbing above the trees. On the opposite bank of the river sandstone already shimmered. She nudged Rhees, who opened his eyes.

'Maybe they've all migrated,' she said.

Rhees said, 'It's not the catching that counts, Amanda.'

'Tell me it's the waiting.'

'The waiting's part of it, sure. But there are other

factors: how to contain a sense of expectation, an ability to be alone with your own thoughts.'

'It's a whole fishing philosophy,' she remarked. 'I bet it's called pisceology or something like that.'

Rhees smiled at her. 'This is more to do with self than landing a fish.'

'Do you charge by the hour?' she asked.

'Just watch the float.'

'I haven't taken my eyes off the float. My whole life is centred around the goddam float. I'll dream floats tonight.'

'Think about this as part of a simple healing process, if that helps.'

A healing process. A life lived away from all the old stresses. No pressure, Rhees had said. She returned her eyes to her line and watched how it rippled in the movement of water. She envied Rhees's ability to drift into contented torpor. He could switch off his engine any time he liked.

She lit a cigarette. A bad habit, one she wished she could abandon, but you didn't win all your victories at once. It was a sequence of steps, and being up here in the deep isolation of the forest was just one of them. Being here on this granulated riverbank, staring at the float, trying to think of nothing, seeking, as Rhees might have said, an inner zone of quiet, a place where you might find all the hairline cracks in your psyche fixed.

She felt him touch the nape of her neck. Her hair, pinned back and held by a black clasp, was brown, flecked with touches of red. Wisps of it always strayed from her head. She had problems with hair management, and she knew Rhees found this disarray touching. He was in love with her flaws. There was a sweet easy flow to life with him. Six years along the road and she could barely remember past lovers except for the weird coincidence that at least three of them had been named Robert, and they all wanted to be called Bob. Plain old Bob.

Even their faces were spectral in recollection. If she considered them at all, she could recall only a sickly medley of deodorants and skin oils. Funny, her past love life reduced to a distillation of odours from bottles and spray-cans, and no memory of any one lover who transported her to a place where comets crashed through the skies and the earth reverberated underfoot. No interplanetary dare-devil Bob.

She lay back, finished her cigarette and stared at the sky. Rhees kissed her cheek, laid a hand gently on her breast. She felt the sun hot against her face. The warmth had a certain tranquillity. She thought how easy it would be to slip into a light sleep, lulled by the fluting of the river. Four weeks up here and she was already becoming accustomed to the luxury of dozing off at odd moments.

Rhees stroked her breast again.

'Somebody might come along, John,' she said.

'Way out here? I seriously doubt it.' He slid his hand under her cotton shirt and she turned her face towards him. The kiss, Rhees's mouth, his breath, the intimate locking together of familiar parts. She imagined a day might come when familiarity novocained passion and everything became jaded and repetitive, but it hadn't happened that way with her and Rhees.

'Listen,' she said. She turned and looked through the trees behind her. The gear-grinding sound of a vehicle was audible in the woods.

'I hear,' Rhees said. 'It's probably a gang of good old boys in a jeep. A keg of Bud and a cassette of Garth Brooks's greatest hits and it's party time. Whoop-de-doo.'

'If that's the case, we'll go back to the cabin,' she said.

'And finish what we were just getting into?'

She smiled at him. 'I thought you were a master of contained expectation.'

'Up to a point,' he said.

'You're such a fraud at times, John.'

She stood up, brushed specks of sandstone from her cut-offs, then turned once again towards the trees. She could see the vehicle between the trees now, a Bronco that kicked up fine coppery dust as it churned and laboured along a very narrow track. It emerged from the woods in a flurry of broken branches and scattered pine needles and came to a halt on the bank about 20 feet from Amanda and Rhees.

There was no gang of good old boys. The big man who stepped down from the cab had plump benign features and his plaid linen jacket was crumpled. He wore sunglasses and moved with a limp – a familiar figure – but his unexpected appearance was baffling.

'Willie?' Amanda said.

'I know, I know. The last guy on earth you expected to see,' and he smiled, slipping off the shades.

Rhees was curt. 'Rephrase that, Lieutenant. The last guy we *wanted* to see.'

Willie Drumm glanced at Rhees, nodded, then shook Amanda's hand two-fisted. He had big soft hands and they dwarfed hers. 'You're looking good,' he said.

'It's this simple life, Willie.'

'Agrees with you. Anything running? Rainbow? Catfish?'

'Not that I've noticed,' she said. 'They must be keeping a low profile.'

Willie Drumm gazed at the river. There was a moment of uncomfortable tension. Amanda knew what Rhees was thinking. Drumm belonged firmly in the past, and he wasn't welcome because the past had no place here. He wasn't a part of her life any more. Those days were dead and buried. Rhees regarded Drumm as a dangerous gate-crasher, a homicide cop from the grim abattoir of the city. Somebody who dragged this environment on his shoulders like a bag stuffed with soiled laundry.

Drumm said, 'Boy, this ain't the easiest place to get to.'

'That's the whole idea,' Rhees said.

'Yeah well. Sure. I finally found the cabin, saw your car parked there, figured you couldn't be far away.' Drumm fidgeted with his glasses. He was uneasy.

'You're a detective, after all,' Rhees remarked. 'A piece of cake for you.'

This sour note in John's voice. Amanda felt a shadow fall across her mind, provoked by Drumm's arrival.

'You haven't come all this way to pay a social call, have you, Willie?' she asked.

Drumm looked at Rhees before answering. 'I'd be lying if I told you that.'

Rhees said, 'She quit, Willie. Q–U–I–T. She's no longer involved. She's out of it.'

'Yeah, I know, John. I just figured she'd be interested in what I have to say, that's all.'

'Maybe you figured wrong,' Rhees said, and slung an arm around Amanda's shoulder, a protective gesture. He wants to keep the world away from me, she thought. Especially that part of it where Willie Drumm belonged, that greased slope into despair. He doesn't want me sliding back down into that abyss.

She said, 'Willie's come a long way. It would be bad manners, John.'

'Far be it from me to be uncivil,' Rhees said. He stared at Drumm, who was wiping his wide forehead with a handkerchief.

Drumm said, 'Lookit, I don't mean to cause a problem, John. This is awkward.'

Amanda said, 'It's OK, it's OK.'

'Oh sure, it's just fine. Amanda says so.' Rhees stepped away from her. With his hands in the pockets of his jeans, he slouched, staring at the ground.

'What's on your mind, Willie?' she asked.

Drumm said quietly, 'Something connected with our old friend Sanchez.'

'Sanchez?' She had an odd experience of darkness, as if the shadow she'd felt a few moments ago had lengthened in her head. A sensory malfunction. There was a kind of faltering inside her. *Sanchez*. The chill claustrophobic space of a courtroom entered her memory and she heard refrigerated air rush from a wall-duct and the sharp knock, knock of a judge's gavel and the quiet tapping of the court reporter, babble she didn't need, but it filled her head regardless.

She fumbled out a cigarette and lit it, aware of Rhees frowning and jingling coins loudly in his pockets.

Drumm said, 'I didn't want you seeing this on the eleven o'clock news before I had a chance to tell you in person.'

'Tell me what?'

'Something's turned up. Literally.'

'Explain, Willie.'

'I'm talking a fish,' he said. 'A very big fish.'

3

IT WAS 23 MILES TO THE MORGUE IN FLAGSTAFF. WILLIE Drumm drove slowly out of the pines. 'John was pretty steamed up back there,' he said.

'He worries about me. But he gets over things quickly,' she said. Where was the conviction in her voice? Rhees had stomped back to the cabin, having registered a couple of protests. *Butt out of this. This hasn't got a goddam thing to do with you any more.* She imagined him walking up and down the small rooms, burning off his funk. The wonder of Rhees was his inability to maintain a bad mood. He might go through the motions, but he didn't have the heart to keep a bad humour alive for long.

Drumm said, 'I still feel like the guy who turns up at the banquet too late to tell everybody the soup was laced with arsenic.'

'You were talking about a certain fish,' she said.

Drumm slowed at a yield sign. 'Right. Washes up in a shallow tributary of the Little Colorado River. No ID, nothing. Gunshot wound in the heart. So the body comes under the jurisdiction of the Navaho cops, but Sergeant

Charlie House isn't happy with non-native American bodies turning up on his reservation, so he ships the body to Flag, and a set of prints down to Phoenix. We run the prints, we get a match. Which is why I'm trucking up here to look at the body and talk with the coroner. Meantime, I'm thinking, it doesn't add up. Make any sense to you, Amanda?'

She searched the breast pocket of her shirt for cigarettes and matches. 'Reuben Galindez was supposed to be far, far away. He was supposed to be secure. That was the arrangement.'

'Right. So what's he doing in a river in northern Arizona? And who shot him?'

She lit a cigarette, shrugged the question aside. The morning had taken on a fuzzy dreamlike quality. One minute you're fishing and the day's sweet and rich with promise, the next you're cruising off to the morgue to look at the face of a dead guy, and the axis of reality tilts and you wonder if this is hallucination. Who shot Galindez?

'I couldn't begin to guess,' she said. She wasn't sure if she even wanted to try. This wasn't her business any longer – so why had she agreed to accompany Drumm to the morgue? Curiosity? A sense of disbelief that Galindez had turned up in a place where he didn't belong? That maybe the ID made from a set of fingerprints was a mistake and the corpse on the slab would turn out to be that of a stranger?

Drumm drove a mile or two in silence, a toothpick parked at the corner of his mouth. 'The only way I can figure this is that Sanchez is behind the slaying. Galindez turns State's evidence and Sanchez gets a room in the Death Row Hilton. He's going crazy in there, so he gets a message out and somebody does a number on Galindez. Revenge being sweet and all.'

24

'Yeah. Just try proving it,' she said.

They were in downtown Flagstaff now. The main drag was motels advertising waterbeds and cable TV, stacked alongside an abundance of fast-food franchises. Plastic flags hung motionless in the sunlit air outside car dealerships. Drumm rolled down his window and the smoke from Amanda's cigarette drifted away.

He parked the Bronco and turned to gaze at her. 'You don't really need to come inside.'

'I've seen dead men before, Willie.'

'It's up to you, Amanda.' Drumm got out of the vehicle. Always courteous, he stepped round and opened Amanda's door.

The room was chilly and windowless, lit by a grid of pale fluorescent lights. Charlie House was there, an enormous copper-faced Navaho whose tan uniform was immaculate. The deputy coroner, wearing a badge that identified him as T. Lavery, was also present. He was a lean man dressed in a starched lime-green smock.

It was Lavery who slid open the drawer and said, 'Step right up, folks. See Moby Dick.' He had an irksome chuckle. He'd clearly developed a barricade of insensitivity against death.

Amanda hesitated a moment before she looked at the bloated corpse on the metal slab. There was a hole in the area of the heart. Ragged, cleansed over and over by the river, it suggested a large embittered mouth. The left eye was blood-red, the right gone entirely. The socket was filled with sediment from the river. The lips and cheeks and throat had been gnawed and slashed by predators – rats, vultures, whatever. The man's hair had the slimy texture of strands clogged in a shower-drain. On the middle finger of one plump, water-puckered hand was a ruby ring embellished with miniature gold leaves.

She looked away. She felt more tense than she'd expected. The smell of death became trapped in the back of her throat, a raw flavour of chemicals and decay.

Drumm said, 'Galindez.'

Amanda thought, Galindez, beyond doubt.

'Half his face is missing,' Drumm said.

'Sure, but you don't see a ring like that every day of the week,' she said. She remembered the item of jewellery, the habit Galindez had had of twisting it. Ruby and gold, flashy. He'd told her during one of their reviews of the testimony he planned to give that he'd won the ring in a game of poker with some fast company in Bullhead City. What the hell was he doing lying here in a morgue in Flagstaff?

Lavery said, 'The way it looks, he'd been in the water maybe two or three days, could be more, could be less. A single gunshot wound to the heart. Size of the wound, I'd say it was a forty-five. A secondary wound, left arm. Killed upriver, floated down. Speed of the current, he might have been shot 30, 40 miles away from where Charlie found him.'

Drumm asked, 'Anything else you can tell me?'

Lavery said, 'I'll give you a copy of my report. There's nothing out of the ordinary here. Clothes washed clean, no clues there. Shoes missing. No unusual detritus under the fingernails. Facial lacerations consistent with predatory animals: buzzards, coyotes for sure. They made a meal of him when he washed ashore. Speaking of food, if you're interested, this guy's last meal was spaghetti and meatballs with a side salad that included radishes.'

Drumm said, 'You don't happen to know anything really useful, do you? Like the name of the restaurant?'

Lavery smiled and gazed down at the corpse. 'Give me a few more days, Lieutenant, I might be able to tell you not only where he ate but also how much of a tip he left.'

'Droll,' Drumm said.

'In this job, droll's useful.'

Charlie House looked at Drumm and smiled. 'He's all yours, Lieutenant.'

Drumm said, 'A gift from the Navaho nation.'

'Render unto Caesar,' House said.

Lavery asked, 'Anybody mind if I stick·Moby back in his box? These outings seem to fatigue him.'

Nobody objected. Lavery slid the drawer shut. Amanda heard the faint squeak of metal on metal. She thought of Galindez floating downstream, ferried by currents, spinning and spinning, and she wondered how far his body had really travelled.

Lavery said, 'Next time you figure on sending us something, Charlie, make sure it doesn't smell this bad.'

'I got enough on my hands without corpses that come floating into the reservation from outside,' House said.

Lavery looked at Willie Drumm. 'I need you to sign some papers, Lieutenant. Papers, always papers, a goddam ocean of papers.'

Drumm followed Lavery out of the room.

Alone with Amanda, Charlie House asked, 'You were the prosecutor in the Sanchez case, right?'

'Right,' she said. She was cold to the marrow. She moved towards the door that led out of the morgue and the big Navaho came up behind her.

'I read you'd quit,' he said.

She stepped into a corridor. It was air-conditioned space, but warmer than the morgue.

'Yeah, I quit,' she said.

'Weary?'

She turned and looked at Charlie House. He had sympathetic eyes the colour of roasted coffee. Death was jarring. She hadn't come all the way up here from the city to look at a corpse, especially that of Reuben Galindez.

27

She'd abdicated her old life and was waiting, as if in a state of suspension, for a new one to present itself. She wanted to be weightless, unshackled by pressures, free of the past. When you don't like your life you change it, Rhees had said to her about a month ago. Which was what she'd been trying to do, a purifying process, a reincarnation, a new Amanda restored from the ashes of the old.

But a dead man had been washed out of a river, a man who should have been somewhere else and long gone, renamed and reinvented, hidden in the secret places of the Federal Witness Protection Program.

'Weary's close enough,' she answered House finally, and she heard a strange lifeless quality in her voice.

4

SHE THINKS, I NEED WHEELS. SHE'S NEVER STOLEN ANYTHING in her life, she doesn't know how to begin. She's imagining unlocked doors, keys dangling inside, maybe somebody running an errand inside the shopping mall, a forgetful person. Theft's wrong, but maybe not when your life's at stake, maybe there's some kind of' forgiveness under special circumstances and God makes allowances.

She walks up and down and she's dog-tired and scared because she doesn't know how long she's got before they find her. And she's sweating, she's melting away under the hot noon sun. It ain't pleasant, she needs a bath and a shampoo and perfume.

She stops, pretends she's fumbling inside her bag, a canvas thing that holds all her sorry belongings. O Jesus, she's come a long way down from the time she shared the big house in Carefree with Ángel, and the rooms all tiled blue and white, and fans that turned beneath the ceiling. And the greenhouse, the *conservatory* Ángel called it, where there were rows and rows of green foliage in pots, and the air was scented with herbs. But this is like a memory

29

she stole from somebody else, a memory of mint and coriander.

She fumbles inside the bag, trying to look busy, because there's a security guy in a blue uniform standing at the entrance to the mall and gazing out across the parking-lot and his gun shines in his holster. He's all glinting metal and his sunglasses are mirrors and she knows, she *knows*, he's watching her as she moves between the cars and glances in each one, looking for keys. She takes a Kleenex out of her bag and raises it to her forehead, and the security guy shifts his face a little. She wipes sweat from her brow and dumps the used tissue in a trash can.

People come out of the mall pushing carts. Kids and women, and she remembers Ángel once said, *We'll start a family*, but that was before it all went to hell, which happened real fast in the end. Now she listens to the clatter of cart wheels and a kid singing a commercial jingle for some pizza joint and a mother calling out to a stray child, 'Come back here, Terry. Don't go wandering away, you hear?'

She watches the mother catch the kid and lift him inside the shopping cart. The security guy is moving out of the doorway and coming across the lot, and this is exactly what she *don't* need. She rummages inside the bag again for something to do, and wonders if she looks like a bum because her hair's not combed and she don't have make-up on, or if she looks suspicious. What's she doing in Farmington, New Mexico anyway? She holds her breath. She hears the guard's boots on the tarmac; clack, clack, clack. She wonders what he wants. She wonders how long she's got before they catch her up. You wonder a whole lotta things when you're scared.

The guard says, 'You OK?'

She looks at him through her grease-smudged sun-glasses. 'Yeah, yeah fine.'

'I been watching you,' he says. 'You look kinda distressed.'

'Distressed?' She says the word *deezteressed*. Her pronunciation, it's like giving something away. It's all fear and sunlight and sweat. Ángel used to say, *Learn how to talk right*. Big shot Ángel, learn how to talk right. I learned how to talk well enough, she thinks. Too well. The sky is coming down on her, blue and heavy, squeezing her dry like an orange in a drought.

The guard says, 'You sure you're OK?'

'Fine,' she says. Go away, she thinks. Quit watching me.

'It's a hot one,' the guard says.

She looks at him again. A hot one. Ah, yeah. He's talking about the weather now, the goddam weather. This is all she needs.

'It's heatstroke weather,' he says. 'Drink lotsa water.'

'Water, yeah.' She walks away, the guard watches her, then he turns and strides back to the mall entrance and she keeps going between the rows of parked cars. She's frantic, caught between the guard and the guys she imagines are maybe only a couple of blocks away. It's like a whirlwind of panic around her and she's dragged up inside it the way a leaf is sucked up in a cyclone.

Find a goddam car.

She crosses herself. Say a prayer. Ask for guidance. The saints are on your side. Except she has a sense they've abandoned her, because she wouldn't be in this shit situation if they were around.

Up ahead she sees an aged Datsun slide into a parking-lot. An old guy gets out. He has a black wood cane with a brass handle and his white shirt-tail hangs out over his black-green herringbone pants and he moves slow, closing the door of his car, then turning and catch-

31

ing her eye and drawing one hand across the stubble on his chin. She looks away.

The old guy goes towards the mall. He uses the cane for support. He calls out to the guard. 'Hot nuff fer you, Jimmy?'

'Nah,' says the guard.

She hears the old guy laugh and say something that sounds like, 'Hot nuff to fry a damn ole egg on the sidewalk fer sure,' and she moves a few feet towards the car, seeing a set of keys lying on the passenger seat.

This is where it goes right or it goes all wrong.

She runs a hand through her hair and waits. The tarmac shimmers. She feels heat rise up through the soles of her shoes. She feels the air is filled with invisible devils. Fuck you, Ángel. You put me in this place, you did that. And I loved you once, I gave you my heart, and what did you do with it?

She touches the door handle of the Datsun. The metal burns right through her. Her skin's welded to metal. She stares in the direction of the guard. The old guy's reached the mall and the guard's laughing at something and she knows she's not gonna get a better moment than this.

She opens the door, gets in the car, picks up the keys, tries until she finds one that fits the ignition, then she turns it and the engine makes a noise like *karam-karam-karam*. If this car had lungs they'd be bronchial. The vehicle shudders, roars into life and belches smoke. She pulls the seat forward, presses a foot on the gas-pedal, sticks the gears in reverse and backs out. She sees the guard come out of the entranceway shouting something, and the old guy poking the air with his cane and the black wood shining, but she's gone, she's gone, she's moving, and although the guard is chasing after her she's out of the parking-lot fast and onto the road. Then she's looking for a freeway sign, even as she knows the demons are congregating in clouds behind her, and her world is about as secure as a house on stilts in a country of earthquakes.

5

ON THE DRIVE BACK TO THE CABIN DRUMM SAID, 'OK, Galindez goes in the Program. Then what? He decides he can't hack the confines of witness protection and wants to get back to his old haunts, only to be dusted by one of his old cronies. Or do we skip that and point the finger of blame directly at Victor Sanchez and consider the possibility that he managed to breach Program security and get Galindez?'

Amanda found herself remembering the sand and grit in the empty socket, the stench of dead flesh. 'I'm not getting clear pictures of how he'd pull that off.' *Breach Program security.* She didn't want it to be that. Something at the back of her mind was sending up pale smoke signals she didn't want to read. 'How would he get inside information? How did he make the arrangements?'

'First he'd need a paid informant with Program knowledge,' Drumm said. 'After that, a hired gun.'

Amanda gazed at the pine forest on either side of the highway. A paid informant, a hired gun. She felt the sun strike her face through the windshield. 'I don't want to go in this direction, Willie. It makes me queasy.'

Drumm looked regretful. 'I'm sorry I dragged you into this. I don't know why I didn't go straight to Flagstaff, and why the hell I took a detour to find you. I guess I wasn't thinking straight.'

'You didn't exactly press-gang me.'

'That's not the point,' Drumm said. 'You don't need good old Uncle Willie dumping the recent past on your doorstep. It was piss-poor judgement on my part.'

Amanda dismissed Willie's remarks with a motion of her hand. She looked from the window, saw that the Bronco had left the highway. 'What's your next move?'

Drumm shrugged. 'About all I can do at the moment is make out a report and send the paperwork down the line and it'll eventually land on the desk of somebody in the Program. Trouble is, the Program works in deeply mysterious ways which makes it tough for your average joe homicide cop to get a foot in the door.'

Deeply mysterious ways, she thought. Secrets that should have been impenetrable – except they weren't.

The cabin came in sight, located among dense trees. It had been constructed in the Seventies by Amanda's father, Morgan Scholes, who'd bought 150 acres of pine forest and spent weekends building his sanctuary. He'd worked with the devout concentration he brought to all his activities, sunk a well and installed a generator. Two tiny bedrooms, a kitchen, toilet and shower. A phone line had been brought in five years ago, a convenience Scholes had paid for handsomely. The number was unlisted. The cabin was a capsule that could be reached only by means of a narrow dirt track through the forest, an isolated retreat from the grind of the city and the red-hot freeways.

Drumm parked near the cabin, but didn't switch off the

engine. 'I don't think I should come inside, Amanda. Two acts of trespass in one day, serious overkill.'

She opened the passenger door and stared at the windows, looking for a sign of Rhees.

'I miss seeing you around,' Drumm said.

'The same for me, Willie.'

'I hear they already gave your old job to Dominic Concannon.'

'He's OK,' she said. 'He's a decent lawyer, if that's not an oxymoron.'

'But he's not Amanda Scholes.' Drumm placed a hand on her shoulder. 'Words of wisdom for you: put all this shit out of your mind.'

She stepped out of the vehicle and stood staring up at Drumm. 'All of it?'

'Every bit. Forget I ever came here. Just get on with your life.'

She shut the door, rapped her knuckles against it and watched Drumm swing the Bronco round and head back down the track. When it had faded out of sight she turned and walked towards the cabin. She hesitated a moment before going inside.

Rhees sat at the table, which was covered with his papers and poetry books. Last night he'd been preparing his lecture material for the Fall semester. His notes were written in a minuscule hand she couldn't decipher.

She had an affection for Rhees's quiet world of poetry. He wrote some himself on occasions, such as her birthday, when she'd find a short poem sealed inside an envelope and attached to a gift. Glasses halfway down his nose, he laboured over his verse like a man with a scalpel. Sometimes he hummed old Welsh tunes quietly. There was a bardic streak in Rhees.

Without raising his face from his books, Rhees said, 'You just had to look, didn't you?'

She needed coffee. She spooned three scoops into the basket then plugged the percolator into the wall. She noticed her hand trembled a little.

'Why?' he asked. 'You like morgues?'

'No, I don't like morgues. I wanted to be sure.'

The coffee began to perc. Amanda played with a wayward strand of hair. She noticed a grey streak.

'Galindez was scum, Amanda,' Rhees said.

'Yeah, I know what he was,' she said. 'I became very familiar with his rap-sheet. A nasty murder in Tucson, reduced through the usual legal legerdemain to a manslaughter rap. Early parole. A couple of rape charges, but he walked on those because nobody wanted to talk. Assisting Sanchez in gun-running to some very peculiar people in Mexico.'

'So a violent man comes to a violent end. Poetic justice.'

Amanda took a fresh pack of cigarettes from a drawer and tore off the Cellophane. She stood with her back to the sink, smoking, smelling the coffee.

Rhees said, 'Look, you were the one who decided you'd reached the end of the line. You wrote the letter of resignation. There was no gun to your head.'

Amanda poured two cups of coffee and carried them to the table. 'And I'm happy with the decision,' she said.

'But something clings to you,' he said.

'I don't want to think so.'

He looked at her over the rim of his cup.

'It just bothers me, John.'

'You're carrying useless baggage.'

'I'm not going to get involved again,' she said.

'Then drop it. Because Galindez turns up dead, suddenly you're ticking over.' Rhees waved the fumes of her cigarette aside. 'I wish you'd quit smoking.'

'It's on my list to stop.'

'This list of yours. Two things you haven't crossed off: smoking's one.'

Amanda put the cigarette out in an old jamjar lid filled with stubs. 'Galindez happens to have been a major witness I used. Without him, Sanchez might be a free man. You think *Galindez* was scum? He was a minor demon compared to Sanchez. But Galindez makes a deal. I wasn't exactly over the moon with that—'

He interrupted her. 'A month ago you were a very unhappy human being. Insomnia, immune system precarious, prone to flu bugs, eating junk food, chewing down Dalmane every night like it was going out of style. You walked round like a ghost evicted from a house she was haunting. You were wandering the borderline of a nervous breakdown. Remember?'

'I don't really need reminding, thanks.' The sense of living on an edge. The feeling that panic was always somewhere nearby. Shallow sleep overflowing with bad dreams. A deep dread she couldn't define. She'd felt fractured, falling to pieces. Now she couldn't even remember the words she'd written in her letter of resignation, only how Luke Basha, the State Attorney-General, had counselled her to think again. *All you need is a vacation*, he'd said. *You've been working too hard.* It goes deeper than that, Luke, she'd said. It goes a long way down. She couldn't recall the press conference either, the way she'd answered questions about her resignation, what reasons she'd given. She only remembered the popping of cameras and sounds coming out of her mouth and a dark jagged pain in her head.

Rhees said, 'We talked it over, Amanda. Your state of mind. Your health. But the decision was yours in the end.' He tapped the back of her hand in an agitated manner. 'The law sucks. Your own words. Just look at the way you've been this last month. Colour's coming back to your face. Sex-drive restored. You sleep nights for the first time in an age. Life's worth living again. The question is, does the law suck enough for you to cross it off this list of yours?'

She walked round the tiny kitchen and paused at the window. Sunlight sloped through the pines. Why couldn't she just enjoy all this and forget everything else? She approached him, placed her hands on his shoulders.

'Look, it's not like I'm reversing a decision I already made. I want to stay up here. I want to make myself feel, what's the word . . . *clean* again. I just happen to think I ought to talk to Lew Bascombe myself.'

'Who's Bascombe?'

'He's the liaison guy with the Program. I'll tell him he should look into a possible breach of security.'

'I don't understand why you can't get Drumm to do that.'

'Because I'm better acquainted with Lew than Willie is. I'll just dump it on Bascombe's desk.'

'And leave it there?' Rhees looked doubtful.

'Yeah, I'll leave it there. I'll drive down to the city tomorrow. You want to keep me company?'

'On one condition. We get back here by bedtime.'

'I promise.'

She opened the kitchen door and stared out into the pines. Deep in the reaches of the forest, coyotes howled, then there was the babylike cry of something dying. A small deer, a stray cat, something.

Amanda shuddered. 'I hate that.'

'Serenity has its downside,' Rhees said.

The whimpering died and silence closed in again. She imagined coyotes feeding: a flurry of blood and fur. She remembered Galindez and she drew closer to Rhees.

'Let's go to bed and get into something passionate,' she said.

Rhees shut the door. 'I just remembered,' he said. 'I left my fishing-rod on the bank.'

'It's not your fishing-rod I have in mind, John.'

6

THE WOMAN READS THE GREEN SIGN THROUGH THE BUG-
smeared window of her car. Tuba City.

Chooba City. Where the hell is that?

There's a coffee-shop up the street with a light blinking.
I'll stop there, I gotta stop somewhere. She's exhausted,
she feels the weariness in her bones, deeper than that,
deeper than the marrow even – in her heart, what's left of
it. She parks the car behind the coffee-shop so it can't be
seen from the main drag. The night is dark and hot and
dry and she feels like a landslide victim, smothered and
blind and struggling for something to breathe.

She goes inside, takes a table away from the window
and watches the waitress walk towards her with a pad in
her hand. The waitress has this slinky sideways manner of
walking, like an old beauty queen, maybe Miss Tuba City
1964, something. The light in this place is bad, low-
wattage.

'Coffee.'

'Coffee. We got some nice Danish, you interested?'

'Just coffee. No cream. Please.'

Coffee – black and strong. She knows she needs to move again, get back in the car and drive, because no place is safe. She looks at her watch, but what's the point? Time don't matter, time don't have a significant meaning, only distance, distance is everything.

She opens her purse, sees the sealed envelope with the scribbled note inside. She wonders if her handwriting is readable, if she's spelled things the right way. She doesn't have a home address, only the office. If it goes to the office, they'll forward it. What if they don't?

The coffee comes. She sips it, taps her fingers on the table, watches the window, sees cars passing down the strip, cars heading out into the hot dark night, cars going everywhere and nowhere. She takes a napkin from the dispenser on her table and crumples it in her hand. Gotta go, keep moving, because you don't know what's behind you. Only one thing you know, the men are back there in the dark and they're coming. Only thing you can be sure of.

The men.

The napkin falls into the coffee and she pulls it out. It's sodden and brown and she makes a wad of it in her fist. There's no ashtray so she drops the wet thing on the floor, but now her hand is wet and she has to take another napkin from the dispenser to dry her palm. All this fuss, these napkins all joined together coming out the slot. She can hear the sound of herself falling apart.

She covers her eyes with her fingers. She needs sleep, she needs to put her head down and sleep. How long since she lay on that narrow iron bed in the mildewed motel room with the broken-down swamp-cooler? Her hand is shaky. She wonders if anyone notices, but nobody's looking at her. They don't care in a roadside place like this, nobody cares, nobody cares anywhere, no matter where you go it's the same thing.

She finishes the coffee, gets up, walks into the rest room

and washes her face, avoiding the mirror. She doesn't want to see her reflection: a ruin. The rest room smells of heather or lilac, she can't tell which. It all comes out of an aerosol can anyway, it's all chemicals. She goes back into the coffee-shop.

'There a phone?' she asks.

The waitress points with a yellow pencil to the far side of the room.

'Thanks,' she says.

She goes between tables to the pay phone, closes the door and digs coins out of her purse. This is another thing on top of everything else: running low on funds. She picks up the receiver, something happens inside her head, like an echo, like a ghost whispering in her skull. It's because she needs sleep, she can't keep going like this. You get hallucinations. You see stuff ain't there. You dream except you're not sleeping.

What she sees are flashes of light in the dark. She pushes the memory away, but it comes back immediately. How the night changed and the temperature tumbled to zero.

Coins in the slot. What's the number, remember the number: 6035 something, something, something. She punches the buttons and shuts her eyes. *Let her answer, let her answer.*

It rings and rings. She thinks of an empty house, the phone ringing and nobody to hear.

OK, she tries the other number. It's the same guy as before that answers.

'Are you the woman who called yesterday?' he asks.

'I'm calling from Chooba City,' she says, and wonders why she gives out this information. Off-guard, going round in a trance, fear makes you crazy.

'Listen, I'll give you the number where—'

She hangs up, a clattering sound. The man – she don't

know who he is, could be anybody. Another trapdoor you fall through. She cries, salt liquid fills the back of her throat and sinuses. She weeps with her face pressed against the phone.

The letter. She opens her purse and she walks to the waitress, handing her the crumpled envelope. 'Please. Can you mail this for me?'

The waitress says, 'It ain't stamped, honey.'

She presses a couple of quarters into the waitress's hand and hurries out of the coffee-shop. She's still crying as she rushes to the parking-lot and unlocks the car and gets behind the wheel. There's a stink of fried-food wrappers.

Drive, just drive, don't think. Make-believe you're maybe on vacation, a woman just touring here and there, some carefree divorcee. She turns the key in the ignition. How far away are the men? she wonders. How far?

7

THE CITY IN THE DISTANCE WAS THE COLOUR OF A DULL
penny in the afternoon sun. On either side of the freeway
heat shimmered in dry brown hills. Amanda opened the
sun-roof of the VW and a warm breeze ruffled her hair.
'Bascombe said he'd see me at three – in and out. Also I'd
like to stop a minute at the house before we head back. I
need to pick up some books.'

'What books?'

'A biography of Lincoln I was reading before we rushed
off to the mountains. Also a saga I'm halfway through. It's
nice to read something that isn't a legal brief.'

Rhees studied the road and said, 'Maybe we should
drop in on your father.'

'Why not? He's always liked you, John. He likes to
think you're a good influence on me.'

'A man of impeccable judgement,' Rhees said.

Amanda had her arm across the back of the driver's
seat. She watched Rhees's face for a time, the line of his
lean jaw, the thoughtful grey eyes. There was a reliability about that face. He'd never disappoint, never betray.

She felt safe with Rhees.

The freeway sliced through the heart of the city. To the left were the spires of downtown, concrete and glass shining. On the right, in purple shadows, were shacks and shanties and laundry hanging motionless on lines. Beyond, suburbs stretched away into a muslin haze.

Rhees said, 'We could live year-round at the cabin. I could easily cram all my classes into two days a week, if I grovel in front of the department chairman.'

Amanda glanced at him. He was perfectly serious about this. A permanent move to the cabin. He'd mentioned it before. 'What would I do with my time?' she asked.

'Read, learn how to fish. We'll get a snowmobile and you can whizz across the landscape.'

'I'll think about it.'

In truth, she hadn't given her future much thought. She had space in her life for the first time in years. She woke mornings knowing she didn't have 200 appointments and interviews with cops and the mind-numbing stress of courtroom appearances. Liberty exhilarated her, but it was a condition she suspected couldn't last. She'd worked too hard for as long as she could remember – law school, two years in a firm where she'd shuffled corporate papers, three years in a DA's office in southern California, another two in northern Arizona, then eight years in Phoenix, the last three of which she'd spent as Special Prosecutor in the State Attorney-General's crime task force. Her CV was overloaded.

'I'd probably feel guilty not doing something,' she said. 'Anyway, I'm not sure I approve of the idea of you supporting me when my savings run out. I'd feel like a kept woman.'

'A kept woman. Has a sexy ring to it.' Rhees smiled and headed downtown. He found a parking space a couple of blocks from the Federal Building.

She suddenly remembered she'd dreamed last night of Galindez, his body rocking through black water, creatures feeding on his flesh. She wished he'd been washed down another river in a state 1,000 miles away. She wished she and Rhees had been in Hawaii or Fiji when Willie Drumm had appeared. Wish, wish, wish.

And now she was back in the city where there were too many reminders of the job she'd walked away from, the work that had squeezed her dry.

The law sucks, she thought. She'd been wrong when she'd said that. It was the way law was manipulated that had depleted and disenchanted her, the sleaze of bargaining with defence attorneys in the fashion of dope merchants squabbling about the price of coke, the lack of any moral coherence underpinning the decrepit machinery of justice. A sense of morality was unfashionable, derisory even. To get a conviction, you had to sleep with the enemy. You had to make all kinds of deals and some churned your stomach, others dripped like acid on your heart – like the commitment she'd made to Reuben Galindez. Give me everything you know about Sanchez, Rube, and in return you'll get a new life. Manslaughter? Rape? Illicit traffic of weapons in contravention of federal laws? Hey, no problem. Testify against Sanchez and *presto* you get a new identity and a house in a distant state and enough money to kick-start you. Welcome to the Federal Witness Protection Program, Mr Galindez.

She opened the passenger door, but didn't get out at once. 'Sometimes it just blows me away to remember how naïve I was,' she said. There was a trace of sadness in her voice. 'I used to believe the law had a purity of sorts, but every shitty deal you cut clouds the picture and diminishes your faith. Finally you become a non-believer.'

Rhees was quiet for a time. 'You really sure you want to see this guy Bascombe?'

'It's no big deal. In and out toot sweet.'

'I'll find a bar and have a beer,' Rhees said.

'Let's meet back here in half an hour.'

He kissed her. She wolf-whistled him as he walked away and he turned back, smiling. He was dressed in a beige linen jacket and black jeans and his skin was lightly tanned. He looked luminously attractive. Six years and her heart still went into orbit.

'Take care,' she called to him.

She went in the direction of the Federal Building, where she walked through the metal detector, then stepped past the armed guards and headed for the elevators.

8

'I HAVEN'T SEEN A POLICE REPORT YET,' LEWIS BASCOMBE SAID.

Amanda said, 'Drumm wouldn't submit it directly to you in any case. It would go to Chief Kelloway. You'll get it through whatever your regular channels are.'

Bascombe tapped his desk with a ballpoint pen which had on it the legend, '*Shop'n'Go 24 Hrs*'. Sunlight was thinly sliced by the drawn slats of a blind. The walls of the office were bare except for a photograph that depicted Bascombe and former President Bush handshaking.

Bascombe was an unimposing man with a toupee the colour of a mouse. 'The guidelines say I need a copy of a police report, Amanda. I need confirmation.'

'*Confirmation?* Of what? The body was definitely Galindez, and he'd definitely been shot. What is this, Lew?'

'I have to have a report from a law enforcement officer.'

'Lew,' Amanda said. 'Why can't we skip your guidelines here? If there's even the *slightest* chance of a security screw-up, you can't fart around waiting for a report.'

'I'm not saying I doubt it was Galindez, and I'm not

going to shed any tears over him, but put yourself in my place.'

'I spent the best part of my career bending the law to make it work. If it didn't fit, I had to twist it, and if that didn't work, I had to tweak it again. One thing I know about guidelines. They're malleable.' She was impatient. 'All I'm asking is that you notify the proper authorities immediately, Lew.'

'You don't have official status these days, Amanda.'

'So call me a concerned citizen, if that makes it easier for you.'

Bascombe appeared to consider this statement. Amanda couldn't tell anything from Bascombe's face about his inner world. Maybe he didn't have one. Maybe he was all surface, the bad wig and the sweat-rings in the armpits of his shirt. He liaised between the US Marshals Service and the Department of Justice in the operation of the Federal Witness Protection Program, which meant he worked in a secret hinterland, an altogether cloudy place. Maybe his lack of expression was a prerequisite for the demands of this shadowy territory.

She said, 'I placed Galindez in the Witness Program, Lew. He turns up dead in a place he should never have been, so naturally I'm concerned. If the Program's fucked we should know about it.'

Bascombe continued to tap his pen. 'Presumably you considered the possibility that Galindez left the Program of his own accord?'

'Of course I considered it, but I don't gamble when it comes to people's lives. Do you?'

'I work in the dark, Amanda. My job is to make sure witnesses are well protected before and during their testimony. After that, I don't know where they go, and I don't want to know. They're taken into custody by US marshals and then they vanish inside the Program in accordance with Title 18, *Crimes and Criminal Procedure*, Section 3521, *Witness Relocation and Protection*. The less I know the better for my own safety and for security in general.'

'Lew, don't go spouting title this and section that at me.'

Bascombe rolled his pen back and forth across his desk. He had stubby fingers. Amanda glanced a moment at the photograph on the wall. Former President Bush was smiling like a man trying to hang tough through a prolonged bout of constipation.

Amanda sighed. 'All I want is for you to make contact with the Program, tell them about Galindez. A favour to me, that's all. And if you won't do it, if you *can't* do it, give me the name of somebody I can contact personally.'

'A name?' Bascombe shook his head, as if Amanda's request were too preposterous to consider. 'The story going around is you'd lost your enthusiasm, Amanda. Turned your back on things.'

'I think of it as lawsick.'

'For a lady with no appetite, you sound pretty keen to me.'

'I don't like the idea of a leak, Lew.'

Bascombe nodded his head slowly. There was a bovine quality about the gesture. He studied the logo on his pen. 'OK. OK. I'll send along the message on Galindez today, but I think what we'll find is that he made the stupid decision to go walkabout and found his way back among his old cronies, and one of them administered the *coup de grâce*. Criminals have shit for brains, Amanda, as you well know.'

'I appreciate this,' Amanda said.

'And if anything comes up you need to know about, I'll be in touch,' Bascombe said.

Amanda gave him the telephone number at the cabin. Bascombe scribbled it down on a piece of paper and stuck it in the drawer. 'Something else on your mind?' he asked.

She hesitated, then shook her head. Nothing, she thought, just some vague unfocused disturbance way at the back of her mind, like wind blowing on a distant lake. The feeling faded as quickly as it had come.

She rose from her chair. 'When did you meet Bush?' she asked.

'About nine years ago.'

'Likeable?'

'A regular guy,' Bascombe said. 'But I didn't vote for him.'

'Why not?'

'I didn't vote period,' Bascombe said.

'Undemocratic of you, Lew.'

Bascombe said, 'You might not believe this, but I have a quiet rebellious streak deep inside, and sometimes it just bubbles up.'

'You're a dark horse. You take my breath away, Lew.'

9

ANTHONY DANSK WAS ATTENDING EARLY EVENING MASS
when the cellular phone buzzed in his pocket. He shut it
off at once, but not before it had drawn the attention of
other worshippers, some of whom turned to stare. The
priest heard it and frowned across the faces of his congregation.

Dansk slid out of the pew and walked up the aisle. In
the vestibule, he pressed a button on the phone and said,
'I can't talk now, McTell. I'll get back to you.'

Dansk severed the connection and glanced at leaflets
tacked to a bulletin-board. Hot-line numbers for manic
depressives, alcoholics, battered wives' support groups, a
schedule for a kindergarten class. He also noticed dust on
ledges and an old cobweb with a skeleton of an antique fly
hanging under Christ's armpit.

He stuck the phone in his pocket, re-entered the church
and slipped quietly into a pew at the rear. Churches
impressed him: he liked the majesty and the mystery. His
mother used to tell him he was a mote in Jesus's sunbeam.
For years he'd thought of himself as a fleck floating in

mid-air, with only Christ keeping him from falling. The things you believe.

He watched the priest, the rose-coloured scalp glowing under subdued light. Dansk pondered the concept of chastity, what it would be like not to get laid. Unreal. Pecker forever in your pocket, unless you had a taste for choirboys and indulged yourself with much fumbling of cassocks in the quiet of the sacristy.

When Mass was over Dansk walked outside and lingered on the sidewalk. The other worshippers drifted out. They were a well-scrubbed crew: wives with sculpted hair, men in suits. These people had homes to go to, kids to look after.

The priest appeared on the steps and looked at him.

'Visiting?' the priest asked.

'Yeah, more or less,' Dansk said.

'I thought your face was new.'

'New? It's thirty-five years old.'

'Pardon?'

Dansk said, 'A joke. You said new.'

'Oh, right. Yes. Forgive me.'

'Me forgive you? Shouldn't that be the other way round, Father?'

The priest laughed this time, but uneasily. Dansk often had an unsettling effect on others. He'd recognized this in himself long ago. People he met sometimes sensed a nebulous danger in him, a dark core. It was as if they were receiving vibrations that unhinged them a little. He considered it a kind of power he had. He fingered the Swiss Army knife in his pocket.

'Good Mass,' he said.

'We have a nice bunch of people here,' said the priest. 'My name's Father Hannon. Brian Hannon.'

'Anthony Dansk.'

'Are you staying long in our city?'

54

'It depends on business.'

'Ah. A man of commerce.'

'Commerce, right.'

'Well, if you decide to worship with us again, Anthony, you know where to find us. Just remember to switch your phone off next time.' The priest wandered off to chat with members of his congregation.

Dansk walked to the end of the block where he'd parked his rented car. He sat behind the wheel, took out his phone and punched the button that connected him with McTell.

'OK,' Dansk said. 'Talk.'

'We traced her.'

'You traced her before, I seem to remember,' Dansk said.

'This time's different.'

'It was different before,' Dansk said.

'I know, I know. But this time. I swear.'

'What are you swearing to, McTell?'

'She gassed her car on Thunderbird about forty-five minutes ago.'

'Thunderbird. What is that?'

'Name of a road. The guy filling her tank said she was unglued. Dropping coins, crying, the shakes, talking to herself. The guy figured a loony.'

'And?'

'Pasquale is on her.'

'Even as we speak?'

'Yeah,' McTell said.

Dansk considered this. 'I don't want you calling me later just to hum the same old tune, McTell. Don't get in touch unless you can sing me a lullaby.'

Dansk cut the connection. Through the windshield he watched Father Hannon shake hands with his departing flock. Dansk thought about white suburban houses and morning newspapers landing on porches and cookies baking in ovens and kids laughing in backyards. This life he led was one of hotels and endless highways and greasy spoons open all hours and lonely demented strangers.

He changed the angle of the rear-view mirror and looked at himself, the thick red hair, grass-green eyes, lips almost cherubic, pale skin. Thirty-five. He could pass for twenty. Baby face.

He twisted the mirror away, shoved the phone inside the glove compartment, then locked it. What he'd do was go back to his hotel downtown and wait for McTell to call again.

He glanced along the sidewalk at the priest. *Commerce my ass.* You don't know, Father, he thought. You probably think computers or life insurance or hotel supplies.

Wrong. My commerce is darkness without end.

10

MORGAN SCHOLES SHOOK RHEES'S HAND EFFUSIVELY, THEN embraced Amanda. He had thick white hair cut short. He smelled of Old Spice, a scent Amanda always found comforting.

Morgan Scholes said, 'I keep telling you, Mandy, marry this man. You don't, one day he'll just slip through the cracks.'

'I don't think I'm about to slip anywhere, Morgan,' Rhees said.

Amanda said, 'We've discussed matrimony, Dad. It's a subject we circle warily.'

'Nonsense,' the old man said. 'It's an ocean, and you plunge in head first and go with the tides. Is it cocktail hour yet?'

'There's a perfectly plausible theory that it's always cocktail hour somewhere on the planet,' Rhees said.

'See, Mandy. This is my kind of guy.' Morgan Scholes clapped Rhees on the shoulder. 'First time I ever liked any guy you brought home. Some of the cretins you used to hang out with, all those upwardly mobile types with one

eye on their portable phone and the other on my money –
I could sniff those guys a mile away.'

'Hey, they weren't all fortune-hunters,' Amanda said.

Morgan Scholes uttered a dismissive snort. 'They were
wimps, girl. Transparent as all hell.'

She saw no point in pursuing the matter of old
boyfriends, so she let the topic slide. Morgan's opinions
tended to be cemented in his brain and therefore unshak-
able anyway. Besides, she knew that the matter of her past
lovers, even if they meant zip to her, wasn't high on
Rhees's list of favourite conversation subjects. He had an
endearing insecurity at times.

She followed Morgan inside the house, which clung in
defiance of gravity to the side of a mountain, and consisted of three wings built around a central courtyard
where a clay mermaid lay in a fountain. There were
arched walkways, open spaces. In the sunken lounge,
stained-glass windows hand-crafted in the Baja filtered
and changed the late afternoon sun. Traditional Western
art hung on the walls: cowboys in glossy wax coats, a
chuck wagon by camp-fire.

'Gin and tonic OK?'

The old man, dressed in grey slacks and sand-coloured
shirt, made the drinks. He passed them out, then sat down
next to Amanda and said, 'You look good in white. Like
an angel.'

'Flattery, Dad. The old silver tongue.'

'Flattery doesn't enter into it. I never lied to a woman in
my life. Made it a rule. Broke it only once and that was
when your mother asked me outright if her disease
was terminal. I told her no, said she'd get well. Three
weeks later, dead.'

'An excusable lie,' Rhees said.

'You don't look the woman you love in the eye and tell
her she's dying from cancer.'

Amanda tasted her drink. What she remembered of her mother was the voice, soft and Virginian. She'd died when Amanda was three. After that, there had been a series of 'companions' who came and went quickly because they couldn't compete with the dead. Morgan was more interested in the brutality of business than the delicate structures of relationships anyway. He'd made a fortune pioneering greetings cards with high-art reproductions on their covers. He'd parleyed this into even greater wealth in a series of speculative land deals in the days when property could be bought one morning and sold the next for fabulous profit.

'It was a damn good marriage,' the old man said.

'You were fortunate,' Rhees said.

'Sure I was fortunate. I used to wonder about remarrying, having more kids. Then I'd think, hold on, I've probably used up a whole lifetime's luck with Amanda's mother. You two staying for dinner?'

Amanda said, 'Not this time. We want to get back before it's too late.'

'That cabin grows on you,' Scholes remarked. 'I think you did an admirable thing when you quit, Mandy. You don't like what you're doing, dump it. Move on. You're young.'

'Relatively.'

Morgan Scholes waved this aside. 'Forty-two.'

'Three.'

'Three then. That's young. Right, John?'

'Absolutely,' Rhees said.

'And if you get bored at the cabin, enrol in some college courses, study something different – economics, business. Something practical. It's not like you have money problems.'

'I have some savings,' Amanda said.

'Pah. Nickel and dime. I'm talking about your inheritance. I shuffle off, you're a very rich woman.'

'Let's not talk about shuffling off,' Amanda said.

'There's nothing wrong with inheriting money, Amanda. What do you want me to do with it? Leave it to some charity? I don't understand why you're always so damn narrow-minded and Bolshevist about it. It's not like it's tainted, for God's sake.'

The subject of her inheritance, which Morgan raised at every opportunity he could, made her uncomfortable. At some point on the graph of her life, she'd decided it was an injustice that one person should inherit another's wealth because of an accident of birth. During her years at law school in Los Angeles she'd worked nights and weekends as a cocktail waitress in a Brentwood hotel, instead of accepting her father's persistent offers of tuition and expenses. It came down to the fact that she wanted to be her own person, not the brat offspring of a rich man.

She didn't need her father's money, and she didn't like the way wealth influenced Morgan's life. He was always consorting with ossified people who just happened to be as rich as himself, industrialists, powerbrokers, men whose wives were face-lifted and ditzy and spent their days in listless shopping or fund-raising for Third World countries they couldn't find on a map if they tried. Wealth bred in some people a kind of blind ignorance, isolated them in a cocoon.

The old man, in a rare display of tact, changed the subject. 'You're better off out of law anyhow. It's a joke in this country, unless you've got money to burn. Lawyers like only one thing, and it's the folding green. Justice? What's that? John deserves better than a lawyer for a wife when you get right down to it.'

'How many times, Dad? We're not contemplating marriage.'

'She ought to have her head examined,' the old man said to Rhees.

Rhees smiled and said, 'I don't think there's much wrong with Amanda's head, Morgan.'

'You always take her side, John. Don't encourage her. I want to be there when you and she walk down that aisle, all sweetness and light.'

Amanda glanced at Rhees over her gin and tonic. 'He doesn't know when to quit, John.'

'Carve that on my stone,' the old man said. He finished his drink and looked at Amanda for a time, then he said to Rhees, 'She's stubborn and strong-willed. Don't know where in the world she gets it from.'

He winked at Rhees, then stood up and laughed. 'Bad habit telling other people what's good for them, huh? Can't break some habits at my time of life.'

'You mean well,' Amanda said.

'But the road to hell is paved, yadda yadda,' the old man said. 'Another drink?'

'I'm driving,' Rhees said.

'Not for me,' Amanda remarked.

Morgan Scholes said, 'I'm in the company of lightweights,' and fixed himself a second drink. Then he looked at his daughter. 'Say. I just remembered. Some woman's been phoning here for you, Mandy.'

'Here? What woman?'

'She called first time two nights ago, then last night again. I must speak to Amanda, she says. I'm in Tuba City, she says.'

'Tuba City?'

'That's what she said. I tell her you're not here, and before I can give her the number at the cabin she hangs up.'

'She doesn't leave her name?'

Scholes shook his head. 'No, she doesn't.'

'Describe the voice,' Amanda said.

'It's low, whispered. Kind of Hispanic accent. She sounds frantic and then she hangs up like she thinks somebody's listening in, or she's in a big hurry. Who do you know in Tuba City?'

Amanda looked down into her drink. Bubbles of tonic popped on the surface. A woman calls and hangs up again quickly. What did that mean? Her mind blanked.

She gazed at Rhees, who was watching her thoughtfully. She saw dying sunlight come in a pale-blue haze through stained-glass. 'Why didn't you call and tell me this, Dad?' she asked.

'I've been pretty busy what with one thing and another,' Morgan Scholes said. 'Who is she anyway?'

She finished her drink. 'I don't know,' she said.

11

'I'M RACKING MY BRAIN,' AMANDA SAID IN THE CAR. 'I
don't know a soul up in that part of the state.' She lit a
cigarette and inhaled smoke a little too quickly. *Frantic*
was the word Morgan had used. *I must speak to Amanda*,
Yours truly, Frantic, Tuba City. *Hispanic accent*. She
didn't want to think.

A shadow rolled through her head, the same smoke
signal she'd expelled from her mind when she'd been discussing Galindez with Willie Drumm, the same little
shiver of concern she'd felt in Bascombe's office. She shut
her eyes. Tuba City, the back-end of beyond. She thought
of an endless arid landscape and a voice travelling through
telephone wires and the way Galindez had been ferried
downstream by the river.

'Why would somebody phone you at your father's
number anyway?' Rhees asked.

'Maybe she tried our home number first, then when she
got no response she looked up Morgan in the book. I
don't know.'

Rhees was driving towards Scottsdale from Phoenix. All

63

that remained of the sun were a few spectacular streaks the colour of blood. Downtown Scottsdale was a sequence of traffic lights, all seemingly red. Rhees took a left turn off the main street. He drove until he reached the cul-de-sac where the house he shared with Amanda was located. He parked in the driveway and Amanda strolled ahead of him, unlocked the front door and turned on the lights.

Inside the air was stuffy. They'd been gone a little less than four weeks and yet she felt like an intruder. She went into the living-room, Rhees followed her. More lights. She looked round the room. Their possessions – books, TV, furniture – had that alien quality you sometimes experience when you come back after a vacation. The geometry of the house was all wrong, ceilings too high, windows too large.

Rhees said, 'Weird.'

'You feel it?'

'Yeah, I feel it.'

'It's like somebody else's house,' Amanda said. 'I expect if we go into the backyard we'll find duplicates of ourselves emerging from giant pods.'

She walked to the answering machine, then remembered she'd disconnected it before they'd left for the cabin, an act of deliberate severance. Kill the machine. *I don't need and I don't want messages.*

'You think this mystery woman will call?' Rhees asked.

'It's a possibility.'

'I need a drink. Want one?'

'Please.'

Rhees went inside the kitchen. Amanda could hear him rummaging for ice. She sat on the sofa, glanced at the Adams prints on the walls, chilly black and white rock formations. Objects formerly charged with easy familiarity were shorn of meaning. Even the framed newspaper and magazine clippings that concerned some of her legal cases were related to a person other than herself. It was as if somebody had come here when the house was empty and stripped away the veneer of recognition.

Rhees returned with drinks. 'We forgot to empty the refrigerator. Something disgusting is growing in there.'

'Sit beside me.' She patted the sofa. He sat down and touched her wrist. She sipped her drink. She was conscious of the silent black telephone located on the table at her back. She was suddenly uptight, jangled. She wanted the gin to relax her, numb her head a little.

In the distance the shrill whine of a cop car was audible. Night in the city. Deaths and accidents. Casual, drive-by shootings. She yearned for the forest.

'We should be heading back soon,' Rhees said.

Amanda didn't move.

Rhees got up. 'Maybe I'll just defuzz the fridge to pass some time while you finish your drink and wait to see if the phone rings.'

He went back inside the kitchen. She listened to the sound of things being clattered around. Jars and bottles, glass knocked on glass impatiently. He didn't want to be here any more than she did. She heard him say, 'Sweet Jesus, was this sodden mass once a bag of carrots?'

Fifteen minutes dragged past before the telephone rang, and when it did Amanda reached for the receiver at once and spoke her name.

The woman said, 'Manda, I been trying to phone for days, I can't get you, Manda.'

For a second Amanda couldn't speak. Electricity spiked through her. She was only dimly aware of Rhees materializing in the kitchen doorway with what looked like green compost in his rubber-gloved hand. She leaned forward on the sofa and tried to keep alarm out of her voice. 'Where are you? Where the hell are you?'

'It's gone wrong, Manda, the whole goddam thing. This

65

isn't the way you planned it. I'm inside this nightmare where I don't belong.' The woman was crying and her words ran into one another in breathless little utterances.

'Just tell me where you are,' Amanda said.

'God, where am I? Jesus, I don't know.'

'Calm down, calm down.'

'They're coming after me, Manda.'

'Who?'

'These two guys, they're coming after me.'

Amanda's fingers were rigid on the handset. 'I'll help, just tell me where you are.'

'OK, where I am, this is,' and her voice faded. Amanda heard the clank of a telephone being set down, then a creaking noise. 'Where I am. OK, this is a place called, wait a minute, I'm looking at the sign, the Canyon Motel, off the interstate. It's got a big blue light outside.'

'Which interstate?'

'What's the one? Seventeen. I-Seventeen.'

'*Seventeen?* You're here in *Arizona*?'

'Manda, help me. Come help me.'

'You're at a pay phone there.'

'A pay phone, right. Say you'll come.'

'Stay where you are. Don't move.' Rhees was looking at her with curiosity.

'How long it gonna take you?'

'I don't know. Fast as I can get there.'

'Hurry, Jesus Christ hurry, please.'

'I'll be there.' Amanda hung up. Rhees was thumbing quickly through the Yellow Pages.

'The Canyon,' he said, reading from the directory. 'It's near Black Canyon City.'

Amanda could hear the motion of her blood. 'Even if I go like a bat out of hell, that's still twenty-five, thirty minutes. Do me a favour. Call Willie Drumm, tell him to meet me there.'

She rushed towards the door before Rhees – who looked puzzled and anxious – had time to say anything. She was all haste, her brain locked in that space where thoughts don't cohere and your head's filled with a strident choir of panic. She blew a quick kiss back at Rhees and said, 'Tell him it's Isabel Sanchez.'

12

SHE DROVE WITH CONCENTRATED URGENCY. THE CITY thinned until there were no more orange lamps, only the unforgiving dark of the desert on either side. She tried to arrange her thoughts, piling them up like building blocks, but they wouldn't balance. Isabel calls from a place called the Canyon Motel on I-17. She's in trouble. Why is she there to begin with? And what had she been doing in Tuba City before that? Think *think* – but the bricks kept slipping and tumbling, and the letters of the alphabet made no sense. The night was cracked, and the pieces didn't fit, and Amanda couldn't make them.

Out into darkness, out into space. Freeway signs that read like gibberish, a cluster of orange lights, then more blackness for miles, and oncoming traffic rushing past her into a void. When she saw the blue light of the Canyon Motel she realized she'd lost all sense of time and distance. She swung off the freeway and raced up the ramp and braked hard inside the parking-lot, opening the door and stepping out in one unbroken movement.

There was a pay phone located outside the motel office.

Nobody was using it, no sign of Isabel. She went inside the office. The clerk, a kid in a baseball cap, stood behind the desk. Willie Drumm was also there, beefy in his usual tight-fitting linen jacket.

'She's not here,' Drumm said. 'She's gone.'

'Gone?'

'I got here a minute ago—'

'You look around?' Amanda asked.

'I only just arrived, Amanda.'

Amanda looked at the clerk. 'Did you see her?'

The kid said, 'There was a woman out there making a phone call about ten minutes ago. Small woman, Mexican looking. She the one you mean?'

'Where did she go?'

'I wasn't paying close attention,' the kid said. He had a plump textbook open on the counter. *Gray's Anatomy*. Amanda glanced at an elongated sketch that might have been a cross-section of gland.

'Pre-med next month,' the kid said. 'I was studying actually.'

Amanda slammed the book shut. 'What the fuck did you see *actually*?'

The kid, who had a sharp little face, looked at Amanda with annoyance. 'Hey,' he said, 'you lost my place.'

'I'll ask again. What did you see?'

'This woman came in and wanted to use the pay phone, so I made change for her, then she went out again. I saw her go to the phone. She seemed sort of wigged.'

'Then what?'

'I wasn't really watching. I told you.'

'After she was finished using the phone, what did she do? Did she drive away? Did she just walk up and down? What did you see?'

'I heard a car start up. I assume she drove away. Then this other vehicle came screaming through the lot.'

'What kind of vehicle?'

'Land Cruiser, something like that.'

'You heard this vehicle immediately after the first car?'

'Seconds, that was all.'

'You happen to see what direction these vehicles took?'

The kid pondered a moment. 'I don't think they headed to the freeway. I got the impression they were going in the other direction. Back there,' and he gestured with his thumb towards the desert.

Amanda looked at Drumm. 'We'll take your car, Willie.'

'Fine by me.' Drumm moved to the door and opened it. Amanda rushed past him. The cop, his right leg stiff from an old gunshot wound, stumped after her.

Amanda was buzzing, uneasy. She opened the door of the Bronco, sat in the passenger seat, watched Drumm lower himself behind the wheel.

'She can't be far away,' Amanda said.

Drumm backed up the Bronco, turned out of the lot, slid the vehicle into the road that ran at a right angle to the freeway, an unlit ribbon of blacktop. The blue neon of the motel faded quickly behind. The city became a remote yellow-orange constellation in the sky. Cacti loomed up in the headlights, some pock-marked by the gunfire of vandals at target practice.

'You want to tell me what's happening?' Drumm asked.

'She called me. She's in a bad way. She said some men were after her.'

'Did she say who these guys were?'

'She wasn't coherent.'

'You think this other car's chasing her?'

'Sounds that way. All I can tell you for sure is she's frightened and I want to find her.'

The Bronco dipped in and out of potholes and Drumm said, 'This road is the pits. You look your side, I'll look mine.'

'I'm doing that.'

'You can't see shit around here. What if she drove off the road? Headed out into the desert?'

'We'll stick to the road for the time being,' Amanda said.

'I don't see what choice we got. We go off the road, what direction do we take? People get lost in the desert all the time.'

Amanda beat a tattoo on the dash. She was trying to release tension, but it wasn't working. She thought of Isabel, tiny out there in the wilderness. Left, right, east, west. Drumm was correct. If they left the road, they'd be going nowhere.

'I thought she was long gone,' Drumm said.

'I thought the same thing,' Amanda leaned forward, scanning the night, the puny reaches of the lights. 'Stop the car.'

Drumm braked. Amanda rolled down her window and listened to a silence as big as a galaxy.

'You hear anything?' Drumm asked.

'Nothing. Drive on a bit farther.'

Drumm slid the Bronco forward. The blacktop narrowed. The desert crowded in. After a mile or so, Amanda said, 'Stop again.'

Drumm cut the engine. Amanda focused on the night, still and enormous. What she longed for were distress flares, great plumes of white light to illuminate the landscape. She listened as she'd never listened before. She heard only absences and silences and the quickened rhythms of her own pulse. The desert was a vast infuriating secret.

She told Drumm to drive again.

Half a mile down the road, Amanda heard dogs barking far off. Drumm slowed.

'Coyotes,' Drumm said.

'They're dogs,' Amanda said.

'I'm a city boy,' Drumm remarked. 'Dogs, coyotes. What do I know?'

Amanda opened the door and got out of the car. She stood on the edge of the blacktop and listened. The dogs yapped and snivelled. Hounds, hunting dogs, excited. She couldn't tell where the sounds originated, how far away they might be. You could drive out there for miles and think you were heading directly to the source and you'd be wrong. Soundwaves zigzagged. There were acoustic distortions.

Drumm stood alongside her and surveyed the dark with a gloomy look. 'What do you think?'

'We may have to drive out there, Willie.'

'Like two blind people.'

'I don't like the sound of those dogs.'

'Maybe some good old boy's out chasing jackrabbits or something.'

'In the dark?'

Drumm shrugged. 'Anything's possible. You want me to drive off the road, I'll do it. Christ only knows where we'll end up.'

Amanda got back inside the Bronco. A mile away, five miles, ten – the dogs could be anywhere. Drumm turned the key in the ignition.

Amanda hung one arm out the window and Drumm swung the vehicle off the blacktop and steered between cacti that resembled stick-figures petrified into stillness by the white slash of the headlights.

13

SHE'S TWISTED HER ANKLE AND A HEEL HAS BROKEN OFF HER shoe and she's running, stumbling, trying all this time to keep quiet, but she makes gasping sounds because her lungs are bursting and her ankle's beginning to swell.

The dogs have the scent of her. They whine and yelp and she wishes she hadn't abandoned the car, even with the flat tyre, because she could have sat tight with the doors and windows locked, but even then, even then what good would it do? The men are following the dogs in a jeep. Always the men, the men.

There's no moon and the stars have gone out, and she finds herself scrambling up a slope. Dust rises into her nose and mouth and stings her eyes, and she wants to cry, but she's been crying too much lately, and she thinks, there's a time when you don't have no more tears.

She climbs up the slope on all fours now. Loose stones slither out from under her, and what she wants is to lie very still and pretend she isn't here and if she makes herself small maybe the dogs won't smell her. She loses her hold and slips a few yards and thinks, the landscape's against her, like everything else.

What she remembers is hitching rides from truckers who took her places she didn't want to go: Gallup then Farmington, New Mexico, the wrong direction, but she wasn't thinking straight for a while, and then she stole the car and drove back to Arizona.

The weariness, the car overheating, the air stuffy and stifling, this is what she remembers. Also how Manda's telephone rings on and on and even when she decided to try the other number all she ever got was a man. Maybe Manda's father. Maybe. You don't know who to trust: cops, strangers, you don't know. It's the world, the way of it.

She should have kept her mouth shut, but she spoke up about Ángel, yeah, *really* bright of her, very smart, Ángel who she used to love. Ángel who screwed her over real bad and treated her like shit and one time, with his razor, cut her in a private place. She doesn't want to think about him because love rots.

Running, driving long hours, panicky, drained, freeway lines painted inside her skull, one night in a small stuffy motel room and not knowing how long she can sleep because the men are always just behind her. She can't stay ahead of them no more and she knows it, and she's gonna die here and nobody gonna find her.

She wishes for moonlight, but then she thinks, maybe she don't want to see what's out there. Let it be this way, this dark. Better like this. She climbs again. Her fingernails are broken. One time she was proud of her nails and how long they were, she'd paint and buff and file them, when she wanted to look good for Ángel, when she loved him. When they had the big house and the *conservatory*, whatever it's called. The plants, she smells the plants, it's a dream of back then, that's all. A dream rotting inside her skull.

Her ankle feels like a crab is pinching. She's dragging the foot and it gets in the way of her movement, and the dogs are coming. She imagines them bounding through the dark towards her. She thinks of their hot breath, paws, sharp teeth. She thinks, the dogs gonna get me, no matter how hard I try to get away, the dogs are coming, and then the men behind them. They're coming at her in the night, and all she did was say what was in her mind, because all Ángel did was cause pain – he deserves what he got. But he don't roll over just because he's been put away, no, he don't do that: he sends out men and dogs to hunt her. Nobody else would send men and dogs after her. She can't think. She never hurt a soul. She was always kind, right from the time when she was a little girl and her grandmother dragged her from town to town selling those crazy herb potions for warts and insomnia and flatulence – dry towns and villages, Camargo and La Esmeralda and Ceballos. She remembers the cracked roads and her grandmother carving strips of yucca and muttering the secret holy words. She remembers the withered old bronze woman saying, *You're a good girl, Isabella. Always say your prayers and tell the truth and brush your teeth. And when a handsome young man talks to you, smile at him like you mean it.*

Manda you promised me. Manda you said everything gonna be OK. Just tell me this one thing, what good are your words now?

She slips again, clutching at nothing. She rolls over and over down the slope and dust chokes her and she's dizzy and the sky's off-centre and the dogs are louder all the time, and she feels the way a hunted rabbit would feel: all fear and wild impulses and thinking how to survive, how to get out of this place and just live.

Then suddenly the dogs are on her, out of the dark they come snarling, and she smells the meaty breath of the animals, and they whine and bark, snapping at skin and clothing, quick and savage. She sees their eyes gleam. She tries to cover her face and kicks at the beasts. The stench of their fur is strong and sickly, their bodies feel moist and hot against her skin. 'Mother of God,' she says. 'Mother of Christ.' Fangs, jaws, saliva, claws. She curls herself up into a ball. The dogs snap and bite and whine, how many: three, four, who can tell? Her leg is slashed, her hands are bleeding, the dogs are crazy for her blood. She tries to crawl out from under the pressure of their bodies, but they cling to her, they dig into her.

The sound of a vehicle. Slamming doors. A man's voice. 'Back, back. Get back.'

The animals retreat, sniffling, whimpering sullenly.

She looks up into the bright disc of a flashlight.

'Bitch,' the man says.

She knows this voice. Knows it.

Another man says, 'End of the road, sweetie.'

The first man says, 'I'll do it myself.'

The other man reaches down, grabs her hair and twists her face to the side. 'You don't look so good any more. You look tired and weary.'

He thrusts her face away. She's on fire where the dogs have lanced her skin. She says, 'You gonna do it, do it quick.'

'Think you're a brave little number,' the first man says. He kicks her straight in the heart and she moans. 'Huh? Huh? I'll show you brave, *conchita*.' He bends, pulls her skirt up, inserts his finger under her panties and thrusts it deep inside her and moves it up and down. Then he laughs and draws his hand away and she hears him sniff his own fingers. He laughs like the dogs bark.

'Get it the fuck over with,' the other man says.

She sees a gun, silver in flashlight. Jesus save me. She crosses herself with one bleeding hand.

76

'*Adiós*,' the first man says, and presses the barrel of the silver gun to the side of her head. And there's a click, a friction between her skin and metal, and then the flash.

14

WILLIE DRUMM SAID, 'I'M TIRED, AMANDA. IT'S GOTTA BE AT least two hours since we heard the gunshot, and I haven't heard the dogs either. The smart thing would be to quit, come back n the daylight with more help, give the area a thorough sea. h.'

Amanda stared into the dark beyond the headlights. Her eyes ached. She knew Drumm's proposal was sound, and if she'd been looking for anyone other than Isabel she would have agreed to call it a night.

'Keep in mind Sanchez was my case too, Amanda, and I worked it long and hard. So don't take what I have to say the wrong way, but some might call this compulsive behaviour.'

'Maybe that's what it is.'

'I know we owe the woman big time. I understand your feelings.' Drumm indicated the wall of dark, moving his hand in a gesture of hopelessness. 'I heard of needles in haystacks, Amanda, but this . . .'

Amanda smoked a cigarette. She'd gone through almost a pack in the two hours since the gunshot. Two hours of ruts and ravines and cacti, 120 minutes or more in which she'd tried unsuccessfully to attribute the gunshot to another cause altogether – some jerk camper's kerosene stove exploding, a demented gold prospector's pick-up truck backfiring. There were all kinds of loonies drawn to the desert in the quest for gain, spiritual or material, God or gold.

But she was fooling herself. It had been a gunshot, unmistakable and dreadful. And just after the shot, she thought she'd heard a vehicle droning in the distance. She'd scanned the night but hadn't seen headlights. The landscape was pocked, hollows and canyons, a million hiding-places.

'I'm getting sick of cacti,' Willie Drumm said. 'They're starting to develop personalities. Any time now, one of them's gonna say *you again?*'

Amanda was hunched forward in her seat. She'd been locked in this position a long time. 'Give it another twenty minutes, Willie. Then we'll go.'

'You think you remember the way back to the road?'

'We'll find it.'

Drumm edged the Bronco between stands of cacti. A jackrabbit ran mazily ahead of them. Once, a cactus wren darted in front of the vehicle, a feathered ball of light. Amanda barely noticed these disturbances. Her mind was elsewhere, probing her own private wasteland.

The Bronco bumped, thudded, bottomed out in a shallow arroyo Drumm had seen too late to avoid. 'Shit,' he said. He backed the vehicle up and the rear tyres span, and dust, thrown up by the wheels, clouded the air.

Amanda saw something then, metal and glinting. 'There,' she said. 'What's that?'

Drumm parked, removed a flashlight from the glove box. He left the headlights on, and they illuminated a late-1970s Datsun with a punctured front tyre. Drumm opened the passenger door and switched on the flash. Inside the car was a clutter of discarded fast-food wrappers and styrofoam coffee cups and empty Camel Light packs and crumpled Kleenex.

Amanda looked at the debris. 'Flash the back,' she said to Drumm.

Drumm moved the beam. In the back Amanda saw a heap of crushed clothing. Some of it was deadeningly familiar. A candy-striped blouse, a pair of jeans with a designer label, a blue T-shirt with a palm tree and the word Malibu.

'Hers?' Drumm asked.

Amanda nodded. She noticed a small pink thing among the clothing and she reached for it and held it in the palm of her hand.

'What's that?' Drumm asked.

'A barrette. A hair-clasp.' Amanda wrapped her fingers round the thin strip of plastic.

Drumm played the light on the ground around the Datsun. 'She had a flat and decided to hoof it,' he said.

Amanda studied the ground. There were footprints scuffed by paw-marks. Drumm was the first to see the shoe, which he picked up. 'You don't run too good in high heels,' he said.

Amanda took the shoe and noticed it was missing the heel. She tried to reconstruct the scene, but she didn't like the pictures she was coming up with. Isabel runs, her heel snaps, the dogs are after her.

'You want to keep going?' Drumm asked.

Amanda didn't. This was a trail she had no heart for. She felt empty and depressed. 'Sure,' she said.

Drumm trained the flashlight on the scuff of prints, Amanda followed. She didn't know how far she and Drumm walked: a quarter mile, a half, more. The desert was beyond measurement.

'She comes this way.' Drumm stopped suddenly at the foot of an incline. There were indentations, disturbances, and blood.

Amanda squatted on her heels, picked up a handful of grainy dust and ran it through her fingers. She saw bloodstains in the grains, wet still.

'This is where it ends,' Drumm said quietly. He swung the flashlight around the general area. 'I see some tyre tracks over there.'

Amanda didn't look in the direction of the beam. She was thinking of dogs, wondering what it felt like to be hunted by them, trying to gauge hysteria, the sense of doom. This is where it ends. Drumm's sentence resonated in her head.

Drumm said, 'The dogs get her, they bring her down, then it happens. The gunman steps in and calls off the dogs. Boom.'

'And her body?' Amanda asked.

'He removes it.'

'Why not leave it here? You couldn't find a more isolated place for dumping a goddam corpse.'

'You got me,' Drumm said. 'What the hell. This whole goddam thing gets me. Two go in, two come out again.'

Two go in, two come out. Amanda listened to the desert, silent now, and eerie, where the dark land seamlessly met the dark sky.

15

DURING THE TRIAL OF VICTOR SANCHEZ, RANDOLPH Hanseimer, defence attorney, had tried to club Isabel Sanchez into submission. His tactics were crude, and once or twice Isabel had closed her eyes and swayed a little in the witness stand as if she were about to faint. *Aren't you just trying to get back at your ex-husband because he left you? Aren't you just mad at him for dumping you because you didn't live up to reasonable expectations as a wife? Isn't this just a seriously malicious case of sour grapes?*

Objection, objection, objection.

Amanda was replaying the trial in her head. She kept seeing Isabel in the stand, clenching her hands into small fists. Hanseimer tried to break her, but she always found the resolve to come back at him. The jury admired her. The jury saw an unassuming young woman abused beyond reason by a husband who was a cold-blooded killer.

Amanda stretched one arm across the bed. Her thoughts raced and her throat was raw from cigarettes and the desert still clung to her, the dread she'd felt, dread she was *still* feeling. Drumm's flashlight, the jackrabbit running, blood in the dust. The dogs, the goddam dogs: she kept hearing the way they yelped and whined. Isabel running from them, that fear, that solitude, just her and terror under an unyielding black sky.

She sat up. 'Two people I entrust to the Program. New names, identities, the whole Federal package. So what the hell were they doing back in Arizona?'

Rhees propped himself on an elbow. 'Maybe they were lured back somehow.'

'Lured?'

'Who would stand to get satisfaction from their deaths anyway?'

'Only Victor Sanchez. Lured though? I don't see how.'

'Sanchez wants revenge, but he wants it in a very special kind of way. What's the point of killing them in Idaho or wherever? That's remote. Better to draw them back here somehow and kill them where they're going to be discovered. Where *you're* going to know about it because it's your state, your own backyard so to speak. He's giving you the finger. He wants to show you he can cut through the Program like cream cheese, but he also wants you to be *aware* of it. He wants you to know that although you have him under lock and key on death row, he can still call the shots.'

She thought about this, then said, 'Explain why we couldn't find Isabel's body. If Sanchez was giving me the finger, why wasn't the body left right there?'

'Maybe you just didn't see it in the dark. Maybe she wasn't killed.'

'Drumm's going back in the morning with some help,' she said.

'Then he'll find her. If she's there to be found.'

Amanda didn't want to think about Drumm and his search-party. She remembered the many hours she'd spent with Isabel in a hotel room on the outskirts of Phoenix, where she'd been sequestered during the trial. Armed guards at the door, unmarked cop cars in the parking-lot. She hadn't been taking any chances. She remembered how fragile Isabel had been. Her small face, dainty in its pale-brown perfection, had been taut most of the time. The atmosphere in the room had been a mix of tension and uneasy allegiance. It had been difficult for Isabel to testify against her husband, because even if the marriage had been a kind of crucifixion, even if Isabel had been hammered nail by nail into the splintered wood of matrimony, and Victor a bundle of unspeakable cruelties, there was still some stunted form of vestigial loyalty. At times Amanda had held Isabel, telling her she was doing the right thing, Victor belonged in jail and she could put him there for a very long time. *Don't think of it as betrayal, Isabel. I promise you'll be safe afterwards.*

Promise. Empty words, dry kindling.

She got out of bed, walked around the room, arms folded. She paused in front of a full-length mirror and caught her reflection in the faint moonlight. She looked frazzled, and she was 4 or 5 pounds too heavy, which was visible even under the oversized black T-shirt she wore. She turned away from the image and sighed.

Rhees was watching her. 'Sanchez has the key to all this. It's obvious.'

'There isn't supposed to *be* a key, John. The doors are meant to be locked tight. Nobody is supposed to be able to open them.'

'Sanchez found a way.'

'How?'

Rhees scratched his jaw. 'Come back to bed.'

'We're talking about something so secret even a guy like Bascombe doesn't know how the machinery really works. We're talking about sealed documents and secret codes.

You don't just pick up a phone and ask for information about the new names and whereabouts of witnesses.'

Rhees flipped the bedsheet back and patted a pillow. 'Lie down,' he said.

'OK. I'll lie down.' She stretched alongside him, held his hand and brushed it with her lips. But she couldn't relax, couldn't *begin* to relax. 'I talked her into it, John. I persuaded her to go into court.'

Rhees stroked her forehead. 'You can't blame yourself.'

'I need to smoke. I know we have a rule about smoking in our bedroom but I'm about to break it.' She lit a cigarette. The sulphuric smell of the exploding match was awful. 'She wouldn't have testified if I hadn't forced her.'

'Forced? It was her decision in the end. Nobody shackled her and led her inside the court, she went of her own free will.'

Amanda shook her head. 'I bought her ticket. I put her on the justice train, which happened to be going nowhere.'

'Now you're choked up with remorse and you want to do something about it. But you'll be a damn sight better off going back to the cabin first thing in the morning and letting Drumm get on with it. Let Bascombe do what he has to do, you're out of it. It's not as if you have an official job these days anyway.'

'Bascombe said the same.'

'He's right. Now try to sleep.'

'How the fuck can I sleep, for God's sake?'

Rhees opened the drawer of the bedside table and removed a prescription bottle, took the lid off, slipped a red and yellow capsule into his palm. 'Take it.'

'I don't want it.'

'Do I have to stuff it down your throat?'

She opened her mouth reluctantly. He placed the capsule on her tongue and gently clapped a hand over her lips. She swallowed.

'Great bedside manner,' she said. Dalmane again. She hadn't used it for weeks and weeks. She'd been working hard to relegate the Sanchez trial to a basement room at the back of her head, and she'd almost managed to bury it.

Rhees said, 'I wonder what she ever saw in Sanchez.'

'That's easy. She was young, naïve and poor, John. Sanchez is a handsome guy, wads of money, knows how to blind her with flash. Flash loses its allure, so he comes up with other ways of getting her attention. He was careless with lit cigarettes when she was around. Once, just for the hell of it, he cut off one of her nipples with a razor blade. This is not a pleasant man.'

She'd seen Sanchez day in day out for the best part of eight weeks in court, and what she remembered was the way he'd stared at her with a concentrated look of contempt. She remembered the trick he had of seeming not to blink. He emitted some very powerful waves of animosity, like a transmitter sending out a constant stream of malice. It had reached a point where she'd dreaded going into the courtroom and feeling the dangerous laser heat of his eyes.

'I don't mean this to sound callous, but you don't owe her,' Rhees said.

'I gave her my word, John.'

'Yeah, but it wasn't you that broke it.'

'That's not really the point,' she said. 'I came to like Isabel.'

'I know you did—'

'She survived a very damaging marriage, and she needed serious reassurance to go in that witness-stand. Thrown together in that kind of situation, you feel close to a person. We talked about a bunch of things: families, friends. We talked a lot about our fathers. I told her about the time Morgan gave me a brand-new car on my seventeenth birthday. The only birthday gift she could ever remember from her father was a cheap plastic barrette when she was twelve, which she kept. That made me feel kind of sad and kind of angry. I had this privileged upbringing I didn't ask for and she had nothing.'

Amanda felt the pill begin to kick in slowly. She could hear a slight echo around the edges of her words. There was a dryness in her throat. Rhees said something she didn't catch because she was drifting towards the peculiar numb darkness of drugged sleep.

She dreamed of Sanchez. She dreamed she was taking his temperature with a rectal thermometer. He was bent over, thighs splayed, and he was grinning, and the grin was terrifying.

She woke at dawn. The sky was the colour of a pale vein. She tossed the bedsheets aside. The inside of her head was like sludge at the bottom of a cafetière, but she knew where she was going.

16

WILLIE DRUMM SURVEYED THE DESERT. THE SUN WAS UP, darkness banished. He said, 'Different place in daylight. Striking, if you like miles and miles of nothing.'

Amanda gazed at shadows in the distant foothills. A hawk crossed the sun with lazy ease. Four patrol cars, doors hanging open, were parked among cacti near the Datsun that contained Isabel's possessions. Uniformed officers stood round in groups and drank coffee from vacuum flasks. She counted a dozen men.

Among them she noticed Drumm's superior, Police Chief Dan Kelloway, long neck and lean concave body and shaven head. A fitness freak, he was reputed to cycle 20 miles every morning before breakfast and survive on a diet of almonds and yoghurt. He was tanned and tall and wore an off-white suit, and his posture was invariably rigid. Between her and Kelloway was a chill zone, a permafrost which had its origins in a bitter disagreement a year earlier over a case Kelloway had been desperate to bring to trial. Amanda had considered the police evidence circumstantial, and the case – involving a young black man with the unfortunate name of Hood, who'd been caught in possession of a gun used in the fatal shooting of a pregnant white woman during a robbery – altogether unworthy of the court's time. Kelloway's frustration and anger with her opinion had been volcanic. He accused her of dereliction of duty, wilfulness, stupidity, hawking up a whole thesaurus of insults. It had seemed to her at the time that Kelloway's vibrating rage went some way deeper than the flawed Hood affair, as if he were driven by other more subterranean resentments she'd never quite figured out and didn't have the inclination to try.

She said, 'The brass is in evidence, I see.'

'Yeah. I guess he wanted to put in an appearance. The mood to get involved overtakes him. When he's not playing Mussolini at the office.'

Drumm ticked out a list on his fingers. 'OK, this is what we got: two shoes, one with a heel broken. One car, flat tyre. Assorted items of junk-food containers. One map of the United States in the glove box. Clothing and more footwear. Some blood in the vicinity, but significantly no corpse. We did find some dog hair, though.'

Amanda was barely listening. She stared at the car. 'New Mexico plates.'

'Yeah, we ran those already,' Drumm said. 'The car was stolen in Farmington.'

'Farmington?'

'What was she doing in Farmington, you wonder,' Drumm remarked. 'I couldn't even hazard a guess. Where she's been, what brought her back here. The only thing I can come up with is maybe she travelled all the way just to see you, Amanda. She was in some kind of trouble and you were the only one she could turn to.'

'She was supposed to be beyond trouble, Willie. That was the whole point.'

'She didn't trust anyone else but you. God knows, I

spent hours trying to get through to her, but she never told me much. Must be the woman's touch.'

'Must be,' Amanda said. A tuft of dog hair, New Mexico plates, a carload of fast-food wrappers – it was like a list of ingredients you could never turn into a digestible concoction. She tried to picture Isabel driving long frantic distances to see her, ending up out here, panicked and forlorn and alone.

A patrol car appeared out on the flats. It kicked up a storm of orange dust as it approached. A uniformed cop, a sandy-haired, square-faced man with a moustache, stepped out of the car. Amanda recognized him as Sergeant Thomas Gannon.

He nodded at Amanda and said, 'Ms Scholes. Nice to see you again.'

'Sergeant,' she said.

Gannon said to Drumm, 'The tyre tracks you're interested in go way out there into that canyon where it's rough terrain, so we're looking at an off-the-road vehicle for sure. I couldn't take the car up there, no way.'

Amanda gazed off into the foothills again where shadows created sinister pools. The sun burned into her eyes and when she turned her face to the side her sight was streaked with zigzagging lines and flashes.

Drumm said, 'We'll send up a chopper.'

Sergeant Gannon said, 'No stone unturned, Ms Scholes.' He laid the palm of his hand on his pistol. 'I liked the woman.'

'Yeah, we were all fans,' said Drumm with a small forlorn note in his voice.

We were all fans. An epitaph, Amanda thought.

Drumm said, 'I know what you're thinking.'

'You know a lot more than me then.'

'We're gonna have US Marshals from the Program coming in droves. Probably guys from Justice. You can count on that,' Drumm said and touched her arm. 'Your best bet is to walk away. Walk the fuck away and keep walking and don't look back.'

'Or I'll be turned into a pillar of salt,' she said.

'Go live your life with John. Get your priorities straight.'

Amanda went back in the direction of the red VW. She was aware of Kelloway approaching.

'Miss Scholes,' he said.

She turned to him. Sun gleamed on his shaven head. He resembled a predatory bird, the nose a beak created for ripping flesh.

'Morbid curiosity bring you out here?' he asked.

He had a habit of attributing sleazy motives to people.

'I'm curious,' she said. 'Morbid doesn't come into it.'

'I don't need to remind you that this is strictly police business,' he said.

'No, you don't need to remind me.'

'I should hang a sign: "Civilians Keep Out."'

'I have a stake in Isabel,' she said.

'*Had* a stake. Had. Past tense. And I don't want you out here interfering with any of my guys.'

He made it sound like she had sexual molestation of uniformed officers in mind. He was more eclipse than human being, she thought. He enjoyed the dark little satisfactions he got from flexing authority.

'I'd love to chat more with you because it's always such a life-affirming experience, Kelloway, but I'm pushed for time.' She moved past him and sat behind the wheel of her car.

He stuck his face close to the window and smiled. He had a gold filling in an upper-left bicuspid. 'You're history, lady. Remember that. Any rights and privileges you enjoyed before, they're null and void. Your visa's withdrawn. Your credit's wiped.'

'Thanks for reminding me,' she said.

'My, do I hear testy,' Kelloway said and brought his face a little nearer. 'Guess what?'

'Astonish me,' she said.

'Our old acquaintance Hood, the one you figured had a halo round his head?'

'What about him?'

'Busted him last night for illegal possession of firearms and conspiracy to distribute crack cocaine.'

She stared straight ahead. 'I hope it stands up,' she said.

'Oh this one's watertight. This one's not falling apart because of some petty misgivings of the lady prosecutor.'

She turned the key in the ignition. 'They weren't petty, Kelloway.'

'They were piss-ant, and you know it.'

'Up yours,' she said.

She turned the car in a circle and headed for the road. She waved at Drumm and then glanced once in the rear-view mirror and saw Kelloway smile, and then he was gone, leaving a reflection of the barren desert. She drove a few miles before she'd shaken Kelloway completely out of her system.

17

SHE FOUND BASCOMBE IN A COFFEE-SHOP NEAR THE FEDERAL Building. He was halfway through a buttered bagel when she slid into the booth alongside him.

'I see our concerned citizen is also an early bird,' Bascombe said. 'How did you track me down?'

'I asked a secretary. You know why I'm here.'

Bascombe finished his bagel. 'I had a copy of a report from the Phoenix PD filed by Lieutenant Drumm. I know about your desert jaunt last night.'

'There was another jaunt this morning,' she said. 'I just got back from it. She's not out there. If she is, she's buried deep. Drumm had a dozen men looking. Including God, in the form of Kelloway.'

Bascombe sipped his coffee and looked impassive.

Amanda said, 'First Galindez, now Isabel. Face it, there's a serious breakdown here. There's a fatal flaw.'

'Yes, yes, there is,' Bascombe said. He rubbed his eyes, which were faintly bloodshot.

'You sent off your report on Galindez?'

'Immediately after you left my office yesterday

afternoon, a fax went out.'

'You've heard nothing?'

'Amanda, they don't break open the brandy and the cigars because Lew Bascombe happens to send a message. A fax comes through, somebody picks it up, then it has to be directed to the person responsible.'

'What about Isabel? Have you reported that? Did you mention the fact that she phoned me last night in a state of distress?'

'Done. Half an hour ago. Another fax.'

Amanda crushed out her cigarette. 'Did you mark it urgent?'

'I drew attention to the fact that both Galindez and Mrs Sanchez were prosecution witnesses in the Victor Sanchez trial.'

'What does that mean? *Drew attention?*'

'It means I pointed out the background shared between Galindez and Mrs Sanchez. I cross-linked.'

'Is this Fed-speak I'm hearing, Lew?'

'You asked me what I'd done. I told you.'

'Drew their *attention*, for God's sake. *Cross-linked?* Why didn't you come right out and say the security's fucked? Why didn't you phone them? Why didn't you speak to a living human being? A fax. You don't even know if anybody ever receives a fax. They can go off into the ether sometimes. Mars.'

'These things are done by the book,' Bascombe said. 'The book says words on paper. The permanence of a written record.'

'Yesterday you were a rebel, Lew. What happened to you overnight?'

'What I did yesterday was a personal favour to you.'

'And I'm grateful.'

'But I can't ignore the guidelines all the time. I can't just disregard them because some former prosecutor with a

94

bug up her ass breezes into my office.'

'A bug up my ass,' she said. 'That's a goddam funny way of describing my reaction to two dead people.'

'One dead anyway. The other isn't so clear-cut.'

'Because there's no corpse? Lew, I *want* to believe she's still alive, but even if by some remote chance she's wandering around the goddam desert barefoot and seeing visions of the Blessed Virgin on account of dehydration, the fact remains – security is shot. That's what this is all about.'

Amanda lapsed into silence. There was a fuse burning in her head. She could hear it hiss. She lit another cigarette. She smiled at Lewis Bascombe and changed the tone of her voice to something more reasonable. 'OK, I'm calmed down.'

'And better for it,' he remarked.

She kept the smile fixed on her face, but *Jesus* it was an effort. 'If security's on the fritz, Lew, you'd think they'd want to act at once. You'd think they'd go like greased lightning. You'd also think they'd be having a quiet word with Victor Sanchez, seeing as how he's the choice suspect here.'

'They'll talk to Sanchez, Amanda. Obviously he'll be top of their agenda. Just because I haven't heard, it doesn't mean they're not doing anything. Of course they'll act fast. They're not obliged to keep me informed of everything they do. In fact, they don't have to tell me a goddam thing.'

'So you sit in the dark, knowing nothing.'

'I'm just the guy who beats a drum. They hear it, they do something.'

'And they don't tell you what.'

'They don't have to.'

'Secrets and more secrets.'

'That's how they designed it.'

'They didn't design it all that well, did they, Lew? Not if somebody can ferret out witnesses—'

'The best-laid plans.' Bascombe picked up the check, rummaged in his billfold, left a five-dollar bill on the table. 'I have to get back.'

'Tell me one thing, Lew. Is this the end of it? Do we never hear anything again? Do we never get to the root of it all? Why it happened. Why these two people weren't properly protected. How security was breached. Is this where it finishes?'

'I can't even answer a simple question like that,' Bascombe said, and moved towards the door.

Amanda sat for a time after Bascombe had gone, then she rose to leave. She had a moment of dizziness when she stepped outside. Too many cigarettes and no food, the way it had been before she'd quit, before she'd decided to make her break for freedom and good health.

Except she wasn't free. She thought she'd dynamited her way out of the cave.

But she hadn't.

18

IN HIS HOTEL ROOM ANTHONY DANSK FLICKED THROUGH A sex sheet, studying the ads for escort services. He liked hookers because they filled up a space inside. Fast-food sex, hygienic disposable wrapper. He liked how hookers didn't linger after, fishing for affection. They came and went with minimum fuss, just a basic lube job and thanks for the business.

When his phone rang he picked it up and heard McTell say, 'I'm in the bar.'

Dansk left his room, stepped along the corridor and decided to skip the elevator and walk down to the lobby. A little cardiac action did wonders. He believed in physical exercise. He was proud of his body.

The bar was shadowy. McTell, bearded and pale, occupied a table in the middle of the floor. Dansk sat and asked the miniskirted cocktail waitress for a club soda. He didn't like alcohol because it kicked the struts out under your judgement.

Eddie McTell said, 'Done. *Finito*.'

Dansk didn't speak. His drink arrived and the waitress

departed, leaving a pleasing mango fragrance in the air. He followed her skimpy little dress and long legs with his eyes, a reflex action.

'Pussy on stilts, hey,' McTell said.

Dansk ignored this.

McTell said, 'We got her. Out in the desert.'

'Spare me the details,' Dansk said.

'The dogs added a neat touch,' McTell said.

'That's a detail.'

McTell shrugged. 'So we can get out of this town now anyway. This fucking heat, you can keep it.'

Dansk sipped his soda. He looked at McTell's thin face. The beard was an attempt to give the face some hint of intelligence, but it didn't work. It looked glued-on, a spy's beard.

McTell picked up his lager. '*Vaya con dios*,' he said.

Dansk watched McTell slug his drink and asked, 'When you were a kid, how did you see your future?'

'My future? You mean, like ambitions?'

'You must have dreamed of something, McTell. Fireman. Engine driver. Superjock, last-minute touchdown, your pick of the cheerleaders. Making it big some way.'

'I used to be a wizard on ice-skates.'

'You thought hockey. A future in hockey.'

McTell shook his head. 'I tried out for a team in Boston one time, but I guess I lacked some quality they were looking for.'

'Maybe it was grace, McTell.'

'Grace. Yeah, maybe. Funny, my first wife was called Grace. Grace Spatsky. Polack broad with tits out to here.'

Dansk had no interest in McTell's matrimonial history. He said, 'I had a notion of becoming a missionary. Doing good. Working in a leper colony maybe. I used to study maps. Places with names like Chad. The Ivory Coast.'

McTell grinned and stroked his beard. 'A missionary?'

98

'You think that's funny?'

'Just that kids think funny things. No offence.'

Dansk wondered why he'd bothered to mention this childhood fancy to McTell. Everything you said to McTell vanished inside a black hole. It was like sending a message into outer space because McTell was an inferior creature, barely a notch above the kind you saw all the time in K-Marts, pushing carts and surrounded by a squabble of snotty-nosed kids and waddling wives, or in late-night supermarkets stocking up on monster frozen pizzas and a gross of Danish. They lived in trailer parks with broken windows and crooked satellite dishes, or in subsidized housing with cockroaches and graffiti. They gorged themselves on Snickers bars and potato chips. They watched Oprah and thought they were checking the pulse of America. These people operated on weak batteries.

The sad thing, they didn't know they were empty and stupid. They had a certain animal cunning, but in reality they were on this earth to run the errands, to do the dark stuff somebody like Dansk wanted done.

Dansk pushed his glass away. He'd had enough of McTell's company. The beard depressed him, so did the light-blue jacket and the necktie the colour of a dead salmon.

Dansk stood up, reflecting on the fact that in this business you had to work with guys like McTell.

'Me and Pasquale, we'll just head out, I guess,' McTell said.

'Go to Vegas, stay at the usual place,' Dansk said. 'I'll be in touch. There's another piece of work coming up in Seattle.'

Dansk turned to leave.

McTell said, 'Oh yeah, Pasquale shot the dogs. Took them somewhere off the freeway and shot them. Smack between the eyes.'

Dansk knew McTell was telling him this because it might rile him a little. He pictured canine heads blown away and bloody fur. He kept going. In the lobby he passed the concierge's desk, stopped sharply and wheeled back round again. He approached the desk.

The concierge looked at Dansk with the general ass-clenched expression of concierges the world over. There had to be some kind of college where these characters learned how to patronize.

'Can I help you, sir?'

Dansk didn't answer. He picked up a newspaper from the stack on the guy's desk. The *Arizona Republic* with the word 'Complimentary' stamped on it.

'Help yourself,' said the concierge.

'Yeah,' Dansk said.

Halfway down the front page, a single column. There it was. A jolt. He walked back inside the bar.

He stood over McTell and said, 'Forget Vegas. Vegas is off the fucking menu.'

Dansk drew up the chair that was still warm from before and stared at McTell.

'Something wrong?' McTell asked.

Dansk tossed the newspaper down on the table. 'I take it you can read.'

McTell looked at the front page for a time without expression. Dansk snatched the paper back out of his hands and said, 'Let's take a stroll. Get some air.'

'I hate the air around here,' McTell said.

Dansk said, 'Move, Eddie. Don't give me any friction, I'm not in the mood.'

Outside in the heat Dansk sweated: the back of his neck and armpits. His perspiration displeased him. Liquid oozing through pores, impurities leaking from the system. He walked, followed by McTell, until he came to a small square on the edge of downtown where office workers,

100

sprawled here and there on the sunny grass, ate health-conscious lunches. Men in white shirts, women in crisp blouses. They had the look of minor civil servants. They were clocking down their time until it was retirement day. Here's your pension. Enjoy.

A guy in wire-framed glasses laughed at something. The girl who kneeled beside him, a half moon of pitta bread in her skinny hand, spluttered. There was a sense of things in their rightful place and lunches that lasted a regulation thirty minutes and amusing office gossip. Let's kill the supervisor. Let's poison his pastrami sandwich.

Dansk drew a hand across his wet forehead and sat under a shady tree. McTell hunkered down on his heels and let his arms dangle between his legs. Dansk had a feeling of anger so intense it seemed a thing apart from himself, a seething *doppelgänger*, another Anthony in another dimension.

He thrust the newspaper under McTell's nose with such vigour he might have intended to shove it up the man's nostrils. 'Quote unquote. "The body of Reuben Galindez, forty-seven, was found in the Little Colorado River on the Navaho Indian reservation by Sergeant Charles House. Police reports blah, blah, blah, gunshot wound blah, blah, blah. Galindez turned State's evidence against Victor Sanchez et cetera et cetera. Homicide detective Lieutenant William Drumm of the Phoenix Police Department attended the forensic examination in Flagstaff rhubarb, rhubarb. With him was Amanda Scholes, the prosecutor in the sensational trial of Sanchez, now on death row. Neither Lieutenant Drumm nor Miss Scholes were available for comment." '

'Yeah, yeah, I read it, Anthony.'

Dansk said, 'I'm seeing Galindez float down a river like driftwood, and I don't like the image. I don't like it from any angle. I don't like any of this. You didn't tell me this was the way it happened.'

101

McTell said, 'Pasquale shot him, but the current was too fucking fast, and it wasn't like there was a full moon or nothing. We figured maybe he'd—'

'Maybe he'd what? Dissolve in the water like goddam Alka-Seltzer? Or were you under the illusion there were piranha in the river and they'd eat him?'

'Piranha?' McTell smiled his dull brute smile. 'More like decompose someplace, the river bottom, like that.'

'Dead people float, McTell. Unless you weigh them down, they have this unfortunate tendency to surface.'

Dansk sighed and looked up at the sky. How high and blue it was. Up, up and away. McTell acted on his thoughts the way a chunk of Kryptonite affected Superman.

'He drifts down the river, and *then* who enters the picture? Look, *look*. Black and fucking white.'

'So what?'

'So *what*? He's only a homicide cop and she's only the goddam prosecutor whose last case was Victor Sanchez. I'm trying to run a discreet little disposal business here. Some business. Galindez floats out of sight down a fucking river and a woman the size of Minnie Mouse has you running your asses off.'

McTell shuffled his feet in the grass. 'Yeah, but we got her, Anthony.'

'Sure you got her. That's what you're paid for, McTell: getting people. Only now we have a goddam homicide cop *and* this former prosecutor bitch, and they're rolling around inside my head like very loud fucking marbles and I'm thinking, Maybe they're not just gonna drop this matter. Maybe they're gonna be intrigued, McTell.'

'Hey, they're a problem, no sweat, no big deal, we can fix them,' McTell said.

'A homicide cop and a former prosecutor and you can fix them, huh?'

'Listen. Anybody can be fixed.'

'All your solutions come down to the same thing: blow somebody away. Here's a problem, let's blast it into oblivion.'

'Saves time and trouble in the long haul.'

Dansk tried to imagine how Einstein felt in a bus station, say, surrounded by morons. How he felt standing in a cafeteria line for a hot dog and fries and listening to empty drones chatter about last night's soaps.

He looked across the grassy square. He admired how the freshiy laundered office workers gathered up their trash before they left. House-trained. Picky-picky. They worked in smoke-free zones and drank bottled water and belonged to health clubs and had mortgages and good credit ratings. They were respectable, central to the way the country worked. The machinery couldn't turn without them. Politicians drooled for their votes.

He found himself imagining what would happen if a passing gunman opened fire on this bunch just for the sport of it. He saw blood spilling across grass, white shirts red, people screaming and diving for cover, total chaos. He thought of snipers in towers and fertilizer bombs in vans parked outside government buildings and deranged sorts in the badlands who were at odds with revenue officials. This is America, bulletproof vest country, where you don't sit with your back to the door. The nation was bent out of shape.

He rose, brushed blades of grass from his slacks and looked at McTell. What was it about killers, why were they so well-endowed in the vicious department and so challenged when it came to brains? You took what you could find, he thought. It wasn't like you could go down to an employment bureau and ask for assassins. McTell and Pasquale came out of sewers. All they knew was death. It was a limited kind of understanding. They enjoyed killing, it thrilled them. It was their own crazed theatre.

He pondered this, what it would be like to buy a ticket and go inside. Snuff scenes at the Blood Bijou. People blown away. Carnage galore. And maybe when you slept you dreamed of human slaughterhouses and corpses hanging upside down from hooks, skinned and de-veined and raw.

He watched McTell yank a daisy out of the ground and destroy it one petal at a time, and he wondered if flowers felt pain and anguish, if this daisy was screaming at some level beyond the range of human hearing. The thought intrigued him. Noises you couldn't hear, a place beyond the net of the senses.

He said, 'We'll wait, keep an eye on the situation, see what comes up. Then I'll decide. It's not like there's any bonus money in it for giving them the ultimate good-night kiss, McTell.'

'No bonus money?' McTell asked.

'None. And if you don't like that, take it up with your union.'

19

THE FIRST THING AMANDA HEARD WHEN SHE RETURNED TO the house was a female voice. Rhees had a student with him in the living-room, a willowy girl with straight, long blond hair. She looked as if she'd strolled out of a shampoo commercial. A yellow nimbus hung about her.

'Amanda,' Rhees said, 'this is Polly Svensen. Polly's doing post-grad work next semester.'

The student smiled. Amanda smiled back. Polly Svensen was, well, simply stunning. She had the kind of astonishing beauty that quickened men's hearts and sent thrilled whispers running through crowded rooms. Her neck's just a little too long, Amanda thought.

'I didn't expect Professor Rhees to be at home. I was just dropping off my paper,' Polly said. 'I heard he was out of town.'

'Lo and behold,' Amanda said, frost in her voice. 'Here he is. The man himself.'

Polly was all false modesty. She knew she was a knock-out. Slender, five-eleven, faded skin-tight blue jeans and a white halter, and her cute little navel showing. She knew she changed the weather wherever she went.

Rhees frowned at Amanda and said, 'We were just discussing the role of nature in Dylan Thomas.'

'Mmm, interesting,' Amanda said. Rhees had access to a surfeit of girls. He met them one on one in his office, tutorial fashion. She wasn't normally threatened by these academic tête-à-têtes, but today things were just coming at her and she felt defenceless.

She said, 'The force that through the green fuse drives the flower, et cetera.'

Polly said, 'Right. You're familiar with Dylan.'

Dylan. Polly was just the type to be on first-name terms with dead poets.

Amanda said, 'A few lines, that's all.'

'He's worth getting into,' Polly said. 'There's this really marvellous deep underlying green thing. "About the lilting house and happy as the grass was green", you know?'

'And all this time I thought he wrote about jerking off. Goes to show.'

Polly had a distinctive giggle. Somebody had probably told her once it was real neat, so she reproduced it whenever she could.

Rhees got up from the table and cleared his throat. He indicated with a gesture of his head that he wanted a moment of privacy with Amanda. He went into the kitchen and Amanda followed. He shut the door and crossed his arms.

'You're being rude,' he said.

'Am I?'

'You know you are.' Rhees reached out and touched her shoulder. 'This isn't like you, Amanda.'

'Well,' she said, and shrugged.

'You sneaked off at dawn without saying where you

were going. I can guess anyway.'

Amanda opened a closet door, rummaged around and said, 'I thought we had some Grahams here. Polly might want a cracker.'

'Unworthy scold,' Rhees said.

Amanda slammed the closet door shut. 'She's young and she's like some goddess. Her hair goes all the way down to her ass, for Christ's sake. What planet's she from?'

'Come here.' Rhees spread his arms and Amanda fell into them and shut her eyes. Rhees, her harbour. 'Polly's mostly bubbles, you're more my ideal.'

'How can I be anybody's ideal? Look at me.'

'You get better all the time, Amanda. I have you up on a pedestal.'

'I'm too heavy for your pedestal. I feel overweight and sluggish. And this.' She tugged at her brown hair, letting it slide through her fingers. 'They didn't find Isabel, John. They looked and they looked.'

'Maybe . . .' he said.

'Maybe what?'

'She's still out there somewhere.'

Amanda remembered the grains of dirt damp with blood. Rhees was trying to force open a little window of optimism in the face of evidence to the contrary. He was good at finding silver linings in the gloom. Please God let this be one of those silver linings. Let her be alive.

Rhees kissed her forehead. 'I'll give Polly the benefit of my wisdom, which should take all of seven or eight minutes, then we're out of here and heading north. How does that sound?' He moved towards the kitchen door. 'Before I forget, some reporter from the *Phoenix Gazette* phoned. Wanted to know if you had anything to add to the story of the Galindez discovery.'

'I hope you told him I was incommunicado.'

'My lips were sealed.'

Rhees left the kitchen.

Amanda's head hurt and she had an acid sensation in her stomach and a general sense of malaise, a weakening inside, as if her immune system was flagging. She looked out into the backyard. Neglected grass grew long in ragged brown stalks and butterflies flapped here and there, settling where the mood took them.

She watched for a time. She thought about Isabel. She couldn't cancel the thought out. She couldn't flutter away from it like one of those mercurial butterflies.

She walked into the bathroom, opened the cabinet, ransacked through a collection of bottles. Say hello to the old gang: ginseng, zinc capsules, iron, the whole spectrum of B-vitamins, garlic tabs, fortified C, some kind of painkiller. It was a regular health arsenal. She scooped out pills and downed them with water.

Then she put her hand in the hip pocket of her jeans and took out Isabel Sanchez's plastic hair-clasp and studied it. It caught the sunlight streaming through the bathroom window. There were people in the world reputed to be able to locate buried corpses by caressing their possessions, but she wasn't one of them.

She had a mechanic's eye, not a mystic's.

She walked up and down the kitchen for a time before she dialled Directory Assistance, and wrote down the number she was given by the operator. Then she dialled it.

A man answered and introduced himself as Donald Scarfe.

She said, 'Don, this is Amanda Scholes.'

'We-ell, Amanda,' Scarfe said, 'it's been an age. What can I do you for?'

'I need to come see you.'

Scarfe said, 'You know the way.'

Amanda hung up. She left the kitchen by the back door, so that Rhees wouldn't see her. He wasn't going to be overjoyed about this stunt.

20

THE WINDOW OF DONALD SCARFE'S OFFICE IN THE FLORENCE facility looked out over a hazy view of desert mountains in the distance. There was another vista directly below: the compound, watch-towers, barbed wire, high walls.

The compound was empty. Amanda glanced down, seeing shadows pressed against concrete. The watch-towers made her uneasy. Guards in shadows with guns. The penitentiary was a volatile place, heavy with violent potential.

'So you think he contracted out a killing,' Scarfe said.

'Everything points that way, Don.'

Donald Scarfe was tall and gaunt and his face had been hammered and dried by too much sunlight. He'd always reminded Amanda of a weathered fence post at the edge of a dry prairie. He wore a white short-sleeved shirt and a turquoise bola necktie, and looked more like somebody's idea of a middle-aged rodeo rider than an associate warden of a prison.

Amanda walked to the water-cooler in the corner of Scarfe's office and filled a dixie cup. She drank hastily. 'Mind if I smoke?'

Scarfe pointed to a no-smoking sign. 'Sorry.'

'It's OK. More and more I feel like a leper anyway.' She crushed the dixie cup and dropped it inside a wastebasket. She looked at Scarfe for a time. She'd met him at various seminars on penal policy and law-enforcement strategies several times during the last few years, and she'd liked his attitude, which was liberal, compared to the prevailing hard-assed positions concerning the treatment of prisoners. Stick them in goddam tents and let them sweat and feed them pig slop.

'I don't have any objection to this visit,' he said. 'I don't know what you expect to come of it, that's all.'

'I'm not anticipating a confession,' she said.

'So what are you expecting?'

'I don't know,' she said.

'You think you can tune into him, is that it?'

'I'm not sure, Don. Has anybody been to see him recently? Any visitors?'

'He doesn't get visitors, Amanda.'

Amanda looked at her watch. It was three-thirty in the afternoon. She remembered what Willie Drumm had said. *We're gonna have US marshals from the Program coming in droves. Probably guys from Justice.* So why hadn't anyone arrived yet? Bascombe's first message to Arlington, concerning Galindez, had gone out twenty-four hours ago. His second must have been received around noon today Eastern Time. And what had Bascombe himself said? *Of course they'd act fast.*

Bureaucrats. They doodled while cities caught fire. They shuffled papers as volcanoes erupted. Perhaps they were still studying Bascombe's messages. Or perhaps somebody was in transit even now. She had no way of knowing.

'Are you up for this?' Scarfe asked. 'You look a little out of sorts.'

'It was a hot drive down here,' she said.

Scarfe shrugged and picked up one of the two telephones on his desk. He pressed a button and spoke to somebody. 'Chuck. Escort Prisoner eight eight sixty around to the interview room, would you? I'm bringing along a visitor. I want an armed guard in the room for the duration.'

Scarfe put down the telephone. He opened a drawer and took out a small laminated badge with the word 'Visitor' on it. She pinned it to her shirt.

'I'll walk with you,' Scarfe said. 'I ought to warn you though. He's been trouble from the start. He attacked another inmate with a screwdriver, which of course can't be proved because nobody saw anything. Punctured one of the guy's lungs.'

'He's a charmer,' she said.

'And last week he torched another guy's cell. He thought it was funny.'

'Offbeat sense of humour.'

'Black, anyway. I guess if you're living where he's living, nothing matters a damn in the end.'

They left the office and stepped into a long chilled corridor. Halfway down, she stopped. She was approaching a transition here, a crossroads, choices. She had only to change her mind, turn round, walk back to the car, drive away and leave things be.

She moved forward.

The bridge was crossed and burning behind her and the fumes had a bitter-sweet smell, and she thought she detected in the smoke the strange scent of her apprehension at the idea of being in the company of Prisoner 8860.

21

THE INTERVIEW ROOM, A TABLE AND A FEW CHAIRS AND A one-way observation window, smelled of floorwax. Overhead was a solitary fluorescent strip. Amanda, glad to see an ashtray on the table, lit a cigarette at once.

The door opened and Victor Sanchez, accompanied by an armed guard, a bullet-headed man with a long jaw, was led inside. The guard took up a position in the corner. Sanchez, with a slow motion imposed upon him by his ankle-shackles, shuffled to a chair and sat facing Amanda.

'The lady prosecutor,' he said. 'Life's all surprises.'

He was dressed in loose prison garb. He was sleek, muscular, handsome, more than 6 feet tall. He had long eyelashes that curled, and eyes the colour of a midnight with no moon. Girls would swoon and drown in those eyes. Isabel had.

'Smoke?' Amanda pushed the pack across the table. Her hand shook a little and she tried to still it.

'I conquered the habit,' he said. 'This a social visit or what?'

'No, not social.' Isabel had often referred to her former

113

husband as Ángel, pronounced Anyel. It was a stretch to think of Sanchez as *anyelic*. He was spun out of darkness, a creature of vicious whim. If he had wings, they took him on flights into dismal regions of his own making. Celestial destinations weren't on Ángel's itinerary.

Amanda glanced at the guard, whose name tag identified him as Holland E. He was staring at a bare wall.

'How's prison life?' she asked.

'It's a ball. We got some real fuckwits there. Real clowns.' Sanchez gave her his withering look. She was determined to hold the gaze and not flinch, even though she was thinking about the border guards Sanchez had executed. He'd made them kneel and then shot them directly into their open mouths. Galindez, whose evasive manner in court had made him a less plausible witness than Isabel, had testified to this. Sanchez had ordered the guards to pray for mercy, then slaughtered them anyway. *Like a coupla lambs. Bleeding all over the place.*

'I guess it's not easy stuck in here,' she said. 'You appealing against the sentence?'

'I'm appealing any way you look at it.' He was amused. His smile was lethal. The sculpted body and the bronze skin were just extra tinsel on the Christmas tree. In another reality he might have been a male model of the Latin variety, white linen suit and two-tone shoes, strutting his stuff on the catwalk.

'What you here for anyway?' he asked. 'Talk about my sentence? Hey, maybe you got a pardon tucked in your pocket. You got a chit from the Governor or what?'

'No pardon, Victor. Just some loose ends.'

'I'm a loose end, huh?'

'Tell me how you got to them.'

'Got to who? You talk in puzzles, lady.'

'You don't have any idea what I'm driving at, I suppose.'

Sanchez laid a hand flat on his thigh. 'I like puzzles. I

got this book with all these scrambled words in them and stuff, also join the dots and get a fucking donkey or eagle. I do crosswords. It gets pretty damn thrilling, I gotta say.'

'It's not crosswords I have in mind,' she said.

'You know what I think of you?'

Amanda shook her head. 'I don't read minds.'

Sanchez moved the hand on his thigh. 'Kinda proper, kinda aloof. But hot in the sack. Whooeee,' and he waved his hand loosely, as if his fingertips had been scalded.

'Games, Victor. I'm not playing.'

'What are you? Fortysomethin'? Late thirties? A lady in prime time, ripe and ready for plucking.'

'Is this the bit where you grab your crotch?' she asked.

'I watched you in court. You gave me these looks.'

'Chief among them was contempt.'

'Contempt my ass.'

'This may come as a surprise to you, but I don't see you as God's gift.'

'Know how many women I fucked in my life? Running close to fifteen hundred.'

'I bet you got testimonial letters from all of them.'

'I got no complaints. Most came back for more of the same, and some screamed with pleasure,' he said.

'Except when you were cutting off their nipples, I guess.'

Sanchez made a snorting sound. 'You believe that cunt's story? She walks into court like a Madonna, and she sits there and every time she opens her mouth out comes another lie.'

'She blackened your character, huh?'

'She fucking charbroiled me,' he said.

Amanda was silent a moment. Sanchez had led her on a detour and she'd followed. She was being drawn into areas of no relevance. She said, 'Let's backtrack, Victor.'

'You were talking puzzles, I remember.'

'You were the one talking puzzles. I was asking you how you did it.'

'I heard that tune already. Did what?'

'Galindez. Your ex-wife. You know what I'm talking about.'

'Pair of fucking vipers,' he said.

'How did you get to them, Victor?'

'Get to them how?'

'How did you have them killed?'

Sanchez pushed his chair back. 'Killed? You're saying they're dead?'

'Galindez for sure. He was shot through the heart. Isabel maybe. That's what I'm saying.'

Sanchez tilted his head back and stared at the ceiling. He moved his feet and the shackles rattled. He laughed, then he slumped back in his chair and his arms dangled at his sides and he looked serious. 'How do you mean Isabel maybe?'

'Just what I said. Isabel maybe.'

'Explain that to me.'

'Your people might have slipped up with her, I don't know yet.' A slim prospect, she thought, but sometimes you grabbed at such things because you wanted to hold on to a belief, no matter how marginal.

'My people? Meaning what?'

'The guys you hired. How did you arrange it? That's what I want to know.'

'Arrange it? That what you think?'

'That's my general inclination, Victor.'

'Look, lady, I sit in a cell and I do these puzzles in the book I got. It's a confined life.'

'Somehow you got a message to somebody,' she said.

'Oh sure, same way they allow me to send out for Domino's pizza and call-girls.'

He propped his elbows on the table and stared at her.

116

Discomfited by the troubling black of his eyes, she was silent a moment. Sanchez lied instinctively. He probably considered truth a form of weakness.

She said, 'You wanted vengeance. You had the motive, Victor.'

'Sure I wanted vengeance. I sit in my cell and I dream up these real slow painful deaths for them, when I'm not joining fucking dots. If dreaming's a crime, I ain't been told. What you gonna do? Slap *another* death sentence on me?'

'They were in the Witness Protection Program, Victor,' she said. 'So how did you reach them?'

'Lady, you got a serious listening problem.'

What could you tell from Sanchez's expressions? What could you read into the body language? She shook a cigarette out of the pack and flicked her lighter. She was getting nothing here. She watched him tap his fingers on the table and had an impression of great energy held in check, but only just.

'For the sake of argument, let's take this big leap and imagine you didn't do it,' she said. 'You got any idea who did?'

He shrugged. 'Nope.'

'Try a little harder, Victor.'

'What you want from me?'

'The truth.'

'The truth is what I been telling you.'

'I wonder why I'm not buying it.'

'Like I give a fuck.'

Sanchez smiled at her. She saw slyness in the expression, complicity even, or maybe he was a mirror in which you saw any reflection you wanted. 'You say I done it. OK, you figure it out, you're the brains. Me, I'm a common criminal. I'm lowlife.'

Sanchez gestured for her to lean a little closer to him, as

if he wanted to say something in confidence. She inclined her head warily and drew her chair nearer to the table. She was conscious of his overwhelming physical presence, the way he projected himself. She imagined how women would go for this. You could look into Sanchez's eyes and see nothing there but romance and sea cruises and breezes blowing through chiffon and prolonged lovemaking, sometimes tender, sometimes brutal, in the penthouse cabin.

His hand rose and his fingertips touched her lips gently, and she didn't move, she held his eyes, smelled cheap prison soap on his fingers. This touch might arouse some kid, a naïve girl like Isabel or the 1,500 others he'd boasted about. She felt the hairs on the back of her neck go cold even as she knew it was important she didn't move away from him, that she meet him as far as she could on his own terms, whatever they were. Then he parted her lips and touched her teeth. He had long fingers. Those same fingers had taken a razor-blade to Isabel's breast. Don't forget that. She hoped he suffered in his cell. She hoped he had times of dread. She wanted him to have bad dreams. Seeing himself strapped down in a gurney and wheeled inside the execution chamber, the IV drip attached to an open vein, the lethal concoction entering his bloodstream, and then goodbye, good riddance.

The maintenance of eye contact stressed her, and suddenly she was plunged back inside that foul courtroom, her head aching, nose stuffy, a drum pounding in her brain and the judge's gavel striking wood.

He whispered to her. 'Say, maybe you could kinda accidentally drop something on the floor, and when you bend down and pick it up you could find some way of entertaining me, then maybe I'll confess to anything you like . . .'

The guard said, 'Hey, Romeo. No contact. You know the rules.'

'Yes*sir*, Mr Holland.' Sanchez drew his hand back with exaggerated slowness. It was the motion of a man who didn't care about a goddam thing, who had nothing but disdain for authority, for the world.

Amanda stood up quickly, walked to the observation window and crossed her arms. She could still feel the lingering impression of his fingertips. *He can get to you even when you despise him*. She ran the back of her hand across her lips: an act of erasure, a small exorcism. But she felt vaguely askew, thrown off centre by Sanchez and that strange unwanted intimacy. The way he'd whispered. The way he'd imposed himself. Drop something, go down on your knees, entertain me while you're down there.

She strolled round the table.

He said, 'I don't have to answer your goddam questions. What's in it for me anyhow? Half an hour's exercise in the yard, maybe my own TV with multi-channels and a remote control? Big fucking deal. Suppose you gimme one good reason I should help you. You put me in this shithole.'

'You put yourself here, Victor. I was only doing my job.'

'Yeah, yeah, yeah, your job. Instrument of justice. Blindfold bitch. Fuck *you*.' Sanchez stared at her, challenging her.

She watched him a moment in silence, but now she couldn't hold his eyes because his look was hard and heartless and impossible to meet. She imagined that same expression on his face when he shot the border guards.

She turned away, feeling a tightness in her head. 'Let's see if we can put together a scenario, Victor. Let's say you managed to acquire some information. You got to some-body inside the Witness Program. Say you dangled the kind of money this somebody couldn't turn down. In return, you get Galindez's location, and Isabel's.'

'And I manage to do all this business from my fucking cell with no phone,' he said.

119

'You arranged it before the trial. You put it all together before the verdict.'

'Wow. And how did I manage all this?'

'I don't know how, but I'm close, Victor. I'm on track. Right?'

Sanchez laughed suddenly, then he stopped and his face was icy. He could go from tropical to arctic in a flash. She looked at him again, but it was still difficult to hold his gaze because it was as if he had some kind of electric force field around him, and if you listened hard enough you could hear a tiny little sizzle of danger.

He stood up and gestured to the guard. 'Holland, I'm through here. Take me home, country roads.'

'Wait,' she said.

'Wait for what? I don't have a whole lotta time, lady.'

She wondered how he could look that good and be so monstrous. Skin deep. Go down through the epidermal layers and keep going and you encounter a black heart, an unlit chamber.

She said, 'Nobody else had the motive, Victor.'

'Motive ain't proof, something you ought to know.'

'You're the only one,' she said.

He looked up at the ceiling a moment, then he moved. She hadn't expected it, nor had the guard. Despite the inhibition of the shackles, Sanchez acted with surprising agility. He lunged, bringing his forehead down hard on Holland's face. Amanda heard bone break and saw Holland drop to his knees, blood pouring from his nostrils. Sanchez turned quickly and with sheer brute strength forced her back against the wall, his solid forearm pressed like an iron bar to her throat. An alarm bell was ringing somewhere in the building. She heard it distantly because the pressure of Sanchez's arm was squeezing the air out of her and there was a roaring inside her head. She beat against the sides of his face with her fists but he wasn't troubled by her efforts, he just kept smiling, his expression one of – what? Some dark joy? A kind of twisted glee? He brought his face down close, his mouth almost touching hers. His breath smelled of toothpaste. She was conscious of how her knees touched his and the way he had his body pressed against her. Weird little lights fizzed in her vision.

He whispered, 'Bad things come in threes, lady. You ever hear that saying? Two down, you can guess the rest. Keep it in mind.'

Holland had recovered his balance and taken his gun from the holster. His face was covered with blood. He said, 'Motherfucker,' and struck Sanchez on the back of the skull, but the blow didn't alter Sanchez's expression. The smile was fixed and immutable and dreadful. More guards were clattering into the room, three or four heavyweight types. One of them applied a stranglehold around Sanchez's neck and dragged him away from Amanda, another battered his ribs with a night-stick. Sanchez, covering his head with his hands, fell to the floor and lay in a foetal position. The guards circled him, kicked him a few times, then hauled him to his feet. His body limp, he looked at Amanda, who was trying to catch her breath and fight against the sensation of blackness that raged in her head.

'Remember,' he said.

She watched him being led out of the room. She heard the rattle and clank of the shackles and the sound of his laughter, then the swift crack of a night-stick, and after that there was silence from the corridor.

Donald Scarfe had appeared. 'Jesus. Are you OK?'

'Shocked, I guess,' she said. She coughed a few times into her hand.

'You need a medic? I'll call for one.'

She shook her head. Her legs felt like they were made of air. 'Nothing's broken. I'll be OK.'

'I was in the observation room,' Scarfe said. 'Then it all happened so fast. I should never have given permission for this—'

'Don, it's OK, I'm *fine*.' But it wasn't OK. She leaned against the table, shaken, light-headed, breathing a little too quickly. She lit a cigarette anyhow, imagined smoke swirling round her lungs as if she were seeing a live-action X-ray of herself.

'You heard the last thing he said?' she asked.

'He says things just to make your head spin.'

'Bad things come in threes. You heard that.'

'I'd take it with a pinch of salt, Amanda.'

Two down, she thought. *Bad things come in threes. You know the rest. Two down, one to go*. She had images of Galindez's white hand and his ruby ring and Isabel's blood and her cheap pink barrette, and she thought of herself lying on a coroner's slab and Rhees having to identify her. Bad things.

In the corridor fluorescent tubes hummed. She felt they were buzzing inside her.

'What now?' Scarfe asked.

What now. She wasn't sure. She felt hot and run-down and something else, something new, *scared*, and she'd have to drive home through relentless sunlight in a world that had abruptly shifted and cracked under her feet. She looked at Scarfe, but she said nothing. She was thinking of the smell of Victor Sanchez's breath and feeling the leaden weight of his arm and how the air had been crushed out of her. And she was hearing his words, over and over.

22

DANSK SAT IN HIS CAR IN THE CUL-DE-SAC AND WATCHED THE house. A dead-end street was a bad environment for surveillance. Traffic entering the street, eight houses on either side and one at the end, was usually local. A stranger who sat too long in his car would draw attention. Somebody would jot down his licence number, maybe even make a phone call to the local cops.

All the windows had little yellow or blue security stickers attached. Some were barred, others had steel shutters. This was profitable territory for the merchants of fear that sold home-safety systems.

The house Dansk watched was the last one on the left. He was parked diagonally across from it. It was the only house with an unruly garden out front. Some care was needed here, a little pride. There were neighbours to think about, the general appearance of the street, property values.

He looked at his watch. He didn't want to spend more than twenty minutes max in this place, any longer was folly, even twenty was stretching it.

He had a clipboard to which was attached a number of invoice sheets with the name of a dummy pharmaceutical company, and he started ticking items off with his pen and trying to seem occupied, like a salesman or a delivery guy catching up on a backlog of paperwork.

It was a strange thing about people. If they saw you with a clipboard they tended to glaze you out, thinking you were on some kind of legitimate business and unthreatening.

His cellular phone rang and he picked it up.

Pasquale had a voice like somebody coming down from a helium infusion: high-pitched, a little husky. 'On the way, Anthony. Maybe two minutes.'

'Right.' Dansk hung up and waited. He saw the car turn into the cul-de-sac, then it passed him and he watched it enter the driveway of the house with the overgrown garden.

He saw her get out.

She wore a navy-blue shirt and jeans. She swept a hand through her short brown hair. There was a slightly distracted frown on her face. Halfway up the path she stopped and plucked a leaf off a eucalyptus tree and sniffed it as if it were a rare perfume. Faces intrigued Dansk. This woman, for example. She wasn't what Dansk would call conventionally attractive. Good-looking in an idiosyncratic way, determined jaw, cheeks a little fleshy. She wasn't the type he went for. For one thing she had tits, and Dansk liked his women scrawny. He liked bones and angled structures and skinny hips. Another thing, she was outside his age limit. He preferred eighteen, seventeen. This one was what – forty?

But you never know. He wouldn't kick her out of bed. An upholstered lady might be a change.

Smile more, he thought. Add a little make-up, change the hairdo, a touch of colour – sienna, say, or something outrageous and bright. Blond with a small pink streak. Turn a few heads.

She needed to pay attention to her posture. Too many years hunched over law books, hunting down precedents. Pick yourself up, inject a little elegance, ditch the blue jeans, and navy isn't your colour anyway. Get the best out of yourself. Nice ass, all the same. Usually at her age asses drooped, but hers looked firm.

He thought, I don't want to bring anything bad into your life, so don't make me. You're probably intelligent, concerned, dedicated. Don't be dedicated to the wrong things.

He leaned forward against the wheel, watching. She'd stopped again, like she was reluctant to go inside the house. What was it? Indecision? A forgotten door key?

A guy came out of the house.

Dansk was surprised because he'd somehow thought the place empty. The man was tall and on the lean side. Black jeans, a white shirt, thick dark hair going grey at the sides. He said something to the woman and she shook her head and Dansk sensed friction. The guy took a few steps towards her. The woman didn't move.

Who was the guy? Her lover?

On the one hand that might be problematic, on the other it might be nothing. It depended on the woman. Everything depended on her.

They were embracing now, repairing whatever was damaged between them. Dansk watched the guy's hand drop to the woman's ass. An easy intimacy. Dansk wondered how her laugh would sound. He imagined smoky and sincere, something you might hear at a crowded party and it would take your attention for a moment because of its hearty, good-natured quality.

Dansk never went to parties, never received invitations. He watched the man slip an arm round the woman's

125

shoulders and then they kissed, which involved an awkward craning movement downwards for the guy. They went inside the house – heading for the bedroom, he imagined. He zoomed in on an image of clothes cast aside, a clasp of bodies, the hot damp flesh of love, and the smells.

He drove out of the cul-de-sac. He went through downtown Scottsdale, took a turn off the main drag and found himself in a street of art galleries. Overpriced canvasses in windows, Native American Indian influence everywhere, Navaho and Hopi art, beads and goodies plundered from the reservations.

He kept driving. The early evening sky was leaking light.

Eventually he found the place he was looking for. It was a bar called Floozies that advertized topless girls. Inside, he found a big gloomy room doing nothing in the way of business – it was too early for the topless crew. The place smelled of spilled beer and the floor wasn't clean. Typical.

McTell and Pasquale occupied a table close to the stage, which was concealed behind a silver curtain decorated with naked women. Dansk sat down near a set of spangled red drums and a Yamaha keyboard.

McTell stroked his beard and said, 'She was at Florence for three quarters of an hour, I timed it. She drove down there on her own. I didn't see any sign of this Drumm character. She went straight inside the slammer unaccompanied.'

Dansk looked round for the bartender and couldn't find him. There was no decent service in this country any more, everything was bad manners and have-a-nice-day insincerity. He said, 'She saw Sanchez.'

'That a question?' McTell asked.

'She goes down to Florence. Who else is she going to see?' He thought of the woman visiting Sanchez. So she

126

was working up an interest. She was pursuing something she should leave alone. Too much persistence. Probably engrained in her. Her world hung by a thread and she didn't even know it. Drumm hadn't gone with her, so maybe she was just poking around on her own.

Pasquale fiddled with a paper napkin. He folded it once, then a second time, and suddenly he had a little paper animal which he set on the table. It might have been a horse or a tiger, you couldn't tell. Whatever, it was sturdy, well-made. Dansk observed Pasquale's dark suit and white open-necked shirt. He had a thick lower lip and was overweight by about 15 pounds. He had long elegant fingers and his hair was grey-yellow, with sideburns. He wore a gold pendant round his neck.

Dansk watched a guy come in and sit down behind the drums. He tapped the cymbals then cracked his knuckles one at a time. Dansk closed his eyes. Here he was in this tit and ass joint in the company of killers and a guy was cracking his knuckles, which was a sound that affected him like chalk squealing on a blackboard. Here he was sitting in a goddam drain with a sleazy curtain tattooed with nudes. He thought, This is what I do. This is how I make my nut.

McTell said, 'Why don't we blow the whole thing off and split? Why are we hanging here anyhow? You said we had other work.'

Dansk's patience was approaching meltdown. 'We need to know what she does, who she sees. How her behaviour might affect us. Information, Eddie. Know who you're dealing with. The more you know, the less likely an error of judgement. Suppose we split right now. Suppose we just get the fuck out. We don't have a clue what she and the cop might get up to behind our backs, do we? You see the problem?'

McTell nodded. He had a flat, almost concave forehead.

He said, 'So she saw Sanchez. What's he gonna tell her? He's gonna laugh right in her fucking face.'

Dansk, hugely irritated by the world in a general way, turned to the guy at the drums and said, 'You intend to sit there tugging on your bones all night, fella?'

The knuckle-cracker had a weak lopsided smile. 'What's that?'

'That knuckle business,' Dansk said. 'It's frankly irritating.'

'Yeah? You got a problem with it?'

'I won't, soon as you get out of my sight.'

The knuckle-cracker looked at Dansk. If he was contemplating a verbal come-back, whatever he saw in Dansk's eyes made him change tack. 'OK, sorry, sorry, man. No sweat. I'll go sit on the other side of the room. Sorry.'

Dansk watched the guy slink away. The world was filled with nuisances, fringe disturbances, little whirlpools of agitation. All kinds of stuff he just didn't need.

He looked at Pasquale and McTell. They were watching him, waiting for instructions.

He said, 'I'll work the woman myself. Pasquale, you stay in your motel and watch cartoons until I need you.'

McTell asked, 'What about me?'

'There's a guy in her life, find out about him. Who he is, what he does. Just go gentle, if you know how.'

'Got it,' McTell said.

'OK.' Dansk rose. He wandered outside into the heat. A mandarin moon was suspended in the sky. He walked to his car, remembering the way Amanda had sniffed the eucalyptus leaf. He wondered if he could change the direction of his life through some perfumed avenue.

Dream on. Once you were in this line of work there was no way out. You made your living out of the dead.

23

THE RESTAURANT IN NORTH SCOTTSDALE WAS FRENCH. RHEES
had suggested the place. He liked his meat rare, bloody
juices swimming on the plate.

Amanda saw a misty reflection of herself in the
mahogany panel behind Rhees's head. They'd made love
earlier and she'd detected in him a certain restraint. He'd
been tense, and the absence of his usual verbal passion
bothered her. Rhees never made love silently. Speech, even
whispered in the incoherent language of lovers, was inte-
gral to the act where he was concerned.

'Are you still annoyed?' she asked.

'Yeah, I'm still annoyed. You sneaked off to see Sanchez
without telling me.'

She looked down at the remains of her saffron rice,
bright yellow on the plate. 'OK, I sneaked off. I knew
you'd disapprove, so I didn't tell you I was going.'

'Share things with me, that's all I ask.'

She rubbed the back of his hand. 'I didn't ask for this
situation, John.'

Rhees folded his napkin and placed it over the lamb

bones and stared at her. 'So why bother with it?'

'Because it just fell in my lap and it's messy.'

'But not your mess. You gave your word to Isabel, fine, admirable, honorable. But she quit being your responsibility as soon as the trial was finished. What were you supposed to do? Hold her hand for the rest of her life? Maybe she should have moved in with us and you could have kept an eye on her twenty-four hours a day. Besides, I seem to remember all you were going to do was talk to Bascombe. In and out, you said. Toot sweet.' Blood seeped through Rhees's napkin. 'What did Sanchez tell you anyhow?'

'Nothing,' she said. She hadn't described the meeting to Rhees because she knew he'd react with horror. She played with a spoon, turning it over and over, remembering the way Sanchez had acted, bringing back the disturbing shock of the moment, focusing on the violence of the encounter: Sanchez forcing her against the wall, the blow of the gun on his head, the rap of a night-stick.

She thought about his threat, and suddenly there was an underlying strata of vulnerability. Faces in this restaurant, for instance. How could she know they were harmless? For all she could tell, at least one of them might be a Sanchez operative, watching, waiting.

She stopped herself. She let Donald Scarfe's words play through her head as if they were a kind of balm. *He says things just to make your head spin. A pinch of salt.* But Sanchez returned unprompted. *Bad things come in threes.* What credence could she give Victor Sanchez's threat?

'He's into games,' was all she finally said.

'Did you expect anything else?'

'Not really.'

Rhees caught a waiter's eye and asked for the dessert menu and chose a meringue basket of pears baked in sherry. Amanda wanted only coffee. The waiter came

130

back and Rhees plunged his spoon into the dessert. She enjoyed watching him eat. He did it with gusto.

'That's a mountain to get through, John.'

'I somehow worked up an appetite earlier.'

Amanda said, 'I don't understand why he hadn't been interviewed by anyone from the Program when I saw him.'

'You're dealing with a bureaucracy.'

'But this is a situation where you'd expect rapid response.'

'Maybe they're talking to him even as we sit here.'

'What I'd really like is to talk in person to somebody who works inside the Program,' she said. 'Get some straight answers, if there are such things.'

'You think that kind of access is possible?'

'Anything's possible if you go at it the right way,' she said. She picked up her napkin and dabbed Rhees's lower lip. 'You've got a stray morsel there.'

'Yes, Mother.'

'I can request a meeting,' she said. 'It's not like I just drifted in off the streets and I'm sticking my nose in. I'm an interested party.'

She dropped a cube of sugar into her coffee and stirred. Rhees said, 'Here, sample this.' He held his spoon to her lips. She tasted, found the meringue sickeningly sweet and the pears heavy on the sherry.

'Unadulterated cholesterol,' she said.

'Clogs the arteries. Slows the rush of blood to your head and makes you sluggish in your thinking.'

'Which is what you want, of course.'

'You know how I feel, Amanda.' He called for the check then went off to the men's room. He was gone a long time. When he came back they walked outside to the parking-lot. The night was filled with hot dark enclosures beyond the beacons of lamplight that streamed up into the palm

131

trees around the restaurant. There was the illusion of an electrified oasis. She didn't care for the shadows between the lights.

Rhees said, 'I think you're happy back in the swing again. The old pizazz. You never really wanted out of it in the first place, did you?'

'I wouldn't be too sure,' she said.

'You haven't forgotten that the razzmatazz comes at a price, sweetheart,' he said. 'Just keep that in mind before you start digging deeper into this whole wretched business.'

Digging: it was what she'd been trained to do in law school. Spade and shovel, examine the debris that came out of the earth, discard what was irrelevant and store what was useful. Legal archaeology. She hooked her arm through John's and, raising her face, kissed him. She found some very slight resistance in the kiss, almost as if he were trying to distance himself from her, but then he yielded, put his arms around her and drew her against him.

24

FIRST THING IN THE MORNING, AMANDA TELEPHONED Donald Scarfe. 'Has Sanchez had any visitors yet?' she asked.

'You were the last,' he replied.

'No requests? No enquiries?'

'None so far.'

'That's all I wanted to know, Don. Thanks.'

'How are you today anyway?'

'I'm over the shock,' she said.

'I still blame myself, Amanda.'

'I absolve you totally, Don. I was the one that asked to go into the lion's den.'

Next, she punched in Bascombe's number.

'I haven't had my coffee,' Bascombe told her. 'I'm a goddam bear before that first cup.'

She was using the phone in the kitchen. The morning was rainy and humid and the long stalks of grass in the backyard buckled. A break in the weather. She liked rain.

'Explain this, Lew,' she said. 'Why hasn't anyone been down to see Sanchez? Has somebody at Program control

133

overlooked the connection between Sanchez and the two allegedly "safe" witnesses?'

Bascombe said, 'I sent the messages, Amanda. I don't have any say in the follow-up.'

'It's not acceptable, Lew.'

'You're speaking with your prosecutor's voice, Amanda.'

She watched Rhees, in a knee-length robe, put two slices of bread in the toaster. He poured a cup of coffee and sat at the table gazing out of the window.

'Lew, you might be quite comfortable working away in the dark, but it isn't a situation I find conducive to my peace of mind.'

'I'm not sure your peace of mind matters a damn to the people in Arlington,' he said.

'Did they acknowledge your messages?'

'We've been here before, Amanda.'

'I understand that. I'm just not very happy. In fact, I'm pissed. I don't like the way this thing works, if it works at all.'

'I hate it when I have to deal with shrill women first thing.'

'I am not being shrill, Lew.'

'Yes you are.'

'This is like trying to get through a brick wall,' she said.

'I can send off another message, see what happens.'

'Make it different this time. Add this rider: the former prosecutor wants a face to face with somebody in the Witness Program admin. And I'm not kidding, Lew.'

'You don't know what you're asking.'

'I know exactly what I'm asking.'

'They'll refuse.'

'Not if you mention that I intend to raise holy hell about the whole thing.'

'Meaning?'

134

She took a deep breath to ease the knot of pressure in her chest. 'It's really simple, Lew. Galindez has already made the papers, but the story didn't say anything about how he was supposed to be in the Program, nice and safe. And Isabel hasn't made the papers at all yet. All it takes is for me to phone some avid journalist and give an in-depth, behind-the-scenes account. Big problem with the Witness Protection Program, it leaks like a goddam sieve.'

'You wouldn't,' he said.

'Oh, try me.'

'You'd be jeopardizing criminal prosecutions all over the country, Amanda. A story like that—'

'A story like that is hair-raising, Lew,' she said.

'A story like that is going to make potential witnesses think long and hard about testifying. You're not giving this proper thought, Amanda.'

'*Au contraire.*'

'You're obsessing over Isabel Sanchez. This is a personal thing and it's also blackmail.'

'It takes what it takes, Lew. Get back to me before the end of the day. That's an ultimatum. I'll be waiting.'

Rhees looked up from his coffee. 'Hardball,' he said, with a sharp little note in his voice.

'What else works?' she asked.

She poured coffee. She felt a healthy vibrancy run through her like the struck strings of a zither. 'Goddam. I can't tell you how satisfying that was.'

'You think it's going to achieve anything?' Rhees asked.

'We'll see.' She clasped her hands round her cup and listened to the rain. It pattered on the roof, slinked over downpipes, stirred the grass. The doorbell rang. The sound made her jump. Rhees went to answer it. She heard him open the front door and after a couple of minutes he came back. 'Some guy selling magazine subscriptions,' he said. 'I felt sorry for him in this rain.'

'They count on your sympathy,' she said.

Rhees smiled. 'I told him I'd take *Sports Illustrated*.'

'You don't like sports.'

'The poor bastard was dripping. Besides, there's always the swimsuit issue. In any case, he didn't have the *New York Review of Books*. So what was I to do?'

'You'd give your last dime to any guy rattling a tin cup.'

'It's called charity,' Rhees said.

She paced the room. She wondered if Bascombe had telephoned Arlington, if she'd made him sweat enough to go that far.

The telephone rang. She reached for it at once. It was her father.

'I tried the cabin,' he said. 'Obviously you haven't gone back yet.'

'Not yet,' she said.

'I go out of town one night and I come back and there you are mentioned in the newspaper. You didn't say anything to me about this corpse.'

'Dad, I'm waiting for a call. I'm going to hang up and I'll get back to you.'

'You're back in business again, right? That's what I smell.'

'No, I'm not back in business. I'm only doing what I think I have to.'

'What is it with you? You got an aversion to peace and quiet? If I was Rhees, I'd stick you in the trunk of the car and drive you back to the cabin immediately and lock you there until you're thinking halfway straight. What's wrong with him anyway? You wrap him round your little finger like—'

'I'm hanging up, I'll call you back.'

'Don't you dare hang up on me, Amanda.'

She set the receiver down. She swept a lock of hair from her forehead. In a way, she liked the feeling of hanging up on Morgan, who longed to think she needed him *and* his money. The telephone rang again. This time it was Bascombe.

'Listen carefully,' he said, 'this is the deal.'

25

BY EARLY AFTERNOON DANSK HAD ALMOST FINISHED GOING through the microfiche material in the newspaper morgue. He zoomed in on a photograph of Amanda taken outside a courtroom. Dressed in a dark suit with a double-breasted jacket, she was smiling into the camera. He gazed into her face. Was that fatigue he saw there? Or relief? He couldn't decipher the expression.

The caption read, SANCHEZ PROSECUTOR RESIGNS.

He skimmed over the story. 'Ms Scholes said she needed time for her personal life . . . looking forward to a vacation but gave no indication of where she plans to spend it . . . delighted the prolonged Sanchez case is finally over and that justice has been served.'

Justice served, and amen.

Behind Amanda in the photograph was a man identified as Lieutenant William Drumm. He had small slitted eyes and a benign smile. He was quoted as saying that the resignation of Special Prosecutor Scholes was a blow to the law-enforcement community. Amanda and the plump cop, a mutual admiration society.

The article also mentioned that Amanda's successor was a guy called Dominic Concannon, a graduate of Columbia. Concannon said that Amanda Scholes had set very high standards, she was a hard act to follow.

She'd had a fair amount of press in her time, Dansk thought. Magazine profiles, newspapers, mainly in-State publications, but also a couple of nationals. She had views on *big matters.* Capital punishment (against in some instances, for in others – cop-killers, child-murderers). Abortion (pro-choice). She was critical of the legal profession, the usual gripes: too many frivolous lawsuits, too many ambulance-chasers, too many deals cut in back rooms.

He left the building, stepped out into the rain, sat in his car, took out his little notebook and leafed through it. This Amanda was one determined woman. She sailed into battle with cannons blazing. In court she harried defence witnesses, squabbled with opposing attorneys, took flak from the bench. Gutsy, and brainy, give her that.

Then out of the blue she'd had enough. Abracadabra, gone. He wondered what lay behind this decision. Maybe she realized she'd chosen a career that didn't fulfil her, which wasn't a decision she'd make lightly. He had the feeling she didn't go into things in a superficial way, she'd figure the angles first, which was maybe too bad – superficial he could deal with.

He flicked the pages of his notebook to the biographical stuff. Father named Morgan Scholes, widower, rich business shark. Amanda had gone to law school in Los Angeles. She'd never married. Probably too busy being Ms Prosecutor, building the career, climbing the glory ladder. The fucking problem with microfiching your way into somebody's life was how you didn't get the full story, only the margins, and they were never satisfying.

For instance, did she have close friends? Old pals from

college? People she'd confide in? People she'd turn to in an emergency? A support group? He wrote, 'friends?' in his notebook.

He gazed out at the rain streaming across the parking-lot. No sun, the city grim, passing cars making spray. Typical, you're in the desert and it rains. He drove back to his hotel, left his car in the underground parking. McTell was waiting in reception. They went inside the empty bar and Dansk ordered a 7-Up. McTell asked for a Coors.

He hunched across the table. 'The guy's called John Rhees,' he said. 'He's a professor. Teaches college here. Poetry or something.'

She'd want somebody smart, Dansk thought. 'Anything else?' he asked.

'According to this busybody neighbour I talked with, they've been living in a cabin up near Flagstaff past few weeks. Seems she was sick or something.'

Sick. Dansk wondered about that. Sick didn't tell you much. He settled back in his chair. 'You've been busy, Eddie.'

'Nice guy Rhees,' McTell said.

'Don't tell me. You talked to him.'

'A few minutes.'

Dansk asked, 'What did you say, you were from the electric company and had to read his meter?'

'Trade secret, Anthony.'

'Did you see the woman?'

'Uh-huh.' McTell stared inside his drink. 'Whaddya think, Anthony? We gonna have to do surgery or what?'

Dansk said nothing. Surgery, he thought. Arteries ruptured, blood pumping.

'We can't like hang out here for ever,' McTell said.

'We like hang out until I say otherwise, McTell.'

McTell blew out his cheeks and looked sullen, re-sembling a puffer-fish in a bad humour.

Dansk pushed his chair back from the table. He thought about the French restaurant last night, the way Amanda and Rhees had held hands across the table. He was aware of a bleak little blue-yellow gas flame of loneliness inside his head. He recalled how she'd leaned across the table and dabbed Rhees's lips with her napkin, the concern that was maternal and sexy at the same time. Concealed behind a vase of carnations, Dansk had picked at his *salade niçoise* without any enjoyment.

He'd followed Rhees inside the men's room at one point and stood at the urinal next to him. In the strained manner of conversations conducted between strangers pissing side by side, Dansk had said, 'It's always a good sign when a restaurant has a spotless toilet.'

Rhees, zipping up, had agreed. Out of casual interest, Dansk had glanced very quickly at Rhees's flaccid penis – circumcized, mid-sized number, nothing to write home about – then he'd washed his hands and held them under the hot-air dryer.

Dansk said, 'Sanitary. Better than towels.'

Rhees said, 'Those gadgets don't dry as well as towels.'

'Towels carry germs,' Dansk had remarked.

Rhees had said, 'I guess it's down to personal preference,' and smiled affably, the smile of a man who knows his love is waiting for his return. Dansk had pictured this lean man with the easy smile fucking Amanda. He'd imagined Amanda's spread thighs and pubic shadows and moonlight on a window and Rhees saying he loved her, and he wondered what that was like, living your life as if you belonged inside it.

Dansk stood up now. Remembering Rhees depressed him. 'I think I'll rack out for a while.'

McTell said, 'Later.'

Dansk took the elevator up to his room. He hung the 'Do Not Disturb' sign on the handle and closed the door.

He started to take off his jacket, then realized he wasn't alone. The man who sat on the bed wore a long black overcoat and a black cashmere beret. His breathing was shallow and laboured.

Dansk didn't move, didn't say anything. He was surprised by the guy's appearance, conscious of turbulence in his head. He had his jacket halfway off, an empty arm dangled at his side.

The man covered his mouth with a black-gloved hand and coughed a couple of times. His eyes were bloodshot and runny and, Dansk thought, disgusting.

The man opened his briefcase. He produced a thick wad of crisp banknotes, set it on the bedside table and said, 'Payroll time for your guys, Anthony.'

26

SHE ENTERED THE BILTMORE AT 10 P.M. *IT'S CLOAK AND dagger*, Bascombe had said on the phone. *It's the only way they'll agree. Be punctual.*

The only way, she thought. What was wrong with a little openness now and again? They were infatuated with secrecy. They liked nocturnal meetings and whispered conversations in secure rooms.

She surveyed the reception area. This place, all the rage in the years after Frank Lloyd Wright had designed it, was past its shelf-date. Women with bad face-lifts dined here, balancing awkwardly on high heels and hanging on to the arms of silver-haired men who looked like traumatized bankers or golfers from the age of knickerbockers. There was the perfume of old money and the musty smell of quiet power. It was the kind of place where her father occasionally dined.

Amanda approached the desk. She asked a clerk for the key to room 247, as she'd been instructed. *Do it exactly the way you're told*, Bascombe had said. The clerk was supercilious. He pushed the key towards Amanda as if he thought she was here for the purpose of an illicit assignation. She wondered if her clothes were suspect. The knee-length black skirt and matching jacket didn't strike her as the garb of a working-girl. You couldn't tell, she supposed.

She took the key and walked towards the stairs. On her way up she encountered a party of old dowagers chattering among themselves like so many fluttery birds descending in a wave of chiffon and the choking smell of Chanel No. 5. Amanda sidestepped, let them creak past her on their way down, then continued up.

She clutched the key in her warm hand. *Go into the room. Somebody will meet you there.* For an uneasy moment she suspected some kind of trick or trap. It was groundless, a case of nerves. She was going to have a quiet word with a grey-faced bureaucrat, that was all, somebody who'd allay her fears with a few appropriate phrases and maybe a lie or two thrown in for good measure. Somebody who'd tell her that the situation had been investigated and the repairs made, the holes sealed, it couldn't happen again. Sorry about Isabel Sanchez, by the way.

But still.

She walked down the corridor, searching for the room number. She reached it, paused, then kept walking. This affliction of nerves was downright stupid, so why didn't she just turn around, slip the key in the door and enter the goddam room? This is what you wanted, she thought. This is what you asked for.

She walked back. She looked at the key a moment, then she opened the door. She stepped inside the room. It was empty. She checked the bathroom, also empty. She went to the window and gazed out, seeing falling rain caught in the lamplight on the lawn. Somewhere a band had begun to play, a tinny sound heavy on drums, music for people who wanted to shuffle through a geriatric foxtrot.

OK, so the Program representative was late, flight delayed, traffic jam, all kinds of reasons. She sat down in front of the dressing-table and caught a glimpse of herself in the mirror. A little make-up, a touch around the eyes, the lashes, the lightest of lipstick, hair sensibly brushed and in place. She'd wanted to look down-to-business serious, the kind of person who wouldn't be swayed by platitudes and excuses.

She heard a key turn in the lock and the door opened. The man who entered the room came across the floor towards her. 'Amanda Scholes?' he asked.

She noticed tiny spots of rain in his hair. He reached inside his raincoat and said, 'Let me show you some ID.'

'Sure,' she said.

He handed her a laminated badge. She saw the words 'Department of Justice' and the guy's photograph and a thumb-print and a name typed just beneath it: 'Anthony Dansk.'

27

HER FIRST IMPRESSION WAS OF A MAUVE BIRTHMARK, suggestive of a truncated map of Italy, situated between Dansk's jawline and ear. And then his eyes: greens were often restful, but not the green of Dansk's eyes, which had the sharp, just-too-bright quality of a traffic signal located on a lonesome road in the deep heart of nowhere. His hair was thick and red and healthy, brushed back and straight, and a faint gingery down fuzzed his cheeks. He wore a neat single-breasted grey suit and grey shirt and a black and grey necktie. His body was trim: clearly he worked out. He looked way too young, she thought, but so did a whole lot of people these days – physicians, cops, lawyers. They were like kids dressing up. You go over forty, and suddenly the world's filled with children running the show.

She lit a cigarette. She was still a little tense.

'I'm late,' he said. 'Flight schedules don't mean a thing these days. I wonder why they even announce them.' He sat, frowning at the smoke drifting from her cigarette.

'Yeah, I know. The health warning's on the pack,' she said.

Dansk said, 'What people inflict on their bodies is their own business. They want to take risks, it's up to them.' He leaned back in his chair. He smiled very briefly, which in that split second softened the starkness of his eyes and dimpled his cheeks unexpectedly. She could imagine him as a boy, apple-cheeked and freckled. He had perfect teeth. He puts a lot of effort into dental maintenance, she thought.

She looked for an ashtray. A length of ash dropped in her lap and she brushed it off, leaving a grey smudge on her skirt. Clumsy. Dansk watched her without expression.

'Do I call you Amanda or are we doing this on a formal basis?'

'Amanda's fine,' she said. 'So where do we begin?'

Dansk clasped his hands together. Well-manicured, except there was no nail on the pinky of his left hand, just puckered skin. 'Your concerns about the Program,' he said.

'That's a start,' she said.

He wandered over to the mini-bar, removed a can of Diet Dr Pepper and popped it. 'Under one name or another – Silencer, WITSEC – the Program's been around for thirty years, give or take. And you can't run something this sensitive for that length of time without the occasional mistake, a lapse here or there.'

'I don't call the fact that Galindez is dead a lapse,' she said, 'and I certainly don't call the likelihood that Isabel Sanchez is dead a lapse either. Euphemisms give me heartburn.'

He leaned forward in his chair. 'What I'm saying is, people are fallible, they get greedy. An official takes a bribe in return for somebody's address, then a witness you thought was well-protected turns up in the trunk of an abandoned car. I expect we'll find a bribe was involved in the situation with Galindez and Isabel Sanchez. We need some time to work on it.'

'How much time?'

'Impossible to estimate. These things have to be done very carefully. You don't want to alert the culpable party that he or she is under scrutiny.'

'How many people have access to the kind of information we're talking about?'

'I'm not allowed to divulge that.'

'What exactly are you allowed?'

'Try to understand, Amanda, the heart of this Program is secrecy.'

She said, 'Look. The glaringly obvious place to start is with Victor Sanchez. I already went down to Florence and gave it a shot, not that I achieved anything.'

'What impression did you get?'

'He's involved up to his neck, I just can't figure out how he penetrated your security. Also he threatened me.'

'Threatened you?'

'He said I was next on his hit list.' She made a slashing motion with her index finger across her throat. 'Which wasn't pleasant.'

'You think he was serious?'

'It's something I don't take lightly,' she said. 'He scared me.'

Dansk was quiet for a moment. 'We've arranged to interview him.'

My heart beats easier, she thought. 'You're finally getting around to that, are you?'

Dansk seemed impervious to her sarcasm. He said, 'My advice to you would be take a vacation and don't tell anyone where you're going. You'd be safer far away from here. Let me get on with my business, it's in good hands.'

'Funnily enough, I told Isabel Sanchez the very same thing,' she said. 'You're in good hands, sweetie. But I keep hearing the goddam dogs in my head.'

'The dogs, right,' he said. 'How close were you to them?'

148

'Hard to say. A mile, two, maybe more.'

Dansk looked pensive. 'You responded to a phone call from Mrs Sanchez, I understand.'

Amanda nodded. 'I was too late to help her.'

'What did she say exactly?'

'Didn't you see the report?'

'Sometimes the reports I get leave things to be desired.'

'She was scared. Men were coming after her.'

'Did she know these men?'

'She didn't say.'

'She mention how many men?'

'Two she said.'

'Descriptions, anything like that?'

'No, no descriptions.'

Dansk shook his head. 'It's a bad business.'

A bad business was an understated way of putting it, she thought. 'I'm curious. She was in Farmington, New Mexico, then Tuba City. Finally she comes back here to Phoenix. Where did you relocate her?'

'I can't answer that, sorry.'

'What the hell *can* you answer? Galindez is dead, Isabel's missing and you come waltzing down from God knows what cubby-hole in Arlington or Washington or wherever, and you're condescending. Oh, we're taking over, Amanda, why don't you go on vacation.' She checked herself, the way her voice was rising. She didn't want to alienate Dansk, because he had the power to close doors on her.

'Condescending?' he asked. 'I flew all the way down here to set your mind at rest.'

'And what if my mind isn't at rest? What if it's like a jumping bean?'

Dansk strolled across the room and sipped his drink. He switched the subject suddenly. 'You talked about going to the newspapers, I believe. I don't think that would be smart.'

149

'Is this some kind of warning?'

He sat down again and drew his chair close to her. Their knees were almost touching. 'All I'm telling you is this: if you decide to have a word in the ear of some inquisitive journalist – cases collapse because witnesses are too scared to talk.'

'But would you gag the journalist?'

'You think we have that kind of power?'

'I don't know exactly what powers you *do* have. I'm supposed to mosey off into the sunset while you people get on with your business.'

'You agree to stay out of this business entirely, and in return I'll let you know the outcome.'

'I stifle my curiosity while you get to work.'

'One other condition is you don't talk with journalists.'

'I see a problem,' she said. 'You could come back to me in a couple of days, a week, a month, and you could tell me anything you please, and I'd have to buy it.'

'That's not my style,' Dansk said.

Amanda stood up. She had pins and needles in her legs. 'You're asking me to trust you.'

'I'm asking you to be reasonable,' Dansk said. His voice was suddenly chill in a way she didn't like. 'I don't have to tell you anything.'

She turned and looked out of the window and saw Dansk's can of soda glint in the rainy pane. She watched his image move a little closer to hers.

'What if you don't get in touch with me? You're not going to give me a phone number where I can reach you any time I want, are you?'

'I don't want you to walk out of this hotel feeling you've just talked with somebody who's going to vanish inside some – what was the phrase you used – cubby-hole in Washington?' Dansk took out a notebook from his pocket and scribbled something on a sheet. 'I'm going to be in town a couple of days at least. Here's a number where you can reach me.'

'You're not staying here?' she asked.

'This was just for the purpose of meeting you.'

A secure room, she thought. Cloak and dagger. They did it in style. She wondered if people whose profession revolved around secrecy became addicted to it, if a life of secrecy was like being immersed for a long time in a sensory-deprivation tank. If that numb, lonely suspension did something to the way you viewed reality.

'And when you leave town, where can I call you?'

'I'm adding another number. This one's highly confidential. I'm not always behind my desk, but you can leave a message and I'll get back to you as soon as I can.'

'I have your word on that?'

'Of course.'

She wondered about the value of Anthony Dansk's word. Then she thought, I'm judging him too harshly. He has his own code of rules and regulations, he has to play by the book the way it's written. And she ought to feel some gratitude towards him for flying 2,000 miles just to talk to her – even if she'd had to apply pressure to get him here.

'Are we agreed?' he asked.

She thought a moment and then said, 'We're agreed.'

'Maybe a drink on the deal would be nice.'

He sounded like a kid asking for a date, she thought. He was watching her with a certain expectation she found vaguely embarrassing, and for a moment he reminded her of the high-school loner who could never get a girl, the one who stood on his own at the edge of a crowded prom, clip-on bow-tie askew, eyes shyly scanning the dance floor.

She glanced at her watch. 'Why not. Gin, if there's any, and tonic.'

He walked to the mini-bar. 'There's no ice.'

'That's OK,' she said.

Dansk brought her the gin and tonic.

She sipped the drink and looked at him over the rim of her glass. She noticed he had a habit of turning his face to one side every now and then to hide the birthmark from sight. He had to go through life that way, she thought, his face forever turned a little to one side. The birthmark obviously burdened him.

He said, 'Why did you quit law?'

'You've been researching my background, Anthony.'

'I'd hardly call it research. When I knew I was coming to meet you, I figured I ought to know who I was talking to, that's all. Your resignation's no big secret.'

'Why I quit law. Too many reasons. Mainly I was becoming polluted after years working with liars and flim-flam artists and human eczema. I'd reached an unhealthy level of toxicity, and I wasn't prepared to go on paying the price.'

'Human eczema,' he said.

'Suppurations masquerading as people.'

'Harsh words.'

'You asked.' She listened to rain spray against the window. A wind was getting up and the trees shook outside, flickering the lamps.

She finished her drink. 'I have to be going.'

She shook his hand, then he opened the door for her in such a way that she had to duck under his outstretched arm. She stepped into the corridor.

She said, 'I was a little overheated before. I apologize for that.'

'Already forgotten, Amanda. I'll be in touch.'

'I look forward to it.'

'Meantime, you'd be wise to get away for a while. The rest is under control.'

She went down the stairs, crossed the lobby and walked

outside. She sat in her parked car and looked out at the night and realized she didn't like the dark. Rain drummed on the roof. She'd done her duty, she'd dropped the whole mess in somebody else's lap. At least it would make Rhees a happy man. She turned the key in the ignition just as Dansk came out of the hotel and walked in a sprightly way across the parking-lot. He passed within 20 yards of her car, but his range of vision was limited by his big black umbrella, and he didn't see her.

For some reason she had an urge to follow him, but she resisted it.

28

IN HIS OWN HOTEL ROOM, DANSK UNDID HIS NECKTIE AND hung it just so in the closet. There was a knock on his door. He went to answer it. The girl was about nineteen and waiflike. She had big brown eyes and a tiny oval face.

'You're expecting me,' she said. 'Chaka? From Romantic Liaisons?'

'Yeah, come in, come in.'

She asked him what he wanted and he said, 'Nothing exotic.'

'You got it,' she said. She undressed in front of him, stepped out of her white miniskirt, slid down her tights and her black panties. She wore no bra: she didn't need one. She lay on the bed and he placed his hand on her taut belly. Navels intrigued him. A navel was like a tiny eye of flesh.

She smelled of talcum powder. Her armpits had been shaved. Her pubic hair had been razored also. Vaginal topiary. He'd once seen a hooker in El Paso with her pubes cut heart-shaped, like a furry valentine between her legs.

He took off his pants and folded them over a chair. Chaka was watching him and waiting, checking her internal meter. Tick, tick, time is money. He removed his shirt. She put her hand inside his yellow and white polka-dot shorts and stroked him for a while.

'I don't feel anything stirring in here,' she remarked.

A breakdown of the machinery was the last thing he needed. He wanted release, his valve opened, pressure let out. The girl propped herself on an elbow and looked at him.

'You wanna watch me jerk off, get you going?' she asked.

'Sure.' His head wasn't sending signals down to the central furnace. Boiler-room failure. What's going on here, he wondered.

She spread her legs and rubbed a finger in the slit of herself. Her nails were red. Her little mouth was open. Dansk could see her fillings way back and the dark cavity of her throat. And then suddenly he was out in that goddam desert and he was wondering how close Amanda Scholes had been to McTell and Pasquale and their hounds. She'd said a mile, maybe two. Some margins were way too narrow.

Easy, easy, Anthony.

The girl had her hand inside his shorts again. 'I guess my charms ain't doing it for you. For extra, I could blow you.'

Dansk didn't like putting his cock in anybody's mouth. He'd tried it but he'd felt uncomfortably vulnerable, thinking what would happen if the woman had a brainstorm during the act, or some form of feminist-bitch revenge agenda, and decided to bite a chunk out of his dick.

Suddenly he caught her hand and squeezed it. Her bones were tiny. He imagined he had a small delicate bird

155

trapped in his closed palm and how simple it would be to crush it. Squeezy-oh and snap.

'Ow,' she said.

For a moment Dansk found himself contemplating the notion of pulverizing the hooker's small hand. He thought of the noise the bones would make as they broke, a bag of brittle little sticks. As a kid, he'd once shot a pigeon with an air rifle, and he remembered how it dropped off a ledge and lay broken-winged and bloody on the sidewalk, a sickly substance oozing out of the beak. That bird had been a long time dying, spasming on the ground. His mother had told him, *You don't kill God's creatures, Anthony.*

It's only a pigeon, billions of them in the world, and God cares about one?

His eye is on the sparrow, sweetpea.

'Hey, *hey*, you!' the girl said, tugging to be free of him.

He released the girl's hand. He felt lopsided. The zip of the air rifle, the pigeon falling, what had he experienced at the time? A little surge of power or some kind of regret, he couldn't target it now. A kid blowing a bird away for the hell of it, just because the boy had a weapon and the bird happened to be where it was at that particular moment in time. Things converge, eddies of pure chance, like Galindez in that goddam river. Some things you can't foresee.

The girl rubbed her knuckles and said, 'I bruise easy, mister.'

Dansk gave the girl fifty bucks, two twenties and a ten. She was still rubbing the hand he'd squeezed and giving him a wary stare. He had an urge to grab her again and this time press his fingernails into her veins until he'd drawn blood.

She dressed. She had it down to a quick-getaway art as a safeguard against loony clients. He turned aside from

156

her. He listened to all the sounds she made, the snap of panty elastic, tights rolling over flesh like a second skin, the meshing of a zipper.

'You're a real dipshit, buster,' she said.

Dipshit. He had an image of Amanda Scholes's face, and he wondered if there was some bizarre connection between his failure with the hooker and the encounter with the lady prosecutor, a distraction on a level he hadn't been aware of. He thought of the Sanchez woman phoning. OK, so her state of mind was one of dislocation, but that wasn't the point. She might have been lucid. It was no way to run a business like this. You couldn't depend on luck. You had to shape your destiny.

He walked quickly across the room. The girl had the door halfway open. He kicked it shut. 'Dipshit, huh?' He realized he was breathing a little too hard. He gripped her shoulder. He could feel bone and imagined he heard her heart beat. Anger foamed through him. He wasn't thinking, he was listening to this tide and the persistent voices it carried.

'I'm a dipshit? That what you called me? A dipshit?'

She said, 'Don't fucking touch me, I warn you.'

The girl tried to shrug his hand away but his grip was too tight. Just do it. *Do it, Anthony.* He punched her in the mouth, slammed her against the wall, punched her again and her head snapped back, but somehow she managed to get her teeth round his wrist, nipping his flesh with her teeth. It was like the pain of catching your skin in a zipper. He pulled his arm away and grabbed her by the hips and spun her round, striking the side of her face with an open palm. She crumpled into a crouching position. He stared down at her and the tide receded in his brain and then there was hollow silence.

The girl looked up at him. Already there was a discolouration around her mouth. He made a slight motion of his hand and she flinched, pulling her head to one side.

He turned away from her, didn't look as she got to her feet and opened the door. He heard a quick intake of her breath, as if she were struggling against tears. He studied his hand. He thought, You move certain muscles and a hand becomes a fist, a weapon. You give in to an impulse and discipline dies inside you. A moment of rage.

And here's the kicker: *weirdly pleasant.*

He heard the door close. She could go to the cops, he thought, but she wouldn't, not in her profession.

The problem with rage is you can't focus it: it overflows, goes in all directions, you strike out at whoever's within range. But you don't need rage. Everything's under *control.* You were Mr Smooth. You set out your wares and the former prosecutor, a discerning customer, listens to your pitch, and before she knows it she's buying. She's buying your plastic, your whole story, and then she's homeward bound, carrying her stack of purchases from Honest Anthony's Bazaar. She's home safe with her lover, her worries alleviated, her concerns eased.

But . . .

You never really know. Other people are mysteries, planets unto themselves. *I'm at a loose end right now,* she'd said. This bothered him. A bright woman, formerly very busy, with too much time on her hands. A little bored. She wouldn't be the type to sit around crocheting or inclined over a cookbook studying a recipe for fucking bouillabaisse. And you couldn't see her serving soup in some tent-town for the homeless roaches of the nation. So what does she do with her time?

Dansk's Law: You can never sit back and get complacent. Another person's life was alien territory and you needed to map and monitor it until you were absolutely certain. And if it came right down to it, you needed to bring pressures to bear.

He was a master at pressures.

He walked up and down the room for a time, turning possibilities round and round. She'll drop it, she won't drop it. His fingers were beginning to ache from the impact of his punches. It wasn't a bad sensation.

He picked up the phone and dialled the number for the decrepit motel in south Phoenix where McTell and Pasquale were staying. It was called the Hideaway Knolls, situated on a busy intersection with nothing remotely resembling a knoll in miles.

McTell answered, first ring.

Dansk said, 'She was in the desert, McTell. The prosecutor was in the goddam desert at exactly the same time as you and your dufus associate. Have you any idea how close you came to having an eyewitness? She heard the *dogs*, McTell.'

'She see us?' McTell asked.

'You got lucky. But that's not the point, the point is carelessness. The point is keeping your eyes and ears open and making absolutely goddam sure there's nobody around when you work.'

'How were we meant to know somebody was out there? It's a big dark fucking place, the desert.'

'You don't pay close attention, Eddie. You smell blood and everything else flies out the window – like the possibility of an eyewitness. I'm trying to run this business in a professional way. *Professional*, McTell. You know that word? You heard it before?'

McTell said, 'I don't unnerstand your beef, Anthony. If she didn't see us where's the hassle? It's history. I still say surgery's the answer.'

Dansk ignored this. 'I want you and Pasquale to meet me. There's a Denny's joint off the interstate on Thomas. You'll find it. Forty-five minutes.'

He hung up and stepped inside the bathroom. He

159

wanted to shower. He wanted the good feeling that came when pressurized water tingled against your body and all the grime and germs you'd accumulated during the day went swirling in grey-white foam down through pipes and into the rancid labyrinthine dark of the sewers.

29

AMANDA DROVE UNTIL SHE CAME TO A COCKTAIL BAR ABOUT
a mile from her house. She parked outside, thinking about
Rhees, who'd be in bed reading some heavy academic
tome through the little half-moon glasses that made him
look ecclesiastical. She went inside the bar, which was
deep in shadow. A few lonesome drinkers, a mulatto girl
playing the piano and singing 'I Got You Under My Skin'
in a feathery little voice.

She asked for a gin and tonic, fidgeted with a coaster,
rolling it round between her fingers. She looked around
the room. A sign in one corner read, 'Rest rooms.
Telephone.' She didn't move at once. This behaviour
came firmly under the category of sneaky activity, but
the idea of further disapprobation from John didn't
enchant her.

She scanned the bar again: shadowy faces, strangers,
the girl at the piano. She was thinking of Dansk's advice.
Take a vacation. Go far away. She tried to imagine his
investigation, but she had no idea what it involved, and
this niggled her. She was beset by an incomplete feeling,

like a Scrabble tile she couldn't use, a solitaire card that wasn't playable.

Go ahead, *satisfy yourself*. Cut off that troubling little hangnail of doubt you have. She walked in the direction of the telephone. She took from her jacket the sheet of paper Dansk had given her. She fed a coin into the slot and dialled the number.

A woman's voice came on the line and said, 'The Carlton. How may I help you?'

'Anthony Dansk,' she said.

'One moment please.'

Amanda listened to the ringing tone. Dansk answered, a little breathless.

'This is Amanda Scholes,' she said. 'I hope I didn't wake you.'

'I was just getting out the shower.' He sounded cheerful.

'I realized I didn't give you our phone number,' she said.

'I figured you'd be in the book.'

'We're in the Phoenix directory, but you might need the out-of-town number, which is unlisted.'

'You've decided to go away?' he asked.

'We have a cabin upstate.'

'Sounds nice. OK. Pencil's at the ready.'

She gave him the number. He said, 'Got it.'

'Don't forget me,' she said.

'No chance of that, Amanda.' He said good night.

She hung up the phone, lingered, tapped her fingers on the directory. *No chance of that, Amanda.*

She picked up the handset again and hesitated, then she pushed a handful of coins into the slot. She imagined a twenty-four-hour hotline, an operator who would pick up. Instead, she received a recorded message uttered by a man who sounded as if he had severe laryngitis.

'Department of Justice. You have reached the office of

Anthony Dansk. Mr Dansk isn't available to take your call at present. Kindly leave a message. Your call will be returned as soon as possible. There is no need to leave the date and time of your message because this is automatically recorded. Thank you.' She put the phone back. An answering machine with a croak in its throat. The desk of Anthony Dansk. The recorded message in a voice that wasn't his.

She wondered about this all the way back to her car.

30

SHE WAS AWARE OF SUNLIGHT AGAINST HER CLOSED EYELIDS and the sound of the doorbell ringing. She heard John get out of bed and leave the room. She drew a bedsheet round her face and tried to get back to sleep, but Rhees returned and said, 'You've got a visitor.'

She opened one eye. The sun was a slit of revolting light. 'Who?'

'Dom Concannon,' he said.

'What ungodly time is it?'

'Eight-forty.'

'What the hell does he want at eight-forty?'

'Who knows? I'll brew some coffee,' Rhees said.

Amanda sat up. She dragged herself slowly inside the bathroom, brushed her teeth, ran a comb through her hair, then decided she didn't need to look her best. It was only Concannon, after all. She entered the living-room in her robe and blinked at Dom, whom she liked well enough except for the fact that he was always bright and switched-on, irritating if you'd only just awakened.

He was sitting on the sofa, long legs stretched out. 'Got you out of bed, eh?'

She said, 'Just don't do your stage Irish bit, promise me.'

'And here I was practising bejaysus.'

She sat down facing Concannon. He had a big frank face and untidy fair hair. His family had emigrated seventy years ago from Cork. He was an expert on the subject of Celtic religious artefacts. Like Rhees with his sporadic Welshness, Concannon was another herb in the American stockpot.

'Just tink of me as yer postman,' he said.

'You promised, Dom,' she said.

'It comes over me and I can't for the life of me stop. What can I say?'

'As little as possible would be considered a start,' she suggested.

Rhees came in from the kitchen with a jug of coffee and three cups on a tray. He set it down on the table and poured. Amanda sipped and waited for the brew to kick in.

'What's this postman business?' she asked.

Concannon took an envelope from the inside pocket of his jacket. 'This came for you care of the office. It looks like it's been in the wars.'

She looked at the creased brown envelope. Her eyesight was out of focus. 'You didn't come just to bring me this, did you?'

'I've been missing you around and the letter gave me a good excuse, and anyway I happened to be in the vicinity. So, how are you doing?'

'OK for a person whose sleep has just been rudely interrupted by a fake Irishman. Don't you have cases to try or something?'

'Matter of fact, yeah. There's this interesting little thing I've got in court in a couple of hours. Some guy selling

165

humongous parcels of Northern Arizona that aren't his to sell. Complicated fraud, involving misuse of the US mails. The guy says he's been framed by an associate. Same old, same old. Your friend Randy Hanseimer is defending.'

'Kick ass, Dom.' She took another mouthful of coffee and turned the envelope over in her hand. She still wasn't focusing properly. She made out her name scribbled in caps with a ball-point. The stamp was stuck on upside down.

'Funny business about Galindez,' Concannon said. 'I thought he was protected. The whisper going round is you're worried about witness security.'

She said nothing. She wondered about whispers, leaves stirring on the old grapevine. Gaggles of attorneys gossiping in stairwells, feeding on this snippet of truth or that crumb of misinformation.

'I understand they don't tell you shit, those Witness Program guys,' he said. 'I haven't had a whole lotta experience of them, but from what I gather they run their business like Fort Knox.'

'Allegedly.'

Concannon drew his long legs back and rearranged his sprawl. 'If I can help, let me know. Because if there's a leak in the Program, it's bad news.' He finished his coffee and then stood up. Six feet four and legs like stalks. 'Gotta run. Nail another shithead to the cross of justice. Oh, before I forget, you had a phone call day before yesterday. Bernadette Vialli.'

'Bernadette Vialli?'

'A blast from the past,' Concannon said. 'Said she wanted to talk to you about something. I said I'd have you call her.' He touched his forelock in an exaggerated way. 'Good luck to ye, me dear.'

She picked up a cushion to toss at him, but he'd already slipped out the door and was gone. She wondered a

166

moment about Bernadette Vialli, whom she recalled as a small bespectacled widow with permed hair. She remembered her son, Benny, and the shy way he'd answered questions in the witness-stand. A pale downtrodden kid, he'd directed his gaze somewhere into mid-air, never once meeting the eyes of the two defendants who stared at him with brooding hatred. Both were blood relations, Uncle Charlie Ravanelli and Uncle Giovanni 'Ironhead' Luccini, a couple of funereal mob types who'd seen too many Mafia films and had copied all the moves and the mumblings. Not the brightest kid on the block, Benny had drifted into the old family businesses: extortion, narcotics, prostitution. He was the invisible nephew and nobody paid him much attention. Run here, run there, fetch, fetch, fetch. The eager gofer. But Benny had a memory that was almost photographic, and when his time came in court he was an encyclopedia of names and places, dates and conversations he could remember verbatim. A prosecutor's wet dream.

Rhees said, 'I didn't hear you come in last night.'

'I didn't want to wake you.'

'How was your undercover meeting?'

She briefly told him about the talk with Dansk.

'You're suitably reassured,' he said, 'so now we can get back to the pines?'

'Sure.'

'I'm not hearing absolute certainty,' he said, and gave her a doubtful look.

She gazed again at her name on the front of the envelope and noticed the postmark. She raised her face towards Rhees and felt blood rush through her head, and when she ripped the envelope open it seemed to her that her hands were numb and not her own and a strange wind, like a cyclone twisting through a canyon, stormed in her ears.

31

PASQUALE WAS PARKED ACROSS FROM THE ENTRANCE TO THE cul-de-sac. He had a map spread against the steering-wheel and he was frowning like a tourist who'd lost his way in the complexity of a strange city.

He raised his face and looked towards the cul-de-sac. Nothing moved there. Iffy kind of morning. Bright sun, then clouds, then sun again.

His phone buzzed. He picked it up and heard McTell say, 'Lavatory cleaner. That would be the worst job I could think of.'

This was a game they'd been playing back and forth. McTell was parked a couple of blocks away. They changed locations every so often in accordance with Dansk's instructions.

'It don't beat morgue beautician,' Pasquale remarked. 'Lipstick on corpses, eye-shadow on stiffs, rouge on dead cheeks.'

McTell said, 'Naw, that's kindergarten stuff. Picture this. You come into work and it's the early a.m., you got your brush and your bucket and your disinfectant, you don't know what you're gonna find in the cubicles: vomit, unflushed shit, diarrhoea, piss all over the floor, used condoms leaking, junkie needles. Hey, I just thought of something worse even. A lavatory cleaner with a big momma of a hangover.'

'Pretty gross,' Pasquale said.

'You come up with anything better than a lavatory cleaner with a hangover like death, you call me. What's happening where you are?'

Pasquale said, 'Nothing.'

'I hate this waiting shit. You get all tensed up because you don't know if you're gonna do the job or if you ain't gonna do it. Waiting makes me pissed. Dansk makes me pissed. He wants us to create this . . . what's he call it? A diversion? Create your own fucking diversions, Anthony. Shove them up your ass.'

'He pays good money, plus some nice bonuses. You don't have to like the guy.' Pasquale tore out a square section of his map and began to fold it.

'Sometimes all I ask is some credit,' McTell remarked. 'He treats you like crap. He has you running here, running there, up and down this whole fucking state. He don't give respect where it's due.'

'He likes to think he's perfect,' Pasquale said.

'Perfect my ass.'

'He picks up the tab,' Pasquale said. 'He calls the shots.'

'Oh sure, he *calls* the shots, all right, but we're the ones do the actual *shooting*, Bruno. You don't see Tony Birthmark out there. He's like somebody just dropped in from another planet. You ever see this whole deal he goes through every morning before coffee?'

'No,' Pasquale said, working the segment of map between his fingers. Then he studied the paper dart he'd made, adjusted it and propelled it through the open window. It caught a pocket of air and drifted in smooth flight for some way before nosediving into shrubbery. Kamikaze.

McTell said, 'Check this, it's unreal. First, he flosses with mint-flavoured, wax-coated floss made in Holland or somewhere. Second, he has this Turkish or Indian wooden tongue-scraper that takes all the overnight shit off your tongue. Next, brushes his teeth with Sensodyne. Always Sensodyne. Then he rinses with this stuff, Per something, Peridex, I ain't sure. You'd think that would cover the oral hygiene, right? Uh-uh, there's more. He rounds things off with a salt-water gargle. Always bottled water, never straight outta the faucet, and always sea-salt. He carries round this little salt-shaker kinda thing. I wouldn't wanna be bacteria wandering loose inside Dansk's mouth. It'd be like a holocaust. And I haven't even started on the hair tonic and the whole shaving ritual and the stuff with the fingernails and the hundred quick press-ups.'

'It's what I said, Eddie. Perfectionist.'

'That's one way of putting it,' said McTell.

32

AMANDA SMOOTHED THE PAGES AND GAZED OUT INTO THE backyard without seeing anything in particular, the long grass, the swimming-pool, the young grapefruit trees whose waxy leaves played tricks with the light. What she kept hearing was Isabel's voice, the way it issued from two pages of cheap notepaper.

She lit a cigarette and said to Rhees, 'I know it's too damned early but I need a drink.' She rose from the table, went to the liquor cabinet, poured a shot of brandy, sniffed the fumes and drank.

Rhees was bent over the letter, studying it the way he might study the long-lost first draft of a major poem. She wondered what he saw in it, if he was trying to read between the lines. She thought of the misspelled words, the lack of punctuation and the spidery, back-slanting letters and the curious alignments and how they reflected Isabel Sanchez's state of mind.

She finished the brandy. She'd read the letter again, for the forty-second time, it seemed. She wasn't counting. She walked back to the table. The brandy made a fiery lasso round her heart.

Manda, I hope this gets to you, they're behind me.
two guys take me in this big kinda van

and Galindez is there also and this surprises me –
I don't expect to be traveling noplace with him, he
don't like me.

he sits up front with one guy and Im in the
back with the other and this guy tells me how
Im gonna like my new life

Galindez keeps saying he wishes hed kept
his big mouth shut, so then it gets dark and we're
drivin and then the bad shit happens – the van
comes to a stop Galindez jumps out and the two
guys go after him and

theres gunshots and Im scared and I think the
best thing is for me to get the hell away before the
two guys come back.

I get outta the van and I
hear one of the guys say stoopid motherfucker and
the other says what we gonna do with conchita
now.

I move real quiet into the trees.

I hear one of them calling out
conchita where are you and I dont move, I dont
know how long I lay still.

then here comes a truck and the driver gives me
a ride so I end up in this place Gallup.

Amanda stopped reading and glanced at Rhees. He was
standing framed in the window, watching her with his head
inclined slightly to one side. She picked up the letter and
stepped through the kitchen and out into the backyard.
Rhees followed her. They walked together to the
swimming-pool. On the tiled bottom lay the corpse of a
chlorinated frog, crouched and white. Clouds, stacked round
the morning sun, were like smoke from a crematorium.

She spread the letter in her lap. She didn't want to read it again.

> then I get another ride to farmington – I phone the number you give me only nobody answers and I try the other number and there's a man answers
>
> and I think maybe I better head back to phoenix and get to you.
>
> I steel this car outside a store then I see the two guys again.
>
> I drive fast as I can but theyre behind me all the time except when I lose them near this park where Im writing
>
> and then I see the guys again and this time its outside Tuba city.

Amanda folded the pages. 'I can imagine her driving around in this stolen car, remembering all the promises I made . . .' She felt cold, like the edges of flu. The ice was in her bones and travelling. She gazed at the walls that bounded the yard and she thought, They wouldn't keep anyone out, anyone determined enough to come after her. She imagined shapes in the shrubbery.

She said, 'Galindez decides he doesn't want to participate, so he steps out of the van. The two escorts chase him and gun him down, and he's swept away in the river. Why didn't they just let him go? It's his decision. It's *his* choice. Why kill him?'

Rhees said, 'And because Isabel is a witness . . . what? She has to be killed too?'

'But why shoot Galindez in the *first* place? These guys are US Marshals, for Christ's sake. They're supposed to protect witnesses and whisk them off to a bright new life, not kill them.'

Rhees sat beside her and said, 'It's obvious they're not

Marshals. They carry fake documents and ID good enough to convince anybody that they're charged with taking witnesses into protective custody, when in reality they're people Sanchez has hired.'

Cloud and sun, air heavy and lifeless. Amanda said, 'Why would Sanchez's people go through a charade like this? And why drive up into the boonies of Arizona? His hit men would do the job the first secluded place they came to.'

What we gonna do with conchita? The sun was sucked again behind clouds. The day was intermittent dark and light. She thought about Sanchez. She remembered the strength of his body and the touch of his fingers against her mouth and the smell of toothpaste and bad things coming in threes. How the hell did he get access to the Program? Who did he pay?

'You're trembling,' Rhees said.

'I know. Maybe a bug.'

'Let's go back indoors.'

Inside, she poured another shot of brandy. Booze on an empty stomach, like lighting a fuse. She needed a mega-infusion of vitamins and supplements, protein-shakes and immune-system boosters.

'Call Dansk,' Rhees said. 'Give him the letter, let him deal with it. Let's get the hell out of here and back to the cabin.'

The cabin, right. She was picturing Sanchez in his cell. People from Justice come to interrogate him, Dansk among them. They probe him long and hard. He doesn't have to tell them a goddam thing. He's a dead man, he can say whatever the hell he likes. Go fuck yourselves, he tells them. And maybe Dansk asks something like *Was your threat against Amanda Scholes serious?* And Sanchez just says *Eat shit* and smiles with contempt.

Rhees said, 'Call Dansk, give him the letter.' He picked

174

up the telephone and held the receiver towards her.

She didn't take it from his hand.

'Call him, for God's sake. Arrange to deliver the letter. It's outside your domain. It belongs in the hands of the proper authority.'

Dansk. The proper authority. But Dansk was a stranger. He hadn't spent hours in Isabel's company the way she'd done, hadn't listened to the brutal story of her marriage to Sanchez, hadn't sat up at all hours comforting her, gently prompting her memory, sometimes embracing her while she cried tears of rage and fear.

She's still mine. She's still my business.

Rhees continued to hold the phone towards her.

She turned away. She walked inside the bathroom and shut the door. She pulled on jeans and a T-shirt and stuck Isabel's letter in her hip pocket, swallowed a handful of capsules and tablets, catching the acrid scent of brewer's yeast. Gimme strength. Help me think. She ran a brush through her hair. *What we gonna do with conchita now?* Kill her, what else?

Kill Conchita.

Rhees was waiting for her when she came out of the bathroom. 'Where do you think you're going?'

'I need my sneakers,' and she edged past him. She found the sneakers, put them on and tied the laces. 'I have to go out for a while, there's something I want to check. I won't be long.'

'Let Dansk do the fucking checking. That's what he's here for. What is it with you? What is this need to fly solo?'

She headed for the front door. She was already stepping into the car when she saw Rhees appear in the driveway. She backed out. He had a hand raised in the air, a gesture that meant stop, but she didn't.

She thought, John, try and understand me. You don't

175

belong in my world. She wasn't even sure she belonged in it herself any more. She wasn't sure if she still had the maps to it, if she understood the grids and interstices, or if she was rushing back in the direction of the same head-numbing sickness that had almost engulfed her before.

She drove out of the cul-de-sac, thinking about the last words of Isabel's letter.

> you know sumtin?
> this protection thing
>   it just dont work

33

DANSK, IN BASEBALL CAP AND DARK SHADES, PICKED UP HIS cellular phone on the first ring and heard Pasquale say, 'She just left.'

Dansk said, 'I'll be in touch.'

He was parked outside a Taco Bell. He waited until the red VW appeared, then slid out of the parking-lot and cruised into traffic behind Amanda. The vehicle he drove was an anonymous Buick he'd picked up an hour ago from Budget. He believed in changing cars frequently as a matter of general strategy. He always went for mid-size cars in boring greys or dark blues with unmemorable wheels.

Headlines formed in his brain. FORMER PROSECUTOR KILLED IN FREAK ACCIDENT. You couldn't just bribe a crane-operator to drop a 6-ton slab of concrete on somebody's car. Here's a suggestion for you, lady: why don't you just drive across this construction site and under the crane with the big slab on the hook?

Then he thought, EX-PROSECUTOR DISAPPEARS LEAVING MYSTERIOUS NOTE. *I'm going away, I can't take it any more, forgive me.* But Amanda Scholes wasn't the kind who disappeared.

She was heading towards central Phoenix, high-rises in the distance, craggy brown peaks beyond. Please be doing something perfectly normal: going to the bank, the supermarket, picking up your dry-cleaning. Your everyday activities.

He was still pondering the fact that she'd called his hotel late last night, ostensibly to give him a phone number, but in reality *checking up* on him, which told you something about the way her mind worked. And he was still thinking about her trip to see Sanchez. She picked at fabrics just to see if they'd unravel. Pick, pick, pick.

Oh, lady. Let it be.

Downtown, clouds had lifted, traffic was snarled, drivers hung their shirtsleeved arms out of windows. Cigarettes were smoked, fingers tapped on side-panels. He could see her VW half a block away, stuck like he was. He took off the baseball cap. It was making his scalp itch.

Traffic moved again. The VW made a right turn. Dansk, six cars behind, followed. He wished he had a mask to filter out the fumes that hung in the air.

Amanda had found a parking space and was backing into it. Dansk drove past, reached a busy intersection, made an illegal U-turn and drove back past the VW.

Now Amanda was moving along the sidewalk. She ran a hand through her hair and Dansk thought, Rhees ought to give her a fine brush and comb for Christmas. Silver hair-clasps and a partridge in a pear tree.

He had to find a place to leave the Buick. He entered an alley clogged with cars, then he turned left and slipped the car into a metered space between a U-Haul truck and a busted-up old AMC Pacer with Nevada plates. He locked the Buick. Amanda was about 50 or 60 yards away. She wasn't looking his way. She wasn't looking at anything in

178

particular. She was focussed inward. She was dressed in jeans, white shirt and bleached-out sneakers.

In the French restaurant she'd looked smart and alive and attractive. She had the kind of sexiness that comes with maturity. A woman who knew all the points of the compass on her lover's body. Dansk wondered what she'd been like at seventeen and if he might have lusted after her. Probably.

No, *definitely*. Fucking the younger Amanda. Burying your face between her breasts and her hard darkened nipples in your mouth. Your cock inside her, and yeah, she's coming, she's coming in a noisy way, and you're beginning to feel your own derrick crank, and the geyser is rushing from deep inside you, and she's digging her fingernails into your spine and you can't get your tongue *deep enough* inside her mouth. You want it all, you want to consume her, your tongue all the way down inside her womb, and she's saying, oh oh oh, Anthony, oh, Anthony, and her whole body starts trembling and it's oh ah, God, oh, Anthony, Anthoneee, *do me, do me, do, don't stop, fuck my brains out*.

He could see all this. Smell it.

Slow down, Anthony. The key is detachment.

She paused on the sidewalk, reached inside her hip pocket and removed a couple of sheets of paper. Something in the way she held them struck him as interesting. Tight, possessive, as if they were important to her. From this distance, they looked like nothing more than some sheets ripped from a notebook. Maybe they were insignificant, a shopping list, say, reminders she'd written for herself. Things to do. But why clutch them like they were the secret key to a dead language?

Then one of the sheets slid suddenly from her fingers and a very faint breeze fluttered it along the sidewalk. She reached down quickly to pick it up, but the breeze tugged it beyond her and she went after it with a slight panicky movement, pushing her way forcefully past pedestrians, then trapping it beneath the sole of her foot. When she lifted the foot the paper blew away again, this time coming to rest under a parked car. She went on her knees, groped around, retrieved it, and in a crouching position smoothed the sheet against her thigh. She had an expression of relief on her face, a little half smile.

She remained motionless for a few seconds, as if she were trying to reach a decision. Which she apparently did, because she folded the sheets and stuck them back in her hip pocket and then continued to walk.

The way she'd gone down on her knees to pick up the fallen sheet intrigued him. Whatever the papers were, you could dismiss the idea of shopping lists. Something else, something important to her.

She reached the Federal Building and went inside.

The Federal Building. Well, well. He loitered among pedestrians.

A mime approached, white-faced, a yellow helium balloon attached to a string in his gloved hand. He eyed Dansk a second, then changed direction abruptly and wandered away. Dansk had a serious contempt for these pests. Their plastic flowers that squirted water, the way they pretended they were walking against a storm. There ought to be a law against these assholes, and while you're at it another against former prosecutors who couldn't mind their own goddam business.

34

LEW BASCOMBE WAS CROSSING THE LOBBY TOWARDS THE elevators. Amanda called out his name and he turned.

'The bad penny again,' he said.

'Thanks for arranging the meeting,' she said.

'I trust it was fruitful,' Bascombe said.

'It was fine.'

'Does that mean I can look forward to some peace?'

She laid a hand on his arm. 'One last question, Lew.'

She looked across the lobby. Federal workers went back and forth carrying files and briefcases. An armed guard at the metal detector was quietly whistling 'Danny Boy'.

She said, 'You told me before that you'd passed Isabel Sanchez and Reuben Galindez along to agents from the Program. Right?'

Bascombe nodded his head in a tired way.

'US Marshals, right?'

'No,' Bascombe said. 'SS storm troopers.'

She wasn't in the mood. 'How many Marshals?'

'That's three questions, Amanda. I'm counting. You said you had one.'

'Please, Lew.'

Bascombe said, 'How many Marshals. I can't answer that.'

'But they showed you ID?'

'Amanda, what the hell is your problem? You blackmail me into fixing you up with a meeting with a Program official, which I do. Why didn't you ask him any questions you had?'

'I'm asking you, Lew.'

Bascombe drew her to one side, away from the elevator doors. 'This has got to stop, Amanda.'

'What did they show you, Lew?'

'They have a docket, stamped and authorized. I check the docket against a duplicate supplied to me by Arlington. If it matches, that's good enough.'

'They could be fake papers,' she said.

'I wish I had some kind of stuff in a canister I could spray on you. Send you into a temporary coma. As it is, I have half a mind to get the security people to toss you out on the street.' Bascombe pressed the call button.

Amanda said, 'The whole system sounds porous to me.'

Bascombe shook his head. 'The dockets have to match exactly. There's also a one-off code-number for each case, which is highly confidential. These are the safeguards.'

'OK. They show you papers. Do you accompany the Marshals when they pick up the witnesses, Lew? Make sure it all goes smoothly?'

'The logistics change from case to case, for security reasons. I'm not getting into that area, Amanda.'

She stared at Bascombe. The rug on his skull looked a little maladjusted today.

'Tell me one thing, Lew. Are you straight?'

'Straight?'

'Or are you crooked?'

'I don't think I follow,' Bascombe said.

182

You don't have the face and your hair's wrong too, she thought. You are what you are, a pencil-pusher with a house in the suburbs and two point something kids.

'Forget I ever asked, Lew,' she said.

Bascombe said, 'Now watch, Amanda. See me step inside this elevator. Imagine me rising to my tiny chamber upstairs where I like to be left alone. Got the picture?' He entered the elevator and the doors slid shut.

She turned and walked out of the building and back into the sunny street. She strolled through the crowds. She had a sense of being a cork afloat on an unpredictable tide. She felt the sun on her face and cold in her bones and indecision in her heart.

She moved across the street. She walked to the next intersection where she paused outside a drugstore. She patted her hip pocket, as if to reassure herself that Isabel's letter was still there.

Give it to Dansk. Take it to him now. You're wasting your time, burning up energy. She removed the two sheets, thinking how flimsy they were, feeling the cheapness of the paper, then she stuck them back inside the pocket and walked to a pay phone. She called the Phoenix PD and asked for Willie Drumm. She'd discuss the letter with Willie. He'd know what to do. He'd advise her.

She was informed that he was out of the office. Call back again in an hour or so. She hung up.

She stepped out of the phone booth and the glass door swung and trapped in reflection the face of a man several yards along the sidewalk, and for a moment she wasn't sure if she should turn and walk away. Then she thought, What the hell.

35

DANSK, STUNNED WHEN HE SAW HER STEP OUT OF THE PHONE booth and move towards him, squeezed out a smile.

'Amanda,' he said, 'this is a surprise.'

He was furious with the way he'd allowed himself to be bushwhacked. Your concentration slips a second and suddenly you're on the defensive, only you can't show it, you have to work to keep it out of your expression *and* your tone of voice, and this effort *grinds* inside your head.

'I had some business downtown,' he said. 'You too?'

'Nothing serious,' she answered. 'A chore, that's all.'

Nothing serious, he thought, just a trip to the Federal Building. 'You got time for a coffee?'

'Too busy with this and that. Sorry.'

'You were meant to be smelling the flowers, Amanda.'

'I'm getting round to it.'

Dansk took off his shades. 'You have to catch them at the right time. Summer goes and before you know it, it's Fall.'

'Then it's dark old winter,' she said.

Dark old winter. You got it, lady. 'I had the impression you were going off to that cabin you mentioned.'

'Are you in some kind of hurry to see me leave by any chance, Anthony?' she asked.

'Hurry?' Don't push this, he thought. She's smart enough to sense any urgency in you. 'I just thought you were heading out of town, that's all.'

'I'll go tonight probably,' she said. 'Tomorrow morning at the latest. Have you been to see Sanchez yet?'

'I'm expecting a report any moment.'

'You're not interviewing him yourself?'

'Somebody else does that.'

'You don't do interviews,' she said. 'You don't have the knack for knowing when somebody's bullshitting you.'

'No, I'm not saying I don't have the knack. It's just the way it works. Division of labour.'

She moved a few yards down the sidewalk and Dansk went along with her. 'How did you get into this line of work anyway, Anthony?' she asked.

'Through various channels,' he said.

'You're a load of information.'

'It's a habit.'

'Secrecy, you mean.'

'It's a lifestyle you get used to.'

'Some might say it's a strange lifestyle, Anthony.'

Dansk said, 'It's not what you'd call a sociable occupation. It's not the kind of thing where you have office Christmas parties and company barbecues.'

'Sounds quite lonely,' she said.

He hadn't meant to give an impression of loneliness. He hadn't meant to reveal anything of himself.

'The work has compensations,' he said. 'I'm doing some good.'

'Something for society.'

'We provide a service. We work in the shadows so

185

people like yourself can put criminals where they belong. I believe in my work.'

'I don't doubt it, Anthony. You have a purposeful air about you.'

She looked directly at him. He understood he was being assessed somehow. He didn't like the frankness in her gaze. For a second he had the impression years had been stripped from her face and he was seeing her as she might have been in her early twenties, cheek-bones less well-fleshed, an absence of those tiny lines around the corners of her grey-blue eyes, the eyes themselves bright with the future.

He glanced away, then looked back at her, but she'd shifted the angle of her head and the impression of youthfulness had left her and he experienced a certain relief. She flicked a lock of hair from her forehead and he realized he wanted to do this for her and clenched his hand and held it against his leg. Touching the lady prosecutor. Fixing her hair. Don't start *liking* the woman. Don't get drawn in. OK, you had one of those wayward sexual fantasies before, which meant zero, just random discharges of the imagination. Don't even think in terms of her being a woman, she's the subject of your scrutiny, that's it. She's what you're working on. This is your job. This is what you do with your fucking life, Anthony.

She slipped her hand inside her hip pocket. He thought about the papers she'd treated so preciously. He needed a pickpocket, a deft hand in Amanda's jeans. He needed to see these papers.

She asked, 'Do you ever lose people?'

'Lose people?' Dansk weighed the question. He had the feeling she was asking something completely different. 'You mean, do they ever stray?'

'Maybe,' she said.

'A few. They miss their old hang-outs. They wander off. Not often.'

186

'Are there stats available? How many people have walked away, for instance. What percentage stays with the Program. It would be interesting to look at the figures.'

Dansk said, 'Information like that would be confidential, Amanda.'

'Confidential. Of course.'

He looked at her. *Do you ever lose people?* It was more than simple fishing. Her question was a radar scan of deep waters, a probe for undersea life-forms. She was somehow different today than she'd been during the meeting at the Biltmore, only he couldn't quite figure it. She seemed more confident, self-assured. He wondered why. Maybe she'd stumbled on something by chance. *She knows something.* No way. What could she have found out anyway? There was nothing to find out. This whole thing was watertight, chained and padlocked.

Still.

His attention was drawn to a woman with a small rodent-like dog on a leash. The dog squatted, deposited excrement on the sidewalk, then shook its ass and strutted on.

Dansk stared at the little pile of shit and said, 'Goddam, I *detest* that. People let their dogs mess the sidewalks and just walk away. Morons throw beer cans from cars and pick-up trucks. The freeways are filthy. You find furniture just lying around outside houses. Mattresses, old refrigerators, beds, clothes, abandoned shopping carts. You have to wonder what kind of mentality is at work and why people can't keep the environment clean—'

Stop here, Anthony. Don't take this any further. Quit at this stage.

'This really gets to you,' she said. She looked at him with a little element of surprise.

'Goddam right it gets to me. Doesn't it bother you?'

'Yeah, but I can't honestly say I've given it as much thought as I should, Anthony.'

Dansk took a deep breath. Calm was the important factor here. He was supposed to be *detached*, not the kind of guy who'd get worked up over dog poop. Not that kind of guy at all.

In more measured speech, he said, 'That's just it: nobody thinks any more. They dispose of stuff but they don't do it properly, and somebody else has to come along and clean it up. The seas are filled with chemicals, rivers are poisoned. The air. Everywhere you look there's graffiti.' He ran the back of his hand across his lips.

'You're a tidy freak,' she said. 'You dispose of your own garbage in an orderly way, do you?'

'I try,' he said. 'I don't know about being a tidy freak.' Freak was a word he didn't like. Freak rubbed him all the wrong ways.

'Is this some kind of parable, Anthony?' she asked. 'You complain about litter and pollution, but really you're talking about something else.'

'I was talking strictly about trash.' He laughed. He heard a weird strain in the sound.

She glanced at him. 'Frankly, I'm more interested in other kinds of disposal: Galindez. Isabel.'

The way she said *disposal* – she gave it sly layers of meaning. She looked in a store window. A thousand kinds of old-fashioned candies in jars, stripes and swirls and a sense of rainbows trapped in bottles. She said, 'Fudge, look, butterscotch fudge.'

She entered the store and Dansk followed. The air was heavy with vanilla and cinnamon. Dansk studied an array of lollipops and liquorice laces and jaw-breakers. He was brutalized by scarlets and greens and screaming yellows. He'd never had a sweet tooth, and this kind of place made him feel as if silver foil had been placed directly against a metal filling.

Amanda bought a bag of butterscotch fudge. She

popped a piece in her mouth before they were even back on the street.

'Want one?' she asked.

'No thanks.'

'Butterscotch fudge is my secret weakness,' she said. There was a bulge in her cheek. 'Do you have one, Anthony?'

'You mean a secret weakness? I don't think so.'

'Let me guess,' she said. 'Your secret weakness is so secret you don't even know what it is.'

Dansk smiled. She's playing with me. She's going too far. He thought, My finger's on the button.

'We were talking about your investigation,' she said.

'Right, we were.'

'This anticipated report concerning Sanchez may tell you nothing.'

'You never know.'

'And then what? Back to HQ?'

Dansk nodded. 'Right.'

'Back to your internal investigation. And when you learn something, I get to hear about it.'

'That's still the deal, Amanda. We shook hands on it.'

'Right, we did.'

'Call me old-fashioned, but a handshake means something to me,' he said.

'And to me, Anthony.' She rattled the paper bag containing the fudge. 'My secret weakness is really pretty tame when you think of what I could get up to.'

'What could you get up to, Amanda?' he asked.

'Oh, mischief, I guess.'

He looked at the slender little chain she wore round her neck and visualized twisting it until her eyes popped and her tongue hung out and that was the end of her. Then he imagined burying her alive. Soil falling on her face and darkness coming down on her, her hands upraised against the relentless rain of dirt. How she'd scream until her mouth filled up with earth and sand, and nothing to mark the grave, nothing to say, 'Here Lies The Lady Prosecutor'. Then he thought of her catching fire, burning. He imagined the air filled with cinders. *I have power over you, lady. I can fuck with your life like you wouldn't believe.*

They strolled until they came to an intersection. Dansk had a feeling of ropes tightly knotted inside his skull. *You're keeping me stuck in this burg when I have other places to go, other business elsewhere. I can't spread myself thin like this, lady.*

She said, 'My car's over there. This is where we part company.'

'I guess so.'

She shook the bag of fudge again. 'Sure you won't try one? Last offer.'

'You're persistent.'

'Oh very,' she said.

She opened the bag and he dipped a hand inside and came out with a crumbling brown cube, which he placed on his tongue as if it were nuclear waste. She smiled and walked to her car, and as soon as her back was turned he spat the candy from his mouth.

She drove past him and honked the horn twice and waved. He waved back. The sickly flavour of the fudge adhered to the back of his throat like sweetened chalk. He watched the VW disappear round a corner.

He went back to his car and sat behind the wheel. There were tracer bullets screaming in his head. His brain was a war zone. Trenches, casualties, men rushing with stretchers, the rumble of cannon, the dead littering the field of battle.

Mischief, he thought. I'll show you some genuine fucking mischief, toots. You have Anthony Dansk's personal guarantee. He had an image of his hand hovering over a control panel, lights blinking, his index finger poised, the pull of Amanda's gravity drawing his fingertip down and down to its destination.

One touch. Smithereens.

He phoned McTell.

36

SHE DIALLED DRUMM'S NUMBER FROM A PAY PHONE AT A filling-station. He was still unavailable. She left a message to say she'd called, then decided to phone Rhees. She watched traffic slide past and wondered if Anthony Dansk was nearby, if he'd really followed her downtown and seen her going inside the Federal Building, if he was following her still. Watching her moves. *You were meant to be smelling the flowers, Amanda.*

She'd surprised him when she'd popped out of the phone booth. He'd made a big effort to seem unflustered, but he'd reacted like a man caught in an act of voyeurism, an eavesdropper surprised behind a door, a whole flurry of give-aways: scratching his birthmark, nibbling the tip of his pinky. And then out of the blue the whammy, the bizarre diatribe against litter, white flecks at the corners of his lips.

A dog craps on a sidewalk and Dansk reacts badly. A neatness freak. Captain Hygiene. The thing that bothered her was the voltage in his eyes as he spoke. It was a zealot's intense stare, unblinking and focussed on some remote place only he could see. The eyes had become hard bright emerald stones, and spooky. He meant what he said. He was a man who'd gone up the mountain and come down with a big-time revelation. Keep America clean.

No, it was more than that, more than litter and graffiti and shopping carts left all over the place. She had a low allegory threshold in general, but it seemed to her that he was saying, in his own roundabout way, something about the condition of the country. What? The heart of the nation was trashed? As a people, Americans had drifted too far towards a disregard of law and order, as evidenced by their tendency to litter the streets and let their pets shit anywhere they liked?

She wasn't sure, but his sudden outburst had made her uneasy, more than uneasy. There was clearly a very strange and worrisome compartment in Dansk's head, and for a moment she felt an odd sense of vulnerability, as if inside the phone booth she presented a clear target for a sniper nearby, her skull in somebody's scope, a nicotined finger on a delicate trigger. She looked across the street. The stucco building opposite was an office block, four storeys, blinds in windows, a solitary date palm outside. She gazed up at the roof, thinking, This is absurd. Dansk might be more than a little weird and scary, but he is an agent from the Justice Department, he is supposedly on your side . . .

And yet. She felt pressured by menace.

Rhees answered the phone.

She said, 'It's me.'

Rhees was quiet for a time. 'Where are you?'

'Glendale Avenue,' she answered.

'You're on your way back, I hope.' He sounded sullen.

'I didn't mean to rush out like that, John.'

Rhees said, 'You never *mean* to rush, Amanda.'

'I'm sorry,' she said.

'Now I'm hearing the contrite bit,' he said.

'OK, I'm contrite.'

'And furtive. I hate furtive.'

She felt a tense band across her forehead. 'Truce?'

'You can't just say that word and think it makes everything peachy. Have you contacted Dansk?'

'I saw him.'

'Tell me you gave him the goddam letter, Amanda. That's all I want to hear.'

'I think he's been following me, John.'

'*Following* you?'

'Watching me.'

'Why would he do that?'

'He wants to make sure I leave town. He doesn't want me hanging round. I also get the strong feeling he's a carrot short of a coleslaw.'

'So he's following you. He's watching you.'

'That's a gut instinct, I can't be sure—'

'But you're saying you don't trust him.'

She answered quickly. 'Yeah. I don't trust him.'

'You don't trust him to be honest with you? Or you don't trust him period?'

'Period,' she said.

'Why don't you just come home and we'll discuss all this face to face. Meantime, I'm still waiting to hear about the letter, which you managed to sidestep quite neatly.'

She was quiet a moment. 'It's in my pocket,' she said. 'I'd like to discuss it with Willie before I do anything else.'

'Drumm, Dansk, I really don't give a shit who you give it to just as long as you get it out of our *lives*.'

He hung up. He'd never done that before. He'd never once just hung up on her in all six years of their relationship. She stuck the handset back. She felt slightly fragmented, as if some mild explosion had occurred inside the phone booth.

She stepped out and the hot sun zapped her and she suddenly remembered she was supposed to return Bernadette Vialli's call. She went back to the pay phone, searched through the tattered directory and called the number. There was no answer.

She walked to her car, drove a little way, checking her rear-view mirror, wondering how she could tell if she was being tracked through the stream of traffic. She steered into the parking-lot of a shopping plaza, killed the engine and then she sat for a time, staring through the windshield and watching traffic come and go. So many cars, so many people, all movement eventually fusing together in one unbroken sunlit glow that after a time became surreal.

Her thoughts drifted to Sanchez, to the threat she could hear echo and roll inside her. She thought of shadows and stalkers, the possibility of harm lurking behind the glare of light.

Dansk.

Or somebody else, somebody hired by Sanchez.

How could you *possibly* know if anyone was following you through this crazy bright urban nightmare? And by the same token, how could you know the plastic Dansk had flashed at you was genuine issue? What evidence did you *really* have that he was who he claimed to be?

None.

37

RHEES WAS KILLING TIME FISHING DETRITUS FROM THE POOL –
dead butterflies, limp insects, leaves – when the telephone
rang inside the house. He laid the net on the ground and
walked into the kitchen. He half-expected to hear
Amanda again, but it was Morgan Scholes on the line.

'Is she around?'

'Not at the moment,' Rhees said. He looked across the
backyard at the cedar fence. Water reflected by sunlight
rippled against the wood, a dappled effect. A few yards
down the alley beyond the fence a telephone lineman in a
white hard hat was climbing down from a ladder propped
against a pole. He vanished out of sight and Rhees heard
doors slam and the sound of a van start up.

'You there, John?' Scholes asked.

'I'm here.'

'I call her, she says she'll get back to me, I don't hear a
goddam thing.'

Rhees said, 'She's running an errand, Morgan.'

'Don't tell me. It's this stiff in the river business she's got
herself into, right?'

'You know what she's like,' Rhees said.

'The back of my hand,' Morgan Scholes said. 'You're too soft on her, John. Who's in charge there anyway? You or her?'

Rhees said, 'We're equal partners,' and wondered how true that was. Sometimes he thought of Amanda in terms of a storm, a river suddenly flooding. His role was to stack sandbags along the banks and wait for the waters to recede.

'Equal, I don't think. She has you by the short and curlies.'

'That's not true, Morgan.'

'I blame myself. I gave her too much freedom when she was a kid and what good has that done? I should have laid down the law more.'

Rhees glanced at the kitchen clock. Half an hour had passed since he'd hung up on her. Maybe she was sulking somewhere, taking her time coming home, trying his patience.

'I don't think this has to do with you giving her too much freedom, Morgan,' he said.

'No?'

'One minute she wants the cabin and peace,' Rhees said, 'the next she's not sure it's inactivity she's really after. She's always had goals in the past. Now . . . I guess it's a question of redefining herself, which isn't easy for her.'

Morgan Scholes said, 'She's old enough to make up her mind, John, and you ought to tell her that.'

Rhees said, 'I'm trying.'

'Get her to phone me when she comes in.'

Rhees said he'd pass along the message.

He hung up, wandered through the house, room to room, restless. In the bathroom he looked inside the medicine cabinet. He had an urge to gather together Amanda's vitamin supplements and immune-system

197

boosters and just dump all that quackery in the trash. He studied the labels: dried seaweed, powder derived from a green-lipped mussel, whatever the hell that was. He imagined plants and creatures fished out of the deep sea, ground down and then stuffed into capsules.

There were a couple of prescription medications: Diazepam, Dalmane. Downers she'd used during the Sanchez trial when she'd needed to sleep, when she was fraught and wound too tight, and it was three a.m. and she was collating material or studying Isabel Sanchez's testimony, or poring over transcripts of her interviews with Galindez. When she was fraying at the edges.

And now, now she'd said Dansk was following her. Her gut feeling, she'd said. She usually had good instincts, but this time he had to wonder if she was interpreting the signals accurately, or if she was creating her own little melodrama because of Isabel.

A touch of paranoia? Possibly.

He shut the cabinet. He listened to the silences of the house. He wished she'd come through the front door and he could hold her and say something like, I'm sorry I hung up on you, let's talk. Let's clear the air about everything.

He walked into the kitchen. The door to the backyard was open. He thought he'd closed it. No, he *remembered* closing it to keep the cold air from the air-conditioning escaping—

He saw the tyre-iron but couldn't move out the way before it smashed into his ribs with an impact that forced all air out of his lungs, and he staggered, clutching the area of pain, aware of light being sucked out of the room, and he had the sensation of plummeting down a greased cylinder. The second blow struck the side of his head and the sense of slipping inside a darkening tube was even stronger now, and he gave up trying to keep his balance and went down on his hands and knees.

He raised his face. He made an effort to get up by clutching the edge of the table, and that was when the third blow was launched, sharp and dreadful, metal coming down so hard on his left hand that he could hear the sound of his finger-bones breaking. He slumped and the room was like one of those deranged rides at a carnival when you went spinning round and round in the air and the spectators far below you were just a sea of faces in white light. He rolled over on his back and dimly saw two guys wearing ski masks. He launched a foot, the best effort he could make, and struck one of the guys in the groin.

'You mother*fucker*,' the guy said.

The tyre-iron cracked against the back of his knee and he was dragged across the kitchen floor and out into the yard towards the swimming-pool where his head was forced underwater and held there, and all he could see were pale red bubbles rising from his mouth. Drowned, he was being drowned. He wanted to scream, but then his head was yanked up from the water and the sunlight was blistering against his eyes and he was whacked again, this time across the shoulders. And then his face was forced underwater a second time, or maybe a third, he couldn't count, he was beyond making elementary measurements. Now the pain came roaring through him, gathering strength, but that was only the first stage, because after that he found himself entering a place of pain beyond pain, where a deep burgundy tide hurried into his brain.

38

AMANDA DROVE INTO THE CUL-DE-SAC. SHE SAW NOTHING out of the ordinary. There was no sight of Dansk or anyone else, no car behind her. She parked in the driveway.

OK. Time to get practical. Go inside the house and call the Justice Department in Washington, and ask through the central switchboard to be connected to Anthony Dansk. The private number he'd given her could be *anything*. If she found herself connected to his extension, then at least she'd know he worked for Justice. If the operator told her there was no listing for anyone called Dansk – but she wasn't ready to think this through to a conclusion.

She got out of the car. She turned and looked the length of the cul-de-sac. It was calm and somehow completely unsettling. It was as if a cortège had recently passed, leaving behind a somber pall of silence. No kids, no pedestrians, no lawnmowers roaring, nothing. It was wrong, only she couldn't think why. Some form of charged static hung in the still air, like the atmosphere before a storm.

She opened the car door, glanced at the house, saw the

sunstruck windows. Fiery glass blinded her. She walked to the house, unlocked the door and entered the hallway, where the shattered mirror on the wall reflected her face in a series of jagged slivers.

She didn't move. She understood at some level of memory activity that there was a procedure to follow in situations like this, you were supposed to back out of the house at once and call the police, you were advised not to run the risk of confronting the intruder if he was still on the premises, there were rules to follow if you wanted to survive. Rules didn't enter her head.

She took a step forward. Broken bits of mirror crunched under her sneakers. She glanced through the open doorway of the living-room. A typewriter lay upturned on the floor. The drawers of Rhees's desk hung open. Papers were strewn all around.

Terror comes in variations on the ordinary. Papers where they shouldn't be, a typewriter lying upside down, a broken mirror. She edged closer to the door, conscious of the way a deep silence was clinging to the house, all noise vacuumed out of the place, dead space, just this void. She was numb, circuits down.

She entered the room.

'John,' she called.

His books were scattered. His files lay in utter disarray. A chair was overturned, a lampshade trampled and bent. No sign of Rhees.

'John!'

She moved to the kitchen doorway. No Rhees. On the kitchen table a jar of beets had been toppled and dark purple liquid dripped to the floor like a strange wine.

She was finding it hard to breathe. The space through which she moved was viscous. Go back, turn, get out of here. She walked to the half-open kitchen door and gripped the handle.

'JOHN!'

The yard was silent. Butterflies flapped over the long grass and her own voice returned to her as an echo she couldn't identify. Blue sky, frail bright wings, an echo dying. She went through the grass, drawn for some reason towards the pool, then stopped dead. The sun darkened.

He was seated motionless on the steps in the shallow end. His head was inclined forwards against his chest. His eyes were shut. The water, which rose as far as his waist, was ribboned with spirals of red.

This happens, this kind of thing, you read it every day in the papers – home invasions, suburban terrorists, dopers looking for quick cash, fix-money. This is the way it happens, only it's supposed to happen next door to somebody else, not to you.

No way. Never to you.

She rushed to where Rhees sat and, bending at the knees, gripped him under the shoulders, and then she pulled until she was breathless and her head was burning with a kind of fever and she'd hauled him out of the water and the air smelled of chemicals and damp clothing.

A mosquito landed on John's face, humming its blood song.

39

DANSK STEPPED INSIDE THE CONFESSIONAL. HE NOTICED A scab of pink chewing-gum pressed to the wall and a crayoned item of graffiti close to the floor: 'Jesus Saves at Citibank'. And here on the floor was a wrinkled condom dumped by some moron with a distasteful sense of humour. These signs of decline in the national fibre were everywhere – in churches even.

'I've sinned, Father. Fornication, hookers, call-girls.'

A thread of sunlight sneaking from somewhere illuminated the priest's skull on the other side of the grille, outlining a frizz of white hair, a halo effect. Dansk heard the priest yawn. Even priests suffered from the general malaise of things.

He thought of his mother and her unlimited piety. She lived in Patterson, New Jersey, occupying three brown twenty-watt rooms over the workshop of a blind violin repairman called Chomsky. To the accompaniment of plucking sounds coming up from below, she prayed a lot in front of a plaster statue of the Virgin that stood on top of the TV. Under the base of the statue were the words,

Souvenir from Knock, Ireland. You grow up, Anthony, be an accountant, an optometrist, something people will respect.

Respect was her mantra. And always go to confession when you can.

Three or four times a year he phoned her, told her he was moving around from place to place, going where the oil company sent him in his capacity as a surveyor. He made up names for things that didn't exist. The *calsidron* broke down yesterday. There's one site near Amarillo that's probably the world's biggest deposit of *vobendum*.

His mother never asked questions, not even if he had a girlfriend and if she could look forward one day to being a grandmother. Whenever he thought about her he saw her stooped in front of that statue with her eyes shut, praying for her dead husband, Albert, who'd succumbed to a cardiac arrest on Dansk's fourth birthday. All Dansk could remember of his father was the smell of fried food that clung to his clothes from the fourteen-hour days he spent as a short-order cook in a truck stop on the edge of Patterson. Some memory. Some life.

'Do you believe in God?' the priest asked.

'I believe,' Dansk said. Confession boxes made him apprehensive. They were filled with the echoes of millions of sins, ghostly voices asking forgiveness.

'Ten Hail Marys,' the priest said.

Dansk said, 'Thank you, Father.'

'Bless you.'

Business done. Religion was a hurried affair like everything else in these days of acronyms and sound bites and nobody with the time to listen. Dismissed, Dansk stepped out of the box. I pay for sex, I consort with call-girls. I'm Chief Surveyor for Transamerica Explorations Inc. A man to be respected in spite of his sexual inclinations. I have nothing to do with death.

Ten Hail Marys, low-impact aerobics for the soul. You wouldn't even break sweat. He dropped some coins in a collection box for a Patagonian mission and went out to the street. He moved towards his car where a tall black man was leaning with folded arms against the hood. Dansk kept going, slowing his pace just a little, hearing the drone of imminent danger.

'You Dansk?' the man asked.

Dansk reached the car. He studied the man quickly. Black silk bomber jacket, black polo-neck, the face with the monstrous overhanging brow, huge hands, no rings. Dansk had the general impression of brutality.

'I wanna word,' the guy said.

Dansk said, 'I don't know you.'

'You're about to,' the guy said.

Dansk could feel it in the air around him, a kind of static, and somewhere in his head a sound that reminded him of Chomsky stretching a violin string to breaking-point.

The black guy had his hands clasped in front of him. 'Let's you and me walk over there,' he said.

Dansk looked, saw an entrance to an alley, dumpsters, plastic sacks, one of which had broken and disgorged its contents. He saw chop-bones and a lettuce oozing brown slime. 'I don't walk into alleys with strangers,' he said. 'Rule of mine.'

The black man said, 'We can do this right here on the street.'

Dansk gazed the length of the street. He saw quiet houses, empty sidewalks, palm trees, and a few blocks beyond, the high-rises of downtown. Nobody moving. This was one of those upmarket streets, reclaimed from disrepair by lawyers, ad executives and local media types.

The black guy prodded Dansk's chest with a thick finger.

'This a mugging?' Dansk asked.

'You're gonna wish.'

Dansk looked into the man's eyes, which were the colour of smoked oak. What he saw there was a palpable dislike. 'So it's personal?' he asked.

The guy kept prodding, and Dansk backtracked.

'What you done to that girl's fucking shameful. Cretins like you need some serious discipline.'

The call-girl, Chaka, Dansk thought. She runs to her personal enforcer. She sets free the brute from her zoo. Dansk stepped a few paces back but the guy kept prodding. Keep this up, Dansk thought. I'm in the mood, and I'm one fit son of a bitch.

'The alley or right here. You choose,' the guy said.

'Touch me one more time.'

'And you're gonna what, Dansk? Slap me? Punch me a coupla times? I ain't some skinny little whore, if it ain't escaped your notice.'

The guy stuck his finger in Dansk's breastbone again. 'The joke's over,' Dansk said.

'Ain't no joke, asshole.'

'See if you find this funny.' Dansk had the Swiss Army knife out of his pocket in a flash, and before the big man could react he'd stuck the corkscrew attachment directly into the guy's right eye, hearing it puncture the gelatinous orb, a squelching sound. The guy said, 'Oh Jesus fucking Christ' and Dansk twisted the corkscrew round then pulled it free and the big man took a couple of unsteady steps to one side, his hand clamped over his eye and blood seeping between his fingers. Dansk kicked the guy's legs out from under him and he went down like an axed tree. He lay rolling around on the sidewalk and Dansk dragged him into the alley.

'What you need is a matching pair,' Dansk said.

The black man raised a hand to protect himself, but

Dansk was way too fast for this cumbersome *asshole* and was already driving the corkscrew into the left eye, where he twisted it as if he were opening a bottle of cheap wine. The guy dropped his hands from his bloodied face and turned his head this way and that, his mouth open, no sound coming out, unless you counted the weird noise that suggested difficulty in breathing, some kind of shock reaction to his pain.

Dansk stood up, stepped back, feeling very calm, very detached. 'You fucking pimp,' he said. 'You piece of shit, worthless maggot.'

The guy started to groan. Bewildered, he stretched his hands out as if to grab something solid. Dansk crushed one hand with his foot, stomping it into the ground, then he walked to his car. Inside, he cleaned the knife with a tissue and stuck the tissue inside the ashtray.

He rolled down his window and called to the guy, 'You can always find work as a trainee violin repairman, jack.' He drove away amused, pleased with himself. He looked at his reflection in the rear-view mirror and laughed.

His phone rang, it was Pasquale. 'You oughta see her, Anthony. Pacing round outside the hospital and looking like her womb just fell out. It's a picture would break your heart.'

A picture.

'You know what to do next,' Dansk said.

'I'm moving.' Pasquale cut the connection.

Dansk laughed again and looked at himself laughing until all sense of self-recognition had left him and he was looking at somebody else, a roaring wet-eyed red-haired stranger, hugely satisfied with the day's work so far. A guy on a roll that didn't end here.

40

THE PHYSICIAN WAS A STERN YOUNG WOMAN WHOSE NAME-
tag identified her as Dr Clara S. Lamont. She wore her
hair in the tight bun of a pioneer's wife. She clearly didn't
consider sympathy an implement in the practice of medicine. She spoke like someone reciting from a low-budget
mail-order catalogue.

Two fractured ribs. Broken humerus. Three fingers of
the left hand broken. Haematoma in the knee. A few
blows to the head, but no internal damage. The patient
would recover, given time and rest. He's not going to be
mobile for a while. Clara S. Lamont had obviously seen
every kind of human disaster and been numbed by
calamity.

Amanda asked if Rhees was conscious and whether she
could see him. Clara S. Lamont told her it might be hours
yet and suggested Amanda make herself comfortable in
the waiting-room.

Make myself comfortable, Amanda thought. Tell me
how, doc. Guide me a little before it's screaming time.

She watched Lamont turn and walk down the corridor.

The hospital was a maze of passageways and rooms painted in pastels designed to minimize the dread inherent in these institutions. The colour scheme didn't work for Amanda. This was no nursery. This was a place of pain and death, where screens were drawn round beds and people were rushed on rattling gurneys to operating rooms to be cut open and sewn up again. Two fractured ribs. Three fingers of the left hand broken. Haematoma. She thought about this, a subcutaneous swelling filled with blood, the pain of it.

She was aware of nurses and orderlies, but only in a dim far-away fashion. She slouched towards the waiting-room where a strict no-smoking policy was in force. This was useless to her in her present state. She needed nicotine, vast quantities.

She went outside, and with a hand that trembled, lit a cigarette. She thought of the ambulance that had brought her here with Rhees. Rhees lying in silence, the orderly checking his pulse and blood pressure and flashing a light into his eyes, the slackness of Rhees's eyelids, the pupils that looked dead, the whites bloodshot.

I'm coming apart, she thought. Rhees is broken, and so am I, just in a different way.

The uniformed cops who'd come to the house had asked some questions in a manner that might have been desultory or delicate, she was too stunned to tell the difference. Had she seen anything? Did she know anything? Was anything missing?

Like I have time to search the fucking place looking for missing baubles, she'd said. Shock stripped you of basic manners, atomized your responses. You were raw all over.

The cops had talked to Clara Lamont, and then somewhere along the way they'd contrived to disappear. Reports to write. Narratives in triplicate. Get down the details while the blood is still fresh.

She walked up and down. She smoked and squinted into the sun. She sat on a wall, hands dangling between her knees. She couldn't stop herself shaking. What were you supposed to do in a situation like this anyway? How were you supposed to comport yourself? *Endure.* She closed her eyes. She didn't see Willie Drumm approach.

'Amanda.' Drumm's expression was sympathetic. He put his arms around her shoulders and she pressed her face into his plaid jacket. It smelled of dry-cleaning solvents.

'I came as soon as I heard. What's his condition?'

Amanda said nothing.

'The two uniforms say he took a bad beating,' Drumm said. 'You got any idea who'd do something like that to him?'

Amanda's mind was sand and silence, her own little Kalahari. She hadn't collected enough strands of herself to even think of apportioning blame. She shook her head and looked at Willie. She couldn't talk.

Drumm said, 'Hang in there, kid.'

That's what you're supposed to do. That's the phrase for every rotten situation. Hang in there. But what were you meant to hang from?

Drumm stepped back from her, a hand on her shoulder. 'You came home and found him, I understand.'

She nodded.

'Is he conscious?' Drumm asked.

'No, not yet.'

'When's he expected to be in a condition to talk?'

'I don't know. I'll wait. For as long as it takes I'll stay right here.'

'You got anything of value in the house, Amanda?'

'I had, only he's in this goddam hospital now.'

Drumm was quiet a moment. 'Things: jewels, money, that kind of stuff.'

She thought about the house and found she couldn't remember it exactly. How many rooms it had, what they contained. She knew it intimately but she couldn't force it into her head.

Drumm said, 'Maybe we should sit inside.'

'No. They don't let you smoke. I need to smoke.'

Drumm tapped a foot on the ground. 'People going round breaking into homes, beating the shit out of some poor bastard. It's an epidemic.'

Amanda looked up into the sun. It was strange to be part of the world and yet not, as if you were in a purgatory where you waited for Christ knows what. The sun in the sky, for instance, looked odd to her, shaped like a lozenge. And why did it make her feel this cold? She shivered and said, 'I can't get a handle on it, Willie.'

'Here.' He took a little pack of Kleenex out of his pocket and gave it to her.

She blew her nose and said, 'I can't get my head round it.'

Drumm was of the old school that believed in the mystical power of blowing your nose to feel better. He eased a fresh Kleenex into her hand. He was being kind and it touched her.

'John wanted to come with me when I left this morning,' she said, 'but I drove away. I just drove away. I should have taken him along, Willie, then this wouldn't have happened.'

'You don't have a crystal ball, Amanda. You couldn't predict anything was gonna happen to him.'

Amanda walked in tight little circles. It was movement, something to keep the circulation going. 'I've been neglecting him lately. I haven't been paying attention to him. It's not like he demands much from me.'

Drumm took her hand. His palm was unexpectedly soft. 'Let's go inside, Amanda. Maybe we should think about talking to one of the doctors. Get something to settle you down.'

She allowed herself, without resistance, to be led back inside the hospital. Drumm told her to sit in the waiting-room while he went off in search of a physician. She glared at the no-smoking posters and a diagram of a human skeleton that adorned one wall. She looked at the word humerus, known also as the funny-bone. She imagined it was Rhees's skeleton. Poor John. He'd never hurt anyone in his life. He wasn't at war with anybody.

Fuck the warning sign. She lit a cigarette.

The only other occupant of the room, a man with an insurance-collar, said, 'I don't mind, you smoke all you want.'

Amanda said, 'I intend to.'

The man got up and set an empty Coke can on the table beside Amanda and said, 'Here, use this as an ashtray.'

'Thanks,' she said.

'I'm here on account of this neck.' He sat alongside her and leaned across her lap to adjust the position of the Coke can. His hair smelled faintly of crushed grapes. There was a brief contact of bodies she didn't like.

'Happened in a work-related incident,' he said.

'Really,' Amanda remarked. She didn't want to hear the guy's medical history. She looked elsewhere and edged slightly away from him.

'I'm suing because it wasn't my fault.'

'Good for you.'

'That's what the law's for,' he said.

The guy smiled at her and went out of the room. A moment later Drumm came back carrying a dixie cup of water. 'Here.' He gave her the cup and a small blue pill.

'What's the pill?' she asked.

Drumm said, 'The nurse said it would calm you.'

'Assuming I want to be calm, Willie.'

212

'Take the damn thing.'

Amanda stuck the pill in her mouth and washed it down with a sip of water. 'I want to see John,' she said.

'So do I,' Drumm said. 'Meantime, let's wait here.'

He patted her arm. She sat in silence for a long time, and when the pill kicked in she felt lethargic and light-headed. She must have dozed for a while because the next thing she knew Drumm was shaking her shoulder and saying, 'We can see him now.'

She was dry-mouthed and groggy, and when she stood up she was a little unsteady. She followed Drumm down a corridor to an elevator.

'You OK?' he asked.

OK in what way? she wondered. Physical mental spiritual. Delete what doesn't apply.

She stepped inside the elevator. Drumm said, 'He's in room three sixty. We've got five minutes, doctor's orders.'

She listened to the quiet whine of machinery and pulleys. She wondered about the kind of noises Rhees had made when he was being attacked. She didn't want to think. Some things were located just outside the scope of your imagination, like shadows beyond the reach of a camp-fire.

41

RHEES HAD A ROOM TO HIMSELF. HE WAS PROPPED UP IN BED with his eyes shut. The shades had been drawn against the sun and the only light came from a low-wattage lamp in a corner. Amanda went close to the bed and Willie Drumm lingered behind her.

'John,' she said.

His head turned slowly. 'I am *high*. Great drugs in here.'

She smiled at him even if it was the last thing she felt like doing. His left arm was in plaster. His left hand too. His face was bruised. His knee was an angry scarlet colour and bloated, and the ice-pack that had been wrapped around it had slipped out of position.

When he spoke, his words were lifeless, as if they'd travelled a very long and awkward distance to reach his mouth.

She wanted to touch him, she wasn't sure where. She decided on the back of his right hand, where she placed her palm gently.

Drumm asked, 'Can you answer a couple of questions, John?'

Rhees shut his eyes again. 'There were two guys, I think.'

Drumm waited. Amanda rubbed Rhees's hand. She wanted to tell Drumm that this wasn't the right time, Rhees needed to be left in peace.

Rhees said, '. . . in ski masks.'

'Ski masks, OK,' Drumm said.

Rhees started to add something but his voice dried up. Amanda held a container of water to his lips and adjusted the angular straw for him. She thought about ski masks. A terrorist nightmare in your own house, your backyard.

Drumm leaned closer to the bed. 'Did they say anything, John?'

Rhees opened his eyes. His pupils were black and enormous. 'Nothing. They had a . . . tyre-iron.'

This was the first time Amanda had thought about an assault instrument. It had been an abstraction before, but now Rhees had identified it, she could picture it rising and falling on his face and body. The brutality of it, the destruction of bones and tissue.

Rhees turned his face to the side and for a second it seemed he'd drifted off into sleep, but he hadn't. He looked into Amanda's eyes. She saw in his expression stress and puzzlement, only slightly obscured by the glaze of painkillers. She experienced a flutter of anger. Rhees had been reduced to this wrecked figure lying in a hospital bed. He'd been traumatized and diminished, and for what? Money probably. Credit cards. *Stuff.* Anything of value.

Rhees closed his eyes and this time didn't open them again.

'He's out,' Drumm said.

Amanda held his hand a moment longer before she stepped back from the bed. She leaned, kissed Rhees on his forehead, then walked into the corridor.

Drumm said, 'It sickens me to the gut. What do you do?' He shook his head in a slow side-to-side manner.

Amanda looked up at a fluorescent strip on the ceiling. A voice was issuing through the sound system: 'Dr Strapp to Emergency. Dr Strapp to Emergency'. More casualties. More damaged humans swept in from the streets. Smashed cars, bullet-wounds, stabbing victims. What do you do? Drumm had said. You went up to the mountains, was the answer. You ran off up into the pines and you never came back, and if everything was going to hell in the city you didn't give a damn. You stayed where it was safe and the nights were as deep as all the oceans.

The elevator arrived. She and Drumm got in and rode down in silence. She slipped her hands into the back pockets of her jeans, thinking of Isabel's letter, expecting to encounter it with her fingers. She wished she'd never received the goddam thing. She wished it had been lost in the mail system, overlooked, shredded inside a franking machine, anything. She wished she'd never heard of Isabel Sanchez.

The letter wasn't in either hip pocket, and it wasn't in the front pockets.

She searched again, fumbling among keys and a bashed cigarette pack and a crumpled receipt chit from a Walmart and three washed-out dollar bills that must have gone through a laundry cycle.

No letter.

'Looking for something?' Drumm asked.

Without answering, she got out of the elevator and walked towards the waiting-room, thinking she might have left the letter there, tugged it out of her jeans along with her cigarettes. She checked the room, saw the Coke can she'd used as an ashtray, but no sign of Isabel's two pages. Just an empty room painted lavender and grey.

Drumm, who'd limped behind her, asked, 'Lost something?'

She didn't reply.

42

WILLIE DRUMM WALKED AHEAD OF AMANDA INTO THE HOUSE. She was reluctant to enter. She was picking up on echoes, hearing the noise of Rhees's funny-bone snapping.

In the living-room Drumm circled the fallen typewriter, the scattered papers and books with broken spines. 'They did a number here,' he said.

'I can't deal with this,' she said.

'A quick look round is all,' Drumm said. 'See if anything's missing. You keep jewels in the house, Amanda?'

'Any jewellery I had was in the bedroom, except for this silver chain I wear.' A gift from John, she remembered, with one of his poems attached.

'What about money?'

'John might have had a few dollars. We weren't planning to stay here.'

'Where's the bedroom?'

She showed Drumm the way. The closet had been ransacked. Her underwear had been rummaged through like lingerie at a frenetic post-Christmas sale. Panties in a heap, some of them flimsy and silken, sexy gossamer items. She thought of strangers crudely handling these intimacies and making off-colour jokes.

The drawers of the dressing-table lay open. 'There should be a small black velvet box with a string of pearls inside,' she said.

'I don't see it, Amanda.'

'So they stole the pearls. I never wore them anyway.'

Drumm peered inside the bathroom. 'They didn't bother with this room,' he said.

She followed Drumm into the kitchen. He bent, picked up something and held it carefully, dangling it between thumb and index-finger. It was John's brown leather wallet. He flipped it open. 'What did he keep in this?'

'An Amex card, a Visa, a couple of library cards. Probably some cash.'

'All they left were his library cards,' Drumm said. He wrapped the wallet in a sheet of waxy kitchen paper and stuck it in his pocket, then he stepped into the backyard and wandered off through the long grass, skirting the pool. She puzzled over what kind of inventory he was making. *One wallet, empty of cash and credit cards. One jar of beets, spilled. Frog in pool, deceased.* This wasn't his regular field of inquiry. He was here as a favour she hadn't asked for.

He came back indoors. 'They steal some jewels and a couple of credit cards and a negligible sum of money,' he said, 'but they don't take the PC or the TV and they don't rip off your expensive stereo system. That's a little strange. Usually it's the kind of stuff they make a beeline for.'

'They're not interested in carrying things,' she said. 'Maybe they're worn out by the physical exertion of beating up on John.'

Drumm laid a hand on her arm. 'I'll get some fingerprint guys in. And when John's feeling up to it, he might have more information we can use.'

219

She sat down at the table and looked through the kitchen door into the backyard. The setting sun was an otherworldly gold. A postcard. Wish you were here. Miss you.

She pressed her fingertips to her eyelids to ease the headache that was threatening. She glanced down at the puddle of beet juice. 'What makes them choose one house instead of another anyway? Why not the house next door, or the one next door to that? Is it like some kind of violent lottery, Willie? Spin the wheel, come up with an address?'

Drumm said, 'Sometimes.'

'Our house is the only scruffy one in the street. The yard's a mess. It doesn't exactly shout prosperity.'

'Exactly what makes it so attractive. Nobody comes to mow the lawn or clip the trees. Thieves watch a place. Who comes, who goes. They get the impression of vacancy and they think an easy score.'

'They watch,' she said.

'Sure they watch.'

They watch. They monitor. They drive past in the night, doing quiet U-turns in the cul-de-sac.

Anthony Dansk sailed into her mind.

She needed air. She walked out of the house and went to the bottom of the driveway and looked the length of the cul-de-sac. She glanced at parked cars. She moved until she came to the corner of the through street. Here, vehicles were tightly parked all the way along the sidewalks. Street lamps had come on, globes of orange-yellow light.

She stood on the corner, looking left and right, not at all certain what she expected to see. Maybe a guy behind a wheel, a woman staring idly into space, a man deep under the hood of his car, pretending he had engine trouble. Potential disguises were unlimited. Any innocent presence or movement was open to sinister interpretation.

She tried to imagine Dansk sitting in the vicinity, watching her coming and going, maybe even parked in the cul-de-sac itself now and again, brazenly observing the house. And if not Dansk, somebody who reported to him. And if not that, maybe Sanchez's people.

She went back, pausing in the driveway to look inside the VW, wondering if she'd dropped Isabel's letter on the floor. She checked under both front seats and found only a discarded Tab can. She flashed on the empty Coke can in the hospital waiting-room, the guy in the insurance-collar, the way he'd sat down right next to her and how a certain amount of fumbling and body-contact had gone on while he'd adjusted the position of the can for her. *I don't mind, smoke all you want.* The memory was smudged. She hadn't been in a frame of mind to register details.

Drumm was standing in the doorway. 'What are you looking for, Amanda? You were looking for something at the hospital too.'

She leaned against the car and gazed up at the dusky sky.

Drumm was silent for a time. 'You still interested in the Sanchez matter?'

'I don't know what I'm interested in any more. I'm not thinking clearly, Willie.'

'A little bird told me you went down to Florence. You saw Sanchez. He became violent, made threats.'

'You've got good sources,' she said.

Drumm said, 'We sent up a chopper.'

She thought of the desert, Isabel's broken shoe, the shadow of a helicopter.

'The pilot found nothing,' Drumm said.

'Why didn't they steal the goddam TV and the stereo?' she asked. 'You said yourself it was unusual.'

'Back up. We were talking about the Sanchez thing.'

She looked at her watch. 'It's time I phoned the hospital.'

'Amanda. What do you know that I don't?'

'I just want to call the hospital.'

'You're being evasive. You don't trust me?'

'What kind of question is that?' she answered.

She went inside the house and Drumm followed. She called Directory Assistance, got the number of the hospital and dialled it. She asked to be connected to the nurses' station on the third floor. Immediately a woman answered.

Amanda said, 'I'm calling about a patient, John Rhees.'

'And you are?'

What was the appropriate word? Lover? Cohabitant? 'His fiancée, Amanda Scholes.'

There was the sound of a keyboard being tapped. 'He's stable, Miss Scholes.'

'When's the earliest I can see him?'

'Visiting hours are from ten a.m. until noon.'

Amanda thanked the woman and hung up. She looked at Drumm and said, 'He's stable. That's hospital-speak.'

'*He's* stable. What about you?'

'I can't stay in this place. I'll check into a hotel for the night.'

'Smart idea.'

'Pack a few overnight things, I'm gone.'

Drumm caught her hand. 'Look. If there's something you're keeping back, this is as good a time as any to tell me. You left a message for me before. What did you want to tell me?'

It was an invitation to talk. Fine, why not? Break the goddam lid off the box and let the contents fly. She looked into Willie's eyes. There was never any guile in that face.

'This isn't for public consumption, Willie. This is strictly between you and me.' And she told him. About the letter, and the loss of it. The way she'd coerced the Program into

222

sending Anthony Dansk to Phoenix. When she was finished, she felt vaguely relieved. She'd shifted a burden even if she hadn't removed it.

'Sweet Jesus,' he said. 'What I wonder is how in God's name Sanchez pulled it off. I mean, you're talking fake papers, funny badges, serious access to the inside track, knowledge of the MO of the Program, the location of witnesses, et cetera. You're talking more than a leak, this is the whole dam.'

'That's what it is,' she said.

'And this guy Dansk says he'll fix it.'

'That's what he says.'

'He never saw Isabel's letter?'

She shook her head.

'And you've no idea where you lost it?'

'None.'

'So Dansk says he'll investigate and let you know how it comes out. You got a problem with that?'

'Yeah, but my head's like a carousel going round and round and I can't get it to stop long enough to think clearly.'

'Talk to me some more, Amanda.' He put his hand under her chin and turned her face slowly towards his own. 'Unload. Dump the rest on me.'

Dump what? All she had was instinct, vague and fuzzy, like a photograph screwed up in the dark-room. All she had were reverberating doubts and the conviction that Dansk was seriously missing a hinge, and that made him dangerous.

'He has me under surveillance, Willie,' she said.

'You know this for a fact?'

'Not for a fact,' she said. It sounded, she thought, loopy. 'Next I'll be hearing voices.'

Drumm didn't smile. He'd always given her the courtesy of taking her seriously. 'OK. He wants to know what you're up to. What's he so lathered about, Amanda?'

'I made a threat about speaking to the newspapers, which went down like the Hindenburg. I guess he's uneasy because he can't be one hundred per cent certain I won't go through with it. He doesn't enjoy the possibility of me trespassing where I don't belong. Namely, Program security.'

'Program security seems a little thin on the ground at present,' Drumm said. 'Maybe he's covering his ass because he's got something to hide.'

'For example?'

Drumm took a toothpick out of his breast pocket and placed it between his lips, moving it from one corner of his mouth. He tilted his head back. She knew this ruminative look so well she could practically hear wheels turning in his head. 'I'm just thinking out loud. Sanchez penetrates the Program, right. But he needed a whole lotta help. What if . . .' Drumm snapped the toothpick in two. 'What if he hired this character Dansk?'

'Sanchez hired Dansk?'

'Keep in mind, I'm only saying what if, that's all. Dansk is running around doing some damage limitation on a situation he created himself. The monster he built for Sanchez is roaring out of control. He's got nothing to do with the Program. He's a freelance operator—'

She interrupted Drumm. 'And somebody else *inside* the Program is providing him with information?'

'Maybe. Just maybe.'

She pondered Drumm's speculation. Suppose Dansk's performance was all some elaborate masquerade. She remembered calling the number Dansk had given her, and the taped message in a voice that wasn't his. *You have reached the office of Anthony Dansk. Mr Dansk isn't available to take your call at present.* She wondered about this, tried to imagine the location of his office, and if

Dansk really had any connection with the Justice Department. The office could be anything, rented space, an answering machine in an empty room. But whose voice was recorded on the machine? Then she remembered her earlier intention to telephone Justice, but when she'd entered the house and found chaos the notion had been swept out of her mind like debris in a flash-flood. And something else, another phone call she'd meant to make, but it evaded her. What the hell was it? She searched her shook-up memory.

Drumm said, 'What I can do is poke around, ask a few questions about this Dansk and see what comes up. A cop's badge still opens some doors, remember.'

'What doors do you have in mind?'

'For starters, Lewis Bascombe's,' he said.

'Bascombe? He's probably the most secretive man in this city,' she said. 'I don't know what you'll get out of him, even if he agrees to see you.'

'I'll kick my way in,' Drumm said and smiled.

'And wave your thirty-eight in his face?'

She couldn't imagine Drumm getting anywhere with Lew Bascombe. She shut her eyes a moment. *Bernadette Vialli, of course*. That was the missing thought. Like so much else, it had drifted away from her.

'Do me a small favour,' she said. 'Remember the Vialli case?'

'Scorched into my memory,' Drumm said.

'Benny's mother tried to get in touch with me. I'm not in the mood for calling her back right now.'

'You any idea why she phoned?'

'No.' Amanda looked at John's typewriter on the floor and the scattered papers and books and all at once she heard a low-pitched humming reminiscent of wasps disturbed and zooming in crazy disarray. She recognized this anger, a delayed reaction to the fact that her world had been chopped like kindling, and somehow Dansk was the one with the hatchet, and a lit match in his fingers.

'You want me to contact the woman,' Drumm said.

'Would you?'

'No sweat,' Drumm said. 'Any favour you need, come to me. Night, day, it doesn't matter. You got that?'

'Bless you,' she said. She kissed him on his plump warm cheek. Direct this animosity, she thought. Harness this rage.

'Meantime, I suggest you try and get a good night's rest,' Drumm said.

A good night's rest. It was the last thing on her mind.

43

AT 7.30 P.M. ANTHONY DANSK AND EDDIE McTELL STOOD IN A park where a floodlit softball game was going on about 200 yards away, a serious affair played with raw enthusiasm between one team in blue shirts and another in orange. The guy on strike had a massive roll of rubbery white flesh that leered between his shirt and waistband. A small crowd was gathered behind the wire fence at the catcher's back.

McTell asked, 'You uh like this game, Anthony?'

'I'm no big fan,' Dansk said. 'I just like to see people at their leisure, because I forget what leisure is.' He watched the fat guy swing and miss. Americans at play. An innocent contest under the lamps. Also shadows beyond the outfield where anything might lurk. A perv offering some seven-year-old a Snickers-bar bribe for a blow-job, or a sick dickhead junkie shooting up.

McTell stroked his beard. 'What's on your mind, Anthony?'

'A burden the size of a cathedral,' Dansk said. He handed two sheets of paper to McTell, who held them angled towards the distant floodlights.

McTell read, then raised his face and gazed at the soft-ball field. 'This is from . . .'

'You know who it's from. She sent it to the lady prosecutor and the lady prosecutor read it.'

'It don't name names,' McTell remarked and went into a defensive slouch, like a tired pugilist.

'And we're thankful for small mercies,' Dansk said.

'How did you get this letter?' McTell asked.

'Pasquale let his fingers do the walking.' Dansk took the letter back. 'I'd like to be happy, Eddie. Instead what I get are problems and headaches.'

'And you're blaming me and Pasquale, right? I gotta say this, Anthony, you never have a good word. You never say we did this right or we did that right.'

'What are you looking for, Eddie?' He raised both arms in the air and made a salaam motion. 'The mighty McTell, praise his name.'

McTell said, 'A kind word now and again is all. Instance. We did some terrific work on Rhees. You lay into a guy with metal, you run the risk of maybe punc-turing a lung or breaking the skull and then it's serious. But we did it the way you wanted it: delicate, Anthony. Like fucking artists.'

Dansk stared at the softball field. Artists. McTell and Pasquale were up there with Van Gogh and Reubens. He pondered the letter. 'The lady's learned something she wasn't supposed to learn, McTell.'

'Ask me, I don't see where she's learned anything,' McTell said.

Dansk thought of pushing the corkscrew of his Swiss Army knife into McTell's brain. 'Show me where the fuck it's written that you're paid to make judgements, McTell. You're reimbursed to kill, I'm the one paid to think and organize and forecast. And the problem here's not so

228

much what she's learned as what she *thinks* she's learned, what she believes. Her brain's on overtime.'

'She don't even have the letter,' McTell said.

Dansk said, 'No, but I'll bet good money she showed it to Drumm.'

'So she tells this cop. What's he gonna do? Drag Sanchez outta his cell and interrogate him day and fucking night? Who did he bribe? Who did he buy? That kinda thing. And what's Sanchez gonna say? Jack shit.'

Dansk said, 'You're not taking into account the woman's persistence. She's like a termite. She's not happy unless she's nibbling away at timbers.'

'What you do with a termite is you drop poison.'

'Poison,' Dansk said. He felt entangled in a variety of possibilities suddenly. The softball game seemed very far away, miniature figures participating in a meaningless ritual under the lamps. His lips were dry. He took from his pocket a tube of salve and applied it. He tasted lemon.

McTell's voice was surly. 'So beating up on the guy was a waste. All that labour for what? Shit?'

'Without this goddam letter, she'd have withered on the vine, McTell. She'd have shrivelled to a puckered substandard little raisin. Without this hysterical fucking note from the runaway señorita, she'd have dropped out of sight and done her Nurse Nightingale bit and tended to her lover's wounds. But the letter arrives and she reads it and her head starts running and she can't stop it.'

McTell had a look that might have been exasperation. 'So what now?'

The phone in Dansk's pocket went off. He felt it vibrate against his hip. He flipped the device open and heard Pasquale say, 'I lost her, Anthony.'

'Lost her?'

'She was in the house with this cop Drumm for maybe an hour. He leaves and a coupla minutes later she comes

229

outta the house and gets in her car. I follow her along Lincoln Boulevard, she pulls into a Circle-K, goes inside, ten minutes pass and she still hasn't reappeared. So I look in the store, only she's not there. I figure she's using the john, but when I take a look-see the john's empty and she's nowhere around. I walk back outside. Item, her car's still there. No sign of her.'

'So she slipped out the back?'

'Item, I go round the back. There's this alley. No sign of her. I check the front and her goddam car is still there. So I check the streets round the store: nothing. Then I haul ass back to the store again. Her car's *still* there. I can see it from where I'm sitting.'

'So this is like some magical illusion? She vanishes into nothing?'

'I don't know where she went.'

Dansk thought for a moment. 'Here's what I want you to do. Take her car, and don't tell me you don't have the keys and can't get it started. I'll call you back soon.'

Dansk snapped the phone shut and shoved it back in his pocket. She knew she was being followed, so she took steps to lose Pasquale. Nice. Did she ease through the back door of the store and into a maze of suburban streets? Stroll until she found a gas station where she could phone a cab? This lady has more than a degree of cunning.

'She skipped,' he said. *After talking with Drumm.*

'Anything you want me to do?'

Dansk was silent a moment. 'One thing,' he said.

'I'm listening,' said McTell, and inclined his body forward, his head tilted in what he considered his concentration mode.

44

FROM THE WINDOW OF THE HOTEL AMANDA COULD SEE THE freeway, the lights of the suburbs stretching towards darkness. She drew the curtains briskly, dumped her overnight bag on the bed and opened it. *The motions, remember the motions. Focus.* She worked fast. She dressed in the suit she'd worn at the Biltmore. She went inside the bathroom and applied thick make-up. She painted her lips a high gloss red and drew exaggerated lines around her eyes with a fine brush, then sprayed gel into her hair and ran a comb through it. The glistening look. She walked back inside the bedroom and varnished her nails a dreadful nuclear pink that would glow in the dark.

A new Amanda. Overstated.

She opened the mini-bar and took out several miniatures of liquor, mainly brandy and gin. She loosened the caps a little and stuffed the tiny bottles in her purse, along with cigarettes and all the rest of the junk she'd need.

Then she thought of the car that had been following her along Lincoln Boulevard. When she'd slowed down, so had the car. She pulled into the parking-lot of a convenience store. The car had sailed past the store and then hung a U-turn at the next lights and come back. She'd stepped inside the store, walked towards the john and kept going, pushing the metal crossbar of the delivery door at the rear, and then she was running.

I can't go through with this. This loony plan. This trip to the moon. Drumm would disapprove and Rhees would have a cardiac arrest, but they don't know what I'm doing.

You're not even sure yourself.

Yes you are. This is called focussing your rage.

She felt an inner tremor, a doubt. Shove it aside, cast it off. No time for indecision. She let her hand hover above the telephone. Her fingernails looked like they belonged to somebody else's hand.

She picked up the telephone and called the operator. 'Connect me to Anthony Dansk,' she said.

'Hold.' Ringing, ringing, ringing.

'I'm sorry, the room isn't answering. Is there a message?'

'No message,' Amanda said.

She put the telephone down. How much time, she wondered. She couldn't begin to guess. She slipped her feet inside her black shoes, picked up the bulky purse and headed for the door. She rode the elevator downward to the reception area where a great chandelier spiked the air with light at all angles, like a wayward laser.

The concierge's desk was unattended. At reception there was only the young man who'd checked her in earlier. He had a smile designed to please.

'How can I help you?' he asked.

'I'm supposed to meet somebody here, but he hasn't shown up,' she said. 'He's a guest.'

'You know his room number?'

'I think its eight seven three four. I'm just hopeless with

232

numbers.' The helpless shiny lipsticked smile.

'His name?'

'Dansk. Anthony.'

The clerk punched his computer. 'You certainly are hopeless with numbers,' he said, still smiling.

'Did I get the room wrong?'

'Miles out.'

'Typical. What is his number anyway?' she asked.

'Sorry, I can't say. Security reasons.'

'Makes sense these days,' she said.

'I'll call the room for you.' The clerk picked up a phone.

Amanda thought, Do it now. Do it before you lose whatever momentum you have.

She tipped her purse and it spilled open, tubes of lipstick, eyebrow pencils, a compact, a bottle of liquid hair gel, everything rolled across the surface of the desk in a variety of directions.

'Oh, Christ, clumsy me,' she said, and then the cigarettes followed, and six loose tampons, and the miniatures of liquor, which scattered across the desk leaking brandy and gin. 'Shit, shit, shit.'

The clerk said, 'It's no problem really.'

'My friends all call me Amanda Accident,' she said, in a bubbly airheaded fashion. 'I guess you can see why.'

'I'll just clean it up.' The clerk took a linen handkerchief from his pocket and began to swab the desk like a cabin-boy. Booze was soaking through the tampon-wrappers, making rainbow puddles around the eyebrow pencils and the tubes of lipstick.

'Jesus, it's a mess, it's a terrible mess. I'm sorry,' she said.

'It's nothing, really. I can clean it up in no time.'

'Let me help,' she said.

'I don't need help, really,' the clerk said.

'No, I insist.' She reached across the desk to retrieve

233

some of the spilled items and she struck the computer screen with her elbow and it swivelled slightly towards her, even as a few of the cylindrical beauty enhancements dropped on the clerk's side of the desk and booze dripped onto his paperwork.

'Now it's all over your papers. I'm so damn sorry, really I am. I shouldn't be allowed out.'

7320.

'I'm fine, I'm absolutely fine,' he said.

Bless his heart, he was still smiling. Slapstick, she thought. I have a knack for it, a clown's gift.

The clerk had collected everything together in a wet mound on the centre of his desk. 'There, I think that's most of it. I guess you want me to dump this stuff.'

'Would you please,' she said.

'No problem.'

'You're very understanding,' she said. 'I come in here and before you know it, disaster.'

'I'm trained for emergencies, large and small,' he said.

She fished a wet five-dollar bill from her purse. 'Here,' she said.

'That's not necessary,' he said.

'Call it guilt money,' she said.

He took the bill tentatively out of her fingers.

She walked quickly out of the reception area. Act one over. She was conscious of time again.

She rode up in the elevator to her room. She looked at the room-service menu, picked up the phone and said, 'This is Mrs Anthony Dansk, seventy three twenty. Send up a Union Jack burger and fries. How long will that take?'

'Ten minutes, ma'am.'

She checked her watch. Ten minutes. Mrs Anthony Dansk, she thought. She wondered if Dansk had a wife. She couldn't imagine it.

234

She walked up and down the room. The slapstick was over. The next part was different. She sat on the bed, but her heart was like a racehorse and she had to get up again. She went inside the bathroom and looked at her face in the mirror. The surge of nervous energy that had transported her through the comedy of errors at reception was still flowing vigorously. All the time at the desk she'd wondered what would have happened if Dansk had chosen that moment to enter the hotel and he had seen her. A sliver of luck. You needed it now and again.

Let it hold.

She checked her watch again. She took off her shoes and left her room. She rode the elevator down and stepped out on the seventh floor. She found room 7320 and she waited outside the door. Ten minutes since she'd ordered from room service. Eleven. Twelve. This is no way to do things, the heart flat out. Dansk could appear. Dansk could materialize in the corridor. And then what? Hello, Anthony, I was just in the neighbourhood.

She heard the elevator in the shaft, the clank of cutlery. She saw the room-service waiter come into view with a tray balanced on one hand. He was a tall black kid in a striped vest. She smiled at him as he approached.

'I know, I know, you're gonna think I'm a total moron,' she said. 'I locked myself out. I'm not even wearing my shoes, for God's sake. I thought I heard somebody at the door, so I went to see, the door swung shut behind me. What do you put on the hinges here? Electromagnets? Now I'm standing here like an idiot.'

'Happens all the time,' the kid said.

'It does?'

'Oh sure.'

'So do I eat my dinner out here in the corridor or are you going to be like my knight in shining armour and let me back inside my room?'

'You're a damsel in distress,' the kid said.

'Distress is right. I think I'm beyond the age of damsel, though.'

The kid laughed. 'I never heard of an age limit to damsels.' He slipped a keycard from his shirt pocket.

'Will that work?' she asked, looking at the card and thinking, Hurry, hurry.

'This is a magic card. One size fits all.' He slid the card into the slot, turned the handle and said, 'See? Open sesame.'

She walked ahead of him into the room. He set down the tray and gave her a slip of paper to sign. She wrote *Mrs Anthony Dansk* and added five dollars in the gratuity column.

'Thanks a lot,' the kid said.

'You deserve it.'

The kid left the room, closing the door behind him.

She thought, *I'm in*.

45

DANSK, STEPPING OUT OF HIS CAR IN THE PARKING GARAGE, saw the man emerge from the shadows. Long black coat, beret, black gloves even. The man was seized by a fit of coughing and dug inside the pocket of his coat and came out with a small chocolate-brown bottle which he uncapped and held to his lips. He took a swig and stuck the bottle away again. His eyes watered. He looked as if he'd hawked up a chunk of diseased lung and was sickened by the taste in his mouth.

'What is that shit you're drinking, Loeb?' Dansk asked.

'Morphine in a syrup base.'

'Morphine?'

'Whatever it takes,' Loeb said. 'Anybody ever tells you there's dignity in pain is talking unadulterated crap. Let's get some air.'

They walked together through a door marked EXIT and entered an alley at the back of the hotel where Dansk saw dark-green plastic garbage sacks and cardboard boxes, all very orderly.

In his beret Loeb resembled a raddled, hollow-faced

1950s poet, a guy sitting outside a café on the Left Bank or in Greenwich Village, scribbling intense odes and drinking cheap red vino. 'I was wondering about our lady,' he said.

'This is territory I work my own way. This is mine,' Dansk said, keeping his voice in check.

'Yeah, it's your domain all right. But this work can contaminate a man. I've seen people get a taste for death. They develop a jones.'

'Oh spare me the fucking lecture,' Dansk said.

'Sometimes enthusiasm's great, Anthony. Other times it fogs a man's judgement.'

Dansk said, 'There's nothing wrong with my judgement, Loeb.'

Loeb said, 'You're so damn defensive these days, I wonder if you aren't just losing the place a little. I worry about your detachment.'

'I'm detached,' Dansk said.

'Maybe. But this work can get to you in such a way you wouldn't even notice it happening.'

'I'd notice,' Dansk said.

'So tell me about her. Share, Anthony.'

Dansk laughed. 'Share? What is this? Like a counselling session?'

'Carry too much inside, you get stressed, Anthony. I attend this group in Fairfax, it's people like myself living with a death sentence. And we talk things through, and it helps, because you realize you're not entirely alone in the universe.'

Dansk imagined a room filled with dying people. Incurables Anonymous. 'I don't need to share,' he said. 'I'm not the one sick.'

'Pardon me, I forgot, you're invincible. Captain Fucking Marvel. The occasional services of a hooker and a whistle-stop tour of a church or two, and suddenly you're walking on water.'

'Don't give me static, Loeb.' Dansk was irritated with Loeb prying, carping, carrying that dark bloom of death. He didn't want to be in Loeb's company. Hanging round terminal people was depressing. Even if you couldn't catch the other person's disease, you were vulnerable to the despair they hauled like leg-irons.

'She goes here, there, so I track her movements and I try to read her mind and see how much of a problem she is.'

'How much of a problem is she, Anthony?'

'I'm tired. This has been a long day and I feel like one of those plastic sacks there. There's grime attached to me, which I don't like. I need to shower.'

Dansk moved a few steps along the alley. Loeb followed, catching him by the arm. 'You think you can handle her, Anthony?'

Dansk shrugged the hand aside. 'I can handle her.' He thought about the letter in his pocket which he had no intention of showing to Loeb. Why give the nosy old fart something to criticize?

Dansk kept walking. He stopped only when he heard Amanda's voice:

'*Oh God, this is an emergency I need an ambulance and police, and I need them five minutes ago.*'

'*Give me your address and the nature of your problem, please.*'

'*The address is three six one Kennedy. That's Scottsdale, near the Civic Center.*'

'*And the problem, miss?*'

'*My boyfriend . . . I think he may be dying . . . somebody came in the house and he's beaten up and I found him in the pool and—*'

'*Try to remain calm. I'll have somebody with you as fast as I can.*'

'*How fast is fast?*'

'*As fast as possible.*'

'*Hurry, for Christ's sake . . .*'

Enraged, Dansk said, 'Jesus, you got a wire on her *fucking* phone.' He felt he'd been cuffed around the ears and the inside of his head was ringing, his skin stinging.

Loeb had a tiny cassette player in his hand. He said, 'Listen some more.'

Amanda's voice: '*I'm calling about a patient. John Rhees.*'

'*And you are?*'

'*His fiancée, Amanda Scholes.*'

'*He's stable, Miss Scholes.*'

'*When's the earliest I can see him?*'

'*Visiting hours are from ten a.m. until noon.*'

Loeb shut off the machine. 'And that's what you ordered, Anthony? You had the shit kicked out of her boyfriend?'

'It was a simple diversion,' Dansk said.

'Is that what you call it?'

'You had absolutely no goddam right, Loeb,' he said.

'No right to run an eye over your operation?'

Dansk said, 'The deal was you don't interfere, you don't question my decisions.'

'I question this one. Rhees is one half of a couple. You've trespassed into some very dicey emotional territory.'

Dansk said, 'Emotional territory? Where did you get your psychology degree? Some school in Guatemala that advertises on the back of matchbooks?'

Loeb looked morose. 'You didn't take into account the obvious thing, Anthony. You've only tossed more kerosene on the woman's bonfire.'

Dansk said nothing. He was seething at the idea of Loeb criticizing him.

'You never used to put a foot wrong, Anthony, but what you didn't take into account is the fact that other people

240

have strong feelings, and sometimes those feelings lead to unpredictable responses. Am I coming through to you on any known frequency?'

Dansk was silent. Let Loeb drone on.

'The question is, what's your next step, Anthony?'

'I go up to my room and I take a shower.'

'About the woman,' Loeb said.

Dansk said, 'I can take care of her.'

Loeb looked infinitely weary and sad. 'God knows why, but I'm your friend, Anthony. Maybe the only one you've got.'

'I don't need friends that go behind my back,' Dansk said. He listened to Loeb's ruined breathing. 'You know what I think? The drugs have addled you. You're stoned morning to night. You can't make judgements.'

'I don't believe I've ever seen the world more clearly in all my life,' Loeb said.

'Drugs'll make you believe anything,' Dansk said.

Loeb folded his arms and leaned against the wall. Under his eyes were dark sooty rings. 'This work we're doing, we're pushing boulders up mountains, and there's always more boulders. There's a job in Seattle should have been taken care of yesterday. Another in LA.'

Open-mouthed, Loeb was sucking on shallow pockets of air. 'What I'm saying is we need to get the business done here because we're falling behind. I need to know you can finalize things in a straightforward way. I need to believe that this business you engineered with Rhees was just some brainstorm along the way.'

'I can cope,' Dansk said. Brainstorm, he thought. Loeb didn't appreciate intricacy. He didn't like filigree. Angles baffled him, curved surfaces bewildered him. His was the geometry of a wasted old pen-pusher. X belongs in this box, Y belongs in that. There's only one road from A to B, and that's the straight and narrow. Maybe for you, Loeb.

241

Loeb looked bleak. 'I don't want an extravaganza, Anthony. I don't want to hear about diversions. Give me quiet, and don't leave any mess. Bury your litter.' Loeb turned and moved in his slow-footed manner down the alley. He stopped and called back, 'I'm trusting you, Anthony. Just don't go off at tangents.'

Tangents. You brain-dead fuck. Dansk chewed on the small finger where no nail grew, a nervous mannerism he'd acquired in fifth grade. A brutally dumb kid called Skipper Klintz had smashed his pinky with a claw-hammer. It was all on account of Skipper's need to assert his tribal superiority over Dansk, whose birthmark rendered him odd and imperfect, and consequently a victim. The nail had never grown back again. Two weeks later, on a bleak sub-zero night, Dansk had waited in an alley for Skipper and battered his head with a baseball bat. He could still feel the whap of the bat in his hands and the crack of Skipper's skull. A home run and the crowd going crazy in the bleachers and the electronic scoreboard popping.

Now he watched Loeb go, a sick shambles of a guy shuffling away, dying with every step he took. *I'm trusting you.* Bugging phones behind my back, you call that trust?

Dansk walked to the end of the alley, reached the street where the hotel sign created a soft yellow glare and a uniformed doorman stood motionless on the steps, misted by the light falling all around him.

46

AMANDA FOUND STACKED ON DANSK'S BEDSIDE TABLE THE following: a map of Arizona, a paperback entitled *Guide to Restaurants in the Valley of the Sun*, and an inky copy of something called *Phoenix After Dark*, which was a list of swingers and spouse-swappers, strip joints and gay bars and escort agencies. Dansk had circled some of these agencies in red ball-point. Romantic Liaisons. Sweet Dreams. Phantasy Chix. Some had come-on lines, like, 'Meet Miss Foxxy Foxx and get out of that rut.' 'See Petal, ripe for plucking.'

In the drawer of the table she found a packet of condoms, a set of old rosary beads and a plastic wallet-insert that contained a series of photographs.

She glanced at these snapshots. Dansk was unmistakable in each of them. Some depicted him as a kid, others as a teenager. A woman figured in every shot. In some of them she had an arm round Dansk's waist or a hand on his arm. Amanda guessed Dansk's mother because there was some slight resemblance. Touching, she thought. He carries pictures of Mom. And the beads. She tried to imagine him smoothing them with his fingertips but she couldn't.

She opened the drawers of the dressing-table. The potent aroma of sandalwood emerged from a sachet that had been placed over a neat stack of boxer shorts. She dug around the polka dots and the paisleys, noticing how fastidiously they'd been ironed and arranged. The next drawer down contained a couple of shirts, still in their Cellophane packages, and a half dozen pairs of socks, coupled and folded. The third drawer was empty.

She walked to the closet and checked the clothes that hung meticulously on hangers: two suits, both designer labels, two sports coats, a couple of pairs of shorts. The pockets were all empty. They yielded nothing, not a coin, a scrap of paper, not even lint. What did he do? Vacuum them?

On the closet floor was a combination-locked aluminium case. She picked it up, shook it and heard what sounded like papers sliding around inside. She longed to open the case, but it was useless. She set the case back.

She entered the bathroom. Toilet items were lined up just so inside the cabinet. Aftershave, hair lotion, a mouthwash she'd never heard of and a toothbrush designed to reach the deepest recesses of the gums and God knows where else. A nail-file with a genuine ivory handle, a heavy-duty nail-clipper, a container of floss, a tortoiseshell hairbrush in whose bristles a matching comb had been inserted, and a wooden spatula-like device whose purpose she couldn't begin to guess. On the sink was a bottle of Italian mineral water and a razor and shaving cream in a tube.

And a salt-shaker. Did he gargle with brine?

This is what Dansk came down to. Expensive toiletries and empty pockets and a locked case and the fact that he used escort services.

Who the hell are you, Dansk?

She went back inside the bedroom. A printed card on top of the TV provided the information that guests could access a computer that would provide them with a detailed account of their bill. She aimed the remote at the screen, turned the TV on, selected Channel 22 as the card instructed. The name popped up: ANTHONY DANSK

Then:

ROOM RATE $175 TAX INC.	TOTAL $875.00
ROOM SERVICE	TOTAL $63.00
PHONE CALLS	TOTAL $4.25
LAUNDRY	TOTAL $48.50

She studied the room rate figure a moment, calculating. He'd been here five nights. He hadn't just come to Phoenix to meet her some twenty-four hours ago. *I flew all the way down here to set your mind at rest*, he'd told her. But you were already here, Anthony, already in place. Why the lie? Why go through that rigmarole?

You lie when you have something to gain.

Or something to hide.

She stared at the menu along the bottom of the screen and pressed sixty-seven on the remote, which gave her access to an itemized account of telephone calls.

PLEASE WAIT. TRY OUR YUCCA ROOM ON THE MEZZANINE FOR FINE WESTERN CUISINE!

Then:

DANSK, ANTHONY 7320

What followed was a list of calls he'd made. He'd

245

placed four, all local, three to the same number. She wrote the numbers down on a scratch pad that lay on top of the dressing-table, then she folded the sheet and stuck it in her pocket. She switched off the TV.

It was time to get out of here, and yet she had the feeling she was overlooking something, she hadn't explored deeply enough. But what was left to explore? Hotel rooms like this one didn't have a surplus of hiding-places. There was an air-conditioning duct, but she didn't have either the time or the tool to unscrew the grille. There was also the chance of something concealed under the carpet, but the task of searching would take too long. Down on her knees, hauling at the rug, popping tacks.

The mini-bar was the last place left. It was stuffed with miniatures, a half bottle of Californian Chardonnay, a jar of macadamia nuts and a tube of Toblerone. She rummaged, found nothing unusual and shut the door. Leave, she told herself. Leave now. You've already pressed your luck to its limits and then some.

She took a last quick look round the room and then stepped towards the door, and halfway there the mercurial bird of good fortune abandoned her, and she heard *click* as the coded key card was inserted into the lock and the door opened.

'Interesting,' Dansk said.

47

SHE RAISED ONE HAND TO HER HAIR IN A FLUSTERED MANNER, her nerve-ends jumping. The atmosphere around her had a tense zing to it, like the vibration left by a tuning-fork. She moved, standing with her back to the window, crossing her arms in a defensive way. She was aware of the peripheral blackness of night behind her, and she imagined Dansk strolling towards her and casually pushing her through glass, and then she was falling, storey after storey, to the sidewalk.

She walked away from the window and thought, Nobody knows I'm here.

Dansk said, 'I guess there's a good explanation for this.' The letter from the señorita. That's what brings her here. She's shovelling and she doesn't know what lies underneath the soil. And if she knew, she wouldn't be here. 'You looking for anything in particular? Or was it just a general sniff around, see what you could find?'

She could still hear the air vibrate as if a huge menacing bird had just passed close to her face. When she spoke her voice sounded cracked. 'You've been following me.'

'I didn't hear that. Louder.'

She cleared her throat and said it again.

Dansk looked annoyed. 'Following you? Is this because I bump into you by chance on the street and you construct a whole weird scenario around that encounter? Why would I follow you, Amanda?'

He undid his necktie and it dangled from his hand.

'You know why,' she said. She noticed how the silver tie caught the light and resembled a loose metal chain.

'You're speaking a foreign language. Translate for me.'

'You're running surveillance on me because you know I'm not buying into your deal.'

'Where is all this coming from, Amanda?'

'Rhees is in hospital with broken bones.'

'Rhees?' he asked. 'I don't know any Rhees. You can't just toss out a name at me, Amanda.'

She saw from the window the lights of radio masts perched on mountains in those black distances where the city faded. The anger and adrenalin that had driven her appeared to be slipping, and an edge of dread had replaced it. She felt very alone all at once. She looked at Dansk's reflection in the pane. He seemed to exist simultaneously in different dimensions, behind her in solid form, floating in front of her in a fuzzy spectral framework.

Why hadn't she told Willie she was coming here? Anything could happen to her and nobody would know. She turned, bringing Dansk back into focus. 'Rhees wasn't any part of this—'

'I'm hearing foreign still.'

'You didn't do it personally. You paid for it to be done.'

'Paid who to do what?'

'It was meant to look like robbery with serious violence thrown in. But it was badly stage-managed. Thieves *steal* things, Anthony. You should teach your thugs that.'

'I don't even know Rhees, so let me hear one good reason why I'd want him harmed.'

'As a warning to me.'

A warning, he thought. If she wanted to think it was something that crude, let her. People often misconstrued his intentions. Even the smart ones, like Amanda. They didn't set themselves demanding standards.

'You're off in the twilight zone, Amanda. I'm hearing that dooda-dooda tune. You just break in here and lay this shit on my doorstep and you don't have one solid thing to back it up. This is unlawyerly.'

'I'm not a lawyer these days,' she said. She stared at him. He gazed back, nonchalant, running the necktie through his fingers.

'You break in here and make a wild accusation. Is that normal behaviour?'

'You're familiar with normal, I suppose.'

He didn't like this remark. It rubbed him in all the wrong ways. He walked towards her and looked at her bright lipstick and polished nails. She wasn't cut out for these gaudy adornments, they cheapened her. 'What the hell is your *problem*? You break into my room, presumably you rummage through my belongings. What did you expect to find here? Spell it out for me. Tell me what's really on your mind.'

'Your Program. The way it leaks.'

'And that's all.'

'That's all.'

'I think it's more. You're unhinged on account of Isabel Sanchez and whatever it was happened to this guy Rhees,' he said. 'And now you're imagining funny things.'

There was an alteration in his mood. He leaned forward, placed his palms against the wall on either side of her face. She was imprisoned between his outstretched arms. She felt she was seeing him through a microscope.

The fuzz on his cheeks, the ginger eyebrows, his pores, the birthmark, everything was blown-up in unnerving detail. She anticipated violence. She imagined Dansk striking her. She felt an inward flinch.

'Talk to me,' he said.

'I don't have anything else to say.'

He looked into her eyes and it occurred to him that he could strangle her with his necktie. The idea strobed through him in black and white flashes: the lethal laying on of hands, the deadly intimacy of it all, her eyes darkening as she died. Killing somebody, the way McTell did, or Pasquale. How it would feel. He imagined numbness, the heart anaesthetized, a plunge into a bewildering madness. He didn't want McTell or Pasquale involved when it came to this woman, he didn't want them getting within a mile of her. He wanted her for himself. But not here in this room, because even if she died without a sound there was still the daunting prospect of dragging a corpse into an elevator and out through reception, past clerks and porters and guests and security people. Unrealistic.

And then there was Rhees. Any final solution had to involve him too, because he and Amanda had probably discussed the letter together. They were lovers, and lovers should die together.

He noticed the room-service food on the table. The hamburger smelled cold and the fries were limp.

'You haven't eaten your food,' he said. 'Lost your appetite?'

'I'm not that hungry.'

He gazed down at her feet. 'Lost your shoes as well?'

'I like not wearing shoes,' she said.

She looked at the sweat on his forehead and wondered where he'd been for the last twenty seconds or so, because he'd misted over like a window under a layer of condensation, and his jaw had set in a purposeful way and the muscles in his cheeks had been working as if he were chewing gum. He'd vanished in front of her eyes.

'Eat. You ordered the stuff.' He caught her wrist and tugged her towards the table. 'Sit down.'

'I don't want to sit,' she said.

He pulled back a chair and forced her into it. '*Now eat.*'

'I don't—'

'Eat,' he said.

He whipped the top off the bun and she found herself looking at a dollop of ketchup on the browned meat.

'Try the burger,' he said. His voice was chilly and brittle and angry.

She lifted the burger reluctantly. It fell apart between her fingers and she watched it drop on the plate, a soggy bun disintegrating and a crumbling disc of meat smeared with sauce. Dansk was hovering just behind her.

'Clumsy, clumsy. You need some help.'

He scooped up a handful of meat in his palm and held it to her mouth and she turned her head to one side and said, 'I'm not fucking hungry.'

'Kids are starving all over the world,' he said. 'And I hate waste, I hate the way people don't think about others less fortunate.' He pushed the meat forcefully into her mouth, and she shoved his hand aside.

'I don't *want* the goddam food,' she said.

'You *ordered* it,' he said.

Dansk could smell her perfume. He could smell fear on her too, and he had a sense of power flowing through him. He was wired to this woman in some fashion and he was draining energy out of her battery and it made him giddy. He reached down to the table and picked up a fork, speared an onion and raised it close to her face and let it dangle just in front of her.

She gazed at the hanging strand of onion and tried to shove her chair away from the table but Dansk obstructed her. He let the fork fall, placed his hands back on her shoulders and felt her shiver.

'I scare you,' he said.

'I'm not easily scared.'

He wanted to keep his hands on her. Suddenly he didn't want to release her, he wanted to open the buttons of her blouse and lay his head between her breasts. He kept the pressure on her shoulders. He thought, This is a step too far. So fucking what? He couldn't stop himself. He wanted to taste her breasts – a crazy idea, she meant nothing, she didn't even attract him that way, and in his head she was already a corpse. He reached over from behind and lowered his hands and fumbled with the buttons of her blouse and she didn't move, and he thought, She wants this. He slid a palm inside her blouse and felt the silky material of her brassière and slipped his fingers under it. Then he was touching her warm breast and it was a good feeling, the softness of her skin, her acquiescence, the power he had over her.

She moved abruptly. She swept the food and the plate from the table with a speedy motion of her hand and she picked up a knife, which she jabbed hard into his knuckles, and he stepped back. She rose, colliding with the table and toppling it over, then she spun round and held the knife towards Dansk, who held out his hands in a gesture that might have been one of appeasement, but it wasn't, because there was a vicious light in his green eyes. She was aware of the knife shaking in her fist and how breathless she'd become.

She could still feel the pressure of his fingers on her shoulders and the way he'd slipped his hand inside her blouse and how the ice-cold palm had covered her breast, the whole ugly violation of the moment.

Dansk casually examined the back of his hand where she'd jabbed it. 'What we have here is a slight misunderstanding,' he said. 'I guess I imagined ... some carnal agenda.'

'*Carnal* agenda?'

'You turn up in my room. What am I supposed to think?'

'You don't think ...' She wanted to laugh at his supposition, but she knew laughter would provoke him. Still holding the knife in front of herself, she moved towards the door and hurried out of the room. She ran along the corridor to the elevators, half expecting Dansk to follow her, but he didn't. She entered the elevator and pressed the button for her floor and realized how tightly she was holding the knife in her tensed hand. Dansk had dragged her down to the place where he lived, his world of brutality. She entered her room, shut the door, slid the bolt in place and stood with her back against the wood, trying to catch her breath and steady her nerves.

Sweat stuck Dansk's shirt to his flesh.

He thought, She's past the point of no return. She's a long way past that.

He pictured her moving somewhere in the night. (Shoeless. Why shoeless?) He pictured her in bed, waiting for the hour to roll around when she'd visit Rhees in hospital. And then what? She'd sit beside him, feeling bad. She'd reproach herself. And what next?

He lay back and closed his eyes. He smelled the hamburger again, the stone-cold French fries. He looked at the overturned table, the scattered food, little globs of mustard and ketchup on the carpet. Messy, Amanda.

He lifted the phone and called McTell.

McTell said, 'I picked him up when he was leaving his office.'

'And?'

'OK. He drives to the suburbs, somewhere, north

Phoenix, I dunno exactly. The streets look all the same to me round here.'

'Then what?'

'He parks outside a house surrounded by all these palm trees and yuck plants, yucca, whatever they're called—'

'Skip the garden tour.'

'He goes inside, stays a half-hour.'

'Whose house?'

'The name on the mailbox was Bascombe.'

Dansk was quiet for a time. 'Where is he now?'

'OK. He left Bascombe, stopped in a diner for some apple pie, cream, the works—'

'The point, McTell.'

'He's in another suburb, looks exactly like the last one. He's parked outside a house.'

'You got the name of the occupant?'

'I'm waiting to check the mailbox. You don't just walk up to it, Anthony: there's neighbours, a guy walking dogs—'

'Call me back when you know.'

Dansk hung up. He took Isabel Sanchez's letter from his pocket and stared at the scribbled words. He struck a match, applied it to the sheets and dropped them into an ashtray. He stirred the ashes with a fingertip, imagining they were the cremated remains of some tiny creature sacrificed, and then he opened his case and removed a bunch of faxes. He set these on fire too. Flame purified.

His phone rang. McTell said, 'Check this out. The name on the box is Vialli.'

Dansk said, 'Stay right where you are, McTell. Don't move an inch. I mean that.' He got up and started gathering his clothes together. He swept all his toiletries inside a leather bag and closed it. The sound of the zip closing

254

reminded him of flesh tearing, of a sharp instrument slicing a vein.

He thought, This Is Your Life, Amanda Scholes.

The beginning of the end of it.

48

DRUMM RANG THE DOORBELL, WAITED, SHIFTED HIS WEIGHT
a little. His leg ached from an old wound inflicted on him
during the course of a liquor store hold-up when he'd
been a rookie. He remembered the shock of the bullet ripping through his flesh and exiting along with tissue and
blood and a chunk of bone. The ache was more pronounced at times of stress, such as now. He attributed the
stabbing pain to his meeting with Bascombe. Talk about
pulling teeth. Lew Bascombe was a dentist's nightmare.

A porch light came on and he blinked.

A woman's voice from inside: 'Who's there?'

'Police,' Drumm said. Even pleasant suburbs had
become shotgun territory, he thought. People lived with
guns in nightstands, guns in closets. Villains roamed the
streets. Look at Rhees.

'Police?'

'I have ID,' Drumm said.

The door opened an inch. There was a chain between
door and jamb. Drumm held out his ID card. The woman
peered at it. 'This is kinda late to be calling,' she said.

'I apologize,' Drumm said.

'You better come inside,' she said. 'You know, I think I remember you. You were at the trial of Benny's uncles. Right?'

'Right.' Drumm stepped into the hallway. There was an overload of floral arrangements on various surfaces. The woman led him into a sitting-room suggestive of a funeral parlour, more flowery arrays, mountains of lilacs and lilies, stacks of greenery in baskets.

'Sit, sit down, Lieutenant.'

Drumm lowered himself into a plump easy chair. The leg stabbed. Bernadette Vialli wore a blue robe. She had thick little fingers. The lenses of her glasses were grey-tinted, matching the colour of her short permed hair. She was a small woman and her feet barely touched the carpet when she sat in an armchair facing Drumm.

Family photographs hung on almost every available wall space, interrupted by a couple of paint-by-numbers water-colours. Drumm saw Benny Vialli in some of the photographs. Benny as a kid, Benny as a teenager. He had protruding ears and a cheerful smile.

'I'm here on Amanda Scholes's behalf,' Drumm said. 'You called her, I understand.'

'Yeah. A few days ago.'

'She asked me to follow up,' Drumm said.

'It's real nice of you to come in her place, except now I wish I hadn't called her. It's a waste of your time.'

'You must have had some reason when you phoned her.'

'I'm a mother. Worry about this, worry about that, then you're out of control before you know it and imagining all kinds of things.'

'I don't have any children, Mrs Vialli,' Drumm said. 'My wife died a few years back. We just never got round to kids.'

'I'm sorry,' she said. She took off her glasses. There were red ridges on either side of her nose.

Drumm thought about his little downtown apartment and the pantry loaded with Campbell's soup, individual servings in small cans. Jeanette, God rest her, had been some kind of cook. But that was past. He didn't dwell on her absence except when he had a can-opener in his hand and was wondering whether to choose the cream of asparagus or the cream of mushroom even though they tasted exactly the same: of corn-starch.

'Kids are a joy. Also a heartbreak.' Mrs Vialli rose and adjusted flowers, gathering bright clumps of petals between her hands. She did this for a while as if she had in mind some ideal arrangement she couldn't actualize. 'I got to thinking about Benny, that's what happened.'

'What about Benny?' he asked.

'It's just so . . . it's nothing.'

'I'd still like to hear.'

Mrs Vialli gave up on the flowers. 'Benny and me, we were real close, until his uncles hired him down to Tucson. With relatives like those guys you wish you could pick and choose your family. I hope they goddam rot in jail. They had Benny going like, yeah, a yo-yo. Drive this guy, drive that, deliver this package, deliver that. I don't believe he ever thought he was doing anything illegal. I'm his mother, and I love him more than anyone in the world, but he's always had this kinda lost thing about him. Day he was born, I took one look at his face and I thought, This world's gonna be a rocky ride for you, darling.'

Drumm heard the sadness in the woman's voice and it touched him. Mrs Vialli opened a cabinet and took out a small cassette deck. 'The battery's probably weak on this.'

She pressed PLAY. Initially there was hissing. The voice that eventually issued from the cassette sounded as if it had travelled from an abandoned space probe.

'Ma, it's Benny. I wish you was (*inaudible*) got (*inaudible*) two but (*inaudible*) I'm doing (*inaudible*) these guys are (*inaudible*) they say I can't call you (*Insert another seventy-five cents please*) Ma, I'm outta time, I'll call again real soon.'

The tape stopped dead.

Mrs Vialli said, 'That was two days after he went away. I've listened to it fifty times at least. I try to imagine where he was phoning from, what kind of place, what he was wearing, was he getting the right food, you know? He never did call back.'

Drumm thought the room felt like a box wrapped in Cellophane. One of the paintings on the wall depicted a harbour and a small anchored sailboat and gulls that were no more than a haphazard series of Vs.

I'll call again real soon. And he never had.

'My hobby,' Mrs Vialli said. 'Water-colours.'

'Very nice,' Drumm said. His thoughts drifted to Bascombe's hobby, the balsa-wood Messerschmitts and Spitfires he built in a workshop that smelled of glue and chemicals. He was some kind of World War Two airplane buff and he laboured in grim patient silence. His tiny models hung from nylon strings tacked to the ceiling. *I don't like being interrupted in my own home*, Bascombe had said. *Make an appointment at my office.*

Mrs Vialli said, 'Benny's gone, and my husband passed away eight years ago. I miss the boy. It's a hole in my heart.'

'I'm sure it is,' Drumm said.

Mrs Vialli said, 'You got time to look at something?' She moved to a writing-bureau and opened it, and from a small drawer took out a white envelope. She handed it to Drumm.

'Go ahead, open it.'

Drumm took the message card from the envelope. It

259

had a red heart on the front and the words 'HAPPY BIRTHDAY TO MY BELOVED MOTHER'.

Mrs Vialli said, 'The card was attached to a buncha roses. There's a message inside. Read it if you like.'

Drumm flipped open the card and read the message, written in featureless block capitals with a ball-point pen. 'Dear Mom, I miss you very much, love, your son.'

'One quick phone message and flowers and that card in more than six months, nothing else,' Mrs Vialli said. She sat down and frowned. 'It's not much. I know, the Program protects him, I know the rules, but it's still not much. And there's something about the birthday card worries me.'

'What?'

'You have a kid, he's like this book you can always read, you just know how he behaves. And one big problem I have with this card is . . .' She paused and looked at Drumm. 'I know this is gonna seem very small to you and maybe you'll leave here thinking I'm a little crazy, but I'll tell you anyway. You heard the tape, he called me Ma. You read the card. How does it begin? Dear Mom, that's how. Dear Mom.'

'And?'

'When he was a very young kid, just starting to talk, he always called his grandmother Mom. Poor little guy couldn't get his mouth around the word grandma, I guess. Anyway, it was always Mom. I kept telling him life was gonna get confusing for everybody if he went round referring to his grandmother as Mom, so he called me Ma.'

'Always?'

'He'd come home from school and say what's that cooking in Ma Vialli's kitchen. What's that good smell, Ma. You change Ma to Mom, why it's like somebody who's called you Jack all your life suddenly deciding to call you John. Where's the sense of it?'

Mrs Vialli was right, it *was* a small thing, it was microscopic. But Drumm wasn't inclined to dismiss small things, because he understood from years of experience that they sometimes had significance way beyond their size. A fibre from a rug, a single pubic hair, a speck of dust, stuff like that had sent some people to jail, others to death row. You never overlooked small. He had a bad feeling, only it wasn't his leg this time, it was closer to indigestion, an eruption in his intestines, gassy heat round his heart. *I can't talk about the Program*, Bascombe had said.

This is serious, Lew. This is a homicide investigation and I'll be damned if you stand in my way.

'So if he calls me Ma every day of his life, how come all of a sudden it's Mom?'

'I don't know.'

'It crossed my mind . . .' Mrs Vialli let her sentence die.

'You can tell me.'

'OK. Maybe somebody else sent the flowers. Somebody made it up and sent it to me. And the question I keep coming back to is real simple: Why? If Benny didn't send them why not? Which is why I called Amanda Scholes.'

'Amanda resigned,' he said. Officially, he thought, but her heart had never quit.

'Resigned? Oh.'

Drumm nodded.

'Maybe *you* can help me then, Lieutenant. I'd like to see Benny, even for a couple of minutes, and if that's impractical, then maybe just to hear his voice on the phone, or a letter at the very least. I don't even need to know where he is, nothing like that.'

Drumm said, 'Have you written to the Program?'

'I've begun letters I don't know how many times. Then I thought of Amanda. She was the prosecutor in the case, she must have connections. It's depressing when you don't know about your own son. Probably I'm making a mountain outta nothing, but it would be a relief just to know that.'

Drumm rubbed his leg. Goddam switch-blade of pain. He rose from his chair. *Tell me about this guy Dansk, Lew.*

He said, 'I'll look into it, Mrs Vialli. I promise.'

Her glasses reflected lamplight. 'Listen. You want some coffee? Maybe a slice of pie? I'm forgetting my manners.'

Drumm thanked her, but said no. He stepped into the hallway, and a weariness descended on him. Ma, Mom. What's in a name? Maybe a whole lot. Maybe everything. Flip the coin, maybe nothing.

He turned to Mrs Vialli, who'd followed him along the hallway. 'Leave this with me. I'll be in touch.'

He stepped out of the house. Mrs Vialli called good night to him. He heard her shut the door and slip the chain back in place. He wandered down the path to the sidewalk. As he opened the door of his car, he sniffed the night air, which had the smell of week-old fish covered with fat blue flies.

49

MCTELL DISLIKES THE CREEPY-CRAWLY HUSH OF THE SUBURBS.
He prefers downtown life and crowded streets and honky-
tonks and pussy joints. He'd rather be in New Orleans or
Chicago than this place. Better still, give him Tijuana,
where it's lawless and anything goes.

He sits in his car for a while, surrounded by the big
silence of it all, and sees the cop drive away.

Minutes later, McTell gets out and strolls half a block
through the warm dark. He pulls on a pair of leather
gloves as he moves. They make his hands sweat.

He pauses. Looks around. Sidewalks empty. Keeps
going. Busy night doing Dansk's work. Yessir, Anthony.
Yessir, Mr Birthmark.

You got another disfigurement, Dansk. Inside your
head is where.

He raises one hand and pats the perspiration from his
brow. He checks his pockets. He's got everything he needs.
He walks down a driveway and presses a doorbell. An
outside light comes on.

'Who is it?'

McTell clears his throat and says, 'Drumm again.'

'You forgot something, Lieutenant?'

'Right.' Cough, cough.

He hears the chain slide back. The door's opened a slit. The woman is dressed in a big blue robe and has cold cream on her face. She looks like a wary raccoon.

She blinks and steps back, mouth turning into an o of disbelief. McTell sticks a hand across her face and spins her around. She kicks against him. He forces her to the floor and goes down on his knees and still holds one gloved hand clamped across her lips. He grunts and the woman's dumpy little legs kick in the air, and her hands thrash and cold cream adheres to McTell's glove, white and greasy. He keeps one hand across her face and from his pocket draws out a plastic bag, which he pulls over her head. Suck this air, lady, he thinks. She struggles, her little fingers turning into useless blunted claws, her legs still thrashing up and down and she's gasping inside the plastic bag.

She dies in a matter of minutes with her body angled in a position close to foetal. The plastic bag's been sucked a few inches inside her mouth and her eyes are open. She looks like somebody staring out of a rainy window at some horrible accident in the street below.

McTell wipes sweat from his face and gets to his feet. He's short of breath. He glances at the stairs and contemplates the next task. With some difficulty, he drags the woman upstairs, thump thump thump. Her head rolls from side to side.

He pauses halfway to get air into his lungs, then keeps going. Inside the bathroom he sets her down on the tiled floor. He runs some cold water, splashes it across his face, then he checks the shower-curtain rail. He grabs it and pulls hard. It doesn't budge. It's been screwed deeply into the wall by somebody who knew his job. Unusual in this day and age.

He raises the woman into a sitting position and props her against the side of the stall. He removes the plastic bag and her head tilts towards her chest. He takes a length of rope from his pocket and prepares a noose that goes round her neck. The other end of the rope he tosses round the curtain rail.

Now pull.

He raises Mrs Vialli up from the floor inch by inch. Hard fucking work. The curtain rail trembles but doesn't pop loose from the wall.

He pulls until she's about 24 inches from the floor, then he makes a knot and watches the woman hang, her body turning very slightly. She brushes the edge of the shower curtain which makes a tiny creaking noise. Her big bunny-rabbit slippers are wet with piss which trickles down her legs. McTell has seen a lot of effluence in his time.

He finds a chair in a bedroom and carries it into the bathroom and places it on the floor under Mrs Vialli's feet. He wads sheets of toilet paper together and steps up on the chair, then he cleans the goo of cream from the woman's face.

He steps down, flushes the papers and makes sure they've been sucked away, then kicks over the chair.

Check-list.

Climbs up, *tick*, hangs herself, *tick*, knocks chair over as she chokes, *tick*.

Anything else?

He looks round the bathroom and goes down the stairs. He puts the chain back in place and turns off the hallway light, then walks with the aid of a pen-sized flashlight through the kitchen to the back door. He opens it, steps out, pulls it shut again behind him, hears the Yale snap at his back. No sign anywhere of forced entrance. No intrusion.

Just a very depressed woman hanging in her own bath-room.

50

AMANDA, WHO'D SLEPT BADLY, DREAMING AGAIN OF Galindez turning over and over in black waters, drank a quick coffee in her room at 7 a.m., then checked out of the hotel. She rented a Ford from the Avis office in the lobby. She drove past plazas and shopping-centres not yet open. The world was uncontaminated in the early sunlight.

She entered a parking-lot, idled outside a Walgreen's emporium, checked the street. The only vehicle that came along was a beat-up old van with the logo PEACE and a hippie floral design peeling from the body. Time-warp travel. Groovy.

She drove again. When she reached the Hideaway Knolls Motel she parked and sat looking at the jaded two-storey cinder-block construction. This was the motel Dansk had telephoned three times, according to the information from the hotel computer system. The other number he'd called turned out to be an escort service called Romantic Liaisons. A receptionist with a voice like smooth ice-cream had told Amanda, 'We can help you in ways the Red Cross never dreamed about, honey.'

Amanda lit a cigarette. The dashboard clock read seven-forty. Dansk had phoned the Hideaway Knolls three times. Who does he know here? She got out of the car. She'd sit in the coffee-shop and wait until it was time to visit Rhees. She put on a pair of sunglasses, walked inside and took a table in a far corner with a view of the door. She skipped quickly through the menu, ordered coffee and gazed round the room. This could be nothing, a waste of time.

The place was crowded. Some of the customers had the stunned dead-eyed glaze that comes when you're crossing the continent with your possessions in a U-Haul and wondering what your new lives will be like when you get where you're going.

New lives. Just what the Program offered.

She looked through the window at sun glaring off the pavement. She saw her image reflected in a knife on the table and she thought about Dansk and the sickening sensation of his fingers on her breast.

The waitress came with her coffee.

What was she expecting to discover in this place anyway? Dansk phones here, but you could hardly go from table to table asking people if they knew a man called Anthony Dansk, any more than you could trek from room to room knocking on doors. She went to the telephone and called the hospital. Rhees was fine and alert, the nurse said. He'd passed a comfortable night and eaten a good breakfast.

She walked back to her table, finished her coffee. She looked at her watch. Eight a.m. She wondered what Rhees might need, if there was anything she could take to him at the hospital. Reading material, maybe? Clean underwear for sure. Fresh clothes in the unlikely event they decided to discharge him in her care—

The door of the coffee-shop opened.

Startled, Amanda held the menu close to her face. *Don't panic.*

The man who came inside sat up on a stool at the counter and yawned. He checked the room with a casual movement of his head but he didn't see her. He wasn't wearing his neck brace, but this was the guy from the hospital waiting-room. This was the one, she thought. This was who Dansk phoned here.

The thought raced through her mind that he might also be one of the pair who'd attacked Rhees. He resembled an athlete who'd let himself go: muscled, but slackly so. She watched him as he blew on the surface of his coffee. She looked at his yellow-grey hair and sideburns and his crumpled dark-blue suit. He turned to survey the room again and she laid the palm of one hand like a mask against her face, something to reinforce the dark glasses and the menu held in mid-air.

She couldn't play this hiding game indefinitely.

He was hunched on his stool, staring into his coffee. He yawned, stretched his arms, performed some business with his hands, applying the force of one against the other in a form of callisthenics, fingertip pushed upon fingertip. He tugged a tissue from the dispenser and in an absent-minded manner stroked it with his fingers.

It disappeared a second between his palms, and when he opened them the tissue had been transformed into a shape like the head of a white rose.

He pushed it across the counter towards the cashier, a teenage girl who smiled and said, 'Hey, neat little party trick you got there.'

There was an unusual grace and suppleness about those hands. They could play a cello, shuffle cards as if they were lubricated, conjure hankies or rabbits out of top hats, pick locks.

Amanda thought, Wait. Rewind all the way back to the

moment when he'd leaned across her at the hospital, the soda can he'd suggested she use as an ashtray. The memory was like a scene filmed through cheesecloth, muted halos, soft edges.

Hands like those could pick more than locks. They could slide inside pockets, deft and weightless, they could remove two sheets of paper from the hip pocket of a highly distressed woman in the space of a breath. Two sheets of paper, gone in a whisper.

It was possible, more than possible.

He steals the letter. He slips a hand inside her back pocket and steals the goddam letter. She didn't want to think.

She dropped a couple of dollar bills on the table and hurried outside. Her dark glasses slid off her face and fell to the pavement and she stooped to pick them up. The left lens was cracked. She moved in the direction of her car. The world through cracked plastic. The tinted sun had a spidery fracture.

She reached her car and sat behind the wheel. OK, you didn't lose the letter after all. And all the time you were in Dansk's company, he knew you'd read it, you'd read Isabel Sanchez's hasty words that had dynamited the bunker of Program security.

She backed up the car into a green plastic dumpster that rocked to and fro, then she edged forward into the traffic flow. She avoided the clogged freeways. It took her twenty minutes driving along suburban back streets to get to her house. She parked and went indoors. She didn't look at the mess. She walked quickly inside the bedroom and found a freshly laundered shirt and a pair of jeans and clean socks and underwear, gathered them together hastily, then turned around to head back out again.

The telephone rang. She was tempted to let the answering machine pick up, but she reached for the handset

269

before the recorded message kicked in.

It was Willie Drumm. 'Next time you go to a hotel, leave me the name of the place,' he said. 'That way I can reach you.'

'I wasn't thinking straight, Willie.'

'Whatever. Here's the run-down on my activity.'

'I'm listening.'

'First Mrs Vialli. She hasn't heard from Benny since he went inside the Program, except for some flowers on her birthday and a card she feels isn't kosher.'

'Not kosher how?' She clutched Rhees's clothing against her body as if she were holding the man himself.

Drumm told her. She listened carefully through an unexpected flutter of static on the line. She imagined Mrs Vialli reading and rereading a terse message she considered fake and replaying a taped phone message and thinking odd thoughts about a bunch of flowers long-since withered. She remembered Bernadette and the way she'd embraced her son outside the courthouse after he'd given his testimony, how she'd wept because she knew he was going away.

Amanda thought about this a moment. 'What are we saying here, Willie?'

'Maybe only that Benny's less loving and attentive than Ma Vialli wants to believe. She reads something into a message that isn't there. I don't know.'

Amanda thought Drumm's voice lacked conviction. 'When I spelled out for Benny what it would involve going into the Program, the only thing that bothered him was leaving his mother, nothing else. They're pretty close all right.'

'There's a note in your voice I don't like, Amanda. What are you thinking?'

'We know security's screwed-up. So . . . maybe there's some kind of connection between the apparent dis-

270

appearance of Benny and the Sanchez-Galindez affair. Something we haven't thought about.'

'I don't see how there could be a connection,' Drumm said. 'Two different cases six months apart with nothing in common.'

'Except me, the prosecutor,' she said.

'So somebody's got it in for you personally? Dansk, say.'

'Until a few days ago I didn't even know he existed, Willie. I'd be inclined to dismiss anything personal.'

'If it's not personal, what is it?'

She didn't have an answer. Her brain was scurrying here and there, but coming up with nothing. 'I don't know what it is, Willie.'

Drumm was quiet a moment. He said, 'Speaking of Dansk. Let me just shift the scene to Bascombe a moment. This is a sensitive area, he tells me. Highly confidential. I tell him I don't give a rat's fuck how sensitive it is or who he works for, he's got no right to stand in the way of a homicide investigation. I mention Dansk's name has cropped up.'

'And what does he say?'

'Never heard of the guy. Total blank. So I press him just a little. He says he'll run a check on the name and get back to me this morning.'

Amanda let John's shirt slip to the floor and stooped to pick it up, balancing the handset between jaw and shoulder. 'That's the best he can do?'

'He says. I get the funny feeling he's gonna come up with nothing, even if he comes up with something. You know what I'm saying? He guards his territory like a killer Dobermann. He'd prefer to bite your face off than give you any information. I think it's time I had a word with Dansk in person.'

'You'll find him at the Carlton.'

'I'm also going to call Justice, check if they have anybody called Dansk.'

Something she'd meant to do. 'Contact me at the hospital as soon as you can.'

'Will do. Say hi to John for me.'

She hung up and left the house, stepped inside the car. She felt a shivery motion at the back of her mind, dark gauze shimmering in a draught.

Say hi to John for me.

It occurred to her then that if Dansk knew *she'd* read Isabel's letter, he'd assume Rhees had *also* read it. It was something she hadn't considered before, an oversight she attributed to the way events had whirled and jigged around her, but now she found herself worrying about hospital security and if Rhees might be in even more danger because he'd seen the letter, and in Dansk's distorted view of the world that made him a threat as much as herself.

She had a feeling of sinking through a sudden quicksand of panic. She thrust the key into the ignition and roared out of the cul-de-sac.

51

DANSK STARED THROUGH THE WINDSHIELD OF HIS CAR AT THE huge pink and aquamarine hospital, which bore some resemblance to a massive birthday cake. He turned to look at McTell in the seat. 'I want a gun, Eddie.'

'Say?'

'Something out of your private arsenal.'

'A gun,' McTell said and smiled in an uneasy fashion. Suddenly, outta the blue, Dansk wants a gun. Dansk's head was red flags, bad tides, No Swimming Beyond This Point.

'What kind of weapon can you give me?'

McTell said, 'I got a nice Heckler & Koch P7M8. Also a Ruger P89. You sure about this, Anthony?'

'I'm sure.'

'It's just when it comes to guns, me and Pasquale usually—'

'The Ruger,' Dansk said. He imagined the gun in his hand, the weight of it, the deadliness. He pinched the bridge of his nose. He was stuffed-up on account of this city air. His head ached, he was probably coming down

273

with desert fever or whatever evil spore floated in from the hot canyons and clogged your nostrils and rooted itself like a fungus in your lungs.

McTell said, 'The Ruger's a joy. Square post front sight, square notch rear adjustable. It comes in blue steel, but I always had a soft spot for the stainless version.'

Dansk watched visitors getting out of cars and strolling towards the entrance with their flowers and candies. There was a certain type of person who thrived around sickbeds. They drew up their chairs and flashed their own epic scars. Here's where they did the bypass, a quadruple job, and down here's the appendectomy.

He looked for Amanda and saw no sign of her. Maybe she'd enter the building another way, a side door, a rear door, thinking she was being clever.

There's a note in your voice I don't like, Amanda. What are you thinking?

We know security's screwed-up. So ... maybe there's some kind of connection between the apparent disappearance of Benny and the Sanchez-Galindez affair. Something we haven't thought about.

Dansk thought about the tape that had been delivered to his hotel at 9.15 a.m. just as he'd been finishing his press-ups. A brown padded envelope, no message. It hadn't needed any message. It was Loeb's way of telling him things had drifted too far. Well fuck you Loeb, I do this my way. Who needs a dying man's shit? He remembered sweat falling on the envelope. He'd called Pasquale immediately. His hand had left smudged prints on the phone.

'Is the gun handy?' he asked McTell.

'It's in the trunk of my car over there.'

'Get it for me.' Dansk watched McTell walk to his car, unlock the trunk and take out a brown-paper sack. McTell returned to the car and gave the sack to Dansk, who placed it in his lap, peered inside and saw the Ruger.

'Tell me about Mrs Vialli,' he said.

'What's to tell? It went off OK.'

Dansk said, 'You looked in her eyes, Eddie.'

'I don't think much about these things.'

'What did you see?'

'Like in her eyes?' This is Dansk. Dansk who never wants to hear details. All of a sudden he's interested. 'She just looked kinda surprised. She wet herself. She had on these furry slippers. Big fluffy things with like rabbit ears.'

Dansk thought of fuzzy dampened ears, the body discharging piss. He said, 'Here's what I want you to do, Eddie. Check the room Rhees is in.'

'Then what?'

'Just look inside, that's all.'

'That's it?' McTell opened the door and stopped halfway out. 'And if she's there with him? I just kinda look and walk away?'

Dansk said, 'Right. Buy a bunch of flowers, they'll make you appear legit. Go inside. Make it seem like you got the wrong room.'

'Rhees is gonna recognize me from that time we spoke.'

'Let me worry about that.'

McTell shrugged, stepped out of the car and walked across the lot.

Dansk regarded himself in the rear-view mirror and noticed a small brown wad of his morning toast stuck between his front teeth. He picked it out with his finger then wiped the finger on a Kleenex, a pop-up box of which he kept on the dash. Amanda Scholes had good teeth, he remembered. Strong and clean, healthy gums.

Good teeth. Everything decays though.

The hospital shimmered in front of him. All that sickness wrapped in a huge blue and pink cake. Terminal

275

cases attached to machines, bony old women hunched behind screens.

On an impulse, he picked up his phone and called a number in New Jersey. He heard his mother's voice, faint and far away. Spectral.

'Anthony? That really you?'

'Yeah, really me. How are you?'

'It's been a while.'

'I've been busy, Ma.'

'Mr Chomsky was just asking after you,' she said. She had a quivery voice. It kept fading in and out.

'Where you calling from, Anthony?'

'Las Cruces, New Mexico.'

'You coming this way?'

'Soon, Ma.'

'I miss you.'

'Listen, I met a girl.'

'Yeah?'

'Nice girl, you'd like her. Maybe I'll bring her up there. Introduce you.'

'What's her name?'

'I can't hear you, Ma.'

'What's the girl's name I asked.'

'Amanda,' he said.

'Pretty name,' she said.

'Yeah, nice lady. Works for the same company as me.'

'I'll light a candle for you,' she said.

'You do that, Ma. I gotta go now. Talk to you soon.'

'I love you, Anthony.'

Dansk put down the phone on the passenger seat. The call would make the old woman's day, brighten her calendar. Sometimes you did what you could to spread a little cheer. He could see her hurry down the narrow gloomy stairs to the violin repairman's rooms where, surrounded by ancient amputated fiddles and a mountain

276

of pegs and coiled strings, she'd tell Chomsky she'd just had a phone call from her son. He's got a girl called Amanda. She'd build it up into a big thing, a church wedding and decrepit Father McGlone conducting the service, and old Chom would tip his head in the manner of a blind person listening, and he'd smile in his gap-toothed way and say, 'Miracles happen when you least expect 'em. You gotta believe.'

Dansk leaned forward against the steering-wheel. You tell a lie or two and they bring a little happiness. Where's the harm?

Amanda. It was the first name that had sprung to mind. He wondered about that, then decided it was on account of how much she occupied his thoughts, the way she eclipsed all other business. In one bizarre sense, he was more intimate with her than he'd ever been with any other woman in his entire life. He looked at the back of his hand, seeing the red mark left by the knife she'd used against him. Pathetic.

So somebody's got it in for you personally. Dansk, say.

Until a few days ago I didn't even know he existed, Willie. I'd be inclined to dismiss anything personal.

Personal, yeah. It hadn't started out that way, but somewhere along the line it had changed.

Dansk opened the paper sack, dipped a hand inside and gripped the Ruger. It had a lovely gravity. It seemed to emit a low humming sound, like a machine plugged into a power source. He took the gun out, passed it from one hand to the other, over and over. This killing device. This snuffer of human candles. He imagined saying, Open your mouth a little, part your lips just enough for me to slide the gun inside your mouth, Amanda. Let me bring an end to your troubles. The gun is foreplay. The rest is darkness.

He shut the sack. She was nearby and he knew it, he

277

could sense it. He was tuned into her frequency. She was a clear image on his radar screen.

The wedge of pain had shifted to the front of his brain, and when he looked at the hospital it seemed to him that the edifice was disintegrating, like an ice-cream concoction melting in the heat.

A pigeon flew from the roof, flapping into the sun. Dansk watched it climb. He tightened his hold on the Ruger and imagined shooting the bird out of the sky. This was an unsettling junction where past and present intersected, and for a moment he seemed to hover outside himself, looking down and seeing a red-haired man sitting in a car with a gun in his lap and a freckled kid in the back seat clutching an air rifle. Both had murderous expressions.

52

SHE PARKED AT THE BACK OF THE HOSPITAL IN ONE OF THE slots reserved for physicians and, wearing her cracked sunglasses, walked quickly between a fleet of ambulances. She went inside the building through double doors marked DELIVERIES, expecting to be challenged by hospital security guards. Nobody appeared.

She found herself in a wide corridor leading to the laundry. She passed a glass-panelled door, behind which she saw industrial washing-machines, enormous dryers rumbling, people in white smocks ironing and folding bed sheets. She took off the glasses when she reached the service elevator and punched the button for the third floor, where she emerged into a warren of corridors stretching into great pastel infinities. She took a left turn. Two security officers in chocolate-brown uniforms were talking together. They gazed at her, a moment of professional assessment, then turned away. She'd passed their scrutiny. A woman in a dark business suit, not worth challenging.

The door of room 360 was open.

He was propped up against pillows. His face was pale and swollen, his plastered arm in a white sling. His eyes were lacklustre. She drew up a chair to the side of the bed and Rhees managed a smile.

'How are we?' she asked.

'Prodigious amounts of Percodan in my bloodstream,' he said. 'I feel like a passenger on a slow-moving train crossing Kansas.'

She held his good hand between her own. Her and Rhees and nothing else. If only that small world could be restored. She watched him tilt his head back against the pillows. She wanted to protect him, make him safe. She wished she had the magic to turn back clocks.

He cleared his throat and said, 'Coughing's the real killer.'

The real killer, she thought. She looked at the window, seeing the frazzled morning gathering the kind of momentum that would lead to 100 degrees and change, mercury exploding in glass tubes.

She said, 'I don't think they were burglars who came to the house, John. Dansk sent them.'

He looked at her for a time. 'He gets to you through me. Is that the idea?'

She looked round the room, the walls the colour of mango flesh, the wheelchair in the corner. 'I'm sorry for this, all this.'

'What's the point? I don't think you can help yourself. You're programmed to run in a certain direction, Amanda. It just happened that this time you ran into a bad place.'

'I might have disconnected the program,' she said. 'Ripped out the logic board. Anything.'

'You might have, but you didn't, and I didn't do enough to stop you.'

'I look at you and I feel like shit,' she said.

He closed his eyes and turned his face slightly away from her.

She said, 'Dansk got Isabel's letter from me.'

'How?'

'I was distracted. The point is he got it, he read it, and I think he knows you read it too. I don't know what conclusion he imagines I've reached.'

'Have you reached one?'

'I wish I could say yes. Willie's helping now.'

'You finally enlisted him? That's a step forward.'

'One I might have taken sooner,' she said.

Rhees flexed the fingers of his undamaged hand. 'How safe are we in this place?'

She looked through the door towards the corridor. People passed carrying flowers, bags of fruit, paperback books, magazines. People visiting the sick. She wondered about them and their credentials, whether at least one of them had a hidden purpose. She walked to the window and gazed down at the parking-lot. The roofs of cars were like tinted mirrors. Tension was rising inside her.

She was aware of Rhees watching her. 'Well?'

'I don't think we're safe, John.'

'Where is Drumm right now?'

'He said he'd call me here.' She looked at her watch. Ten-thirty. She had no idea when Willie would contact her. He'd talked about going to see Dansk, an idea that seemed to her suddenly loaded with menace.

Rhees said, 'You know what would be nice? A little protection. A cop posted outside the room. Somebody handy with a gun.'

A man appeared in the doorway. He was dressed in an open-neck shirt and held a plastic-wrapped bouquet of mixed flowers to his chest. He wore tinted glasses and his beard was neatly trimmed.

Jangled, Amanda rose immediately from her chair.

'This three zero six?' the man asked.

Amanda stared at the bouquet. Bright petals, green stems slick with water. They seemed fake, pressed out of synthetic materials. Anything could be hidden in those flowers. Plastic crackled against the guy's shirt and Amanda thought of explosives detonating miles away, like something you'd hear in the background of a TV broadcast from Bosnia or Sarajevo or wherever the world was at war.

'Three six zero,' Amanda said. This is what your condition comes right down to: a place where guns might be hidden in flowers and you hear bombs in the crackle of plastic.

'I guess I got the wrong room,' the guy said, and drifted back into the corridor.

Rhees was staring at the empty doorway. 'Last time I saw that guy he was selling magazine subscriptions on our doorstep. I signed up for *Sports Illustrated*.'

'That's the *same* guy? You're sure?'

'No question. We chatted a few minutes. It was raining and I felt sorry for him. It's no coincidence he's here, is it?'

'Dansk wants us to know how exposed we are,' she said.

'I guess that answers my question about safety. Call Drumm, Amanda. Do it now. Get him to come here.'

She lifted the handset from the bedside table. She punched Drumm's number. A woman answered and introduced herself as Sergeant Betty Friedman.

Amanda asked, 'Is Willie available?'

'He's out of the office,' the sergeant said.

'If he calls in, get him to phone me at the Valley of the Sun Memorial Hospital immediately. My name's Amanda Scholes.'

'Amanda Scholes?'

'Scholes. You want me to spell it?'

282

Betty Friedman said, 'No, I'm pretty familiar with your name. It's funny though, because I saw Willie about twenty minutes ago and he was rushing out, and when I asked him where he was buzzing in such a heart-attack hurry, he said he'd received a message to meet you.'

'A message to meet *me*?'

'What he said.'

'I don't know anything about any meeting. Did he say where it's supposed to be?' Something caught and fluttered in her throat.

'He just boogied out the door. I guess maybe some wires got crossed along the way if he isn't with you.'

'Do you know where the message came from?'

'He never said. I'll see if I can find out. You want to hold?'

Amanda said, 'Sure.' A message, she thought. A message she'd never sent. She stared at the open door. People still passed back and forth along the corridor, a shuffling procession, funereal in its lack of energy.

Sergeant Friedman came back on the line. 'Nobody seems to know who received the message, Miss Scholes. Could be the officer has gone off-duty.'

'Can you contact Willie?'

'If he's not in his car, it's a problem. He carries a cellular, but he keeps it switched off when he feels like it. He says a man needs some private space, time to think.'

'The number here is nine four nine seventy seventy, extension three eight nine eight,' Amanda said. 'I need to talk with him – badly.'

'I'll get back to you.'

Amanda put down the receiver.

Rhees said, 'Problem?'

'Somebody left a message for Drumm to meet me.'

'We don't need three guesses, do we?' Rhees said. 'Dansk can predict your future. He knows you'll call on

Drumm for help, so he lures Willie away with a story.'

She thought of Dansk trespassing in her head, forecasting her moves. He'd sent a message luring Willie away. Something about this bothered her. *Luring Willie away.* Before she could think it through any further, the telephone rang. She picked it up and heard Betty Friedman's voice.

'Sorry, I can't raise Willie,' she said.

'Please keep trying, it's important.'

Amanda hung up. This wasn't going to do it. Waiting here balanced on a piano-wire, waiting for Drumm. She couldn't just linger until some totalitarian head nurse told her visiting hours were over and ejected her, and she couldn't go, leaving John on his own. She'd left him once before and she wasn't abandoning him again. Ever.

'Who else can you call?' he asked. 'What about Drumm's boss. What's his name?'

'Kelloway's a hard-ass who doesn't like me.'

'The Irishman then. Maybe he could help in some way.'

'I don't see Concannon walking into a situation without knowing how the odds are stacked. What am I supposed to tell him? We need your help but it might be dangerous?'

'So we're in a box and it's just you and me,' Rhees said, 'and either we stay inside it or we try to get out.'

Amanda thought, This is no longer a hospital, but another kind of institution altogether, one of danger and high risk where a surgical mask might conceal a killer's face, a rubber glove a murderer's hand. She searched her mind for a small pocket of clarity. She thought of the parking-lot at the back, getting John to the car, getting him away without being seen. She thought of waiting here in the hospital for Drumm to call. Inside outside, a bind.

'I'll get you out of here safely, John. I swear.'

'Then what? The house is out of the question. The drive to the cabin in my present state would be gruelling, and we can't go to your father's, because I don't see any reason to drag him into all this.'

Her father. She hadn't had time to think of him. She owed him a phone call, but this wasn't the moment. 'Then we drive downtown. The mountain goes to Muhammad.'

Rhees said, 'I hear the click of the little steel ball in the roulette wheel.'

'What you're really hearing is my heartbeat,' she answered.

53

SHE PUSHED THE WHEELCHAIR CLOSE TO THE BED. 'WE'LL DO this as quickly as we can. First the shirt.'

She slipped the hospital gown from Rhees's upper body and looked at his strapped ribcage. She draped the clean shirt she'd brought loosely around his shoulders. 'I need your legs next.'

Rhees groaned when he swung his legs in stilted fashion towards the edge of the bed. 'Jesus *Christ*,' he said.

She bent, drew the jeans over his bare feet and rolled them halfway up his legs. His bloated knee looked raw and awful. 'I've got to get you into the wheelchair, so I need you to stand up. I know it hurts. Grab my shoulder with your right hand.'

He reached out and moaned. His fingernails dug into the flesh around her shoulder. He was halfway up, his body bent forward awkwardly.

'I'm tottering, Amanda. The knee's fucked.'

'You can't afford to totter. Come on.'

He was upright now, all his weight on his good leg. She eased him into the wheelchair. She drew his jeans to his waist and buttoned them quickly and slipped his bare feet inside his canvas espadrilles.

She wheeled him to the door where she looked for the guy with the flowers, but didn't see him, which didn't mean he wasn't around somewhere, lingering, watching, waiting. Her whole life was a book lying open and somebody with the power of life and death was reading the pages.

Rhees had his upper body angled forward. His breathing was shallow. She tried to remember the way back to the service elevator. Her memory skipped a beat. Blank. She took a chance, turned right, then glanced back the way she'd come. An overweight woman in a baggy hospital gown stood propped up by a walking-stick, a kid with a bandaged head bounced a rubber ball on the floor, an old guy in a walker was being helped along by an elderly woman who had one leg in a metal brace. It was like the Lourdes Express had just disgorged its passengers.

She rolled Rhees through a door and faced another corridor. She recognized the colour scheme ahead: sky-blue and lemon. Quick, quick as you can. The service elevator was about 20 yards away. An orderly was waiting outside the door. The elevator arrived, the orderly held the door open for them and Amanda pushed the wheelchair inside.

The orderly looked at Rhees and said, 'He OK?'

'He's fine,' Amanda said.

The elevator started to descend with a cranking sound and a shudder. Rhees had his eyes shut. 'Looks like he needs rest,' the orderly said.

'I want to get him out of here.'

'Yeah, this hospital experience can really be a major bummer.' He was skinny and whitefaced and had the look of a guy who spent all his leisure time travelling the deepest arteries of the Internet until his eyes popped.

'Say, you taking this guy out without authority? This some kind of escape from the Gulag?'

'In a sense,' Amanda said.

'Cool. Anarchy.'

Amanda had the slight suspicion that this orderly had been dabbling inside the pharmacy, maybe a little speed to propel him through the day.

'I wonder if you'd do me a favour,' she said. 'My car's parked out back. Would you get it for me? Reverse it right up to the back doors, so I don't have to push this wheelchair all the way across the lot?'

'You're asking me to assist you in an unauthorized escape?'

'I guess I am.'

The orderly said, 'Sometimes I kinda imagine this whole place is a penal colony floating in outer space, you know? Like the patients are really prisoners of some oppressive regime that injects them with experimental drugs? And I'm on this secret mission to scope out the truth.'

'Outer space, huh,' Amanda said. Boy, you really know how to pick them. 'Maybe you can pretend my car's some kind of mini space shuttle.'

'Yeah, I could get into that.' The elevator stopped, the door opened. 'Just gimme the keys and point the way.'

'It's a yellow Ford parked near the ambulances.'

She pushed Rhees in the direction of the sign marked LAUNDRY. The laundry door was open and steam floated out and fogged the air. The exit was just ahead.

'Back the car as close as you can possibly get,' she said.

'Gotcha.'

She looked in the direction of the Ford, 30 yards away. She scanned the parking-lot and saw a crew of guys washing ambulances. Pressurized water whizzed from black hoses, smacked against the panels and gathered in glittering oily puddles. BMWs and Jags were parked in the physicians' slots. No sign of the bearded guy with the flowers, and yet everything was charged and tense, as if somewhere nearby, perhaps inside a trash can, perhaps stashed under the chassis of an ambulance, there was Semtex attached to a ticking clock muffled in old newspapers, or someone hidden in the shadows with a gun.

The orderly walked to the Ford, got in and backed up at speed, docking the shuttle.

He squeezed the car all the way inside between the open doors, a narrow margin. He got out and surveyed the distance separating car and door-frame, a matter of maybe a foot on either side.

'That close enough for you?' he asked.

'Terrific,' she said.

'Lemme help you get your friend in.' He opened the passenger door. There was just enough room for Rhees to slide in, but it was a difficult manoeuvre, even with the orderly's assistance. They raised Rhees out of the wheelchair, but when he had to bend to get into the passenger seat, he gasped.

'I think we'll rip off the wheelchair,' Amanda said.

'I'll fold it for you,' the orderly said. He collapsed the chair and placed it behind the front seats.

'What's your name?' Amanda asked.

'My earth name's Jonas.'

'Jonas, I owe you.'

'Consider me an agent of justice,' he said.

She got behind the wheel and slammed the car into the great bright vacuum of the day, tall date palms whipping past in a blue-green blur, groves of citrus trees flaring under the withering masonic eye of the sun.

'I don't recognize the car,' Rhees said.

'It's another story, John.'

He sat with his head against the back of his seat. 'It's going to get worse,' he said.

She wasn't sure if he was referring to the heat or his pain or something else altogether.

54

WILLIE DRUMM WAITED OUTSIDE THE SHOPPING MALL. HE drank coffee from a cardboard cup and checked his watch every so often. He was a patient man by nature, but this situation was beginning to test him. The message on his desk had read, 'Meet Amanda Scholes, Metrocenter, 11 a.m.' It had been received by a young cop called Lazarus, whom Drumm barely knew. Lazarus had gone off-duty, so Drumm hadn't been able to question him about the message. Had it come directly from Amanda? How had she sounded? Did she say anything else?

It was eleven-twenty now. He wondered how much longer he should give her. She'd always been a stickler for punctuality, at least when he'd worked with her. Her resignation had created a void in his life. He'd enjoyed the regular leisure hours they'd spent drinking, chatting, talking cases, crimes, the state of the nation.

He wandered up and down, scanning the parking-lot. It was packed with cars, people hurrying out of the sun and inside the mall as if this was the last shopping day in the history of the universe.

He realized he was hungry. Inside, you could get pizza, kebabs, stir-fry, anything you liked except it was all indigestible. He didn't want to go in and grab a sandwich because he didn't want to run the risk of missing Amanda when she showed up. He didn't like these consumer malls anyway. He preferred corner grocery stores and small family operations, when you could find them these days.

He strolled up and down. He'd give Amanda five more minutes then he'd call in and check his messages. She might have cancelled. He tapped the face of his watch.

This wasn't his day so far. He'd gone to the Carlton only to find that Anthony Dansk had checked out fifteen minutes before. No forwarding address, and now here he was waiting for Amanda.

She'd said she was on her way to visit Rhees, and that he should telephone her at the hospital after he'd seen Dansk. Maybe her plans had changed for some reason – hence the message, maybe she'd been delayed somewhere. He took the mobile phone from his pocket. He couldn't stand these things, they made him feel like a late-blooming yuppie. He didn't like electronic doodahs. Computers and modems and e-mail and all the rest of it were beyond him. Another world altogether.

Drumm punched the buttons and got himself connected to Betty Friedman.

'Finally,' she said.

'Why? You been looking for me?'

'Your friend Amanda called. Says it's urgent you get back to her.'

Drumm had an odd little feeling: somebody walking on his grave.

'She's at the Valley of the Sun Memorial. Got a pen, I hope?'

'I got a pen.' Drumm went through the pockets of his

jacket and found a toothmarked stub of pencil attached to a frayed loop on his notebook.

Betty Friedman read him the number and the extension. He wrote it down.

'When did she phone?' he asked.

'About half an hour ago.'

'She sound OK?'

'Odd you should ask. She doesn't know anything about this meeting with you. It was news to her.'

'She didn't *know* about our appointment?'

'Nope.'

'That's weird.' More than weird, he thought. He had a prickling sensation in his bad leg.

'Call her. You're supposed to be in the business of clearing up mysteries, right?'

Drumm hung up. He dialled the number of the hospital. It was a while before anyone answered. You wouldn't want to be in the throes of cardiac arrest, gasping your last. Eventually an operator came on the line and Drumm asked for the extension number. It rang unanswered.

The operator broke in and said, 'That number doesn't reply.'

Drumm hung up and called Betty Friedman back. 'You sure you gave me the correct extension?'

'I told you what Amanda Scholes told me, Willie. Extension three eight nine eight. You probably wrote it down wrong.'

Drumm checked his notebook. No, he'd written 3898 exactly the way Friedman had given it to him. He dialled the hospital again – the switchboard took a long time to pick up this time too – and repeated the number. There was still no answer. Baffled and irritated, he called Betty Friedman yet again.

'I'm still getting no response from that number,' he said.

'Maybe the room's empty. She might have checked Rhees out.'

'He didn't look like a guy who was going anywhere when I saw him yesterday. I ought to get over to the hospital.'

'Willie, a moment's logical thought, huh?'

Drumm said, 'You're gonna tell me what to do. I can hear it coming, Betty.'

'A suggestion is all. She's bound to call here sooner or later, so it makes sense for you to come back to the office instead of wandering around a hospital she may have already left. At least you'll be here to take the call, right?'

'I hate sensible,' Drumm said.

'Men always do. See you.'

Drumm hung up the phone. Funny about that message. If Amanda didn't know about it, where the hell had it originated? But this whole business was funny, beginning with Dansk. Dead witnesses. A protection program that didn't protect. A mother worrying about her kid.

He tucked the phone away, scanned the parking-lot and tried to remember where he'd left his car.

55

DANSK SAID INTO HIS PHONE, 'GIVE HER BONUS POINTS FOR trying.'

McTell, driving behind, said, 'I guess.'

Dansk leaned forward against the wheel and watched the small yellow Ford ahead. He thought, She knows I'm behind her. She knows I'm in the vicinity. She might pull some utterly predictable stunt, like a sudden U-turn, but she'd have to dig deep inside her box of tricks to shake me off now. And it isn't going to be easy with the invalid on board. Rhees isn't exactly flexible.

When she'd roared from the rear of the hospital, McTell had picked up on her and Dansk had slipped in behind McTell. Sometimes he'd overtake Eddie, other times he'd let him lead. Alternating strategy.

'I'm enjoying this,' he said to McTell.

McTell's words floated on a ragged cushion of interference. 'This what?'

'This. This whole thing. Everything. The way you flushed her and Rhees out.' Dansk took the shooter out of the paper sack and laid it in his lap, fingering it with one hand. The day was vibrant all around him, a shade too bright, like a soap opera on Mexican TV, but he had a charge of exuberance going.

'This Ruger's sweet,' he said.

'You really sure how to handle it?' McTell asked.

'I didn't spend five years with the US Marshals making paper-clip chains,' Dansk said.

'Five years,' McTell said.

'Five years. I even represented DC Metro in a target-shooting competition in 1992, and came second.'

Inside his car, McTell thinks how little he knows about Dansk's history. Like he gives a shit anyhow. Dansk presses buzzers and you jump, end of story. He wants a gun, so he gets a gun. He always gets what he wants. McTell would have done it differently: straight inside the hospital, big fat silencer screwed on, perform the surgery fast and beat it outta this place where sunstroke was always 2 or 3 degrees away. But no, Dansk has to get intricate. Dansk has this game he's playing with this woman, he wants her to run and sweat and squirm through hoops. But sometimes you could cut somebody too much slack and then you had a major problem reining them back in.

What is it with Dansk? This business of flushing the man and woman out. He'd never mentioned that was his purpose. Just go in, McTell, check the room, carry flowers. But Dansk is devious. And why? *Because he wants to do the surgery himself!* He wants to pull the trigger, thinks he's got what it takes for the job. Doesn't want to do it inside the hospital, has some other place of execution in mind. Let it go. This is the Anthony Dansk Show. He's the star and you're just Eddie McTell, warm-up comedian.

McTell said, 'If I was her, I'd head for the nearest precinct house and tell them I'm afraid for my life.'

'I'd do the same thing myself,' Dansk said.

'And this, like, don't worry you?'

'You don't see it, Eddie. You think if she wanders in off the street and pours out her yarn to some hard-assed cops, they'll sit around hanging on her every word? They'll listen, oh sure, because she used to be connected, but they'll be tapping their pencils slowly on their desks and thinking this lady's turned into a class-one conspiracy freak, this one's all the way from Woo-Woo Central. What a sad sight, emotionally unbalanced by recent events. Boyfriend battered and that poor Sanchez woman God knows where. She doesn't have a goddam thing to back up any suspicions she has. It's beayoo-tiful. So let her strut inside some precinct house and say what she likes. Here's a news flash for you, McTell, sooner or later, she's gonna have to come out again.'

And I know where she'll go then, he thought, because I know what I'd do in her position. I'm scanning you, Amanda. It was like being twinned in some way, a bizarre kind of affinity, an intimacy. Like two lovers kept apart by fate and time.

'Drumm'll listen to her,' McTell said.

'Drumm, sure. Drumm'll listen. Right. He's Mr Empathy.' Dansk laughed, cut the connection and focussed on the Ford that glowed bright yellow in the sun. He imagined Amanda's hands sticky on the steering-wheel. Your nerves are puppy dogs in a canvas bag on the way to the river to be drowned, sweetheart. You're running and running. You and your invalid lover running to see good old Willie Drumm for sympathy.

Sympathy. Right.

Ahead, the Ford was turning towards downtown.

56

THROUGH THE WINDSHIELD OF HIS CAR, PASQUALE WATCHED the cop cross the parking-lot of the shopping mall. The guy had a slight limp. He was hurrying in an odd hip-hop fashion.

Pasquale drove slowly in the cop's general direction, then braked. The cop vanished between a line of parked cars a moment and Pasquale, tapping his fingers on the wheel, waited for the guy to step back out into full view. He didn't like this situation, this waiting, all these shoppers going about their business. Waiting frayed his edges.

The cop re-emerged between a parked camper with a bumper-sticker saying DIVERS DO IT DEEPER, and a flashy new pick-up truck painted in blue and burgundy streaks. Pasquale remembered he'd had a bumper-sticker one time with Bruce Springsteen's face on it and an electric guitar. An old Camaro he'd owned when he was nineteen. Nice car. Babes liked it. Not like this one he was presently driving. This car was a total fuck-me embarrassment. It wasn't the kind of thing he'd want acquaintances to see him cruise around in.

He watched the cop pat the pockets of his jacket like he was looking for something. Shoppers walked in front of the car. One little kid stared at him and made a face, poking his ugly nose out of shape with a middle finger and pulling down the flesh under both eyes.

Pasquale rolled the window down. 'Your face'll stay that way, asshole.'

The kid flipped him a finger, then skipped away. Brat. Pasquale revved the engine. The cop was in open space, a bunch of keys in his hand, and Pasquale pressed his foot down on the gas pedal.

Go. This is your best chance.

The cop seemed oblivious to the car. He was elsewhere, wrapped up in his thoughts.

One hit, Pasquale thought.

He was a couple of hundred feet from the cop, who was still unaware of the car bearing down on him. It's gonna be one of those last second things, Pasquale thought, the cop raising his face just before impact, fear and surprise thundering through him when it was too late to take evasive action.

Pasquale floored the gas pedal.

The cop turned. His face had a stricken look, like this was all some kind of mistake or a sequence in a very bad dream.

You're not dreaming, buster.

The car struck the cop and tossed him in the air, and Pasquale felt the crack of impact and saw the guy tossed to one side, plaid jacket open and flapping in a draught of air, glittering coins falling from his pockets, a clutch of keys seeming to hang like a small silver kite.

In his rear-view mirror Pasquale saw the cop land on his side and roll over and then – holy shit! – he was raising himself up on one knee. His jacket was covered in blood and he was shaking his head in a dazed, pained way, clutching his arm, which had to be broken because it was bent at a weird angle, and his mouth hung open and contorted.

A fuck-up, Pasquale thought. Big time. He stuck the car into reverse. No other way to do this, Bruno. He tightened his grip on the wheel and zoomed backwards fast, before the cop had a chance to react, and he heard the crunch of the rear wheels against the cop's body and the car rose a foot, suspension swaying, exhaust discolouring the air. He kept backing up, and then when he'd driven the front wheels over the cop he stuck the gear into first and rolled quickly over the guy again.

He looked in the rear-view mirror.

The cop wasn't moving now. He was lying there in sunlight and blood.

Pasquale hammered the car forwards and screeched across the lot and out into the street. It was two miles before he felt he'd covered enough distance from the shopping mall and it was safe to pull over. He parked in a street of tract homes and sat motionless, his breathing heavy.

He noticed a streak of blood on the lower right-hand corner of his windshield, a dark smear already drying in the hot air, and when his phone began to ring he let it go unanswered for a time, because it could only be Dansk checking how things had gone. Dansk, always Dansk.

He picked it up on the tenth ring.

It wasn't Dansk and it wasn't McTell.

It was a guy he'd never heard before, a guy with a deep cracked voice and a wild hack of a cough.

57

STUFFY INSIDE THE FORD, RHEES IN PAIN, EYES SHUT, LIDS fluttering every now and again. Sometimes he'd lick his dry lips and try to dig out a small smile from a place far inside.

Amanda said, 'I'll stop someplace, pick up some aspirin. They might help ease the pain.'

'I'm more in a morphine mood,' Rhees said. 'Forget the aspirin. Don't stop, just keep going.'

She looked in rear-view and wing mirrors, but it was the old story: you needed to know what you were looking for before you spotted it, unless it was obvious, like the car that had tailed her a little too close along Lincoln Boulevard. But here traffic was glutted and cluttered and you couldn't single anything out.

A pick-up swerved directly in front of her and she wondered if the movement was designed to impede her. She changed lanes to avoid any possibility of impact, but the truck – booming hard-core Nashville, driver in a stetson with a long bright feather in the hatband – gathered speed and went past her and a Pabst beer can was tossed languidly from the cab. She imagined Dansk's disapproval: the world's a mess, the ozone layer's disappearing and the oceans are dying.

And so are people, she thought. Disappearing and dying, and not just because of harmful rays or seafood spiked with mercury.

She rolled down her window, lit a cigarette, then remembered what Dansk had said about smoking during their first meeting in the Biltmore. *What people inflict on their bodies is their own business. They want to take serious risks, let them*. She realized now he wasn't just passing a casual opinion on the perils of tobacco, he had in mind other kinds of risks more immediate than the long-term effects of cigarettes.

Rhees turned his face towards her. 'Doesn't it strike you that the guy with the flowers had the perfect opportunity in the hospital? You and me together in the room. All he had to do was shut the door, whip out a pistol. Why didn't he?'

She looked at Rhees. 'My guess is it's something Dansk wants to do himself.' And she wondered why she hadn't tried to plunge the knife into Dansk's goddam heart last night, why she hadn't at least attempted that last act. Because he was strong and would have disarmed her easily, because even with the knife in her hand she was afraid of him, just as she was afraid of him now.

She gave the car more gas, cutting in and out of the traffic flow. She headed south, neglecting the futile mirror checks now. Fear reduced everything to driving, just driving, concentrating on the distant towers, the heart of the city. The few clouds that drifted on the blue horizon were like smoke left by old cannon-fire.

Rhees asked, 'Are we close yet?'

'A few blocks.' Seventh Avenue and Washington, that was the place. Not far now, she'd see it any moment: the big beige building, patrol cars parked outside, cops coming and going. She'd park at the front and she'd ask a cop to help her get Rhees out of the car and into the wheelchair and she'd wheel him inside, and if Drumm wasn't there she'd ask for Betty Friedman. She had this much planned. Thinking your movements through brought an illusion of control.

She saw a clutter of cruisers, a few cops talking together and laughing, a hive of law-enforcement activity. Guns and protection, the safest place she could imagine. She parked the Ford as close to the building as she could, a no-parking zone, then she opened the door and stepped out. Her clothes stuck to her. She ran a hand through her damp hair.

She looked at the entrance to the building, saw the huge circular concrete flowerpots designed to prevent motorized assaults by madmen on the front doors, then lowered her face to check on Rhees, who was gazing at her listlessly. The line of her vision was drawn away from him and up, up over the roof of the Ford to the other side of the street, where she saw Dansk pass slowly in a car, wearing dark glasses and grinning at her, his hand hanging arrogantly from the open window, as if he were no more than a tourist driving idly through town, with nothing more than time to kill.

58

BETTY FRIEDMAN HAD STRONG SQUARE HANDS AND SHREWD brown eyes that didn't miss much. 'Willie called,' she said. 'He oughta be walking through that door any moment. You want coffee, tea, anything while you wait?'

'Water, please,' Amanda said.

Rhees sat to one side of the sergeant's desk in the wheel-chair. 'Water's fine,' he said.

She filled two dixie cups from the cooler and passed them out. Amanda gulped hers down. It had a faint chlorinated taste, but it was wet and welcome.

Rhees asked, 'Would you have a painkiller handy?'

'I got some codeine somewhere.' Betty Friedman, who wore her dark hair in a tight curled perm, rummaged in the drawer of her desk, opened a bottle and tipped out a couple of white pills. Rhees washed them down with his water.

'That message business is pretty weird,' Betty Friedman said.

'Yeah, it is,' Amanda said. She thought of Dansk driving past and the way he'd grinned, and she wondered why he hadn't looked unhappy to see her outside the Police Department HQ, why he wasn't worried by the prospect of her walking inside the building. Because he's tricky, he's made a move I haven't taken into account, he's shuffled the deck and come up with a different hand. But what?

She felt she'd been manipulated, except she couldn't figure how. It was almost as if he wanted her to come to this place.

Because.

'Any idea who sent the message?' Betty Friedman asked.

Amanda said nothing. Dansk lures Willie away because – no, this was one of those roads she didn't want to travel. It went straight to a black destination.

'I guess it's something you'd prefer to share with Willie,' Betty Friedman said. 'Fine by me.'

Amanda looked at the clock on the wall. 'How long since he phoned?'

'Twenty-five minutes about, from Metrocenter.'

'He should be here by now.'

'Any moment. Relax.'

Amanda was thinking of Drumm out there in the city, maybe bogged in traffic, delayed by roadworks, something. *Any moment*. He'd come through the door and he'd believe her story and he'd say *leave it to me* and she'd walk away from the whole thing, back to a private life. Mountain air, owls flying into the moon.

Any moment.

She looked at Betty Friedman and said, 'Try to reach him, please.'

The telephone on the desk rang then and Betty Friedman picked it up, and Amanda watched her face go through various stages of change, from disbelief to shock, and then to some other expression, a kind of puzzled vagueness, an emptiness, spirit draining out of her.

Amanda couldn't sit, she had to move. She rose from her chair and paced the room and felt a disastrous darkness beat against her. *She knew*. She tried to distance herself from the external world, to silence extraneous sounds and sights, but she could hear Betty Friedman's voice anyway, scratchy and thin, like somebody on an ancient record. 'Did anybody get the goddam number? Sweet Christ, I can't take this in. I don't believe it, I talked to him maybe half an hour ago.'

Betty Friedman had put down her phone without hanging up, and the line beeped like the sound of an electrocardiograph emitting the bleak whistle of fatality. Surgeons took off their masks, sighed and washed blood from their hands. She pushed her chair against the wall and tilted her head back and appeared to be looking at the ceiling.

'It's Willie,' Amanda said. 'Something about Willie.'

Betty Friedman said, 'Run down by a car.'

Amanda flattened her hands on the surface of the desk and leaned forwards, and Betty Friedman said again, 'Run down by a car.' Her eyes had a far-away look. 'DOA.'

Rhees shifted his wheelchair a little. There was the sound of rubber tyres on the floor.

'Somebody,' Betty Friedman said, but her sentence gathered no momentum and she gave up on it and looked at Rhees as if his presence puzzled her. She picked up the handset but didn't hang it up. 'Some bastard,' she said. 'Some bastard hit Willie then backed up over him to make sure and then drove away and . . .'

Amanda felt like a long steel needle had entered her heart, an emotional biopsy. We need a small sample, Miss Scholes, to check your condition. Killed by a car. DOA. Betty Friedman got up and dropped the handset and it slithered from her desk and swung back and forth on its cord, a pendulum measuring nothing. Watching it,

Amanda thought of Willie, and the image she received was of Drumm being struck and thrown, a killer's face in shadow behind a windshield, metal cracking bone, Drumm jolted, damaged by the impact, and then the car reversing over him. *Just to make sure.*

This is going to go away. Somebody will touch your shoulder and say it's time to get up.

She looked at Rhees. She went towards him and he caught her hand and held it against the side of his face. Betty Friedman had knocked over a waste-basket and papers spilled across the floor. She had all that unfocussed energy of grief, the kind that burns without purpose. 'In the parking-lot at Metrocenter, and all we got is a colour, and that colour's red, and a partial of the licence number, that's all. That's all we got. Just D–O–A.'

Betty Friedman drew the cuff of her shirt across her face. Amanda moved away from Rhees and reached out and touched the woman's arm. Whether she meant to comfort Friedman or comfort herself, it didn't matter which. A red car at Metrocenter and Willie's dead. Rushed to a hospital, the scream of an ambulance, Willie dying with an oxygen mask on his face and maybe blood spurting against the inside of the mask, and Willie's hands clawing air, life flying out of him.

And somewhere a man in a red car.

One of Dansk's people, she thought. One of Dansk's people sticking the hook into Willie's flesh and hauling him up out of the water.

Betty Friedman stared at Amanda in a hollow way and asked, 'Where the hell did that message come from?'

59

AN ELEVATOR RIDE, BETTY FRIEDMAN WHITE AND MUTE, Rhees hunched in the wheelchair, Amanda beset by a sense of sluggishly wading through water. A walk along a corridor to an office, a big room of panelled walls hung with various awards and civic honours.

Dan Kelloway stood behind his desk, sleeves rolled up to the elbows, arms burned brown, shaven head suntanned and gleaming. Another cop was present, a guy in a double-breasted suit and a lapel badge that identified him as Lt. Wom, S. He had Asiatic features, tiny hands and small feet in black patent-leather shoes. He lounged in the corner of the office, half in shadow, motionless.

Amanda thought, I don't know if these people will listen to me, and even if they listen whether they'll believe. But the telling of her story had become more important than how she gauged the mood of her audience, and even though she wanted Willie she couldn't have him, and that was something she couldn't change.

Kelloway told her to sit. Betty Friedman must have picked up on some sign from him, because she went out of the office, closing the door quietly.

Kelloway looked at Rhees. 'Who's this?'

Rhees introduced himself. Kelloway frowned and turned to Amanda. His voice was like an old-fashioned razor drawn across a leather strap. He sat down behind his desk, white shirt phosphorescent. 'OK, I'm listening.'

Amanda hesitated. She felt the solid wall of Kelloway's hostility. He had that hard-bitten scepticism common to career cops, and he had it in spades. You might have been a shit-hot prosecutor once, but you're history, and your history with me is a bad one.

She remembered Willie's kindness at the hospital, the depths of his concern for her, her face against his shoulder and the faint scent of dry-cleaning chemicals from his jacket, and the way he'd pressed Kleenex into her hands. She heard the room roar in her ears and saw Kelloway clasp his hands on the desk. 'We're waiting. You got something to say, Miss Scholes, say it.'

When she spoke she had no fluency, she fumbled over names and episodes. It didn't take long to tell the story – five minutes, ten, she wasn't sure. Neither Kelloway nor Wom moved. Kelloway watched her without expression, Wom studied his fingernails. She was dry-mouthed when she finished. She wanted to smoke, but it wouldn't have been allowed in Kelloway's sanctum.

Kelloway glanced at Wom. Wom shifted his head a little. Some kind of exchange passed between them. It was hard to tell what it meant. She didn't feel good about this little signal, whatever it was. She felt suspended, awaiting judgement.

Kelloway said, 'Pity about that purloined letter.'

Amanda didn't like the spin he gave the word *letter*. 'I wasn't the only one who read it,' she said. 'So did John.'

'I'm not denying it existed,' Kelloway said. 'All I'm saying is it would be useful to have.'

308

Wom spoke for the first time. His accent was East Coast clipped, maybe Boston. 'You say this guy Dansk is a resident at the Carlton downtown.'

'He is. At least last night he was.'

Wom picked up a phone on the desk and turned his back. He dialled a number and conducted a conversation in a low whisper. While Wom was on the phone, Kelloway said, 'What you're telling me is that Dansk is part of some corruption inside the Witness Program, and he's on the Sanchez payroll. And you also think this same Dansk is behind Willie's death because Willie was conducting an investigation Dansk didn't like.'

'Right,' she said. Her thoughts drifted to her last conversation with Willie, and she remembered Mrs Vialli's concern about her son. 'Willie talked to Lew Bascombe, also to Bernadette Vialli. My guess is he was followed to both places—'

'You told us that already.' Kelloway looked at Rhees. 'You were attacked by associates of Dansk, right?'

Rhees nodded.

'How do you know they were his associates?'

Rhees turned his face to Amanda for help. She read a certain helplessness in his expression.

Kelloway said, 'You're only going on what Miss Scholes said. Have you ever seen Dansk? Ever laid eyes on him?'

'No, never.'

'What are you getting at?' Amanda asked.

'I wasn't getting at anything, Miss Scholes. I just want to know if Rhees has ever encountered Dansk.'

Kelloway had a way of staring that made you want to turn your face aside, but Amanda held his eyes. She was damned if she was going to relinquish any of her territory to this hard-ass. 'I'm getting the strange impression you don't believe Dansk exists,' she said.

Kelloway said, 'You're overreacting.'

Overreacting. She liked that. Drumm had been killed and Dansk was out there scheming, and she was overreacting.

'You just jumped to the conclusion that the people who attacked your boyfriend are associates of Dansk? Maybe the same people that shot Galindez and chased after Isabel Sanchez? Maybe even the same people that ran a car over one of my most experienced men? And one of these quote unquote killers is a resident at a place called the Hideaway Knolls, but you don't know his name.'

'I don't need your *scorn*, Kelloway. I come here, I tell you something is totally fucked inside the Protection Program, and you treat me like I'm some drooling idiot that just wandered in off the streets, instead of getting up off your ass and being practical.'

Kelloway was unaffected by her. He clasped his hands behind the back of his skull and cracked his finger-joints.

She said, 'Begin with something indisputable and work from there. Galindez and Isabel Sanchez – both protected witnesses, allegedly.'

Kelloway nodded. 'According to the elusive letter, Galindez was shot by the people protecting him and Isabel Sanchez ran away, et cetera. After that, what have you got? Some vague reference to Benny Vialli, which is a case I remember real well, but it doesn't seem to fit anything I can see.'

It doesn't seem to fit, she thought. Willie had said much the same thing. What was she doing? Looking for connections where none existed? Inventing structures that couldn't support any weight? And yet she was trying to forge something out of Bernadette Vialli's story, even if she wasn't sure what. I put Galindez and Isabel into the Program. I placed Benny Vialli in the same custody and nothing's been heard of him since. A kid out there somewhere – maybe he'd fallen in love, married, forgotten his

310

mother. Maybe he'd found an altogether new life and the past was something he didn't want to resurrect.

No, she knew that wasn't true. It didn't square at all with the impression she'd had of Benny Vialli. But why did he send those flowers and the message that Bernadette thought was a fake? Answer: he didn't, somebody else did. Because Benny was in no position to send anything, because—

Wom hung up the phone and said, 'A man called Anthony Dansk checked out of the Carlton this morning.'

'Big surprise,' she said. Checked out and gone, she thought. Perfect timing. Dansk disappears into the sewers, planning to re-emerge when he's ready.

Kelloway said, 'Here's something puzzles me. If you know so much about Dansk, how come you're walking around to tell the tale? Why hasn't Dansk sent a car to run *you* down or get one of his killers to blow *you* away? Why didn't he stop you before you reached my office?'

Amanda looked into Kelloway's sharp blue eyes. 'Maybe because he's self-confident in a way neither you nor I understand. He lives in a demented world we can't quite fathom, Kelloway. And maybe he has other plans for me.'

'What kind of plans?'

'I can't read his mind, I doubt if anyone can do that. I only know his plans are lethal, whatever they are, and I'm feeling vulnerable because he's out there somewhere.'

Kelloway's phone rang. He picked it up, listened, then he rose. He said to Wom, 'Back in a second, Sonny,' and went out of the room.

Amanda heard the door close. She looked at Wom and said, 'I bet he stuffs dollar bills into collection boxes for religious missions in Patagonia. I bet he's active in the Big Brothers organization.'

Sonny Wom said, 'He's not a happy man today. None of us are.'

311

'Is he ever happy?' she asked.

Wom didn't answer. Kelloway came back into the room, carrying a piece of paper he spread on the desk. His skull shone like a hazelnut. 'What kind of car do you drive?'

'Car? A VW.'

He read something scrawled on the back of the paper. 'Registration number 4KL580?'

Rhees said, 'That's the number all right. Why?'

'Colour red?' Kelloway asked.

'Where is all this leading?' Amanda asked.

'It was your car that ran down Willie.'

'My car?'

'We found it abandoned a couple of miles from Metrocenter. Front seriously dented, blood on the windshield, plus a strip torn from the sleeve of Willie's jacket stuck to a broken front light.'

Her own car. Willie's torn jacket. She couldn't think around this. 'I left that car last night outside a convenience market on Lincoln,' she said.

'By left, you mean you just walked away from it?'

'Somebody was tailing me. I decided to skip.'

'Who was tailing you?'

'One of Dansk's people,' she said.

'Naturally,' Kelloway said.

'So I dumped the car.'

Kelloway said, 'And somebody came along later and drove it away. And somebody sent Willie a message, using your name. And Willie walked into a trap.'

'Not somebody. Dansk.' How many ways could she tell Kelloway the same thing?

Kelloway tossed the sheet of paper aside. 'A suspicious person could look at all these things and interpret them in a dark way, Miss Scholes. A message you say you never sent. The fact your car was used in a hit and run.

Somebody could add these things up and you'd come out looking murky.'

Rhees said, 'Crap, Kelloway. Are you accusing Amanda of something?'

Kelloway said, 'I'm just looking at the angles.'

'With some offensive results,' Rhees said. He sounded angry, even in his pain. Amanda rose and stood directly behind him, laying her hands on his shoulders. She felt heat rise from his body.

'I *saw* that goddam letter,' Rhees said.

'Did I say I disbelieved you?'

Amanda stepped in front of Kelloway's desk. Calm was the important thing. An air of reason. 'Don't you see what's going on, Kelloway? Dansk is stirring the pond, he's making the waters muddy. He leaves a message for Willie in my name, he uses my car, it's all diversionary stuff designed to confuse.'

'It's confusing all right. I grant you that.'

'He knows how to hide and he knows how to manipulate. Look, I don't have any motive for fabricating this story. I don't have anything to gain from making up fictions.'

Kelloway shrugged. 'I never accused you of making up fictions. Did I, Sonny? Did you hear me accuse Miss Scholes of that?'

Wom said, 'No, I missed out on that.'

Amanda smiled thinly. 'The pair of you are missing out on quite a few things, not least the fact that I was very close to Willie Drumm, and it hurts like fuck to think about what happened to him.'

'You're grieving,' Kelloway said.

'Goddam right I'm grieving.'

Kelloway tapped the surface of his desk. His tanned hand was bony. He looked at Sonny Wom and said, 'This lady won a few cases in her time. She came in for some

313

courtroom glory. Sent some real bad guys away. She didn't do it all by herself, of course. No, we did all the shit work, built good solid cases for her. I don't think she ever once went into court on wobbly roller-skates. And the press she got. Jesus, you wouldn't believe it. Like a movie star. Cher or Michelle or somebody.'

Amanda asked, 'What am I hearing, Kelloway?'

Kelloway continued to address Wom. 'She had these profiles in the newspapers, Sonny. Magazines. How sharp she was. What a legal brain. Strange thing is, I never saw much mention of the back-room staff, the guys that lit the stage for her. The scriptwriters, the researchers, the little guys. She hogged it.'

Amanda stared at Kelloway. *The penny drops.* 'Oh Christ. How long have you been breast-feeding this grudge?'

'Grudge? What grudge?'

Exasperated, Amanda said, 'OK, I confess. You handed me cases on a shiny silver platter. Some of them were perfect, beyond perfect. Is that what you want me to say?'

Kelloway said, 'I'm not asking you to say anything, Miss Scholes.'

'Because you didn't get your share of the spotlight, you want to make life awkward for me,' she said.

'Awkward?' Kelloway feigned surprise. 'My department has always been the soul of co-operation, Miss Scholes. You'd agree with that?'

'Wholeheartedly,' she said.

'You'd also agree my people always walked the last few yards for you. Always.'

'More,' she said. She considered Kelloway's ego and what a delicate thing it had to be. Female prosecutor gets headlines and stories, macho Chief Kelloway gets none. So this was the source of his attitude: he was crying out for attention and he wasn't getting what he wanted and he

314

was stamping his feet with a petulance that had been festering inside him for a long time, a resentment out of control. If you added to this the rancour he still hauled around because she'd refused to prosecute the Hood case, you got a guy who was a twisted bundle of bitterness.

'And now you need my help,' he said.

'Yeah, I need your help.'

Kelloway got up from his chair. 'Get one thing straight, Miss Scholes. The only important factor for me in all this is Willie Drumm. I'll have a man visit the Hideaway Knolls and check out the guy you claim pilfered the letter, so we'll need a description from you. I'll get in touch with Justice and see if we can arrange a meeting with somebody who knows about the Witness Protection Program, and we'll sit down together and look at this thing closely.'

Somebody who knows about the Witness Protection Program, she thought. The phrase created disturbances inside her. How could Kelloway know this somebody was trustworthy? And when it came to the question of trust, how did she know she could put any in Kelloway, riddled as he was with pettiness?

'As a bonus, we'll also talk to Mrs Vialli who's so worried about her kid. You see how co-operative we are.'

She said, 'I want you to understand one thing. I didn't write those goddam interviews. I didn't go out looking for publicity, and I still think the Hood case was too damn weak to take into court.'

'I don't actually give a shit who wrote them any more than I give a shit about Hood,' Kelloway said, and adjusted his belt buckle. 'I'm a mean-spirited bastard and I just got what I wanted.'

He smiled at her fiercely, an expression of satisfaction and voracious spite. She heard the whirr of feathers, wings ruffling then settling back in place. Lay an egg, Kelloway. Lay it so it chafes your ass.

315

60

DANSK CHECKED INTO A HOTEL FIVE MILES FROM DOWN-town. The place was a dump but he didn't plan on staying. It was a base, nothing more, a place to freshen up. The porter who touted for Dansk's case wore grubby black shoes and a tacky brocade vest with a grease-stained pocket.

Dansk chilled the bag-man with a stare, and got his room key. He went to the pay phones and opened a Phoenix directory. He found what he wanted and scribbled the information down inside his notebook.

He went up to his room. Stuffy. He opened the bedroom window just as his cellular phone rang.

Pasquale said, 'It went off OK.' He had a sullen distance in his voice.

'Go to a place called the Sidewinder on McDowell. You'll meet McTell. I'll be in touch.' Dansk cut the connection and looked out the window. Something was smouldering in the distance, a garbage dump, maybe garden trash. A stack of thin white smoke rose into the sun, like a pope had just been elected.

This would be a great room if you were thinking of suicide: long drop. Jumpers heaving themselves over the ledge, air whining in their ears as they fell, maybe even changing their minds halfway down, when it was too late to reverse the polarity of the situation.

Like it was too late for Amanda.

Amanda, Amanda. You got a guy that loves you. A guy you love. Life should've been more precious to you, but you took a wrong turning.

He picked up the telephone and dialled a number.

'Phoenix Police Department,' a man said.

'Put me through to Lieutenant Drumm,' Dansk said.

'He isn't in the office at the moment.'

I bet. 'When do you expect him?'

'It's hard to say.' This guy was following the official line: no death announcement at the moment. Keep a lid on it. 'Maybe somebody else could help you,' he said. 'I'll connect you.'

A woman came on the line and introduced herself as Sergeant Friedman. She sounded dispirited.

Dansk imposed a little authoritative weight into his voice. 'This is Morgan Scholes. Amanda Scholes is my daughter. She left a message on my answering machine, something about how she was going to see Lieutenant Drumm, something about Rhees being hurt and hospitalized. Is she around? Can I talk to her?'

'You just missed her, Mr Scholes.'

'Father and daughter, we're like ships in the night. You any idea where she went?'

Betty Friedman was quiet a moment. 'She left the building with Chief Kelloway and Lieutenant Wom.'

'She say where she was going?'

'All I know is they went to interview somebody.'

'What hospital is Rhees in?'

'He's here in the building at the moment. A physician

317

gave him a painkilling injection, knocked him out.'

'This world,' Dansk said. 'What the hell's it coming to when vandals can just go inside somebody's home?' He made a clucking noise of irritation and bewilderment. An older man's sound of bafflement at the condition of today's society.

'You wanna leave a message you called? If I see her I'll pass it along.'

'Don't bother. She'll be in touch with me soon, I'm sure.'

So, they were going through the motions, interviewing somebody. He guessed Mrs Vialli. Who else? Running a check on her. *Some flowers on her birthday and a card she feels isn't kosher*. Loeb's fuck-up, he thought. Correspondence was Loeb's department, but he'd failed to keep track of nuances and quirks and simple stuff like accurate birth dates. Ma. Mom.

And Rhees was drugged and dozing inside the police building. He'd wake soon enough and he'd have to come out, and Amanda would be pushing him in the wheelchair, very touching, lovers looking out for one another. Be my valentine.

He remembered he'd received a valentine once in his life. Aged twelve, a giant red rose and the words, 'You Are My Secret Love.' Unsigned. He'd wondered about the sender, hoping it was Louise Andersen who wore her yellow hair in Nordic braids and dressed in pretty frocks, who'd been the inspiration behind his first masturbation when he'd sat on the john with his underwear round his ankles and thought of what lay under her frock and her panties, and he'd jerked off and nothing was the same ever again. That feeling, that hot eruption, the discovery that you had fluids inside you never even knew about.

But when he'd looked at the handwriting on the

envelope he'd recognized it as his mother's. A valentine from his own goddam mother.

He took the Ruger from his case and studied it. The exactitude of the architecture was impressive. You could lose yourself in the interior of the weapon, like you were something very tiny strolling a vast tubular passageway and the cartridges were the size of nuclear warheads.

He stuck the gun in his waistband at the base of his spine. His jacket concealed it neatly. He thought, Life can be good, Anthony. Life doesn't have to be pity valentines from your own mother.

He looked at himself in the full-length mirror.

Babyface Dansk.

He was ready now.

61

BERNADETTE VIALLI WASN'T ANSWERING HER DOORBELL. HER maroon Toyota was parked in the garage and Kelloway was trying to open the door that led from garage to house, but it was locked.

Sonny Wom, who'd disappeared round the side of the house to peer through the windows, returned and said, 'I can't see anyone inside, and the back door's locked. Place feels empty.'

Amanda smelled the hot air of the garage, motor oil and a scent of paint-stripper. She moved outside and stood under a sumac tree and looked at the upper windows of the house, where curtains were drawn across what might have been Mrs Vialli's bedroom. One-thirty in the afternoon, curtains still shut. Maybe she popped sleeping-pills and slept through the sound of her phone ringing and straight into the early afternoon.

Kelloway emerged from the gloom. The temperature was well above a hundred. 'We'll give this one last try.' He laid a fingertip on the bell and left it there. You could hear the constant maddening chimes indoors.

Amanda gazed again at the curtains, thin and floral-patterned. She imagined light passing through the flimsy material and into the room. She moved out of the shade a moment but withdrew as soon as she felt the full force of the sun. The world was burning up. This climate lashed and punished you.

A scrawny woman dressed in Bermudas and a baggy silk blouse appeared on the edge of Mrs Vialli's lawn. Her mouth was set in a suspicious pucker. 'Is there a problem here?' she asked.

Kelloway showed her his identification, which relaxed her up to a point. She introduced herself as the next-door neighbour, Mrs Christian, spelled as in Jesus, she explained solemnly. 'Something wrong with Bernie?' she asked.

'She usually sleep this late?' Kelloway asked.

'She's normally up at the crack.'

'You happen to see her today?'

Mrs Christian shook her head.

Kelloway said, 'Her car's in the garage and she's not answering the doorbell.'

'Maybe she's sick,' said the woman. She fell silent a moment, making a worried sucking sound on her grey dentures. 'You need to go in and have a look, I got a key. Bernie likes me to keep an eye on the place if she goes away. I water her plants. Keep an eye out.'

'If it's no problem,' Kelloway said.

'Always help the police. Rule of mine.' The woman dug a cumbersome clutch of keys from her pocket. She separated one from the bunch and handed it to Kelloway. He turned the key in the lock and stepped inside the house. Amanda and Wom followed, but Mrs Christian, looking wary, lingered on the threshold.

The house had a moody silence. Amanda stood at the bottom of the stairs while Kelloway and Wom explored the ground-floor rooms. Her eye was drawn up to the shadows at the top of the stairs. Hot air was trapped in the house.

'Nothing,' Kelloway said.

Wom was already climbing the stairs, Kelloway followed. Amanda came behind, thinking of the room with the closed curtains.

Kelloway went inside the bedroom. The bedsheets were drawn back and the pillows indented, but Mrs Vialli wasn't there. He opened the curtains and the room burst into brightness. Amanda blinked and stepped back out into the hallway where Wom was already opening another door leading into a room that had obviously been Benny Vialli's once upon a time. Sports posters on the walls, Magic Johnson frozen in mid-flight above a hoop, a couple of dated rock posters, Madonna clutching her groin, a shot of The Rolling Stones before they became raddled capitalists.

Amanda wandered away from Benny's old room. Across the landing the door of the bathroom was open a couple of inches. Damson tiles, peach-coloured towels on a rack, a mirrored medicine cabinet that reflected a small area of the room's interior. Amanda moved towards this door and stopped. She saw something reflected in the mirror. A shower rail at a bad angle, a shower curtain twisted. Kelloway appeared at her back. He moved past her and stepped inside. Wom, directly behind him, blocked Amanda's view.

'Eureka,' Kelloway said.

Amanda shifted her position slightly, glanced over Wom's shoulder and saw how the shower rail had broken free from the wall at one end and the curtain was crumpled. A length of rope had been twisted round the rail and Bernadette Vialli lay in the centre of this tangle with a noose round her neck and an overturned chair a few feet away.

322

Amanda pushed past Wom into the bathroom. Kelloway, stretching out an arm, tried to hold her back, but she was already past him and kneeling over Bernadette Vialli, whose mouth was open, tongue swollen. Her robe was damp and her big silly slippers had slipped off her white feet to the floor.

Amanda looked at the nylon rope, the knot, the way it had cut into the dead woman's throat, the angry purple abrasions created by the tension of the noose. Kelloway, leaning forward, touched Amanda's shoulder and said something about how she shouldn't be looking at this. But Amanda ignored him, her attention fixed on the woman's open eyes, the whites bloodshot and a smear of cream that had adhered somehow to her eyelids and the darkness in the pupils. She found herself wondering if it was true that the eyes retained an image of the last thing a dead person had seen, or if that was just nonsense, a fantasy, and what did it matter anyway? Something about the cream bothered her.

'She got up on the chair and kicked it over,' Kelloway said. 'I guess the rail held out long enough for her to choke.'

'I don't buy that,' Amanda said.

'Let me guess. You think she was murdered and then strung up,' Kelloway said.

'That's exactly what I think.'

'By the mysterious Dansk.'

'Or one of his minions.'

'There's no sign of forced entry,' Wom said. 'No broken windows, smashed locks, anything like that.'

'So she opened the door to somebody she knew,' Amanda said, and finally looked away from Bernadette Vialli. She thought, A crushed plastic shower curtain with the tiny label 'Kaeskoo Products, Seoul' wasn't much of a shroud.

Kelloway asked, 'You're saying she knew her killer? How come?'

Amanda rose. 'I don't know how come.'

Kelloway was quiet a moment.

She thought of Dansk, the way he'd tracked her. He must have watched Drumm come to this house, and the idea of a conversation between the cop and Mrs Vialli worried him to the point where he'd ordered the deaths of Willie and Bernadette. Let's just close this situation down, he might have thought. Let's nip this in the heart of the bud.

Amanda stepped out of the bathroom. She felt unwell, giddy. Kelloway followed her. Wom remained behind, notebook in one small hand, a scribe of death.

'No way was it suicide,' she said.

'Convince me,' Kelloway said.

'She's got some traces of moisturizing cream round her eyes. You think she slaps cream on her face before she hangs herself?'

'You're talking a trace, that's all. Maybe she started to apply the stuff then changed her mind. What the hell. I've seen suicides in tuxedos. You'll have to do better.'

She struggled against her dislike for this cop. But she had to accept the fact she needed him, she was dog-tired of going it alone, and he had behind him a large law-enforcement organization whose help she wanted. His scepticism, his abrasive manner, she'd tolerate these until it became impossible.

She stopped halfway down the stairs. A uniformed cop appeared in the hallway. It was Sergeant Thomas Gannon, whom she'd last seen during the fruitless search for Isabel in the desert. He touched his little moustache, nodded at her, then looked directly past her at Kelloway.

'I went to the Hideaway Knolls,' Gannon said. 'The only guy vaguely resembling the description Miss Scholes gave checked out this morning. He'd registered under the name of John J. Coleman.'

Kelloway looked at Amanda. 'Dansk checks out of his hotel, now this other character checks out. These people have quite a knack for timely disappearances, don't they?'

Amanda had a stifling sensation. She was caught up in filaments that, no matter how hard she tried to claw them from her skin, still clung to her. People check out, from hotels, from life.

Gannon said, 'I also have a message for you, Chief. Somebody from Justice will meet you at five in your office.'

'Quick response,' Kelloway said.

'Apparently this guy happened to be in LA and your enquiry was forwarded to him and he caught the first plane,' Gannon said.

'Lucked out,' Kelloway said.

Lucked out, Amanda thought. Mrs Vialli hadn't lucked out.

She reached the foot of the stairs and strolled past Gannon into the harrowing sunlight. She lit a cigarette and sucked smoke inside her lungs and wondered where Dansk was, what crevice of this city concealed him, what step he was planning next.

62

EDDIE McTELL AND BRUNO PASQUALE SAT IN THE BIG DRAB empty lounge of the Sidewinder Motel, a room that had the ambience of a charity clinic run by an indigent religious order excommunicated long ago.

McTell said, 'I've had it to the scrotum with crummy joints like this. Gimme Tijuana. Lead me to a bordello. Slamming tequila with some hot-blooded little chickadee sitting in my lap. Way to fucking go.'

'I never been in Mexico,' said Pasquale.

'I'll take you there one day, Bruno. Who needs shit places like this? The pits. Christ.'

Pasquale leaned back in his chair. He had a cinematic notion of Mexico, musicians with guitars strolling under fancy wrought-iron balconies. 'I hear they got cock-fights down there. I never seen one.'

'It's all blood and feathers and flying guts. You'd enjoy it.'

Pasquale was quiet for a time. 'I'm still thinking about this guy Loeb I met. He showed me some heavy ID, I mean, *impressive*. He's like up there. Way up. He knows

326

everything going on, Eddie. You name it, all the work we done for Dansk, he knows about it. And it goes back a ways. I'm not just talking about recent stuff. And we're supposed to keep him posted on the moves Dansk orders, except Dansk ain't to know.'

'What I think it is, he's checking up on Tony Birthmark,' McTell said. 'Like a performance evaluation, something. How Dansk is handling the job. Maybe Loeb's got some doubts, which wouldn't blow me outta my chair with astonishment.'

'I don't like going behind anybody's back, Eddie.'

'If this Loeb's the big chief, you forget any doubts you might have.'

Pasquale said, 'He gave me his phone number, and we're supposed to call and keep him informed.'

'I don't have a problem with that,' McTell said. 'Dansk's head is wired all the wrong way.' He tapped the side of his skull with a fingertip. 'You ask me, the Birthmark Boy's got a fixation type thing about this broad. The way he talks about her, he gets this buzzing in his voice. Sometimes I think he's a death junkie and he wants to take a walk on the dark side, see how guys like you and me live. Only he hasn't admitted it to himself and now this woman comes along and stirs his juices and suddenly he's out of the closet and trigger-happy. It's like he's got a hard-on for her, swear to God.'

Pasquale played with a paper napkin, folding it, tearing it here and there, then spreading it open so it looked like a line of chorus girls. 'I didn't like the hit and run shtick,' he said.

'A cop into the bargain,' McTell said.

Pasquale said, 'A target's just a target. I don't have any hang-ups who I work on. It was that dumb-fuck little German car in broad daylight.'

'You mentioned this hit to Loeb?'

'No. You think I oughta?'

'Loeb wants the skinny, you give it to him, man.'

'So I tell Loeb, you're saying.'

McTell sipped his lager and nodded. Pasquale placed a beer coaster on the edge of the table, smacked it with his hand and watched it rise in the air. He snatched it on the way down like a frisbee. 'I don't feel good about going behind Dansk's back.'

McTell shrugged. 'Me, I wouldn't think twice about talking to Loeb. Fact, you want to give me his number, I'll call him myself, because I got more than a few comments to make about Dansk.'

Pasquale plucked a slip of paper from his wallet and put it down on the table. 'Here.'

'You wanna go first?' McTell asked.

'After you, Eddie.'

'That's me,' said McTell. 'Always the guy that breaks the ice at parties.'

63

IN THE BACK OF KELLOWAY'S CAR AMANDA THOUGHT ABOUT
Willie Drumm and Bernadette Vialli. She pictured those
little war monuments you saw sometimes in the leafy
squares of backwater towns, the names of men and
women who'd died in far-away wars for what was
commonly referred to as democracy and liberty. No such
rhetoric attached to the deaths of Willie and Bernadette
Vialli. They'd been killed for reasons that had nothing to
do with patriotism or honour or whatever pumped-up
nonsense words were carved into granite to cover the fact
of human sacrifice and blood-letting.

They'd been killed because of Dansk, because of
Dansk's business, which clearly wasn't limited to Sanchez
alone. Because if that were the case, Bernadette Vialli
would still be alive in her split-level suburban home.

Something else, she thought.

Willie had speculated about a personal motive, but she
wasn't buying this. It was more than that, but it was just
beyond her reach, whatever it was, something she
couldn't focus on. She wished she had Willie to talk it

through with her. She wished for a resurrection.

She turned her face and looked from the window. Outside the car the city was a blend of glass and brick. Between the buildings were forlorn blue shadows. Wom was driving, Kelloway sat in the passenger seat, his body turned towards Amanda.

Kelloway said, 'You mentioned Mrs Vialli had a birthday card from her son, also a tape. We couldn't find either.'

Amanda said nothing. She looked at the windows of tall buildings. She imagined the sniper again, a telescopic lens attached to his high-powered rifle, a bullet slamming into her skull. Welcome back to happy hour for paranoids, when uneasy feelings were two for the price of one and the bartender had Dansk's face. She stared at the unusually deep cleft in the back of Kelloway's neck.

'Willie talked with Lew Bascombe about Dansk,' she said. 'That's an avenue you should be exploring.'

'You don't mind if we do this my way, do you?' Kelloway said.

'Bascombe was supposed to do some checking and get back to Willie—'

'My way,' Kelloway said. 'I mean that.'

Amanda lapsed into silence. Why not go direct to Bascombe now? Why not squeeze him hard? She wondered if there was any future in talking to Kelloway. He seemed to hear only what he wanted.

She looked at the digital dashboard clock. Four thirty-two. Somebody was coming from Justice at five, somebody who'd answer questions and allay the fears and suspicions. Yes indeed.

Wom parked the car in the lot of the Police building. Amanda stepped out into the volcanic afternoon. She didn't want to enter the monolithic beige-coloured building. She didn't want to see this somebody from Justice

330

who'd have a plausible multi-layered story and a nice white shirt and the speech patterns of a real-estate salesman.

She followed Kelloway and Sonny Wom into the cool interior. 'I'll check on John,' she said.

'Sure.' Kelloway led her along a corridor to a tiny room. He opened the door. Rhees lay on a narrow cot. She entered the room alone and approached the bed. Rhees was drowsy from painkillers.

'How are you?' she asked.

'I was having this dream we were in Fiji drinking coconut milk, only it wasn't milk, it was ink. You see any symbolism in that?'

'No, not really. How's the pain?'

'Numbed,' he said.

'I've got a meeting with some person from Justice shortly.'

'And then?'

She didn't know how to answer. She said, 'We'll see.' She ran a hand lightly across his face.

'Get brochures,' he said. 'Glossy ones from a travel agent . . .'

He closed his eyes, slipping into sleep. Ink and coconut milk, cave-writing on the walls of the unconscious. Rhees had hopes of blue distances and vacations, getting away from nightmares. She kissed his lips, then left the room.

Kelloway and Wom were waiting in the corridor.

'We'll go up to my office,' Kelloway said.

They rode an elevator in silence. When the doors opened Kelloway ushered her out. The corridor was quiet. A sense of bereavement hung in the air. A few cops sat at their desks and shuffled paperwork without interest. Here and there, in doorways and around a water fountain, they stood in small sombre groups. The fact of Drumm's death

331

had permeated the building and alerted officers to the notion of their own mortality.

Amanda felt the heaviness in the atmosphere. The only thing missing was Willie's body inside a coffin on a plinth surrounded by floral tributes.

Kelloway entered his office with Sonny Wom. He went behind his desk and vigorously rubbed his arm with the palm of his hand. Amanda sat, struggling against her tension. Relax. Somebody from Justice is coming, the world is going to be set right, explanations will be forthcoming.

There was a knock on the door.

Kelloway said, 'Come.'

The door opened. Amanda didn't turn to look.

She heard a man say, 'I'm on time, I trust.'

Kelloway moved out from behind his desk to welcome the visitor and Amanda changed the angle of her head and saw a man dressed in a black suit and white shirt with a black tie. Over one arm he'd slung a coat. His hair was white and sparse and he moved across the floor in a shuffling way, no elasticity in his muscles.

I'm on time, I trust. Amanda had a sense of backtracking, rolling in reverse on some kind of memory monorail through a tunnel filled with echoes.

'Chief of Police Kelloway?' the man asked.

'Right.'

'This heat,' the man said and smiled. 'How do you cope with it?'

'You get used to it,' Kelloway said. 'After twenty years, give or take.'

The man sat. He set a briefcase on the floor beside his chair. Amanda stared at him. His eyes were watery. She was still travelling backwards, still trying to compartmentalize something that had strayed out of place. But what?

The man opened a wallet and held out his ID. Kelloway looked at it, nodding his head.

The man turned to Amanda and asked, 'And you are?'

She spoke her name quietly. It had come back to her. It had come rolling all the way back to her.

She thought, This is wrong. This is out of tune.

64

AMANDA ASKED, 'YOU JUST FLEW IN FROM LOS ANGELES? Weather nice out there?'

The man said, 'Sunny like here, but less hot.'

Kelloway said, 'What's the weather got to do with anything?'

'Just curious.' Amanda noticed the darkness under the man's eyes, the lack of colour in his lips. 'What airline did you fly?'

'America West.' His voice was like grit inside a cat-litter box, cinders rolling back and forth, and he breathed with difficulty.

Kelloway said, 'Mr Loeb hasn't flown in to discuss weather or airlines.'

'Ralph,' Loeb said. 'Call me Ralph.'

'Last time I was in LA, I stayed at the Marmont,' Amanda continued. 'Were you staying in a hotel?'

'No, with a friend in Westwood,' Loeb said.

Sonny Wom slipped out of the room quietly as if he'd received one of Kelloway's imperceptible signals. Kelloway was rising from behind his desk. His irritation was palpable. From the corner of her eye Amanda was aware of his bronze skin and white shirt.

'This chit-chat's entertaining, I'm sure,' he said. 'I'd like to see us get to the point, Scholes.'

Plain old *Scholes* now. Amanda ignored the cop and asked, 'How did you receive the message that brought you here?'

'Carrier pigeon,' Loeb said. He smiled thinly. 'By phone, of course.'

'In LA. At your friend's house in Westwood.'

Loeb faced Kelloway and asked, 'Am I under oath?'

'What's the point of these questions, Scholes?' Kelloway asked.

Amanda stepped a little nearer to Loeb. 'Who was it that telephoned you in Westwood?'

'A colleague in Washington,' Loeb said with a certain patience. 'Let me take you through the steps, Miss Scholes. Chief Kelloway contacted the Justice Department with an urgent request to meet somebody connected to the Witness Protection Program, and his enquiry was passed along to me because, A, I'm associated with the Program, and B, I was less than an hour away by plane. That answer your questions?'

'Does this colleague have a name?'

Kelloway looked at Loeb and said, 'I'm sorry about this, Ralph. Scholes was a prosecuting attorney until recently, which she thinks gives her a licence to come off like the Grand Inquisitor.' He turned to Amanda, and his stare was unpleasant, and just for a moment Amanda had the tiny flash of a feeling that Kelloway and Loeb weren't entirely strangers to one another. But the sensation was smoke, and it dissipated as quickly as it had arisen, blown out of her head by the sharpness of Kelloway's angry voice. 'Ralph isn't here to play Trivial Pursuit, Scholes, and this isn't a court of law, in case that had slipped your mind.'

335

'I asked a simple question—'

'An irrelevant question,' Kelloway said.

Loeb smiled and said, 'You ought to have Miss Scholes fitted with an emergency brake, Chief.'

Kelloway said, 'I think it's a muzzle she needs more.'

Amanda said to Loeb, 'I can understand you might not want to tell us the name of your colleague at Justice. Confidentiality and so forth. What about your friend in LA? What's his name?'

Kelloway had his hand firmly on her elbow now. 'Outside,' he said. 'I want a word.'

She allowed herself to be led into the corridor, where she yanked her arm free of Kelloway's flinty grip.

'What the fuck are you playing at?' he asked.

'He's not on the level, Kelloway.'

'How do you figure that?'

'Because I recognize his voice.'

'You're losing me.'

'Dansk gave me his private number to call in Washington. When I called it, I got an answering-machine, and the voice on the machine was Loeb's.'

'You phone Dansk and you get Loeb's voice on a machine. What's the big deal?'

'The big deal is they're in this together. Dansk and Loeb. They're *partners*, for Christ's sake. He's here to feed you bullshit. He'll tell you exactly what Dansk told me. He's going to talk about an in-house investigation of security leaks in the Program. He's going to tell you how they're in the process of being sealed. I've heard it before and it all sounds very plausible, but I'm not sitting through it again, thanks.'

Kelloway clenched a hand and tapped it like a mallet against the side of his leg. 'So you don't trust Loeb. Maybe you don't trust me either, huh?'

Amanda gazed along the corridor. A bubble rose inside

a water-cooler and popped on the surface. She turned her face to Kelloway, whose sarcasm made her feel isolated. *Maybe you don't trust me either, huh?* Trust was fragile scaffolding and it swayed when you climbed it.

She said, 'All I'm telling you is that Loeb and Dansk are involved in this thing together, and Loeb's going to try and pass you off with pap. Christ, they've got it *sewn-up*, Kelloway. It's neat. They've got it nicely self-contained. Call Dansk and you get Loeb's voice. Messages for Dansk never go any further, they're always intercepted by Loeb.'

'So what have we got here? Guys that have entered into some sinister compact to bury a couple of witnesses on behalf of Victor Sanchez?'

'Exactly. Check Loeb's story. You can find out what flight he claims he caught from LA and the name of the friend he says he stayed with in California. My bet is he's covered his ass and you'll get nowhere. He can arrange well-rehearsed associates to back up anything he says. A flight attendant who seems to remember him, an old pal in LA who's going to tell you Loeb was his house guest.'

'Check Loeb's story. This is your best advice?'

'It's my only advice. This is a labyrinth. One wrong turn and you're lost.'

'Did you ever drop tainted acid back in the old days and every now and again you have weird flashbacks?'

'Acid scared me, so I left it alone.'

Kelloway rolled up a sleeve that had begun to slide down his arm. 'You should have stuck to that principle, Scholes: leaving things alone.'

Sonny Wom came along the corridor and said, 'He checks out. He's with Justice all right.'

'Fine. Go back and keep him occupied, Sonny. I'll be with you in a minute.'

Amanda remembered Willie Drumm's speculation about Dansk. *He's got nothing to do with the Program. He's a freelance operator*. And somebody on the inside is feeding him information, somebody bought and paid for by Sanchez. Loeb.

It had to be. A sinister compact.

Kelloway said, 'So Loeb's the genuine article.'

'He works for Justice, which doesn't mean he's on the—'

'He's on the level until I find out otherwise, Scholes.'

'OK, OK, OK. Play it by your rules.'

'You still don't want to hear what he has to say? You're walking away?'

'First I have to think of someplace to walk,' she said. 'I don't like the idea of the streets. I don't know what's out there in all that sunlight.'

Kelloway said, 'Maybe that's all there is, sunlight and nothing else.'

'I seriously doubt it.'

He was quiet a moment. 'Why don't you ask me?'

'Ask you what?'

'Don't go coy. You need a favour.'

He reminded her increasingly of a hawk hovering in the still air above hot canyons, scanning for soft prey. 'I don't expect favours from you,' she said. 'You don't like me. The chemistry between us is like frozen tundra.'

Kelloway shrugged. 'I have powers. You want to get out of here safely, don't you? And there's Rhees to think about.'

'There's Rhees, sure,' she said.

'But you don't like the idea of just walking away. Feisty lady prosecutor suddenly backed into corner, doesn't know who to trust. Injured man on her hands, serious limits to her freedom of movement.'

'You want me at your mercy,' she said.

'It's an appealing notion. The cops step in where the former angel of justice fears to tread.'

338

'You're an asshole, Kelloway.'

'Assholes can be powerful.'

'Power comes and goes.'

'Yeah, but right now I happen to have it, which is why you need me.'

'What are you offering?'

'You believe you're in danger. OK, you need protection. I'm thinking of offering you Thomas Gannon.'

Protection. Kelloway was right about one thing: Rhees restricted her activities. But if she walked away, it meant leaving everything to Kelloway. He inherited it all.

'Why the helping hand?' she asked.

'Willie Drumm thought the world of you. He talked about you like you were his favourite niece or something, and that counts where I'm concerned, because I liked Willie. Surprised?'

She tried to find a tiny kindness in his face at that moment, an underlying gentleness, but the face gave away nothing. It was all suntanned surfaces and hard angles. Whatever feelings he had were encased behind barbed wire, deep inside, where you couldn't get a glimpse of them.

'I'm wondering if you'll follow through,' she said. 'Or if you'll just buy Loeb's version and let everything slide away into obscurity.'

He drew a hand across his face. 'Let me explain something to you. When you say Willie was killed because this Dansk wanted him dead, I'd be remiss if I didn't look into your story, right? So that's what I'm doing: looking into your story. And meantime giving you protection. Doing my job.'

'I sit in the bleachers and you play the game,' she said. 'And Gannon is my guardian angel. Which is also pretty convenient for you, because he can report on me if I decide to step out of line.'

339

'That's what it comes down to. Pick a safe place.'

There was an echo here she didn't like: Dansk on their first meeting. *You agree to stay out of this business entirely, and in return I'll let you know the outcome.* Things had changed since then. Her world was haywire and she didn't have the resources to straighten it out on her own. A woman with a fractured lover: What could she do? Her boundaries had narrowed, her options diminished.

'Well?' Kelloway asked. 'Do I hear a thank you?'

She was thinking of the forest and the estuaries of darkness, the howl of coyotes and the sorry little pipsqueaks of their victims. She wasn't in the mood for expressing gratitude because she didn't feel any. It was another feeling she had, a kinship with those creatures of the pines that lived in fear of nocturnal predators with a craving for easy blood.

65

DANSK PARKED ON THE SIDE OF THE MOUNTAIN WHERE A paved road had been laid close to the edge. Up here, people who'd accumulated great wealth built houses with amazing views of the city spread below. This was a place where you could stand on your balcony and sip your freshly squeezed orange juice on sunny mornings and say, Thank you, God, I've arrived. And maybe you'd spare a thought for the peasants toiling in the city far below, street-cleaners and janitors and maids, all the peons and wetbacks who laboured down there so you could live up here just a little nearer to heaven.

He got out of the car and walked through dusky light to a set of iron gates. He could see a house at the end of a driveway of rose-coloured gravel chips. The gates weren't locked. Up here, maybe people felt immune to the brigands in the city. Up here where private security cars patrolled back and forth, maybe they felt superbly secure.

Dansk pushed the gates open and heard his feet crunch on the gravel.

He heard an electronic beeping sound emerge from the

house, faint but audible. He figured he'd set off an invisible alarm when he'd come through the gates. The sound stopped and a man appeared outside the house. He was dressed in neat brown slacks and a white cotton poloneck. He had grey hair, well-trimmed. Dansk smiled and kept walking towards the man.

About six feet away, Dansk stopped. The guy had a stern look, slightly canine. Dansk tried to see some resemblance in the face to Amanda, but he couldn't find one. He remembered from his background research that Morgan Scholes was a widower and wondered how long ago his wife had died.

Dansk said, 'Sorry for the intrusion.'

Morgan Scholes had white hair on the backs of his hands. 'There's a sign at the gate,' he said. 'It says no trespassing, and that's precisely what it means.'

'I must have missed it,' Dansk said. Morgan Scholes's voice was authoritative. He gave an impression of crabbed impatience, belligerence held in check. A ruthless business type, Dansk thought, steamrolling the competition, amassing enormous amounts of cash and breaking bones along his merry acquisitive way.

Dansk kept smiling. 'My ID,' he said.

Morgan Scholes looked at the Justice Department credentials. This appeared to make him less aggressive. 'What can I do for you?'

'It's about your daughter,' Dansk said. 'I just want a quick word.'

Morgan Scholes said, 'Let's get out of this damn heat first.'

The house was all arches, Mexican tiles, ceramic pots and Western art. Dansk followed Scholes into a room filled with oil-paintings of cowboys.

'Sit,' Scholes said. 'Drink?'

'Maybe a soda,' Dansk said. He didn't sit. He never sat

on command, that's what dogs did.

Scholes went into the kitchen. Dansk examined some framed photographs on a sideboard: Amanda on graduation day, gowned and mortarboarded and ready to shake plump fruits off the tree of the world. She looked fresh and innocent, hatched only minutes before. Her mouth had a slight enigmatic smile, but there was latent determination in the expression. He ran a fingertip across the glass, thinking he could almost feel the warmth of her flesh, the soft mouth. The next picture was that of a woman in a swimsuit. The resemblance to Amanda was obvious, so this had to be the dead mother. She had provocative lips and was staring evenly into the camera, like she was daring the photographer to disrobe.

Morgan Scholes came back carrying two ice-cold cans of root beer. He gave one to Dansk.

'So, what's this daughter of mine up to now? She's drawn into situations like a fly to horse-shit. Quits her job one minute, the next she's running around doing God knows what because of some stiff in a river. Too busy to speak to me on the phone, that's for sure.'

'The independent type,' Dansk said. He sipped the soda. Chemicals and carbonation.

'Independent wouldn't be my first choice, more like mulish. Gets her feet planted and won't budge. So what's happening?'

'I need to ask her a few questions,' Dansk said. 'Some clarification concerning the dead body, that's all.' This amazing calm he felt. It was like his heartbeat was down to five a minute and his nerves narcotized. 'But I'm having a problem trying to locate her. I tried her home in Scottsdale.'

'Welcome to the club.'

'You any idea where she is?'

Morgan Scholes shook his head. 'Not a clue.'

343

Dansk said, 'I understand there's a cabin someplace up near Flag.'

'I've been trying that number too. No luck.'

'Where is the cabin exactly?'

'Why? You think she's up there not answering the phone?'

'Maybe she's *en route*,' Dansk said. 'I don't know. I have to cover the possibilities.'

'I built that cabin, you know. With these,' and Morgan Scholes raised his hands in the air. 'The idea was a retreat away from everything.'

The self-made man, Dansk thought.

'Except I never spent much time at the goddam place. Too busy. Story of my life.'

Dansk wondered how long he could maintain the smile. He was beginning to feel lockjaw. 'I was thinking I'd take a run up there. If she shows up, fine.'

'If she's not there, you've driven a long way for nothing.'

'I'll take the chance,' Dansk said. 'What I'd like is the location of the cabin.'

Scholes looked hesitant. 'It's damned hard to get to.'

'I understand that, but it's important I contact her, otherwise I wouldn't be here bothering you.'

Scholes rose from the arm of the leather chair. He stared at Dansk, a look of assessment. Just for a moment it seemed that the old guy was about to resist giving out information.

'You'll need a map,' he said finally. He went to a desk, took a sheet of paper and a pen from a drawer.

Dansk watched him draw neat lines on the paper.

'Leave Flagstaff on Route Forty heading west. Go about thirteen miles. You'll come to a track on the right that's poorly marked except for an ancient sign that says "No Hunting". The letters are faded. I'll mark that with an X.

Go down this track about five miles. Two miles down the track you'll come to a bridge over a creek. I'll mark that B. Go slow there because that bridge is shaky. On the other side there's a path which isn't easy to find because it's overgrown. I wouldn't be taking any car of mine beyond that bridge unless it was four-wheel drive. It's rough.'

Dansk gazed at the map. X for turning. B for bridge.

'You follow the path for a mile, and you come to a fork. You keep going right. See this line I'm making? Follow that. It's the only access track to the cabin, and it's damn narrow, so stick to it. Go left and you're lost.'

'So I keep going right at the fork.'

'Exactly. You won't see much in the way of landmarks except a million trees that all look the same. I'm marking this C for the cabin. And if you run into my daughter, tell her I'm not too pleased with her right now.' Scholes handed the sheet of paper to Dansk.

'I'm obliged,' Dansk said.

'If Amanda happens to call in the meantime, I'll tell her you're looking for her. You got a number where she can reach you?'

This tricky moment. Dansk had been waiting for it, expecting it. Say Amanda phones her father. Her father tells her somebody called Dansk has been asking for her. It couldn't be allowed to happen that way. His heart accelerated and the edge of his vision dimmed and he stared at Morgan Scholes who seemed surrounded by a sudden mist.

'Something wrong?' Scholes asked.

Dansk thought, Do this thing, do it now.

He whipped the Ruger out of his waistband and from a range of 6 or 7 feet he shot Scholes in the head. He felt the kick of the pistol in his fist, and it reminded him of the sting of the baseball bat when he'd hit Skipper Klintz. He flashed back all those years, down through the fogged passages of time, and even as Scholes staggered back it was Skipper Klintz Dansk saw, a thick-skulled kid with a crew cut and snow falling lightly in the dark and blood in the snow and a scared cat screeching out of a trash can. Dansk lowered the gun to his side and stepped closer to Scholes, who'd fallen against his desk and knocked over a limestone paperweight decorated with some Navaho conceit. It had broken clean in two.

When you take your seat in the Blood Bijou you break some things, Dansk thought.

The map Scholes had sketched for him had half a dozen spots of blood on it. He picked it up, walked to the door, hesitated, then took Amanda's graduation photograph. He left the house and walked down the pathway, and this time he didn't hear the crunch of gravel under his feet. Goddam, goddam, he was thinking.

He reached his car. He sat without moving and stuck the gun back inside the paper bag. The picture of the young Amanda lay in his lap. He looked into her face. Amanda in my lap. Amanda lying near my groin. He nibbled on his pinky. I killed a guy. He stared down in the direction of the city, the layered pall of pollution. Suddenly street lamps came on. Scholes's light went out and the street lamps were switched on, like illuminations to mark the old guy's demise.

His phone rang. He picked it up in a hand that felt numb.

McTell said, 'She left the building. With Rhees.'

Dansk felt removed from himself. The building – the word seemed to have cast off meaning. He had to remind himself. The building. Police HQ.

McTell said, 'Minor problem, Anthony. She's in one of those four-wheel-drive Broncos with a cop driving. Looks like she got herself a little protection.'

Protection. Dansk closed his eyes. 'Any backup? Any other vehicles following?'

'None I can see.'

'Is Rhees with her?' *I killed a guy and I don't feel a goddam thing.*

'Yeah, he's with her. So how come she's got protection, Anthony? Cops believe her story after all? Something you didn't anticipate?'

Dansk heard a note in McTell's voice, an undercurrent of what – gloating? 'If they bought her story, they'd give her more than one cop inside the Bronco, McTell. Believe me. You'd also see a backup car you could spot a mile off. She's being patronized. The cop's like a condom she can wrap round her fears.'

'If you say so,' McTell remarked, that funny note still in his voice.

Dansk was jazzed a little, thinking about this unexpected cop. The lady had low-level protection, a fact of life you had to deal with. Things came up and you coped with them. Dansk's Law.

One cop wasn't a disaster. McTell and Pasquale could deal with the cop at the right time. The rest was his own business. Shapes formed and fell into place. Everything had its own little slot. The future was no mystery.

'Where are they exactly?'

McTell said, 'They're driving on I-Seventeen. Passing the Thunderbird exit.'

'Stay with them.'

He punched in Pasquale's number and asked, 'Where are you?'

'I'm on, lemme see, Indian School Road approaching the interstate.'

Dansk took a map from the glove compartment. He moved a fingertip directly north. It was just as he'd figured: she was see-through. *I know you, babe. In* another reality we might have been close and this affinity would have had a different outcome, but now I sit with a Ruger in a brown-paper sack and your face in my groin and think of unhappy endings.

'McTell says they're in a cop vehicle. I don't like that,' Pasquale said.

'Just keep going, Pasquale.'

Dansk drove for a while. The matter was settled in his mind, only the mechanics remained.

He called McTell back. 'Still no sign of backup?'

'Nothing I'd point a finger at.'

'Where are you now?'

'The sign I just passed said Flagstaff one hundred and eighteen miles.'

She was still on course. She'd feel safe now. She had a cop with a gun to comfort her. She'd be letting down her defences a little, saying soothing words to Rhees, holding his hand. Tra-la-la, everything in her garden was beginning to bloom again. She thinks.

He drove about 10 miles. Much of the traffic was out of state, sun-seekers from the Dakotas and Nebraska who lumbered south in bulky motor homes, exchanging monotonous wheatfields for the furnace. The landscape reverted to desert. Cacti blazed gold out on the brown-red flats and the sun was dying in an extravagant palette of pinks and purples and yellows.

His phone buzzed and he picked it up, expecting Pasquale or McTell, but it was Loeb, sounding like a man trapped in a barrel of molasses.

'We need to talk,' Loeb said.

'What's on your mind?' He didn't like the idea of Loeb contacting him. Especially now, when he was pre-occupied.

'Face to face, Anthony. I don't like talking into these gadgets. I know they're supposed to be secure, but I have a suspicious nature. Where are you?'

'The middle of nowhere,' Dansk said.

'Specifically,' Loeb said.

'There's some kind of road-house coming up,' Dansk said, spotting a ratty wooden tavern overlooking the interstate. An orange neon sign was lit. JACK'S DINER. STEAKS. RIBS.

'Is this important, Ralph?'

'Just tell me a place we can meet.'

Dansk pulled off the freeway and into the parking-lot and explained where he was. 'Give me thirty minutes,' Loeb said.

66

JACK'S TAVERN WAS CRAMMED WITH GOOD OLD BOYS HEE-
hawing and playing eight-ball with cigarette packs tucked
in the sleeves of their T-shirts. Country music came
wailing from the place. Dansk walked up and down the
parking area. The music annoyed him.

The sun had gone when a green Nissan entered the lot
and parked. Loeb stepped out, his face dark and
aggressive. 'What the fuck game are you playing,
Anthony?'

'Meaning?'

Loeb expelled air in a choked manner. 'I just spent half
an hour with the cops.'

'And?'

'The lady goes to the cops. The cops call Washington. I
get an intercept. I meet the cops. The lady is present in the
room for a time.' Loeb shivered although the night air was
hot.

'They're not going to believe her,' Dansk said.

Loeb placed a hand on Dansk's sleeve. 'First off, she
recognized me. Soon as she looks at me, I hear the whine

of her brain hydraulics. She starts in with sharp little questions disguised as innocent enquiries. How do you suppose she knew me?'

Dansk said, 'Maybe she saw you talking to me somewhere. Maybe she did some spying.'

'What it comes down to is you were supposed to do the business with her, but there she is in the cop's office. No holograph, Anthony. The woman in the flesh, and not very happy.'

'I work my own way,' Dansk said. He was walking the boundaries of sheer displeasure now, staking little fenceposts of irritation on the perimeters of his property.

Loeb said, 'Work? What you're doing is building some Byzantine edifice. This isn't a fucking mosque under construction, Anthony. I told you before, no tangents. And suddenly there I am face to face with the woman.'

'The cops won't buy her story,' Dansk said.

'They shouldn't have been given the goddam opportunity to *hear* her story! You let her get to the cops. You allowed that. Fuck only knows what's going through your head. I can't keep track of you any more, Anthony.'

You'll never know what goes through my head, Loeb. 'So she talked to the cops, and you talked to the cops. What do they think of her story?'

'They think it's fluff. At least that's what they say.'

'I rest my case,' Dansk said. He looked at Loeb and out of nowhere he had the feeling the old guy wasn't being absolutely honest about something. He wasn't sure what.

'Premature, Anthony. Maybe in normal circumstances they'd cross the street to avoid her because she reeks of paranoia, except for a couple of important things. One of them is this dead cop. Cops don't like their colleagues dead. They become very tetchy. Small things get blown out of proportion. Fluff goes under the microscope, Anthony, and suddenly everything's complicated.'

Dansk looked at the night sky. You want to talk complicated, Loeb, lift up your eyes. Check out the firmament.

'A dead cop,' Loeb said, 'and a letter from Isabel Sanchez. A letter you didn't bother to mention to me.'

'There's no letter,' Dansk said, which was true, if you looked at it a certain way.

'Not according to what the prosecutor told the cops.'

'The prosecutor's full of shit,' Dansk said.

'Shit to one side, the cops think about their dead colleague and wonder about the contents of the alleged letter and suddenly they've got questions, and I'm the one who has to sit there and come up with answers, not *you*. You're too fucking busy playing your games. Life isn't a theme park somebody put you in charge of. I asked for simplicity. I asked for no funny sleight of hand.'

Dansk didn't say anything. He was wondering if stars emitted noise up there. If there was whistling and crackling in the galaxy or if it was just eerie silence to the end of the universe.

Loeb sighed. 'A dead cop, Anthony. For Christ's sake, why?'

Dansk felt a weary superiority. Grandmasters probably experienced the same feeling facing some patzer across a chessboard. 'I took him out of the picture because he was a sympathetic ear Scholes could rely on. Then when she comes in with her story, there's no Drumm to tell it to. It's called isolating your target.'

'Isolating your target.'

'Hanging it out exposed.'

'Exposed.'

'You don't see the strategy here, Loeb. You're on a whole different wavelength from me.'

'Everybody's on a whole different wavelength from you.' Loeb stared at Dansk in silence for a time. 'You got the tape I sent you. You heard the lady and Drumm

352

discuss a possible connection between Galindez and Isabel and Benny Vialli.'

'Pure fucking speculation,' Dansk said. He was above all this petty shit.

'Yeah, but dangerous speculation, Anthony. The one plus is she obviously didn't mention this conversation to the cops, because they never raised it with me.'

'She's groping, Loeb. She's playing with mysteries. She's out of her league.'

Loeb said, 'Then your name came up. The cops asked if I'd heard of you.'

'My name was deleted,' Dansk said.

Loeb looked morose. 'Erasing your name from the computers is the easy part, Anthony, but you can't do the same with people's memories. The cops ask the lady prosecutor for a description of you and one of their artists comes up with a likeness. Then this picture goes out to such places as the FBI, Justice, the US Marshals Service, and somebody's going to say, "Hey, I know this guy, a US marshal. Wasn't he the one took compassionate leave from the Service a coupla years back on the grounds of depression caused by the death of his mother?"'

'My *mother*?' Dansk asked, jolted.

'Your mother. Slain by scumbag junkies for the few bucks in her purse. Remember?'

Scumbag junkies? What was this shit Loeb was talking? The old guy's marbles were broken and scattered. 'I talked to my mother on the phone this afternoon. She's absolutely fine. I never heard her better.'

'You *talked* to your mother? Is that what you're telling me? You actually talked to her. Talked? As in held a conversation?'

'Yeah, as in held a conversation.'

Loeb looked for a while into Dansk's eyes, then said

quietly, 'Oh, Jesus.' He shook his head from side to side very slowly.

'What's your oh-Jesus problem, Loeb?'

'No problem, Anthony. Honestly. I'm glad she's in good shape. I mean that. I'm happy.'

He stroked his cheek with a fingertip. He looked past Dansk at the neon sign above the tavern. His expression was contemplative. His face had an unhealthy tangerine glow. 'It's over, Anthony.'

'What's over?'

'This. This work. I'm bringing down the curtain.'

'No way. No goddam way.'

'I can't let you . . .' Loeb smiled at Dansk in a soft sad manner. 'Look, Scholes has planted a seed and there's a chance it could grow up to be a plant, and the cops study this plant, and before you know it, it's got leaves and branches. Suddenly the cops are wondering how to classify it, because it's not in the usual books.'

Dansk said, 'Spare me the horticultural story, Loeb.'

'You kill the prosecutor, I'll tell you what happens. The plant just bursts into an amazing flower, Anthony, and the gardeners are swarming all around it. They're analysing the roots, and that's the last thing we want, because the roots go places we don't want anyone finding. Kill the prosecutor and the cops are gonna take her story with a whole new level of seriousness.'

'Killing the prosecutor's the whole goddam *point*, because she's gonna keep prying and prying until she finds what she's looking for. You can't walk from that fact.'

Loeb gestured firmly, his hand slicing the air. 'Covering our tracks is the whole point now. The only point. We shut the book, we burn it and we try to make sure the goddam ashes don't blow all over the place.'

'The only thing we burn is the fucking woman,' Dansk said. His voice sounded thundery inside his head. He could hear his mother somewhere in all this ruckus, the mother Loeb said was dead, the mother he'd phoned that afternoon. Loeb was spaced on drugs. The prospect of death had unbalanced him. Sand was running out his egg-timer. A man looking down the tunnel of doom had to have profound difficulties concerning reality. You couldn't take him at face value, you couldn't trust anything he said. This story about his conversation with the cops, for instance. It didn't ring true. It had a counterfeit sound, like he was making some of it up.

'Let it sink in nice and slow,' Loeb said. 'We're shutting down, Anthony. Out of business. Trading conditions are adverse. We're looking at a whole dismantling operation because it's not secure any more, it's not like it used to be. I'm taking it apart brick by brick by brick. No more death. You following me, Anthony?'

'This is my work, Loeb. This is the way I live my life, and you want to close up my shop. You're out of your mind.'

'The work's devoured you, Anthony.' Loeb placed a hand on Dansk's shoulder, a gesture of comfort Dansk didn't need. He knocked Loeb's hand away.

Loeb said, 'Look, we accomplished a lot of what we set out to do back in the beginning. Remember that.'

'So it ends here,' Dansk said. 'Just like that. Just like that.'

'You'll be looked after,' Loeb said. 'I wouldn't leave you hanging, you know that.'

Dansk listened to the voice in his head. *Get people to respect you, Anthony. Don't get pushed around.*

'It ends here all right, Loeb, but not for me.' He reached quickly inside his car, stretched a hand across the framed photograph of Amanda, took the Ruger from the paper sack and turned and fired one shot into Loeb's forehead. Loeb collapsed slowly, his coat a tent about him. He lay like an old crow with spread wings. Dansk looked down at him. Blood, turned to orange by neon, flowed from Loeb's face. Dansk thought of juice squeezed out of oranges.

He got inside his car. Look on the bright side, Ralph, you don't need morphine now.

He picked up Amanda's photograph from the passenger seat and then, with a barely discernible notion of regret for things that might have been in an alternative dimension of dreams, he tossed it out of the window a few miles along the highway. He heard glass shatter and he thought, Goodbye, lady.

And good night.

67

NIGHTFALL AND DARKNESS. AMANDA SAT IN THE BACK OF THE Bronco with Rhees. Rested, more alert, Rhees seemed to have negotiated a very fragile truce with his pain. Up front, Gannon drove with consideration, slowing when he came to bends.

'How you both doing back there?' he asked.

Amanda said, 'Fine,' but it was a lie, she didn't feel fine. It wasn't the fact that Kelloway had taken control of things, although it annoyed her to think of the way she'd been obliged to buckle and step aside. No, this was something else. *Pick a safe place*, Kelloway had said. Instinctively, she'd jumped at the idea of the pine forest as a secure destination, but now a dismaying sensation the colour of squid-ink was spiralling inside her head.

She said, 'Stop.'

Gannon pulled the vehicle over.

Rhees asked, 'Why are we stopping?'

Amanda looked at his face, then her vision drifted past him towards the empty blacktop. Clouds trailed across an insipid vanilla moon and the desert on either side of the highway was a landscape patched with tiny areas of spangle and shadow.

'The cabin,' she said.

'What about it?'

'I just have a bad feeling.'

Rhees said, 'You think Dansk knows about the place? Even if he does, it's not easy to find.'

'He *probes*, John. He's got the instincts of a psychotic proctologist, and somewhere along the way he finds out we've been living in a cabin near Flag.'

'You're saying he'll follow us,' Rhees said.

'He's driven. He has a relentless streak. He isn't going to drop this. He isn't about to let you and me off the hook.'

Gannon, who had a shotgun balanced against the passenger seat and a Colt .45 in a holster, said, 'Listen, I only know what Chief Kelloway told me. I drive you both to the cabin and play bodyguard until I hear otherwise. Now you're saying you don't want to go there because you're worried about this guy.'

Amanda pictured the small rooms of the cabin, but the intimacy of the place had dissolved, the idea of sanctuary had eroded. She was going passively back to the forest, and it was the wrong move. Unless she could somehow turn it to her advantage.

Traffic appeared on the highway, a cluster of four or five cars, bright lights. She wondered about their occupants. If Dansk was nearby, if he'd tracked her from Phoenix. A cop vehicle wouldn't deter him, she knew that. He'd consider it a minor nuisance.

Gannon asked, 'Is this guy working alone, or are we talking numbers?'

'Including Dansk, three at least,' she said. 'There might be more, I don't know.'

Gannon said, 'Nobody's told me the whole story here,

358

but the buzz I hear is that this Dansk is connected some way to the death of Willie Drumm.'

'Connected some way is right,' she said.

'I don't like losing friends,' Gannon remarked.

'And I don't like running away from things,' she said.

Gannon said, 'Look, my brief is to guard you. Kelloway never mentioned anything else. Just keep an eye on the pair of you, he said.'

'The Colt .45 and the shotgun, what are they for? You need permission from the bald eagle to use them?' She listened to her own voice and how bellicose it had become. It was like the voice of a different person.

Gannon said, 'If there's a life-threatening situation, first thing I reach for is my friendly Colt, believe me. I don't stop to ask permission, Ms Scholes.'

Rhees shifted his body slightly and said to Amanda, 'I know what's running through your mind. You're wondering if Dansk can be trapped.'

'Maybe,' she said.

'No maybe, Amanda. I know you. You're wondering if he can be trapped and caught.'

'I don't like the direction of this,' Gannon said.

Amanda said, 'He killed Willie Drumm, Gannon. Your colleague. Your friend. My friend.'

'My instructions don't include capturing Dansk or anyone else.'

'I'm not asking you to disobey,' she said. 'You just do your job the way Kelloway wants it done. You protect us.'

'I have every intention,' Gannon said.

Rhees said, 'A trap needs bait. What bait are we talking about here?'

Amanda said, 'It's a risk.'

Rhees looked at her for a long time. He shook his head. 'No way. Absolutely no way. I don't want to hear the rest of this. Forget it.'

'Like I said, it's a risk.'

Rhees said, 'No. End of subject.'

'You can't just make Dansk disappear, John. If Kelloway's investigating, it could take days, weeks. Even then there's no guarantee he's ever going to get to the truth. He'll be shunted between Justice officials, US Marshals and God knows who else in the Federal machine. This guy Loeb who came from Justice, for instance, he and Dansk come out the same damn pod.'

Rhees said, 'We could go somewhere—'

'And hide? I can't live that way, John. Sorry.'

Rhees sighed. 'It's in the hands of the cops, Amanda. That's what really riles you. You've been decommissioned.'

'No, what riles me is the idea of doing nothing,' she said. 'And with respect to Sergeant Gannon, I don't feel very secure.'

Dansk's presence in the pines, his head filled with murderous notions, birds disturbed, wings suddenly fluttering through branches – no, she couldn't go through with that, waiting and waiting.

Gannon alone wasn't enough. She'd need more than Gannon's shotgun and the Colt in his holster before she could feel remotely secure. 'Pass me your mobile.'

Gannon handed her the unit with a little gesture of reluctance.

Rhees asked, 'Who do you intend to call?'

Amanda began to tap numbers. 'I want Dansk out of our lives, John. I want to hand him over to Kelloway and say, Here, here's the elusive Dansk for you, Chief. Why don't you grill him for answers? Why don't you shine a big bright fucking light in his eyes and make him talk? I just want things back the way they were before.'

Rhees said, 'Before? Remind me, Amanda. Refresh my memory.'

'It was a good life and I want it to be good again. It's that simple.'

'What is it really, Amanda? You feel you have some kind of appointment with Dansk you're desperate to keep?'

An appointment with Dansk, that was one way of putting it. But it had to be on her own terms and her own territory. 'I'm not running from this situation. Somebody else might, but not me.'

Rhees's voice was dry and flat and suffused with resignation. 'It's all or nothing with you, Amanda. It's always been that way.'

'You get to a point where you're sick of fear, and I've reached that point, John. I've reached it and I've outstripped it and I'm tired.'

She finished punching in the number that would connect her with Kelloway.

68

DANSK FELT THE DARKNESS WAS FEVERED IN SOME WAY. IF THE night was a human being, it would be running a temperature. He glanced at the Ruger on the passenger seat. The power of a gun. The stunning velocity of a bullet, the implosion of an eye, the demolition of brain tissue, flakes of bone spitting through the back of Loeb's head into the tangerine light, Morgan Scholes crumpling like an empty grocery bag. Death delivered in an instant. Life and death locked in an ammunition clip locked in a chamber locked in your fist. All that lethal energy. Death compacted and compressed in pointed cylinders.

You killed Loeb. You killed Morgan Scholes. No inner turmoil, no conflict with your conscience, no great upheaval of the heart. Just point the gun and pull the trigger. Real easy.

Somewhere far to his right a firework went off. A solitary burst of bright purple light, then a fine spray as the power ebbed out of the thing and it fell to earth. Some kid with a firework he'd probably smuggled back from Mexico. Dansk retained the impression behind his eyes for a few miles, a firefly flutter of powdered light.

He pulled into a gas station, got out of his car and approached the office. The old guy who appeared in the doorway had a discoloured glass eye. Dansk noticed the fake eye was blue-grey and the white around it viscous, milky.

"Bout to close up,' the old guy said. 'You got me just in time.' He shuffled out to the pumps and began to fill Dansk's car. 'See some eejit set off a firework. You get these drunk kids out in the woods. They don't think fire hazards. You just passing through?'

For ever, Dansk thought. He said, 'Yeah. Passing through.'

"Bout all Flag's good for these days, passing through. One time it was different. Air up here used to be sweeter than honey in my day.' He closed the gas cap.

Dansk followed the man inside the office, which was also a storeroom. It smelled of grease and rubber and stewed coffee. He spotted a Coke machine that issued soda in glass bottles. He asked for change and inserted enough coins for two bottles. He looked round the place, bought a flashlight, a box of Kleenex, 36 inches of clear plastic tubing, a bottle-opener, a disposable lighter and the largest wrench he could find.

The old guy rang the items up on his cash register. Dansk paid. Outside, a car idled near the darkened pumps, then drove away quickly in a squeal of rubber.

'I guess that's one fellow decided he don't need gas,' the old guy said, 'or else he's in an almighty hurry, like everybody else these days.'

Dansk stepped outside, clutching his purchases, seeing tail-lights glow like cast-off cigarette butts down the highway.

69

INSIDE McTELL'S CAR PASQUALE SAID, 'I GOTTA CALL LOEB, tell him it's done.'

'You attached it OK?' McTell asked.

'While Dansk was in the gas station. The thing's magnetic.' Pasquale removed his phone from his pocket and dialled Loeb's number. There wasn't an answer. He let it ring for a while. 'Funny, he said he'd wait to hear from me.'

'So he split. Back home probably. It's no big deal.'

'This whole thing's gone weird,' Pasquale remarked.

'You get new orders direct from Loeb, you go through with them. Nothing weird about that.'

Pasquale sighed. 'Loeb isn't a healthy guy, Eddie. I never seen a human look like that since my Uncle Bill on my mother's side croaked from pneumonia. He's like this zombie colour.'

'The only colour interests me is money,' McTell said.

Pasquale took a thick white envelope from the inside pocket of his jacket. 'Twenty thou in crisp hundreds. Severance pay, Loeb calls it. We get the second instalment afterwards.'

'Yo, May-eee-co,' said McTell. '*Arriba arriba!*'

'Yeah,' said Pasquale, 'it's gonna be a change.'

McTell said, 'I hate Dansk like a tumour in my chest, like a thing I gotta cut out at the root. It's got to where I can't hack the sound of his voice even, that little nasal thing he's got sometimes.'

'Tell you what I hate,' Pasquale said. 'This feeling of treachery.'

'You'll get over it, Bruno. Down in Tijuana the Birthmark Kid's gonna fade to black.'

Pasquale said, 'The thing is, I was inside the Protection Program, sitting in fucking Buffalo and bored outta my skull and just fucking *aching* for some action, and he rescues me from that meat-packing plant. He pulls me outta that situation and puts me back to my own kinda work. So I still feel I owe him, Eddie.'

'Listen, I was twice as bored in Pasadena managing a laundromat and sniffing all those fucking cancerous chemicals they got in them places,' McTell said, 'but I don't figure I owe Dansk a goddam thing. I'm sick of his shit attitude and the way he does things.'

McTell drove in silence for a time. 'Let's see the gadget.'

Pasquale removed a black plastic box from his right side pocket. It was about 4 inches by 4, battery-operated. He flicked a switch and a panel lit.

'Who made that box?' McTell asked.

'Who what?'

'There a manufacturer's name?'

Pasquale turned on the map light and studied the box. 'Cisco Electronics Inc., San Luis Obispo, Cal, it says here.'

'American. Call me a patriot.'

Pasquale peered at the red digital numbers on the box. 'The only condition Loeb laid down is we got to do the thing in an isolated place.'

'No problem,' McTell said. 'It's a big empty state, Arizona.'

70

AMANDA KICKED OFF HER SHOES, CHANGED HER CLOTHES from the business suit to jeans and a long-sleeved shirt of John's. She lit a cigarette and drew smoke deeply into her lungs. The nicotine didn't relax her. The palms of her hands were damp and some kind of nerve worked like a pulse in her throat. The unlit rooms of the cabin cramped her. The night was all tension and expectation, the silence that of a very delicate cease-fire. The dark had a heavy stillness and the air smelled like a pine coffin and the moon was behind cloud and sailing.

She crushed her cigarette in the fireplace and thought of Gannon strolling quietly round the cabin. She'd called Kelloway and badgered him into contacting the Flagstaff PD to see if members of the local force might provide more backup, and he'd been grudgingly obliging. A mile down the path, two cops armed with rifles and night-scopes watched and waited for unusual sounds and sights in the dark, and another, a deputy called Clarence Griffin, was posted close to the old bridge.

And now she wondered if she'd done enough or if her

idea was flawed, or if she should have listened to Rhees and changed tack and gone to another destination far away. But she'd made this decision and she couldn't back out even if she'd wanted to, and she didn't, despite the menacing quiet of the forest and the arrhythmic nature of her pulses.

She lit another cigarette. She tilted her head back and realized she was listening as she'd never listened before in her life. If a pine needle drifted from a branch she'd hear it. If a grass snake stirred, she'd register the whispered slither of its movements. She was fine-tuned to whatever happened outside the cabin.

She sat on the floor, her back propped against the wall. She studied the dim shape of Rhees in an armchair on the other side of the room. He'd defiantly refused the wheelchair. He'd turned down the suggestion of going to a motel room and waiting alone. He'd been adamant and unusually stubborn, as if he felt a need to match her determination with his own. If he couldn't make her change her mind, then he'd stay with her and to hell with his pain.

He sat in shadow and said nothing, and she wondered if there was reproach in his expression, or fear, but she couldn't see his face, just the pale outline of his plastered arm and the sling, and the white stripes in his shirt.

She flicked her cigarette into the fireplace. 'You OK?' she asked.

'You're whispering,' he said.

'Yeah, I guess I am. You think this is a bad move, don't you?'

'When it comes to you, Amanda, it's like being caught up in a whirlwind, and I don't see much point in criticizing a force of nature.'

'You didn't have to be here,' she said. 'You had choices.'

'The only feasible choice was to stay with you, at the eye of the storm.'

'You haven't answered my question,' she said.

'It's a bad move if it turns out wrong. It's a good move if it works.'

'Fence-sitting,' she said.

Rhees said, 'I'll tell you something I'm a touch more certain about: you don't *really* want Dansk captured, you want him gunned down by one of your posse out there. This notion you have about handing him over to Kelloway is one you'd *like* to believe in, but I get the sense you want blood. Tell me I'm wrong.'

Dansk's blood. Maybe there was a truth in Rhees's words she didn't want to acknowledge. Maybe a hardening had taken place inside her and she wanted him dead. But there were mysteries still, and they confounded her.

'I want him any way I can get him.'

'Dead or alive,' Rhees said.

'I'd prefer alive,' she said. 'The other way, he can't answer any questions, and I have a few I want answered.'

She lit another cigarette, masking the flame of the lighter in her hand.

'He kills Willie and Mrs Vialli. Willie, OK, I can understand. He's a cop poking around asking questions. But Bernadette? Your average suburban widow, for God's sake . . . except for one big difference. She happens to have a son in the Protection Program and she's not happy because he's been silent too long. And when he does get in touch, it's in a form she finds iffy. Question: Where the hell is Benny?'

Rhees said, 'For God's sake, leave it to Kelloway, Amanda.'

She walked the room quietly, window to door and back again. She stopped behind Rhees and laid her hands on his shoulders and a dark thought formed in her brain.

'Benny's dead,' she said.

'You can't *know* he's dead, Amanda.'

'Benny's dead and Dansk's responsible, and the only goddam reason I can think he'd have for killing her was to keep her from discovering the fate of her son.'

'I don't know where you're going with this,' Rhees said.

The patterns in her head kept spinning and shifting. She heard herself say, 'Why wasn't Bascombe high on Kelloway's list of people to talk to? Lew was supposed to be digging up information for Willie, after all. So why did Kelloway call Justice first? And Loeb – what did the big Chief learn there? When I phoned him to beg for more bodies, he didn't mention his talk with Loeb. Why? Because it amounted to nothing? Because Loeb fobbed him off? Why?'

'Leave it,' Rhees said.

Leave it. Leave it all to Kelloway. Hail to the Chief. Her thoughts were greyhounds on a slippery track, and she couldn't follow them and the hare they chased was out of sight.

Rhees said, 'There's the more pressing matter of Dansk. If he's out there, he isn't going to walk blindly into a set-up, Amanda. He'd *know* you've got cops staking the place out. He may be outnumbered for all we know, but maybe he hasn't been out-thought. Which scares me more than a little.'

Amanda heard the sound of Gannon's quiet footsteps on the porch. She inclined her face, bringing the surface of her cheek against John's. 'I wish,' she said.

'Wish what?'

'Forget it. It doesn't matter—'

'Wish I wasn't here? Wish I'd stayed in some nice safe motel room so you didn't have to take any responsibility for me?'

'Yes. No. I'm not sure.'

He touched her hand. 'If there has to be bait, you'd rather it was just you dangling.'

'I want you to be safe, that's all. I don't want anybody to hurt you again.'

'Eye of the storm, Amanda. It's no place to be alone.'

'There's protection,' she said. 'I wouldn't be alone.'

'Four cops. An army would make me a little less uneasy.'

She kissed him. He rested his hand against the curve of her hip. She drew the flat of his hand across her stomach, and for a second she thought it was possible to believe nothing had altered. And then the telephone rang, harsh and unexpected. She picked it up on the first ring.

Dansk said, 'Nice quiet countryside, Amanda. Nothing moving except a few old raccoons, unless you count me.'

She didn't respond. Her hand on the receiver was stiff and suddenly she was cold.

Dansk said, 'The woods are lovely dark and deep, et cetera.'

She still didn't reply. She realized she was holding her breath.

Dansk laughed. 'You figured it all out yet, lady?'

71

DANSK LEFT HIS CAR HIDDEN UNDER SHRUBBERY A QUARTER of a mile from the old bridge, and moved through the trees, ducking now and again to avoid low-hanging branches. You had to be careful what was underfoot: roots, rotted trunks, gopher holes. He went cautiously, but with a certain ease. He'd backpacked in rough places, he'd put in hard time on survival courses courtesy of the US Marshals Service, spent weeks alone in remote Appalachian hill country where all you got was a knife and a box of matches and a length of twine and a safety pin, and fend for yourself, buddy. And I did it, he thought. With flying colours. This was a walk on the beach by comparison. Easy-peasy, watch where you step, *concentrate*. Listen to the language of the pines, what the landscape is saying. He stopped moving, crouched low, studied the darkness.

In the right-hand pocket of his dark-blue jacket he had a Coke bottle into which he'd siphoned gasoline from the tank of his car. He'd stuffed the neck with wadded Kleenex. He had a second bottle in his left pocket, also filled with gas and similarly fused. In his right hand he carried the hefty wrench he'd bought at the filling-station, the Ruger was in his left. He'd tucked the flashlight in his belt and the mobile phone was in his back pocket with the ringer switched off. The last thing he needed in the stillness of the night was a call from McTell or Pasquale, the sound of buzzing in the pines.

If they phoned.

Earlier, he'd tried to make contact with them from his car, but neither had answered. He'd assumed at first that they'd made a rendezvous, and maybe they'd left their cars to take a leak at the side of the road, but ten minutes later he was still getting no answer from either. One possibility was that they'd stopped for pizza or to grab a hamburger. They were always chowing down unhealthy fast-food fodder. Another was that they'd crapped out, decided to quit, go their own way. But they'd never run from a situation before, so why start now? Afraid of the cop presence?

Or something else.

Such as what? He wondered if maybe Loeb had contacted them, ordered them out of the picture, part of his dismantling operation. We're shutting down. We're hanging a sign in the window: Out of Business.

They'd both been off-centre recently, McTell more than normally sullen, Pasquale remote. Fuck them. Dansk was only half interested anyway, inclined to dismiss them. It was a shabby world. You can't trust people, they disappoint. What it comes down to over and over is that there's only one person to rely on in the end: Anthony Dansk. Your good self.

He didn't need McTell and Pasquale. He was weary of dumb killers and their idiot resentments. They were like boulder-filled baggage he had to haul, directing them to do this, go here, go there. They couldn't think for themselves, they didn't have enough brains to boil a fucking egg. He was better on his own because he'd always preferred his own company. Maybe he should have worked alone from the beginning, doing the surgery by himself. God knows he was capable of it, and he was comfortable with it.

He kept moving. It was surprising how little sound you made if you concentrated, if you were aware. The darkness was a warm embrace. Come on in, Anthony, there's nothing to fear.

The forest filled his head like sweet music. McTell and Pasquale would've been noisy, crushing twigs and cones underfoot, disturbing birds and alarming skunks. They wouldn't have heard the music.

Come in, keep coming, Amanda isn't far away.

He thought of her in the darkness ahead. Her and Rhees. He pictured her when she'd plucked the eucalyptus leaf outside her house. He saw Rhees's hand dropping to her ass. Oh that intimacy. He remembered the way he'd grabbed her wrist in the hotel room and forced food to her lips, and the feeling of power that spiked through him and the warmth of her breast.

He also remembered calling his mother to tell her about a girl named Amanda. His mother seemed very far away from him at this moment, a distance greater than 2,000 and something miles. She seemed locked inside the prism of his memory like a butterfly pinned in a glass display case.

He stopped suddenly, alert to a slight alteration in the melody in his brain. A change of modality, major to minor. He stood very still under a tree that oozed a resinous odour. The sound was faint but he zoned in on it. He recognized it as the noise made by somebody's stomach, a churning of intestinal juices.

The source of the sound was somewhere to his right, 5 or 6 yards, maybe more. You had to make allowances for the way noise carried here. There was barely any light. The moon was shrouded by thick strands of cloud.

He stepped to his right. He had the sensation of floating just above the ground. He weighed the wrench in his hand, 12 inches of hard steel, something you could believe in. That's what you needed in life, something to believe in. Like this work Loeb had wanted to close down and walk away from. Close the book. Burn it. Leave the prosecutor alive and look after our own asses.

Right, rob me of my life, Loeb. No way.

The man in the trees was about 6 feet tall and wore a dark windcheater and black jeans. He had a holstered weapon on his hip and he was standing very still. Maybe he'd sensed something, aroused by a faint instinct to the fact that there was a change in the atmosphere, only he couldn't quite pinpoint it.

A guard, Dansk thought. He wondered if this was the cop who'd driven Amanda and Rhees up here from Phoenix, or if Amanda had managed to stock the woods with reinforcements. It was the kind of move she'd make. You see one cop in the Bronco, but what you don't see are the others in the pine forest. Just keep coming, Anthony. I have a few tricks left.

I'm ready for you, lady. Always have been.

He edged forwards. He felt a weird tingle in the tips of his fingers, as if the steel of the wrench had turned to ice and welded skin to metal, like the effect when you took something out of the deep-freeze.

The man turned his head a little, away from Dansk. Dansk stepped forward and swung the wrench with all his strength and felt it split the skin and sink into the base of the man's neck. The man went down at once and Dansk straddled him, noticing that one of the guy's eyelids quivered uncontrollably as if a circuit of nerve-links had been severed with the blow.

374

'How fucking many of you?' Dansk whispered.

The guy rolled his face to the side. Blood was flowing from the place where neck and shoulder had been punctured, and the eyelid kept flickering open and shut. Dansk brought the wrench down a second time into the side of the guy's neck.

Pine needles adhered to the guy's lips and teeth. 'Go fuck yourself,' he said.

Dansk was centred, he'd found a balance in himself. He hammered the wrench into the guy's head with controlled force. 'How many, fella?'

The guy moaned and said, 'Three . . .'

'Three where?'

'Two . . . a mile up the path.'

'And the third?'

'The cabin.'

'Thanks,' and Dansk smacked the wrench down again and again, three times, four, he lost count, it didn't matter. And then it was no longer what you'd call a face, it was bloody and broken and ugly, hard steel had splintered bone and demolished the skull and mouth and blinded the eyes.

Dansk stopped, listening for the sound of breathing. He heard none. This one was gone. Like that. Life battered out of him. Face, skull, blood pouring from shattered veins. Life is a skinny thread, snip.

He reached down and touched the guy's groin, wondering if there was a discharge of piss, but the guy was dry.

Dansk stood up and his eye followed the overgrown path as far as he could see in the diminished light. He was conscious of the scent of gasoline from one of his pockets, where a bottle had tilted a little and fuel soaked the wadded tissue.

Two other guards a mile along the path, and one at the cabin. Amanda and Rhees inside.

I'm coming, I'm on my way. There's no stopping me.

He went between the trees with the blood-wet wrench in his right hand, and he walked as close to the path as he could. It was choked with fern and stunted bushes and scrub. Here and there stray pine saplings had taken root but, overshadowed by the density of older trees, they grew stilted and starved. Survival depended on how much territory you could claim for yourself.

I claim this forest. This whole goddam thing and everything in it, especially the former prosecutor. This is my dominion. McTell and Pasquale could never have understood this.

The only thing they knew was thuggery. They didn't understand the true nature of killing, they thought of it as simple disposal. But you weren't just ending the life of somebody, no way, you were changing history. A man beaten to death was no simple brutal act, it had consequences you couldn't begin to foresee – bereaved wife, orphaned children, an empty chair at dinner, a coffin, lawyers checking last wills and testaments, insurance agents scanning policies. Killing was a form of re-arranging the patterns of reality, breaking a sheet of stained glass into a sudden amazing kaleidoscope in which you could watch all the coloured flecks revolve in an infinity of configurations. Even on a simple level, the dead guy's clothes would need to be stacked inside boxes and donated to Goodwill, and somebody else would go round wearing them, unaware of the fact that they'd once belonged to a guy battered to death in a pine forest by a wrench.

You don't touch just one life in killing. It was a stone dropped in water: the rings spread and all kinds of people were changed, some in big ways, others in small. Some were heartbroken, others got used Levis from a charity store.

On your own you can change the world.

He kept going, his body hunched a little, shoulders down. He wasn't thinking now. He was all motion and hard focus and silence. He'd stepped up a gear. He was cruising through the trees, sensing treacherous dips in the earth before he reached them. His night vision was acute, vulpine.

He stopped.

There were two of them just ahead. There was also a vehicle of the jeep variety. One of the men was moving slowly round the vehicle, the other, smaller and younger, leaned against the door panel. They had rifles and wore uniforms.

Dansk calculated the distance to the vehicle: 50 yards, maybe less. He lowered himself to the ground and watched. To see without being seen. Invisibility was a kick. The cop leaning against the door sighed quietly. He didn't know somebody was out among the trees watching him.

Dansk moved closer.

The older guy stopped beside the younger and whispered something Dansk couldn't catch. The young cop shook his head.

Dansk got a little closer still.

The moment.

Showtime.

He removed the Coke bottle from his right pocket. The stench of gas was strong, but there was no breeze to carry it in the direction of the cops. The night was like a deflated lung. He hunkered down behind a bush and took out the cheap cigarette lighter he'd bought.

He adjusted the little lever to low before he applied his thumb to the lighter. He pressed down, got a tiny eye of flame from the plastic cylinder – and now this had to be quick. Lighter-flame to tissue, just a touch, then he stood up and tossed the bottle through the air and heard the musculature in his arm ripple. He watched the bottle rise and fall in a lit arc, spinning and turning as it fell, then exploding against the windshield of the vehicle, and instantly the air was luminous with flame and the younger cop, seared by an outburst of fire, screamed. The older guy had dropped to the ground, his flesh pierced with spears and shards of glass, and he was moaning about his eyes, how he couldn't see *a fucking thing*, and the young cop just kept screaming, rolling over and over in an attempt to douse the fire that melted his clothes to his skin.

Polyester shirt and pants, Dansk thought. Man-made fibre. Never trust it. He lit and threw the second bottle. It struck the jeep, which exploded. The force of the blast made Dansk step back into the trees. The jeep combusted in blue and yellow flags of fire and the air was bitter with the smell of rubber and gasoline.

A thing of great beauty, this conflagration. Your own private war zone. Dry pines began to crackle, flame created sudden bridges through space, the forest was lit and the darkness dissolved. Birds shaken out of branches were turned gold and red by reflected fire, transmuted from ordinary bluejays and ravens into creatures with exotic plumage. The night burned and burned and burned.

And Dansk was already moving again, and thinking.

Of the cabin. Of Amanda.

72

BAREFOOT, SHE HURRIED OUT TO THE PORCH, WHERE Gannon stood with his shotgun against his side, the barrel directed downwards. She'd heard somebody scream and then the explosions rocked the night and she'd seen unidentifiable debris rise and fall through the air. Now she stared at the fire half a mile away and watched it spread like an apocalyptic false dawn. Then Rhees was standing just behind her in the doorway, breathing hard and leaning against the frame for support. The heart of the fire was the place where the two cops had been parked.

Rhees said, 'The Bronco's parked out back. We could try to drive out of here.'

Gannon shook his head. 'Too damn risky. The path's blocked by fire, there's a good chance we'd fry, and there's no way to drive out except that path. You couldn't get a vehicle through the trees. Too dense.'

Amanda resisted panic. Be calm in the face of adversity. Dansk and his thugs had pierced the thin defences she'd arranged, which meant they'd got past the deputy Clarence Griffin at the bridge, then blown up the cop vehicle. They'd created this light show, all these special effects, and now they were moving somewhere in the shadows between the flames towards the cabin. As for Griffin and the two cops – this was an area she didn't want to enter.

Gannon said, 'One stroke of luck is there's no wind. The way the fire's spreading I'd say we have maybe thirty minutes or more before it reaches this far.'

Amanda looked towards the pines that edged the path. They were burning, dry sticks in a bonfire. The scent of smoking wood drifted through the air, sweet, narcotic. But there was a secondary smell, a noxious undercurrent of plastic smouldering, oil on fire.

Amanda said, 'So either we sit here and barbecue or we get the hell out. Turning to hamburger doesn't attract me, and if we can't drive, we hoof it out of here and head away from the fire in the direction of the river.' She turned to Rhees. 'There's not a multitude of choices, John. You think you can make it?'

'Like you say, no choice.'

Gannon seemed suddenly decisive. 'OK, let's do it. Let's go for it.'

'Once we're about a mile clear of the cabin there's a dry creek surrounded by scrub, which might give us some cover for a time,' Amanda said.

'I know the place,' Rhees said.

In another lifetime they'd made love in that arroyo, she recalled, spontaneous and urgent in spite of the grit and the pestering flies.

She remembered she was barefoot. She stepped into the cabin to fetch her shoes. The reach of firelight hadn't penetrated the rooms, so she flipped a switch, saw the shoes near the fireplace and slipped her feet into them.

He was standing by the open window on the other side of the room. His face was smoke-stained, his jacket was smeared with soil and pine needles, and there was blood on the back of the hand that held the gun. He was about 6 feet away and reeked of gasoline.

'Say nothing, Amanda,' he whispered.

She registered the open window, the bits and pieces of forest that clung to Dansk, who resembled some creature long dormant, emerging from an underground cavern, half human, half some other kind of being. He stepped towards her, caught her and turned her around, and she felt the pressure of his body against her spine, the gun and his breath upon the back of her neck.

'The door,' he said.

He forced her outside to the porch.

Rhees leaned against the rail, and Gannon stared at the flames like a man trying to gauge the rate the fire was spreading. She thought of giving a cry of warning, an elbow smacked into Dansk's ribcage, into his heart, a sudden turn and a rake of his face with her fingernails, trying to grapple the gun away from him. Then she felt Dansk's mouth against her neck, his lips, teeth. A kiss.

Rhees turned his face and said, 'Jesus.'

Gannon looked round then, but it was too late for him, the shotgun he held was pointed downwards and he didn't have time to bring it up into a firing position, and even if he'd had days to figure out a move he couldn't have fired because Amanda was a shield protecting Anthony Dansk. Dansk levelled the pistol, his hand an inch or so above Amanda's shoulder. She tried to lean into him, collide just enough to force him into an erratic shot, but he was too quick, he'd already fired the gun and the sound was like a land-mine in her ears. She felt sick in her stomach and sour saliva came flooding into her mouth. She thought she heard Dansk say, 'Not very smart, Amanda,' and then she was conscious of how Gannon was thrown back against the rail and the shotgun fell out of his hands. The rail yielded and Gannon dropped out of sight through wood that had snapped with the impact of his body.

Rhees, dragging his useless leg, took one halting step forwards, as if he were considering an act of bravery. She told him to stay where he was in a voice that was thick and half audible to herself.

Dansk laughed. 'Listen to the lady, Rhees.'

Rhees said, 'Let her go.'

Dansk laughed again. It was a quiet laugh, restrained. 'Let her go?'

Amanda stared at Rhees. His face was illuminated by flame, his expression was numbed. And all the time there was the deafening roar in her head of the gun firing and the pine trees crackling.

'You thought you'd be nice and safe here,' Dansk said. 'A flash for you. Nowhere's safe. It's that kind of world.' He surveyed the fire a moment. 'It's time we got out of here.'

'Where?' she asked.

'To a place where all your curiosity ends.' He looked at Rhees. 'It's a rough walk for you, I guess. Maybe you'd prefer to stay? Or maybe you're just as curious as your lady here.' He pointed the Ruger at Rhees.

Rhees said, 'I go where she goes.'

'Figures.' Dansk released Amanda and gestured with his head towards the forest. 'We'll go round the flames back to the bridge.'

'And then what?' she asked.

Dansk seemed not to hear her question. He said, 'Pity about the trees. You take something out of nature, it disturbs the balance of things. I don't like that.' There was a look of mild regret on his face. 'Now walk. Just walk. I'm right behind you.'

73

THEY MOVED BETWEEN TREES, ALONG THE EDGES OF FLAME, past the burning jeep. She saw no sign of the cops and hoped they'd somehow managed to survive, but she knew this was a dim prospect.

The going was rough on Rhees. Amanda had to take his weight against her body, an effort that confined her thoughts to the immediacy of things around her: the sound of Rhees's breathing, the architecture of fire. She had no sense of a future. It was a matter of walking out of the forest, and wherever they went next was up to Dansk. This place he had in mind. *Where all your curiosity ends.*

Rhees said, 'I need a moment.'

Dansk prodded Rhees in the back with his gun. 'You don't have a moment. Keep moving.'

Amanda looked back and saw sparks float above the core of flame and up into the night. Sooner or later the cabin would be destroyed. Sooner or later she and Rhees would go the same way. No escape route came to mind. Dansk had the gun and the gun was the future.

'Over the bridge, cross the road,' Dansk said. 'Hurry. Move, move, move.'

The bridge was made out of wooden struts, decaying under a layer of moss. Amanda felt the structure sway when she and Rhees stepped onto it. Beyond the bridge, Dansk herded them to the right where his car was concealed under shrubbery. Behind, the fire roared with the noise of a small sun exploding.

'You're the designated driver, Amanda,' Dansk said. 'I'll just keep Rhees company in the back. I think that's the best arrangement.'

Amanda helped Rhees into the rear seat, then she sat behind the wheel. Dansk got inside, handed her the keys and said, 'Go back to the main highway, I'll give you directions along the way.'

She backed the car out from the shrubbery. When she reached the intersection of the highway, Dansk told her to turn left. She glanced at Rhees in the mirror.

Dansk leaned forwards. 'Keep your eyes on the road at all times, lady.'

'I was checking on John,' she said.

'John's fine. John's just hunky-dory back here. Right, John?'

Rhees said in a flat way, 'Sure, fine.'

'See? Don't worry about John.'

She stared ahead into the dark. Moths and bugs loomed up in the headlights and perished against the windshield. Mucus stains, broken wings trapped and flapping under wipers, a glass cemetery of dead insects. The road filled her vision, the white line bisected her head. Concentrate, figure a way out of this if you can: crash the car, swerve off the road, slam the brakes, anything you like. It didn't matter, because she had no doubt Dansk would shoot Rhees if she deviated by as much as a yard.

Dansk said to Rhees, 'This is nice, the three of us together like this. Cosy. I feel like I'm with old friends. We met before, John.'

'Did we?'

'In a French restaurant. We pissed side by side and talked about the merits of towels against forced-air hand-dryers. We discussed germs.'

'It escapes me,' Rhees said.

A French restaurant, Amanda thought. Was there any place Dansk hadn't followed her? His fingerprints were all over her life.

Dansk reached forward and touched her neck with the barrel of the handgun. She felt the metal against her skin and she remembered Dansk's distasteful kiss and moved her head just slightly. Dansk laughed and said, 'We're all happy. We're happy travellers. Right, John?'

Rhees said, 'I'm happy.'

'This is what I like. The only thing missing here is a picnic basket stuffed with goodies. A little roast chicken, a couple of cold brewskies to wash things down.' Dansk made another little move with the gun, some pretend fumbling, letting the weapon slip through his hands to his lap. 'Whoops. Gotta be careful. Don't want this to go off, do we?'

'Don't point that at Rhees,' she said. Dansk having fun with his gun, she thought. Dansk tightening the screws.

Dansk said, 'You hear that, John? Lady's worried in case I just happen to make a fatal slip. Zip. One bullet into the brainbox and goodbye Rhees. This concern's touching. I'm moved. I'm hearing the voice of love.'

She said, 'You don't know shit about love, Dansk.'

'Do I hear the expert's voice?'

'Death's what you know,' she said. 'All you know.'

Dansk made a mock sound of disapproval which sounded like choo-choo-choo. 'You're no slouch in that department yourself, sweetheart. Check the destruction in your own wake before you pass judgement on me. You're like some kind of fucking Typhoid Mary spreading a deadly plague. Instance, Bernadette Vialli. Instance, Willie Drumm.'

She said nothing, but kept her eyes on the road, as if all she wanted in the world was to get away from Dansk's voice. He was shifting blame. He was sprinkling fertilizer in the hope guilt would bloom in her.

'You want more, Amanda? Three dead guys in the woods, right? Who invited them in the first place? And the cop on the porch? Even poor Rhees here – he'd be in a damn sight better condition if it hadn't been for you. You drag death and pain behind you like luggage on a trolley, and the only thing I ever asked of you was to stay out of the way. Simple, but you didn't listen. Dumb, dumb, *dumb*.'

'I didn't kill those people, Dansk,' she said. Three men dead in the woods – people who'd come to protect her – and Thomas Gannon lying beneath the broken porch rail.

'You didn't pull any triggers, right. You just put certain people into lethal situations. I wasn't the one who did that.'

'You can't blame me for their deaths,' she said.

She was flooded with anger, but she couldn't tell if it was directed entirely at Dansk or whether some of it was channelled back in on herself. She recalled those moments when she'd thought of pulling out of the situation, when she might have chilled her mind and stilled all her impulses. But the tide had long ago gone out on those possibilities and the beach was a vast empty strand.

The road in front of her was empty.

'Where are we going anyway?' Rhees asked.

'A place. A couple of hours away.'

'What kind of place, Dansk?'

386

Dansk didn't answer.

A fire-engine, blue lights flashing and spinning, came out of nowhere and zoomed past the car in the opposite direction, and then there was a State police car, sirens going.

Amanda thought, Stop. We need your assistance. It's not only the forest that's burning. But the fire-engine and the State police car were already gone, and the road in the mirror was as black as the future.

74

PASQUALE SAID, 'THESE DIGITAL NUMBERS GIVE YOU THE location of Dansk's car and how far away it is and the speed. Right now it's three point two miles north of here and travelling at sixty-four m.p.h.'

McTell glanced down at the box. The numbers kept flickering. Pasquale said, 'You don't want to get too close to him.'

McTell nodded and said, 'That fire. Holy shit.'

'You figure he had something to do with it?'

McTell shrugged. He remembered being parked between trees just off the main highway and then whoom, all hell. 'All I know is what we saw. The whole place went up in flames and then the car's driving away and the woman's behind the wheel with the crippled boyfriend in the back.'

Pasquale said, 'I never figured he had the balls to go in and snatch the woman.'

'Balls,' McTell said, with some scorn.

Pasquale said, 'You think the woman and her boyfriend are a problem?'

'Nope,' said McTell.

Pasquale regarded the red numbers on the little black box. 'You know, Eddie, I think I'm over my doubts.'

'Sure you are. I told you they'd go away.'

'Dansk rescued me, OK. He gave me some purpose. But the way I'm beginning to see it, I paid that back with interest. I wonder what he thought when we didn't answer the phones.'

'Who gives a shit?' McTell glanced down at the black box. 'What's the numbers now?'

Pasquale examined the meter in his hand. The numbers went crazy suddenly. According to the digital register, Dansk's car was now 97 miles away due west. Impossible. Pasquale tapped the box.

'You got a problem with that?' McTell asked.

'It's acting funny.'

'Funny?'

Pasquale gave the box a shake. The red numbers changed again. *5.8 m N 67 m.p.h.* 'No, it's OK now. Maybe there was some kinda interference.'

'A quirk,' McTell said.

'Yeah, a quirk.'

'Made in America, man. It's reliable.'

Pasquale said, 'Here's what I'm wondering. Why didn't he finish his business in the forest?'

McTell was silent, watching the dark highway. The trees had thinned, then vanished, and the landscape was desert again.

He snapped thumb and forefinger together in a click of realization. 'Forget that electronic box you got. I know where our boy Anthony's headed.'

75

THE LAND STRETCHED BARREN AND FLAT ALL THE WAY TO
the horizon where dawn was a few pale streaks. Dansk
imagined this place in winter, a numbing wind howling
over wasteland, the frozen bones of tumbleweed blowing
across the narrow icy highway. Around here the season
was basically always the same: dead.

He said, 'There's a turn coming up. Slow down.'

Amanda touched the brakes. The landscape was lunar
and malignant in its indifference. She'd spent the last 100
miles or more ransacking her brain for ways she could
shake off Dansk, but the ideas that came to her were fruitless. She was conscious of time seeping away. Only one
thing was certain: Dansk hadn't brought her and Rhees
out here for a barbecue.

Dansk had a map open under the rear light and one
fingertip pressed to the paper. There were no colourful
Native American attractions anywhere near here, Navaho
rain ceremonies or Hopi dances, no trading post to attract
tourists with trinkets and postcards. This was beyond
nowhere, awesome in its desolation, perfect.

'Hang a right here,' Dansk said.

No track, landmark, sign. She felt the car rock as she turned off the highway. She wondered if she might find a ravine, hammer the car down it and hope for the best, but there were neither gulleys nor fissures deep enough for any action that desperate.

The dark was disintegrating. Dust blew from under the wheels, spreading a thin ashen film on the windows of the car. Dansk leaned towards her and said, 'You're looking pale, Amanda. She look pale to you, John?'

'A little,' Rhees remarked.

'She's wondering where we're going and how she can get out of it, except there's no way, not even for the lady prosecutor.'

Dansk tapped his gun a couple of times on Rhees's plastered arm and Rhees winced. 'Two professional types, and all I had was high school and two years in some sleazoid community college with metal detectors in the hallway.'

Dansk sat back again. Two educated characters, degrees and diplomas up the kazoo, and he had them helpless, playing a glissando on their nerves. They were afraid of him. This was a high. Watch me fly, Ma. *The respect I'm getting*.

He looked from the window. Out here was a hell of a place to die. Fifteen miles from the highway and you were in the heart of a zero state nobody claimed, nobody wanted.

The car swayed across ruts. Amanda's hands on the wheel were as white as her face. Dansk saw her eyes in the mirror. Our Lady of the Sorrows. She was no longer the smart-ass Amanda with the precious letter in her pocket. She was broken, afraid of where she was going and what awaited her when she got there. *Afraid of knowing*.

He remembered the way he'd kissed the back of her

391

neck, prompted by mischief, but he'd liked the contact, the taste of salt and sweat on her skin. He'd imagined sliding down her jeans and fucking her from behind, right there on the porch with the gun in the back of her neck, and Rhees watching helplessly and the fire ripping through the pines. Little erotic signals from nowhere. The mind beamed out strange notions and impulses like a cock-eyed lighthouse in your head. He didn't want to fuck her, he wanted her dead. That was the square root of his desire.

'There,' he said, and pointed a finger. Strands of rotted wire hung between posts which rough winds had battered out of position. A sign, tilted backwards, bore a bleached message illuminated by the headlights of the car. All that was left to read were the meaningless fragments of words. *S DEP F AG RE.*

'What is this place?' Amanda asked.

Dansk said, 'Some kind of agricultural station once. I guess they were trying to develop a sturdy breed of soya bean or some such shit. They gave up twenty years ago. Nothing grows here. Drive between those posts.'

She drove where Dansk had indicated. Her heartbeat was violent and she couldn't slow it down. She turned and glanced back. 'John doesn't belong here,' she said.

'I've been waiting for that one. Oh, please, Anthony, let John go. Weep, weep.' Dansk gave his voice some falsetto, made a sobbing sound and pretended to wipe a tear away from his eye.

Rhees said, 'I'm here. I'm not going anywhere, Amanda.'

Dansk said, 'What a downright loyal guy.'

Amanda braked. 'Let him go,' she said.

'You heard what the professor said. Just drive.'

'This is just between you and me, Dansk.'

Rhees said, 'Don't, Amanda. Drop it.'

'See,' Dansk said, 'he's here for the duration. Now drive.'

Amanda clamped her hands on the wheel and stared ahead. 'Drive yourself.'

Dansk raised the gun to the side of Rhees's head. 'You don't drive, and guess what, Amanda.'

Her obstinacy against Dansk's gun, a serious mismatch. From the time Rhees had been beaten and hospitalized, Dansk had had the upper hand.

Dansk pressed his gun into Rhees's jaw. Rhees was maintaining a look of very quiet dignity. She wondered whether it was simply resignation or a façade he'd built against terror. She took her foot from the brake and the car slid forward. She stared through the dusty windshield. What had she expected from Dansk anyway? Compassion?

'Very sensible,' Dansk said. He lowered the gun. He'd wanted to blow Rhees's head away, but not in the car. He didn't need bloodstains in a rental car.

'Over there,' he said.

The structure was the colour of the land around it, camouflaged by years of exposure. It was a windowless wooden rectangle about 50 feet by 30 with a roof of rusted tin.

'Park,' Dansk said. 'Give me the keys, then step out the car.'

Amanda switched off the engine and handed the keys back to Dansk, who stuck them in a pocket. She opened her door and got out, then helped Rhees from the back seat.

Dansk was already outside the car, gesturing towards the building. She didn't want to go inside. The absence of windows enhanced the general sense of doom, even with the rim of the dawn sun pale on the horizon. You could run, if Rhees was fit and healthy, if running could get you anywhere.

'Open the door,' Dansk said.

She didn't move. She looked at Rhees but she couldn't read his expression. Six years of living together had come down to this moment when he seemed remote. She walked a few feet, Rhees at her side. She wanted to say something but words wouldn't come. She took his hand. His skin was cool.

'Push it,' Dansk said.

She touched the door and it swung open. Beyond, she was aware of dark space, nothing else. Dansk came up behind and nudged her forward, then he edged Rhees inside. Dansk fumbled against the wall, pulled a handle, and after a moment there was a creaking sound that changed to a deep rumbling, a groaning, and the whole structure trembled. A strip of overhead light flickered a couple of times and then was steady but gloomy. The noise, Amanda realized, originated from an old generator reluctantly coming to life somewhere. It whined and rattled, complained and chugged.

Amanda looked round. One large room, 300 square feet or more. Dust was everywhere: between rotted floorboards and on the shelves that lined the walls and clinging to the yellowy light-strip overhead.

Then she noticed the drums, dark-blue metal cylinders stacked on the shelves, layered with the same dust as everything else. She saw stencilled letters on the sides of the drums: DANGEROUS. TOXIC WASTE MATERIAL. Drum after drum, each about 2 feet tall, perhaps thirty-five or forty of them, and they all had the same warning in silver letters.

Dansk said, 'Toxic waste.'

The sound of the generator roared in her head. She watched Dansk walk to the nearest drum, saw him reach out and tip it forward at an angle. The lid came off and went spinning away like a wheel beyond the reaches of the light, and landed, still spinning, in the shadows. Toxic waste, she thought. She realized she didn't want to see, didn't want to look at the drum Dansk was tilting downwards from the shelf.

The drum fell. The generator changed pitch a moment and the overhead light flickered a couple of times, and then the machine was rumbling again wholeheartedly, making the floor shake.

Dansk said, 'There's a profitable sideline in jewellery, money, whatever these people had. It's like a bonus system. This watch I'm wearing, for instance,' and he held up his wrist. He might have been talking to himself. 'A perk. Usually I don't touch any of the stuff, it goes to people of minimal sensitivity who aren't fussy about the previous owners, but this took my fancy. I'm just a little wary of the karma that might be attached to it. It's a nice watch though. I figured, take a chance, karma's a lottery anyhow.'

Perks. A bonus system. Karma. Dansk stared at the spilled contents of the drum, and Amanda turned her face aside. She felt her heart drop and go on dropping like a stone down a well whose depths were beyond measurement.

'Don't be queasy,' Dansk said. 'Professors and prosecutors, it doesn't matter. This is what we all come down to.' He was sifting through the stuff that had spilled from the drum. 'After we incinerate them, they're delivered here in these drums. We stash them and then dump them in the sea when air transport's available. Some of the work isn't up to scratch. Look at this.' He held something out in the palm of his hand.

She turned her face. She was aware of Rhees watching, his body hunched a little. Her eyes moved to Dansk and she stared at what he held in the centre of his palm.

'Now this is part of a fingerbone. See?' He plucked

something else from the grey-white heap of human remains. The bone was charred and blackened and about 2 inches long. 'Looks like some spinal debris,' he said. 'Maybe even Benny Vialli's, huh?'

Benny Vialli's.

'Or maybe it's Isabel's,' Dansk said.

She'd known Isabel was dead, of course she'd known, but there must have been a level where she hadn't altogether accepted the fact, because she felt nausea. She folded her hands over her stomach. 'What else do you do? Wrench out the gold fillings, Dansk?' Her voice was dry. Her throat was parched. There was no oxygen getting to her lungs. Her heart seemed to have stopped pumping blood and she was outside of herself in a strange disconnected way.

'You make me laugh,' Dansk said. 'You've got this warped *thing* about justice. You go in a court of law and you think you're hot stuff, setting the world right. Bad guys go to jail, good guys don't. Except you have to make deals with some serious lowlife forms to get what you want—'

'It's the system,' she heard herself say. She was dizzy and there seemed to be ash in her mouth, a fine film of human ash.

'The system's fucked. But you were a serious player in the game. And there are people out there who ought to be behind bars or sucking on cyanide fumes, only they turned into songbirds singing tunes prosecutors need to hear, and you reward them by shipping them back out into society, which has rules and laws these lowlives have never paid attention to since the fucking day they were born. You think because they're in the Witness Protection Program they're all of a sudden saints? They go to PTA meetings and join the church choir? Make me laugh. They're shit on the sole of my shoe, and I wipe shit off.'

396

'They had guarantees,' Amanda said. She shut her eyes and swayed a little. Her stomach pitched, as if she was riding a boat on a very rough sea.

'Not from me they didn't,' he said.

'You're above the law.'

'There's more than one law in this great land, lady. You did your stuff on the surface where it shows and looks good. I'm the guy underground, I'm the miner working the dirty shafts all hours. You give your guarantees and I pop up and invalidate them. The scum you need to get your convictions, they don't deserve freedom. There are some evil fuckers wandering around out there, courtesy of people like you.'

'You select your . . . candidates and you bring them here, you take them into permanent custody—'

'That's how it works, and it's beautiful. They go into the Program, they disappear and nobody ever comes looking for them, and even if somebody does get nervy – like Mrs Vialli say – there's too much security to get through. And if these people persist, hey, we solve that problem.'

'What in God's name did Benny ever do to deserve this?' She had her hands clenched so tightly she was stemming the flow of her circulation and her knuckles were white.

'Guilt by association. He was tainted.'

Tainted. It was lunacy. No, it was out there beyond lunacy in a place she couldn't describe.

'As for your pal Mrs Sanchez, she was also scheduled for disposal, except she happened to split, which caused some needless delay, as you know.'

'All Isabel ever did was testify against her husband, she wasn't a criminal—'

'She married one. She knew what Sanchez did for his money, but she went on living the life of luxury anyhow on the proceeds of his work. Then, when it suited her, she walked away and became one of your little songbirds, lady.' Dansk laughed. 'And all this time you figured Victor Sanchez was the one pulling the strings, didn't you?'

'You're cleaning up the country, Dansk.'

'I'm the Rotorooter man with a fucking vengeance,' Dansk said.

She stared at the drums and wondered how many had ended up in this place, sealed in cylinders, their names lost, their identities gone. Her brain was leaden. You couldn't take this in.

'I like my work,' Dansk said, and let ash sift through his fingers and looked thoughtful, maybe even a little serene. 'Some people came to me and told me I was the kind of guy they needed for this kinda operation. These are people who believe the Witness Program pumps megadoses of poison into the arteries of the nation. People who ask, What the fuck are we doing helping out the scum you lawyers pass down the line? People who say the whole thing is shaky on the morality issue – *aside* from the fact that it's costing millions and millions of dollars. And for what? To keep a criminal element safe and well? We've got thieves and killers receiving monthly federal pay cheques and job-training and relocation at the taxpayer's expense, and all this at a time when budget deficits are out of sight, and decent ordinary people can't find work and their fucking homes are being repossessed by banks?' Dansk, whose voice had been rising, stopped in an abrupt way. She heard the sound of his hand running across his wet lips.

She thought, Budget deficits, unemployment, the country stretched on a rack of cosmic debt, and certain people looked around for programs to slash. It didn't matter which ones, just cut the numbers. School lunches, kindergarten classes, welfare hand-outs, the Federal Witness Protection Program, wherever, it didn't matter.

Dansk said, 'These people felt a line had to be drawn somewhere, and this is the line right here, lady.'

'These people,' she said. 'Some of them work in Justice, some in the US Marshals Service. Places where ID cards can be made up in the blink of an eye, and messages intercepted, and official papers obtained without question.'

Dansk said, 'Where they work, what the fuck does that matter? The whole point is, what I do has moral merit. People like you leave a mess and I'm the guy who cleans it up.'

Moral merit. Morality was modelling clay. Shape it any way you like. Dansk had rationalized his role on the grounds that the Protection Program was wrong, but she guessed that whoever had dreamed up the unholy idea in the first place were more likely to be spreadsheet types on an economy drive than philosophers fretting over an ethical dilemma. She pictured memos going out in droves to assorted Federal agencies. She saw them landing on the desks of various department heads in these agencies. She imagined they all carried the same vaguely innocuous message, written by some bland bureaucrat in the Office of Management and Budget. 'At the present time, the condition of the general economy necessitates a reduction in Federal spending, consequently you are requested to analyse those areas of your operation where budgetary measures might be taken . . .'

And a devious functionary in Justice, Loeb say, had scanned his domain and seen the bloated form of the Protection Program, and he'd had a bright idea which he'd whispered to somebody else: here's a place where we can put the knife in, provided we go about it a certain way. So a sick scheme is born in furtive whispers and quiet consultations, and a few people like Dansk are recruited to implement it, people who lived on a dark rim of experience and who weren't particular, and they were issued cards that identified them as marshals or agents of the Justice Department. And money could be saved in accordance with the vague suggestions of the memorandum, and where there was money moral problems were nuisances that had a way of dissolving like a skeleton in acid.

She wondered about the mechanics. You didn't need hundreds of people to work it. You needed only some killers, a couple of supervisors in Arlington, two or three computer operators to falsify data, two or three insiders in Justice. Guys like Loeb.

Then, without any warning, Rhees moved, urgently and recklessly. As if he'd decided that his own pain was irrelevant, he grunted and threw himself against Dansk, who stepped effortlessly to the side. Rhees fell without making any contact and was lost a moment in shadows, and when he tried to get up again Dansk kicked him in the ribs and Rhees clutched his side and groaned.

Dansk said, 'They always say it's the quiet ones you need to watch. It's the bookish types you need to keep an eye on.'

Amanda went to Rhees. His eyes were bloodshot and his face had shrunken in the bewilderment of pain. The generator faded, the rumbling was less intense, and the overhead light dimmed. She wished it would die completely so she'd be blind, immune to her surroundings. This place where all your curiosity ends.

She could smell death, death packed inside drums, and she wondered how many people had been brought here, 300, 400, and the process of flame they'd gone through, the furnace that had reduced them. She imagined rings and watches, lockets and ear-rings removed from limp bodies, ghouls sifting the possessions of the dead. She wondered about bank accounts and houses, and how monies must have been plundered and ownership documents transferred, and how many 'For Sale' signs throughout the country stood on posts outside homes where the lawful owners were never returning because they'd been shot and burned and brought here.

Dansk stepped towards her and placed a hand under her chin. 'Look at me,' he said. She kept her eyes shut.

'Look at me,' he said again.

But she didn't.

He thought, You don't want to see the face of your executioner, lady. You don't want me to be the last person you'll ever see. Carrying Anthony Dansk's image all the way into eternity with you.

She was thinking of dying. She'd hear the explosion of the gun. She wasn't sure. How could she know what she'd hear?

'Fucking look at me,' Dansk said.

'Dansk,' Rhees said hoarsely. 'Wait—'

'For what, John? The lady dies, then it's your turn. These are the facts. Face them.'

She felt the gun against the centre of her brow. She was linked to Dansk and the gun was a bridge. She heard the sound of the generator, the clunking and the asthmatic whirring noise which sometimes flared into a roar. Or maybe it was just the noise created by the broken dynamo of her brain. Outside, inside, there wasn't any difference, you knew you were going to die, you knew this was an ending.

She raised her face and looked at him finally.

He gazed into her eyes and saw what he wanted to see there, and it excited him. Defeat and despair, the pits of anxiety. It was how you looked when you turned the last page in your own history book.

'This is where curiosity gets you,' he said. He was the dispenser of darkness, the tourist guide to the other side.

'*Hey, Anthony! Check this out!*'

Surprised, Dansk turned. Amanda looked towards the

doorway, dropped to the floor and shut her eyes.

The sound of automatic gunfire roared, shot after shot kicking up clouds of dust and splintering the wall behind Dansk. Amanda lost count, confused between the gunfire and the echoes it created. There was no spatial logic to the acoustics, just noise and more noise, until the place sounded like a shooting-gallery where all the clients had gone insane. Dansk was punctured everywhere, arms, legs, chest, skull. He took a series of staggered steps, and when he fell he rolled over and over, and was finally motionless a few feet from Amanda.

Two men in shadow. They walked to where Dansk lay and studied him, as if they half expected him to have survived the fusillade. One of the men kicked Dansk in the chest. The other said, 'Hey, enough.'

She couldn't see their faces. She didn't want to see them. The generator failed. The big room was suddenly quiet and dark, and the silence was strange and terrifying.

One of the men said, 'We ought to do surgery on this pair, you ask me.'

The other said, 'That ain't the way it was spelled out by Loeb.'

'No names, asshole.'

She heard them walk to the door where they stopped. She held her breath because she knew they were going to turn back and use their guns against her and Rhees. A bad moment, dust in your throat and the bitter taste of panic, but they stepped outside. Then a minute later she heard the sound of a car kick into life and then fade in the distance.

She moved to Rhees and held him for a long time, his face against her body, her arm round his shoulder. She sat until her body was numb and the sun had climbed high enough to send light through the open doorway into the room.

She wiped the gritty ash from her clothing and went to where Dansk lay. She searched his jacket for the car keys but didn't find them. Instead she found a notebook held shut by a thick red rubber band. She removed it, then rummaged in the pockets of his pants and found the keys, which were wet with blood.

The side of his skull was shattered. She could see bone and more blood than she would have thought possible. She had the impression he was turning to liquid. Hair sodden, mouth open and crooked. The eyes stared into nothing, but were curiously bright. A strange vigilance. She imagined some elementary form of life lingered in Dansk, that he was watching her, that when she turned and walked to the door with Rhees he was still following her movements and somehow in his ruined brain recording them.

She wondered how long it would take to liberate herself from this feeling, or if it was going to stalk her a long time. But she knew.

It wasn't going to go away.

76

RHEES SAT IN THE PASSENGER SEAT WITH DANSK'S NOTEBOOK in his lap, flicking pages in a listless way she found distressing, as if he'd used up too much of himself and had nothing left inside to give. The small arid towns they passed through had an air of despondency. In Holbrook they used the rest rooms of a gas station to clean themselves up. In Winslow she bought a pair of sunglasses and telephoned Kelloway from a pay phone outside a liquor store.

'I've been waiting,' he said.

'Let's meet in Flagstaff.'

'What's wrong with Phoenix?'

'Because I don't think I can make it without falling asleep at the wheel. I'm a road hazard, Kelloway.'

'Yeah, you're a hazard all right. Forest fires, serious loss of life. Name a location.'

'The airport.' It was the first place that popped into her head.

'I'll be there in a couple of hours,' Kelloway said.

She hung up and went back to the car. She sat behind

the wheel. Weariness was like woodworm tunnelling through her. But you're alive because Loeb had issued certain instructions. Maybe he'd come to the conclusion that enough was enough, no more killing after Dansk, because the whole sick clandestine business was coming apart.

Rhees hadn't even raised the subject. He seemed to accept the fact that he was alive without any curiosity. He was slowly turning the pages of the notebook as if he were reading text in a language he didn't know, one that held no interest for him.

Dansk's notes were centred on the pages, framed by sequences of tiny crosses and arrows and jagged lines that suggested thorns. One page contained a single word with a question mark: 'friends?' She couldn't imagine Dansk having friends.

Rhees continued to flick pages and sometimes read Dansk's notes in a disturbing monotone. In obscure ways, in phrases and fragments, Dansk had recorded his impressions. People were referred to by initials. L had to be Loeb. Dansk had written, 'I wish I could cut L's fucking throat like a pig.' She had no notion of the identities of Mc and P, initials that recurred. Willie Drumm's name was inscribed inside a rectangle, like a crude coffin.

Pages were crammed with letters, followed by abbreviated place names. BNDenv McKSeat FSaltLk RMDenv QDalbu RDalbu PROgd JROgd. In the back, the pages were covered with a series of digits, some of them phone numbers, others that looked like PIN codes for bank cards. You needed a key to unlock the significance of all these numbers. You needed another kind of key to reveal a different kind of accounting: the numbers of the dead.

A cryptic notebook, a cryptic life. She wondered what could be deduced from these pages, from the abbreviations and the numerals, the mysteries in Dansk's world.

Something slipped out of the notebook into Rhees's

hand. It was a folded newspaper clipping. He opened it.

'What's that?' she asked.

Rhees gave her the clipping and she read it.

LOCAL WOMAN SLAIN. Under this headline was a terse story:

> Mrs Frederica Danskowski, aged sixty-seven, of 2343 Drake, was killed yesterday by unknown assailants in broad daylight outside her apartment building. She was stabbed several times. She was taken to County Hospital, and pronounced dead on arrival. Police are asking for information from anyone in the vicinity of Drake Street between three and three-thirty yesterday afternoon to call the Patterson Police Department. Mrs Danskowski is survived by one son, Anthony, a surveyor for an oil company.

It was dated April 1994. A surveyor, she thought. She remembered the photographs Dansk kept. Mother and son. Anthony Danskowski, shortened to Dansk, a surveyor.

Somewhere between Winslow and Flagstaff she drove 100 yards off the road. She got out, opened the trunk, found Dansk's case and set it down. She battered it open with a tyre-iron, sweating as she smashed the lid, the hinges, the lock again and again. She went down on her knees in the dust and rummaged through the contents, looking for papers, documents, files, any text of substance that might yield intelligible clues to Dansk's world. All she found were his clothes, folded neatly. His toiletries. But no papers. She kicked angrily at the stuff, scattered it around, then went back to the car. Sweat dripped into her eyes, blinding her.

She took the notebook from Rhees's slack hand, shut it and imagined this simple act might silence Dansk's voice, which had seemed to issue from the pages in whispers and incomprehensible asides. But it didn't quieten Dansk at all, because she could still hear him. *Check the destruction in your own wake before you pass judgement on me. You're like some kind of fucking Typhoid Mary spreading a deadly plague.*

Flagstaff marked a change, mountains and high green forests and a soft breeze. Amanda drove a mile or so beyond the town, where the airport was located. A small terminal, it served mainly short-hop commuter flights north to Las Vegas or south to Phoenix. A couple of picnic tables were situated at the edge of the parking-lot.

She parked and bought two large sodas in the cafeteria and took them to one of the tables. Rhees sipped his in silence. Amanda smoked a cigarette and watched cars come in and out of the lot. A Cessna rose up from the runway. She imagined being inside the small plane, floating in a kind of light membranous sac through blue skies, where consciousness was suspended and amnesia a possibility.

She saw Kelloway step out of a car. He noticed Amanda and Rhees immediately and walked briskly to their table. He sat, waving smoke from Amanda's cigarette away from his face. She removed her sunglasses and looked at him, searching his expression for an indication of his mood. It was hard to tell.

'OK,' he said. 'Let's start with Tom Gannon.'

'Dansk shot him,' she said.

'And the other cops?'

She didn't say anything. She felt an unexpected reluctance to tell Kelloway anything else, but she wasn't sure why. Speech was an enormous effort suddenly. Words congealed and darkened like scars in her head.

'So he kills four cops in one swoop and burns down half a forest,' Kelloway said.

Amanda looked beyond Kelloway a moment. The breeze fluttered briefly, then faded. The wind-sock nearby deflated. This situation had the pitch of a dream, or of that moment when you experience the first slide towards sleep.

'And then where did he go?' Kelloway asked.

Rhees said in his flat way, 'Dansk's dead.'

'Dead?'

'There were two gunmen,' Rhees said.

'Where?'

Amanda said, 'A place we never want to go again.'

Kelloway looked into her eyes. 'What place?'

'I'll draw you a map,' she said. But all she could remember was wilderness and gunfire. The geography was missing.

Kelloway leaned forward, elbows on the table. 'These gunmen shot Dansk and left? You saw their faces?'

'It was dark,' she said. 'We couldn't see them.'

'So you can't identify them.'

Amanda said, 'Frankly, we weren't really looking. My best guess would be they were the same pair who attacked John.'

'Dansk's own people turned on him.' Kelloway swatted a fly from his arm. 'And left you two alive?'

'Maybe Loeb can explain that,' she said.

Kelloway made one hand into a tanned fist. 'Loeb was shot at close range outside a roadside tavern on I-Seventeen. We don't know who killed him. Nobody in the tavern heard any gunfire. You never find witnesses in these sawdust joints.'

She absorbed this information. No witnesses, she thought. No Loeb to answer questions. No Dansk to interrogate. Silenced voices. 'How much background have you looked into?'

'Ralph Loeb was with Justice for sixteen years. Terminal

lung cancer, so he was going to retire one way or another pretty soon. I imagine he expected to croak in a hospital bed with tubes up his nose, but fate's a real joker. He told me he'd never heard of Dansk.'

'Surprise.'

'I have calls into various people. Top guys in Justice. The US Marshals Service. The Director of the Witness Protection Program. I'm also talking with the State Attorney-General's office. I have forensics examining the late Mrs Vialli for exact cause of death. The description of the guy you saw in the Hideaway Knolls has been circulated.'

'You've become a believer, have you?' she asked.

'Let's say I'm leaning,' Kelloway said, 'but I need anything you can give me by way of solid evidence.'

She thought of Dansk's notebook. She thought of the drums and the labels on them. She had the unsettling feeling that Kelloway was keeping something back from her and Rhees. She didn't know what.

Her attention was drawn to a car entering the parking-lot and cruising close to the table. She saw the driver's face half in shadow, and she had a sense of recognition. The car moved past, then slid into a space about 50 yards away and the door opened.

The breeze came up again. The man who stepped out of the car put a hand to his scalp. His necktie, caught by a current of air, flapped up against his face and he smoothed it back into position. In his left hand he carried a brief-case.

Kelloway said, 'I'm looking at the possibility of a serious investigation here. One that's also very delicate.'

Amanda turned away from the man fidgeting with his necktie. 'Does the prospect scare you, Kelloway?'

'I don't scare, Scholes. I've got balls of steel. All I'm saying is, this isn't your run-of-the-mill affair. This is something you piece together, and if there's a case I'm gonna have to convince some pretty influential people I've got something worth pursuing. This one leads in all sorts of directions. Justice. The US Marshals Service. I can see FBI involvement. Beyond that . . .' He shrugged.

Amanda stared past Kelloway at the man who was struggling once more to keep his tie in place against the renewed mischief of the breeze. When he reached the table he smiled at Amanda.

She said, 'Lew Bascombe. Got a plane to catch?'

'No, no plane,' Bascombe said. He sat, opened his brief-case, took out an opaque plastic folder and laid it on the table. It was red and shiny, buttoned shut.

Kelloway nodded at Bascombe, then said to Amanda, 'I want everything you can tell me. A to Z.'

She wondered about Lew Bascombe's presence. She looked at the red folder. Lew was drilling his fingers on it. She leaned back, sluggish. When Kelloway spoke his voice came from a cloud of ectoplasm. 'I got some real thick doors to knock on and some heavyweight characters I'm gonna have to talk to. I need good stuff to show them, and where am I gonna find this stuff if I don't get it from you and Rhees? Not from Loeb, and not from Dansk, that's for sure.'

She said, 'Loeb and Dansk weren't working alone: they had support. People with access to information. People who knew what buttons to push on their keyboards. Others who specialized in violence. I don't know how many or how deep this whole sickness runs.'

'These are exactly the people I want to fucking nail.'

'Have you thought that Loeb had time to start covering his tracks before he died?' she asked. 'Maybe he made a few phone calls right after his talk with you. He realized things were beginning to fall apart, so he sent out messages. Eliminate certain files and records, et cetera.'

Kelloway said, 'You can't wipe out *everything*, Scholes. There are always traces left somewhere, and I'll find them. When I get my foot in the door I'm like some fucking Jehovah's Witness on Benzedrine.'

Kelloway looked at Bascombe, who unclipped the folder and opened it. He started to pull papers out.

Bascombe said, 'I've arranged a complete set, Amanda. Two birth certificates, two social security cards, two driver's licences issued by the State of Arizona. Two credit cards and a cheque-book from a bank in Yuma. The key to a house in the same city, address attached. You'll see we've described you as married. I picked the names myself. Erika and Robert Bloom.'

'Wait,' she said.

Kelloway said, 'I can't begin to build a case without you two and I want to be one hundred per cent goddam sure any witnesses of mine are in protective custody—'

'*Wait*,' she said again.

'I want you both safe and sound while I work this business out. We have our own in-State witness protection program—'

'I'm aware of that—'

'It's small-scale compared to the Federal one, but at least it's secure, and I know where I can contact you when I need you. I can guarantee total safety, round-the-clock protection, a direct line to my office open all hours.'

Amanda looked at the birth certificates, the credit cards, the cheque-book. They appeared to vibrate in her vision. 'You're asking us to drop out of sight for God knows how long and assume new *identities*?'

'Nobody's gonna come looking for you. You don't have to live with an ongoing paranoia. You'll be safe in my care.'

Safe in my care. 'Is this mandatory?' she asked.

Kelloway shrugged and raised his eyebrows. 'Let me tell

411

you what's gonna happen if you don't accept: you'll spend a whole lotta time looking over your shoulder. When the sun goes down, you'll wonder what lies out there in the darkness. When the doorbell rings, you'll jump. When somebody comes to fix your garbage disposal, you'll be reaching for a Valium or a gun, whichever's closer. And then there's Rhees to consider. He needs rest, time to mend.'

He'd fingered her weak point. She stared at the wind-sock and watched it fill with air. She listened to the breeze as if she expected to hear a message of guidance rustle out of the trees nearby, reliable counsel voiced by the shaken leaves.

'Maybe you don't trust me,' Kelloway said. 'But you have to trust somebody somewhere along the line. Begin with me. Who was it that gave you Tom Gannon for protection? Who was it offered you that? And those other cops? I walked that extra mile for you.'

She looked at Rhees, whose drawn face seemed to recede from her. Trust somebody somewhere.

Rhees said, 'Robert and Erika Bloom,' as if he were checking the flavour of the names in his mouth and didn't like how they tasted, but his voice was odd and lifeless.

She heard another small plane rise off the runway.

'Well?' Kelloway asked.

She raised her face and watched the craft, a dwindling gleam of quicksilver in the sun. The sound of the engine dropped a half-tone. She put her sunglasses on and the gloss of the day dimmed to an acceptable level. She looked at Kelloway, who was less harsh, less predatory, in reduced light. Then she stared at Bascombe for a long time. That bland face, that bad wig.

'What do you think, Lew?' she asked.

'I think you should go for it, Amanda,' he said.

'Just like that,' she said.

Bascombe said, 'I've already agreed to co-operate one hundred per cent with Dan to get this whole goddam business cleared up. I believe you should do the same.'

The same, she thought. Christ, she was weary, weary. She wanted a bed and clean sheets and a cool dark room. Above all else she wanted Rhees to be safe. She looked at Bascombe and remembered Willie Drumm. 'Tell me, Lew. Did you ever get around to checking on Dansk?'

Bascombe said, 'Of course I did.'

'And?'

'Nothing,' he said. 'He wasn't employed by Justice. He wasn't employed by the Marshals Service. He came out of nowhere.'

Zero, she thought. A mystery. Now he was dead and she should begin the process of imposing amnesia on herself. She saw a State police car enter the parking-lot.

'Is that our transportation, Kelloway?'

'Only if you accept,' he said.

She glanced at Rhees again. He made an indeterminate movement of his head. She knew what it meant: I'm in too much pain to think.

'What about my father?' she asked. 'He's going to wonder. I owe him a call.'

'Later, when you're relocated, we'll arrange for you to phone him. We're not talking for ever, Amanda. Three months, six, it depends on what I find. I might get lucky sooner, you never know.'

She closed her eyes against the light and finished the last of her soda. She thought of Morgan and his hacienda in the hills, Morgan waiting to hear from her. Later, like Kelloway had said.

Life was going to become a series of postponements and abdications. She removed the sunglasses and blinked.

'There's a notebook you're going to need,' she said.

77

KELLOWAY WATCHED THE STATE POLICE CAR DRIVE OUT OF sight. Neither Amanda nor Rhees looked back at him. He turned to Bascombe and said, 'Where the hell did Loeb dig up a psycho like Dansk? What was the old clown dreaming of? He must've known the risk he was running trusting a guy like that. OK, so Dansk was a US Marshal with special undercover status, big deal, but Loeb should've checked on his mental stability, for Christ's sake.'

Kelloway picked up an empty soda container from the table and crumpled it in his hand. 'Then, lo and behold, Loeb changes tack and decides he wants Dansk dead because the guy's outta control and it's panic stations, and all the evidence has to get swept under the nearest rug immediately, and Scholes goes home happy and content because she imagines her personal nightmare's finished . . . A dying man finds some mercy in his heart. You think it was something like that with Loeb? Or did he just lose his nerve?'

'It doesn't matter much now,' Bascombe said.

Kelloway had a hard purposeful quality in his expression. 'No more fuck-ups. No more of Loeb's misbegotten judgements. No more Dansk.'

Bascombe smiled, a humourless effort. 'This wide-ranging investigation of yours. When does it begin?'

Kelloway said, 'What investigation?'

'I'm sorry for the woman, kind of,' Bascombe said.

'Save your sympathy, Lew. She got herself into this. She had her chances to back out. More than a few times.'

'Her father . . .'

'Tough one,' Kelloway said. 'But you can't have guys like Dansk doing this work. He fiddled around and he blew it, and along the way some unhappy sacrifices had to be made. Jesus, I hate losing men. It's a total waste.' He was silent a time, staring towards the trees. 'OK, I figured Dansk was deranged enough and determined enough to get through to the cabin, but fuck, I really missed out on Loeb's misguided charity. Maybe the old fart saw Scholes's reprieve as an act of atonement or something, or maybe all the death just sickened him to the heart, which I could understand, believe me.'

'Who knows,' Bascombe said.

'Sometimes I get depressed and I think this operation's too much. The pressure-cooker syndrome. The whole act you have to go through: containment, keeping secrets, all the lies. Then I swing the other way and it looks good again, it feels right, it's running like a well-oiled clock and God's got a grin on his face. You think I need Prozac maintenance, Lew?'

'Drugs don't keep a man's head clear.'

'Whatever,' Kelloway said. 'She's all mine.'

'I don't have to ask what you intend to do with her, do I?'

A sparrow landed on the table.

Kelloway stretched a hand out and said, 'Boo,' and the

415

frightened bird flew upward in a nervy flapping of wings and disappeared like a puff of woodsmoke or a dead soul in the direction of the freeway.

BLACKOUT

For Roy Stevenson,
fisherman, bookman, friend,
and for Stephen Black for his help

This stuff will probably kill you
Let's do another line

– Tom Waits, *Heartattack & Vine*

1

THE JACKRABBIT, FROZEN IN TERROR BY THE HEADLIGHTS OF
the car, appeared abruptly out of nowhere. Samsa – even
if he knew it was completely the wrong response in heavy
rain, that a jackrabbit's life wasn't worth a nickel in
the larger scheme of things – slammed his foot hard on the
brake.

Pure blind instinct.

The car went immediately into a searing skid on the
slick blacktop and plunged off the road down an incline,
overturning. Samsa found himself suddenly in a jarring
upside-down world, an inversion of black sky and black
rain glittering in the headlights, the passenger door bursting open and the girl screaming as she fell out, as if she'd
been sucked into another dimension.

The girl. Oh, dear Christ.

He twisted the wheel, imagining there might be some
corrective maneuver he could perform, but the car kept
sliding on its roof across greasy terrain. Only the buckled
seat belt, digging into his chest, kept him in place. The
hazard lights came on, blinking and clicking crazily, and

the Billie Holiday tune playing on the tape deck slurred to a halt. He heard the malevolent roar of the useless engine, and the wheels spinning overhead as the car scudded along. A half-empty vodka bottle shattered the windshield, and Samsa had the frightening impression he was seeing the night through an opaque clutter of plastic packing pods, or in a spidery dream that obscured a terrifying mystery.

There was a stabbing pain in the region of his shoulder and the seat belt felt like a band of iron. But these sensations came to him dimly because of a whine deep inside his skull, and his heart was very loud, and he could still hear the echo of the girl's scream and feel wet air flood through the open passenger door. The car churned up soil and kept plowing forward and Samsa thought for the first time of a possible explosion, a punctured gas-tank, an electrical spark from somewhere, and boom.

Because of a goddam jackrabbit traumatized by headlights, because of some misbegotten respect he'd entertained for the sanctity of life, here he was in this upturned car, fighting panic and powerlessness and wondering how far the car might travel before it finally ground to a halt, or whether it would combust first. Stricken by an assortment of acute fears, he groped for the seat belt with the idea he could free himself and open his door and roll out of the vehicle, but he was fumbling, and his hands couldn't work the buckle, and the car was shuddering in a way that suggested it was about to fall apart in a disconnected series of bits and pieces, broken wing mirrors, hubcaps, misshapen engine parts. He imagined a field strewn with such things, like the horrific wreckage left by an airplane that had fallen out of the sky. Bodies burned beyond recognition. The sifting of charred bones.

He thought, *I'm dying, this is it. Big time.* Blood zoomed to his head, an almighty roaring.

And then it was over, the car struck something hard and spun round once and stopped. The engine died. Samsa clawed free of the seat belt and slid out into the rain.

Smoke hissed through the shattered radiator grill. The headlights, which somehow hadn't died, picked out the shape of the tree the car had hit. A leafy branch, bark violently stripped and raw, lay across the chassis. On his back in the wet grass, Samsa moved away from the vehicle. He was aware of how the wheels still turned in diminishing whispers, and of the sound of rain falling through leaves, and the odd silence that lay in a spectral place just beneath these noises.

He got to his feet. His legs trembled. The girl. Where was the girl?

His mouth ached. He must have broken a tooth along the way, although he couldn't remember how. He had to find the girl. Spitting out the gritty debris of the tooth, he walked the field in the direction of the blacktop, listening for some sound of her. But there was nothing except the goddam rain and mud sucking at his shoes.

When he came to the foot of the incline where he'd skidded off the road he stopped. For a time he didn't move, paralyzed by aftershock. His system shut down. A collapse was taking place inside. He shivered, closed his eyes, and the scary incident replayed itself in his head. He had to shake off this numbness and find the girl, nothing else mattered. He moved, lost his footing, went down in the grass. Pain penetrated his shoulder – a torn muscle, a dislocation maybe. He could tolerate that. He'd known worse. He got up again and called the girl's name a couple of times.

No answer.

She's unconscious somewhere nearby. Blacked out, lying in the warm rain. Yes.

He felt the need to check the time, anchor himself in the

familiar, the quantifiable. He glanced at his wristwatch, but the face was cracked and the hands bent and the luminous dots meant nothing. A wind came up and gathered the rain together and blew it directly into his eyes. Where was she – this girl he barely knew? He remembered her waiflike face and the detachment in her eyes and her long legs under the short blue velvet skirt, the white shoes with the thick clunky heels. He remembered how she'd drunk vodka like there was a new Prohibition Law about to be enacted. Sometimes she'd tried to make a fluting sound by pressing her lips against the neck of the bottle and blowing. He'd seen the shape of her mouth by the lights of the instrument panel and been distracted by it. Or enchanted. It didn't matter which anymore. Because of that fucking demonic jackrabbit.

'Say, where you taking me?' she'd asked.

And he'd talked vaguely about some place he knew, although in reality he wasn't thinking of a particular destination. His head was filled with motels. A key to an unfamiliar bedroom, a double bed and white sheets, a corny painting hanging on the wall.

His lightweight summer suit was soaked and clung to him like a second skin. He was oblivious to his discomfort. He was starting to experience another kind of panic now, different from the one he'd felt hanging upside down inside the car. This had its origins in a place less primal, that civilized intersection where you were supposed to know right from wrong. But he'd overridden all the internal controls that regulated everyday behavior. And now he wished he could turn the clock back to the point where he'd first decided to switch off these instruments and just go go go with his gut feelings and his needs.

Jesus, his needs—

He stumbled into her. She lay half submerged in a

hollow of water maybe five or six inches deep. He bent down, gripped her by the shoulders and raised her up a little way. Rain fell into her short soft hair and ran down her face, and mascara tracks that resembled some kind of weird shorthand message slid across her cheeks. His throat was dry as cinder.

There was a lawful procedure to follow, regulations to obey. He knew all that. You reported the accident and a cop duly arrived on the scene, and you uttered the details of the incident in the flashing glare of a patrol car's roof lights.

But he couldn't do that.

Not immediately.

His shoulder throbbed. With the tip of his tongue he explored the stub of the broken tooth and tried to gather his thoughts, but they were in disarray.

2

'TAKE A PEW, LEE,' JIMMY PLUMM SAID.

Lee Boyle, who hated being ordered around, sat down. The room was lit only by a single green-shaded lamp on the desk, which had the effect of making Plumm appear like something you'd encounter on a bad trip. He had enormous glowing green eyebrows and shoulder-length hair the same color. He wore a faded monogrammed smoking jacket that had the look of a garment passed down from one generation to the next, as if to impart the impression of a decayed English aristocrat who'd sold off the family estates and hocked the crested silver years ago.

Boyle knew better. He knew for a fact Plumm had been born and raised in Long Island. The closest he'd come to England was probably a travelogue about the Lake District on TV, or maybe some groveling documentary on the House of Windsor.

Plumm said, 'I do very much like that little gold doodah round your neck, Lee. Set you back a good sum, I imagine.'

'I got it pre-owned,' Boyle said.

'Pre-owned, eh? Good shoes, too,' Plumm remarked. 'Top of the line, if I'm not mistaken. Also used?'

'Who wears used shoes?' Boyle said. He didn't like the notion of Plumm running an inventory. He considered it an invasion of his private space. Plus, the obvious subtext here was criticism of his spending money he didn't have. And he didn't need to hear that either.

'Well, then,' Plumm said. 'Where exactly do we stand?'

'Basically, I need more time,' Lee Boyle said.

Plumm raised one of the big eyebrows. 'Let me guess. You're going through a bad spell.'

'Business sucks.'

'If I believed every sob story I heard I'd hang one of those sweet little Gone Fishing signs on my door.'

'I wasn't giving you a sob story, Jimmy. I'm only saying there's this cash flow problem, which is inconvenient and embarrassing.' Boyle leaned forward in his chair. He knew Plumm found him attractive – gays were always drawn to his yellow-haired blue-eyed looks and his physique, the good Aryan template that probably fueled decadent fantasies of a sado-masochistic Nazi nature. But when it came to business, Plumm's bottom line was cash. You owe. Pay up. Plumm's equations were very simple and sometimes vicious.

Plumm rose. He was massive, six-five at least, and broad-chested. He stepped round the front of his desk and looked at Boyle for a time. Rain swept against the window beyond the curtains. The summer night was profoundly foul.

'You do have somebody you could ask, of course,' Plumm said.

Boyle shook his head. 'Get real.'

'I am *being* real. Very much so. Dear old Daddy.'

'Dear old Daddy doesn't talk to me,' Boyle said.

'I hate to hear of estrangements in families. A

rapprochement would be in order, given the circumstances.'

'Daddy doesn't believe in forgiveness, Jimmy. You only get one chance with him, and if you fuck up you're through. And I fucked up years ago as far as he's concerned. End of story.'

Plumm didn't move for a while. He appeared to be considering the situation, sifting courses of action. Then he reached out and gripped Boyle's upper lip between his thumb and index finger and pulled on it hard. Boyle felt himself being drawn forward, his face level with Plumm's crotch. This was humiliating and disturbingly intimate. Nobody – *nobody* – treated him like this.

'My advice is simple, friend. Go to good old Dad,' and Plumm twisted the upper lip with nasty vigor, holding it a moment. Just as Boyle had had enough of this fiasco and was raising a hand with the intention of hammering Plumm's fingers away, the big man released him.

'What the *fuck*,' Boyle said.

'You don't like physical?' Plumm asked.

'I prefer to choose who touches me. And I don't remember giving you a free pass, Plumm. Don't *ever* pull that kind of stunt again. I mean that.' Boyle, who stored grudges the way some people accumulated price-saver coupons, sat back in his chair and thought murderous thoughts. He thought about the gun in his apartment, a Llama Compact .45 he kept stashed in the cabinet under the bathroom sink, concealed behind Almond's tampons and toiletries, and he imagined pressing the barrel into this phony's huge forehead just to watch the bozo sweat.

'I was only trying to emphasize my point. Go see Daddy,' Plumm said.

'I already told you, Jimmy. No can do.' Boyle's lip hurt. 'Daddy's not Santa nowadays.'

'Then Daddy and I have something in common,' Plumm

432

said. He sat behind his desk, opened a folder and lowered his head. Without looking up he added, 'The sands of time are just running and running, love.'

Love. 'How fast are they running?'

'Oh, let's say three days, shall we? I'm in a charitable mood.'

'Three days? Three whole days? Gee.'

'Don't tell me you have a problem with that.' Plumm flapped a hand.

Boyle realized he'd been dismissed just like a Domino's delivery boy. He walked to the door and looked back. Plumm was making a scratchy sound on paper with a pretentious gold-nibbed fountain pen, like he was answering an invite to tea from an imaginary fucking duchess or something.

Asshole.

Seething, Boyle let himself out and stood at the top of the stairs. Through the glass panel of the door below he could see rain brightened by street lights. He went down quickly, two steps at a time. On the sidewalk he hauled his jacket up over his head and hurried through the downpour. Halfway along the block he ducked inside a bar called Chang's, a big white-walled room decorated with pink plaster-of-Paris flamingoes, scores of them.

Busy place. Escapees from the weather crowded the joint, cluttering all the available floor space and tables. Raincoats had been hung over some of the flamingoes. The air stank of damp clothing. Boyle scoped out the faces, recognized a couple of dopers looking strung-out, and a few small-time hoods planning low-grade scams that were doomed from conception. A bunch of losers.

He eyed the women as he usually did. He didn't see Almond anywhere. He pushed his way across the floor, tense, hands knotted. Plumm might be a faggot and a fraud, but that didn't alter the fact he was a tumor

433

inside Lee Boyle's head and had to be excised somehow.

He made it to the other side of the room, where he took a pack of Camel Lights from the pocket of his jeans and lit one with a Zippo on which his name was embossed. Almond had given him the lighter on his last birthday. She'd wrapped it in tissue and put it inside a little cardboard box with a ribbon stuck to it. 'The big three-oh,' she'd said at the time. 'You're getting up there, babe.'

Where the hell was she? He touched his lip where Plumm had yanked it and he thought, *Three days and counting*. He gazed into the Zippo flame.

A girl in tight leather pants stepped out of the toilets. 'Hey, good-looking.'

She had a gaunt face, a little heavy on the make-up. He knew her as Krystal with a K. Her real name was probably something like Darlene. She had an accent that might have been prairie.

'What's happening?' Boyle asked.

'I'm thinking you need, uh, like a snorkel to work in this weather. Maybe a tank of oxygen strapped to your back.'

'Innovative stuff.'

'I'm running,' she said. 'See you around.'

'Say, Krystal. You seen Almond anywhere?'

'I saw her yesterday, I think. Maybe the day before. I never keep track of time, Lee. You know me. I'm scattered.'

Boyle watched the girl vanish in the crowd. He considered hanging around for a while, wait for Almond to show. Then he thought he'd go home instead. He made his way to the front door, working his elbows into a few spines and ignoring complaints – 'Hey, buddy, watch where you're going' – with a scowl. His car was parked in an alley about a hundred yards away. He ran splashing through puddles. At the end of the alley a solitary light hung above the back door of a seafood restaurant, illuminating the black dumpsters where he'd left his old Porsche. He took the key from the pocket of his jeans. He didn't see the man emerge from the cover of the doorway.

'Lee.'

Still cowled in his jacket, Boyle turned. The man stood under a black umbrella. He had a huge punched-out face and one bad eye that looked like somebody had used white-out on it. Tom Raseci, known as Bigshoes, was about the same height as his employer Plumm, except he'd gone to fat. He was carrying about 300 pounds of blubber.

'What is this, Tom? I just talked with your lord and master. Didn't he tell you?'

'Fine car,' Raseci said. 'Classic.'

'You want to make small talk in this weather? I'm going home.'

'Not in that car you ain't.'

Boyle looked at Raseci. 'Why? You intend to confiscate my vehicle as collateral, Tom?'

Tom Raseci shook his head. 'What I'm trying to say is, your car's got a problem.' He approached the vehicle, nodded at the front right tire. 'You ask me, I'd say somebody came along and slashed it.'

Boyle went down on one knee and fingered the soft rubber, feeling the ragged slit and getting angry. 'Nice fucking work, Tom.'

'You think I did that?'

'Yeah, I think you figured a little vandalism might hassle me. Keep the heat on.'

'More like some passing moron resented your Porsche, I'd say. You get guys like that. They work out their envy with a knife.' Raseci came closer. 'Myself, I'd never stoop that low. I appreciate classic cars. Hell, I wish I could *afford* one. But it's the upkeep. The specialty mechanics.

The spare parts. Must break your heart at times.'

Boyle stood upright. He looked into the other man's face. The weird thing about Raseci's bad eye was the way you were drawn to it, fascinated by the milky quality. You could imagine stirring your finger in it.

'Tell your boss, Plumm, to go fuck himself,' he said.

'Smart messengers don't deliver bad messages, sonny.'

Boyle gazed again at the trashed tire. The anger foaming through him had its sources scattered all over the place, the constant debilitating lack of cash, a sky that had been pissing rain for days and days, and the absence of Almond. And now this act of mutilation on his Porsche, which was one of his few assets at present.

'Got a spare?' Raseci asked.

'It's flat.'

'You'll need a ride home. My car's round the corner.'

'I'll walk.' Boyle turned and moved to the end of the alley.

He heard Raseci call out. 'Hey, rich boy. Maybe you could phone Papa and have his limo pick you up. *Har-har-har.*'

436

3

DARCY STARED AT HER SCRABBLE TILES. Q E K E L M I.

Milk, she thought. Or *meek*. Otherwise, what these letters looked like was the name of some Libyan despot.

On the other side of the coffee table Nick was wearing his smug expression. *I've got a great word.* She could see it in his eyes. Maybe he had a seven-letter beauty he could get out. He arranged his tiles just-so. The game had begun to drag on her, but she knew she'd keep playing because it occupied him; it kept his mind off his groin, which was where his thoughts tended to drift. She got up, slotted a CD into the deck. She was into her classical mode. Brahms.

'I don't know what you get out of that stuff,' Nick said after a while.

'Just listen,' she said.

'I've been listening and I still don't get it.'

'Try using both ears.'

Nick, handsome in a dark, gipsy kind of way – as if he knew ancient secrets, which wasn't even close to the truth – gazed at her across the table. 'It's not like you can dance to it, Darcy. You can't even tap your feet.'

'I'm trying to upgrade you,' she said.

'And I'm trying to downgrade *you*,' Nick said. He stretched out his arm and laid his hand on the back of her fingers. He had soft hands. They felt like cotton handkerchiefs that had been dried outdoors on a spring day. He was eighteen and on his way to college in the Fall, and when he graduated he'd work in the family company, which produced something Darcy thought totally boring – paper products: napkins, towels, what have you.

She tried to imagine being married to him. Mrs Darcy Doily.

Nick's whole life was set out in front of him, predetermined and immutable. He'd never dream of straying off the path and going in an unexpected direction. All the Mancuso brothers worked in the family business. Nick, the youngest, would start out as a regional salesman, driving long distances to show samples of patterned paper plates to department-store buyers in towns bypassed by freeways long ago.

She felt him stroke the palm of her hand. What he wanted, she knew, was to make love to her. Desperately. There had been a series of urgent clumsy encounters in the back of his car, sweaty moments when she'd *almost* been swayed – more from curiosity than any lust, or affection even. In the context of her world, she and Nick were 'going steady'. They hung out together at school. They held hands at ball games and in burger joints. 'Going steady', that quaint phrase, seemed to her a suffocating kind of business. People made assumptions about you. *She's screwing Nick. She's gotta be.* Darcy Doily, prisoner of conjecture.

She liked Nick well enough. He had good qualities. Reliability. Generosity. But.

She stood up. She looked at the clock on the mantelpiece. Ten thirty-eight. Alongside the clock a sequence of family photographs had been arranged. She glanced at one of her mother, then turned away. Nick was watching her. He had the air of a faithful dog about him. Something that was always under the kitchen table or lying around by the sofa, waiting, hoping to be tossed a scrap. Or better still, stroked nicely.

Dream on.

Nick rose and stood directly behind her now, his arms crossed over her breasts. His breath was warm on the back of her neck. He eased his fingers between the buttons of her shirt, reaching for a breast. He was hard as a rock. She could feel it against her. He had only to come within an inch of her and his motor cranked up.

There was an intimacy here she knew she was supposed to enjoy. Sometimes she did, sometimes she didn't. Her feelings came and went for no particular reason. Fickle little breezes: yes, no, I don't want to, I'm not ready, I don't think I love you, I don't know what love is, Nicky, I'm too young.

She drew away from him. 'We were in the middle of playing Scrabble, I remember.'

Nick looked let down, slightly martyred. He shrugged and went back to the table to examine his tiles. At least he didn't pull the predictable crap – I can't go on this way, Darcy. It hurts a guy, you know? You get a pain in the groin. A knot.

She gazed at her letters. 'I'm not one of those . . .'

'One of those what?'

'Cockteasers.'

'I never said you were.'

'I think you sometimes *think* I am.'

Nick shook his head. 'I love you,' he said.

Love was supposed to light up in your heart like a big neon arrow. But the electricity just wasn't getting to her.

There was no real juice unless you counted the occasional little spark. And that wasn't enough for her.

'I figure you'll come round,' he said.

'Pretty sure of yourself, aren't you?'

'I'm a patient guy, Darcy.'

She pushed her fingers through her dark-brown hair. Patience, sure. He had it in spades. Another of Nick's qualities. Look on the bright side. He could be ugly, geeky, like one of those Internet chat-room addicts, a snail with myopia and acne. Instead he was easy on the eye, gregarious, polite to his elders. He didn't smoke cigarettes, didn't touch drugs. He played tennis and basketball. He was every father's ideal. Her own father, for one, approved of Nick Mancuso. 'Nice kid,' he'd said. The unspoken declaration was that she could do a whole lot worse.

She thought: *Just do it and get it over with, why don't you, Darcy? What are you saving it for?*

He played his tiles on the board slowly.

CUNT.

'That's the only word you can come up with?'

'Yeah,' he said.

'A suspicious person might say you're trying to tell me something, Nick.'

'I'll show you my other letters if you don't believe me.'

She pushed her tiles away. She was suddenly tired. It was ten forty-six on the clock. Where was her father at this time of night? Busy guy. Out there doing all the stuff he did. She moved, sat in Nick's lap, curled up against him, enjoying a sense of comfort. He seemed quite content just to hold her. He smelled of deodorant and aftershave and the underlying musk of the permanently horny adolescent. *He's a kid, really. A big kid.*

The telephone rang. She climbed out of Nick's lap and answered it.

'Darcy? You okay?' Her father, voice fuzzy, speaking on his cellular phone.

'Fine. Nick's here.'

The frazzle of static, and her father's voice fading in and out. She heard the word 'accident'.

'I can hardly hear you,' she said. 'What accident?'

There was a moment of clarity. 'I'm not hurt. I don't want you to worry.'

'What happened?'

But the connection was lost entirely and the sound Darcy heard in her ears reminded her of a locomotive vanishing down a long black tunnel.

4

THE COP WHO ARRIVED ON THE SCENE WAS A STATE TROOPER wearing a name-tag that identified him as Trope, Frederick. Samsa, who'd never seen or heard of Trope before, showed the trooper the place where he'd gone off the road. Trope, a gangly man in a glossy rainslicker, wrote a few words in his notebook.

Samsa mentioned the jackrabbit, knowing it sounded foolish. But sometimes when you admitted your own idiotic behavior you gave yourself a certain authenticity: people were inclined to believe you when you put yourself in a bad light. He was apprehensive anyhow, even though he'd rehearsed himself. What to say. How to act. He'd been over all that, checking the angles. But there were tightropes in his head and not one was entirely secure.

'You braked for this rabbit?' Trope asked.

'Stupid, huh?'

'Reflex action,' Trope said. 'Happens.'

'Still pretty stupid,' Samsa said. 'A rabbit. Jesus Christ.'

'You need medical attention?'

Samsa said, 'I broke a tooth and my shoulder's probably bruised. Nothing serious.'

'You might want a couple of X-rays to be on the safe side.' Trope turned his flashlight on Samsa's face at a considerate angle. 'Let's take a look at this car.'

They went down into the wet field and walked to where the overturned Chrysler lay against the tree. Samsa had turned off the headlights earlier.

Trope peered inside the wreck, working his flashlight into black crannies. *Looking for booze*, Samsa thought. Samsa hadn't drunk more than a mouthful of the vodka and he'd disposed of the broken bottle. He'd fly through any sobriety test, if it ever came to that.

'You're a lucky guy,' Trope said, and strolled round the car. 'So you overturned and slammed down the slope and traveled – what – about five hundred yards. I seen people croak in cars that looked a damn sight better than this. She's pretty smashed up.'

Samsa said, 'I guess my number wasn't written on this one.'

'With your kind of luck you ought to play the State lottery this week. Course, maybe you used up all your good luck right here.'

Samsa saw his dark muddy hands by Trope's flashlight, and streaks of dirt on his suit. He gazed at the big tree, the naked bruise where the branch had snapped off. He heard the sound of the girl's scream inside his skull and for a moment imagined he saw her trapped in the car.

He'd dreamed all that in a nightmare and now he'd come out the other side and everything was going to be okay. Everything was under control. Right.

Trope asked, 'You got any idea what time you skidded off the road?'

'Ten, maybe,' Samsa said. 'Earlier. Later. I'm not sure.'

'You called in at ten fifty-three.'

'I wasn't exactly thinking about time,' Samsa said.

'That's understandable,' Trope remarked. 'It's not important to be one hundred per cent precise. This is just for the incident report.'

'I used my cellular phone to call. But my watch is busted.'

'So you go off the road around ten and you report the accident at ten fifty. You black out for a while?'

Samsa said, 'I guess so. I don't remember much after slamming into the tree.'

Trope, who had an Adam's apple the size of a mandarin, again wrote something in his notebook, which he held protectively under his slicker. 'Where were you headed?'

Samsa hadn't expected this question. A cop being nosy, he figured. Gathering and storing snippets of intelligence for future reference. You never knew what might come in handy. Trope the trooper, doing his job.

'I was just driving around. Thinking. You ever do that?'

'I do my thinking in bed mostly,' Trope said.

Samsa had a sudden fierce urge to say to Trope, it was like this, Fred. Something happened. But Trope didn't have a confessor's face, and Samsa saw no chance of understanding there. Nor absolution.

'I need to see some ID,' the trooper said.

Samsa took out a wallet from the inside jacket pocket where he also kept his phone. He showed his driver's license. Trope looked at it, gave no sign of recognition. *He's a new kid on the block*, Samsa thought.

'I think the best thing is for me to drive you home nice and safe, Mr Samsa.'

'I'd appreciate that,' Samsa said.

'Sure you don't want to stop at the County Hospital first?'

'I don't think it's going to be necessary. But thanks anyway.'

444

They walked back across the field, and Trope placed a hand under Samsa's elbow, as if he expected him to collapse suddenly on the way up the incline. *I might just do that*, Samsa thought. The night was filled with invisible weights and burdens and they pressed down on him.

They climbed to where Trope's car was parked on the edge of the blacktop. Trope held the front passenger door open and Samsa got inside. He inclined his head against the back of the seat and tried to think his way into another state of mind. A well-regulated place where gravity wasn't defied and cars didn't slam down inclines and doors didn't burst open.

What you need is instant amnesia.

He turned to the trooper. 'You must have been cruising pretty close,' he said. 'I was expecting city cops.'

'I just happened to pick up on the call. I was in the vicinity. I've only been on the job two days, so I wasn't sure if I should leave this for the boys downtown.'

Two days and you're keen, Trope. Samsa shut his eyes briefly when the car moved forward. He didn't want to look out across the big field.

He looked anyway.

The land, some twenty acres clogged with weed and dandelion and untrimmed shrubs, and bisected by the blacktop, belonged to a family called Purchase who'd lived in the state since the turn of the century. It was used by people walking dogs, trysting lovers, kids firing air rifles, nocturnal junkies. He'd heard that the city council had tried to procure the property from the family with the intention of turning it into a park. But the Purchases wanted more money than the city could afford. It was a wilderness.

Beyond the trees that marked the boundary of the land he could see the lights of the Chackstone Acres subdivision, which was screened by a cedar fence. The houses

445

were too far away for anyone to have heard anything. Too far away for anyone to have *seen* anything either, unless some amateur astronomer happened to be adjusting his telescope. On an overcast rainy night like this?

The only telescope was the one in his imagination.

Trope said, 'You want to give me directions, sir?'

'Sure.' Samsa leaned forward. 'Turn round first chance you get. Go back toward downtown. I'll direct you from there.'

There was a wasplike hum in Samsa's head. *I wasn't thinking straight.*

I wasn't thinking at all.

He clenched his hands in his lap and listened to the rain drumming on the car, imagining it falling through the branches of the tree and over his ruined car and all the way across the tangled field to the subdivision, and beyond that into the deepest stretches of the night. His thoughts were all wild stampeding horses.

5

LEE BOYLE WALKED ABOUT A MILE, HIS MOOD FESTERING. HE passed steel-shuttered store fronts and a building site surrounded by a high fence. Urban renewal. There was no doubt some of Daddy's money was involved in this prettification. Hugh, bless his glacial heart, had built a pyramid of investment corporations and subsidiaries, through which he owned shopping malls in Alabama, a dumb country-western theme park in Tennessee, a marina in Southern Cal, and fuck only knows what else. Hugh's money was insomniac. It buzzed day and night, swelling as it moved.

All I need is a lousy twelve grand, Boyle thought. Which is beer money for old Hugh. Twelve grand! He'd used the cash borrowed from Plumm to settle some long outstanding debts, the bulk of it to dealers, but also his landlord, collection agencies and sundry other demanding bastards.

On a plot of flattened land a crowd of bums huddled around a blazing oil can that sizzled in the rain. People with sodden newspapers folded on their heads. One old guy with a sad broken umbrella. Boyle glanced at the flames. *If you're not careful, this is the kind of place you might end up.* It was the kind of thing Hugh would have said in the days when he acknowledged his son's existence.

He found a payphone, stuck a quarter in the slot and called Rudy Vass.

Rudy Vass said, 'I was just about to truck on over to your place.'

Boyle explained he was stranded.

'I'll come get you,' Vass said. 'Tell me where you are.'

Boyle mentioned the location, then hung up. He waited in the grubby glass phone booth. *While I sheltered in this archway from a day of driving showers.* He couldn't remember who'd written that. Sometimes things escaped him. He smoked cigarettes and wondered about Almond. Occasionally she disappeared for a day. Now and then she had an all-nighter. But she was supposed to have met him in Chang's. Where the fuck was she?

He didn't like to think of her wandering beyond his lines of demarcation. He had boundaries, strictly imposed. One time she'd said, 'You want to keep me in a goddam straitjacket, doncha?' He'd laughed and slapped her straight in the mouth, because what it all came down to in the end was control. She couldn't just go dancing off into the darkness unless it was on his say-so. You had to lay down the law every now and then.

His Nikes squelched. His green silk bomber jacket, acquired from a mail-order company by means of a bogus credit card, was ruined. Water from his gold necklace dripped down his chest. He suddenly thought about The Kid, popped another coin inside the slot and punched the numbers. All he got was an answering machine with The Kid's faggoty drawl. 'I can't come to the phone right now. Don't hang up without speaking. Your call is

448

important to me, so please leave a message and I'll get back to you. Pax.'

Pax. The Kid was damn hard to reach. He'd need to go over there, wait outside The Kid's apartment. But he didn't have time for hanging around, he needed to score, he needed hard cash. And quick. Like now.

Rudy Vass's battered pick-up appeared. Boyle climbed inside the cab, which smelled of damp dogs. Wet dog hairs stuck to his black jeans. 'You want to invest in one of those deodorant tree-shaped things you hang on the mirror, Rudy.'

'The smell get you down? Funny, I don't notice it.'

Vass, a lean man with a goatee that gave him the look of a redundant hippie, changed gear and the old pick-up groaned. Empty beer cans rattled around in the back, where Vass kept a puzzling array of stuff: rope, a winch, hubcaps, discolored tools, dog bowls.

'Your place?' Vass asked. 'I got the goods.' He tapped the breast pocket of his leather jacket.

Boyle thought, *Tempting, very tempting*. He looked at the empty streets, scanning for Almond. Here and there the feeble lights of a bar or coffee shop burned.

'There's a guy I want to see first, Rudy.'

'Who?'

'Crassman.'

'Crassman? That guy with the funny leg?'

Vass snorted into a suspect old handkerchief he'd pulled from his pocket. He had a bronchial problem exacerbated by the fact he didn't look after himself. Boyle had once tried to impress upon him the merits of vitamin supplements. 'Fuck vitamins,' Rudy had said. 'Vitamins are so goddam bourgeois. Only the demented want to live for ever.'

'That raunchy trailer park,' Vass said. 'I hate going over there.'

449

'Take a few minutes, that's all. You got a gun on you?'

'Yeah I got a gun but—'

'It's only for show, Rudy.'

'Guns are never only for show,' Vass said. 'Forget Crassman, Lee. Let's go to your place and do this shit that's burning a hole in my pocket.'

Boyle said, 'It'll keep.'

Vass revved up the truck and drove through a variety of suburbs to the trailer park where Crassman lived in a camper shell supported by cinderblocks. He'd attached a half-assed wooden extension to it, which he used as a kind of living room. You didn't need planning permits for anything at Shadow Oaks. The place was a poorly lit slum filled with a jumble of trailers, campers, pick-ups, jeeps. There were always snot-faced screaming babies here, oversized women in baggy cheap floral dresses, and a range of animal life, some domestic, some not.

'This is the pits,' Vass said. 'Makes my place look like a goddam show home.'

'Everything's relative,' Boyle said. Vass lived in a converted gas station. He'd turned the interior into a workshop, and when he needed cash he carpentered furniture in blond Scandinavian style and sold it.

'Over here,' Boyle said.

Vass parked outside Crassman's place. A mutt chained to a metal pole barked a couple of times and then was silent. Shadow Oaks gave Boyle the impression he'd entered the sludge at the bottom of American life. You looked at the windows of campers and trailers and you couldn't help feeling that the people inside were busy rehearsing heavy family traumas – incest, repressed rape memories – in case they got the call from Oprah.

He stepped down into mud. Vass followed him reluctantly along the path to Crassman's front door. A light was visible in the wooden extension.

450

'You bring the gun?'

Vass patted his jacket. 'I'm a walking felony, man.'

Boyle slapped his palm on the door.

Crassman was a long time answering. The door opened a slit. The man's face was tiny and oval, his nose sharp. He reminded Boyle of a cross between a human and a ferret, the offspring of a bestial coupling.

'Why, hey, Lee,' Crassman said.

'Bad night,' Boyle said, and shoved the door and stepped past Crassman. Shrugging, Vass followed.

'Let's go inside this living room of yours,' Boyle said. He kept moving. The camper shell was cramped, the ceiling so low you had to stoop. The extension wasn't much higher. It had a sofa and an old velvet armchair. A lava lamp bubbled on a wooden packing crate.

'Look at this, Rudy,' Boyle said. 'When did you last see a lamp like this baby?'

'I read someplace they made a comeback,' Vass said. 'You don't keep in touch with trends, Lee. Retro, they call it.'

'You saying Crassman's at the cutting edge of style?'

'I don't know shit about style,' Crassman said. 'I got it at a garage sale.' He rubbed his hands together nervously. He had a gloss of sweat on his upper lip. 'Figured it was kinda nice. Cost me two bucks.'

Boyle picked up the lamp and watched the colors expand. 'You think it's nice, Rudy?'

'I covet it,' Vass said.

Boyle set down the lamp and surveyed the room. The paneled walls were buckled and the air smelled of kerosene. Copies of *Ring* and *Hustler* were scattered here and there. Crassman's fly was halfway open.

'I hope we didn't interrupt you in any self-administered five-fingered massage,' Boyle said.

Crassman tugged up his zipper. 'Nothing like that, Lee.'

'Tell me, sport,' Boyle said. 'How's your wallet?'

'Things ain't so good,' Crassman answered.

'How bad are they?'

'This leg's been acting up.'

'Oh, yeah, right. The hunting accident.' Boyle looked directly into Crassman's eyes. 'You ran into a stag with an Uzi, I remember.'

'Ha ha. You know damn well I shot myself in the knee,' Crassman said. 'Rainy weather affects it, Lee. So I can't go out and find work.'

'You never worked in your life. You're a welfare artist.'

'Now, Lee, that ain't exactly true—'

'You know every welfare scam going.'

'They tightened up on all that,' Crassman said.

'My heart is bleeding,' Boyle said. 'How about you, Rudy?'

'I'd be crying in my beer if I had one, Lee.'

Boyle stared at Crassman. 'It's payback time, sweetheart.'

'I'm not in a position—'

'Don't fuck with me,' Boyle said. He wondered if Plumm felt this way, if he had this same kind of exuberance going through him when he threatened one of his tardy debtors. This little rush of power you felt when you knew you had somebody by the balls. 'You owe me one thousand dollars, which I was foolish enough to loan you three weeks ago because you said you had this deal with a quick turn around that was going to net you *beaucoup* bucks. And my thou was going to grow like some magic mushroom into fifteen hundred overnight. Funny thing is, you don't answer my calls, you don't show up at my place with cash, you don't phone.'

'It didn't pan out, Lee. Some things went wrong.'

'Figures. So how much can you pay back?'

Crassman looked trapped and miserable. 'God's honest truth, I'm down to my last twenty.'

'Twenty? *Twenty?*'

Crassman tugged a crumpled bill from his back pocket. 'Here. Take this on account, Lee. Go on. Take it.'

Boyle knocked the bill from Crassman's outstretched hand. 'Pass me your gun, Rudy.'

'Lee, come on,' Vass said. 'Let's blow this place.'

'Give me the goddam gun, Rudy.'

'Gun?' Crassman asked. 'You don't need no gun, Lee. I swear I'll get the bread for you.'

Lee Boyle took the gun from Vass's hand and pointed it at Crassman's head. Crassman's expression was a mixture of despair and incredulity. Boyle poked the end of the barrel into Crassman's chin. *There was a pecking order of things*, Lee Boyle thought. Plumm picks on me. I pick on Crassman. Who does Crassman pick on? His mutt in the yard? A few harsh strokes of the whip?

'Twenty's a fucking insult, Crassman,' he said.

Rudy Vass made a clucking sound of disapproval. 'Be careful with that gun, Lee.'

'Give me one good reason I shouldn't just blow this roach into the promised land, Rudy,' Boyle said. He pushed the gun into Crassman's larynx.

'Because homicide's a very bad rap,' Vass said. 'Just take the guy's twenty, Lee.'

Boyle smiled at Crassman. 'So, Crassman. Do I take the twenty or pull the trigger? You see my dilemma.'

'I can raise another hundred tomorrow,' Crassman said. 'Somebody owes me, Lee. He's good for it.'

'I hate this shit. Somebody owes you. You owe me. I owe somebody else. I swear to God, I really hate these chains of debt. I gave you a grand in good faith. You exploited my generosity.'

Lee Boyle increased the pressure on Crassman's throat. 'Down on your knees, champ.'

'Good Christ, Lee,' Crassman said.

'Down.'

Crassman went into a supplicant's position. *This was it*, Boyle thought, *the undiluted essence of glee*.

'Please, Lee. Look, I can probably raise two, two hundred tomorrow.'

'Spare me the mumbo-jumbo,' Boyle said.

'Maybe even three. I don't know yet, I gotta do some chasing around.'

Lee Boyle struck Crassman's skull with the gun in a swift downward motion. Crassman pitched forward, covering his head with his hands and whimpering. Boyle stepped back. It wasn't enough. He felt unfulfilled. He grabbed Crassman's collar and hauled him halfway up, and this time hammered him with the butt of the gun across his nose. It made a hard cracking sound, steel on bone. Blood flowed from Crassman's nostrils. Boyle drove his knee into the guy's chest and Crassman slumped to the floor.

'This is only minor violence, Crassman,' Boyle said.

'Lee, forget it,' Vass said. He'd picked up the twenty and was holding it out to Boyle.

Boyle ignored the offering. He grabbed Crassman's hair and yanked it, forcing the man's face up into the purplish light from the lava lamp. He picked up the lamp and brought it down on Crassman's head and the glass cracked and warm colored liquid spurted out. The light went out and now the room was lit only by a bare bulb overhead. Crassman lay face-down in a small pool of his own blood and liquid from the lamp.

Rudy Vass said, 'This is a bad scene, Lee. Come on.'

Boyle squatted alongside Crassman, and with the tip of his finger opened the guy's left eye. 'I'm taking the pitiful twenty, Crassman. But if you don't call me tomorrow with some good news about a sizeable installment, you don't get off so lightly in the future. *Comprender?*'

Crassman's eyelid fluttered.

Lee Boyle gave Vass his gun back and went outside to the pick-up. Vass came behind him, blowing into his handkerchief. They got inside the truck.

'That was cruel, Lee,' Vass said.

'Yeah, well, I'm desperate,' Boyle said.

'You were crazy to invest in any scheme of his.'

'A moment of unjustified optimism, Rudy.'

'You know what I think? You don't like your life. That's what I think.'

'So it's not exactly a pleasure dome.'

Vass drove for a mile in silence. Then he said, 'I remember a time when you wouldn't even have considered doing that violent shit.'

'In my glorious yesterdays,' Boyle said. 'When I was a college boy and the world was all sunshine and I could get high on Keats and Shelley. When I didn't need substances. Yeah yeah yeah. *I am not the buoyant thing I was of yore*, quote unquote.'

'Fuck it. Let's just get wasted, Lee.'

Boyle thought about Crassman's blood, streaks of which dampened the twenty-dollar bill he held in his fist. Blood money.

'Yeah. Let's do exactly that.'

6

SAMSA ENTERED THE HOUSE QUIETLY. HE WENT AT ONCE UP to his bathroom, where he removed a bottle of painkillers from the medicine cabinet and shook a couple out into his hand. He dropped them on the tiled floor, stooped to gather them up, swallowed them with water. Then he swirled Listerine round in his mouth, and when he spat it out he saw dark metallic pieces of an old filling.

He tried to avoid his reflection in the cabinet mirror. Blood had darkened and dried on his lips, and there were bruises and streaks of dirt on his face. He was white and unrecognizable, his eyes lackluster, as if somebody had turned out the lights behind them. His thick graying hair was wet and plastered flat across his skull, and his cheeks, normally full, appeared deflated.

This doesn't look like me. This isn't Greg Samsa.

He took off his shoes, undressed, stuffed his clothes in a closet alongside other garments he'd gathered to take to the dry-cleaners, then stepped inside the shower, where he worked a lather of warm soapy water into his face. He scrubbed his hands and fingernails briskly again and again with a small hard-bristled brush, and ran shampoo through his hair. Wash, dry, put on a robe – it was a series of steps and tiny performances. Pantomime. Doing normal things. Looking the part. He was operating in a haze and it terrified him, and he couldn't allow himself to feel that way.

He heard Darcy's voice beyond the bathroom door. 'Dad?'

He said, 'A minute, honey.' He knotted the belt of the robe before he opened the door.

'You look bad. Are you hurt?'

'You should see the car,' he said.

'*Seriously*. Are you hurt?'

He placed a hand on her shoulder. 'I could use a drink.'

'What happened exactly?'

'Skidded,' he said. 'Off the road and into a field.'

'Where?'

'You know the old Purchase property?'

'What were you doing over there?'

'Just driving,' he said.

'I bet you were driving too fast. You always do.'

He thought how little he could see of Harriet in her. She had his coloring, his very dark-brown eyes, the same slightly stubborn set of mouth – but softer, infinitely more attractive. It was as if Harriet's involvement had stopped at the birthing process. She'd left no mark on this girl. Here's our daughter, Greg. She's all yours. I'm empty now. And she'd stayed that way.

They walked downstairs to the living room. He went to the liquor cabinet and poured himself a large cognac, noticing the Scrabble game on the coffee table. 'Nick gone home?' He needed to make small talk. Where you didn't have to think. As if you were concussed.

'A few minutes ago.'

He swallowed some of the brandy. He sat down, and

457

the room rushed at him all at once as if it had turned over just like the Chrysler. He was dizzy and faint and felt like an astronaut inside a space capsule. There were inversions, strange flips, optical illusions. A voltage spike on the graph of perception. Photographs turning over, Harriet's lovely face upside down on the mantelpiece, the hands of the clock hurrying backwards.

His fingers shook. The brandy in the glass rippled. He closed his eyes. What he saw behind his eyelids was the shallow pool of water and the broken branch and something black flapping in the air like a predatory bird, eyes lethal.

'Are you really okay?' Darcy asked.

'A little shook up. It'll pass.'

'I'll call Pascal if you like.'

'I don't need a physician, honey.'

'How do you know you don't? There might be internal bleeding or something.'

'I'd know,' he said.

'Okay, okay. I'm only trying to help.'

How can you help, dear Darcy?

He opened his eyes. The room had readjusted itself, but seemed to exist precariously in an unfamiliar dimension. Darcy began to stack the Scrabble tiles inside the box. He watched her. Fifteen, full-breasted, suffused with the confidence of youth and yet riddled at the same time by insecurities, the whole all-out nuclear rage of her hormones. Fifteen, a young woman, time flying away, and Nick Mancuso sniffing round her. He felt love and sadness simultaneously.

He finished his cognac. He needed another to blunt his mind.

'Your hand's shaking,' she said. 'Maybe you should take a tranquilizer.'

'What I need is another brandy,' and he rose to pour himself one.

It happened then, a zap out of nowhere, a crushing sensation around his heart, breathlessness. He reached out, supported himself against the liquor cabinet, thinking coronary, meltdown in the aorta. *Does she have parents somewhere wondering about her? In some faraway house in another part of the city, another part of the nation, were two people waiting for the phone to ring and a daughter to say, Hi, I'm fine, I'm doing okay?*

He raised the bottle. He could hardly hold it.

'Here,' Darcy said. 'I'll do that. You'll spill it all over yourself.'

He watched her pour into his glass. He said, 'That's a miserly amount.'

She added another tiny drop. 'It's all you're getting.'

'Come on,' he said. 'This is cruel and unusual punishment for a guy that just survived a car wreck.' He attempted to infuse a certain flippancy into his tone, but it was like trying to maintain a shuttlecock of lead in the air.

'Drink it slowly. I'm going to find you a pill. There's some upstairs.'

'Darcy, I don't want a pill,' he said.

But she was already gone from the room and he could hear her hurrying up the stairs. He imagined her rummaging in the medicine cabinet among the tablets Harriet used to take. He wondered why he'd never gotten round to throwing the entire pharmacy out. For the same reason he'd kept all her clothing, all her jewelry, he supposed. Whatever that reason was called. Something the heart stoked up. The demands of love, the deranged idea that you kept the essence of the person by hanging on to their possessions – as if one bright afternoon she might just materialize under a halo in the doorway and say, Sorry I left you alone this long, my love. He didn't need this and he didn't need to look up at Harriet's photograph either, goddamit – that oval face and those solemn eyes with melancholy secrets hidden in them, things she'd never explained, couldn't have explained, monsters trapped in the dead-end labyrinth of her mind.

You drifted from me, he thought. *And I fill the cold emptiness any way I can.*

Darcy came back in the room. 'Here.' She was holding out a pill to him. 'I'm not sure it's the smart thing to take it with brandy,' she said.

He looked at the sky-blue tab. It was called Limbitrol, he remembered. It was only one of a bunch with names that rolled easily off the tongue. Elavil and Surmontil. They sounded like futuristic candies. Here, kids, chew these down. Try some Prozac while you're at it. They'd done nothing for Harriet except drive her deeper into that impenetrable pocket where she'd lived her life. He placed the pill in his mouth and swallowed it with brandy. Quickly. He didn't want the taste of it.

The telephone was ringing. The sound, shrill and un-expected and yet so goddam commonplace, went through Samsa's head like a vibrating ice pick. Darcy answered, then handed the phone to him. He heard Eve Lassiter's voice.

'The grapevine's buzzing. You hurt?'

'No. I'm fine.'

'This is what comes of driving on slippery roads in the rain,' Eve Lassiter said. 'You were brooding again, right? You were in a funky mindset and not paying attention. You took your eye off the ball, didn't you?'

'I confess.'

'What you need is a refresher course in careful driving.'

'Is this going to be a nag, Eve?'

'A half-nag, I'd say. Not the whole thing. If you were feeling low, why didn't you call me? Tell me it just never crossed your mind.'

'It never crossed my mind,' he said.

'A hundred times I've told you, Greg. You feel low, you phone me. You never listen.'

Samsa could hear noises in the background. A jukebox, the click of pool balls. Eve was having a late drink in a bar she liked, because she said she enjoyed the attentions of the young studs that hung out there.

'Go back to your beer and your boys,' he said.

'I'll come over if you need company.'

'I'm going to sleep.'

She was quiet for a moment. 'Okay. Sweet dreams.'

He put the handset down.

'She's got the hots for you,' Darcy said. 'She sees you and her mouth just kind of hangs open.'

'The hots? *Eve?* I don't think so.' He pulled his daughter toward him and held her, smelling a trace of herbal shampoo in her hair.

'You're going to meet somebody one of these days,' Darcy said.

'It's only been a year,' he said. 'One year ago to-morrow.'

'I'm having a problem breathing, Dad,' Darcy said.

He released her. 'I think I'll go upstairs,' he said. He kissed her cheek.

She asked, 'You sure you're okay?'

'Yeah. Don't worry about me.'

He went up to his bedroom, climbing slowly. His shoulder ached and he rubbed it. 'Sweet dreams,' Eve had said. Tell me how.

Restless, he rose and walked the room for a time. *His shoes. He had to do something about his shoes.*

He heard Darcy in the kitchen, the clack of a plate in the sink, water running. Then she was climbing the stairs to her own room. Her door closed. She sang a couple of phrases of some popular song. She had a good clear voice, but now the sound struck him as discordant, like an untuned harp randomly plucked.

He waited, then went inside the bathroom, where he picked up his shoes, carried them down to the kitchen and wrapped them inside a plastic bag he found in a drawer. He stepped out of the house. He dropped the bag in the trash can, rearranging garbage, concealing the bag under a pile of withered carrots and browned lettuce leaves and ancient celery. He stuck the lid on the can, went back inside the house and climbed once again to his bedroom. *I'm thinking like a goddam criminal.*

He walked to the window and parted the curtains and looked down into the street. Empty. A couple of lamps shining between the trees along the sidewalk, a nocturnal suburb. He watched the still scene for a while, expecting – expecting what?

He didn't know.

Something bad. Something that formed in the shadows.

He let the curtain fall from his hand and sat on the edge of the bed. Then he pressed his knuckles to his lips, as if to hold back a cry rising inside. He lay on his side and tried to eclipse everything from his mind. A process of emptying himself, draining the battery of his memory until it was dead.

7

RUDY VASS SAT ON BOYLE'S SOFA AND SAID, 'NOW THIS IS what I call great shit.'

Boyle was peering through the slats of the blind down at the street below, feeling the edge of paranoia he associated with speed that had been stepped on. He strummed the slats with his fingertips and chewed on the inside of his mouth, where he had a tiny ulcer. He'd been forgetting his vitamin regime.

His apartment was situated over a pawnshop protected by steel shutters and a state-of-the-art alarm system. Directly below he could see three brass balls glistening in the rain. 'It's cut with something. I don't know what,' he said.

'No way,' Vass said. 'It comes from my regular guy.'

Vass's regular guy was a postgrad chemistry student named Stretch, who paid his tuition by making up batches of drugs – speed, downers, hallucinogens – now and again.

'I'm too jittered,' Boyle said. His pulses were at the races. His head was out of touch with the rest of him.

'My guy doesn't mess around with his basic recipe,' Vass said.

'Then how come I'm feeling like this?' Boyle asked.

'Maybe it's your mood.'

'My mood's okay.'

'Not from where I'm sitting, Lee. That number you did on Crassman. That was *unreal*, man. There's a mean streak in you wasn't ever there before.'

Boyle popped a can of Coors and gulped it back. He studied his answering machine, stared at the zero in the little message window. Almond was out there somewhere. The rule he'd laid down was for her to call him every three hours, no matter what. He hadn't heard from her since – since when? Yesterday afternoon? The idea she might have acted independently was an insult to him.

Rudy Vass sipped from a bottle of Southern Comfort. 'You want to sit, calm down a little.'

'I don't know why I shoot myself up with this shit when it gets me so goddam *amped*,' Boyle said. He let his arms hang at his sides, loosened them up, did a couple of neck rolls.

'Drink some of this, take the edge off,' Vass said.

Boyle took the bottle and sipped. It tasted sour. He set it back down on the coffee table, which was littered with paraphernalia. Rigs, a little plastic baggie of speed, a few sparkly crystals that had spilled. There was a packet of Rizla and a small vial of Lebanese grass and a half-dozen tabs of pink downers made up by Stretch to a formula he'd concocted himself. The shooting-works to take you into orbit, the calming agents meant to restore equilibrium. Sometimes they didn't work and you just zoomed into a place in the ether, where you were frazzled and unglued.

Vass was rattling on about his opinion of Boyle's life. 'You want to bring your problems into focus and get a handle on them, Lee. Once upon a time, as I remember, you were going places. You had smarts galore. You might have become a fisher of men.'

'You're going to tell me where all that good stuff vanished. Right?'

Vass tugged his beard. 'You developed a fondness for this drug. You started to get like you just don't give a fuck about any goddam thing: where you're headed, what you're doing. You could still build a whole new life for yourself, Lee. I'm looking to give you advice. We go back a long way, you and me. Eleven years.' Vass ticked each item off on his fingers. 'One, give up the drugs, clean up your act. Two, this stuff with the chick. Set her loose, Lee—'

'Set her loose? She brings in around two thou on a good week, Rudy.'

Vass had veined eyelids and his cheeks were sunken. His pallor was like classroom chalk dust. 'It's a moral consideration. I remember we outlawed slavery way back. Lincoln et cetera.'

'Slavery my ass. She does her thing for me willingly. I tell her, do this, do that, she does it. I don't call that enslavement.'

The telephone rang. Boyle picked it up at once. He expected it to be Almond, all sweet and contrite. Instead he heard a man's angry voice.

'I been waiting at this hotel an hour for your girl, Boyle. Where is she?'

Boyle couldn't think a moment. 'She didn't show?'

'If she showed, would I be calling?'

'I don't understand,' Boyle said. Losing his grip here. Had he made an appointment for Almond through one of the phone services? He couldn't remember. His mind was in hyperdrive. He didn't even know this guy's name, and the voice was strange to him. He had the glimmer of a suspicion that maybe this call was some form of sting operation engineered by the vice cops. They were always trying to set up capers that were forever being tossed out

465

of court on the grounds of illegal entrapment.

The guy said, 'I'm out of here in ten minutes if she don't show. And I'll tell you this, Boyle, it's the last time I contact you. This is a waste of my time.' The guy hung up.

'Your little chickadee didn't keep a date?' Vass asked.

'Apparently not.' Boyle walked round the room, trying to remember. But it was gone. Slipped down some crevice. *Jesus. Where do lost memories go anyhow?* He checked the view again, a forlorn street of shuttered storefronts and apartments poised above them, and everything seemed to pulsate feebly like a light flickering on and off in a dying man's eyes. He didn't belong here.

'How much does she keep out of what she earns?' Vass asked.

'Enough.'

'You throw in what, nine or ten grams of *el cheapo* coke a week? You buy her some clothes now and then, you feed her when she feels like being fed, maybe some pocket money. Most of the time she's too zoned to give a rat's ass.' Vass sucked on the Southern Comfort and dragged his shirt cuff across his lips.

'She does all right,' Boyle said.

Vass said, 'It blows me away, Lee. The blue-eyed boy turns pimp.'

'That's a loaded word, Rudy.'

'It's your fucking *job* description. How would you describe what you do?'

'I'm in the lubricants business.'

Vass laughed. 'You're still a pimp. You lost your way. You detoured down some weird highway, and now you don't know what the hell you're doing with your life. I mean, you're even entertaining some weird-ass notion about going into the blackmail business with that guy you call The Kid, whatsisname. That is totally off the wall, Lee. And then there's this money you owe to Plumm,

466

who's a ghoul. I swear I saw him in *Friday the Thirteenth Part Three*, man. When I think of the way you used to be . . .'

Boyle tuned Vass out. This was the point when Vass usually started to ramble about the old days. How he and Boyle met at the U of Penn, where Boyle was skimming through Eng Lit like a genius and Vass was losing his struggle with the mysteries of physics. How Boyle, despite his high grade-point average and his penchant for asking intelligently contemptuous questions at lectures, was obliged to drop out in his freshman year because Daddy Boyle didn't like the inauspicious reports of his son's activities, which included such misdemeanors as stealing the dean's car and screwing the dean's daughter in the back seat of it, no less. A dishonorable discharge from academia for young Lee, and no more of Daddy's money for future scholastic purposes. Vass himself had quit school after a weekend retreat, when he'd tuned into a message from a Nepalese guru. Set yourself free, young man, walk away from the chains of organized education.

So I took up my hammer and saw, Lee. And I kept on drugging. Ah, sweet Christ, I wish I'd been at Woodstock. Born too late. Vass kept coming back to this speech every time he was speeding.

Boyle, cresting the crystal arc at a slippery point, was thinking about that phone call again. If it was a set-up, it meant his name was in somebody's black book. He thought about a sleazy vice cop called Stephen Rebb who'd hassled him a few times in the past. Maybe Rebb, an altogether objectionable character, had set something up. Lee Boyle didn't like this possibility. He tried to maintain a very low profile. He wasn't one of those movie-type caricatures in a long fur coat and blinding jewelry and a broad-brimmed hat and bimbos hanging on both arms.

467

He picked up his telephone and unscrewed the mouth-piece.

'What are you doing?' Vass asked.

'I'm wondering about bugs, Rudy.'

'As in *listening* devices?'

Boyle nodded. He looked at the wiring. What could you tell from that? A listening device could be anywhere: under a table, inside a lampshade, in his bedroom. He had an urge to start dismantling things, stripping them down to basics. He'd get his screwdriver and go into the ventilation duct. Take apart the answering machine. On one level he understood this was speed causing havoc. On another it was all very real.

'Lee, nobody's got your place bugged.' Vass took the phone out of his hand. 'There's nothing wrong with this goddam phone. You're small change in the big network of sexual commerce, man. The idea of anyone taking the time and trouble to bug your apartment, hey, that's down-right laughable.'

Boyle walked to the sofa and sat and drummed his fingertips on his knees. He tapped one foot rapidly on the floor. He couldn't quit doing it. Moving, shaking, tapping. He flashed on The Kid, pictured his sweetly cut sandy hair, those floppy fag sweaters he always wore with the sleeves rolled up to the elbows, his ever-so-nice manners. *I'll get you something solid, Lee, it just takes a little time.* He thought about phoning him, but even though Vass had said the telephone was okay, Boyle didn't trust the god-dam thing.

'Pop one of those pink babies,' Vass said.

'This shit's cut with something,' Boyle said. 'I'm telling you, Rudy.'

'Just take one of the pinks.'

'How do I know what's in the pill?'

'Don't go all funny on me now.'

Boyle stuffed his hands in his pockets and rattled coins vigorously. 'I ought to go out looking for her. Hanging out here's a waste of time.'

Vass said, 'Let's just stay right where we are, Lee. She'll show. You know she'll show.'

'What if she doesn't?'

'Then you're out of a bad business. Or else you'll have to get yourself another girl.'

Boyle listened to the rhythms of his blood and the wild timpani of his heart, and he wondered if this speed was taking him to outer space. It was a long trip back from there, crashing down through one depressing level after another. Grinding your teeth, chewing the inside of your mouth, pacing up and down.

'Tell me this,' Vass said in a quiet voice intended to soothe. 'You ever get it on with this girl?'

Boyle's scalp was tingling. It's all too much now: huge rushes of unfocused energy, thoughts that don't gell, collisions between what's real and what's not. Bugged rooms, people watching from the shadows of doorways, Revenue guys going through his canceled checks on microfiche at the bank, special warrants signed by judges – you could imagine the whole works.

'Well? Did you?' Vass asked.

Boyle scratched his head. 'No. I never did. But I was sorely tempted.'

'You had the will-power to resist.'

'You don't mix business with pleasure.' He remembered seeing her step out of his shower, and her supple little nut-brown body glistening with water, her hard flat stomach damp. She'd looked at him standing in the doorway. 'You like what you see? Come on, Lee. Do me.' And so he had, right there on the bathroom floor among damp towels, a sweet grappling, not once, twice, but three times. His own desire was a fever. And if she was faking passion, she was one hell of an actress. 'I don't do this for the tricks, Lee. This is special.'

Why had he lied to Vass about it? Some vestigial shame? *I don't feel shame*, he thought. Shame's what happens when you hand a megaphone to your conscience. And conscience was a loud-mouthed luxury.

Vass was quiet a moment. 'What age is she?'

'She could pass for twenty,' Boyle said.

'Yeah, but how old is she?'

Boyle stood up. 'You stay here if you want. I'm going out.'

'Wait—'

'Don't stop me, Rudy.' He was all haste now, looking for a jacket, shoes, rummaging around. It was important to hit the streets. When I find her, she's in serious trouble.

Vass said, 'You didn't answer my question.'

'Okay. Thirteen. One three.'

'*Thirteen?* Unlucky number, man. Real evil vibes.'

8

THE MAZE OF BASEMENT ROOMS BENEATH CITY HALL ALWAYS
smelled of mildew. Damp infiltrated everything. Papers
curled round the edges and folders felt gummy to the
touch. Eve Lassiter had once found a fuzzy white mold
growing on the wall behind one of the old-fashioned
steam radiators. It became known in the department as
The Blob. For a while it was an object of curiosity and a
certain indignation. Sergeant Duff had taken a Polaroid of
it with the intention of showing it to the mayor as proof
of the inhospitable conditions in which the city's downtown cops were obliged to work. But the fungus had been
forgotten in the flux of business.

Samsa found himself remembering the growth, thinking it might be expanding there still. He had an urge to
get up from his desk and check it out, but instead he
shifted papers from his in-tray to his out and back
again. The muscles at the nape of his neck ached. That
morning, shaving, he'd seen blue and yellow contusions
on his shoulder, a whole map of discoloration as sharp
as a new tattoo. The thought had occurred to him: *I*

carry a bad sign on my body.

He rose, walked to the water-cooler, filled a dixie cup, swallowed a couple of aspirins. He was conscious of activities going on all around him – John Cullinan, an odd soul with a haunted look, muttering to himself at his desk, 'People don't have a fucking clue what it's like down here, what the hell ever happened to the new building the so-called city fathers promised.' Duff politely talking down the phone to some lunatic, 'You say you actually saw your husband being beamed up inside this craft, Mrs Gogarty, and the craft had a swastika sign on it. So what is it, like a Nazi from outer space?' Fogue lighting up one of his foul cheroots in flagrant disregard of the department's no-smoking policy.

Babble echoed down the interconnecting rooms.

Samsa went back to his desk, which was partitioned off from the hoi polloi. *Three hundred and sixty-five days ago. A year almost to this very moment.* He sat, gazed at some paperwork, feeling detached from his purpose in this place. Overhead, the fluorescent strip hummed. No natural light penetrated these rooms.

Eve Lassiter put her head round the door. 'Surprised to see you this morning, Lieutenant. Shouldn't you be taking it easy?'

'Why? I'm functioning.'

'I hear the car was a write-off. You look like a write-off yourself.'

She was tall and slim-hipped, thirty-three years old. She wore her red hair straight to her shoulders. She had green carefree eyes – some Irish filtered through her ancestry. You could imagine her playing a harp with those long fingers. Around the department she'd acquired a minor reputation for picking up younger men in a certain bar she frequented. Samsa considered this rumor for the most part macho talk down among the lockers. So she had a casual dalliance now and then, that didn't make her a nymphomaniac. She was young, she had appetites.

Needs. He knew about needs. Where they led you.

'I slept badly,' he said.

'You sound a little off-key,' she said.

'I keep thinking . . .' He paused. There was a doorway here he couldn't open in a hundred years. He wanted to, he wanted to go inside that room and say, 'This is what happened, Eve. Try to understand. I took a very wrong turning.' It was the same feeling he'd had with Trope.

'Thinking what?'

'That car. I see that car slamming off the road.'

'Post-trauma,' she said. 'You'll have flashbacks.' She approached the desk. 'I have a suggestion. Why don't we have dinner at my place one night?'

'We'll do that,' he said.

'I'm not being pushy or anything. But when do you have in mind?'

He shrugged. 'Some night next week.'

'I've heard of pulling teeth. What night?'

'Whenever—'

'Enthusiasm would be a step forward, Greg.'

He raised a hand to his head. Pick a day. Any day from the deck.

'Wednesday,' he said.

'Okay. Seven suit you?'

He nodded. She said, 'I do good Creole. Tex-Mex, if you like that. I can cook. Really.'

'I believe you, Eve. I look forward to it.'

She leaned across his desk. She looked very young suddenly. He imagined her as a teenager, gawky and unco-ordinated. She spoke in a quiet voice. 'Know something, Greg? There's this sad streak in you that really bothers me.'

'Sad streak?'

'I'm not saying it very well, I guess. A kind of lost quality. You're like an explorer who's mislaid his compass.'

'You want to mother me, Eve?'

'Shit, no. I'm not the mothering type. And I don't ever fall for any of that little boy lost jazz. I only want to feed you. I think you need it.'

'You can feed me Wednesday then.'

'Deal.' She turned to the door, then stopped. 'The Leeson case, by the way. I'm meeting with a guy whose phone number we found scribbled on a scrap of paper in Leeson's bedside drawer. I'm heading out to see him now. He didn't sound exactly over the moon to hear from me. Why don't you come keep me company? You look like you need just about any old excuse to get out of here.'

Samsa thought about Anthony Leeson, a retired pharmacist who'd been stabbed to death a couple of nights ago by an assailant in a frenzy. Zane, the coroner, had counted twenty-four stab wounds. The murder had all the hallmarks of a homosexual-related slaying. Leeson's neighbors were quick, indecently eager even, to point out that he'd often been seen bringing young boys back to his apartment.

'It's your case, Eve,' he said.

'I could use some help with it.'

He was reluctant. He wanted to stay behind his desk and shuffle papers and keep his head down until kingdom come. He'd given the Leeson case to Eve because he'd been entangled in other matters, and, anyway, he knew she was capable. There had been thirty-two homicides in the city during the last four months. It didn't compare with certain other cities, but it stretched the resources of the department.

Samsa spent too much time juggling manpower and schedules and asking the chief, Al Brodsky, for more qualified people. 'I've talked to the mayor,' was Al's stock response. The mayor's response was also stock: 'I'll look into it and get back to you, Al. It's a matter of money we just don't have at this point in time. We went way over budget building the new precinct house on the East Side, and refurbishing the South Side was more than we bargained for. You know how it goes, Al. The city's impoverished.'

Yackety-yack.

The mayor's idea had been for the bulk of the downtown cops to be moved to the new East Side precinct, but the building, incompetently constructed, had problems with the refrigeration system, the elevators were unreliable, the sewage pipes constantly backed up, and – a true brilliancy in planning – an inadequate number of phone jacks. Samsa remembered a time when the department had thirty precinct houses throughout the city, but policy – which he thought misguided – had dictated closing these houses and cramming as many cops into as few boxes as possible. Bigger boxes, sure, but better service?

A fortune spent nationwide on extra cops, on new jails. But very little of it seemed to be coming this way, to the hub downtown, this fetid basement that housed a total of 233 cops in the course of different shifts. This hell.

Eve said, 'I could use your input. You're sharp when it comes to assessing what people say. I'm still a little naïve.'

'Naïve? *You?* I don't really think so, Detective.' Samsa got up anyway, took his jacket from the back of his chair and slowly followed her. Naïve wasn't a word that came to mind in connection with Eve. She was sharp and persistent, qualities that had led to her promotion to detective only last year. Okay. She wants your company. She thinks you need to get out. And you don't have the energy to resist.

Fogue, a plump bald figure blowing perfect thick smoke rings, looked up from behind his chaotic desk and said, 'Hey, Lew Tenant.' Fogue always made Samsa's rank sound like a man's name. 'Heard you lost your bearings last night.'

'I had an accident, Billy,' Samsa said.

'You ever hear the theory there's no such thing as an accident? I read this guy, forget his name, says accidents are things you actually want to happen. No kidding.' Fogue laid a hand on his heart.

'Bullshit,' Cullinan said. 'All I hear in this place is bullshit. All I smell in my nostrils is this damp.'

'Hey, it ain't my theory, Cull. Can I help it if I'm well read?'

To the tune of 'Smoke Gets In Your Eyes', Cullinan sang to himself, 'Damp gets in my bones.'

Fogue said to Samsa, 'Seems you go out actually *looking* for accidents. Least, according to this guy I read.'

'The man cracks open a book and listen to what comes out,' Samsa said. 'One thing he hasn't read is the No Smoking sign.'

'Unconstitutional discrimination,' Fogue said. 'I belong to this group. Rights of Smokers in America. ROSA. We're fighting back against all those puritan clean lungs suckers.'

Samsa moved toward the stairs that led out of the basement. Eve walked just ahead of him. She had a loose-limbed motion, hips swinging just a little, her ass firm under her tailored black slacks. He thought, *I've never looked at her before from this perspective.* A little surprised, he lowered his eyes.

Fogue called out. 'Anybody searching for you, Lew Tenant, what'll I tell them?'

'Say I'm up to my neck,' Samsa said.

'In what?'

Samsa didn't respond. He listened to the sound of his footsteps click on the old marble floor of the entrance to City Hall, with its high neo-Gothic ceiling in need of a paint job. Upstairs were courtrooms and the DA's office and the mayor's staff. The place was riddled with dry rot and the marble was engrained with dirt, and in winter the outmoded boiler failed to send heat through the veins of the building.

Outside on the street he felt clamminess in the sunshine. It was one of those mornings when the atmosphere would agitate asthmatics and swamp-coolers stifle rooms. *Say I'm up to my neck*, he thought. That would be the truth.

Eve tugged his arm. 'You coming or not?'

He must have been standing motionless without realizing it. He had to prevent traffic jams in his head. Curtail them somehow. The plan, if he really had one, was simple: concentrate on what he was doing at any given time, rein in wayward thoughts and dispel tiny seizures of drift. It was more than just going through the motions. It had to be an act of belief. He had to get inside the memory banks and delete whatever he didn't need.

Accidents are things you want to happen.

He didn't believe that for a moment, because it implied some kind of ludicrous collusion between himself and a hapless jackrabbit on a highway.

He found himself moving slowly through the molasses of air. His mind was filled all at once with alternatives too late to deploy. *She was a hitch-hiker I picked up.* But she didn't look like a hitch-hiker. She looked exactly what she was. There would be suspicion, innuendo.

Okay. She was a hooker. And that's against the law.

Yeah, but why this particular hooker out of so many, Lieutenant? Why did she catch your eye?

She was somebody I was bringing in for questioning.

In connection with what, Lieutenant? What particular

case? Did you suspect her of something? Let's hear your story for the record.

'Greg,' Eve said. 'Are you orbiting the planet or is there some way I can connect with you? You're miles away.' She unlocked her car. 'You *sure* you didn't bang your head last night?'

'I'm sure,' he said.

She sat behind the wheel. Samsa lowered himself into the passenger seat. He felt the car slide forward out of the parking lot. He thought, *Maybe all our lives are lived through acts of dishonesty. The only way we cope is by lying to ourselves.*

He turned to look at Eve. 'I'm a good cop,' he said.

She glanced at him. 'Is that a question?'

'I've always been a good cop. It's all I know how to do.'

She said, 'What is *bothering* you?'

'Maybe it's a mid-life crisis.'

'Maybe it's loneliness,' she said.

He looked through the window. The city rose in a haze of towers, stacks of concrete and glass. In the downtown acre of greenery called Patriot Park, there was a birdshit-smeared monument to the man, Barnabas Sullivan, from Limerick, who'd first built a settlement here in the wilderness in 1835. All that energy and optimism only to have your effigy covered in droppings. Welcome to neglect.

It was still a fucking wilderness out there. It was just the savages that were different now.

Eve said, 'I didn't have any right to say that, Greg. About loneliness.'

'It's probably true,' he said.

'It's none of my business. I've never lost a spouse. I can't even imagine what that grief must feel like.'

Grief, he thought. Grief was like plugging into a connection that ripped the heart out of you. It was a demon

478

you hadn't summoned, but it came without invitation, a gargoyle that gatecrashed your life.

Don't dwell on this. You don't need it.

He continued to gaze from the window. They were driving through an area on the edge of downtown that was seedy, old warehouses and dilapidated factories. It was a grim neighborhood. Early twentieth-century signs were still barely visible in dirty brick: 'Carstairs Mattress Manufacturing Company'. 'McPherson's Grain & Feed'. The area was known as Flesh Row. Sometimes Skin Street. At night this was the neighborhood where bodies were traded, boys and girls pacing round under weak street lights and cars cruising back and forth. This was the place where you came if you were lonely and your appetites had gone beyond any consideration of consequences.

'I'd like to see all this razed,' he said. He heard a little note of anger in his voice. 'I'd like to see them come in with a crew of wreckers.'

'No way. It's historic. If anything, they might pump some money into cleaning it up and preserving it. It has character. With a little work, maybe a few cafés and bookshops, it might even have charm.'

'Charm? I doubt it. It's always going to be sleazy.'

'Let's agree to differ,' Eve said.

She patted his knee a second. 'And, yes, you've always been a good cop. In my book, the best.'

'Thanks,' he said.

'Dignified and emphatic,' she added.

'Enough already.'

'And honorable.' She smiled. 'I hope I grow up to be just like you.'

'Yeah? Just be careful what you hope for, Eve.'

9

IN GINNY FLAGG'S BEDROOM, DARCY SAID, 'I THOUGHT YOU were supposed to be sick.'

'I am sick,' Ginny said.

'You don't look it.'

'I feel fluey.'

'Sure you do. You haven't prepared for Hump's test, have you?'

Ginny Flagg, a tiny girl with a red-dyed streak in her cropped black hair, took off her glasses and wiped them on the edge of the bedsheet. 'All that geography stuff is too, I don't know, blah. Like I need to know the capital of the Ukraine? I don't know where the Ukraine is even.'

'It's a former Soviet state,' Darcy said before she could stop herself.

She had a memory that was sometimes a curse. Everything got stored automatically inside her head. She could remember the names of minor actors in forgotten B-movies. She could tell you the line-up of rock bands and who split to form another group. She remembered all the things they crammed into her at school, even when they weren't interesting or useful. Lately she'd begun to let her mind stray in class, as if to spite this gift of recall. Besides, school had started to drag on her – the gossip, the day-after-dayness of it all. She'd found herself daydreaming and drifting, impatient to put the whole place behind her and move on to something else, even if she didn't know what.

Something exciting. It had to be that, at the very least.

Ginny's bedroom had black walls and glossy yellow furniture. The blinds were drawn, giving the place the feel of a cave.

'You on your lunch break?' Ginny asked. She ripped a pink Kleenex out of a pop-up box on her bedside table and held it to her nose.

'Yeah. I thought I'd just drop in and catch you slacking.'

'I am not slacking.' Ginny smiled and put her glasses back. She had a face like a myopic pixie. 'I was watching a video actually. Wanna see?'

'I don't have time.'

Darcy glanced at her watch. She supposed she could skip PE and get back for Hump's test. Ginny zapped the remote. A videotape clicked into play. Darcy looked at the TV in the corner.

'He's dreamy,' Ginny said. 'He's still the dreamiest babe imaginable.'

James Dean in *Rebel Without A Cause*. Darcy remembered that Ginny belonged to a group in school called The James Dean Appreciation Society, a cult of about ten girls who were enraptured by images of a dead man. They met regularly to watch the few movies Dean had made, and on the anniversary of the actor's death they wore black clothes and mooned around sadly and held a day-long wake. She could see Dean's appeal up to a point, but not the way Ginny did.

'Tell me he doesn't turn you on,' Ginny said.

Darcy shrugged.

'Come on. Look at those eyes. Look at that mouth.'

Darcy said, 'He's okay.'

'*Okay*? He's got something Brad Pitt doesn't have. He's got something Val Kilmer would *murder* to have,' Ginny said. 'You just want to get him in bed and make love for hours and then, when he's hungry afterwards, you'd scramble him some eggs and bring them on a tray. Like a love slave with an offering.'

Darcy stared at the screen. She thought Dean too moody, as if he was in a place he could never be reached. Maybe that was his attraction on celluloid. He was aloof, mysterious, and his death in real life had added to this allure. Now he was truly inaccessible.

'I'd be his love slave,' Ginny said. 'He'd only have to snap his fingers and boy I'd be there. Who am I kidding? He wouldn't even *need* to snap his fingers. He'd only have to give me one of those real cool looks of his and I'd wither, I swear to God.' Lips slightly parted, Ginny gazed at the picture, then pressed the remote and froze the image. 'Look at the way he wears his jeans. The way he stands, kinda hunched like that. If that's not a turn-on, I don't know what is. Okay, so it's Fiftyish, it's ancient, but that doesn't take anything away from the guy.' Ginny sighed and laid a hand on her heart. 'He's immortal. He's like some god. He knows something you don't. He's got secrets. You just wish he'd share one of them with you. He's so goddam romantic it's practically *unbearable*. It ought to be outlawed, for Christ's sake.'

Darcy propped her elbows on her knees and leaned forward. The static image of Dean flickered a little, traversed by lines of video interference.

'You also get the feeling he knew how to treat a girl,' Ginny said. 'He had to be a great lover.'

Darcy remembered reading somewhere that Dean was either homosexual or bi, but this wouldn't have made any difference to Ginny or her fellow members of the Appreciation Society. He was beyond criticism, beyond judgement. Beyond death even. The eternal lover. The endless dream. She could see the romantic strain in this notion. The guy you could never get. The one wasted before his time. The tragic figure.

'Is Nick a great lover?' Ginny asked suddenly.

This question bothered Darcy. It wasn't Ginny's curiosity, but more the casual assumption behind it. Nick and Darcy, Darcy and Nick. They were a couple, they had to be making out on a regular basis.

'Why don't you ask him yourself, Ginny?'

'Yeah. Right. I'll just walk up to him and say, ' "Hey, Nick, how are you in the sack?" '

'Maybe he'd answer you.'

Ginny plucked a Kleenex from the box. 'He's studly,' she said. 'I know a few girls that think so.'

'But I'm the lucky one he picked,' Darcy said.

'I hear a funny little note in your voice, Darce.'

'Like what?'

'Like you're not absolutely sure what you feel about this thing between you and Nick.'

'I guess maybe I don't,' Darcy said.

'Hey, if you ever dump him, let me be the first to know.'

Darcy smiled and looked back at the screen a moment. 'I have to run,' she said.

'Run,' Ginny said, and touched the remote. James Dean's image was reactivated. 'Who needs you for company anyhow? I have my boy, Jimmy.'

Darcy let herself out of the house. The noonday heat was a heavy shroud that hung over everything. She moved along the sidewalk, dragging herself through the humidity in the direction of school.

Get educated, her father had always told her. Like he really believed it was a key to some bright shining future. Ever since her mother's death, though, he'd lost a lot of his interest in her report cards. He'd lost interest in a whole bunch of things. Over the past two months he'd taken to driving alone at nights, never saying where he'd been when he returned, or whether his voyages into the dark were work-related or some solitary nocturnal way of killing time.

He'd become a mystery.

And last night he'd crashed, and this morning he'd been weird, scowling into dead space over his coffee, then for no apparent reason playing silly knock-knock jokes with her. Oscillating between moods, between sounds and puzzling silences. These were signs of some kind. Was he falling apart a year after his wife's death as the recognition finally socked him that he'd never see her again for as long as he lived?

But then she hadn't been present in any real sense for years before her death. She'd lived in a zone of withdrawal. Physicians had run brain scans that revealed no abnormality. Then they'd put her on drugs. But nobody had a connection to her head or what she was thinking. Her father had spent a great deal of time trying to coax her back into the world. He'd sit for hours on the edge of the bed and stroke her hand and whisper to her. Harriet had gazed vacantly into the distance most of the time. Sometimes at night she walked through the house like she was in a dream.

One time Darcy had found her in the kitchen and she'd asked, 'Is there any way out of this place?'

You found a way in the end, Darcy thought. She drew a hand across her sticky forehead. She thought about Eve Lassiter, whom she'd met a dozen times and liked. Why didn't her father just get it on with her? Why didn't he grasp the fact, so obvious to Darcy, that Eve had a *thing* for him?

She reached the entrance to the school, then stopped. She realized she didn't give a damn about Hump's test. She turned round and walked away.

10

LEE BOYLE DRANK THREE CUPS OF COFFEE IN QUICK SUC-
cession inside a café downtown. It was located in a new
pedestrian precinct cobbled in red stone, fancy black
wrought-iron street lamps here and there, flower boxes,
boutiques galore.

He was sweating under the whirring ceiling fan and
conscious of potted ferns made to sway by the breeze of
the blades. A minute ago he'd thought somebody was
watching him from behind, but when he swiveled his head
all he saw was one of the ferns shimmering. He wondered
about plant sensibilities – a random notion that just
chugged into his head.

He sucked urgently on sugar cubes and smoked cigarettes and made an inventory of his long trawl through the
city. Here, there, looking for Almond. Clubs, late-night
dives. Nobody had seen her.

He remembered going back to his apartment at some
point and opening the *Yellow Pages* and calling round
motels and hotels, asking if they had a guest called
Almond – which was pointless, because she wouldn't be

registered under that name. She wouldn't be registered at all. Night clerks tended to hang up on him when he started to describe her – beautiful little girl, about five-two, maybe eighty-five pounds, dark hair, kind of Latino looks, you'd remember if you ever saw her. But nobody wanted to get into long telephone conversations with a guy that sounded desperate and incoherent. *Well, fuck you, I happen to be looking for a missing person*. Click. Dead connections.

Somewhere in the course of all these phone calls he'd also tried to contact The Kid, but he didn't get anything except the answering machine again. He left a message instead of just hanging up. 'Hey, this is Lee. You got anything I can use? I need something, man. Anything. Get back to me.'

He'd snorted more of Stretch's powder, instead of mainlining, and it had burned his nasal passages like he'd inhaled Comet, but *Jesus!* the boost was there. Then he'd gone out and walked around some more in the dawn light, driven by manic energy, but the dives were all closed and the kind of people who might have seen Almond had gone underground. They were people of the night, couldn't hack sunlight, vampires. He'd left messages everywhere he could. Tell her to get in touch. Like immediately.

What he needed was sleep. But his mechanism wasn't even *close* to shutting down. He knew this condition. Restless, marginally demented. He tapped his fingers on the table.

The waitress, a fat girl with healthy rose-colored cheeks, came with the coffee pot. 'Another refill?'

'Sure. Why not.'

She leaned over and poured into his cup. He had a desire to engage her in conversation, but she'd already drifted away among the greenery. He drained the coffee and left, walked back in the general direction of his apartment.

Almond. *Beautiful little girl, about five-two, dark eyes.* He had only to snap his fingers – like so – and she'd do whatever he wanted. Because she adored him. Because he was good to her, in his fashion. But strict, because she needed that.

He turned a corner and entered a street of derelict office buildings. His mouth was dry. He knew if he looked at his tongue it would be the color of coffee. He came to a cross street and popped inside a bar, thinking of ice-cold lager going smoothly down his throat. It was one of those Irish pubs of the 1930s immigrant school, dark and unfriendly – no plastic shamrocks here, no furry little leprechauns for tourists who'd lost their way.

He asked for a Heineken. He drank half of it, *aaah*, then scanned the clientele, a few pre-noon dark-faced boozers, who sat hunched over their drinks like men communing with private gods. He finished his drink, ordered another, chugged it. He liked the glorious icy feel.

He noticed a payphone by the door and he thought, *Why not? Why the hell not? Because he despises you. He sees you as a wastrel. Somebody down the tubes. A young man who didn't know what to do with the silver spoon.* In his present frame of mind, one of whirlpools and agitations, Boyle wasn't convinced that these were sufficient reasons, so he fished coins out of his pockets and went to the phone. He remembered the number, dialed it. He felt a great surge of confidence suddenly, above the hubbub of everyday life.

'Yes?' Always the same brittle response.

'It's Lee here.'

A silence you could cut with a chainsaw. Lee Boyle imagined his father behind the big walnut desk inside the fancy house on Cable Hill. The high-ceilinged rooms, cornices restored by craftsmen imported from Milan, antiques up the ying-yang.

'Lee,' Hugh Boyle said. The tone was deep-freeze.

'I just thought I'd give you a call,' Boyle said. 'It's been a long time. Last time we spoke was at Monique's wedding.'

'How dare you bring up Monique's wedding?'

Trying to ease his way back into his father's favor, Boyle realized he'd need one of those ice-cutting ships that negotiated the Antarctic. 'We talked about stuff.'

'What "stuff" exactly did we talk about, Lee?'

'I remember you—'

'Stop. Let me tell you what *I* remember. You got outrageously drunk and fell face-first into your poor sister's wedding cake. You brought with you – entirely uninvited, I might add – a couple of underdressed young women of dubious vocation, and that wretched crony of yours, Vann, Vass, whatever he's called. Your little crew then proceeded to disgrace itself. Do I have to go into detail? There was blatant evidence of drug-taking in a bathroom. A valuable hand mirror was shattered. Sexually explicit graffiti was lipsticked on walls. Sums of money and credit cards mysteriously disappeared from the pockets of coats in the cloakroom. I am not speaking of an isolated prank, Lee. I'm looking back over an entire history of misdemeanors, some of them utterly appalling.'

'You ought to let all that water flow under the bridge,' Boyle said. 'It's past. It's gone. I've changed my ways. I've just spent weeks in a rehab clinic. I'm clean. I've been doing social work.'

'I think I've heard this one before. It's the angular approach to asking for money.'

'Did I mention money? Did I *mention* money? You're the one that brought it up. Not me.'

'You're an embarrassment, Lee.'

The jay makes answer as the magpie chatters. W. Wordsworth. It was weird what kept coming back to him across the years.

'Goodbye, Lee. Don't call again. Do you understand me?'

'I need a little help here, I'm tapped out, I'm having difficulties, it would only be a loan, you'd get it back at twenty, twenty-five per cent interest, I *mean that*.'

He was talking into a disconnected line. He slammed the handset back in place, raging. He cut me off. His only son. An embarrassment. Well, screw you too, Hugh. You'll get yours.

He must have been speaking very loud because the drinkers were watching him. He returned to the bar. He was burning up.

The barman said, 'You okay, fella?'

'Nothing a chilled brew won't cure,' Boyle said.

The barman, who had fat tattooed arms, slid a green bottle across the countertop. Boyle felt the urge to talk to this guy, explain his outburst on the phone. 'I don't get along with my father,' he said. 'Oil and fucking water.'

'Mine's dead,' the barman remarked.

Boyle leaned across the bar. 'You know what name he gave me when I was born? Huh? Lee Harvey Boyle. Lee *Harvey*. You carry that round and see where it gets you. You know why he did it?'

The barman shook his head slowly. 'Tell me.'

'Because Lee Harvey Oswald shot John F. Kennedy, which made Oswald a big-time hero in my father's book. He hated Kennedy. Loathed him.'

'The name's a weight all right,' the barman said.

'Fucking right it's a weight.' Boyle felt spit gather like cotton at the corners of his lips. 'My fucking sister, little Miss Precious, she gets Monique, ooh la la, and what do I get? Huh?'

'It's a hard road any way you travel it,' the barman said.

Boyle poured his lager into his glass. He wanted to forget Monique, and all of his family, but sometimes Monique's face came drifting up to him, out of the shallows of memory, pale and pretty and utterly despicable. Her and her fucking wedding to that geek stockbroker type called Austin Arganbright. What kind of name was that? It sounded like a goddam mouthwash.

He said to the barman, 'All I want is *Love in a hut, with water and a crust*. Keats. You know what I'm saying?'

'Keats,' the barman said, like a man chewing on an unexpected bit of tofu.

Boyle took a great swallow of his lager, then asked, 'Where's the toilet?'

The barman pointed to the other side of the muggy brown room. Boyle crossed the floor, entered the john. It was scented with pine, but that didn't disguise the fact that somebody had recently taken a highly fermented dump in one of the cubicles. He unzipped, leaned against the urinal, cursed his father.

Lee Harvey Boyle. The gunman in the book depository in Dallas.

He looked at the stream of his urine. *That goddam Almond*, he thought. *Had she just upped and left town? That was like giving him the finger. He'd get to the bottom of it. He'd track her down. She wasn't getting out from under him. And if she thought that—*

'Hey. You. Bright boy.'

Boyle, lost in his roiling thoughts, hadn't heard anyone enter the john. He turned his face round. There were two guys. One was tall and ponytailed and wore a leather jacket, the other was short and thick-necked with an off-center mohawk that gave his skull the look of a lopsided skunk. Bad hairdos, both of them. The one with the

491

slanted mohawk was carrying a lead pipe, maybe a foot long.

Uh-oh. Boyle zipped up quickly.

The guy in the leather jacket had a severe case of acne. 'You know Vern Crassman, I understand.' He had a country twang to his voice, maybe hick Kentucky. It was a voice Boyle associated with mangy dogs, tar-paper shacks, haggard old women shucking corn.

He turned from the urinal. He was thinking rapidly. 'Crassman,' he said. 'Vern Crassman. Umm. Do I know Vern Crassman?' He glanced at the lead pipe. Mohawk was holding it against his side and emitting unambiguous rays of impending brutality. From the corner of his eye Boyle realized the john had no window. Ergo, no escape route. So it was down to him and these two bad-looking hillbillies Crassman had despatched. The prospect of pain sizzled in the air.

The one in the leather jacket said, 'You hurt Vern, buddy.'

'There might have been a minor fracas, I guess,' Boyle said. 'Some kind of misunderstanding.' He wondered how long this pair had been following him.

'A fracas,' the guy with the lead pipe said.

'Yeah, a fracas,' Boyle said. He looked at the squat man, who was overweight and probably ponderous in his movements. He was the kind of guy who always got the heavy shit to lift when you needed something moved. Here, grab this grand piano, Mohawk Man. All dumb strength, a real grunt.

Boyle walked to the washbasin and turned on a faucet. Thinking, thinking. He wasn't going to be able to schmooze his way out of this situation because neither of these guys looked like a good listener. They'd been sent by Crassman and they were here to redress the balance of things, plain and simple. Violence begets violence.

The one with the ponytail suddenly grabbed the lapel of Boyle's jacket.

Boyle said, 'Take care. This is an Armani, friend.'

'It don't look it.'

'Like you'd know?' Boyle asked.

'Armani. This is a fucking rag, what it is.' The guy tugged hard, bringing Boyle's face close to his own, affording Lee Boyle a close-up of acne pits, pustules, blackheads. It was like the surface of some hostile planet.

Boyle pulled his face back. He heard stitches pop in his lapels and he was aware of the squat fellow with the lead pipe coming up from behind.

This is total squalor, Boyle thought. *Violence in this shithole.* He knew there was a better life. If this was the best the human condition had to offer, somebody had a whole lot to answer for.

He said, 'I do judo. Be warned.' It was worth a try.

The mohawk snorted. He probably thought judo, like Armani, was another fashion designer, a Jap one.

The lead pipe was raised in the air and coming hard and fast toward Boyle's skull. He reacted without any thought, because the time for thinking was past, everything was measured in microseconds, and the idea of a lead object embedded in your head concentrated your goddam mind like nothing else. He made a great effort to free himself from the grip of the guy in leather, twisted his face to one side, and the pipe whoomed past his head and crashed against the sink, cracking the ceramic. Boyle saw his lapel come away and saw the guy in leather holding a strip of what had once been a fine jacket. So the jacket was a write-off, but on the plus side he was free, he could move now, he could act. He felt energy come up from his feet and rush through his body. He was spiked.

The mohawk made a snarling noise and drew the

pipe back up a second time. 'Judo my pecker,' he said, and the pipe began its spooky descent.

Boyle's perceptions were suddenly unlimited, as if he'd just become plugged into an all-encompassing awareness he never knew existed. He was conscious of a flood of brilliant light. Watching from a place above, he saw himself bring his knee up into the pipe-wielding guy's groin and, in almost the same instant, headbutt the one in leather and watch him stagger back against one of the urinals, while the mohawk – squawking – was doubled over like a constipated man with his asshole stitched shut. The pipe had rolled out of his hand and Boyle bent down to pick it up and whacked it against the mohawk's head. Next he turned to the guy in leather, who was crouched in a urinal, holding his face in his hands as water flushed automatically down the tiles and diluted his blood, turning it pink like the juice from certain grapefruits.

What the hell. Sweating, heart roaring, Boyle smashed the guy's kneecaps with the lead pipe.

The guy went all the way down. His mouth was open but nothing was coming out. He was in that place where pain made you mute. Boyle turned and gazed at mohawk, who was flat on his back and gazing up at the ceiling with a deeply dazed expression. He wasn't seeing anything except maybe his own private planetarium.

It was a moment of huge satisfaction. *Incalculable* satisfaction. Boyle pondered some extra violence, but decided the best idea was to blow this place entirely. He tossed the lead pipe inside one of the cubicles, walked out the john and through the bar to the street. He went several blocks in his ruined Armani, but, hey, what was a jacket? You kicked ass, Lee. You took the pair of them and you *destroyed* them. What you ought to do next is go over to the trailer park and have a word with Vern Crassman. Surprise the hell out of him. See Crassman cower.

494

It was only when he'd made it back to his apartment that he felt the symptoms of collapse. He looked at the drugs on the coffee table and contemplated the notion of dabbling in just a tad more, enough to get him through the rest of the day so he could continue to look for the bitch.

Runaway.

His hands were wet and they'd begun to tremble beyond all social acceptability, and when he shut his eyes he could see that lead pipe smash the mohawk's head and he could smell the rancid stench of the toilet. *You got lucky*, he thought. *It could have gone the other way: your skull caved in, your all-American looks demolished.*

He went inside the bathroom, dipped his face under the cold-water faucet. The inside of his mouth tasted foul. He walked back into the living room and surveyed the crystals of speed.

You don't need it, Lee. Yes you do. That little nagging voice in his ear.

He wandered to the answering machine. The message window read '2'. He pressed playback. Almond. Let it be. But the first voice was Jimmy Plumm's. 'I hope I'm not pressuring you unduly, love. But time is passing. Time is indeed passing.'

The second message was uttered in a hushed voice he recognized immediately.

'Lee, you old speed-freak, I hear you're looking for your little Almond,' it said. 'Maybe I can be of some tiny assistance?'

11

EVE SAID, 'I'M DETECTIVE LASSITER. THIS IS LIEUTENANT Samsa.'

The young man, Joshua Gold, stood in the doorway of his apartment and looked defensive. 'I was under the impression you were coming alone, Detective.'

'The lieutenant doesn't bite, Mr Gold.'

Gold held the door open and, frowning, indicated that Eve and Samsa come inside.

Samsa surveyed the living room quickly. An aquarium stocked with salt-water fish occupied one corner. Flutters of yellow and green, translucent flashes. The filter pump throbbed. The walls of the room were covered with photographs of young men, some of them naked, others in briefs. They weren't beefcake shots. They were *artsy*, young guys with broodingly sensitive expressions. On the bottom of each framed photograph was the signature J. Gold in copperplate.

Gold, who wore a purple cotton shirt and white cut-offs, said, 'Sit, if you like.'

Eve sat on a beige leather sofa. Samsa remained standing, watching Gold. He was a pretty kid, Samsa supposed, slim, with very fine hair that he kept sweeping back from his forehead. His legs were suntanned, his feet bare. He wore a slender silver bracelet around one ankle and a small pearl earring. He sat down on the arm of the sofa with his knees clamped together and his long fingers intertwined. Then he got up and walked to the aquarium, where he lounged with a fretful expression.

He stared at Samsa. 'Anyone ever told you you have a lived-in kind of face? Faces are like houses, I always think. Some occupied a long time, others just sort of blank and *totally* without soul. You have soul, Lieutenant.'

'Is that a good or bad thing?' Samsa asked.

'Oh, I think it's good. It's very good.'

Samsa gazed at the young man a moment and then, for a reason he didn't understand, had to look elsewhere. Perhaps it was the way he felt Gold was studying him. Whatever, he was uncomfortable. He looked down at the smooth pine floor, so highly varnished it created reflections. He saw himself there, his image distorted in glossy wood. *I have soul.* Or maybe I traded it away, made a deal with my own personal devil.

Eve opened her notebook and tapped it with a ballpoint pen. 'Let's talk about Anthony Leeson,' she said.

'I told you when you phoned, Detective. I gave him my number. That's all.'

'In what circumstances, Joshua? You ran into him in a bar, something like that?'

Gold was hesitant. He strolled the room, tapping his hands against his thighs.

Eve said, 'I don't have to remind you that this is a homicide inquiry, do I, Joshua? You don't keep information back when it comes to murder. It's not very bright.'

Gold stood still, took a couple of deep breaths. 'Okay. I sometimes go to a certain . . . *risqué* area close to

497

downtown, which I guess I don't have to spell out for you, do I?'

Samsa listened to the filter. He gazed at the fish. Bubbles rose spiraling in the water.

Gold was saying, 'I was very strapped for cash, you understand. I do mean *strapped*. So I did what I sometimes do when the old bank balance goes into the red and that nasty manager writes me shit letters. I know I shouldn't go down there, but I do it anyway.'

'Let's just say you were looking for companionship,' Eve suggested.

'And then what?' Samsa asked, turning to look at Gold.

Gold said to Eve, 'I think your lieutenant is judging me, Detective. I feel a condemnation coming on.'

'I am not judging you, Joshua,' Samsa said.

'He isn't usually the judgemental type, I promise you,' Eve said.

'Well he's certainly shooting me some pretty dark *looks*,' Gold said.

Eve leaned forward on the sofa. 'Just tell us what happened, Joshua.'

'Do I really have to?'

'You have to,' Samsa said. 'Get it through your head.'

'See,' Gold said. '*More* dark looks.'

'Forget my looks,' Samsa said. 'Just answer the questions.'

'I'm not terribly proud of some of the things I do,' Gold said.

'Your pride isn't our concern,' Eve said.

Gold pressed his hands to the sides of his face. 'About a week ago I went down to that particular stretch of town we're talking about and I hung out for a while, which I don't like, because you do get some terribly sick boys and girls round there. There's one girl with full-blown Aids, my God. She's literally *dying* on the sidewalk—'

498

'The point,' Eve said.

'Okay. This green car comes along. It pulls up beside me, I get inside. The man behind the wheel takes me out to his apartment in the suburbs.'

'And this man was Anthony Leeson?'

'Right,' Gold said quietly.

'And you spent how long with him?'

'Most of the night. He was quite a gentleman. I suspect he wanted company as much as, you know . . . And I left, oh, just as it was getting light. He asked for my phone number and I wrote it down for him.'

Samsa stared into the tank of water, and suddenly remembered how her mascara had run. *What the hell did I think I was doing? Where was my fucking head at the time? What lunacy afflicted me?* A terrible fear descended on him. There was pressure behind his eyes. He forced himself to concentrate on the conversation between Eve and Joshua Gold, but he'd missed some part of it already. You have to pay attention. You have to believe the world goes on and you're an active participant.

'So when you went back downtown again on the night Leeson was killed, you saw him, but he didn't pick you up this time,' Eve was saying.

'Right. He drove past, signaled to a boy a little way down the block, and this kid got in the car. And off they went.'

'This kid – you ever see him before?'

Gold shook his head. 'Never. And the next day they found Anthony slaughtered. I read about the knife wounds and I freaked, I just *freaked*. And I thought, *Nobody's safe down there*. Not if there's somebody going round with a knife.'

Samsa said to Eve, 'Let's take him downtown.'

'*Downtown?*' Gold was horrified. 'Am I a suspect?'

'We need a description of the kid you saw, Joshua,'

Samsa said. 'You get to sit in a room with a very patient man who'll show you a book of facial characteristics and you'll tell him what you remember. And he'll come up with a composite.'

'You haven't answered my question,' Gold said. 'Am I a *suspect*?'

Eve said, 'Nobody's saying you're a suspect, Joshua. Anyhow, yours wasn't the only phone number in Leeson's possession. We have to check them all.'

'But nobody's ruling me out either, are they?'

Eve said, 'We're only asking for your co-operation at this stage.'

'At *this* stage? What does that mean? Is there a *next* stage where you try and pin this murder on *me*?'

Eve spoke with great patience. 'Joshua, I have no reason to consider you a suspect. You say you saw somebody get into Leeson's car, fine. I have to take that as a truth unless I find out otherwise. I *could* say it worries me a little that you didn't report the fact you saw Leeson on the night of his death – but I'm giving you the benefit of the doubt where that's concerned. Obviously you don't want it known what you do on your nocturnal jaunts.'

'Damn right I don't,' Gold said.

'And I understand that,' Eve said. 'So let's co-operate on this description.'

'It was so dark,' Gold said. 'I don't know if I can do it.'

'You'd be surprised what you can remember,' Eve said, and closed her notebook. She got up from the sofa.

'When do you want me to do this thing?' Gold asked.

Eve put a hand on the young man's tanned arm. 'How about coming in now?'

'Now? I always visit my mother at lunchtime. She's in St Jude's, poor dear. If you ever need to put your mother in a nursing home, I certainly *don't* recommend St Jude's. The nurses are absolute Fascists.'

'After lunch then,' Eve said. 'Say three? I'll set it up. It won't take more than thirty minutes or so.'

'You're sure this isn't some kind of devious ploy to get me downtown and interrogate the hell out of me?'

'We don't need ploys to do that,' Samsa said. 'Believe me.'

'Okay. Three o'clock.'

Gold showed them to the door. As Samsa stepped past him, the young man said, 'Have we ever met before?'

'I don't think so,' Samsa said. 'Maybe I remind you of somebody else with a lived-in face.'

Gold tapped a fingernail a little nervously against his teeth. 'Could be,' he said. He stood behind the screen door after Samsa and Eve had stepped out.

The interior of Eve's car was like a sauna. Samsa rolled down his window, slipped the knot of his necktie, undid the top button of his shirt. This air was unbreathable. He heard something click in his shoulder and experienced a short thrust of pain. *Have we ever met before?* He felt the pinching movement of dread in his heart. Dread was new to him. He didn't have a place where he could store it.

Eve said, 'I don't quite see Gold stabbing Anthony Leeson. He doesn't strike me as the homicidal-frenzy type somehow. But you just never know, do you?'

Samsa said nothing. He gazed up at the red-brick apartment building. He thought he saw Joshua Gold watching from behind a window on the third floor, but he couldn't be sure.

Eve laid her hands against the steering wheel. 'If I'm wrong, forgive me, but I'm getting the distinct impression this case doesn't entirely intrigue you.'

'Why do you say that?'

'Normally you're more animated. More alert. You didn't seem too interested in Gold. You had an elsewhere kind of look on your face.'

'I don't have high expectations of him, Eve. You heard him. It was dark, and he's not sure he can come up with a description. I don't rate him as a suspect either—'

'That's not the point I'm making, Greg. There's some other thing troubling you. And whatever it is, it's been bugging you all morning. So why don't you just take a chance and tell me—'

'Look, if I wanted advice I'd go to a fucking therapist.' It was out before he could stop it, the snappy remark, the uptight tone. He was sorry immediately.

Eve stared at him with a look of annoyance. 'Fine, *fine*. There's nothing on paper that says you have to tell me anything, Lieutenant. Let's just drop it, okay? I'm sorry I bothered.'

'Eve,' he said. 'We're good colleagues, we're friends—'

'I always thought so.' She turned the key in the ignition.

'Okay. I'm not myself. I've been thinking a lot about Harriet these last few days.'

Eve leaned back in her seat. 'God. It's been a *year*, hasn't it? I totally forgot, Greg. I'm so sorry.'

'There's no reason you should remember this particular anniversary,' Samsa said. 'I've been reliving some things, that's all . . . You know what the worst thing is? I'm never going to know why she did it in the end. For the rest of my life, it's going to be one big mystery. The physicians and the shrinks talked about clinical depression, but that doesn't begin to explain anything, Eve. That's just a god-dam label they hang on something they don't understand.'

Eve touched his hand sympathetically. He looked into her candid green eyes. He could read the message there: share this with me, Greg. He felt fraudulent and cheap. He was stealing from her fund of compassion. Of course he thought about Harriet, because there was hardly a moment when she didn't come into his mind, and he was choked with memories of the better times before she plunged irretrievably into her own black world – but he was cheating Eve by omission.

'I'm glad you told me, Greg. I thought maybe it was something like that. I wasn't sure.'

He shrugged. He had a sense he was melting, changing forms, turning into something else. 'Let's get back,' he said.

She drove most of the way in silence. At one point she talked about what she might cook for dinner next Wednesday, and he understood she was trying to lift his spirits. She had a generous uncomplicated heart.

She parked in the lot behind City Hall. They walked together down to the basement. Eve vanished in the maze of rooms, saying she was going to look for Ross, the guy who put together the faces from his big book of features.

Samsa entered his office and switched on the tiny portable fan on his filing cabinet. He stood close to it, letting the blades blow directly into his face. The air churned but didn't cool.

Al Brodsky, Chief of Police, appeared in the doorway. 'I heard about the bust-up, Greg. You hurt?'

Samsa said, 'Nothing serious. I broke a tooth.'

Brodsky had a big round face and slitted eyes. He was an untidy man, his neckties always loosely knotted and hanging wrong, his suits crumpled, usually a shoelace undone. He was sharp where it mattered, though. He had a mind like a carving knife and a low-key ability to terrify interviewees, whether they were suspects in a crime or cops who'd transgressed. Fogue had nicknamed him Brodsky the Blade, and it had stuck. Samsa had a genuine fondness for the man. Their relationship went back years.

'How are you getting along otherwise, Greg?'

'I'm fine.'

'How's Darcy?'

'She's doing all right at school.' Brodsky's questions, he knew, were not entirely idle. The chief was checking on him, because he wouldn't have forgotten the anniversary of Harriet's death. He'd have it memorized.

'She's a bright kid,' Brodsky said. 'She'll go places.'

'The right ones, I hope,' Samsa said.

Brodsky placed a hand on Samsa's shoulder, an affectionate little contact. 'You're a good father. Always have been.'

Samsa adjusted the fan, but it didn't help. Sweat ran from his scalp down his face.

Brodsky asked, 'How's your caseload?'

'Heavy enough.'

'Anything new on Leeson?'

'We might have a witness. Then again, we might not. There's also the Dell thing, which isn't going anywhere.'

'Homicides involving transients are goddam knots. Drifters kill other drifters, then they just keep drifting right along.' Brodsky leaned toward the fan, running a finger under his collar. 'The Gavency case looks pretty good. I've been reading the reports.'

'It's taking shape,' Samsa said.

'He killed his wife. I don't think there's any doubt. A sweet little confession might be welcome.'

'And we might just get one, Al,' Samsa said. This catalogue of murders dismayed him. He remembered a time when he'd done the work and it hadn't touched him quite this way. Sure, he'd always felt a certain shock when he thought about what humans inflicted on other humans – the extremes of brutality were appalling, deadening – but you dealt with that, you just closed down part of your heart and went about your business. Only it was getting more difficult. It was like a long slope and all you could see at the very bottom was darkness.

Brodsky was observing him. 'We don't have the one-on-ones we used to. We ought to have a couple of beers one of these days.'

'I'd enjoy that.'

Brodsky moved toward the door, then stopped. 'Say. What about tonight?'

'Tonight?'

'Unless you've got something else going on.'

'My calendar isn't cluttered, Al.'

'Your place around eight thirty? I'll bring some of that foreign beer you like. Grolsch?'

'Right.'

'Fine, I look forward to it, Greg. There's something I want to discuss with you anyway.'

Samsa watched Brodsky go out of the room. He stood a few moments longer in front of the fan and then, thinking of Darcy, feeling an urge to talk to her, picked up the telephone and dialed his home number. The phone rang unanswered.

He looked at the travel clock on his desk. Two thirty. It was too early for her to be home from school. He hung up, wondering what it was that Al Brodsky wanted to talk to him about.

12

LEE BOYLE LAY ON HIS SOFA AND HUNTED SLEEP, BUT HE WAS too whacked, too *spun*, and a line of Shelley's kept going round inside his head. *The awful shadow of some unseen Power, Floats though unseen among us.* Tell me something I don't know, Percy.

He heard the sound of his door buzzer. He was drymouthed, and when he rose his legs were stiff. The buzzer went on and on. Whoever the stubborn fucker was down in the street, he sure as hell wasn't going to give up and go away.

Boyle entered the kitchen. Tiled surfaces gleamed and there were no dirty dishes in sight. The pine-top table had been scrubbed. He'd done all this cleaning in an energy fit before trying – fruitlessly – to get some sleep. Buzzing round the kitchen with Spic 'n' Span and two whole rolls of paper towels. He swallowed a handful of vitamins, washed them down with a glass of water. Finally he flipped the intercom switch. 'Yeah?'

'Tom Raseci here. Open the door, Lee.'

'I'm just leaving. I have an appointment.' He looked at

the kitchen clock, a Bart Simpson timepiece Almond had hung. Three forty-three. He had to be somewhere at four-thirty.

'Buzz the fucking door, I said.'

'Is this some rough-house stuff, Tom?'

'The rough stuff don't start until your clock's run out, Lee.'

Boyle pressed the button that unlocked the street-level door. He heard Raseci climb the stairs. Bigshoes. What was he here for? Boyle opened the door and Tom Raseci entered the apartment.

'I never been here before,' he said. He sniffed around, touching this, that, like a goddam landlord checking out the condition of his property. Boyle kept the lid tight on his resentments.

Dressed in an expensive black linen suit, Raseci stared at a couple of titles on the bookshelves. 'What's all this shit you read. *The Mirror and The Lamp*. Is it some kind of thriller or what?'

'I've never met anybody who thought so,' Boyle said. 'It's a book about poetry.'

'Poetry, huh? I wandered lonely as a daffodil, har har.' Raseci tugged a volume off the shelf and flicked the pages. '*Culture and Anarchy* by Matthew Arnold. You got some high-tone tastes, Lee.'

'Souvenirs of a gentler time, that's all.' Boyle hadn't looked at his books in years.

'Hey hey. Now this is more like it. *Confessions of an English Opium Eater*. What is this? Like a how-to manual?'

'You want to come to the point, Tom?'

Raseci sat on the sofa and sifted through the drug para-phernalia on the coffee table. He pushed the hypodermic needle aside with a look of distaste, then rubbed some spilled crystal between thumb and forefinger. 'Speed?

507

Can't get off it, huh? I was hooked on dope one time. Then I discovered Narcotics Anonymous. Changed my life around.'

'My name is Tom R and I am a drug addict,' Boyle said.

'Don't knock it. It worked for me,' Raseci said. 'This shit must cost you.'

'I get high with a little help.'

Raseci held up the baggie in which the crystal sparkled.

'Be very careful with that,' Boyle said. He took the baggie from Raseci's hand and put it in the pocket of his crumpled shirt. He was feeling sluggish, bottomed-out. 'I was just leaving, Tom.'

'What it is, Jimmy Plumm hears the word going round that you've misplaced your little income machine. Which doesn't make him happy. He was figuring maybe this chick would be good for some of the money he's got coming from you. She's a working girl, after all. Not all of the cash, but a little. A thou, say. A gesture of goodwill that might just buy you another day. *Might*. Mr Plumm doesn't really *want* to see you damaged, Lee. I think he kinda likes your face. So it worries him when he learns your main asset appears to have taken a hike.'

'That's street gossip. You don't want to listen to that stuff. I have that girl where I want her.'

'So you say. But Mr Plumm keeps an ear real low to the ground. He's a guy that don't let anything escape him. And what he hears is that you've been running round like a headless chicken looking for your little meal ticket.'

'Untrue,' Boyle said. 'She was doing some high-paid out-call work, that's all.'

'Yeah? So explain how come you been asking for her all over the place.'

Boyle nodded at the table. 'Blame the drugs, Tom. Sometimes they make you forgetful. I sent her someplace, only I don't remember where exactly.' He laughed at his own carelessness. Silly me. He wondered if his lie had any plausibility. Raseci's discolored eye fixed him without expression.

'You're saying she'll be back soon.'

'Right, right.'

The big man rose from the sofa and wandered the room. He gave Boyle the impression that he was looking for something to break, preferably a visible part of Lee's anatomy. 'What I've done in the present uncertain circumstances, Lee, is I've sold your Porsche.'

'Sold it? *Sold* my car?'

'Following Mr Plumm's instructions, you understand. There's a guy paid two grand for it.'

'Sold my goddam Porsche for *two grand*? It's worth seven or eight.'

'There's widespread body rust. The engine needs work. Two grand was the top offer. That cash goes directly to Mr Plumm. Comes off your debt, see. Now you're down to ten. And if your little squaw shows up, let's just hope she has some bread for you. Which you'll hand right over to Mr Plumm. This way the debt is whittled down. And you get some breathing space.'

Boyle thought about his Porsche. He tried to reduce its loss to the simple proposition that it was only a car, just metal and wheels and an engine and shit. That didn't make it any easier, though. He'd had that Porsche five years. And now it was gone, and he was embroiled in the crazy world of Jimmy Plumm's bizarre accountancy system. 'So what are you saying, Tom? I have an extra day on account of the Porsche.'

'That depends on if your girl shows up.'

Boyle felt he'd entered an area of total perplexity. Plumm's world, he understood, was whimsical, his calendar capricious. What Plumm was doing was fucking with

509

his head. You get an extra day, you don't get an extra day. Plumm, fraudulent Englishman, played master of the cosmos. He could give you time, or take it away from you.

'Yesterday I had three days. What have I got now? What's the bottom line here?'

'You're down to two and a bit. That hasn't changed. Unless the girl shows up with an installment. Or, alternatively, you come up with the whole ten grand, which is what is left after taking the Porsche into account.'

'Who bought the car anyway?' Boyle asked. It dawned on him immediately that the question was dumb. He knew the answer and it riled him. He stared hard at Raseci. 'I hope you get into a serious wreck when you're driving it. I hope you become one of those veggies on a life-support system.'

'Tut-tut.' Raseci produced a familiar set of keys from his pocket and dangled them. 'I'm keeping the Porsche keyring too. Comes with the deal.' He rattled the keys in a hugely aggravating manner. Chinkety-chink.

'I have to run, Tom. So if you don't mind?'

'So long as we're straight on a few things.'

'Yeah. We're straight.' Straight as you could be in Plumm's bent universe anyway. Two days and a bit and the sands running. Sweet Jesus. *My heart beats loud and fast.*

Raseci went to the door, opened it. He turned to look at Boyle. 'One last thing, Lee. Don't even *think* about splitting. Because it's a very small world and Mr Plumm has friends in a whole lot of places. See you.' Raseci went out, closing the door quietly.

Boyle stripped, showered, shampooed, gargled with a vile-tasting substance reputed to have a curative effect on mouth ulcers. He took a pair of clean blue jeans and a fresh shirt from his closet, where some of Almond's clothing hung. He fingered the dresses, the skirts. *It doesn't make sense,* he thought. *These things hanging here like this. Abandoned.* A strange kind of loss hit him, made him a touch sad. Where the hell was she?

He brushed his hair. He contemplated shaving, but decided against it. He didn't trust his unsteady hand with a razor. Looking in the mirror, he remembered that years back some drunken old biddy in a bar had told him he was a dead ringer for a long-ago movie star. Tab somebody. Or was it Troy? He couldn't recall. A lot of his memories must be wandering the back roads of his head like lost orphans crying for attention.

He cleaned the drug paraphernalia off the table, scooping it inside a leather shaving bag which he squeezed under the sofa. Then a quick snort of Stretch's crank – *whooo* – and he was out of here. Zip and into the street. No Porsche. No wheels. He felt stripped of citizenship. The disenfranchised American. Take a man's car away, you might as well take his goddam democratic birthright to vote while you were at it.

He looked for a cab, but they rarely cruised this neighborhood. He walked several blocks quickly, then he was into the heart of downtown, passing between office towers. Men and women hastened here and there with briefcases, lawyer types and cops entering the hive of City Hall. *The everlasting universe of things flows through the mind.* He wondered if Shelley had ever shot himself up with speed.

The air he moved through was lifeless. It was like walking inside the cellular structure of a warm wet sponge. He glanced back the way he'd come, scanning quickly for a sight of anyone following him, perhaps a reappearance of Crassman's ruffians, maybe somebody Plumm had tailing him. *It's a small world.* Crowded sidewalks, how could you tell? He skipped past a guy selling hot dogs under a colored umbrella. The stench of onions assaulted him. He

511

turned a corner where a blind man seated on a soapbox was playing saxophone.

He saw the silver and maroon canvas awning of the Rialto Hotel, formerly one of the city's classiest gathering places, but fallen now on tough times. The Rialto wasn't exactly a flophouse, but all its airs and graces were threadbare, and the doorman – who had a rummy's cracked red nose – was missing a brass button.

Lee Boyle went through the revolving doors into the empty lobby. He headed across the faded red carpet and into the coffee shop. It was a big room and there was only one customer and she was sitting in the far corner wearing shades and a black velvet jacket. Her hair matched the color of the jacket. Her make-up was white. She gave Boyle the impression of somebody returned from the grave on a temporary visitor's pass.

Boyle sat facing her. She wore an assortment of crosses round her neck, which were mainly Celtic and chunky.

'Warding off the evil spirits, I see,' he said.

'Plenty around.' She slipped her glasses down her nose and gazed at Boyle briefly before she replaced them. Her eyes were a very pale blue, which he'd always found unsettling, like looking into a couple of dyed ice cubes. 'You look as handsome and edible as ever, Boyle. Save for those dark puffy things under your eyes.'

'I work hard for these dark puffy things, Sartora.'

'I'm calling myself Cass these days, Boyle. As in Cassandra.'

Before Sartora, she'd been Divina. Before that – what? He couldn't keep track.

'You gotta keep altering yourself,' she said. 'I'm a work in progress.'

'Aren't we all?'

'I'm into things like shape-shifting,' she said.

This babe had a quality Boyle found oppressive, and he

512

didn't want to linger discussing her weirded-out belief system, so he didn't ask for details about shape-shifting. He tapped the face of his wristwatch and was conscious of the jerking movement of the second hand.

'I got your message,' he said.

'Oh, yeah, that. The message.'

Don't go vague on me, Cass, he thought. He leaned across the table. The ashtray was crammed with hand-rolled black-paper stubs.

'Are you carrying?' she asked.

'Sorry,' he said. 'I could probably find you something in an hour or so, Cass.'

'I'd appreciate it, Boyle. I really would.'

'No problem. Now this message.'

'Ice,' she said. 'I want high-class ice.'

'I hear you,' Boyle said. *Jesus Christ, tell me about Almond.*

'The best, Boyle. I'm running on fuck knows what adrenalin. And the gauge is way low. So I'm antsy. Also there's an affair of the heart that's a total fucking *disaster*. Which isn't contributing to my well-being.'

'I'll *deal* with it, Cass. Can we talk about this message?'

She examined her black-glossed fingernails, one of which was broken. 'She got in a car, Boyle. This was around nine-thirty last night. Quarter of ten.'

'You know the driver's name?'

'I look like a fucking phone book to you?'

'Okay. What did he look like then?'

Boyle had known Cassandra a long time. She'd stripteased, worked as a call-girl in a few ritzy resorts out west, then slithered somewhat from that summit. She was queen of vague. She perceived the world through a sensory net that was like a blackout blind. He'd hung out with her for a while a year or so back, a casual thing, and although the sex was good and hungry, she was too spacey for his liking, and, besides, commitment – which she valued and needed – was a major chuckle from his point of view.

'I didn't actually see any of this *transpire*, you understand. My days of hanging out in certain places are past, Boyle. I know what's good for me.'

'Listen, Cass. I don't need a guided tour of your learning graph. I need to find the girl.'

'The person that saw her said she got inside a dark-blue car.'

'A dark-blue car. That's truly helpful, Cass. Who was this eyewitness?'

'You don't know this individual, and I'm not revealing my sources.'

'Fuck. Now you're a journalist with privileges.' Boyle had a sudden flash. *Goddam! She was the fucking eyewitness*. Nobody else. She was back hitting the sidewalks and she didn't want him to know, so she'd dreamed up this fictional observer. Well, well. There was pride at work here. In a calmer state of mind Boyle might have found this little act of deception touching.

She said, 'Now don't go all wigged on me, Boyle. I'm trying to help. You score me some dope in return for info. Scratch my back.'

'I'll score you the goddam dope, Cass. But I need more than a dark-blue car, you see. The world is filled with dark-blue cars.'

She said, 'My nameless friend remembers a detail of the license plate. It was nine two K something.'

'Nine two K something. That's all your nameless friend got?'

'That's all, Boyle.'

Boyle asked her for a pen, which she took out of her cavernous purse. He scribbled '92K' on a paper napkin. It was a beginning. How much of one, he wasn't sure.

'Meet me back here in an hour and I'll have what you need,' he said. He started to rise from the table. 'Incidentally, you didn't happen to see the guy's face, did you?'

She stared at him. 'Oh, fuck you, Boyle.'

'Old dogs and new tricks, honey. I don't think this shape-shifting shit is working for you.'

'Fuck you again.'

'I take that as, no, you didn't see his face.'

'Take it any way you like. Just bring me ice, Boyle.'

He was about to step away from the table when he was assailed suddenly by an unexpected sense of doom. It was as if a hood had been pulled over his head and he was being smothered. This goddam tricky powder that fueled you. He breathed deeply a couple of times and the bad sensation passed. *Scary Moments in Lee Boyle's Life*.

'My pen,' Cass said.

'Almost forgot.' He dropped the pen on the table.

'One hour,' she said. 'Don't pull a stunt on this, Boyle. I'm in serious need.'

He pointed a finger at her – *okay, babe, you got it, you got Lee Boyle's word, the ice-man will returneth* – and then he took a few steps across the room. She called out to him. 'Hey, Boyle. One last thing. The car was a Chrysler.'

13

DARCY WAS WAITING OUTSIDE CITY HALL WHEN SAMSA emerged at ten past six.

'Surprise,' she said.

'What are you doing down here?'

'I ditched my afternoon classes. Don't you ever get one of those days when you just don't feel like doing what you're supposed to be doing?'

'Sure. All the time.'

'But you're too conscientious to defy expectations,' she said. 'You don't break the rules.'

She linked her arm through his and they moved along the sidewalk. Downtown was beginning to empty, stores were closing, office workers were calling it a day. *You don't break the rules.* 'So what did you do instead?' he asked.

'I hung out. I just walked around downtown. Looked in some store windows. Nothing special.'

Samsa thought how ordinary this was, a man and his pretty daughter strolling along a city sidewalk in the early evening sun. The proud father smiling. A casual observer might think, *That's nice. I seek the ordinary*, Samsa thought. The commonplace. That elusive place where life is humdrum. And secure.

'So you're a little down?' he asked. 'Is that the message I'm getting?'

'I don't know what message I'm sending,' she said.

She looked gloomy. He wondered if her mood had anything to do with Nick, if something had gone wrong there, but he'd never intruded on that area of her life. Maybe he should have established better links of communication, because love alone wasn't ever enough. He often thought that Harriet's years of silence and withdrawal had established a pattern, and Darcy had grown up accustomed to the impotence of language.

'Sometimes I get this feeling of confinement,' she said.

'We all get that, Darcy.' It wasn't an adequate response. He knew that at once. Maybe what was really bothering her was this wretched anniversary. It was bound to be somewhere on her mind.

'Other people expect things from me,' she said.

'Like what?'

'Let's start with good grades.'

'And this is a burden I impose?'

'Yeah, a little. But mainly it's teachers,' she said. 'There's other stuff. Like Nick.'

He wondered if she was still a virgin. It was a question he'd relegated to the back of his mind, where he didn't have to deal with it. Some horny young guy fucks your daughter, how are you supposed to react to that anyway? Outrage was old-fashioned. The age of the shotgun was dead. And he couldn't summon up shock. He had no rights in the matter.

'Sometimes he stifles me,' she said.

They were in the parking lot now. Samsa had borrowed a car from the department pool. It was a late-model beige

517

Chevrolet in need of a wash. He unlocked it.

'New wheels,' Darcy said.

'Temporary. I'll work out a hire car with the insurance gangsters. I just haven't gotten round to it yet.'

Darcy sat in the passenger seat. 'Ooo-eee. Tobacco Row,' she said, and made a face. The ashtray, stuffed with butts, hung open.

'If Nick's stifling,' Samsa said, 'maybe you should think about cooling the whole thing.'

She slumped back in her seat, hands in the pockets of her jeans. He could tell from her expression that the subject of Nick was closed for the moment. He saw a distance in her eyes. She was so damn *changeable*. One moment up, the next down. One minute she was all hugs and kisses, the next she was about as approachable as frozen tundra.

'I have an idea,' he said. 'Let's go eat at that place you like.'

'Lucky's?'

'We'll pig out.'

She turned her face and there was a trace of a smile. 'I'm sorry if I'm moody. I don't mean to be. It's just stuff, that's all. I'll deal with it.'

'Sure you will.'

He drove through the stop-start traffic of downtown. Darcy fiddled with the radio, found a rock station. She was tapping her fingers on the dash, animated all at once, the funk sloughed off. Moods were like clothes she tried on, then discarded.

Beyond the city center Samsa headed north through suburban streets, passing gardens where people clipped hedges or dug out weeds, and kids played frisbee along sidewalks. Ordinary life as it was lived.

Lucky's, formerly a branch-line railroad station, had been converted a few years back when the railroad company was going out of business. It prospered as a restaurant whose clientele was mainly young and noisy. Samsa had never felt comfortable there. Always geriatric, over the hill.

He parked in the busy lot and went inside with Darcy, and they found their way to a table overlooking the rusted old rail tracks. The floor was strewn with sawdust for a rough-hewn rustic look, and the air, stirred by huge fans, was heavy with the smell of meat charbroiling. Most of the tables were occupied. Teenagers, twentysomethings.

A waitress brought menus, talked her way through the specials – 'Try the crab claws in lemon butter, they're scrumptious' – then left. Darcy studied her menu a moment before shutting it. 'How's the homicide business these days, Dad?'

'There's no danger of it slacking off. You can count on that.'

'Anything juicy?'

He thought juicy a peculiar choice of word. 'There's Anthony Leeson. If you're into blood and gore.'

'I read about that one. You got any clues?'

'We had a guy who said he might know something. It didn't pan out.' Joshua Gold hadn't been able to remember much when it came right down to it. Too dark. Not sure about the guy's height. Couldn't say he'd noticed any special characteristics. But Eve, tenacious as ever, wasn't going to let go of young Joshua just yet. She had other plans for him.

He said, 'You slog on these cases and sometimes you don't turn up a thing. So what happens? You become weary and frustrated, and you start wishing it was like a cop show: everything neat and tidy in the end.'

'Bad day, too, huh?' she asked.

What else could this day be? 'Yeah,' he said, and examined the menu.

When the waitress returned they ordered ribs with barbecue sauce, fries, Diet Cokes. Darcy looked out of the window at the tracks. She plucked a straw from the container and unwrapped it, rolling it back and forth across the table.

Samsa watched her for a while, then cleared his throat and asked, 'You miss her?'

Darcy didn't look up at him. 'She was never really there, Dad. I don't mean that to sound cruel or anything. She was like this presence that was always around, but that was all. Know what I mean?'

He reached for her hand and squeezed it. 'I know,' he said quietly.

'It's not like we were bosom buddies. I couldn't sit down and talk with her about things. I couldn't say, Hey, what do you think of this haircut? Or this shirt? Or these sneakers? What do you make of Nick? Could I?' Darcy picked up a napkin and held it against her face. 'I mean, really. *She was just never fucking there.*'

Samsa had a sensation of ice packed round his heart. This was too painful: her words, the look on her face. If he could defuse the anger and disappointment in the words and alter that expression, what fortune wouldn't he give? He loved this child to the limits of himself. 'She was sick, Darcy.'

'I *know* she was sick. Why didn't you send her away where trained people could look after her properly? And I don't mean that to sound cruel, either. Why did you have to take on the burden by yourself?'

'Because I kept thinking, one day she's going to snap out of it. Misguided optimism. Faith. My foolish heart. Call it what you like.'

'And all her stuff is still in the house. I mean, why are you keeping it? It's unhealthy. Spooky.'

'I'll get rid of it, if that's what you'd like,' he said. He thought of cardboard boxes, filling them with forsaken possessions, the attachments of a life cast away. He wondered if there was any activity more emotionally brutal than sifting the belongings of the dead.

'And you found her. You were the one that found her. Jesus Christ, I can't even *begin* to imagine how you felt.'

'I try not to dwell on it,' he said.

Darcy blew her nose. 'Let's drop this subject, Dad. Why don't we just stuff ourselves with ribs and make a really gross mess on the table?'

'And spill stuff on the floor,' he said.

'And make loud chomping noises like two animals in a zoo.'

The waitress came with stacks of ribs in a glutinous dark-red sauce. Samsa stared at the food. His appetite, small to begin with, had shriveled. He watched Darcy pick up a rib and chew on it, then she let the stripped bone sink inside her finger bowl, where it left a slick of red grease. *Pink water in the bathtub*, he thought. *Stained scissors lying on her stomach. Her hair, razored and chopped brutally short, sticking up from her scalp*. He felt haunted, ghosts stalked his life. What he needed was an exorcism. But incantations and the sprinkling of holy water weren't going to do the trick.

Darcy stared at him over the mound of ribs. 'I have a question for you. When you go out nights, where do you actually go?'

'Mostly it's work,' he answered. He chewed slowly on a fry.

'You don't have a woman you're seeing, do you?'

'No. Did you think I might?'

'You just get up and go, you don't say where you're headed. It can't be night shift all the time.'

'Homicides happen round the clock, which is inconvenient.'

'When it's not work, where do you go then?'

He picked up a rib, but he couldn't bring himself to taste it. 'I like the feeling of solitude I get in a car at night. There. Does that answer you?'

'I guess,' she said. 'I don't know why you sound so defensive, though.'

'I wasn't aware of it, Darcy. I get in the car and it's dark and I look for quiet roads. It's a peaceful sensation.' This intricate web of fabrication. Once you'd started to spin it you couldn't stop, because the strands would strangle you.

Was he supposed to tell her the truth? He could hear gates clang shut inside himself. He was barricaded behind his own evasions and lies. Gregory Samsa, a cop for twenty-one years, twenty-one fucking years of completely honest uninterrupted service to the inhabitants of this gritty threadbare city. Never on the pad, never on the take, never a goddam hint of graft or corruption; he slips up one time, he makes a serious error of judgement—

He crumpled his napkin with a violent gesture and pushed his plate aside briskly. *I was sick to my heart with solitude, Darcy. Can you understand that?* He wondered how he looked to his daughter, if she could read anything in his face. But she was staring into her food, wasn't even looking at him. He gazed round the room, experienced a great rushing blur of sensory impressions, then he remembered the feeling he'd experienced last night when he'd stared at the street from his bedroom window.

Something bad was coming down.

Something he'd be powerless to prevent.

He picked at a couple more fries, but that was all he could manage. Darcy, too, seemed uninterested in eating. *A flop*, he thought. Pigging out together. There had been a breakdown of sorts. It felt like a party where all the balloons had deflated and hung wrinkled.

'If you're finished, I'll get the check.' He looked at his

watch, remembered that Al Brodsky was dropping over. He raised an arm to attract the waitress. He paid the bill with a credit card. On the way out he noticed that Darcy had disappeared inside herself again. She looked distant and secretive.

We all have secrets, he thought. *It's how we handle them that matters. Or if we handle them at all.*

14

LEE BOYLE LOOKED OUT OF THE WINDOW OF VASS'S PICK-UP, which was rattling down a pocked road of old row houses. This was flinty blue-collar territory. Since the steelworks had shut down and the power plant replaced half its workforce with silicon chips, most people in this neighborhood were on welfare and hard times. Politicians didn't give a damn. That's what politicians were for anyhow. Vote for me, I won't do shit. But I'll do it better than the other candidate.

'So where does this guy live?' Boyle asked.

'It's not far.'

'And he can do the job?'

'In his sleep. It's nothing to him.'

'You known him long?'

'A few years,' Vass said. 'I met him through Stretch.'

'You can vouch for him.'

'Fuck's sake, relax.'

Boyle thought, *92K, 92K*. It was like a mantra going round in his head. He gazed at the dreary little houses. Old men, most of them black, sat on porches and read newspapers back to front, then started the whole process all over again. Boyle had a sense that there were drawers inside these houses stuffed with losing lottery tickets and unopened brown envelopes with windows.

'We there yet?'

'You're like a kid who sits in the back of his Daddy's car and can't keep still, Lee.'

Anxiety, Lee Boyle thought. *Time on whirring wings.* He remembered he was supposed to meet Cassandra at the Rialto, but he'd let that slide. He might not run into her again for weeks, months, by which time she'd have forgotten the deal anyway. You could count on that.

'This guy really calls himself Data?'

'Thirty-seven and a Trekkie to the max. You meet him, just don't mention Captain Kirk or that bald guy Picard, or *any* of those assholes, or it's going to be a long night listening to some very tedious details about the righteousness of the Federation.'

Vass slowed the truck, turned a corner, braked outside a row house painted battleship gray and peeling like bad skin. Boyle got out and followed Rudy Vass to the front door. Vass pressed the bell. The guy who answered had a shaved head. His eyes were stone-colored.

Vass said, 'Data, my man.'

Data had a smile like a crack in a rock. 'You're late, Vass.'

'Traffic's a nightmare,' Vass said. 'This is Lee. Lee, Data.'

Data's voice was deep, out of his chest. 'Before you come inside, you oughta know I have two strict rules in here: no smoking, and no drinking anywhere near the equipment.'

Data opened the door a little wider. Vass and Boyle went inside the house, which consisted of small

525

interconnecting rooms, drab and dark and steamy. There was a smell of wood polish or air freshener, Boyle wasn't sure which.

A woman's voice, emerging from one of the tiny rooms, called out, 'Don't go making loud noises up there, Joe.'

'Right, Ma,' Data said.

Data reached the landing and opened the door to a room that burst on Boyle like a *Star Trek* museum. Posters depicted Spock and Kirk and others whose names were unknown to Boyle – he rarely watched TV, it was a foreign country to him – and a whole array of books, magazines, fanzines, miniature replicas of alien life forms, copies of Trekkie weapons. It was some kind of sorry shrine. Joe, aka Data, thirty-seven and still lives with his mother in a *Star Trek* alternative reality. All this kid stuff. Boyle had an urge to say, Look, I'm goddam serious. This isn't some space soap baloney.

'Rudy explain the fee?' Data asked.

'Twenty-five bucks,' Boyle said.

'That's the going rate,' Data said. He was wearing Osh Kosh overalls with big patchy pockets. His arms were hairy and muscular. Boyle drew crumpled notes from his jeans, counted out twenty-five dollars in fives. He wondered if he had anything left in his bank account. Fifty, sixty dollars tops. He knew he had about a hundred bucks in a coffee can stuffed at the back of a closet. His nest egg. Peanuts. All the money you spent down the drain of your veins or up your nose, and nothing to show for it but a serious taste. You've got a Mercedes, a speedboat, and probably a goddam Lear jet lost in your bloodstream.

Data pocketed the cash and walked to a table in the corner of the room, where a black laptop computer was located. It was attached to a box Boyle had no way of identifying. He was computer illiterate. He wasn't one for zipping along the information autobahn.

A tangle of wires dangled from the table and out of sight. Data sat down in front of the computer and pressed a button. Boyle heard a whir and then a series of beeping sounds, followed by what seemed like a strange hoarse wind blowing out of the laptop.

'Okay,' Data said. 'Rudy tells me you want some material outta the Department of Motor Vehicles?'

'I've got three digits of a license-plate number, a make and a color.'

'Shoot,' Data said, his hands poised over the keyboard.

'Ninety-two K. Chrysler,' Boyle said. 'Dark blue.'

'Ninety-two K.' Data's fingers tapped quickly. Boyle watched Data lean back in his chair while the machine whined.

'What's that box attachment?' Boyle asked.

'You never seen a *modem* before?' Data had a look of bewilderment, like he considered Boyle some primeval life form. 'This box connects to the phone lines. Which means the whole wide world.'

Boyle said he saw, but he didn't really, and, besides, he didn't give a damn. He was nervous. Because of the crank. Because of sleeplessness. *The modem's connected to the phone line, the phone line's connected to the phone poles, the phone pole's connected to the exchange.* He understood that in Data's world this was a holy moment, like making contact with God.

'Right, we're in,' Data said. Boyle saw what seemed to be names and numbers scrolling across the screen. Data leaned forward toward the monitor.

'Already?' Boyle asked.

'I got three Chryslers here, all Le Barons, all with the same partial, all in the color specified,' Data said. 'Get a pen and paper and write down this info.'

Vass took from his pocket a Bic, which he handed Boyle, who couldn't find anything to write on except for

527

a hard-top pack of Camel Lights. He scribbled the names and addresses quickly in tiny crabbed handwriting, a kind of shorthand he hoped he'd be able to decipher later. Data pressed a key and the screen blanked.

'I told you he was good,' Vass said.

Boyle stuck the pack in his pocket. 'He's good all right.'

Data rose. Business concluded. 'I'll show you guys out.'

They went down the stairs and toward the front door. 'You don't know me,' Data said to Boyle. 'We never met.' He eyeballed the street, presumably for a sign of alien life forms, then quickly shut the door.

Boyle and Vass walked back to the pick-up. When he was inside, Boyle sat with his head slumped back. 'She vanishes inside a Le Baron and nobody's seen her since,' he said. 'And that makes me feel a tad uneasy.'

'I still say she split,' Vass said. 'She wanted a clean break.'

'Hey, I know this girl. No way would she just up and vanish on me.'

The pick-up shuddered over a pothole in the road. Bumping up and down in his seat, Vass said, 'What now?'

Boyle took a cigarette from the pack of Camel Lights and lit it, gazing at the names and addresses through strands of smoke. 'Check out these names, what else? One of these cars is the only connection I have to Almond.' And he thought of the small girl with the lovely Latino features, damp towels on his bathroom floor and her glistening pubic hair and the sweet honeyed taste of her kiss, and he felt bereft, as if she might somehow have slipped through a crack in the earth's crust, forever lost to him.

15

DR LEWIS DICE WAS A PINK-SKINNED INDIVIDUAL WHO HAD A local reputation as something of an oddball on account of his hobby: taxidermy. Kids brought him dead animals – roadkill, creatures blasted by gunshot – and he restored the more salvageable specimens with a needle and surgical thread, then stuffed and mounted them in glass cases and contributed them to auctions for charitable causes. He had a squeak of a voice. At times he sounded like Mr Rogers through a flute. He wore flip-flops and Bermuda shorts and a Miami Dolphins T-shirt that revealed scrawny nut-brown arms.

People who visited his home invariably noticed such things as the severed heads of birds suspended in jars of preservative and the kitchen sink, usually filled with pale-green fluid, in which organic matter floated. His neighbors sometimes referred to him as Doc Dicenstein.

With a pack of big plastic Ziploc bags under his arm, Dice strode in his purposeful way out through the door in his cedar fence and headed for the great open field that bordered his property, where weeds and tangled thickets of long grass grew riotously. Every now and then he paused to contemplate an unusual arrangement of daisies or dandelions or wild flowers. He disturbed a red admiral on a grass stalk still moist from last night's rain. The butterfly took flight, fluttering past his face, color in motion.

He heard in the distance the *pock* of a rifle. He winced. A second *ping*, then a third. Why did parents give their children air rifles? And why did the children use these weapons for what they called sport? Killing wood pigeons, shooting cats, crippling wildlife. Where was the sport in that?

Shielding his eyes from the setting sun, Dice watched the butterfly go. Then he stared across the meadow, his attention drawn by the sound of machinery. A truck with the sign 'MARTIN'S 24-HOUR BREAKDOWN & RECOVERY SERVICE' was hauling a car from the base of an old tree. The car, strangely enough, was upside down. Men were busy attaching chains to the overturned automobile. A winch began to grind.

Some gosh-darn fool had smacked into the tree, Lewis Dice thought. A drunk in all probability. He looked in the other direction, noticing flattened grass and threadbare places and seeing, at the place where the incline rose to the road, a darkened area of churned ground. The hapless driver had come off the blacktop, *whoopsadiddley*, and slammed several hundred yards into the tree.

Upside down. My lord.

Lewis Dice approached the truck. 'Was anyone hurt?' he asked.

The two men from the recovery service were taciturn. They regarded Dice, with his high-pitched voice and baggy shorts and funny sandals, as if he were some crazy old coot who'd wandered away from an old folks' home without written authority.

'Don't rightly know,' one of them said. 'We just pick 'em up and drag 'em off, dude.'

'It's in bad shape,' Dice said. He looked at the car, the passenger door of which was unhinged and buckled. 'I've seen plenty of accident victims in my time. I spent a few years in ER. I'm a physician, you know. Was. Retired.'

'Zatso,' said the younger of the two men, a boy in his late teens. He had brown teeth. Dice, senses honed by a lifetime of abstention from drink and cigarettes, could smell tobacco on him.

'When did this happen?'

'Dunno. We just haul 'em away,' the kid said. He wore big leather mitts. 'Zatsall we do.'

Dice lingered a few moments and, since the likelihood of further conversation was clearly nil, walked off through the grass. He thought of all the casualty cases he'd attended: the gunfire victims, people with third-degree burns, folks hauled from car wrecks.

Pitiful situations.

Ah – what was this?

The dead swallow was delicately balanced on a pyre-like arrangement of grass. Dice went down on his knees and picked the creature up very carefully and placed it inside one of his plastic bags. The bird was riddled with pellets. Those boys with goddam airguns – why didn't somebody drum into their fat heads that people and creatures shared this planet, that respect was due every living thing?

He sealed the bag, rose and continued to walk. He scanned thickets, looking for casualties. Some days he found none, others he picked up two or three. A few he could repair and stuff, most he rejected as beyond restoration. Now and again, driven by the curiosity that had propelled him all his life, he performed very delicate post-mortems on his kitchen table.

He came upon an umbrella on the ground, one of those plastic transparent jobs people picked up cheaply when they were caught in an unexpected rainstorm. He gazed at it a moment, then walked on. Utterly disgraceful what he came across out here at times. Junkies' needles, shriveled condoms, used tampons, sometimes discarded underwear, shoes, a pair of jeans once. The place was a dumping ground.

He kept going. Grass grew in places as high as his thighs. The air was richly scented with wild flowers. A barbed growth snagged his shorts and retarded his progress a moment. He freed himself carefully and continued, and the stalks of long grass parted reluctantly as he moved. What one really needed here was a machete. Chop chop, slash slash, clear a path. Slice and hack, hack and slice. He hummed a remembered snippet from *The Pirates of Penzance*. Many years ago he'd played the role of the Pirate King in an amateur production staged by the staff of St Dominic's General Hospital, and he'd been good, very good.

He stopped suddenly in front of a thick stand of unruly bushes. A rat, sleek and gleaming, scampered out of the undergrowth and startled him. He watched it vanish, thinking there was something odd about the creature's appearance, something he couldn't put his finger on immediately.

He frowned, bent down, peered through the impenetrable tangle of leaves and limbs.

What was it about that rat?

Its whiskers, *of course, of course.* Wet, stained as if by red wine.

It had been disturbed in the act of feeding. *On a dead bird,* Dice thought. Some fledgling fallen from a nest, perhaps. A defenseless little thing. An innocent. Such was the cruelty inherent in nature.

He reached forward and parted the strands of shrubbery with his hands.

16

_____

AL BRODSKY ARRIVED PROMPTLY AT EIGHT THIRTY, CARRYING two four-packs of Grolsch in paper sacks. Samsa opened two bottles, handed one to Brodsky. Inside the living room Al sat down close to the fireplace, where the last of the sun created a fuzzy yellow rectangle around his feet.

'Cheers, Greg.'

'Better days.' Samsa sipped the Czech lager. What was it Brodsky needed to discuss?

Brodsky stretched his legs out, relaxed. 'Darcy around?'

'Out on a date.'

'Who's the boy?'

'A kid called Nick Mancuso. He's at the same school. A senior.'

'Nick Mancuso . . . Isn't he the kid of that guy who's big in the paper products line? Bobby Mancuso?'

'That's him,' Samsa said.

'Is it serious?' Al asked.

'She says he stifles her.'

'She's young.' Brodsky slipped off his shoes. He had a

534

hole in the heel of a sock. He studied it a moment, then said, 'It gets easier, you know. In time.'

For a second Samsa thought Brodsky was referring in some oblique way to Darcy, but then realized Al had just skipped to the subject of Harriet. 'Tess has been gone five years now. I still catch myself talking to her. There's an absence. But the pain dims to a minor ache.'

Two widowers examining grief. Terrific. Was *this* what Al had come here to speak about? Samsa didn't want to talk about the dead. He wanted another kind of conversation: feathery, inconsequential. Department rumors. Dumb jokes. Anything.

He stood at the window and stared out into the street. The sky was suffused with yellows and pinks. A few stray clouds hung in the still air. *I want to be free of myself*, he thought.

Al said, 'After a while, you have this need to socialize, check what's happening, what you might be missing. Then, one day, a lady catches your eye.'

'And that's happened to you?' Samsa asked.

'More than once.' Brodsky smiled. The small slitted eyes disappeared in the folds of his face. He looked jovial. 'I can still get it up. It's a bit of a crank, I admit. But the machinery's basically sound.'

'I hadn't heard any rumors about you and women,' Samsa remarked. 'Either I'm sleepwalking through the department or the grapevine's shut down.'

'Maybe I'm just discreet in my old age.'

There's a future, Samsa thought. *That's what Al is trying to tell me.*

'Off the record, are you handling things okay?' Brodsky asked.

'Department things? Personal things? Which?'

'Either. Both.'

'I'm doing just fine, Al.'

Brodsky had a stare that at times could penetrate. He fixed you with those small eyes and they bored into your head like two power-driven diamond drill bits. 'You sure?'

'Sure.' Samsa had the sudden thought, *Al knows something*. But that was ridiculous. What was there to know? Everything had been dreamed, everything was effluence that had seeped from his head.

'I want to ask you something,' Brodsky said.

Samsa was holding his breath. This sudden tension was an arrow in his throat. He touched the edge of his broken tooth with the tip of his tongue.

'I'm thinking of the internal reorganization. I'd like your feedback on how it's going.'

Samsa relaxed now, drank some beer. Internal reorganization. That was easy. He could deal with that. He could talk about that all day long. All night.

'I can't think of any problems,' he said.

'You're getting total co-operation?'

'Total.'

Brodsky looked a little doubtful. 'Charlie Bird and Casey are coming through for you?'

'Religiously,' Samsa said.

'I just figured there might be some envy, that's all. When you got Charlie Bird working the East precinct, and Jack Casey the South, you worry about empire-building. They're good guys, don't get me wrong. But if there's the smallest sign of private fiefdoms I want to know about it. I don't want any hostility to get in the way of shared information, because it means the chance of something vital getting lost in the shuffle.'

'I get daily updates on the homicide investigations being conducted by Bird and Casey. They file copies of all their reports with me. I see something I don't like – work duplicated, fruitless inquiries, guys going off at stupid tangents – I talk with Charlie or Jack and we try to fix the situation. That was the mandate you gave me, Al.'

'Charlie Bird wasn't happy in the beginning,' Brodsky said. 'Three months ago, when I told him I was re-organizing homicide, bringing it under one roof so to speak, he pitched a fit. "So Downtown controls everything," he says. "Downtown wins the blue ribbon and Samsa gets to be like the guy on top of the pyramid. What does that make him? Some pharaoh or something? Samsa the First?"'

'Charlie's been with the department longer than me,' Samsa said. 'He had every right to feel aggrieved.'

'The only thing really aggrieved him was the fact he knew you were better equipped for the job than himself,' Brodsky said. 'He doesn't have your . . . call it diplomacy.'

'I never thought of myself as diplomatic,' Samsa said.

'With a slight edge,' Brodsky remarked.

An edge. Samsa wondered about this, whether he'd lost that edge, if it had become blunted by circumstance. He wasn't sure.

He was ready for another beer. He moved toward the kitchen. Al Brodsky, shoeless, followed him. Samsa opened the refrigerator, removed two Grolsch bottles.

'Understand, Greg. The first time you think there's any blockage in this pipeline, you come to me. No hesitation. No misplaced cop-loyalty crap.' Brodsky sat on a kitchen stool. He could look intensely serious, as he did at that moment.

'No, the co-operation's fine,' Samsa said. 'The only draw-back from my point of view is strictly personal. I don't spend enough time with Darcy. She's at a strange age.'

'Show me an age that isn't strange,' Brodsky said. He wiggled his toes inside his dark socks, staring down at them. The heel that showed through the hole was like a small albino eye. 'Are you saying in a coy roundabout way that you wished you'd never assumed this responsibility?'

537

'No, nothing like that, Al.' Samsa had the feeling he was being challenged, pinned. *I'm not the man for this job. It's some kind of sham. But life goes on, you told yourself that already. You're swimming, you have to keep your head above the turmoil of the waters. Everything is dandy.* It was a world of appearances. *I'll continue to be the good cop.*

He said, 'If it was the kind of thing that kept me tied to my desk, it might be different. But I still get out. I have cases I work.'

'I never saw your role as administrative,' Brodsky said. 'But any time you think it's too much, or you start to get that *stuck* feeling, say so. Jesus Christ, we've known each other too long to go beating about bushes, Greg. What is it? Seventeen years?'

'About,' Samsa said. *That stuck feeling*, he thought. The glue on the surface of fly-paper.

Brodsky knocked his beer can against Samsa's bottle and smiled. 'Seventeen years, Greg. Weddings and funerals and kids growing up. Laughter and grief. The whole damn thing. And here we are, a couple of hardened survivors.'

'Just about,' Samsa said. 'Let's go back inside the living room.'

Shadows had lengthened, the sun had almost entirely gone. Samsa switched on a lamp. The telephone rang and he picked it up. It was Eve Lassiter.

'I'm hitting the streets with young Joshua,' she said.

'I figured you would.'

'There's always a slight chance he'll see this kid he says Leeson picked up. If that happens I want to be there.'

'You're dressing for the part, I assume,' he said.

'Short skirt, long boots, very glossy. This little blouse you can just about see through. I don't want to be conspicuous. I'm wearing *mucho* make-up too. Master of illusion.'

Samsa imagined her in short skirt and boots, face made up, strutting her stuff like a hooker.

She said, 'Have you decided if you're joining me or not? All you'd have to do is park your car in the vicinity where we can keep in touch. And if anything happens, I know you're there.'

'Take Billy Fogue.'

'Fogue's loud and sexist. I'd prefer you, Lieutenant.'

'Get Duff then. He's on duty.'

'I'll get Duff if you're chickening out.'

'I'm not chickening out. I've got company.'

'Female by any chance?'

'The chief.'

'Oh, hobnobbing.'

Samsa caught his own reflection in the darkening window. 'I'll be home all night if you need me.'

'I wish you could see me in this outfit. You'd froth at the mouth.'

'Are you flirting with me, Eve?' Darcy had said Eve had the hots for him. He thought about that. Out of the mouths of kids.

'Could be. Or maybe I'm getting inside this role,' she answered. 'I might enjoy trawling the sidewalks. I might just quit the department and take up hooking.'

He pictured her strolling the night, looking provocative but hanging back from the action, turning cars away on some pretext when they approached her. 'Take good care,' he said.

'I always do.'

He hung up, feeling for some reason a little empty.

'Eve Lassiter?' Brodsky asked.

'Yeah. She's working the Leeson case.'

'From what angle?'

Samsa told him.

Brodsky said, 'That neighborhood's a blight. Vice

539

rounds these kids up, they're back on the street next day. What can you do? Eve's a resourceful girl. She just needs a little looking out for. You get along with her pretty well, I hear.'

'Is there gossip?'

'Not so much gossip, more a quiet underswell. You have to listen real hard to pick up on it. They say she's fond of you. Ditto for you.'

'I like her,' Samsa said.

'You got something stronger than beer? I'm starting to get into the mood.'

'Vodka, cognac.'

Brodsky wanted vodka. Samsa went to the liquor cabinet and poured a glass. Brodsky took the vodka and tasted it, then settled back in his chair with his hands clasped across his stomach. Facing him, Samsa thought, *This is a pleasant illusion. This is how it's meant to be: two old colleagues having a drink, comrades in arms, old times, weddings and funerals.* Somewhere there were photographs, Brodsky stiff and ludicrous in a tux, standing directly behind Samsa on the day of his marriage to Harriet. Happy days. Better times.

He turned to the window just as the street lamps came on and cast their customary dullish yellow glow. He drew the curtain, enjoying the idea of keeping the outside world at bay. Nothing existed beyond these walls.

Brodsky said, 'I'll help myself to some more of this vodka,' and he walked to the liquor cabinet.

Al was a lightweight when it came to drinking. He held it up to a certain point, but he reached that borderline fast, and then he became loquaciously sentimental – which meant he'd begin to trample through the undergrowth of the past, and next thing he'd want to drag out the old photograph albums. Remember that time, Greg? You and me and Harriet and Tess, that day on Lake

540

Maska when we hired a boat that almost sank? Remember?

I don't want to go there, Samsa thought. There were too few pictures of Harriet involved in any kind of activity, outdoor or in. She'd passed through the world like a pale shade, leaving barely a fingerprint.

'You ought to take it easy, Al,' he said. 'If you're driving.'

'I'm over the limit, I'll call a cab.'

Samsa was restless suddenly, thinking of Eve Lassiter, the dark places, the headlights of prowling cars. He understood he should have gone down there to provide back-up. Eve was his protégée. He'd taken her under his wing when she'd first joined the department. He'd recommended her for promotion.

But. *Have we ever met before?*

Brodsky appeared somber all at once. 'A year ago already. Hard to believe.'

Here we go. 'Al, I don't want to talk about it.'

'Sometimes you got to air the linen closet, Greg.'

'I just don't want to talk about it.'

Brodsky was going back for more vodka. On the way to the liquor cabinet he ran his knuckles across the keyboard of the piano. The sound rolled around the room. Samsa heard the strings vibrate under the lid, the afterwhisper of notes struck randomly. *This house*, he thought. *This whole goddam house whispers. It never stops. Day and fucking night I hear it.*

He opened the front door and stepped onto the porch where the air was muggy. Brodsky came after him, glass in hand.

'I'm out of line,' Brodsky said. 'I know it.'

'It's not that, Al. It's me, it's my fault. Sometimes I think I have a grip, and then it just goes, and fuck it, *fuck* it.' Samsa quit talking. He looked the length of the street, seeing hordes of moths dart and flutter under the lamps. A million potential suicides. The air was strong with the scent of cut grass and chlorine from neighborhood pools.

Al clapped him on his bruised shoulder. 'I get maudlin. You don't need to tell me—'

Samsa heard the car before he saw it, a patrol car that loomed out of the dark, roaring down the center of the street, roof lights slicing the night. It drew up at the end of Samsa's driveway, and the first thing that came into his mind was the idea that something had happened to Darcy. An accident, Nick Mancuso's frail little VW convertible had crashed, and his head was crammed with pictures of blood and emergency rooms, doctors and orderlies, nurses hurrying with IV drips. Everything hasty. Everything out of control. Madness.

'Sweet *Christ*,' Brodsky said. 'Is there never any peace?'

A cop Samsa recognized as Randy Harrilyn got out of the cruiser and moved up the driveway to the porch.

Don't let it be Darcy. Don't let it be.

Harrilyn was a tall man with a tendency to stoop. He reached the porch steps and looked up, his face the color of a tangerine in the porch light. He stared at Samsa. In that moment, for no good reason he could think of, Samsa knew that Randy Harrilyn wasn't here on account of Darcy. He just knew, and his heart flopped over into a void, and he was hearing an old Billie Holiday tune slurring and dying inside a cassette deck.

17

IT WAS A LONG HAUL FROM ONE SIDE OF THE DARKENING CITY to the other, and Lee Boyle felt a persistent jumpy urgency and the occasional haphazard skip of his heart. It was weird how the mind had a wayward life all its own and thoughts roared around in a carousel of graphics and bizarre sound effects that eventually distilled themselves in the repetition of one word, one picture – Almond, Almond, Almond. *She left me at the silent time.* Yes indeed, Percy. She left me.

Only I don't believe that. I don't believe she'd *ever* do that. So where the hell is she?

Vass slowed the pick-up, checking street signs. 'This is Oakleigh,' he said. 'What number are you looking for, Lee?'

Boyle flicked on the interior light and studied his ciga-rette pack. 'Eight three six,' he said. 'Guy's name is Silas Goba. Or Gora. I can't make out my own goddam hand-writing.'

Vass drove slowly along the street of frame houses. This was one of the city's older neighborhoods, *circa* 1950.

Dense trees camouflaged the homes, and great branches reached out luxuriantly, blocking street lights. A phantasmagorical effect, a jungle suburb. *Trippy*, Boyle thought. He half expected neon parrots to come screaming out of the leaves, like beasts from some acid flashback occurrence.

'Let's hope this is a better candidate than that last one,' Vass remarked. 'She must've been pushing a hundred, man. She'd never driven that Le Baron further than the local mall, for Christ's sake.'

Boyle pondered Mrs Clyde Fodor, whose Chrysler – license plate 92KB67 – had been parked in the driveway of her home out in Stanhope on the eastern edge of the city. Mrs Fodor, all glassy old skin and liver spots and knobby bone, had bought into Boyle's story that he and Vass were landscapers – well, artists, to be frank – scouting commissions. Boyle, who'd pitched his floral notions with extravagant enthusiasm, had an expression he could do in his sleep. It was one of wide-eyed purity, and it charmed birds from their nests and had old ladies wet-eyed and reaching for photographs of sons who'd vanished in the vastness of the continent, with new wives, new jobs, grandkids who existed only in color snapshots, phone calls at Thanksgiving. *You okay, Ma? I've been kind of busy.* Boyle touched their hearts in a mysterious way.

Picture this, Mrs Fodor, a whole bed of azaleas over here, maybe a fine array of marigolds there. The whole thing kind of bound together with a charismatic carpet of, shall we say, snowdrops? Babble babble, envisage the flowery magnificence.

It was bullshit, but he'd even begun to believe it, which was the real secret of any con. He'd put a slight fag spin on his words: *I can just imagine a tiny pond, too, lily pads, a frog or two croaking. How very bucolic, Mrs*

Fodor. While the old lady had considered Boyle's panoramic concept, Vass had sneaked off to check out the Chrysler, whose odometer had a grand total of 905 miles on it.

Mrs Fodor, a lonely soul, enjoyed company. She offered tea and a whole family history to go with it. She was a widow. Dear Clyde had died last year of complications arising from diabetes. Their only son lived in Europe. She didn't get out much. Didn't do a whole lot of driving. Eyesight failing. In an innocent way Boyle had asked if she'd ever loaned the car to anyone, a neighbor, say, or a friend, but the old lady told him she'd never done that. End of story. *Come back soon and talk to me about begonias*, Mrs Fodor had said when they were leaving. *I just love begonias.*

Right, Mrs Fodor. We'll be back.

One down, two to go.

Vass parked the pick-up. 'This is the place. You want to do the landscape shit again?'

Boyle opened his door, stepped down. The sticky night air had the stealthy feel of a mugger's breath. 'Let's play it by ear until we get a sense of this guy.'

He walked under a canopy of branches toward the pathway. Vass, hitching his jeans, followed. Number 836 Oakleigh, a somber brown house, was surrounded by garden gnomes. Jesus Christ, there must have been thirty-five of the squat fuckers on the lawn. Plaster-of-Paris elves skulked in the poor light, bearded leprechauns with pipes. Cute, if you liked little stone squadrons. Boyle found it unsettling, those expressionless eyes watching him as he moved in the direction of the porch. He half expected sudden animation, elves creaking to life, leprechauns deciding to form a debating society. Speed made you imagine all sorts of stuff out of the corners of your eyes.

A Chrysler was parked in the covered carport. Boyle

was about to step toward it when a porch light came on and a man appeared behind the screen door. Boyle couldn't quite make out his features.

'Help you fellas in some way?' the man asked.

Boyle, trying to think on his feet, detected unmistakable hostility flowing out toward him. He moved a couple of yards toward the porch. 'Mr Goba?'

The guy said nothing. He pushed the screen door open a few inches. A hinge squeaked. Boyle considered the idea of saying he was a lover of garden gnomes and had heard about this amazing collection, which he simply had to see for himself, but there were some kinds of bullshit that just coagulated in your throat. In any event, he didn't feel like going through another faggoty act, swishing and swooning over the clay figures like a queen of kitsch.

'I understand you have a Chrysler for sale,' Boyle said.

'I don't know where you heard that, fella,' the guy said, 'but you got the wrong information.'

'This is eight three six Oakleigh, and you're Silas Goba, right?'

'You got that right. But I don't have any car for sale.'

'You're sure?'

'You hard of hearing, fella?' The man stepped out under the porch light. He wore a white T-shirt. He was big, beef-bellied, no neck. His hair was marine-style crew-cut. He had the look of a man who ate light bulbs for breakfast and then, still hungry, chomped on razor blades. 'You know what I think? I think you and your buddy there come round thinking this place might be empty, might be an easy score.'

'No way,' Boyle said.

'I had this house burgled two times before, jack. And I swore to God I wasn't gonna be ripped off a third time, because I had it up to here with thieves. Take a hike, get the fuck off my property.'

546

Boyle didn't move. The air was alive with atoms of potential violence. He tried to imagine Goba picking up Almond. He pictured this: Almond steps inside Goba's Chrysler. Her neat little body settles in the passenger seat. A transaction is discussed, terms agreed. Does Goba fondle her knee? Slip a hand under her skirt? Delve inside her panties? Is he businesslike about it? Does he slobber? Is there the strained desperation of a rock-solid hard-on? Can't wait to get Almond to spread her legs, show him her cunt? Does she go down on him in the car, her beautiful little face in his fat lap, and his fly undone and his boxer shorts open?

Boyle had an awful moment, a sharp racket in his head, a small steel ball rattling through a variety of hooped circuits, as in one of those noisy Japanese pachinko arcade games. He drew a hand over his face. His fingertips were numb and his scalp tingled. *Rush this guy*, he thought. *Rush him and bring him down and stomp the truth out of him.*

'What you're telling me is the car's not for sale,' he said.

'You're real quick on the uptake,' Goba said. 'Lookit. Just get the fuck off my property. Don't make me come down these steps to you, fella. I got a short fuse.' He moved in an off-center way to the edge of the porch. He'd clearly been drinking. Boyle pegged him as the kind of solitary sociopath you sometimes saw sitting alone in bars, whispering menacingly to themselves.

Boyle glanced toward the Chrysler, which gleamed dully in the carport. If he opened the car and scoped it out would he find some evidence of Almond? A heart-draining trace of her perfume, say? A cigarette butt of the brand she smoked? An earring on the floor? Something tangible. He heard Rudy Vass sigh, a let's-blow-this-place sound. But Rudy, old friend that he might be, didn't have a vested interest in Almond, didn't worry about her the

547

way Boyle did, didn't have bad feelings of the kind Boyle was beginning to experience just about now.

She's hurt.

And then he thought, *This goon Goba fucked her and murdered her. This sick sack of shit maybe choked the life out of her and stashed her in the trunk of this fucking Chrysler in the carport. Her lithe body twisted, her face bloodless, her dress crumpled.*

Suddenly these possibilities took on the patina of absolute certainty, and Boyle, who didn't give a damn about Goba's threats, walked directly to the car.

'Hey,' Goba said, and came down from the porch to intercept. 'Don't you listen, fuckface? Ain't you heard a goddam thing I been saying?'

She's in the trunk, Boyle thought. *She's under a threadbare plaid travel rug. She's entombed alongside a spare tire and a jack and cans of oil and all the other greasy crap people store in their cars.* He'd never been so sure of anything. He saw the license plate number. 92KC700.

Goba shoved him in the chest with the flat of his fat hand and said, 'You're outta line here, fella.'

'Don't touch me again,' Boyle said.

'Don't touch you? Don't *touch* you? You're trespassing, shithead. I got rights.' Goba pushed a second time.

Boyle couldn't stop thinking about the trunk. It consumed him. It became a vast space inside his head. He stepped to the side, tried to pass Goba, who grabbed him by the arm and twisted it at a painful angle. Boyle, smelling a serious stench of whisky on the man's breath, made a huge effort and wrenched himself free.

'Where is she, Goba?'

'Where's who?'

'I want to see inside the trunk of that goddam car.'

Goba looked at Vass, who was standing back from the situation. 'Your pal outta his mind or what?'

Vass took out his handkerchief, coughed into it and said nothing.

Boyle reached for the trunk lid and Goba, coming up from behind, seized him, wrapped his thick arms around his ribs and squeezed. Lee Boyle felt air being forced out of his lungs and dizziness descend on him. He slammed his elbows with as much force as he could gather into Goba's ribs and the big guy slackened his hold and Boyle spun around to face him.

'You picked her up and you fucked her, and then something snapped in your sick fucking head and you stashed her in the goddam trunk—'

'Jesus, Lee,' Vass said.

Goba took a step back from Boyle and asked, 'What'n hell you talking about?'

'Absolutely no way she'd have vanished without saying anything to me,' Boyle said, vaguely aware of slippage inside, like he was sluicing down a water slide with no bottom in sight. 'She wouldn't have left her clothes behind. She liked the stuff I bought her. She liked those goddam clothes. You understand what I'm saying?'

Goba looked at Vass again. 'What is this guy *on*, for Christ's sake?'

Vass looked slightly tubercular in the poor light. 'He's worried sick,' he said.

'I don't know about worried, but sick, yeah, I grant you sick,' Goba said.

'I'm opening the trunk,' Boyle said.

'You think there's a *body* in there?'

'That's exactly what I think,' and Boyle turned back to the car. He couldn't get the trunk to budge and wondered if maybe it only opened if you pressed a button or pulled a lever inside the car. He beat the palm of his hand on the lid.

'Let me get this straight. You're saying I picked up some

chick and then . . .' Goba tossed back his head, and when he laughed his belly shook. 'Is this some kind of put-on, buddy?'

Boyle hated the sound of that laugh. He glared at Silas Goba. 'Open the trunk,' he said.

'Piss off.' Goba looked at Vass. 'Why don't you do your pal a favor and drive him down to the psycho ward at St Dominic's? Because if you don't I'm gonna rip his goddam face off.'

Boyle noticed a wrench lying on the floor of the carport, and he stooped, picked it up and held it out in front of Goba. The tool was rusty and brittle and might snap if he struck Goba with any force, but since it was the only possible weapon to hand what choice did he have? Unless he hefted one of the gnomes and used it to launch an assault on Silas Goba, a notion that struck him as only slightly plausible. MAN STRUCK BY GNOME-SHAPED MISSILE.

Goba smiled at the wrench and said, 'Hotshot, huh? Tough guy, huh? Come on. Come on. What you waiting for, asshole?' He made beckoning gestures, inviting Boyle forward even as he struggled to maintain his own balance.

Vass said, 'Lee. Let's get out of here.'

Goba said, 'Yeah, Lee, why don't you listen to your friend?'

'I want that fucking trunk opened,' Boyle said.

Goba took up the stance of a prizefighter and feinted to one side, tossing out a telegraphed punch that flicked past Lee Boyle's face. Boyle swung the wrench and missed, thinking how all of a sudden this little outburst of violence had the dreamy feel of a quiet foxtrot to it. Each movement might have been plotted by a choreographer on ludes. Goba, an adherent of the Marquess of Queensberry rules, sneaked in a stiff uppercut that went whooshing close to Boyle's chin, creating a warm updraft of air. Boyle raised the wrench, brought it down, caught the back of

Goba's wrist. Goba grunted, shadowboxed a few moments, shuffling his feet back and forth like a sand dancer in a ridiculous old vaudeville routine, but he was visibly losing energy.

Boyle considered the diversity of violence. Sometimes it was hard and sharp and brutal. Sometimes it just iced the breath in your throat. Other times it was almost hallucinogenic. This situation between himself and Goba belonged in the dreamlike category, slow slow slow, elementary box-steps at the Arthur Murray School of Terpsichorean Violence. This was burlesque.

'For Christ's sake,' Vass said, stepping between Boyle and Goba, who was breathing hard. Boyle shoved Rudy aside, thinking, *Goba is all huff and puff and threat. He doesn't have the stuff it really takes. He's a drunk windbag.*

Boyle swung the wrench again, this time in an angular fashion, and it struck deep into Goba's ribcage. The big man moaned and went down on one knee, clutching his side. Boyle had the urge to drive the wrench into the guy's head and feel the sweet smack of metal on bone, but he was going through a dip in energy, and all he really wanted was access to the goddam trunk. Goba was staring up at him, mouth open.

'The keys,' Boyle said.

'Fuck off.'

'The keys, man,' Vass said to Goba. 'Just give him the keys.'

'You can take a runnin' fuck, too,' Goba said. 'My goddam rib's probably broken. Sweet God.'

'You want your brain stoved in?' Boyle said.

Vass said, 'Best give him the keys. Don't push him.'

Goba said, 'If I was younger, by Christ—'

'Yeah yeah yeah,' Boyle said and held out his hand. This humidity was wilting him.

Goba said, 'One time I coulda had you for a snack between meals, shithead.'

'*The fucking keys!*'

'Crazy bastard,' Goba said, and dug in the back pocket of his blue jeans. He groaned and tossed a set of keys to Boyle. 'Go ahead. Open the trunk. You'll find this chick you're missing all wrapped up in a roll of linoleum under a pile of oil rags and old newspapers.'

Boyle walked to the Chrysler, unlocked the trunk, hesitated.

He felt the full cold terror of awful expectation.

He flipped the trunk open.

The interior light came on, illuminating thick volumes of drapery samples. He reached in, rummaged, threw the books out, yanked the carpet up, saw the jack neatly tucked away, the spare tire in the well, examined the space in the manner of a demented forensic scientist hunting minuscule clues – a pubic hair, a smudge of dirt, anything at all. He saw nothing, no sign of Almond, no tube of lipstick, earring, errant shoe, discarded panties, sweet fuck all. He slammed the lid shut and lowered his face until his forehead touched metal.

'You satisfied now?' Goba said. 'Huh? You happy now?'

Boyle experienced a strange zero condition. The night was collapsing about him, like he was coming undone in various stages, flesh peeling from bone, his gut falling and falling. Speed wearing off. He was crashing like a machine-gunned hot-air balloon.

He heard Vass at his side. 'Let's split this scene, Lee.'

Lee Boyle raised his face, looked at Rudy. 'Maybe he buried her some place. Maybe it was like that. Killed her, dug a hole.'

'Come on, Lee. This guy's done nothing. Look at him, for Christ's sake.'

'Fucking right I've done nothing,' Goba said. He was hunched among his gnomes and leprechauns, rubbing his rib area and looking fat and pathetic. Spit flecked the corners of his slack lips.

Vass said, 'Come on. We'll go back to the truck. Check out this last address.'

Boyle walked to where Goba crouched and stood over him. 'I'm not crossing you off my list, Goba. Understand that. You're still a candidate.'

'I see you back here, it's shotgun time,' Goba said. 'No questions asked. I blast at the first sign of the whites of your goddam eyes.'

'Yeah yeah.'

'I'm fucking serious, fella,' Goba said. 'A twelve-gauge right in the breadbasket.'

Boyle threw the car keys away among the plaster figures, went to the truck and climbed in on the passenger side.

From his shirt pocket he removed the baggie, laid a tiny mound of crank on the back of his thumb and tried to keep his hand still as he inclined his face toward it. He closed one nostril with the tip of a forefinger and snorted up the other, then repeated this with the second nostril. The crystal hit his throat like a rasp of buckshot and his eyes smarted and he tilted his face back and waited for the familiar acceleration, the quick-quick tango of his heart.

18

EVE LASSITER LEANED TOWARD THE GUY IN THE CAR. HE WAS middle-aged, paunchy, looked respectable. He could have been a store clerk. You could imagine him ringing up your haberdashery items on an old-fashioned cash register in a room smelling of sawdust and kerosene. She saw herself through his eyes, thigh-length boots and a criminally short skirt and her nipples visible through her blouse.

'All aboard for the razzmatazz express, sweetie,' he said.

'Sorry. I'm waiting for somebody,' she said.

'Your waiting days are over, sweet thing. Get in.'

'Not tonight, honey,' she said.

'You just out here flashing your ass for the good of your health?'

'I told you. I'm waiting for somebody.'

'This could be construed as false advertising, bitch.' The guy flipped her a finger and drove his car down the block. Eve turned, strolled along the sidewalk. That was the third approach she'd rebuffed so far.

The smell of reefer was strong in the close night air.

Twenty or so girls walked up and down under the street lights. Kids. Difficult to tell their age. They wore heavy make-up, smoked dope, some huddled around crack pipes, some sharing joints. A couple of these kids looked like basket cases, undernourished. A few older professionals hung together away from the dopers. Eve found the situation depressing. The drugs, the cracked sidewalks, lives casually wasted.

On the next block, where the male hustlers congregated, she saw Joshua Gold beneath a street lamp. There was segregation at work here. Females on one stretch, guys on the other. Gold wasn't looking at her.

She walked to the other corner. Ed Duff's car was parked some way down the block. He was a shadow behind the wheel.

She wished it was Greg in the car instead. He was powwowing with the chief, he'd said. Even if he hadn't been, would he have provided personal back-up anyway? You could hardly expect that of him. First, he was *Lieutenant* Samsa, and he couldn't be asked to perform such a dogsbody function, even though he'd generously gone out of his way for her in the past because he felt some touching custodial thing toward her, which caused some minor gossip in the department and a few snide remarks about favoritism. Second, he'd been acting weird all day, understandable in the context of his wife's death. But still, she'd never seen him quite so *uninterested* before. That glazed look. That sense of something smoldering inside him. The way he'd exploded briefly at her in the car.

Not quite right, Greg. Not in keeping with yourself.

She found herself wondering when he'd last been laid. You didn't have to read between the lines to get the picture that Harriet, who'd lived sealed off from the world, God knows where, hadn't been sexually active. *Maybe for years*, Eve thought.

I want to get him into bed. I want to make love to him.
She was tired of self-centered bar-stool cowboys with
great pecs. She was weary of narcissists who were basically fucking themselves.

A limousine with tinted windows drifted past.
Somebody slumming. Somebody looking for a little sleazy
action on the wrong side of the tracks.

She gazed toward Gold, who turned his face in her
direction and made an almost imperceptible shrugging
movement. She'd pressured him into coming down here to
look for the young man he'd failed to describe. The last
person known to have seen Anthony Leeson alive. His
possible killer.

She looked at her watch. Three hours had passed.
Maybe it was time to call it a night. But she didn't like to
think she might miss anything.

Gold was walking away now, drifting along the sidewalk. He turned a corner. She wondered if he'd just
decided to blow the whole thing off. She moved after him,
caught up with him in an alley.

'Taking a break, Joshua?'

He stuck his hands in his pockets and leaned against a
wall. 'This is like a *total* waste of time. This kid Leeson
picked up might just have been passing through. Anyhow,
I'm not really in the mood for being down here. It's a
major bummer.'

'I'm real sorry it's such a drag for you, Joshua. But I
want you to stay down here with me.'

'I assume I can't refuse?'

'I might take a very dim view of a refusal,' she said.

He pushed himself off the wall. 'Okay. I wouldn't want
to be an unco-operative citizen, would I? It might make
me look more a suspect than you already think I am.'

'Did I say you're a suspect?' she asked.

'Some things you don't have to say out loud, Detective.'

556

Gold frowned. 'A question for you: am I going to need a lawyer somewhere down the line?'

'You're asking me to predict the future,' she said. 'That's not my line of expertise.'

'Look at me, Detective. Take a good long look at me. Now tell me I resemble the kind of guy who'd slash *anybody* to death.'

'Killers come in all shapes and sizes, Josh.'

'God in *heaven*. I did not murder Anthony Leeson.'

'I don't recall ever saying you did.'

'You know, you have a knack of saying things that don't match the expression on your face. You must play a very mean hand of poker.'

'Sometimes I play mean regardless of the game.'

'I bet you do.'

They walked together to the corner of the alley, where Joshua Gold stopped and snapped his thumb against his index finger. He laughed suddenly in an excited way. 'I just remembered something.'

'What?'

'Your lieutenant. What's he called? Samson?'

'What about him?'

'It's probably nothing,' Gold said.

'Tell me anyway.'

'Oh, gladly, gladly,' Gold said, and laughed again.

19

SHE LAY ON THE GRASS, HER FACE AND LEGS COVERED WITH flecks of dried mud and streaks of black dirt. Her position was fetal, short skirt drawn up to her thighs, panties white and lacy and discolored. Samsa hunched down beside her. *Make her go away*. He'd stepped inside a hinterland he didn't recognize, a place where laws didn't apply, logic had no role.

The little man called Dr Lewis Dice, struggling against hysteria, stood a few feet away alongside Al Brodsky. He'd been out walking with his Ziploc bags, looking for samples. *Ziploc bags*, Samsa thought. *Samples of what?* He wondered how any of this fitted into the scheme of things, or if there even was such a scheme. Or if the world was just altogether random and a person's history nothing more than a series of accidental occurrences.

A half-dozen uniformed cops prowled the area, directing flashlights into the tangled bushes where Dice said he'd discovered the body. A couple of portable lamps had been rigged up, but they failed to penetrate the sheer dark secrecy of the thickets. Beyond the lamps, half hidden in shadow, stood a small gathering of observers attracted to the field by the sound of sirens and the lights. They were silent and watchful. This was better than TV. It was live, unfolding in front of their eyes. Why didn't they just go the fuck home?

Samsa was having a problem swallowing. His hands sweated, his shirt stuck to his skin. He needed air, but there was none to breathe.

You need more than air. You need salvation.

Brodsky came forward, loomed over the corpse. 'Broken neck,' he said. 'And look. I'd say a rodent got at her fingertips.'

The girl's head hung at the kind of angle you never saw on the living. If you raised her face up in your hands, even with the greatest care, it would loll from side to side. Samsa was immersed in feelings he couldn't quantify, couldn't differentiate – a terrifying sadness, a murmur of panic, imminent danger. Faded mascara tracks, zigzagged by rainfall, lined her cheeks. Her little mouth was closed in a kind of pout, and her eyes, mercifully, were shut. He wanted to draw her skirt down, cover the underwear, but he couldn't bring himself to touch her. It was the very last thing he could do.

Brodsky kneeled beside Samsa and spoke quietly. 'There's bruising round the neck.'

Samsa hadn't noticed this. Particulars escaped him. Details he had no eye for. He remembered the contusion on his own shoulder and laid a hand against it, covering it, as if he were afraid that somebody might see it, despite the sports coat and shirt he wore.

He turned to look up at Dice. 'How did you come to find her?'

The discovery of the corpse had dismantled Dice. He was shocked, even though death was an old acquaintance. He related the sequence of events to Samsa, a tale that included a dead swallow, taxidermy, air rifles, altogether incoherent and surreal. But the whole night was surreal: the portable lamps, the mention of Ziploc bags, the creaking noises of cops parting shrubbery and the ghouls watching from the shadows.

And the girl. Above all else.

Samsa glanced at the fingertips on her left hand. Bitten, gnawed. He got to his feet. His legs were stiff. 'You collect dead birds?'

'I do a little taxidermy, you see,' Dice said.

Samsa exchanged a glance with Al Brodsky. 'You stuff *birds*, Dr Dice?'

'Not just birds,' Dice said. 'Snakes. Cats.'

'And this is what, like a hobby?'

Dice said, 'More than a hobby.'

'Had you ever seen this girl before?' It was the kind of question he felt obliged to ask. A cop's question. Let's establish a few things for the record. Let's stake out certain parameters. This is the way the business of homicide is conducted. And I'm all business, Dice. I'm Lieutenant Samsa.

'No, never. How could anyone do . . .' Lewis Dice left his question unfinished.

Bad things happen, Samsa thought. *Would that answer you, Doctor?* No, because it didn't go far enough into the rotted infrastructure of the human heart. The things people do to one another. He remembered suddenly a homicide some fifteen years ago, when a man called J. J. Coleman had stabbed his wife, and then butchered her into pieces small enough to fit inside shoeboxes, which he had sent by special delivery to addresses picked at random from phone directories. Strangers opened the boxes, wondering maybe if they'd won some kind of free gift from a department store or a mail-order house.

Only to find otherwise.

Samsa looked at the girl again, wished he hadn't. He wished for a lot of things: to walk away from here, to travel back down through the crooked passageways of time all the way to last night where he might choose a different turning, to go home and lock the door and draw the curtains and lie down and sleep for ever and never dream.

He stared at Dice's pink face. Taxidermy. He thought of the dead girl filled with embalming fluids and laid out in a coffin. He imagined parents, sisters, brothers. Heartache and anguish, wreckage.

Dice was talking about a rat he'd seen come out of the bushes. Samsa tried to concentrate, but his mind was scattered and circuits were jammed.

'So you found the body and reported it at once?'

Dice said, 'I live just over there,' and he pointed toward the lights of Chackstone. 'I ran all the way back to my house to call.'

Samsa turned and looked beyond the lamps across the great field. He felt unsteady. *How long did you think she'd lie here undiscovered? For eternity? Her bones found a hundred years from now? But you knew she'd be found sooner or later. You were waiting, in a state of fearful suspension, for it to happen. You just didn't expect it this soon, did you?*

He saw the faint outline of the big tree in the distance, then he walked a few yards away from Dice. Brodsky followed him.

'You okay, Greg?' Brodsky asked.

'I'm hot.'

Brodsky sighed. 'So much for a quiet evening's drinking and shooting the bull.'

Samsa smiled in a strained way. He tried to imagine how his expression looked to Al Brodsky. He guessed weak, unconvincing.

'I wonder if she was killed here,' Brodsky said. 'Or if it happened someplace else and she was dumped in these bushes. I don't see any tire tracks.'

Tire tracks, Samsa thought. *Go back across the field, Al, and you'll find tracks that reach from the blacktop as far as that goddam tree.*

Brodsky was gazing down at the ground. 'But we'll find footprints all right,' he said. 'Place like this, we'll probably find more than we need. What I hear is kids come out here with rifles trampling all over the joint. And junkies. Also teenagers with kegs of beer. Party animals.'

He gazed across the property. Samsa thought he could hear things click into place in Brodsky's mind. Before the chief had the chance to state what he was thinking, Samsa said, 'Over there's where I came off the road last night. Straight into that tree.'

Brodsky said, 'I *knew* there was something about this place at the back of my mind.' He took a piece of chewing gum from his pocket and stuck it in his mouth.

'I wasn't in the right frame of mind to notice much of anything at the time,' Samsa said. Make light of this. File it under unhappy coincidence. 'There could have been a whole gang of killers dumping bodies all over the place and I wouldn't have noticed a damn thing.'

Brodsky laid a hand on Samsa's shoulder and squeezed it in a manner that was both friendly and concerned. 'I guess not,' he said. 'You're just lucky you didn't do yourself some serious damage.'

'Lucky is right,' Samsa said.

Brodsky glanced at Dice, several yards away. 'What do you make of our embalmer?'

'Eccentric at least,' Samsa said.

'But no more than that.'

Samsa shrugged. 'I don't know, Al.'

Brodsky looked in the direction of the dead girl. Lamps

562

illuminated her in a cruel way. 'Christ, she's so *young*. What do you think? Fourteen? Fifteen? And the way she's dressed – it doesn't leave a whole lot to the imagination, does it? You think she was hooking, picked up the wrong guy?'

'It's a possibility,' Samsa said. He ran a finger under his collar. He felt like some fluffy whipped-up concoction melting.

What have I done to my life?

It was easy to fabricate excuses: I was thinking of my daughter and how the truth would affect her. I was thinking of the department's reputation.

Bullshit.

You were only thinking of saving Gregory Samsa's ass, except you didn't think it through too well, did you?

Brodsky said, 'Let's play this. Some weirdo picks her up. He breaks her neck, wonders where he's going to stash the body, thinks this is the perfect place. So he drives here, parks his car somewhere up on the road, carries her across the field. Which pretty much rules out Dice, I guess. He doesn't look like he can carry anything heavier than a dead bird in a plastic bag.'

'On the other hand, she might have been dragged,' Samsa said. 'The mud on her clothes and legs could be consistent with dragging.' What was he saying? He realized, with something of a painful jolt, that he didn't *want* to rule out Dice so easily. In some subterranean aspect of himself, some corner he was ashamed to discover, he wanted Dice to be a suspect. But Brodsky was right. If the girl was carried across the field, or even dragged, Dice didn't seem a likely candidate. *What is happening to me, for Christ's sake?*

Brodsky said, 'Let's walk a few yards, Greg. I want a little privacy.'

Samsa strolled through the grass after the chief. He had the feeling of being poised on a needle. A little privacy. What did Brodsky have to say that required privacy? They moved about twenty yards beyond the lamps and Brodsky stopped, took the chewing gum from his mouth and slung it away.

'I know it's basically Charlie Bird's territory out here, Greg, but sometimes I have to think beyond zonal parameters. Social Services and Child Welfare and the good folks of our local press are always griping about how little we do about these kids. They claim we just look the other way when anyone mentions child prostitution. Turn a blind eye, sweep it under the rug, et cetera, which is only a perceived truth. We round them up every now and then, but what good does it do? They get rapped on the knuckles and they walk. A few go to juvey. The rest are just tossed out of court.'

Brodsky was silent. Samsa waited, conscious of his own shallow breathing.

'What I'm trying to say is I think it might be appropriate if you took this one yourself, Greg.'

Samsa closed his eyes for a moment. He wondered if he swayed just a little. 'Appropriate? How?'

'If this kid was hooking, and the head homicide honcho is assigned to the case, I can tell you, without fear of contradiction, that it's going to go down pretty damn well in certain quarters. It shows a caring face. We're not assigning your average homicide hack, we're putting the Man himself in charge. We're not sweeping this one under any rug. We're giving it top billing.'

Samsa thought about things being swept under rugs. Secrets. Lies. Terrors. He couldn't do it, didn't have whatever skills it took for this masquerade Brodsky was unwittingly suggesting. He'd say something wrong, make a slip, damn himself somehow.

564

'Well?' Brodsky asked. 'Give me some feedback here, Greg.'

Samsa stared across the property. He remembered how rain had roared. He remembered the way his body had been stooped as he moved through the long grass.

He remembered the weight of death most of all.

'Charlie Bird isn't going to like it,' he said.

Brodsky said, 'I don't give a shit what Charlie Bird likes. I'm thinking of the department as a whole.'

'This isn't a political campaign, Al.'

'Don't talk political campaign to me,' Brodsky said. 'This isn't about politics.'

'PR then,' Samsa said.

'Beyond PR, Greg.'

'The department with heart.'

'What is wrong with you?' Brodsky asked. 'You know I don't give a fuck about PR. I'm thinking about this kid. There are whackos out there. Guys that don't think twice about wasting a hooker. If I put you in charge of the case, it's like sending a double-edged message. One, we treat all homicides with equal seriousness, whether it's a kid prostitute like this or the president of some goddam corporation. And two, we highlight the tragically real perils of the street.'

Brodsky had it down pat. The quickness of his brain, his agility in seizing upon a situation and exploring its opportunities. You had to admire it. Samsa felt mosquitoes buzz around his face and he swatted them away, but they kept coming back.

'And we score some easy brownie points,' he said.

'Look,' Brodsky said, 'if you don't want to take the fucking case, don't take it.'

'I didn't say that, Al.' He imagined Bird working this homicide, picking over details, sifting the ashes, reconstructing the crime. Bird wasn't smart. He was better than smart when it came to this kind of thing. He was dogged. He couldn't be moved. He caught a whiff and tracked it like a demented hound and pursued it all the way to the gates of hell if need be.

'You never know,' Brodsky said. 'You could even be saving some other kid from ending up like the one here.'

Samsa heard movement and looked back at the crime scene. A photographer had arrived, and so had a couple of guys from the coroner's office. They were kneeling, examining the body. Usually they were chirpy, off-hand, just another stiff, so what. Tonight they were solemn. A flashlight popped and the corpse was captured on film for a new homicide folder. 'I'll just get this from another couple of angles and I'm outta here.' *Pop pop*.

The lights stung Samsa's eyes. The girl was surrounded by retinal disturbances, small prancing glares.

Move. Hadn't he told her that? *Get up and I'll help you out of here. But only if you move. Just give me some goddam co-operation*. And then he'd placed his palms on either side of her face, as if he might somehow realign the broken neck, but her head slid from his damp grasp. He'd never forget that. That was one for his nightmare files.

He was struck by an absurdity. The girl was dead. The jackrabbit was still alive. *The rabbit was running around out there someplace*. Life was a series of cruelties and imbalances. One hapless moment and you're ruined, and there's no way back, no road to the high ground of redemption.

A girl dies in the rain.

You want to scream.

He heard Al Brodsky just behind him and, without turning to look, uncertain of whether he could face Al at all without giving something away, he said, 'I'll do it.'

'Good man,' Brodsky said.

I'll do it, Samsa thought. *For all the wrong reasons, I'll do it.*

And he imagined a killer, somebody who'd prowled the rainy dark with his burden, a murderous stranger it was his job to track down and apprehend.

20

LEE BOYLE SAT IN THE PASSENGER SEAT OF RUDY VASS'S PICK-up, his body hunched a little way forward. He was studying the house across the street. Number 1900 Devine, nice two-story home in a good suburb. Trim lawn, flowers around the porch. A flagpole even. The American Way. But no sign of any Chrysler, 92K something something something.

Where was it? Tucked at the back of the house, hidden from the attention of vandals that might stray through a prosperous suburb at dark? Or was there a garage he hadn't noticed? A beige Chevy in the driveway was the only vehicle he could see.

'So what do we do?' Vass said. 'Wait here until this guy shows up with the car?'

Boyle didn't answer. He hadn't really heard Rudy's question. He was shivery, set apart from the humidity of the night inside his own little cell of frost. He chewed on the soft tissue around the ulcer in his mouth.

With great patience, Rudy Vass said, 'He could be a traveling salesman for all we know. Maybe he's gone on a trip or something. What I'm saying, we could be waiting here a long time.'

Lee Boyle lit a cigarette. He looked at the front windows of the house. The only light he saw was one that burned in the downstairs hall. He stared at the Chevy for a time, thinking of the ludicrous struggle with Silas Goba, the empty trunk, the books of drapery samples. The bad feeling he'd had about Almond hadn't gone away. If anything it was more concentrated now, a calcified deposit that had formed in his brain. He was uptight, gripped by wild notions, tidal anxieties.

Vass said, 'The longer we sit here the more chance of some neighbor calling the cops. Next thing you know, a cruiser pulls up and we're talking to some hard-ass cop who wants to know why we're hanging out on this well-heeled street.'

Boyle said nothing. Rudy was getting on his nerves somewhat. A small patronizing note had crept into his voice, and Boyle wasn't pleased with it.

'We should call it quits for the night, come back again in the morning. I'd be happy to drive you home.'

Boyle didn't want to go home yet. He told Vass so.

'Lee, you can strain friendships, you know. You can ask too much of a person at times.'

'Any time you want to let me out, just say the word.'

'I'm only pointing to a fact,' Vass said. 'I don't remember signing on as your chauffeur. You need some sleep anyhow. The way you acted with that guy Goba. I mean, *a body in a trunk?* Let's get a little reality into the situation.'

Boyle looked at Vass's face, the skin yellow under the street lights. He had the appearance of a man in the grip of a terrible disease. 'Suddenly you know something about reality, huh? What are you telling me? I'm suffering from sleep deprivation and imagining things?'

Vass tugged his little goatee. 'All I know is I'm sitting in this truck twiddling my thumbs on account of you having some great burning need to track down this bimbo.'

Boyle dropped his cigarette on the floor, crushed it. 'Say that again.'

'I take it back, okay? I take it back.'

Boyle said, 'You called her a bimbo—'

'I also retracted, Lee. Okay? I happen to be weary. The shit I do for you. Sometimes I wonder, am I weak? Is this a dependency thing I have? Or is it because I don't want to get on the wrong side of you because secretly you kind of scare me? Do I need your approval? What the fuck is it?'

'I don't want to sit here and dissect relationships,' Boyle said. 'If I wanted that I'd be sitting in an art house watching a French movie.'

Vass was quiet for a while. 'Let it go. Forget the girl, blow town for a while, take a trip, straighten out a few things in your life. That way the girl's out of your system, and you're out of Plumm's clutches.'

'I can't get out of Plumm's clutches,' Boyle said. 'He's like an octopus.'

'You just walk down to the bus station and buy a ticket to Nowheresburg.'

'Plumm's got people watching me.' Boyle took the baggie out of his shirt pocket and snorted, fighting back a need to sneeze. The speed zigzagged to his brain after a fiery detour around his heart. He imagined he could see it traveling in his bloodstream, shooting little trails of harsh white flak.

Vass looked doubtful. 'He can't have you under observation *all* the time, Lee. It's just not possible.'

'It's a feeling I get,' Boyle said.

'You know where that feeling comes from? Out that goddam bag you carry around.'

Boyle ignored this. He didn't need Rudy's disapproval. He didn't need criticism. He was listening to the hue and cry of his pulses. He was hearing Almond call out to him from a deep dark place. *Come get me, Lee. Come find me.*

Vass said, 'Know what I really think? You got a taste for this kid. You fucked her, and you liked it. Did you fuck her, Lee?'

'She's strictly business. That's all. I can't just abandon her.'

'Who abandoned who in this case? I mean, what are we *talking* about here? You're not thinking straight, Lee.'

'Don't tell me how I'm thinking, Rudy.' Boyle thought, *I've had about enough of this.* He grabbed Rudy by the collar of his denim jacket and dragged his face forward a few inches. 'Don't *ever* tell me how or what I'm thinking. You don't have some kind of probe that goes inside my skull.'

'Lee,' Vass said. 'Let go. Don't get into this.'

Boyle saw it in the depths of Rudy Vass's eyes, a judgemental quality. Vass was silently accusing him for the actions of his life. The girl, the dope, everything.

Vass sighed long and deep. 'Take your hand away.'

'You make me.'

'You're in this contrary mood I don't like.'

'I don't give a fuck what you like. The hand stays.'

'So what do we do? Sit here all night like this? This is childish. I don't want trouble with you, Lee. Of all people. I'm about the only friend you got, man. Keep that in mind.'

'I've got scores of friends,' Boyle said.

'Name one,' Vass said.

'You're trying to put me on the spot. I can see straight through you, Rudy. You want to be completely indispensable in my life; Lee Boyle's only buddy. I know him from way back, U of Penn. We hit it off from the start, we're fucking inseparable, we're like *that*, twins. You're possessive, Vass.'

'Christ's sake,' Vass said. 'I can't hack this. You're gonezoid.'

Boyle tugged harder on the collar. Anger *pumped* in his blood. He resented Rudy's self-righteousness. Who did Vass think he was kidding, coming off like he was Mr Twelve-Step, certifiably straight? 'You're up there with your halo on and you're looking down at me and I don't approve of that, Rudy.'

'It's not like that, Lee.'

'It sounds exactly like that to me,' Boyle said. He clicked the glove compartment open, and a tiny light bulb came on and flickered meekly. The gun lay under some documents – vehicle registration papers. He pulled it out, a Colt Government model 38, and turned it over in his hand.

'Just put the gun back, Lee.'

Boyle pushed the barrel into Rudy Vass's cheek. 'You think I'd shoot my one and only friend?'

'This is a rotten feeling, Lee.' Little slicks of sweat ran over Rudy Vass's eyelids.

'I can hear your heartbeat,' Boyle said.

'Loud, aintit,' Vass said. 'So put the gun back and let's get on with our lives and we'll forget all about this little game you're playing. You proved you can scare me, okay?'

Boyle thought of life and death, fragile balances, the way things were poised so very delicately. He thought about pulling the trigger, blasting Rudy's face. Imagining it, the ferocious kick in his fist, Rudy's head all over the place like a pizza splashed against a wall. He lowered the weapon slowly, tossed it back inside the glove compartment, laughed for a time, then couldn't remember why he was laughing. The sound dried and faded in his throat, but he could still hear an echo of it.

'I don't fucking *believe* you pulled a gun on me,' Vass said. 'That's it. I'm out of here. This is the end of the line for me.'

He started the pick-up. Boyle had a moment of indecision. He knew Vass was correct on one level: waiting here could turn out to be pointless, and some snoop neighbor was likely to call the cops. At the same time he was reluctant to leave, because maybe the key to Almond was somewhere in that house across the way. Maybe the solution was concealed beyond that porch, that front door. He listened to the whine of the engine, closed his eyes, felt the lids flicker, little tics, small muscular spasms.

'I don't give a shit, man. But are you coming, or you hanging out here?' Vass asked.

Boyle opened his eyes, looked at 1900 Devine. The house appeared to shimmer in his vision. The light burning downstairs was fragmented, casting pale white splinters. He imagined a bulb exploding and felt shards of flying glass in his scalp like small barbed airborne insects.

'I'm going,' Vass said, and he slipped the truck into gear. It rolled past the house and Boyle turned once to look back. I ought to stay. I ought to wait. He was aware of the neighborhood changing, the freeway approaching, and then Vass was driving down the access road. Boyle saw the lights of downtown in the distance. He had the feeling he'd left something of himself behind on Devine. Something he ought to go back and recover.

He looked at Vass, whose face was stern.

'Pull over, Rudy.'

'Pull over? On the freeway?'

'I don't care where. Just drop me.'

Vass said fuck, he wasn't going to stop on the freeway. He came off at the next exit, and Boyle opened the passenger door and stepped down onto the street outside a twenty-four-hour video store. 'Go home, Rudy,' he said.

'Is that what you want? Me to leave you here without wheels?'

'That's what I want,' Boyle said.

'You're sure?'

Boyle looked along the sidewalk and then up at Vass in the cab. 'I'm sure.'

Vass seemed relieved. He needed a break from Boyle's company. 'Whatever you say, Lee. Whatever you say.'

Boyle slammed the door shut, *good fucking riddance*, slapped a hand against the panel and watched the pick-up disappear at the end of the street. He walked to the window of the video store and gazed through glass at the empty aisles, the glossy displays and posters advertising moronic movies.

The girl at the cash register was reading a magazine under fluorescent light and Boyle thought, *Almond, this is Almond*, and he pressed his face to the pane with his palms flattened against the glass and his expectations soaring into flight, but then the girl turned her face to one side and he saw he was mistaken, he'd forced a resemblance on a total stranger, only the black hair was similar, nothing else. He watched her for a time anyway, until she began to throb and brighten in his vision, as if she were on the point of combustion.

21

SAMSA CHECKED HIS WATCH: 1 A.M. HE FILLED A WAX CUP
with water from the cooler and gulped it. The basement
rooms were stuffy, unbearable. From his position at the
cooler he could see through an open door into another
room, and beyond that another room, and beyond that
yet another. It was like an infinity of reflections in angled
mirrors. He imagined himself trapped in endless boxes,
dwindling in size the further he looked.

He crumpled the cup and dumped it just as Brodsky
appeared. Billy Fogue, white shirtsleeves hanging loose,
stood behind Al. His hairless head glistened. Here and
there other cops wandered back and forth or worked the
phones. The graveyard shift, energized by a fresh homicide.

Al Brodsky said, 'Fogue got a fingerprint match
through the computer.'

Fogue said, 'The girl was one Cecily Suarez, reported
missing by her parents in Denver. Seems she made running
away from home something of a habit. She was thirteen
years of age.'

Thirteen, Samsa thought.

Christ. One-three.

He felt the clamminess of the rooms invade his heart. Cecily Suarez. She'd told him her name was Almond. Two years younger than Darcy, for God's sake. He ran a hand across his face. He was thinking of Zane the coroner, the slab in the morgue where the girl had lain, Zane examining the dead flesh. The cause of death was easy for Zane, who'd seen every kind of fatality. The pattern of bruising appeared to be consistent with the use of a blunt instrument of some kind, and he'd studied what he referred to as 'areas of ecchymosis'.

A blunt instrument, Brodsky had said. *Like what? A rubber hose? A baseball bat? A karate chop?*

Zane, a skinflint with loose opinions and facile conclusions, had simply said, *People just don't realize how easy it is to break a neck.*

The girl had tracks on her arms. Zane had peered at them closely, but with a certain clinical indifference. *I wouldn't say she was a heavy user of a needle. I think we'll find out more about her drug habits when we've examined her nasal passages.* Samsa thought of instruments: steel scalpels, probes, the hard awful tools of Zane's trade.

She's been dead twenty-four hours, I'd say. Somewhere between ten and eleven last night.

Billy Fogue said, 'Let me add this news flash. Our girl was picked up a month ago on a streetwalking charge, fingerprinted and kept overnight in juvenile hall, then released on the order of some bleeding-heart social worker because she promised she'd take the next bus all the way home to Denver. She even bought a one-way ticket to Denver, which convinced the dickhead do-gooder that the contrite young Cecily had good intentions. Cunning little number. Did Cecily, aka

Almond, catch the bus? Oh, yeah, sure she did.'

Samsa thought, *I carried her through the rain, I hefted her wet body on my shoulder and carried her across that field, and even though she weighed practically nothing in life, in death she was heavy.* He shoved the memory away like indigestible food, but it kept coming back, a regurgitation of the slog, the mud, the grass, the jagged highs of panic. He'd thought of burying her, but he didn't have the implements and he didn't have the time, all he'd wanted was to hide her and get out of that field quickly, a vanishing act, oblivion. But there were no guarantees of oblivion.

No guarantees of anything. Not now.

Samsa stared into the middle distance, as if he were trying to distort the focus of his eyesight.

'Rebb is on his way,' Brodsky said. He held a hand in front of Samsa's face and clicked his thumb and middle finger together. 'Are you with us, Greg? You remember Stephen Rebb? Long-time vice cop?'

Samsa said, 'Sorry, I was thinking.'

Brodsky asked, 'Anything you want to share?'

Samsa shook his head. 'Not yet.'

'Give us a holler when you do, Lew Tenant,' Fogue remarked cheerfully, plucking a cheroot from his shirt pocket and then, glancing at Brodsky, thought better of lighting it while the chief was around.

Samsa remembered the thickets, the way he'd placed the girl among them, how he'd protected his hands from barbs by tugging the sleeves of his jacket down over his fingers. He remembered the wild rain slashing at his face. He remembered her on the coroner's slab, and how very young she'd seemed, with all the life gone out of her and the make-up washed from her face. Young and very small and soft. A life unlived, an empty bedroom in a house in Denver. Probably posters thumbtacked to a wall. Maybe a secret diary stashed under a loose floorboard. The relics of a person.

Like Harriet's clothing hanging in closets.

He turned his face as Stephen Rebb came into the room.

Rebb said, 'Whatcha got for me?'

Brodsky said, 'A dead girl.'

Rebb was a walking offense, a tall cadaverous man with sunken cheeks and dyed crow-black hair and a serious case of body odor. He'd worked so long in the world of vice it was as if he'd decided that the smells of dark streets and illegal massage parlors and humid whorehouses were preferable to basic hygiene. Dandruff littered the collar of his black jacket and there was always dirt under his fingernails, which he picked at from time to time with a nail file. He was in search of authenticity with a capital A, Samsa sometimes thought. The underworld man with an almost encyclopedic knowledge of the city's illicit flesh trade. You wouldn't want Rebb in your home. It was hard enough to accept him around the office.

Rebb asked, 'How old?'

'Thirteen,' Billy Fogue said.

'Streetwalker?'

'You wouldn't be here at one in the morning if she was a goddam jaywalker, Rebb,' Brodsky said, with a measure of impatience and distaste.

'So I'm not the best-loved character in the department. I accept that role willingly,' Rebb said. He smiled, show-ing his crooked upper teeth. He courted unpopularity, wanted to be seen as a night creature, a sleazy outsider who operated on the far margins of the law. 'The way I see it, I don't get paid for my charm. I get paid because I'm the only sucker you got who knows what shit really smells like down at street level.'

Samsa said, 'We all admire your talents, Steve.'

Rebb came close to Samsa, leaving a little cheesy cloud

of halitosis in the air. 'I like to be appreciated, Lieutenant. So who's the dead babe?'

The dead babe. Rebb had a way of putting things.

Samsa told him.

Rebb, tapping the side of his nose, made whirring sounds like those of a computer scanning a hard disc. 'She's coming into view . . . yeah . . . yeah . . .'

'Forget the sound effects and cut to the goddam chase,' Brodsky said.

Rebb said. 'She worked for a guy called . . . *got it*, real small-time hustler, name of Lee Boyle. Odd case. Wealthy background – father rich as fucking old John D. – disowned by family, drifted downhill. Drugs, the usual. Excuse me if I don't find it altogether an all-American tragedy, because this Boyle isn't a nice guy.'

'Somebody check Boyle's sheet,' Samsa said.

Fogue said, 'Only too happy to oblige,' and left the room.

Rebb asked, 'How did the kid get it anyway?'

Brodsky told him.

Rebb said, 'Busted neck, huh? I think it's a risk-type thing these lowlifers actually like. Life on the sordid edge. The next trick may be your last, honey. The next blow job might be HIV-pos, the next fuck might have a short-handled ax in the glovebox.'

Samsa said, 'You know Boyle?'

'I squeezed him once or twice for the hell of it. You got to apply some pressure on these guys now and then just to keep them in line. He's strictly from Peanuts Street. Smart, but missing the essential nuts and bolts that differentiate a regular guy from a slimeball. He used to run a girl called Nancy, who took a hike. But Lee didn't take kindly to this. So he tracks Nancy down and kicks the shit out of her, and she goes to County with serious fractures and a face that won't look the same again. But, hey, does she press charges? Does she point the finger at Lee? Fuck she does. I fell down an elevator shaft or I was hit by a goddam car, bullshit stories. See, there's some real off-the-wall loyalty out there at times.'

'Could Boyle have killed Cecily Suarez?' Samsa asked. The question seemed to him to hang in the air a long time. But this is the way it works. The creation of diversions. He was building thoroughfares in his head with no master blueprint, trying to believe they might lead somewhere in the end. Somewhere away from him. He felt shriveled, and wondered if this was what fear and shame did to you. And he remembered his disappointment at dismissing Lew Dice as a suspect. He'd taken Dice aside, questioned him briefly, as if to make sure he could be discounted. The motions of a pointless inquiry. I know you're innocent, Dice. But this is what I have to do. I am the lieutenant. This is expected of me. You don't know you're talking to a shell. You're just an involuntary participant in a drama.

Tell me what it's like to stuff dead animals, Doc. But you couldn't jump from the fact that a guy had a bizarre hobby to the idea he might have killed a kid hooker. Not even in the real world could you make that leap.

Rebb said, 'Could Boyle have killed her? Depends. If the crystal's good and it's coming nice and regular, he's okay. Take away his pacifiers, who knows? Or maybe he shot up one time too many.'

'But it's a possibility,' Samsa said.

'So's the idea of me getting it on with Sharon Stone.' Rebb picked grime out of his fingernails with his nail file and, leaning into the light of a desk lamp, examined it studiously. 'So's life on Pluto.'

Samsa looked at Brodsky, who was gazing at Rebb as if the vice cop were a mutant life form spawned in the sewers under the city. Rebb stuck the nail file into his pocket just as Billy Fogue returned to the room carrying a printout.

'He's been a bad boy,' Fogue said.

'Let me see that,' Samsa said.

Fogue passed him the sheet, which Samsa scanned quickly.

LEE H. BOYLE SOCIAL SECURITY NUMBER 074-05-2515.

One count of grand theft auto, September 1992. Six-month sentence, County jail. Served ninety-seven days.

One count of aggravated assault, January 1993. Thirty-day sentence, County jail. Served thirty days.

One count of possession of forged credit cards, March 1993. One year probation.

One count of possession of amphetamine (9.4gms), November 1993. Voluntary psychiatric counseling for three-month period.

One count of sex with a minor, April 1996. Dismissed. Lack of evidence.

One count of aggravated assault, January 1997. Dismissed. Lack of evidence.

Samsa handed the sheet to Brodsky, who looked at it and said, 'It's penny-ante stuff generally.'

'Aggravated assault twice,' Samsa said. 'Maybe this time he just goes overboard. He crosses the line. Hits a little too hard. I wouldn't mind paying him a visit. You know where to find him, Rebb?'

'Not offhand. He doesn't stay long in one place. I can make a few calls, ask around.'

'Do it,' Samsa said. He thought about Darcy. He walked into his partitioned space and dialed his home number.

She answered on the first ring.

'I'm going to be very late,' he said.

'Is this business or another nocturnal voyage?'

'Business,' he said. 'Are you okay?'

'Sleepy,' she said.

'How was the date?'

'I wouldn't write a book about it. He took me to see an Italian movie because he knew I wanted to see it. Halfway through he fell asleep. "I don't like films where you have to read subtitles," he tells me.'

'You're too bright for him,' Samsa said. 'Listen, sweetheart. I've got to go.'

'Any idea of your ETA?'

'Not a clue,' he said. 'Make sure everything's locked up. Leave the downstairs light on.'

'Done that already.'

'I'll be home as soon as I can.'

'Oh, one last thing. Eve called. No message.'

He blew a kiss down the line. He thought of her in the empty house as he replaced the handset. The empty whispering house.

He looked at Rebb through the open doorway. Rebb was talking into a phone, his voice hard and aggressive. 'Yeah, you say you don't know where Boyle lives, asshole, but maybe I don't believe you. Maybe my instincts are telling me something else. And maybe I just happen to remember those scuzzy videos you're selling out the back of your goddam shop . . . Yeah, the ones with women and fucking camels, dufus, the Egyptian filth that comes to you straight outta Cairo . . .'

Samsa stepped away from his desk and felt suddenly light-headed, thinking of going out into the darkness and looking for a stranger called Lee H. Boyle and wondering if a murder rap could be pinned on him. Where was all this leading him except deeper and deeper into a night-world that had no basis in any reality he'd ever known before? Would his life always be like this now? He saw himself carrying the burden of an enormous lie, an evasion that hummed inside him constantly, like the vibrations of a machine. He suddenly remembered the fungus that had been growing behind the radiator and he wondered if it thrived still, if it was spreading, changing shape as it did so.

22

EVERYTHING IN LIFE GETS TAKEN AWAY SOONER OR LATER.
Your Porsche. Your inheritance from Daddy.
And your girl vanishes.
You don't know where. You don't know why. But a whispery little voice in your head keeps telling you it's bad.

Lee Boyle walked under street lights, aware of the webby effects they created. He passed a half-built apartment complex sealed by boards and wire fences. A large cat thumped past. He wanted to get his gun and blast the furry thing into bits and bloody pieces and see its entrails hang on the wire, brain blitzed and strewn around. But the death of a cat wouldn't cut what he was feeling any more than the act of pressing a Colt into Rudy's face had done – this surging anger followed by weird moments of detachment, then anger again. Then something he couldn't identify, loss maybe, a sense of amputation.

He realized he was in an unfamiliar neighborhood. Old brownstone houses with broken-down stoops and darkened windows and a corner grocery steel-shuttered for the night. He heard the sound of a couple squabbling from an upstairs apartment. All about him the night seemed suspended in a troublesome way, as if the darkness were held aloft on precarious stilts.

I need wheels, he thought. He was weary of walking. Wheels would boost him. He wasn't fussy; he'd take the first unlocked car he found. There was always somebody careless, even in a neighborhood like this. You could bet your ass on it. He moved along the sidewalk, checking the handles of parked cars.

Eventually he came across an old black Pontiac with leprous rust spots. The door hadn't been locked. He slid behind the wheel. The upholstery was stripped down to basic sponge. The interior smelled of sour milk. Toys littered the floor. A GI Joe figure, a broken-headed Barbie, an eyeless dinosaur with the stuffing coming out. The kids that rode in this car were brutal to their toys. Little delinquents.

A brother and sister, he figured. Always at each other's throats.

Like the way he'd been with Monique, back when.

Monique – what a fucking *pretentious* name – Monique, you giggling twat, Daddy's little girl, his favorite. Sit on my knee, Monique. Aren't you pretty? Aren't you cute? Can you sing something for us? *Ask me to sing*, Boyle would say. *I know all the words of 'Dixie' and I'm only five.* And then, always rebuffed by Daddy, he'd appeal with his curly blond-haired drop-dead charm to his mother, a cowed woman of some social ambition, whose marriage to that sphincter of a human being named Hugh had pounded her into timidity and alcoholism. Hugh called her the Gin Queen. Sometimes just Queenie. Here comes Queenie. Doesn't she look a little unsteady, children?

Queenie was wasting away in some goddam drunk

585

clinic the last Lee Boyle had heard. Banished just like himself. Discarded, tossed aside. Hugh had a whole lot to answer for. Hugh damaged people.

Boyle peeled back black masking tape under the dash, exposed the wires and connected them. He'd done it a hundred times before. Straight or fucked-up, he knew what he was doing. Spark and sizzle. The motor rumbled. He drove to the end of the street, the boneshaker spluttering. And then he was back in familiar territory, Central, driving past City Hall and Patriot Park.

He turned down side streets, alleys, parked outside a doorway splattered with spray-painted graffiti. A sign above the door read, 'The Half-Moon'. Boyle went inside, nodded at the big bouncer in the charcoal *Hey-I'm-connected* silk suit and climbed a flight of stairs into a room with black walls. A dilatory jazz trio was taking liberties with 'Every Time You Say Goodbye'.

He walked to the bar, asked for a vodka, slammed it back, repeated the action. This takes the edge off. But it didn't, not really. What it did was deceive you into *thinking* it calmed your system. He lit a cigarette, hand trembling slightly, and surveyed the few customers who sat here and there at tables. No Almond, of course. He hadn't expected to see her anyway. He was beginning to wonder if he'd ever see her again. The thought panicked him. He placed the cigarette pack on the bar and stared at his handwriting.

Mrs Fodor. No.

Silas Goba. Question mark.

Gregory J. Samsa. Who knows?

The file on Samsa. Very thin indeed. Practically empty. House in that neighborhood suggested he was probably employed in something quite profitable: financial consultancy, accountancy, maybe an executive sales position. Income what? $60–70,000 range? More? You could only hazard guesses. *You don't even know Samsa's age, what he looks like. You don't know the first goddam thing about him.*

Boyle pushed the Camel pack back and forth with the tip of his finger. He ordered a third vodka, sipped it, smoked another cigarette and stood against the bar with his eyes shut.

The girl behind the bar, skinny with big hair and a skirt so short it would have caused cricked necks and traffic chaos on Central, leaned toward him. 'You say something, Lee?'

He opened his eyes. 'No,' he said.

'Talking to yourself, huh?'

'I guess I must've been, Kiki,' he said.

'You want to watch that kind of thing,' and she winked. 'They take you away for that, I hear. Padded rooms and such.'

Padded rooms.

He remembered padded rooms.

He remembered straitjacket nightmares where he was clamped to iron beds, and thugs dressed like male nurses sat on his chest and shot him with Dilaudid to bring him out of orbit.

They called it 'voluntary' treatment.

Yeah, I asked for it. Take me in, please.

The resident shrink, Lannigan, had stuck him in a treatment group where you got to sit around and discuss your 'addiction' with a bunch of fucking wasted losers for two hours every day. He wasn't ever going back to that sweat-pit to listen to drained old dopers talking about how they'd bottomed-out, grizzled old farts who droned on about broken marriages and lost kids and ruined careers, and cried into Kleenexes or unintentionally pissed on their paper slippers.

He realized his face was sweating even if he was still

cold. His gold chain stuck to his neck. He wiped his skin with a paper napkin.

He looked at the girl and asked, 'You seen Almond around?'

'You're slipping, sweetie. You came in here and asked me that same question, oh, about twenty-four hours ago.'

'Did I? Premature senility.' He had no recollection of ever having come in here asking for Almond. All he remembered was the relentlessly driven way he'd traveled through the crazed hours of darkness and into the first pale-blue horrors of dawn trying to find her. The bars and clubs he'd zoomed through blended into one another like the elements of a long-lost memory.

'She hasn't shown up, I take it.'

'She will,' he said. 'I'm not worried.'

'Why worry,' Kiki said. 'That's my philosophy of life.'

'Positive thinking,' he replied.

'The only kind.'

He leaned across the bar toward her. He was desperate enough to play a shot in the dark. 'You meet a lot of people, Kiki. Does the name Gregory Samsa mean anything to you?'

She appeared to think for a time before she shook her head and said, 'I don't hear any bells, Lee. Sorry.'

'That's okay. No big deal.'

Samsa, he thought. *Who are you?*

He crumpled the cigarette pack.

Get with the program, Lee.

Take steps. Find out.

He left the Half-Moon, walked to the big Pontiac, fired it up. He drove toward the freeway, took the exit marked Skyville. He found the street, parked halfway down the block, cut the engine. Then he waited, didn't move, checked the area. He contemplated dipping inside the baggie just for a boost, but talked himself out of it. He still had some energy burning.

But the next crash was just around the corner.

He got out of the car and walked quietly to the place he wanted. There was still only the beige Chevy parked in the driveway. No garage. *No fucking garage.* What was this? Your basic home with the no-garage option? Save a few bucks, build one yourself later?

He lingered, feeling just a little cold now. A warning sign. Ignore it, keep going. Poor circulation, something, who gives a shit?

He listened to the neighborhood. The hum of freezers and air-conditioners, all the little clicks that regulated the civilized world. He reached the place where the driveway ended at a fenced backyard. A lamp was lit in an upstairs window, throwing enough light down for him to see that the area behind the house was all lawn.

No Chrysler here.

Suddenly he heard a girl sing from a place above. He couldn't make out the words, but the sound was quicksilver and lovely, and he listened to it with unexpected delight, possessed by the notion that the voice originated from no external source but a place inside himself. And he was reminded of the way life had been once upon a time: carefree, vibrant with rich possibilities, notions of a future. *You're going places, Lee*—

But the mountains were always just too high and the distractions too great, and after a time you got used to the troughs, you became an inhabitant of the gloomy valleys whose slopes were made out of scree you couldn't ever climb because it collapsed and crumbled the more you scratched at it.

This sweet voice. It transfixed him. *What soft incense hangs upon the boughs.*

He collided with a trash can and the lid came off and

rattled on the ground and spun to a standstill, and the singing ceased abruptly.

Lee Boyle holds his breath. He steps back in shadow. The invisible man.

The curtain at the lit upstairs window is parted slightly. A girl's face appears.

The girl with the nightingale's voice.

Her face, half lit by a lamp behind it, is young and beautiful. He can't tell the color of her hair, the color of her eyes, he just has this impression of purity and perfection.

He watched the curtain fall back in place and then he turned and hurried away in the shadows, moving quickly along the sidewalk, the voice still echoing inside him and the vision printed on his brain.

What a divine young thing.

Ripe.

Primo.

23

SAMSA DIDN'T LIKE THE LOFT, THE HUGE UNFURNISHED SPACE, ceilings twenty feet high, the brilliant white glossy walls that reflected light from a series of recessed bulbs of various colors – pinks, oranges, mauves. He had a sense of being dwarfed, as if he were shedding inches, diminishing until finally nothing would be left of him except for a pile of clothing and a pair of shoes.

Fogue and Rebb circled the woman, who sat in the only chair in the room. She was unflustered by the cops' presence. She rolled a cigarette carefully, filling black paper with tobacco. She stuck the cigarette between her lips and leaned toward Fogue, anticipating a light, which he supplied with a parsimonious flick of his lighter. According to what Rebb had said in the car on the way over, this woman had a track record: prostitution, operating a house of ill-repute, a couple of dope misdemeanors. Like Boyle, she was somebody who didn't stay in any one place too long, and Rebb had tracked her through a series of increasingly threatening phonecalls to his network of night animals – a porn-flick merchant, a crack dealer, a guy who specialized in sending pictures of naked infants over the Internet.

'Fatima—' Rebb said.

'You're behind the times. I'm not calling myself that these days,' she said.

'Oh, beg your pardon,' Rebb said.

'Cassandra to you, Rebb.'

'Cassandra, huh.'

'Names are limiting, I find. You get one at birth you didn't ask for. Who says you have to keep it for the rest of your life?'

Rebb said, 'There's no law.'

'*Au contraire*, there are too many laws,' she said. 'We are drowning in laws. There's a fucking tidal wave of laws. Traffic. Vice. Drugs. Let's have some anarchy about the place, for Christ's sake. Let's tear down the structures before they choke us to death.' She stared across the room at Samsa. She had eyes too pale to be described as blue. They had a bleached quality. They might have been fashionable contact lenses with a slick marketing name – Arctic Dawn, Cobalt Innuendo.

'Who's your friend, Rebb?'

'This is Lieutenant Samsa. Excuse my manners.'

'A big wheel,' she said.

'He's the Man,' Rebb said.

'Hey, the Man,' she said to Samsa. 'Do I consider this like an honor?'

Samsa stepped forward a few paces. She blew a stream of smoke in his direction, her head tilted back a little. He noticed discarded black pantyhose under her chair.

'Take it any way you like,' he said.

'That's generally how I take things,' she said.

Rebb said, 'You got to understand, Lieutenant. Fatima here – excuse me, Cassandra – she's got this self-image of a free spirit. Back in the old days she'd have called herself

592

a hippy. I got other names for her, though. Whore comes charging to mind.'

'Tut-tut,' she said, pointing her cigarette at Rebb. She looked back at Samsa. 'You ought to demand a refund from whatever charm school you sent Rebb to.'

'Also a jester,' Rebb said.

Samsa said, 'Rebb's style doesn't include charm.'

She smiled and got up from her chair. Trailing smoke, she walked to a big powerful stereo set against the wall in the corner. She pressed a button and the room filled up with the frantic angry sound of rap. The speakers thudded. The walls shook. Cassandra lowered her head, shut her eyes, clicked her fingers in time to the hefty bass beat, sashayed a few steps across the floor.

'*I hate that shit music*,' Fogue shouted.

She smiled *too bad* at Fogue, waltzed past him, approached Samsa with a flirtatious look. The music, a deafening series of staccato phrases, thumped in Samsa's head, which was already delicate. He watched the woman dance in a circle around him, the cigarette stuck in her mouth. Fogue walked to the stereo and killed it with a hasty gesture, and the room was suddenly silent.

Cassandra said, 'You're a fettered little fart, aren't you, baldy?'

Fogue said, 'I'm not listening to that kill-a-honky-cop crap.'

She took her cigarette from her mouth. 'Why? Does it scare you? What would you prefer? Garth Brooks? Maybe Henry Mancini? I got "Moon River" somewhere.'

Fogue scowled at her. 'My taste in music is irrelevant, lady.'

Samsa had a sense of things going out of focus, the real purpose of being here diffused in assorted squabbles and insults. If you could describe it as real. If anything could be described that way any more. He laid his hands against the back of the chair and said, 'We're looking for Lee Boyle.'

'You're not alone,' she said.

Rebb asked, 'Meaning?'

'Meaning I'd like to see him.'

'I'm hearing irritation,' Rebb said. 'He owes you? Left you holding the bag or something?'

'I didn't say that. I only said I'd like to see him. Sort of for old times' sake.'

'You know where he can be found?' Samsa asked.

'The Man speaks,' she says. 'I hear the voice of authority.'

Rebb said, 'Drop the attitude, Fatima.'

'Cassandra.'

'Whoever. The lieutenant asked a question. Give the man an answer.'

'What's your problem? Lost track of Lee? Why don't you look him up in the phone book?'

'Because he ain't in the phone book, honey,' Rebb said. 'Not under Boyle anyhow.'

Samsa intervened again. 'If you know where he can be found, it's in your best interest to tell us.'

'Why? What's he done now?'

'We want to talk with him,' Samsa said. 'That's all you need to know.'

'He's a persecuted soul,' she said.

'Also a shit,' Rebb said.

'So he's a persecuted shit. He's tormented.'

'Aw, fuck's sake,' Rebb said. 'Don't yank my chain, honey.'

'Tormented and misunderstood.'

'Look, he's a fucking junkie and low-rent pimp, who screwed up his chances in life. You know it, I know it, so skip the crap and just tell us where he lives.'

'What are you hounding him for?' she asked.

Samsa said, 'He's not being hounded. He might be able to help us in certain inquiries. That's all.'

'Ooh, what a phrase that is, covers a multitude of sins.'

'She's got a soft spot for Lee. Screw it. Let's just book her,' Rebb said.

'For what?' she asked.

Rebb said, 'Possession of narcotics. Posing for porno pics. We'll think of something.'

'Your aura's the color of dishwater, Rebb. You know that? You're like a coin: you got two sides. One side works for the heat, flip it and you get total sleaze. You'd have made a great pimp. Also you want to brush your teeth now and then.'

'You got me down pat,' Rebb said.

Samsa didn't like Rebb's confrontational approach. He never had. He said, 'You know where he lives or don't you? It's a simple question.'

She fingered the cross that hung from her neck. 'Am I throwing Lee to the lions if I tell you?'

'Yes or no, Cassandra.'

'There's a kindness in your voice that's noticeably absent from Rebb's,' she remarked.

'Which means what? You'll tell me?'

She walked back to the stereo and switched it on again, then returned to the spot where Samsa stood. She must have been very good-looking at one time, even beautiful. Her bone-structure was exquisite, but little lines spread from the corners of her mouth and her powder-white make-up didn't conceal the tiny incisions of age at the corners of her eyes.

'Is this loud enough for you?' she asked.

'Do you want it to be?'

She touched his arm. 'I don't want to hear what I'm going to say, Samsa. Sometimes I just don't like the sound of my own voice. And sometimes I don't like the infernal noise of my own thoughts. Do you understand that?'

'Yeah,' he said. 'I think I do.'

24

THE TELEPHONE ON DARCY'S BEDSIDE TABLE RANG, AND SHE reached for it, expecting to hear her father's voice. Maybe he was calling to say he was on his way. He'd sounded rushed when they'd talked before. She wished he would come home. She was still thinking about the noise of the trash-can lid falling. Her first thought was that it had been the wind, but the night was perfectly still. Okay, a cat, a dog, maybe even one of those raccoons people said they saw scavenging every now and then. And then the word *prowler* had popped into her head. Somebody out there in the dark.

The voice on the phone wasn't her father's. It was deep and rich, a smooth baritone, an actor's voice. It reminded her of one she'd heard on a hot-chocolate commercial. 'Who am I speaking with?'

'First tell me who *you* are,' she said. She'd been trained by her father, who worried about the possibilities of threats from the criminal community, never to talk on the phone to people she didn't know, especially if they didn't state their name. The number wasn't unlisted, because he had the belief – civic-minded but wrong-headed, she thought – that anyone on the taxpayer's dollars should be accessible.

'You wouldn't know me,' he said.

'Then I'm hanging up.'

'No, don't do that. Don't hang up.'

'Give me one good reason.' Breaking her father's rule: always cut the connection. Don't get involved if you're not sure. But the voice had a pleasing quality, and wasn't menacing.

'Is this Gregory Samsa's home?'

She said, 'Yes. But he's sleeping.' She wasn't about to say he wasn't home. She didn't know this caller and she didn't want him to think she might be alone. You don't take that kind of risk.

'I don't suppose you can wake him up.'

'You suppose right.'

'Too bad,' he said.

'You want to leave a message or call back again?'

'Are you his daughter?'

Hang up, she thought. *Just don't get into this.* 'I don't like questions from strangers in the dead of the night.'

'I was only curious.'

She thought she could hear voices in the background. 'I'm hanging up,' she said.

'Before you sever the connection, do me a favor.'

'What?'

'Tell me your name.'

She stuck the handset down. She lay without moving for a time. Then, a little disturbed by the lateness of the call and the way the guy had asked for her name, she went downstairs. She stared through the kitchen window, which faced the side of the house where the trash was stored.

Darkness. Only darkness.

She flipped the switch for the outside light. In the driveway she saw the unfamiliar car her father had borrowed from the work pool, saw light fall against it and fade out in a feeble fashion among the shrubbery that surrounded the house next door, where the Petersons lived, prissy George the bank manager, wife Millie the social psychologist, their brat twins Leonard and Leonora – those names, *really* – nine years old and always spying on her. She hated the brightly colored plastic dental braces they wore. When they smiled they looked like a pair of stupid stunted clowns.

In the living room she helped herself to a drop of her father's cognac. She liked the way it burned. She gazed at the drawn curtains. She thought about the Italian film and Nick sleeping through it, even snoring at one point.

What she hadn't told her father about the date, what she *couldn't* tell him, was that Nick had detoured on the way home from the cinema and parked his car up near the Purchase property and suggested, with some urgency in his voice, that they *do it*. She'd walked with him into the meadow under a white quarter-moon blurry with moths and mosquitoes. She'd lain on the grass and he'd pushed her skirt up over her thighs and kissed her with such ferocity she felt nauseous, gagging on the deep reaches of his tongue and his fingers roughly inserted in her vagina. And she'd *wanted* to fuck him, but it had all gone wrong because she became *dizzy* with that awful throw-up feeling, and in the end she'd said, *I'm sorry, Nick, this isn't the time. I'm truly sorry.* She'd felt like a bitch-wife with a prophylactic headache. She hadn't meant to come off that way.

The phone was ringing again.

She picked it up.

'Just your name,' he said. 'That's all I ask.'

She slammed the handset back in place, finished her cognac and wished her father would come home.

25

WHEN BOYLE DIDN'T ANSWER HIS BUZZER, BILLY FOGUE picked the front-door lock with a pocket knife and said, 'Easy does it,' and the door opened, revealing a narrow staircase that led to the apartment. Fogue worked his trick a second time on the apartment door. Samsa didn't tell him to stop, that rules were being transgressed, the rights of the citizenry ignored.

Rules. Rules were what you made them. You break one, the rest collapse, the whole damn locomotive comes off the tracks at speed. He stood in the center of Boyle's living room and watched through the bedroom doorway as Rebb and Fogue prowled around, opening and closing drawers and closets.

Rebb found a couple of dresses and held one against his body. 'You think this is me, Billy?' he asked.

'Polka dots, nah,' Fogue said.

'Just put it back, Rebb,' Samsa said, a little sharply, and turned away from the skimpy polka-dot number and tried not to think of the girl dressing and undressing in this apartment, mirror-gazing, applying make-up, brushing her hair, all her little vanities past and dead.

Rebb hung the dress in the closet and shut the door and hummed a few bars of 'Polka Dots and Moonbeams', sounding vaguely like a guy playing a trombone. 'Hey, panties,' he said, dipping his fingers inside a drawer and pulling out scant filmy things in an assortment of colors.

Samsa said, 'This isn't a goddam department store, Rebb.'

Rebb stuffed the lingerie back where he'd found it and said, 'I've always been intrigued by the mysteries of female underwear. Bras especially. Hooks and clips and such.'

Billy Fogue said, 'This place is real clean. You notice that?'

'Speed-freaks have a lot of time and energy to kill,' Rebb remarked.

Samsa watched them go inside the kitchen. Fogue shuffled through the drawers of a cabinet and Reb peered inside the refrigerator, which contained only a few cans of Coors and a bunch of shriveled green grapes.

Rebb said, 'Another thing about speed-heads is they're not famous for having a whole load of food on hand. They got no appetite.'

A herb chart hung on the kitchen wall. Samsa gazed at it. Marjoram, Thyme, Basil. How to Use Them. It was a chart he'd seen in many kitchens. There was also a Bart Simpson clock: 2:20.

He worked his tongue against the edge of his broken tooth. The absence of Lee Boyle somehow reinforced an illusion of his presence. He was missing, and yet he wasn't. He was everywhere in this apartment, among the books on the shelves, the toiletries in the bathroom, the towels placed neatly on the rack.

Samsa wandered toward the books and found himself thinking about the distance between his smashed car and where the girl's body had been found, and he was assailed by the notion that somebody would eventually start to think how strange it was that the lieutenant had wrecked his car at roughly the same time the girl was killed, and only a few hundred yards from where her body was found. An unhappy proximity.

Coincidence. The world was filled with coincidence. Brodsky had accepted that without any problem, Brodsky hadn't been troubled by it at all.

Just tell them, he thought. *Kill this travesty. It cuts against the grain of your whole belief system. If you ever really had one.*

Who are you, Samsa?

He looked at the stereo and Boyle's eclectic collection of CDs. A little jazz, some classical music by composers unfamiliar to him – Schoenberg, Alban Berg – as well as Bach, Beethoven. Eighties pop, Dylan Thomas reading his own poetry. One odd item, a collection of Christmas favorites sung by the Mormon Tabernacle Choir. Was Lee Boyle, pimp, a closet sentimentalist?

He felt like a trespasser, a home-invader. He stared at the coffee table, seeing, under the soft glow of an angular lamp, circular streaks where the wood surface had been cleaned.

He listened to Rebb and Fogue clattering around inside the bathroom, the sound of a shower curtain being slipped along the rail, the chink of tiny plastic hoops. *What the hell do they expect to find in the shower?* he wondered. This was like a recreational outing for them, where they could poke among the stuff of another person's life. They enjoyed being snoops. He understood he should put a stop to it, tell them to cool it until Boyle showed up. They weren't here to ransack his property, they were here to ask him some questions, that was all. But they had a momentum going now and he felt removed from whatever they were doing.

He heard Fogue say, 'Now lookee here, Rebb. You suppose he has a permit for this?'

'Nice little gun,' Rebb said. 'A Lama forty-five. Compact Frame model. The idea of him having a permit is highly implausible, I got to say. A guy like Boyle, he wouldn't be big on paperwork. He's an outlaw. Or he likes to think he is anyway.'

Fogue appeared in the bathroom doorway with the gun, the handle wrapped in tissue. He had a cheroot hanging from his mouth and the smell was beginning to drift through the rooms. A heavy sickening odor.

'Item. One gun,' Fogue said. 'Too bad the little hooker wasn't blown away by this very weapon. Then we'd have something straightforward.'

'I suggest you put it back where you found it.'

'Anything you say, Lew Tenant. Back in the tampon box it goes.'

Samsa strolled the room. He walked to the window and peered into the drab street below. He saw the pawnbroker's sign and wondered what effect it might have on somebody to live above a business that dealt in desperation and poverty, wedding rings hocked, war medals traded away for a few bucks and never reclaimed. Maybe despair seeped through the building like a gas.

He still wore his own wedding ring. He looked at it now, a plain gold band. Why did he keep it anyhow? He had an urge to yank it off. He wasn't married. In a sense he hadn't been married for years and years.

He moved toward the answering machine, and pressed Playback.

The first message was a man's voice with a pseudo-English accent: *I hope I'm not pressuring you unduly, love. But time is passing. Time is indeed passing. Beep beep.*

The second was from a woman. *Lee, you old speed-*

freak, I hear you're looking for your little Almond. Maybe I can be of some tiny assistance? Meet me at the Rialto coffee shop around four thirty, okay? Beep beep. The machine stopped.

He recognized that voice.

Cassandra.

He stood with his hands pressed against the back of the sofa, his legs spread slightly, his head inclined downward. He realized he was holding his breath and his nerves were jangling. Tiny assistance? What assistance could Cassandra possibly give? Did she know something? Had she seen something? Like what? Had she been in the vicinity and seen Almond approach his car? Was that it? But Cassandra had given no indication that she recognized him. Not a flicker, a sign. It had been dark last night anyway, moonless and rainy. And Cassandra, even if she *had* been around the place, couldn't have seen much of anything.

He was jumping to wild conclusions, lost in a fog of possibilities and questions that were like darts. Stakes driven into his heart. His mind scampered this way and that, circled around on itself. Had Cassandra met with Boyle, imparted whatever information she had?

He couldn't let that be true. In this new world of his a fact was no longer a fact, it was something you could twist. He wiped the messages from the answering machine, even as his brain was racing to the notion that there was technology capable of restoring voices from erased tapes, there were instruments and audio experts who could find traces and amplify them to the point where meaningful sounds could be discovered, and if it came to that . . .

He heard Rebb say, 'Anything interesting there?'

Samsa wheeled round quickly, wondering how long Rebb had been standing in the doorway. He wasn't breathing properly. A constriction in his throat, like a cherry stone lodged there. His chest felt tight.

'A couple of messages, nothing that serves our purpose,' he said.

Rebb shrugged. 'I guess all we can do is wait for our wandering boy to show.' He approached the answering machine and stared at it. Just for a moment Samsa thought he was going to press the playback button, and he'd hear only a blank cassette, at which point he'd realize Samsa had been lying when he'd referred to a couple of messages that were of no interest.

But then Samsa would say, I must have wiped them inadvertently.

And Rebb might think, What? Very unprofessional, Lieutenant. Wiping a tape by accident. Clumsy of you.

There's no fucking end to this. It's a maze. At the heart of the maze is a monster with your face.

Samsa said the first thing that came to mind. 'You mentioned Boyle came from a rich family?'

'You ever heard of Hugh Boyle?'

'The tycoon?'

Thankfully Rebb had lost interest in the machine. 'Yeah. He's got this slew of companies all over the place.' He sat on an arm of the sofa, took out his nail file and dug away. 'Hugh's the father.'

Samsa said, 'And he disowned his son.'

'Would you want a kid like Lee Boyle?'

Samsa heard movement on the stairs. He made a shushing gesture, index finger to his lips. Rebb stared at the door. Billy Fogue, wandering in from the bathroom, was also silent.

Waiting, waiting.

A key was turned in the lock, the door opened.

Lee Boyle entered the room.

If he was shocked to find visitors, he didn't show it.

'Gentlemen callers. Including Detective Rebb, unless my eyes deceive,' he said. He walked into the kitchen and came back with a can of beer. 'Beer's there if you want to help yourselves, guys.'

Samsa got up from the sofa and said, 'I'm Lieutenant Samsa.'

Boyle looked at Samsa for a moment with an odd expression, and then smiled. 'Lieutenant. Nice to make your acquaintance.'

'Polite fucker,' Rebb said. 'It's all surface. You see those blue eyes and that face and you smell apple pie. Don't be fooled, Lieutenant. You're looking at low-level scuzz.'

Fogue blew smoke directly into Boyle's face. 'It's question time, buddy. You ready?'

'Is there a prize?' Boyle asked. He seemed undeterred by the smoke, didn't even bother to wave it away. He gazed through the disintegrating little cloud at Samsa and the smile didn't leave his face.

Cool, Samsa thought. *Or acting hard to seem so.*

Fogue said, 'The prize depends on your answers, Boyle.'

Boyle said to Fogue, 'Do I know you?'

'Detective Fogue. Sir to you.' He shoved his cheroot at Boyle like a tiny weapon.

Boyle relaxed against the wall, sipping beer. He looked at Rebb and Fogue, and then his gaze settled on Samsa. '*Struck to the heart by this sad pageantry, Half to myself I said, And what is this?*'

'He memorizes poetry like a fucking parrot,' Rebb said.

Samsa said, 'He's got the poetry down all right. Let's see what else he's got down, shall we? Let's see if he remembers where he was around ten o'clock last night. You recall that, Boyle?'

'Ten o'clock, let's see,' Boyle said. 'I was with a man called Jimmy Plumm.'

'Jimmy *Plumm*?' Fogue asked, and blew more smoke.

Samsa thought how crude Billy Fogue and Rebb could be, compared to Eve.

'Moneybags Plumm will vouch for you, will he?' Fogue asked. 'You into him for some cash? Plumm'll say just about anything to keep you out of trouble if you owe him. Duh. He doesn't make a profit if you go to jail.'

'Jail?' Boyle stared at Samsa for a moment over the rim of the Coors can. The look, which struck Samsa as secretive and knowing, was unsettling. *Had Cassandra talked to him? And what could she possibly have said?* The questions were trapped in the revolving door of his head. The questions were Semtex primed and wrapped in old newspapers.

'Excuse me. What's this talk of jail?' Boyle asked.

'Fogue gets carried away sometimes,' Samsa said. 'What time did you leave Plumm?'

'Around ten fifteen, ten twenty, then I went directly to a bar called Chang's.'

'Anybody see you there?' Samsa asked.

'I ran into a girl called Krystal,' Boyle said.

'Last name?'

Boyle shrugged. 'I wouldn't know her last name. She's a casual acquaintance.'

'Then what?'

'I left the bar. I met a man called Tom Raseci around eleven. We discussed the fact that somebody had slashed a tire on my car.'

'Bigshoes Raseci?' Fogue said. 'This just gets better all the time.'

'Without wheels, I had to contact a friend for a ride home. He picked me up at about eleven fifteen, eleven thirty. Vass, Rudolph Vass. You want his phone number?'

Samsa said, 'We'll get in touch with these people, Boyle.' He shoved his hands in his pockets. His palms were damp and stuck to some coins.

Boyle said, 'I guess you'll also get around to telling me what this is all about?'

Rebb put an arm on Boyle's shoulder. 'Here's the story, Lee. Your little girl was found dead. You know who I mean? Cecily Suarez. Almond by her other name.'

'*Dead?*'

'Murdered. Sorry to break it like this,' Rebb said in such a way that you knew he wasn't sorry at all. 'Somebody snapped her neck.'

'Is this a sick joke?' Boyle asked.

'I wish it was,' Samsa said. 'But it's not.'

'*Murdered?*' Lee Boyle looked as if he'd been struck on the face with a sledgehammer. He slumped, the beer can dangling loosely from his hand. He stared at Samsa, but he wasn't seeing anything, his eyes had a vacancy. A sign had been turned off inside him.

The smile was gone, the face empty. The beer can, angled slightly, oozed foam. *There was feeling here*, Samsa thought. *Something between Lee Boyle and the dead girl. A genuine affection maybe.* The expression on Boyle's face suggested he'd lost more than a hooker he had on a chain, a girl he worked. All right, he was lowlife, his world was one of dope and hookers, he had violence in his history, even so – even so Samsa felt an unexpected twinge of sympathy he couldn't afford. He had to be hard. He had to be made of metal that couldn't be broken. *Boyle's a suspect. Boyle has to be scrutinized.*

A long silence. Fogue and Rebb had subsided surprisingly into quiet. Boyle inclined his head now, eyes shut. 'Where did you find her?'

Rebb said, 'You know the old Purchase property?'

Boyle shook his head.

'That wilderness out near Chackstone,' Rebb said.

Boyle appeared to absorb this information absently. He

crumpled the beer can with a tensed hand. Foam exploded over his fingers.

'Who'd kill her, for Christ's sake?' he asked.

'That's what we're trying to find out,' Samsa said.

Rebb said, 'Which is why we're here, blue eyes.'

Boyle said, 'Why you're here . . . Now wait a minute. Hold on. You think I might have done it? No way. She was just somebody crashing in my apartment.'

'Somebody you took in under your mighty generous wing,' Rebb said. 'Some poor little thing in need of shelter.'

'Yeah, absolutely.'

Some poor little thing, Samsa thought. He was back in the Chrysler and the sky was turning over and his world was hemorrhaging.

'But she turned a few tricks on the side,' Rebb said.

'What she did in her spare time, I couldn't begin to guess,' Boyle said quietly.

Fogue pulled the dead cheroot from his lips. 'You were living off her earnings, Boyle.'

'She contributed to the rent. I never asked her how she earned her money.'

'Ho ho ho,' Rebb said. 'And I'm fucking Father Christmas. See my elves, Lee?'

'Fuck you, Rebb. She was a nice kid. I met her somewhere, she needed a place to live, and I suggested my apartment. Our paths didn't cross a lot. It was a temporary arrangement, that's all. What's so terrible about hospitality?'

'Hospitality's just fine. I just happen to think it's pretty scuzzy putting her to work on the streets,' Rebb said.

'Putting her to work? If that's an official accusation, Mr Rebb, and if you also seriously think I had something to do with the death of this girl, then I'd better call my lawyer. What do you think, Lieutenant?'

Samsa said, 'I think we'll check your story, Boyle. If it

hangs together, then you've got nothing to worry about, have you? If it's got holes, then you can bet your ass you'll be seeing more of us. As for you pimping, I don't give a damn. All I care about is who killed this girl. Nothing else.'

'I think you'll find my alibis are sound,' Boyle said.

'Ain't you the lucky one,' Fogue said.

Samsa felt weariness come down on him, a fatigue in his bones. His shoulder ached. He wanted very badly to lie down. 'We'll call it a night for now.'

Fogue looked disappointed. He dropped his cheroot butt casually on the rug. 'I'm only just getting warmed up, Lew Tenant.'

Samsa walked to the door. Boyle stepped in front of him, collided with him gently.

'Sorry,' Boyle said.

Rebb and Fogue went out. Samsa's way was blocked by Boyle.

Boyle said, 'I didn't catch your name, Lieutenant.'

Samsa stepped back from Boyle a couple of inches. The physical contact with the man discomfited him. 'Samsa.'

'As in S–A–M–S–A?'

'Right.'

'Unusual name,' Boyle said.

Samsa tried to imagine Boyle and Cassandra meeting someplace, whispering, sharing a confidence. *I saw Almond,* she might say. And Boyle would say, *Yeah? Where? Under what circumstances?* And then what?

What did she tell him? What *could* she tell him?

Maybe Boyle hadn't checked his messages, didn't know Cassandra had telephoned. But she'd call again if she didn't hear from him. Of course she would.

This is guilt run riot, Samsa thought. *This is a mind operating on desperation. You're walking through a forest and the trees are whispering your name and the clouds*

*scudding overhead are spelling it out in great unfolding
banners.*

'Do you have a card?' Boyle asked.

'A card?'

'Yeah, you know, if I find out anything about Cecily or
her movements, then I'll know where to reach you.'

Samsa reached inside his pocket and gave Boyle one of
his PD cards.

Boyle said, 'I can't believe somebody would kill her. She
was only a kid.'

Samsa couldn't look at him. He stepped out of the
apartment and moved to the edge of the stairs. Fogue and
Rebb were already halfway down. He could see them in
the pale stair-light, two faint shapes. He paused and imagined he heard a sound like a dam cracking in the
distance, and water, as it gathered force, spewing through.

26

SAMSA WENT BACK DOWNTOWN AFTER HE'D LEFT LEE BOYLE'S
apartment. He sat in his office, listening to Fogue speak
on the telephone outside his door. 'Okay, Raseci, just see
if you can remember the exact time you were with him.
Shouldn't be too difficult if you apply yourself...'
Stephen Rebb was working another phone, calling God
knows what sources in the murky places where Cecily
Suarez had worked.

Samsa put his hands on the desk, fingertips touching,
almost a gesture of prayer. He'd been raised a Catholic,
and in the early days of his marriage – those days before
the darkening shadows began to form around Harriet –
he'd attended Mass regularly with his wife. He'd never
considered himself a deeply spiritual person. At best the
church offered comfort and consistency, the center-stone
of Sunday mornings. Then he'd lost interest during the
years of Harriet's disintegration, and it was a long time
since he'd prayed. But he had the urge now, because he
had nowhere to turn, and if the slightest possibility of a
God of any kind existed he'd run to it, he'd go down on

his knees and ask for guidance and forgiveness.

He thought about Lee Boyle.

He'd come back to that subject later, when he was alone. He'd clear a space in his mind and analyze the situation. He'd try to remember if anyone had seen the girl get in his car: a witness he'd overlooked. But he'd been so fucking *careful,* so *discreet.* He'd driven past in the rain and signaled to her from a block down from the main action, and she'd come hurrying toward the car under her transparent umbrella with the rain slicking off it. The *umbrella.* For one dread moment he couldn't remember what he'd done with it. Then it came back. He'd tossed it away in the long grass as far from the wrecked car as he could.

Right now you're conducting a homicide investigation. That's your priority. Making the moves, sifting, gathering information. Seeing what can be fabricated out of the bits and pieces.

Except you can't forget Boyle.

He felt squeezed, pinched. The room closed in on him. He rubbed his eyes. He thought, *I've never been in a lonelier place.*

On a notepad in front of him were two numbers Billy Fogue had given him. He didn't feel like making either call. He had to raise his energy level, infuse himself with an enthusiasm he didn't have. You have to be keen. You have to maintain a façade of professional devotion. Be determined. A girl is dead out there.

He reached for the phone, picked it up, punched in the digits of the first number. Samsa found himself connected to a certain Sergeant Lucinda of the Denver PD. She had a sympathetic voice. He informed her about the death of Cecily Suarez, and the fact she'd been a runaway from Denver. Sergeant Lucinda said she'd check for an address, then have somebody call on the kid's parents. Samsa

613

imagined a cop turning up on the doorstep of the Suarez household: It's about your daughter. I'm sorry. I have to tell you. I hate to bring this kind of news. There was never anything new to say, never a sentence with a glint of consolation. Words were dross at the bottom of a worked-out mine shaft.

He imagined a mother, imbued her with a sorrowful face, dark hair with a few steely strands. He pictured her walking up and down, chain-smoking and clock-watching, a low humming sound of terror forever in her skull. Imagining she hears Cecily's footsteps on the porch. Never again. The child isn't coming back. He had a curious feeling, something draining out of him. His eyes watered a moment.

Sergeant Lucinda said, 'You got anyone in custody for this, by the way? The parents might ask. They often do.'

'We're working on it,' he said, 'but we don't have anybody yet.' *In custody*, he thought. No, the killer was out there in the night. He was skulking down an alley or he was fast asleep in his bed or he was sitting in some late-night dive. Samsa pictured the murderer through a mist: a guy of about six-one, short black hair, add a scar, maybe a tattoo. The more details, the easier to make-believe. Easier to distance yourself.

'Runaways,' Sergeant Lucinda said. 'Break your heart every time.'

Samsa agreed, yes, they break your heart. Lucinda said she'd get back to him after the parents had been informed, and then there was the question of formal ID of the body by next of kin, so a family member would most likely have to fly out, and transportation arrangements would need to be made if the parents wanted the corpse brought back home for burial. All the usual business of death.

Samsa thanked her, then hung up. He listened to the

fan, watched how it oscillated, like a strange blind metal face scanning for something beyond its range.

He dialed the second number on his notepad. It rang for a long time, and he was about to hang up when the call was answered.

'Yes?'

'Lieutenant Samsa, Homicide,' he said. 'I want to speak to Jimmy Plumm.'

'This is he. You realize you woke me up? You know what time it is?'

Samsa didn't say he was sorry. 'I'm checking on a guy called Lee Boyle.'

'I'm more than a little pissed off by this intrusion,' Plumm said. 'By God, couldn't you have waited until a decent hour?'

Samsa recognized the voice. The first message on Boyle's answering machine. Something about time passing. He'd been too distracted to store the exact words in his memory. According to Fogue, Plumm was a money-lender whose rates of interest were usurious. He backed up his operation with muscle, hard stuff. You don't pay, say goodbye to a limb, an eye, whatever. His main enforcer was Tom Raseci, a name Samsa had heard around, always in association with violence.

'I guess I didn't realize it was this late,' Samsa said.

Plumm made a clucking sound. 'Homicide, did you say?'

'Right.'

'And you want to ask about who? Lee Boyle?'

Samsa rolled a yellow pencil under the palm of his hand. 'When did you last see him?'

'What kind of trouble is he in?' Plumm asked.

'This is routine.'

'Routine? At this hour? Come come.'

'Just answer my question, Mr Plumm.'

615

'I can't remember precisely.'

'Try,' Samsa said.

'Monday night, I believe.'

'At what time?'

'Mr Samsa, I'm a busy man. I run several businesses that make excessive demands on me—'

'I know about your business dealings. Let's skip the detours, okay? Monday night. When?'

'I'm sorry,' Plumm said. 'Maybe eight. Nine. I can't really be sure.'

'But definitely Monday?'

'Yes, Monday.'

'It could have been later than eight or nine?'

'Perhaps.'

'Or earlier?'

Plumm said, 'No, not earlier. It was after dinner, I remember that. I always eat between six and six thirty.'

Samsa said, 'Go back to sleep. Maybe you'll remember more when you're refreshed.'

He replaced the handset just as Rebb stepped into the room. 'You ever get the impression the world's filled with liars? There's hardly a fucking whore or pimp or porn-merchant I don't know in this whole city. I mean, sleaze is my specialty, Jesus – but nobody out there is talking. Nobody is *talking*.'

Samsa could see Rebb took this personally. He was insulted because his channels of information were dysfunctional. He'd spent years building delicate networks in the lower depths. He had his own payroll out there, people he greased. But sometimes grease didn't get you anything more than stained hands.

Rebb said, 'The best flash I got was she was seen checking into a room at the Starlit Lodge two days ago, which is ancient history. The guy she was with registered as Jack

Spratt. Ho ho. I suppose she called herself Mrs Lean. They checked out again an hour later, the clerk says.'

'Go home,' Samsa said. 'We'll pick it up again after we've had a few hours' sleep.'

'Go home?' Rebb asked. He was worked up. His unnatural black hair seemed almost navy in the fluorescent light. 'This is the time when my people are up and around. They don't keep normal hours, Lieutenant. Soon as it's dawn, *poof*, they're gone.'

Billy Fogue appeared in the doorway. 'I can't locate anybody who remembers seeing Boyle in Chang's. I talked to the manager, who wasn't overjoyed to be roused. And I haven't run down anything on this Krystal who Boyle claims he saw.' He looked at a notebook in his hand. 'Rudolph Vass says he picked Boyle up somewhere downtown at about eleven thirty, or maybe quarter to midnight. And Tom Raseci admits he talked to Boyle at some point in the course of the evening, but he isn't sure when.'

'Same with Plumm,' Samsa said. 'He saw Boyle, doesn't remember the time.'

'Plumm's thinking percentages,' Fogue said. 'Boyle's into him for some money, but is it worth perjury just to protect your investment? Right now I'd bet my ass he's on the phone to Raseci and they're trying to find out why we're asking questions about Lee Boyle.'

'So now we just keep backtracking,' Samsa said. 'Who saw her last. Where she was seen. We need a timetable of her movements.' He looked at Rebb, who had an unsettling light of determination in his eyes.

Rebb said, 'I'm hitting the streets. As of this moment.'

Samsa understood he couldn't stall Rebb. Nobody could have chained him in his present frame of mind. Besides, how would it look if Samsa ordered him to go home, start work afresh tomorrow? Illogical. A lack of

617

enthusiasm. Out of focus. *Play the game.* 'See if you can get anything on this Jack Spratt character, Rebb,' he said. 'A make on his car. A description of the guy. Anything.'

Rebb said, 'Spratt's two days old, and that's no fucking good.'

'He might have picked her up again on the night she died,' Samsa said.

'I'll lean on that night clerk at the Starlit. He's a Libyan and he doesn't have a green card.' Rebb turned away. 'See you.'

When Rebb had gone, Billy Fogue said, 'The whole alibi bit is looking damn iffy, I think.'

'For the moment,' Samsa said.

'What else do you want me to do before I collapse?' Fogue asked.

'Get some sleep. We'll let Rebb run with this for a few hours.'

'I can go home?'

Samsa nodded. 'That's where I'm headed.'

Fogue looked pleased. 'Later, Lew Tenant.'

Alone, Samsa stood in his partitioned space. He listened to phones ringing, cops answering. Accidents in the small hours, domestic squabbles, home invasions, violence. It never stopped. The world screamed and screamed. He walked out of his office and remembered as soon as he was on the street that he had no transportation. He'd left the Chevy at home, ridden in the squad car to the Purchase property, then he'd gone to see Boyle in Fogue's Buick.

Boyle. So there were holes in Boyle's story. So what? They were temporary. They'd be patched and grouted. He needed to think harder about Lee Boyle.

But not now. His head was overloaded. He didn't have clarity.

He looked the length of the street. A cab came into view

and he hailed it and slumped in the back seat. He was about to give the driver his home address, then changed his mind. It was very late, and no time to be paying social calls, but he didn't want to go home just yet. He told the driver where to take him, then he sat back, gazing absently at the night. He thought of Darcy. She'd be fine. She'd be fast asleep by this time. The house was secure.

He got out of the cab in a street of turn-of-the-century houses, many of them ornate, a few with elaborate ginger-bread touches. Somebody with vision and an eye for profit had saved these places from the wrecker's ball and restored them, turning them into apartments. The street was leafy and suggestive of a prosperous time in the city's history, when the railroad had flourished and commercial barges hauled huge loads along the canal and factories smoked and thrived. Apart from a brief revival of fortune in the early 1950s the city had been on a general down-ward slope for a long time. It wasn't a terrific history. It was no American success story.

He paid the driver, walked up a driveway, stopped out-side a door and pressed a buzzer. This was a bad idea altogether.

He heard Eve's voice through the intercom. 'Who is it?'

'Greg,' he said.

The door clicked open. He stepped inside a high-ceilinged hallway. Eve, tying the cord of her robe, appeared at the top of the stairs.

'Come on up,' she said.

He climbed, followed her quietly along the corridor at the top. Her apartment was spacious and filled with plants. A few throw rugs and very little furniture – a big sofa near the carved fireplace, a couple of chairs, and that was it. He sat on the sofa and wondered why he'd come here. She stood in front of the unlit fire. The only light in the room came from a lamp close to the window.

'This is a surprise,' she said. She had her red hair tied back. Her face glistened. *Some kind of moisturizer*, Samsa thought. She looked very young without make-up.

'I woke you,' he said.

'I'm a light sleeper.'

'You're alone?'

'I'm alone most of the time, contrary to what you might hear. You want a drink?'

'No, I'm fine.' He tapped his fingers on his knees. 'There was a homicide tonight.' He told her the details, how the body had been discovered, the coroner's interim comments. His narrative was brief and superficial. Whatever had brought him here, it wasn't to tell Eve Lassiter about the dead girl. He had a sense of banishing silences, talking because quiet was intolerable.

She listened. Sometimes she smoothed strands of hair from the sides of her face. She sat alongside him on the sofa, drew her feet up under her body. The robe she wore was cotton, blue-and-white check, and several sizes too big for her, and he wondered if it belonged to somebody else, if a man had left it behind. A lover.

'Thirteen,' she said. 'A child. It's so . . .'

'Yeah, I know, I know.' Samsa made a meaningless little gesture with his hand. 'I heard you called me at home.'

She said, 'I was going to tell you how my night turned out. I can report this much: I don't have what it takes to be a hooker. It's bleak down there.'

'Joshua Gold saw nothing?'

She looked just a little preoccupied. Then she smiled. 'You just came here to pass the time or check on your phone messages?'

'I don't know,' he said.

'You didn't want to go home,' she said.

'It's where I ought to be. It's late.'

'Or early.' She reached out, held his hand and ran her thumb back and forward across his knuckles. The intimacy was easy on him, the contact pleasurable. It rushed into the spaces inside him. He moved his head against her shoulder, smelled the scent of her soap, which was suggestive of crushed Fall fruit.

He could lose himself here, he thought. He could travel this road with Eve and he'd be safe from harm. He saw her undo the cord of her robe, and watched the robe part and the way the lamp shone against her inner thighs and highlighted the soft delicate hairs there. He didn't move, thinking how short the distance between them was. She pulled a pin or a clasp from her hair – he couldn't tell which – and it tumbled to her shoulders. He looked at her face, and how the open robe revealed her breasts, and he grasped the extent of his solitude, the way his life had been for too many years, and the silent disoriented woman who'd been his wife; all the years he'd waited for her to re-enter the world, and she never had. The wrists razored in the bathtub, pink water. That was what she'd left him in the end. She might have been saying, with the inexplicable malice of her derangement, Here, Greg, remember this when you think of me.

He kissed Eve, possessed by an excitement he'd half forgotten, a shadowy fuse from his former life, and his blood changed course, his heartbeat became chaotic. She stood up, took his hand, led him inside her bedroom. A big dark-green room, a brass bed. She told him to lie down, and he did. He was willing, obedient.

She removed his shoes, his socks, unbuckled his belt and said, 'I've wanted you. I've wanted this to happen. You knew that.'

'Maybe,' he said.

'No maybe, Greg.' She undid the buttons of his shirt. He couldn't wait. He couldn't hold back. There was nothing elaborate in his desire and excitement, it was primal and urgent, he wanted to be inside her and discover in the act something of the life he'd lost, and dissolve the whole conundrum his existence had become. It was more than flesh, the conjunction of bodies. He had the sense she could rescue him somehow, that she was an angel who could reach down and bring him back from the place where he'd fallen. He looked up into her face and those disturbingly honest green eyes. She hid nothing. Concealed nothing. He watched her red hair swing against the sides of her jaw, and when she spoke her voice was a whisper. 'You need me.'

'Yes,' he said.

'You need me so badly.'

'Yes.'

He felt himself lifted upward, floating to meet her, sliding inside her. The impact was narcotic. He was suddenly in a dream where no external world existed. It was him and Eve and it was going to stay this way for as long as he could make it. This was real. Everything outside her bedroom was ashes.

She bent forward and her hair touched his forehead, then she swayed back from him and her breasts shook as she straddled him, and he was moved almost to tears by her marvelous tenderness. Her mouth was open, her face angled back now. She was all concentration and purpose, and as he looked at the smooth curvature of her long neck and the tightened veins and the shadows around her throat, he had no idea how long he could sustain this.

Not long, he thought, *not long at all*.

He was lost, frenzied and joyous, and already beginning to fall apart inside. He realized he'd barely understood the real nature of his yearning down the years. He'd been caged, grounded. Liberated now, the air all around him seemingly rocked with turbulence, he felt himself come, a fire searing through him. He was in pieces, and the pieces were burning.

Samsa aflame.

He heard himself call her name out loud.

She collapsed against him, her hair on his face, her mouth locked against his. He thought he could suffocate gladly in this way, expire here and now. Go out on a cloud of brilliant light. He'd recuperated after a long life-threatening illness. He was without burdens suddenly. A miracle. He wanted to tell her all this, but the feelings that ran through him couldn't be uttered.

She was quiet a long time before she said, 'I'm all you really need. And just think, I've been around all this time.'

'Waiting,' he said.

'Not always patiently.'

He stroked her hair, the side of her face, touched a breast. 'I wasn't exactly observant,' he said.

'Blind,' she said.

'Or distracted.'

She reached down between his legs and closed her palm around his cock and held it. 'Also some self-pity.'

'Probably that.'

'I *pushed* myself at you. God. I used to think up ways I could get you into my bed. If this hadn't happened now, it was going to happen next Wednesday anyway, because I'd made up my mind. As soon as dinner was over I had these sneaky plans . . .' She stroked him and he was hard again, and he felt unexpectedly young and vigorous, as if she'd stripped years from his life. He rolled her over onto her back and looked down at her. Gazing up at him she seemed vulnerable. If she was an angel, she was one without defenses.

'Again,' she said. 'I want you again.'

Again. Yes, again. It was a more delicious loss this time,

a shucking off of the self, slower now, carefully rendered. He kissed her throat, shoulders, tasted her skin, her hair, the uncharted territory of Eve. He was a man given the key to a room he'd only heard about before, but never entered. It was a room of flesh and bone and joy and honesty. It was where you went if you wanted unfettered exhilaration.

This time she came, and he understood he was receiving a gift of her most private secrets: the intimate sounds of pleasure she made, the way she buried her face in his shoulder, and how her body went rigid for one breathtakingly scary moment. His own climax, which rocked him to his spine, seemed like a note in a minor key by contrast. She said his name three, four, five times, and each time was a different riff on the same three syllables. She lay very still under him, staring into his face.

'Thank you,' she said. 'Thank you, thank you.'

'I should be saying that.'

She extended an arm in a lazy way across the sheets. 'Let's just say the gratitude's mutual, Lieutenant.'

A lovely sharing, he thought. An end to the winter inside himself. A thaw. He touched the side of her face, realized he didn't want to leave her. The notion of rising, getting dressed and going home appalled him. The reality check, the first light of dawn in the sky, the hideous bright face of the sun and all that it involved. He wondered how long it might be postponed. He wanted to draw the sheets over his head and sleep beside her and never stir again except to make love. He clasped her hand and held it tightly and raised it to his lips.

She propped herself up on an elbow and gazed at him. 'That's one hell of a bruise there.'

'I banged my shoulder.' The bruise on his flesh. 'I guess it happened when I wrecked the car. I didn't feel it at the time.'

She said, 'Say, you want to hear something hilarious? Gold says he saw you trawling.' She kissed his mouth.

'*Trawling?*' He was jolted suddenly, as if the atmosphere in the room had become charged with static electricity. Something very fine but ultimately fragile had been damaged in a matter of seconds.

'As in cruising.'

'Where?'

'Along Flesh Row. Where else?'

Samsa shook his head in an emphatic way. 'He's mistaken, Eve. He's got it wrong. He's way off.'

'That's what *I* told him. He's not exactly a wizard when it comes to ID-ing people, is he?'

'Okay, I might be lonely at times, and I don't deny I get depressed. But Flesh Row. No. No way. Christ, absolutely not.' He closed his eyes, remembering the nights he'd driven down there, the times he'd slowed the car and surreptitiously studied the eager girls beckoning from the sidewalks, imagining what it would be like, and how he'd always changed his mind at the last moment. He remembered the temptation, his nerves jazzed, the curious amalgam of desire and emptiness and self-disgust.

'You have to leave, don't you?' she asked.

'Darcy's alone.'

She placed a finger on his mouth. 'It's okay. I understand.'

He thought he hadn't been spotted. He'd considered himself anonymous, driving along, never stopping to buy. Except once. Just that once. One goddam time.

All your precautions, he thought. But somebody always noticed. Cassandra maybe. Now Gold. There were no hiding places except denial, and that was a besieged fortress. He rose from the bed, feeling desperate.

'I'm here for you,' Eve said. 'Remember that.' She

reached out and clutched his wrist. She released him, then watched as he gathered his clothes.

'You've got a broken tooth at the back of your mouth,' she said. 'I could feel it. Kind of jagged and rough.'

'Another souvenir of the crash,' he said.

'You want to get it seen to, Greg. Before decay sets in.'

27

THE TELEPHONE RANG AT 7 A.M. LEE BOYLE REACHED OUT TO
pick it up. He'd lain on the sofa for hours without catching
even a glimpse of sleep, because his head was a satellite that
wouldn't quit transmitting images of Almond.

'Lee? I got your message.'

'You're a tough sonofabitch to find,' Boyle said. He was
weary, dry-mouthed. The little ulcer in his gum was stinging suddenly. He had layer on layer of black feelings. Was
this how sadness engraved itself? *Mournful surges that
ring the dead seaman's knell?*

'I can't imagine why. You know my haunts, don't you?
Maybe we just kept missing one another.'

'Maybe.' His interest in The Kid had been dwindling
lately. *Almond dead. I can't grasp that one.*

'You want to come out to my place, Lee?'

'I'd prefer if you came down here,' Boyle said.

'No, I'll tell you why. I keep all my stuff here, and it's
just more convenient, that's all.'

'I have to drag myself out there,' Boyle said. 'Is it worth
my while?'

'I think so, Lee.'

'It better be. Give me an hour.'

Boyle hung up. He showered, gargled, brushed his teeth. His mouthwash agitated the ulcer. The tiny fucker throbbed intermittently, like a miniature lighthouse in his mouth.

He'd breakfast out of Stretch's baggie. He considered the needle, but that was a whole ritual, and he didn't feel up to it. He laid out some crystal on a mirror that he placed on the coffee table. This shit, one fine day in the future he'd give it up. But not now. He needed it. Even if he didn't trust Stretch's product, even if it amped him out of control, it was the only game in town right now.

He chopped the speed swiftly with a razor blade until it was a fine powder. He stared at the white mound a moment, wondering how many thousands of times he'd done this over the years, then shaped the stuff with the blade into two generous lines. With a cut plastic drinking straw between his fingers, he lowered his head. He saw sparkle, fragments that glinted. He saw his nostrils reflected in the mirror under the lines. *Gimme glass, I need glass.* These two lines were tracks that would carry him express-style for the next four or five hours.

After he snorted he felt the stuff coagulate in his sinuses. He remembered to take his multi-vitamins. He brushed his hair back, ran a quick mirror check. *You don't look the same, Lee. You look older this morning. Depressed. Something's gone out of you.*

He ransacked a closet in the bedroom, found a blue silk shirt and gray jeans hanging among Almond's clothing. He gazed at her dresses. He imagined her presence. Her white smile. The little generosities she bestowed. Any moment now she'd come through that goddam door and she'd have some convoluted tale about why she'd

628

disappeared. These are dreams, Lee. She's lost to you for all goddam time. She's gone where nobody comes back. So you put the thought away, stuff it someplace.

Don't think sorrow.

Zip. He was out of here. 7.30 a.m. and already on the streets, driving the stolen Pontiac through hard sunshine and heat you could taste. No air-conditioner in this heap.

Gregory J. Samsa.

A cop, for Christ's sake.

Now you know what he looks like anyway.

For the sake of argument, say Samsa was the one that picked up Almond. Not the ponderous Silas Goba, that slob drunk, but Samsa the respectable cop. You couldn't blame the guy for that. Almond made all heads swivel like they were on stalks. That strut she had down to perfection, the pert little breasts, the luscious mouth, the sexual confidence she oozed. He'd seen all that the first time he'd met her in a bar, when she'd been in the city only two days, escaping from some family hell out west, and was wandering like a soul in purgatory.

A week later she was working for him. Mainly hotels, outcall services, where the money was good, 150, 200 a throw. But sometimes the street, although he'd always thought that the saloon of last resort, a place she went when the phone wasn't ringing off the hook. He didn't like her out on the sidewalks.

It was from those black sidewalks that her killer had plucked her. Taken her to the Purchase field. Broken her neck.

Had the killer been Gregory J. Samsa? He fucked Almond and took her down to that unruly place, and then, consumed by an enormous guilt, murdered her.

Just try proving it, Lee.

He rolled down the windows. Muggy air that smelled of gasoline and slow death blew through the car. He wondered if cancer had a scent. If leukemia had its own aroma. He wondered also about rigor mortis and when it set in, and if Almond was stiff and lying in a chilled drawer at the morgue. He had an image of her flesh turning blue, which caused him to sense an impending angry derangement, gray vapors forming around the margins of his vision, and his brain like something in a boxcar hauled by a freight train through bleak railroad yards and alongside drab fields.

This day is unreal. This day is totally fucked before it's even begun. The jitters are arriving in hyped-up droves, like hordes of ravenous black flies.

He drove past shopping malls and through suburbs, his thoughts turning to the nightingale. The chime of her voice. That innocence. *Perilous seas in faery lands forlorn.*

She had to be Samsa's daughter. Who else could she be? Gregory J's little girl.

He looked in his rearview mirror. He didn't believe what he saw.

He pulled the black Pontiac over and, with a feeling of concentrated tension, waited. He heard the flies drone malevolently in his head. He glanced in the wing mirror and watched Tom Raseci step out of the Porsche and walk toward the Pontiac. Raseci, wearing a lurid Hawaiian shirt, stuck his head in the window.

'Nice wheels, Lee,' Raseci said. 'Very nice. Where'd you get them? Gossamer?'

Gossamer Avenue, despite its poetic name, was the pits, a row of sleazy used-car lots that provided their own extortionate credit and specialized in selling junked-out gas-guzzlers to itinerant Mexican workers or deadbeats who couldn't raise a cent from any bank. The guys that ran the lots on Gossamer were always busy repossessing their junkers and making a quick turnover.

'I stole the car, Tom,' Boyle said. 'Happy now?'

Raseci kicked a tire idly. 'I hate to see the mighty fallen.'

'And I hate this shit of being followed around.'

'All that dope's made you schizoid, Lee. I happened to see you boogie past, was all. So I swung round for a better look. Lee Boyle in a beat black Pontiac. What is it? Seventy-four? Three?'

'Who cares?' Boyle said. He didn't believe Raseci had been driving along casually at all. At this time of the morning?

Raseci kicked the tire again with the toe of his size thirteens and the hubcap fell off. 'Not put together real well, is she, Lee?'

Boyle got out of his car. 'Okay, Tom. You've seen the car. You've noted my humiliation. Is there anything else?'

'That Porsche,' Raseci said. 'I had it tuned up. Running like a dream. Real sweet. A Swiss fucking clock.'

'Do we stand around in this God-awful humidity and talk cars, Tom?' He looked into Raseci's face. He couldn't see the eyes because Bigshoes was wearing black shades.

'Hell, no,' Raseci said. 'Let's talk about the morning news, Lee. Let's discuss this fresh-breaking story about how a certain young girl was found dead not three miles from where we're standing.'

Boyle gazed along the street. Boxy houses built too close together, spindly young trees, the roar of a diesel-driven lawnmower. 'What can I say, Tom?'

Raseci said, 'Mr Plumm is very distressed by the news. He had the cops talking to him about your whereabouts at a certain time. So did I, Lee. We're not happy with cops phoning. Especially Mr Plumm. Apart from the inconvenience, he sees an income problem for you now.'

'Her death's a tragedy.'

Raseci took off his black glasses and slipped them into

631

his pocket. His pecs shuddered under the fabric of his garish shirt. He touched his bad eye with a fingertip. His battered nose gave him the look of an ex-slugger, somebody who'd been knocked around a few rings in his time. 'Yeah, it's a real tragedy all right, Lee.'

Raseci suddenly grabbed him, got a tight lock on his neck, forced his face down against the hot hood of the Pontiac and pushed his knee directly into the crack of Boyle's ass.

'Christ, Tom. What the hell are you doing?'

'Consider this a freebie, a taste of things to come.'

'Tom, it's broad fucking daylight, there are people in these houses, you're probably scaring the shit out of them—'

'Fuck 'em, it's you I want to scare,' Raseci said. 'Only you. Dum-di-dum. How's that song go?'

The blow was deft and painful. Raseci drove his big leaden fist into Boyle's back just below the shoulder blades. Then Raseci raised him up from the hood, swung him round, and delivered a second punch with great impact into the solar plexus, that intricate network of nerves and ganglia. Boyle felt as if he'd been vacuumed by a very crude sucking device that also crushed and hammered as it cleaned. A Hoover with attitude. He slumped, slithered against the side of the car and groaned. The pain was excruciating. What made it worse was the fact that Raseci was singing 'Only You' as he worked.

Boyle's head rolled to the side. Dizzy. Seeing swirls.

Raseci picked him up and dusted blades of grass from his silk shirt in a manner that was almost tender. 'Nothing personal, you understand,' he said.

Boyle blinked, groping to make sense of his fractured perceptions.

'I don't *want* to bust your face, Lee. I don't *want* to break bones. But I'll do it with great pleasure in' – he looked at his watch – 'let's say about thirty-eight hours from now. Unless, of course, there's a hefty infusion of money before then.'

'Thirty-eight hours,' Boyle said, dazed.

'Time just evaporates,' Raseci said. He stepped back, gazing at Boyle. 'You feeling okay, Lee?'

'I'll survive,' Boyle whispered. He saw Raseci walk back to the Porsche, get inside and drive away, his big ugly face grinning, and he was filled with assorted notions of getting even.

He edged himself carefully into the Pontiac. He lowered his face against the warm plastic of the wheel and gripped the steering column for support. Even though speed anaesthetized up to a point, this pain was going to take some time to pass away. Time he didn't have. Time was a hummingbird, darting, elusive. Now you see it, now you don't. Thirty-eight hours. Was that all he had left? He needed to move. He felt sick. He opened the door and puked what looked like thin minestrone on the sidewalk, and let his head dangle for a while.

He couldn't linger. He had to get his hands on some hard currency. He was trembling as he wired the car, and there was a painful stiffening in his gut, but this was a trifle compared with the damage Raseci could *really* do.

Blow town. What Vass recommended. Walk down to the bus station and say, I want fifty bucks' worth of motion in any direction, Mr Greyhound, sir. No way, he wasn't going to let Raseci and Plumm hound him, he still had thirty-eight hours, enough time to work something out.

Like what?

Your prospects are zero.

He decided he could live with pain. If you focused it could be controlled. He thought about his gun. If it came right down to it, if he was really backed into a corner and

633

there was *absolutely* no way out, okay, screw it, he'd shoot Raseci, and then he'd go after Jimmy Plumm. He'd do that. He wouldn't even think twice.

He drove, listening to imaginary gunshots and struggling to contain his physical distress, to where The Kid lived. He parked outside the apartment complex and didn't move for a moment. Then he got out of the car and walked toward the entrance. Jesus, there were stairs to climb. He'd forgotten that. Halfway up a flash of pain caused him to pause. His animosity toward the world in general was gigantic. Beyond management.

Die, Raseci. Die, Plumm.

And you, Hugh.

He imagined Hugh lined up with his head in a hood, body staked to a post in a lonely place. *A last cigarette before the ultimate beddy-bye, Hugh?* Except Hugh didn't smoke. It was unhealthy. Jesus, how he loathed Hugh. His hatred was like some heavy mahogany yoke around his shoulders.

He continued to climb, and reached the third floor. His heart was slogging. The Kid must have spotted him getting out of the car, because he was already opening the door and beckoning Boyle inside. Boyle nodded, but didn't feel like smiling. He needed to sit, made it to the sofa, and looked at The Kid, that soft wholesome face, hair light and floppy and no doubt shampooed in gentle herbal matter, the sleeves of his sweater rolled.

'How are you, Lee?'

'I've had better days,' Lee Boyle said, trying to recollect when he'd last been in this apartment. Months ago, when he'd run into The Kid in a bar downtown and they'd drunk a few beers together and smoked The Kid's hash, and then they'd come back here and Boyle had provided a little speed from his stash. The night was spent hatching vague plans and plots, ways of making a quick buck. The stoned babble of mendacious conspiracies. Blackmail, that was the word The Kid had used – *I have it scoped, Lee. Trust me. This is a solid proposition.*

'You look somewhat piqued, Lee.'

More tweaked than piqued, Boyle thought. 'Late nights.'

'Do you know your name means a calm sheltered place, Lee? Did you know that? A lee.'

'I enjoy a little irony this early in the day,' Boyle said. 'You got a cold beer handy?'

'Coming right up.' The Kid vanished into the kitchen, gliding off in his bare feet, then came back with two bottles of chilled Amstel.

Boyle guzzled half of his quickly. He looked at The Kid and said, 'Okay. This better be good.'

'I think we've got something, Lee. You want to come this way?' The young man beckoned to a door. Boyle got up from the sofa, stepped after The Kid into a small room where a blackout curtain was drawn over the window and a light bulb hung with red crêpe paper.

Boyle saw various bottles of chemicals, trays, prints hung on a plastic line with clothes-pegs.

'Now, let us see, let us see.' The Kid began to unhook prints from the line. He cleared a space on his work surface, shoving aside the chemicals, then spread out a bunch of prints. Boyle leaned over them, feeling an ache deep in his stomach. He wondered about internal damage. Maybe rupturing inside. A crab clawed at his intestines. He imagined pincers digging.

'The idea was I'd photograph only those guys that looked respectable, right?'

'Well-heeled,' Boyle said. 'Moneyed.'

'Nice cars. No scrapyard candidates. No riff-raff.'

'Exactly,' Boyle said. He peered closer at the prints, which were generally of a poor fuzzed quality. Mainly they showed shadowy figures of men sitting inside cars, occasionally somebody on a sidewalk.

'These don't look too sharp,' Boyle said.

'Consider the circumstances. I'm working in the dark. I can't use a flash, *obviously*. I have to conceal the camera. You try taking photographs in those conditions, Lee.'

'I'm not criticizing you,' Boyle said. 'I'm not expecting Karsh of Ottawa.'

'They can be enhanced, of course. That isn't a problem.'

'Okay. What am I supposed to be looking at?' Boyle asked.

The Kid, smirking a little, hovered over the spread of photographs like a magician about to play a card trick. He slid two prints toward Boyle. 'Check these out.'

Boyle picked up the prints and moved closer to the light and examined the dark images. It took him a moment before he focused, before he understood what he was seeing. Suddenly he was beyond pain. He was flying where the air was thin and he couldn't catch his breath. It was like hanging by a parachute caught on an updraft and all the green countryside spread out way below you.

Thank you, Jesus. This is what I need. This is *the break*.

The Kid asked, 'You'll see the image in one is sharper than the other. You want me to improve them even more?'

'No need. They're perfect. You any idea what you've *got* here?'

The Kid nodded and looked gleeful. 'Yeah. I know *exactly* what I've got. What happens next?'

'You sit back. I'll take it from here.'

'You walk out with the prints?'

'You got a problem with that?'

'I'd like, uh, some kind of guarantee.'

'Guarantee? What kind of partnership is this?' Boyle asked. 'You don't think I'm running a risk here? I'm putting my neck on the line, and if it goes wrong your name doesn't even come up. That's *your* guarantee. I'm the one burned.' He brought his face close to The Kid's, a belligerent little motion. 'Or maybe you want to do the whole thing yourself, huh? You want to look this guy in the eye? He'd fucking eat you and spit out the bones. You want to mess with that, sport? Huh?'

The young man shook his head timidly. 'I'd rather not, actually.'

'You better believe it, *actually*. So don't give me shit about guarantees. I'm about to commit a felony here. You want to stray that far on the other side of the law? You'd be in way over your head, man. You leave this to me, and I'll be in touch the very moment our ship comes in.' *Some people*, Boyle thought. *They think they have the balls for the real hard stuff. Ooh, taking pictures in the dark, how awfully dangerous.*

Boyle stepped back into the living room. He stared at the fish swimming round in the big tank. 'I'm thinking, if you ever fall on hard times and you're really hungry, Kid, you could stick one of them in a sandwich.'

'You are so *gross*.'

'People eat *sardines*, for Christ's sake.'

'They're pets, Lee. Pets.'

'I don't see any point in keeping pets that don't know you from one minute to the next,' Boyle said.

'I have a dim memory of having this exact conversation last time you were here.'

'I don't remember that.' Another little amoeba of memory destroyed. He realized he'd even forgotten The Kid's real name. He went to the door. 'I'll be in touch.'

'I'll be waiting, Lee. *Anxiously*.'

Boyle went down the stairs and outside. He sat inside the warm car for a time, trying to herd his thoughts. Corral them. Line them up. See what they amount to. Then he drove the dying black Pontiac – he'd have to

dump this wreck soon – until he came to a payphone outside a convenience market. He dropped a coin in the slot,
dialed Vass's number and waited an age for an answer. He
tapped his fingertips restlessly on an empty metal phone-
book container. Come on, Vass. Pick up the fucking
phone.

Vass sounded distant, pissed with him still. 'I'm making
a table, Lee. I'm up to here in sawdust.' A dog barked in
the background, one of Vass's menagerie of mongrels.

'Do me a small favor,' Boyle said.

'Lee, man, I'm busy. Also, I had the cops calling me at
some unholy hour asking about you. What the fuck
trouble are you in?'

'Don't worry about the cops. What I'm asking you will
take about five minutes out of your day.'

Vass said, 'Being your friend isn't the easiest thing, Lee.'

'Especially my best friend,' Boyle said.

'Just spell out the favor, man. And I'll see.'

28

SAMSA DRANK HIS COFFEE QUICKLY. DARCY SAID, 'YOU really ought to eat something, you know.'

'I'm rushed.'

'You need cereal. Fresh fruit. You look wan. You don't get enough sleep.'

The portable TV was playing on the kitchen counter. Samsa saw a picture of the Purchase land and the blonde reporter from Channel 5, Linda Kisminski, talking into the camera. A caption along the bottom of the screen read, 5 LIVE AM in orange letters. He got up to switch off.

Darcy said, 'No, wait. I'm watching this. Is this what kept you out last night?'

Samsa said yes, it was, and fidgeted with his cup.

'How did she die?'

He told her. She made a face and continued to look at the picture. For as long as she could remember homicides had been part of her daily life. Her father never talked about the specifics, the blood details, but he carried the burden of them. You could tell when he was brooding: he'd disappear before your eyes, lost in God knows what investigation, what pieces of evidence, what ambivalent phrase from an interview with a suspect.

'How old was she?'

Samsa drained his coffee before he said, 'Thirteen. She was a runaway.' He looked at Darcy and there was uneasiness in his expression. 'You'd never do that, would you?'

'Run away from home? Come on. I can't imagine the circumstances.'

Linda Kisminski was saying '. . . from the details we've been able to gather, the dead girl worked as a prostitute in the city's sleazy and shameful sex trade, which continues unabated despite local complaints. Unless something is done about the situation, how many more girls like this one will be at risk? I talked earlier with Police Chief Al Brodsky, who says this tragic case has top priority, and the department is – I quote – "determined to find this girl's killer". Linda Kisminski, Five Live a.m.'

Darcy had seen the place, known locally as Flesh Row, sometimes Skin Street. She'd driven past there once or twice with Nick and looked at the girls on the sidewalks, and she'd wondered what they were thinking, what they felt when they were in some stranger's car or bed, if they distanced themselves and everything was mechanical.

'She was on drugs,' Samsa said. 'Have you ever . . . you know?'

She laughed, shook her head, no. It was a lie. She'd smoked dope a few times, and tried cocaine at a party a couple of months ago. She'd gone into the bathroom with Ginny Flagg and a college girl she knew only as Spyder – a Goth with torn black leggings and a pin in her earlobe and scarlet lipstick – and Spyder had produced a little brown bottle and a tiny spoon. For twenty minutes or so Darcy had felt a lift of exultation and energy, but then she'd wanted more. By that time Spyder had disappeared upstairs with a boy.

'Any leads?' she asked.

'Not yet.'

'Some sicko picked her up and killed her,' Darcy said. He rose, touched her under the chin. 'I have to run.'

She sipped her orange juice. She watched her father take his sports coat from the back of the chair.

'You're not cutting classes again, are you?' he asked.

'I'm being dutiful and conscientious today.'

'Good.' He leaned to kiss her on the top of her head. She thought there was something a little tentative about him, a lack of the adrenalin he usually had when a new homicide occurred. Maybe you just got tired of death after so many years. She was about to mention the phone call she'd received last night, but the idea of a stranger calling out of the blue like that would bother him, and he was clearly flustered anyway. Why add to his concerns? The good daughter, considerate to Dad. *Sometimes.*

'I don't know when I'll be back,' he said.

'I'll be fine. Call me when you have a chance.'

He hesitated in the kitchen doorway. 'We should spend more time together, Darcy.'

'Yeah. On your retirement,' she said, and smiled.

She listened to him drive away, dumped her cereal bowl in the dishwasher and threw in a couple of cups and glasses. She brushed her hair in the bathroom. She thought about changing her hairstyle, which she wore short. Let it grow out, maybe shoulder-length. Sometimes you got bored with the same face in the mirror. She thought her eyes her best feature – deep brown, almost black, like her father's. 'Eyes like Hershey pools,' Nick had told her once. Mancuso, master of imagery.

She picked up her books from the table in the kitchen and left the house, locked the door, headed toward the corner of the block where the schoolbus arrived. Lately

Nick had been in the habit of giving her a ride, but she'd told him she'd rather bus it. It was a small act of rebellion and pretty pathetic really, but it was a start. If she was to dig out a claim to her independence and free herself from Nick without cruelty, it would need to be accomplished in small steps.

She heard the car cruising behind her before she saw it. She turned her face. The driver had one arm hanging from the window as he brought the car alongside her and said, 'Lovely morning, don't you think?'

She turned and continued to walk. The car – a pale-blue Mercury, finned, prehistoric – kept pace with her, which she found irritating. She stopped.

'Something I can do for you?' she asked.

'What's wrong with saying a simple hello,' he said.

'I'll tell you what's wrong: I don't know you, I've never seen you before, and you're disturbing me.'

'You going to school? Hop in. I'll drive you.'

Fat chance. She walked a few paces, stopped again and stared at him. 'What is it you want exactly?'

'Why do people always leap to the conclusion that other people always *want* something? It's an unhealthy way of looking at life. It's a sign of the paranoid times we live in. Everybody's scared. Nobody wants to connect. We live in our own sealed boxes.'

She shaded her eyes against the brightness of sun. She saw how sunlight was reflected from his shirt and his hair and the windshield.

'Hey, I'm harmless,' he said. 'Ask any of my friends.'

'I don't know any of your friends.'

'I'll introduce you to some,' he said.

'Yeah, right,' and she turned and kept moving. The car slid along beside her.

She said, 'You're being a nuisance.'

'You want to tell me your name?'

'Wait,' she said. 'You're the one that phoned! I recognize your voice.'

'I didn't phone you,' and he stopped the car and got out, leaving the engine running. 'Carry your books in time-honored fashion?'

'I can manage.' *Just walk*, she thought. *He's lying about not phoning*.

'Your heart is spoken for? Don't tell me.'

'*Jesus*. What business is it of yours?'

'You think I'm too old for you?'

'I think you're goddam presumptuous,' she said.

He was in step with her now. 'You're not exactly keeping company with the Ancient Mariner. So your heart isn't taken, huh?'

'What will it take for you to leave me alone,' she said.

'I'm just compelled by curiosity. You quit being curious, you might as well be dead.'

'This is where I catch my bus.'

'I'll drive you to school in my chariot.'

'Uh, don't think so.'

'Come on. Do I look menacing? Do I look like somebody who goes round offering rides to unfamiliar young women?'

She stared at him. 'Yeah, I think maybe you do.'

'Your father warned you against guys like me. Right? Candies-from-strangers syndrome.'

'I don't always listen to my father,' she said. Why had she said that? Why had she sounded so . . . *defensive*? She could hear the school bus rattling a block away. 'I make my own decisions.'

'I bet you do. So why won't you let me drive you?'

'No way.'

'I am crushed.'

'Good,' she said, and glanced at him.

He feigned an inconsolable look and laid a hand across

643

his heart. He had an expressive face and gestures. The eyes were bright and smart and – yeah, all right – attractive. He exuded an energetic confidence, as if life was something to be taken lightly, nothing was too serious, problems were just tiny obstacles you skipped around.

'Here's my bus,' she said.

'Go,' he said. 'Sit with the clones. Conform. Be like everyone else. Ride the bus. Sit in classrooms. Take notes. Regurgitate. Blah-blah.'

'You don't know the first thing about me.'

'I'd say you're intelligent. You're independent. You don't like school. You know there's more to life than books and teachers. You're a prisoner of the system. You're not free. You haven't tasted liberty.'

She smiled at him, didn't really want to. The way he pinned her down, defined her. Accurate enough.

She said, 'You're guessing now.'

'I'm a great guesser,' he said. 'I do a lot of things well, as a matter of fact.'

The big yellow bus drew up and the doors opened.

'Here,' he said, and shoved a piece of paper into her hand. Puzzled, she closed her fingers around it and boarded the bus, and saw him watch her from the sidewalk with a curious smile on his face as the doors hissed shut.

29

YOU DON'T GET ENOUGH SLEEP. SAMSA, TURNING DARCY'S
remark around in his head, thought, *I'm afraid of sleep,
of dreaming.* He entered City Hall, where Al Brodsky
greeted him and drew him aside from the flurry of clerks
and secretaries, lawyers and municipal officials arriving
for work. It was obvious to Samsa that Al had been waiting for him, and he had the nervy thought, *It's coming
down on me now.* But Al, hands stuffed in pockets and tie
undone, had other things on his mind.

'You want to hear a brand-new twist, Greg? We've got
a confession in the Cecily Suarez business.'

'A confession?'

'I don't know how much water it's going to hold. Come
downstairs and see for yourself.'

'Somebody just showed up and said what? He killed the
girl?'

'Popped in half an hour ago with a *mea culpa.*' Al
Brodsky steered Samsa toward the basement stairway.

'One of the usual nuts?'

'Not this time. This one's new.'

Samsa descended alongside the chief. Homicide cases brought loonies out of the woodwork, people anxious to confess for any number of reasons – attention mainly. Notice me, please. Here I am – deranged persons living bitter lives of excruciating anonymity on the fringes of society. Samsa had encountered a good share of these in his career. Usually you could dismiss them after a few questions. They spoke of demonic connections or mind-altering influences from outer space, or how they were the reincarnations of notorious serial killers, some of whom were still actually alive on various death rows.

Samsa and Brodsky entered one of the interview rooms. Billy Fogue was there, and Sergeant Ed Duff, who looked like a middle-aged Boy Scout, suntanned and healthy, the kind of dependable guy you just knew would have a way with sheepshank knots and how to pitch tents on mountainsides.

Billy Fogue said, 'Lew Tenant. Meet Ryan Pritt.'

Ryan Pritt sat at the table in the middle of the room, his hands clasped in front of him. He was a thin-faced man who wore a plaid shirt and neatly pressed khaki pants and shiny brown shoes. His hair was receding. He had a relaxed air about him, an absence of desperation, distress.

'How are you, Ryan?' Samsa asked.

'It's a load off my mind,' Pritt said.

'You really killed this girl?' *Tell me you did*, Samsa thought. *Prove it to me. Let your story be watertight, Ryan. What am I thinking? I want Pritt to be guilty.*

Pritt said, 'Yeah. I killed her.'

Fogue said, 'Ryan's a construction worker, Lew Tenant. Presently unemployed. Married. Two small kids.'

Pritt nodded. 'Evangeline and Angelique. One's three, the other's five.'

'Pretty names,' Samsa said. He looked at Pritt's hands. The fingers were callused.

Pritt said, 'I got pictures in my wallet, you want to see them?'

'Maybe later.' Samsa sat on the edge of the table. The guy had none of the usual behavioral give-aways of the nut: no rapid speech pattern, no weirded-out light in the eye. 'You want to run through your story for me?'

'I already told these officers,' Pritt said.

'Now you get to tell me, Ryan. Start with when you met her.'

'I picked her up Monday night.'

'Where?'

'That area they all go. You know it?'

'What time?'

'About nine, maybe nine thirty.' Pritt adjusted a cuff of his shirt. 'I drove out of town. Took her out to that field near Chackstone Acres.'

'What did you do next?'

'I don't have to give you all the details, do I?'

'Unfortunately you do,' Samsa said.

Ryan Pritt looked round the room at the faces of the assembled cops. 'I get it. You guys don't believe me.'

'It's not that, Ryan. The thing is, sometimes people come in confessing to stuff they haven't done.'

'That's pretty damn stupid.'

'It happens. Which is why we have to ask questions. We need details.'

Ryan Pritt looked up at the ceiling. 'Okay. We went in the back seat of the car. She gives me this condom. I told her, I don't wear those things. No way.'

'So what happened next?'

'We argued,' he said. 'I wanted it straight. I wasn't shelling out sixty bucks for a condom fuck.'

'And the argument blew out of all proportion?' Samsa leaned a little closer to the man. *Why was he lying? What was in it for him?*

647

'I lost my temper,' Pritt said. 'I exploded, I guess.' He shut his eyes in the manner of a man replaying bad memories. 'She slapped me because I wouldn't let her out the car. She was beginning to scream.'

'Then?'

'I didn't mean it,' Pritt said. He hunched forward, laid his head on the table and began to sob silently.

'Take it easy, Ryan.' Samsa gestured to Duff. 'Get Ryan some water, Ed.'

Duff fetched a cup from the cooler and set it down on the table.

Pritt lifted his head, sipped and said, 'Thanks, thanks.'

Samsa said, 'She slapped you. She screamed. There was some kind of struggle.'

'Yeah, very brief,' Pritt said. He rubbed his eyes.

'You hit her?'

'One time. That was all.'

'Where did you hit her?'

'Here.' Pritt reached back, touched the base of his neck. 'In that area, roughly. First, I thought I'd just knocked her out. I grabbed her shoulders, shook her a few times, but she wasn't coming round.'

I shook her shoulders, Samsa thought. *I shook her shoulders. It wasn't you, Ryan Pritt.*

'So this one blow killed her,' he said.

'One blow, all it took,' Pritt said quietly. 'She was a frail little thing. Tiny . . .' He played with the corner of his mouth, touching it with a fingertip as if he were applying balm to a cold sore.

Samsa walked round the room. 'What was she wearing, Ryan?'

'Oh, real short skirt, a blouse you could see through. You know how hookers dress. Even in the rain.'

Samsa remembered the umbrella she'd been carrying.

How could he ask about that without opening a door he wanted to keep shut?

'Anything else, Ryan?'

'She had this bracelet.'

'Can you describe it for us?'

Pritt shook his head. 'Only that it was big.'

'Did you see the color of her panties?'

'I never got that far.'

'Okay. You hit her. Then what?'

'I found a place to dump her out in that field. I was desperate, I was freaked, you got to understand that.'

'You dumped her. Then what?'

'Then nothing. All I wanted was to get the hell away from there.'

Samsa asked, 'Why did you pick up this girl in the first place? You're married, two nice daughters. Why?'

'My wife's . . . between ourselves, I guess we don't get along in that one area,' Pritt said.

'You often use hookers?'

'Two times a month maybe. At most.'

'Had you picked up Cecily Suarez before?'

Pritt said he hadn't. He leaned back in his chair.

'Why have you confessed, Ryan?' Samsa asked.

'Because it's a burden, Lieutenant. It's like this big goddam cloud inside your head. It's this voice that won't stop talking in your ear. You don't sleep. You go around in a daze. You're scared. You feel like shit.'

Tell me about it, Ryan. 'So what do you want? To sign a confession?'

'Somebody take down my statement and I'll sign it.'

Brodsky said, 'It's customary to ask for a lawyer, Ryan.'

'Why shell out good money to those bandits?'

Brodsky looked at Samsa and said, 'A word.'

They went out of the interview room and stood together in the corridor. The chief asked, 'What's your impression?'

'I don't know.'

'He described the girl.'

'Up to a point, sure. He might be lying. He might have picked her up before.'

'Why would he be lying?'

'Why does anybody lie? Has he been checked out?'

'Cullinan did the background. Construction worker, two daughters. That's all on the level. No priors.'

'Everything he's told us he could have seen on TV, or read in the early edition of the *Gazette*. There's nothing new in his story, Al. There's no big surprise.'

'There's the bracelet,' Brodsky said. 'The way she was dressed. I don't remember these details going public.'

'Yeah, but I still say it's *possible* he picked her up before. She might have been wearing a bracelet then.'

'The gift horse, and you're looking it in the mouth.'

'I don't trust gift horses, Al.'

'Normally I don't trust them either. But this guy seems so . . .'

'Straight? Genuine?'

Brodsky said, 'Ordinary.'

'With a mighty conscience,' Samsa said.

'Some people have such things, Greg.'

'You want to book him?' Samsa said.

'I'd like to hold him until I hear from Zane that the blow on the kid's neck is consistent with what Pritt says he did to her. I also want a psychiatric report.'

'And if it gels, he's our man.'

'You got a better prospect?'

Samsa thought, *This is the easy way out. This is my escape route. But it isn't. It can't be. And you can't tunnel your way to freedom through Ryan Pritt.* 'No,' he said. 'I don't.'

'It's your case,' and Al Brodsky raised his hands, palms outward in a backing-off gesture. 'You play it any way you see fit.'

'I want to talk with his wife. See what his home background is like. I want to know this guy before I reach any conclusion.'

Brodsky said, 'Always cautious.'

'Thorough,' Samsa remarked. 'I'll take Eve Lassiter with me. She's got a light touch with some people.'

They were about to step back into the interview room when a uniformed cop appeared at the end of the corridor and called out, 'Lieutenant? There's somebody waiting for you in your office.'

'Who?' Samsa asked.

The cop said, 'I'm only the messenger, Lieutenant.'

'See who it is, Greg,' Brodsky said. 'I'll keep chatting with Pritt in the meantime.'

Samsa, irritated by this interruption, walked to his office.

The man who stood beside the desk was fingering a photograph of Darcy. He looked at Samsa and said, 'I thought I'd drop in. See what the hive feels like. Maybe talk about this and that.'

Samsa stopped dead. *This is wrong.*

The man set down the photograph. 'Your daughter?'

Samsa nodded. 'What do you want to talk about, Boyle?'

Lee Boyle smiled, sniffed, ran the back of one hand across the tip of his nose. 'One or two things, I guess.'

'Be more specific,' Samsa said. *Boyle shouldn't be here,* he thought. He was uneasy, more than that. He fought back the feeling, the sense of menace Boyle had dragged inside his office. Boyle knows nothing. Absolutely nothing.

'I'm not sure you want to hear what I have to say in this particular environment, Samsa,' and Boyle gestured around the small office, encompassing more than this tiny space – the whole department, City Hall, the corridors of law and order and propriety.

651

Samsa said, 'Say what you're here to say, Boyle.' He couldn't keep a certain thickness out of his voice.

Boyle walked round the desk and settled in Samsa's chair. 'You know what I think?'

'Suppose you tell me.'

'I think you're going through assorted degrees of torment.'

'Why would I be suffering torment, Boyle?'

'Think about it,' Boyle said.

'Think about what exactly?'

'Almond.'

Almond, Samsa thought. *Where is Boyle going with this?* He said, 'First, get the fuck out of my chair.'

Boyle shrugged, rose. 'Like I say. Maybe we should continue this conversation someplace where you won't get so uptight.'

'What's wrong with talking right here?' Samsa listened to phones ringing. He heard Cullinan's voice in an outer office and a couple of traffic cops yack about an accident on the freeway. Phones, voices. These sounds came to him over a great distance, but they gathered intensity as they rolled in his direction. He saw a fly flit dangerously close to the whirring blades of the fan. He imagined the motor set in reverse mode and the fly sucked into the blades and butchered instantly.

'Nothing, I guess,' Boyle said. 'I don't give a shit basically. You want to talk about your accident here or some other place, it doesn't matter to me.'

Samsa suddenly had funny spots in front of his eyes, small dancing stars. Stress maybe. Blood pressure rising. *My accident.* He looked at Darcy's photograph. How bright and sharp she appeared. Her smile was open and innocent and imparted all the optimism of her age. He wanted to keep her this way, protect that innocence for as long as he could in a threatening world.

'Name a place,' he said, even as he knew immediately this was a mistake, a moment of weakness.

Boyle smiled and fingered the edge of Darcy's photograph. 'Now that's what I call good judgement, Lieutenant.'

30

LEE BOYLE ABANDONED THE STOLEN CAR – HIS THIRD IN THE last twelve hours – in a parking garage downtown, and began the search for new transportation. The trick to stealing cars was simple: don't get attached to them. He found a white Ford Taurus parked outside a health-food store in a side street, windows rolled down, keys *dangling* in the ignition. The owner must have stepped inside the store on a quick errand, mung beans or organic maple syrup, back in a flash, no sweat – *no car*.

Boyle drove through downtown, swung quickly past the Greyhound station – a seedy functional box surrounded by a stack of great smoking buses – and out to the freeway, thinking of young Ms Samsa, seeing her face in the photograph on Samsa's desk, the neatly written message she'd inscribed: 'Love to the Best Dad In the World, Darcy.' She had a mouth like a cherub waiting to be kissed. And her teeth, the *gleam* of perfection. It struck him that if you dyed the brown hair black, and the eyebrows, she'd look a lot like Almond, those deep dark eyes were similar, a reincarnation if you thought about it from a certain angle, a restoration of somebody you considered lost.

Maybe.

At her age she was delicately poised between obeying rules and flaunting them. The way Almond had been. Exactly.

Darcy Samsa. *Dar-cee*. Rolled off the tongue.

He was on the freeway a few miles before he took an exit ramp, checking his rear-view mirror. Now his mind went racing to the idea of Raseci, and he wondered if Bigshoes was tracking him. He'd seen no sign of him, which didn't mean he wasn't around somewhere. He'd also have minions who carried out tasks for him, such as surveillance. Boyle wouldn't know their faces or the cars they drove.

But they were there. This was indisputable. Gospel.

The dashboard clock registered 11:02. Time clung to him like a succubus. $10,000. He pondered Crassman briefly. A total write-off. Crassman probably had his guys – those hapless dickheads who looked like they were fresh from some Appalachian hollow where the barber had palsied hands – hanging out at the trailer park, armed and waiting for Lee Boyle to show and muttering about what they'd do to that goddammed *scumbucket* next time.

He wanted to arrive at the appointed place early, check it out. The last thing he needed was to be bushwhacked. He felt nervy, like a man committed to a roller-coaster trip, but midway through the heart-shaking ride wondering if he'd made the correct choice, except it was too late to disembark – unless you stepped out into space.

He parked the car, bought a ticket at the booth and passed through the turnstile. Stub in hand, he walked in the direction of the reptile house. The zoo wasn't upscale. The city didn't have the budget for natural habitats. The polar bear, slightly fortunate, had been given a tiny pit to

himself, where murky water dribbled across a rocky for-
mation. The creature looked mangy and sorrowful, like he
was having dim memories of the carefree ice floes of his
youth, before human assholes came and shot him with a
trank gun and he woke up in hell.

Boyle kept moving, glancing around. A squall of red-
assed baboons picked at each other's butts and chattered.
There were very few customers: a bunch of schoolkids led
by a guide, a couple of solitary browsers. The air was
dead and heavy inside the reptile house, and there was
that stale musk common to places where creatures are
trapped.

Boyle, who found himself alone in the building, stared
at a boa constrictor inside a glass case. Fat and motionless. In the next case rattlers lay coiled. All that pent-up
venom.

At the sound of footsteps Boyle turned his face, saw the
door open and Samsa appear with the sun behind him.
Boyle tried to slough off his tension, tried to be cool, but
the speed in his system jittered him.

The cop approached slowly. One of the rattlers struck
the inside of the case, a whack of tail upon the glass. Boyle
moved away slightly.

'Punctual,' he said to Samsa. 'I like that.'

Samsa said, 'Let's hear what you have to say, Boyle.'

Samsa had one of those thoughtfully still faces that
might suddenly explode in animated expression. He
looked, Boyle thought, a little on the haggard side. You
needed to see under surfaces, though. The dark in Samsa's
eye, presently calm, could smolder and turn to fury without warning.

'I agreed to meet with you, Boyle. I'm here and I'm
waiting.'

'Don't rush me, Samsa. You can't afford an attitude
problem.'

Samsa gestured round the reptile house. 'These some of your relatives?' He tapped one of the cases and a diamondback reared up an inch or so, roused from its torpor.

'You're a wag,' Boyle said. 'Except I'm not the snake here. I wasn't the one who picked up the girl. I wasn't the one who killed her.'

'*Killed* the girl? You out of your goddam mind?'

'Let's run through the facts, Lieutenant. You picked her up Monday night around ten.'

'You've got quite an imagination there, Boyle.'

'Then you drove her out to the Purchase place. You went off the fucking road in your Le Baron. Accident report number six-eight-two-zero, submitted by Frederick Trope, State trooper.'

'You must have accessed a computer to get that information. Initiative, Lee. So I had a car wreck. So what? It's a matter of record. The rest is bullshit.'

Boyle smiled. 'I admire you, Samsa. I'm in total awe of the way you handle two different worlds. One is all nice and respectable and wrapped in cellophane. The other's a black steamy hole. And you think you can keep them apart. You're the one with the bounteous imagination.'

'If this is all you've got to say, Boyle, you're wasting my time.' Samsa turned and took a step away.

Boyle said, 'You were *seen*, Samsa. The girl got into your car. You were spotted. I have an eyewitness.'

'This eyewitness has a name?'

Boyle nodded.

'But you're not saying who.'

'I look like a fool?'

Samsa stared at him hard. 'So all you've got is a wrecked car and an anonymous eyewitness. My guess is your erstwhile friend Cassandra, or whatever she calls herself. Her reputation isn't exactly unsullied, Boyle. You think anybody's going to believe anything she has to say?' Samsa shook his head. 'Your story's a work of sheer desperation. You've got surmise and supposition, which amounts to thin fucking air. What you're doing is trying to divert focus away from yourself with this bullshit.'

'I don't think so, Samsa.'

'No? Let me show you the cards in my hand.'

'I'm all eyes,' Boyle said. So Samsa knew about Cassandra. He'd been digging.

'Your alibi frankly sucks, Boyle. Nobody can place you at Chang's at the time you stated. Your pals Plumm and Raseci don't have precise memories of when they saw you Monday night. They give vague a bad reputation. Rudolph Vass is another one that doesn't know the time of day. Your whole yarn's a sandcastle and the tide's coming in. This is a way of saying you have problems, Boyle. Real problems. In fact, you're up there on the suspect list. Way up. Certain parties downtown would like nothing better than for me to book you and lock you away without further ado.'

Boyle said, 'So book me. What's stopping you? Left your cuffs at the office? Here. Look. I'm holding my hands out. Take me downtown. Interrogate me. Lock me up. I'm a danger to society.'

'Unfortunately the law says I can't throw a guy in jail just because his alibi's like a fucking sieve. I need a little more than that, Boyle. I wish to Christ I didn't, but that's the way it's written. I'll tell you this much, though. It's only a matter of time before I nail you for the girl.'

Boyle thought, *This is your moment. Wipe the look off this fucker's face.* 'I happen to have something else, Samsa. Better than any eyewitness.'

Samsa didn't look interested. Or if he was he had ways of hiding it. Boyle placed a hand inside the hip pocket of his pants and left it there a moment. *I want to watch you sink, Samsa. I want to see the bubbles come up to the surface as you go down and down to where the bottom-suckers live.*

'What's in the pocket?' Samsa asked. 'Or are you trying to keep me in suspense, Boyle?'

'What an insightful guy you are,' Boyle said. He took out a sheet of paper, unfolded it and held it in his hand. 'This is a photocopy. The original is in a safe place. Here.' Boyle gave the paper to Samsa, who took it, gazed at it, then let it flop over in his fingers like something he wanted to drop.

Boyle reached out and retrieved the paper. He watched Samsa a second, then he glanced down at the Xerox.

In grainy light, face hidden slightly by the upraised collar of a sports coat, illuminated weakly by a street lamp, Samsa sits in his car, rolling the window up. The girl, slightly blurred by her own movement, is stepping in on the passenger side. She holds an umbrella at an angle away from her head, like she's about to fold it down. The expression on what you can see of Samsa's face is one of nervous fatigue maybe.

The car, you can tell from the badge visible on the hood, is a Chrysler.

And the girl, even though she's out of focus, is Almond. He knows the shape, the little skirt she's wearing, the chunky big bracelet you can just about see. He remembers her body when they made love on the bathroom floor. He imagines her on a slab in the morgue.

He raised his face to Samsa and said, 'So you see.'

Samsa gazed at a snake slithering across its cage. 'It's not a good image,' he said. 'It's blurred.'

Boyle had the impression that Samsa was talking to himself. His voice was strange and flat.

'It can be improved, Lieutenant. Technology's terrific these days.'

Samsa was still observing the serpent. 'I was running her off the streets, that's all. You see a kid like that cruising, you think of your own daughter . . .'

'I'm moved, Samsa. I'm deeply touched. I'm almost tearful. The lieutenant has compassion for hookers. It's something he doesn't want to discuss in his own office, so here we are in this fucking zoo having a secret meeting.'

'It's not a subject I wanted to talk about back there,' Samsa said.

'Why? Your colleagues might overhear, and they wouldn't understand the sheer fucking depth of your compassion? They'd think more salacious thoughts, huh?'

'Exactly.'

'Fine, fine. So if I show this picture to Fogue or Rebb, you wouldn't mind? If I took it to the Chief of Police, that wouldn't bother you? Is that what you're saying?'

Samsa didn't reply. He had the look of a guy who has just backstepped into a pile of dogshit up over the rim of his shoe.

Boyle laughed aloud. 'I didn't think so, Samsa. Here's another scenario for you to mull over: Almond's in your car, and you go skidding off the road and down into the field. And somewhere in that time frame your passenger, God rest her sad young soul, dies. Maybe she's giving you head as you're tooting along and you lose your concentration. Or maybe she's administering a hand job and your senses are otherwise engaged. Or maybe it's even more devious and deliberate than that. There's this dark side to you because you've been hanging around homicides for too long, and something's rubbed off and it's warped your thinking and you wonder, hey, what's it like to kill somebody, what's it like to snuff out a life, because you're sick—'

'No,' Samsa said.

'And after you kill her you fake the accident—'

660

'*No*,' Samsa said again.

'Whatever it is, *bang*, you go off the road. And the lieutenant, concerned about his reputation as a law-enforcement officer of some standing, has a big-time panic attack. He's got a dead hooker on his hands. But wait. The idea of the century comes to him. Why, he'll just *dump* the corpse and report the accident – minus any mention of the dead girl, of course. So he goes through with this chump scheme, and he thinks he's got his ass well and truly covered. Right? *Right?*'

Samsa pressed his forehead against the surface of a glass case. Sweat filmed his forehead. He had his hands clenched and white against his sides.

'*Right?*' Boyle asked again. 'You dumped the corpse. You falsified an accident report. Oh, you're in deep shit, Samsa.'

Samsa looked at Boyle and was silent for a very long time, as if a prolonged inner struggle were coming to some kind of resolution. 'You can't prove this. It's all guess-work.'

'Okay. I'll take the picture to your boss. You don't have any objections to that, I suppose.' Boyle folded the Xerox and turned away.

He hadn't walked more than a few steps before Samsa called him back. *I knew he would*, Boyle thought. *I see his fear. I can smell it.*

'You want money. It's usually money.'

'Money's always useful.'

'I'm not wealthy, Boyle.'

'And I'm not greedy. I call that serendipity.' Boyle thought a second. Ten thou to get Plumm off his back. Something for himself. 'Twenty-five K should keep your name out the papers.'

'That's a lot of cash.'

'But you're in a lot of trouble.'

'Look,' and Samsa stopped, his face devoid of color.

'I'm looking,' Boyle said.

There was a shiver in Samsa's voice. When he spoke, the words came out of some locked cellar deep inside. 'It was an accident, Boyle, a tragic fucking accident. I didn't kill that girl. I didn't mean for that to happen. Believe me, if I could go back and change things I'd do it. I'd give anything to be able to do that.'

'Nobody's going to give a shit if it was an accident or if you broke her goddam neck with your own hands,' Boyle said. 'It doesn't change the fact that this is an impossible situation for you. And just in case it sneaks across your mind to pull out your gun and shoot me dead in this big empty snake house, remember, you don't know where the original print is. You imagine I came here without taking some precautions?'

Samsa looked as if he was calculating in his head. 'I want the print, the negs, the photocopy or copies. Plural. I want all of that. Because I don't want you coming back at me again. You understand that. I give you the cash, I get the stuff, I never see you again. That's the end of it. You cross my path one more time, I can't be responsible for what I might do to you. You understand that, too?'

Boyle smiled. 'Gotcha.'

'Twenty-five thou. After that, I'm tapped out. I'm empty. Is that clear?'

'Transparent,' Boyle said.

'I can get it this afternoon. Tell me a place we can meet.'

'I'll think about that. I'll phone you at your office. Three o'clock say.'

Samsa said, 'You're scum, Boyle. A real piece of work.'

'You're not exactly a walking paragon of virtue yourself, are you?'

'I make one mistake, Boyle. One goddam mistake and—'

'What was it anyhow? A mid-life crisis? Or is it something you do often – go downtown, slumming for a piece of young ass, a little stroll on the dark side to get your juices flowing? Whores excite you? Blow jobs in the front seat? A quick fuck with the seat inclined? Is it like that?'

Samsa made an angry sound that came deep out of his chest, and he shoved Boyle back against one of the reptile cases. He moved quickly, surprising Boyle with his agility and strength. His eyes were wild all at once, and Boyle, whose antennae were finely tuned to such things, felt the unmistakable buzz of serious danger.

He saw Samsa's hand come up and instinctively he ducked, feeling Samsa's fist skim his scalp and hearing the searing crack of glass in his ears. Samsa's knuckles were cut and blood was running down the glass, and one of the snakes, agitated, flicked a tongue against the splintered case. Samsa drew his hand to his side and held it with the other, and the look on his face was one of raw pain.

'Get the fuck out of my sight, Boyle.'

In the doorway Boyle stopped, looked back, saw Samsa, shoulders slumped, clutching his bloodied hand.

Lee Boyle thought, *You could almost feel sorry for Samsa.*

Almost. But he didn't.

31

RYAN PRITT'S HOUSE WAS LOCATED ON THE EDGE OF THE CITY in a new subdivision where building was still going on. The site had a barren unready feel to it, lawns not yet seeded, cement-mixers and construction trucks all over the place.

These half-made places depressed Eve, a feeling that wasn't alleviated by Samsa's brooding mood. She'd expected something different after last night: a smile, a touch, a reference to what had happened between them, which, in her mind at least, had been a wonderful thing. But he was slippery, hard to read. He looked vaguely *tortured*. She wanted badly to touch him, but she didn't. She wanted to ask about the bandage wrapped round his hand, but she hadn't.

She parked outside the Pritt house. A thin woman in a sleeveless floral dress was standing in the open doorway. Behind her two small girls concealed themselves shyly. Eve and Samsa walked up the unpaved driveway.

Eve introduced herself and Samsa, then asked, 'You're Jody Pritt?'

'Yeah. Come inside.'

The house was open-plan downstairs, with a kitchen situated at the back behind a service counter. The furniture was new, the sofa and matching armchairs wrapped in plastic.

'You want to sit?' Jody Pritt asked.

'Sure,' Eve said.

Samsa leaned against the counter and gazed at the two small girls, who were clutching their mother's dress.

Jody Pritt said, 'I don't understand what the hell's going on. Somebody phoned from the cops and said Ryan had confessed to some murder.'

Eve said, 'And we're checking his confession, Jody. You mind me calling you that?'

Jody Pritt, who had stringy mouse-colored hair of the unmanageable kind, made a small gesture of confusion with her bony hands. 'I just don't see it. I mean, Ryan's no killer. He might be a lot of things, but a killer?'

'When you say he might be a lot of things, what do you mean?' Eve asked. The woman, she noticed, was missing a tooth, lower left of her mouth. Her face was gaunt, almost bone. She had a translucent quality you sometimes saw on the terminally sick.

'He drinks in binges. He's in and out of AA. But a killer? If you saw him with these kids you'd see what a terrific father he is.'

A stale marriage, Eve thought. The roaming husband, the neglected wife. And when he was home Pritt gave all his attention to the daughters. It was a common story, but it didn't go any way to explaining why Pritt would kill. Or, alternatively, confess to a killing he hadn't done.

'He's been unemployed how long?' Eve asked.

'Four months. It's his choice. Look outside at the construction going on. If he'd wanted he could be working there. They offered him a job.'

'He turned it down?' Samsa asked.

'It's like he doesn't want to work,' Jody Pritt said. 'Like he couldn't see any future in it or something.'

'What about the mortgage on this house?' Eve asked. 'How does that get paid?'

'I had some money saved he didn't know about. But mostly that's gone now.' She blinked back tears. 'This dead girl was a hooker?'

Eve said yes, she was.

Jody Pritt picked up the smaller of the two girls and held her. 'I can accept the hooker, okay, because we're not what you'd call intimate much, frankly, and he's got needs I can't satisfy, but the rest . . .'

Samsa said, 'He's desperate to confess, Mrs Pritt.'

'That's what I don't get.'

Eve said, 'I have to ask you this, Jody. Has Ryan ever acted violently?'

The woman lowered the kid gently. The girl, blue-eyed and fragile, had a thumb stuck in her mouth. The other daughter was staring at the floor like a shy fawn.

'When you say violently, what do you mean?' Jody Pritt asked.

'Has he ever struck anyone? You, for instance?' Eve noticed from the corner of her eye Samsa glancing round the room. His impatience was almost palpable. He didn't want to be here. He had something else to do. What was wrong with him, for Christ's sake? He'd been off-key ever since that accident. He hadn't been himself. She had an urge to go to him and hold him and ask him what was wrong. *Open up your heart, Greg. You can tell me anything after last night, don't you realize that?* She pictured his car plunging off the road, plowing through the muddy grass of the Purchase property. The report she'd seen said the car had overturned, hit a tree. Something clicked inside her head, like the sound of a latch opening in a faraway room. She wasn't sure what it was, something to do with the Purchase property, Samsa's accident.

She caught herself drifting. Unprofessional. 'Has he ever struck you, Jody?' she asked again.

'Only when I deserved it. Like when I stepped out of line.'

'What exactly do you mean, stepped out of line?'

The woman ran the palm of her hand across the smaller child's hair. 'When he came home and I didn't have supper ready, for instance.'

'He hit you for that?'

'Or when I had a night out with friends and came back late, like after midnight.'

'Did you report any of these incidents to the police?'

'Report them? No way. They're private. They're part of a marriage.'

Eve thought of all the battered wives she'd known, and how many of them still kept buying into the idea that the occasional lash of violence was a component of marriage, something that happened between husband and wife, an unwritten conjugal law – I got what I deserved. I had it coming to me. He was within his rights. Why didn't they learn they could fight back?

'How often did this happen?'

'I don't know how often. Mainly when he was down about something.'

'How did he hit you? With his fist? His belt?'

'You really need these details?'

'It helps form a picture,' Eve said.

'Okay. He'd punch me. He kicked me a few times.'

Samsa asked, 'And you never thought about reporting him?'

'Like I said, it was between him and me.'

'It's still against the law,' Eve said.

'I didn't see it as being cop business,' the woman said. 'It's not like he's a savage. And he never hit the kids. He'd never lay a finger on them. They're his little princesses.'

They were his princesses and you were his punchbag, Eve thought. She saw Samsa gaze at his bandage and a look of discomfort cross his face. She remembered the gentleness of his lovemaking, those hands upon her body. He was a good man, and a tender one, and whatever was bothering him now troubled her, too.

Jody Pritt said, 'I put some of the blame on the medication he takes.'

'What medication?' Eve asked.

'Those anti-depressant things.'

'You remember what they're called?'

'Ela-something. I don't remember.'

'Elavil?' Samsa asked.

'That's it. He started taking them about three years ago, last time he was out of work in fact. He was moping around, feeling pretty low. Then when he went back to work he just kept on taking them. I think they turned his head around.'

'In what way?' Eve asked.

'For one thing – and I know this is gonna sound damn strange – he suddenly decided one day he'd press his own clothes. He wouldn't let me iron anything. Said I couldn't do it properly. Remember, this is a man who never had any interest in these kinds of chores. He'd even press his shorts, his handkerchiefs, everything. He'd spend *hours* doing it. Then he got real weird about money. He started stashing coins and dollar bills all over the place. I'd find bills inside toilet rolls, coins hidden inside the kids' toys. He'd hide money in old wine bottles, beer cans, and he'd dig these little holes in the yard. I'm talking about pennies and quarters, not just bills. I asked him why he was doing it. He always came up with the same answer. "Because I don't trust the banks," he'd say. "They're in cahoots with the IRS."'

Samsa asked, 'Is he still taking the medication?'

'Yeah. But he added some others. So now it's like he takes three or four different kinds. Prozac. Librium. Something else.' She started to cry, raising her hands to her face and trying, Eve thought, to be brave. 'Sorry, I'm sorry,' and she drew the back of her wrist across her eyes.

'It's okay,' Eve said. 'Look, Jody. If Ryan's innocent, we don't want to see him serve time. That's why we need to discover if there's some reason he felt the need to confess to a murder he may not have committed.'

The woman said, 'They have the death sentence in this state.'

'You don't want to start thinking that way, Jody. Believe me. I'll need the name of his physician.'

'Dr Stanford,' she said. 'He has an office down on Rosemont.'

'We'll find him,' Eve said, and rose from the sofa.

'I have a favor to ask . . . I'd like to see my husband.'

'I can arrange that. I'll give you my card, and you phone me later this afternoon and we'll fix up a time. Okay?'

'Okay.' Jody Pritt took the card as if it were a lifeline to her future.

Samsa said, 'You might want to consider hiring a lawyer, Mrs Pritt. Your husband rejected the idea, but I think it would be in your best interests.'

Jody Pritt appeared not to have heard him. 'Ryan didn't kill this girl,' she said. 'No matter what he says.'

'I hope you're right.'

Eve stepped outside. Samsa followed. When they were back in the car she said, 'Violence and bad medicine. Did the medicine contribute to the violence? Or was he always going to be violent anyway?'

'Chicken and the egg,' Samsa remarked.

'And that manic behavior,' she said. She ran a hand through her hair, feeling strands made damp by humidity.

'Harriet used to take anti-depressants,' he said.

Was that the thing troubling him? More memories of Harriet? She wondered how she could rid him of a ghost. She put her hand on his knee somewhat tentatively, as if this action involved a great risk. He gave no indication that he welcomed the touch. She didn't move her hand away. She'd get through to him. She had great determination.

'What's the bandage for?' she asked.

'I cut my hand on some broken glass.'

She thought about saying something flippant – Let me kiss it better – but she didn't. 'You're out of tune today, Lieutenant.'

'Am I?'

'I imagined you'd be all smiles.'

'Maybe I'm smiling inside,' he said.

'I have a question for you. Is there going to be a repeat of last night? Or was it just a one-off thing for you?'

'What do you want it to be?'

'It didn't feel like a one-nighter from my angle. Or am I being too pushy?'

He placed his unbandaged hand on hers. 'No. It's just me being slow.'

'I enjoyed it. I enjoyed every second of it. I can't remember . . .' She let the sentence float off unfinished. She didn't want to talk about other lovers. 'Take your time, Greg. There's no hurry. No pressure.' He smiled at her and she said, 'You should do that more often. It brightens your face. You're a good-looking man, except when you frown.'

She started the car, drove away from the subdivision, headed through older suburbs toward downtown. She had to remove her hand from his knee to drive – a tiny wrench that took her by surprise: she didn't really want to let him go.

She braked at a red light. 'I think Pritt's a candidate. He's violent. He's clearly whacked-out on those drugs. He's got this manic streak.'

'Sometimes candidates don't get elected,' Samsa said.

She tapped her fingertips on the wheel. 'He loses his temper, breaks the girl's neck, dumps her in that field . . .'

The light changed to green. She edged the car forward, and she remembered that the time of Gregory's accident in the field coincided with the estimated time of the girl's death. And she recalled Joshua Gold's insistence – no, his *certainty* – that he'd seen Greg, more than once, cruising the streets.

But Joshua had been mistaken. Greg had told her so.

She cut this line of thinking dead. She disengaged the connection. It was a cop's habit, adding one fact to another, then to another, and sometimes the end result was all these little building blocks leaning in the wrong direction. *What was she thinking?*

Samsa said, 'I need to stop at my bank.'

'Sure,' she said, and she turned her face, pressed her lips against his knuckles and wondered about love, the way it could bomb you quite unexpectedly out of your senses like an incendiary device dropped from the sky.

32

SAMSA LEFT HIS OFFICE AND WALKED SEVERAL BLOCKS through the sapping heat. His hand ached and his shirt stuck to his skin. The envelope in the inside pocket of his sports coat felt bulky and alien.

Stan Rougier at the bank had asked, *You sure you want all this in cash, Greg?* Samsa wanted to say it's none of your goddam business, Stan. He'd withdrawn $15,000 from his savings account, which left a meager balance of $3,300. He'd also taken $10,000 from Darcy's college fund, thinking he'd replace it if he set aside a good sum from his monthly pay check – on the assumption he kept his job. Vicious circles. You pay extortion so you can keep on working to replace the money extorted from you in the first place. He was assailed by a deep loathing of Lee Boyle.

What could he have done anyway? Refused to pay? Listening to Eve interview Ryan Pritt's wife, a stupid parlor game without purpose – poor Eve going through her Q & A session and not knowing it was a fraud – he'd found himself seriously entertaining the idea of killing

Boyle, luring him to a deserted place and shooting him. But that wouldn't be the end of the whole thing. Boyle said he had a collaborator, and Samsa was inclined to accept this. The guy who'd taken the photograph, for starters. Maybe there was even more than one accomplice.

So Boyle dies, and somebody else steps into the frame and makes more demands. *You killed Lee Boyle, Lieutenant, and now the price has just gone up.*

This turmoil. This being nailed to a cross. He found himself imagining Xeroxes of that damning photograph all over the place, falling into God knows whose hands, and multiplying until everyone in the city had a copy.

Eve senses something isn't right, he thought. He could see the way she searched when she looked into his eyes. Lovely generous Eve – she was toting some of Samsa's burden without knowing what it was.

That's an awful lot of cash to carry around, Greg, Rougier had said.

But Boyle might have demanded more. Tell yourself you're getting off lucky. Of course, Boyle might be greedy, come back again. Confirmed dopers were notoriously twisted.

You'd have the print, the copy, the negatives. Even so, how could you predict *anything* in this strange inverted world? This deal with Boyle was flimsy, he knew that. But he'd bought his ticket and he was boarding the flight, even if he didn't know the final destination.

He turned a corner and walked a few more blocks until he came to a pedestrian precinct, cobblestones and Victorian lamps and expensive little shops. He stepped inside a vegetarian restaurant called the Bounteous Planet. The room, ferny and airy, skylights everywhere, was empty. He sat at a table and ordered coffee from a young waitress wearing heavy-framed glasses that added fifteen years to her face.

He sipped the coffee, his hand a little unsteady. He'd been sleeping badly, a few hours at most. Dreamless sleep, and yet he always woke with the feeling he'd just dreamed something dire. He looked at his bandaged hand, the cotton slightly pink. He remembered smashing his fist into the glass case and the snake rearing up, tongue flashing, eyes resolute.

Boyle entered the room carrying a manila envelope. He crossed the floor in that easy loping walk of his and pulled up a chair at Samsa's table. He had well-muscled arms, Samsa noticed. His body was in good shape, no suggestion of flab.

'How's the hand?' Boyle asked.

'Skip the pleasantries,' Samsa said.

'You might have severed an artery,' Boyle said.

Sometimes I wish I had, Samsa thought. *Sometimes I wish I'd died in that field*.

'Just give me the envelope, Boyle.'

'There's a way of doing these things. You get the envelope *after* I get the cash. It's not that I don't trust you, you understand.'

'But I'm supposed to trust *you*? Is that how it works?'

'That's the situation,' Boyle said. He opened a pack of cigarettes and lit one, despite the No Smoking signs. He flapped a hand to waft smoke away. 'This bothering you, Samsa? Say the word and I'll stub it out.'

'Smoke all you want. You might just get lung cancer one day and die in sheer fucking agony.'

'It's a chance I take,' Boyle said. 'We live in a diabolical age where all our sweet little pleasures contain a kernel of danger. Foods have toxic additives, tobacco's bad for you, booze fucks up your liver. And sex is taboo if you don't take care.'

Samsa looked into Boyle's blue eyes and thought they were just a little too bright, the pupils dilated. The way he spoke was a shade on the rapid side. Speed would ravage his good looks in a few years. He was already showing slight signs of mileage.

Samsa took the envelope from his pocket and slid it across the table.

Boyle picked it up, glanced inside. 'I'm not going to count it,' he said. 'See how I trust you, Lieutenant?' He shoved the envelope in a back pocket of his pants, and Samsa, with a sensation of sinking through tar, thought about Darcy, her college money, her future. His own savings also. Gone in a flash. Gone inside this creep's pocket.

Boyle placed his manila envelope on the table. Samsa didn't hesitate to open it. He saw the print, the creased Xerox, and a negative he held up to the light to make certain.

'You'll burn them, I guess,' Boyle said.

'What I do with them is my own fucking business, Boyle. I paid for them.'

'Tetchy.'

Samsa said, 'Don't cross my path again. You understand that.'

'We agreed that already,' Boyle said. He crushed out his cigarette in Samsa's saucer.

Samsa pushed his chair back from the table. 'One tiny thing intrigues me about you, Boyle. I understand you're from a wealthy family. Daddy's a hotshot capitalist.'

'I have that misfortune.'

'You started out with some terrific advantages, didn't you? So where did you foul up?'

'Who gives a shit. Here I am. As is.'

'A convincing argument for abortion, Boyle.' Samsa stood up. He had to get away. The idea of his cash lying in Boyle's pocket increasingly riled him.

Boyle reached out, clasped his wrist. 'Linger a moment, Lieutenant.'

'We're finished. Take your hand off me.'

The waitress came to the table with the coffee pot in her hand. 'Refill?' she asked.

Boyle switched into sunshine mode, which he could seemingly flick off and on at will. He smiled dazzlingly at the waitress and said, 'My good friend here is in bad need of one. Be a sweetheart and pour me a cup while you're at it, honey.'

The waitress fetched fresh cups and filled them, then wandered off.

Boyle said, 'I just happened to see on TV that you're in charge of the murder investigation. What a convenient situation. You're not about to collar yourself, are you?' He picked up the chunky metal salt shaker from the table, shoved it under Samsa's nose like a microphone and fired a few quick questions in the manner of an inquisitive broadcaster. 'Does some patsy get to take the fall, Lieutenant? Is that how it's going to pan out? Or does Almond get lost in a shuffle of paper? Tell me how you see the situation shaping up. Our viewers would dearly love to know.'

'Get that goddam shaker out of my face.'

'One last thing.'

Samsa waited. A pulse beat in his neck. His bandaged hand felt numb. He could see it in Boyle's expression, something else was coming, it didn't end with the 25,000 bucks, and he'd known that going in. But what were his choices? The only choice that mattered was one he'd already made in a rain-sodden field, and every move after that was forced.

'I need one small favor.'

'Fuck yourself, Boyle. *There's nothing left.*'

'This is a very small thing,' Boyle said.

'Boyle, listen good. I'm walking out of here. I'm going back to my office. We had a deal. I'll regret it to the day I die, but it's done.'

'Uh, it's not that simple, Gregory.'

'I *paid* you, for Christ's sake.'

'And I'm everlastingly grateful to you.'

'My heart is overwhelmed. Now I'm leaving.'

'A killer to catch, huh?' Boyle asked.

Samsa stepped away from the table.

'A killer to catch?' Boyle called out, laughing. 'Or some stupid fall guy?'

Samsa kept moving, seeking the doorway, the street beyond. He wanted the air out there, no matter how dense and polluted. He stopped when he heard Boyle say, 'Things got a bit mixed up, Gregory J. And I'm deeply sorry. But the woeful thing is – there's another print.'

33

JIMMY PLUMM LOOKED AT THE CASH PILED ON HIS DESK. HE slid a hundred-dollar bill from under a rubber band and held it to the light. Then he smelled it as one might sniff a cigar. 'I have to be careful these days, Lee. So many good counterfeiters around. So much sham money.'

'We're clear now,' Boyle said.

'Even steven.'

'Pleasure doing business with you,' Boyle said. 'Except for a little random violence and the daylight robbery of my Porsche.'

'Business is very cruel,' Plumm said. 'A moment, before you go rushing away, Lee. I'm curious. How did you raise this much money?'

Boyle tapped the side of his nose. 'No can say.'

'Daddy come good?'

'Daddy isn't involved.'

'Ah. You have other sources.' Plumm fingered a strand of long hair away from his shoulder.

Boyle was restless here. He didn't like Plumm, didn't like Plumm's office, the heavy brocade drapes drawn against the sunlight and the sense of being imprisoned in some eternal night. The desk lamp threw out a sickly light the color of a withered lime.

'Have a drop of port before you go, Lee.'

'Hate port, sport.'

'A little vino then? This is a red-letter day, after all. And to think I was worrying about you, imagining Raseci ruining that pleasant face of yours.'

Plumm was already pouring wine from a decanter into two glasses. He pushed one across his desk toward Boyle, who shrugged and picked it up.

Boyle sipped and said, 'Nice, very nice. I'd be happy to sit here all day, Plumm, but I have places to go. Do I get a receipt?'

'Very funny, Lee,' Plumm said. 'You won't let me in on the secret of this money?'

'I'll carry it to my grave.'

'Then we'll let it go like that, shall we?' Plumm extended his hand and Boyle took it. The handshake was too firm to be friendly. But you couldn't expect amiable gestures from Plumm. Even a handshake had to establish some kind of supremacy.

Fingers tingling, Boyle walked to the door.

Plumm said, 'Terrible thing about your girl, by the way.'

'Terrible is right,' Boyle said.

'You aren't in trouble with the police, are you?'

Boyle shook his head. 'No sweat.'

'Let's hope they catch the culprit.' Plumm had his glass raised in the air. 'And let's hope you're back in business before too long, shall we?'

'Let's hope.' And Boyle stepped out, took the stairs quickly. He was hyper. He had $15,000 in his pocket and he was free of Jimmy Plumm. *$15,000*. Great score. And so *easy*. Samsa had been backed up, manacled, stripped of options and going round in circles like a blind guy without his stick.

Boyle was *flush*. Money gave him a feeling of invincibility. What to do with all that bread. Out on the sunny street he remembered something Vass kept harping on – 'It's not too late to change your life, Lee.' With the bucks bulging in his pocket he could begin a reconstruction of himself, split from this city, do something with his future. Such as? Go back to college, get a degree? In what? Pharmacology, so you could design your own drugs?

The idea of buckling down and getting the brain refocused was a drag. Why work if you don't have to? When you can get other people to do it for you? Like sad little Almond. Nancy, that *cunt*, before her. And before Nancy, the French exchange student called Paulette, whose only true exchange had been one of body fluids.

Let's hope you're back in business before too long, shall we?

Yeah, let's.

Let's put our mind to work on that one.

He reached the Taurus, parked in the same alley where his Porsche had been vandalized. He got in, spread a little speed on the back of his hand, snorted – up up and away. His stash was practically gone. But he wasn't fazed. Nosiree.

He drove out of the alley, air-conditioner blasting. He headed for the freeway. He turned on the radio, found a Bach cello suite on a classical channel, sweet and deep and melancholic. This fondness for classical music was the solitary debt he owed Hugh, who had thousands of albums he played endlessly, and Boyle in his childhood had developed a liking for it. Which was about the only aspect of his youth Hugh had approved of, albeit grudgingly. Monique, of course, *she* went off to learn the violin at Hugh's insistence, despite having a tin ear and an aphid's brain.

His mind was fizzing. He came off the freeway, approached a stop sign, slowed. This was familiar territory. This was where he wanted to be.

He hung a right, parked under a tree, left the engine running. He was hot. He adjusted the flow of cooled air directly into his face.

There she is.

He saw her step out of a VW convertible a hundred yards away. He watched the guy behind the wheel skip lightly over to the passenger door and follow her up the drive. She turned to say something to him, and the guy reached for her hand and simultaneously thrust his head forward, obviously expecting a kiss, but it didn't come.

Instead she moved toward the porch. The kid, filled with youth's mighty persistence, went after her, caught her by the arm and swung her round to face him and she pulled away. She said something – he saw her lips move but couldn't read her words – and then she entered the house, running fingers through her brown hair as the door closed. Boyle thought he detected a certain weariness in her movements, the way her shoulders slumped.

A boyfriend? Or maybe this kid with the shiny black hair and model looks was just making a play for her, only he wasn't getting very far. The relationship, whatever it might be, had obviously hit some snags, and the young guy was applying pressure. The kid lingered on the shadowy porch a few seconds. Boyle could hear him call out quite distinctly, 'I love you, Darcy.'

She didn't open the door.

The kid charged down the steps and jumped back in his car. I love you Darcy. So that was the kid's pitch. I love you and my hidden agenda is I want inside your pants. And Darcy – was she holding out?

Well well. Young virgins might have visions of delight.

Boyle watched the VW swing in a loop and stream past

him. He slipped the Ford in behind the little convertible and followed it, seeing the cocky way the young guy drove, one hand loosely on the wheel, the other dangling over the side and tapping the panel. Look at me, I'm young and horny and driving this neat little auto, and the breeze is doing these real nifty things to my hair.

Boyle's mood was darkening swiftly. I don't like you. Not even a little. I don't want you getting in Darcy's pants, buckaroo.

He followed the VW several miles. The young guy turned the car into an alley behind a row of houses. He parked, ran a comb through his hair, checked his face in the mirror and then got out, hitching up his jeans with a swiveling little motion of his hips.

Mr Cool. God's gift. You think.

He pushed open an iron gate in a fence and entered a backyard.

Boyle parked the Taurus close to the mouth of the alley, exited the car, strolled to the gate. The yard led directly to the rear of a two-storey house. Boyle saw the kid stand outside a pair of sliding glass doors. He was waiting for something, tapping one foot, whistling, cheeks puffed. *He just exudes confidence*, Boyle thought. *He's young, the world at his feet. Fucking fool. Milk behind his ears.*

The glass doors opened, a girl appeared. She had yellow hair piled high on her head and wore a gray sleeveless T-shirt, cut-off Levis and red and blue starred boots that went halfway up her calves. She had big tits and her mouth was a slash of violet lipstick. Boyle, concealed by shrubbery, saw the girl draw the kid inside and slide the doors shut with a deft movement of her foot.

This is interesting.

First he drops off the lovely Nightingale, then he comes here to visit this chick who looks like she's just failed an audition for lead vocalist in a country band.

Boyle pushed the gate, entered the yard and made his way through the foliage to the back of the house. He edged along against the wall until he was within a few inches of the glass doors. A quick peek was all he wanted. A look inside.

So let's do it.

What's this?

The kid, his jeans rolled down to his ankles, ass bare, was ferociously humping the girl on the floor. She had her legs upraised on either side of him, and her cut-offs had been discarded and her sleeveless T-shirt pushed up around her neck. She was still wearing the tacky boots. They were going at each other like rutting skunks, the kid pumping away, the girl clutching him, her mouth wide open.

This young asswipe was playing goddam games with Darcy. He had his flash blonde cutey he was banging on the side. He dropped Darcy off after school and came straight here to get laid, which *could* mean he *wasn't* scoring with Darcy, who was the kind of girl you'd gladly introduce to your parents.

The bimbo was a dark secret stashed on the side, a girl you'd never take home to Mom and Dad in a hundred years.

Boyle didn't like this *at all*. It offended him deeply. He sometimes convinced himself into thinking he had a tiny pocket of decency left, and it was this fictive moral sense, exaggerated by chemicals, that was outraged by the kid's duplicity. *Fizz fizz.*

The greaseball cheapened Darcy. It was a goddam *insult*. And Boyle was filled with a hot flood tide of anger as he stood outside the doors and watched this savage coupling on the floor and listened to the first orgasmic sounds emerge.

He clenched and unclenched his hands time and again. Sweat poured down his face.

Darcy betrayed, he thought. *By this creep. This cretin.*

He'd open the glass doors and go inside and just do something about this whole goddam situation. But not now, he had an appointment to keep, one he didn't want to be late for.

With reluctance he had trouble overcoming, he turned and went back to his car, thinking of the treachery done to Darcy, and picturing her with her hair colored black and her mouth lipsticked and maybe some shadow under her eyes. *Yeah.*

34

SAMSA APPROACHED THE HATCH AND ASKED SERGEANT Docherty for the key. Docherty slid it across the surface of the counter and Samsa picked it up, closing his fingers around it. He looked along the corridor at the locked door. It was one thing to give Boyle your own money – an act that filled him with resentment so deep he couldn't begin to measure it – but this was something else.

There's another print—

Why had he imagined that Boyle would just take the money and cheerfully crawl away under a rock anyhow? Fear of exposure. Naïve optimism. At bottom, some huge blind primal need to trust, because he *hoped* with all his heart Boyle would keep his side of the deal.

And that, dear Christ, was a monumental stupidity, and he cursed himself for believing it could ever have been otherwise.

He moved along the corridor, thinking of Darcy and the great prairie spaces in their relationship. Quit the job, spend time with her, take early retirement, your pension –

but it wasn't enough to live on, let alone replace the college fund.

He slipped the key in the lock, turned it.

He'd never done anything like this in his life.

Sweat from his fingers adhered to the key. He entered the room, shut the door behind him, pulled the drawstring for the light. He was tense beyond reckoning. He stared around the windowless room, the shelves half in shadow, the piles of stuff stacked there. The air smelled of trapped heat and cardboard.

He'd do it quickly, he wouldn't even think about what he was doing, he'd be out of here in a few seconds, a minute at most. He walked to the shelves, moving past cartons and boxes filled with items wrapped in Ziploc bags – guns, money, clothing. You didn't know what you were going to find here: a bloodstained clawhammer, tufts of human hair, broken spectacles, false teeth.

The evidence room was a museum of horror.

There would be a box somewhere with the name SUAREZ, C, freshly inked on the side with a fat black marker.

The boxes were supposed to be alphabetized, but sometimes people didn't put things back where they belonged. He was searching for a carton marked WEEKS, BILLY LEE. Billy Lee Weeks, a known dope dealer, had been shot through the head in his suburban home six weeks ago by a cheap hood named Clarence Newborn.

Hurry hurry.

He found the carton stacked in the wrong place. He drew it forward, quickly looked inside, located what he wanted and stuffed it in the left pocket of his pants. He pushed the carton back in place—

'I was told I'd find you here.'

Startled, Samsa turned. Eve was standing in the doorway. He wondered how long she'd been there, if she'd seen him rummage inside the box. He felt his tension grow as if it were pushing out barbed new shoots in the depths of himself.

'Eve,' he said. 'You surprised me.' He heard himself laugh.

'You look like a kid caught with a hand in the cookie jar.'

'Do I?'

'How is your hand, by the way?'

'It's fine.' But it still pulsed and he kept trying to ignore it.

She touched it gently and said, 'You need to change that bandage. I'll do it for you, if you like.'

'People are going to start talking if we hang around in here like this,' and he laughed again, thinking how shallow and insincere it sounded.

'People always talk. Haven't you heard I'm the scarlet woman of the department?'

'I don't listen to rumors,' Samsa said. He had an urge to hold her, to bury his face between her breasts. Just to be enclosed by her in a safe place beyond the reaches of the rancid waters rising around him.

'I've been looking all over for you,' she said.

'I was checking on something,' he said. 'It's not important. I can't breathe in this place. Let's get out of here.'

He opened the door, let Eve go out before him. Her scent hung delicately in the air. He locked the door and dropped off the key with Docherty. The narrow corridor, the green walls, the light strips overhead – these things combined to make him feel he was institutionalized, that this was not a police precinct but some hospital where he happened to be a patient whose illness no physician could diagnose.

Eve said, 'The shrink spent an hour with Ryan Pritt. That's what I wanted to tell you.'

'And?'

'According to the good Dr Mcalister, who likes to put things in layman's terms, Pritt is probably schizophrenic, a condition exacerbated by prolonged use of anti-depressants.'

'What does that mean in terms of his confession?'

'Mcalister wants more time. He did venture to say that Pritt's violent tendencies might just edge him in the direction of believing the confession. He emphasized *might*. Mcalister is never happy unless he's sitting on a fence. I also talked with Pritt's physician, who claims he only ever prescribed Librium. Which means Pritt's been getting drugs from other doctors.'

'So we wait for Mcalister to come back to us?'

Eve said, 'I guess we do.'

'And hold Pritt in the meantime.'

'Looks that way. He still rejects the idea of a lawyer.'

'How long will it take Mcalister?'

'He says a couple of days. Maybe more, maybe less.'

They were outside Samsa's office now. Phones were ringing non-stop in the maze of rooms, people hustling, shouting at each other, Billy Fogue blowing smoke, Cullinan complaining about something. For a strange moment all this sound was stilled and Samsa, as if struck by a sudden deafness, felt himself slide into a world of utter silence. It was a weird experience, like a blip on his mental screen. He was dizzy, too, and he had to lean against a filing cabinet. Then the strangeness passed and sounds came flooding in again.

Eve asked, 'Something wrong?'

'No, not really.' He wanted to shout, It's me you're looking for.

'You look white, Greg. Can I get you something? Water? Aspirin?'

'I'm *okay*, Eve.'

'Kind of snarly all of a sudden, aren't we?'

'Sorry, I didn't mean to be.'

She touched his arm and looked mildly distressed. Billy Fogue raised his face from his desk and said, 'Hey-hey, what's going on here? Touchy-feely time, huh?'

'Shut up, Fogue,' Samsa said.

'A *joke*, Lew Tenant. A joke, awright? Excuse me.'

'I'm laughing my goddam head off, Billy.'

'Somebody didn't *get* out of bed this morning, they *fell* out,' Fogue muttered.

Samsa entered his office and sat behind his desk. Eve leaned in the doorway. She looked good, red hair lustrous, those green eyes suggestive of limpid marine depths. She wore a black sports coat, a white T-shirt and gray jeans, all very plain and understated, but she transformed them. He wondered again if she'd seen him pull his stunt in the evidence room, but she hadn't said anything. Maybe she wouldn't mention it anyway. He had every right to be in that room.

But not the right to steal.

Al Brodsky materialized holding a plain brown envelope. 'Hey, Greg. I just got Zane's report here. You want to see it?' He tossed the envelope onto Samsa's desk. 'I don't think you'll find it entirely enlightening.'

Samsa opened the envelope, saw three typed sheets, the bottom corner of each initialed by Zane in purple ink. He always found coroner's reports masterpieces of cold prose. He scanned it quickly, '. . . petroleum-based pro-phylactic lubricant in vaginal orifice . . . evidence of intravenous use of cocaine hydrochloride . . .'

Brodsky said, 'The long and the short of it is she was killed by that notorious old culprit, a blunt instrument. A human hand would be consistent with the bruising, Zane says. Or a fall, if she hit the right object at the appropriate angle.'

Samsa stared at the sheets until all the letters ran as if they were moist. The dead girl distilled in three pages of forensic jargon. An epitaph in a chilly language.

Brodsky said, 'She's got some scratchmarks on her hands. Zane says they could be attributed to the fact that she might have come in post-mortem contact with some jagged "vegetable material". I like the word vegetable in there. Why couldn't Zane come out and say it was thorns, or something like that? If Pritt was carrying her around he could easily have brushed her against a bush.'

Stephen Rebb suddenly appeared behind Brodsky. His dyed hair must have been freshly tinted that afternoon because it was an almost cruel black, the kind you never saw naturally on any human. 'I was out all night,' he said.

'And?' Brodsky asked.

'The last recorded sighting I can find of our little hooker was on the night of her death.'

'Sighted by whom?' Samsa asked.

Rebb said, 'This stripper called Marilyn Cooley, aka Bonny Bodymachine, that works out of a place called the Zoom Boom Room over on Clitheroe, more commonly known as – no prizes for guessing, folks – Clitoris Street. Excuse my language, Detective Lassiter. Bonny says Cecily Suarez came in there around eight, looking to score coke. She was alone.'

Eight o'clock, Samsa thought. *She had roughly two hours to live.*

'Did she score?' Brodsky asked.

'Bonny is coy on that point,' Rebb said. 'She deals small-time, so naturally she isn't forthcoming. The kid hung around for a while, then split.'

'Back to work,' Brodsky said.

'An appointment to keep with her killer,' Rebb said. 'Nobody saw her after that. But those hookers tend to turn a blind eye. They see only what they want, and half

690

of them are wasted anyhow. It's like a Masonic club, and if you don't know the right passwords you don't learn shit. I've been trying, believe me. And if I can't get anything out of them, it's damn sure nobody else can.'

Brodsky sighed. 'So what have we got? Not much of anything, so far as I can see. Unless you count the quote unquote confession. I'd love somebody to pop up out of nowhere and say, Guys, great news, I saw her get into Pritt's car.' He looked at Samsa, eyes suddenly wide. '*Speaking* of said car, has anybody gone through Pritt's? Searched for any trace the girl was ever in the goddam thing? Does anybody even know the *location* of the car?'

Samsa stood up. He'd overlooked this elementary procedure, something he'd normally have delegated without thinking. But it had been crowded out of his mind. 'Jesus,' he said, 'I must be slipping in my old age.' Trying to make light of his forgetfulness even as he wondered if he'd subconsciously ignored such a basic routine – because, God help him, he wanted to believe deep down in some dismal ravine of himself that Pritt was guilty, Pritt would take the fall.

'I'll get it done immediately, Chief.'

Brodsky said, 'Do that, Greg.' There was a stony little tone in the chief's voice, almost a reprimand. Brodsky the Blade. 'Then get back to me.'

Brodsky walked away.

'Oops,' Rebb said. '*Quelle* oversight, Lieutenant.'

Eve said, 'I'll see to it, Greg.'

'No, it's my fault, I'll attend to it myself.' He sat down again. He had a burning sensation in his ears. He looked at Eve. 'Why don't you find out the names of the other physicians who prescribed for Pritt, see if they can tell you anything about why they gave him these drugs.'

She seemed a little disappointed, as if she'd expected a more demanding task. 'Will do.'

Samsa listened to her footsteps in the outer office, and heard Fogue say something like, 'Is he a bear today, or is he a bear?'

Samsa said to Rebb, 'Keep checking.'

'I'll check what's left to check, but the cupboard's just about empty,' Rebb said. 'And that Jack Spratt lead, if you can call it a lead, fizzled out.'

There's a print, Samsa thought. And for a terrible second he thought he'd said it out loud without meaning to, but Rebb had already moved away.

For a time Samsa sat very still. He thought of Rebb snooping the dark streets and trying to reconstruct Almond's movements, of Al Brodsky's unexpectedly sharp little sound of disapproval. He thought about Eve coming across him in the evidence room, and the fact she knew he wasn't operating on all pistons – and he felt he was tangled inside a fabric that was about to unravel. Threads were popping audibly, and it was all he could do to keep them from coming asunder altogether.

He left his office and walked out of City Hall with the pilfered plastic bag in his pocket, his neck scorching his collar and his heart pounding, expecting at any moment to be stopped and interrogated and eventually disgraced.

35

BOYLE HEARD SAMSA'S VOICE THROUGH THE INTERCOM. HE
pressed the buzzer and listened to the cop climb the stairs.
He opened the door and Samsa entered the room and
said, 'I want in and out of here quickly, Boyle. Where's the
print?'

'First the stuff,' Boyle said.

Samsa took a plastic bag from his pocket, handed it to
Boyle, who dipped a fingertip inside and raised a small
quantity of the powder to his mouth. It had a rich bitter
taste.

'Now the print,' Samsa said.

'One crucial little test and the print's yours.' Boyle
removed another small amount of the powder and spread
it out on a mirror that lay on the coffee table. He chopped
it with his razor blade. This sacred ritual. He raised a
quantity on the tip of his finger and held it to his nose. It
roared into his bloodstream, no afterburn, no clogged
sinuses. 'I declare this is the goods, Gregory J.'

He went to the bookshelf, opened a copy of Coleridge's
Biographia Literaria, and slipped the print out from

between the pages. He gave it to Samsa, who folded it angrily in half, then folded it again and put it in his pocket.

'This is the end of it,' Samsa said.

'Totally.'

'You said that before.'

'I don't have another print. I just happened to kind of overlook the fact I had a copy. Confusion, probably.' This speed of Samsa's was brilliant. No bathtub crank. Boyle was riding a big smooth Cadillac through a sunny landscape.

Samsa walked to the window, looked down into the street. 'You had the second print all along, but I was dumb enough to think you'd keep your word. What the fuck does that make me?'

'That *rara avis*,' Boyle said. 'A trusting soul.'

'A fool,' Samsa said.

'But with honor, Gregory.'

Samsa turned from the window. He had a gun in his hand. He'd slipped it out of his holster and was pointing it at Boyle.

'You're not going to use that.'

Samsa held the gun level. 'I might, I swear to God, if I'm pushed another inch.'

'Nobody's going to push you again,' Boyle said. 'It's over.'

'This time I'm supposed to believe you.'

'There's no logic to gunplay. You're overlooking the fact I have at least one partner in this enterprise.'

'What if I suddenly decide there's only you and the rest is bluff?'

'I told you I don't work alone. When it comes to a camera I'm a buffoon.'

'And if I have a sudden brainstorm, say I lose control, the gun goes off. One dead small-time pimp. The world isn't going to attend your funeral, Boyle. Not many people are going to be crying into their hankies.'

'It's a big gamble,' Boyle said, wondering just how demented Samsa might be. 'You shoot me. An associate of mine shows up. You shoot him, too?'

'Maybe.'

'And then let's say, for the sake of argument, a third associate pops up. You do what? Just keep on killing?'

Samsa stepped across the room. He pointed the gun at Boyle's chest, and in that moment Boyle knew he wasn't going to pull the trigger. Something just yielded in the cop's expression: his purposeful look dissipated, his eyes lost their hard sheen. Boyle thought, *A scare tactic, a desperate little piece of improvisational theater*.

'Why kill me anyhow, Gregory? I'm the only guy you've shared your secret with, right? And if you think about it, that makes me your confessor. Stuff like that gets you all choked up – and stress is a killer, Lieutenant. I saved you money you'd have wasted on a fucking therapist. Look at it that way.'

Samsa let the gun hang at his side. 'My confessor,' he said. 'A pimp and a blackmailer and a speed-freak.'

'Life's like that, Gregory. Sometimes you just don't get to choose your confidantes.'

Samsa looked into Boyle's eyes, as if he were looking for something he needed to find. Boyle knew what he wanted: *reassurance*. No more demands. This was the final hook. The last print had been handed over and all the rest was silence. Welcome to hell.

Boyle felt the familiar mind-rush, the pulse-beats, words coming in a streak. 'Let me tell you how it's going to be, Gregory. You'll have some sleepless nights for a time, a few bad dreams, and you'll wake up sweating, and now and then you'll feel a little twinge of pain and guilt. But that's going to fade. Believe me.'

Samsa was concentrating, and even if his expression was one of distaste, you could see he wanted to buy into this picture of salvation. He wanted to believe Boyle was painting a true portrait of a guilt-free future.

Then Samsa shook his head in exasperation. 'What the fuck am I doing listening to *you*? Jesus Christ.'

'I'm only laying it out so you can look at it,' Boyle said. 'Anyway, from what I see on the TV you're off the hook. According to the intrepid reporters on the evening news, somebody's already confessed.'

'That confession's going to fall apart sooner or later.'

'Let's say it holds.'

'That's hypothetical, Boyle.'

'I'm fond of dickering around with the hypothetical. If it holds, do you go along with it?'

'Which is what you'd do in my position,' Samsa said.

'I wouldn't give it a second thought. I'd grab this sucker's confession with both hands, man. I'd fall on my knees and give thanks to the one upstairs, I'd stuff all my spare change in mission boxes for isolated priests baptizing savages in the jungles of Peru, then I'd go down the church and light a thousand candles. People in the wax business would be working night shifts. Wick-makers couldn't meet their quotas.'

Samsa said, 'You turn my stomach, Boyle.'

'I affect different people different ways, *amigo*.'

Samsa holstered his gun, then moved toward the door. Watching him, Boyle detected some slight resemblance to Darcy.

Samsa opened the door. His shoulders seemed to sag a little. 'I never want to see you again, Boyle. Under any circumstances. Not in the street, not in a bar, not in a restaurant. *Nowhere*.'

'Hey, I'm your genie, Lieutenant. Your wish is granted.'

'Enjoy the speed,' Samsa said. 'In fact, why don't you

do the whole three ounces in one swoop? Have yourself a hell of a trip, Boyle.'

Boyle smiled and said, 'One thing you might consider in future, Lieutenant.'

Samsa moved to the stairs. 'And what's that?'

'Save yourself further hassle and stay home with the little woman at nights.'

Samsa turned. He looked as if somebody had thrown a blazing firework into his eyes. He stepped away from the edge of the stairs, moved quickly and shoved Boyle against the door jamb, elbow pressed into Boyle's neck.

Boyle could see great heaving currents of hatred and hurt in Samsa's face. The pressure from Samsa's elbow was giving him trouble breathing. He flattened a hand against Samsa's chest and tried to push the cop away, but Samsa was like a stone wall leaning against him. What raw thing have I touched? he wondered. He smelled a faint medicinal odor rising from Samsa's discolored bandage, some kind of anti-bacterial cream maybe.

'Hey,' Boyle said, struggling a little for air. 'This is becoming a problem, Gregory.'

'*Never mention my family*,' Samsa said. He squeezed the words out angrily between clenched teeth. 'You understand that, Boyle? *Never, ever mention my goddam family.*'

'Jesus,' Boyle gasped.

Samsa relaxed his arm, drew it back to his side and moved toward the stairs.

Boyle shut the door, rubbed his throat and coughed. His telephone was ringing. He thought about ignoring it, but in the end he picked it up. It was The Kid. *Joshua* – the name came back to him now.

Silver? Or was it Gold? What did it matter?

'Anything nice happening?' Gold asked.

'It's too soon,' Boyle said, wishing he'd let the call go

unanswered. 'These things take a little time.'

'I guess. I was checking, that's all.'

'Listen, I have company. I'll call you back.'

'Can you give me, uh, an estimated time?'

'Later.' Boyle put the handset down. He didn't need to be hassled by The Kid. It could become a regular thing, The Kid calling to know what was going on. He might give him 500 bucks, keep him quiet. He might not.

He had to get out of here. Time was a force.

He rubbed his neck again and noticed the lit message digit on the answering machine. He pressed Playback and heard, *I don't know why I'm doing this, really I don't. I don't even know you . . . but you gave me your number and I figured, oh what the hell, I'd call . . .*

36

EVE LASSITER PARKED OUTSIDE THE APARTMENT BUILDING, and for a time didn't move. This was a tangent she really didn't need to explore. She remembered Greg in the evidence room, the way he'd spun round in astonishment when she'd spoken, the sense she'd had of just missing out on something – that tingly feeling of entering a space where some furtive activity has happened a split second before your arrival.

She opened the door of her car, got out and entered the building.

The carton she'd seen him shoving back in place was marked WEEKS, BILLY LEE. She was familiar with the case. A dealer shot in his home – banal, commonplace. Ed Duff was in charge of the homicide and Greg's involvement a supervisory one. What had he been looking for?

She felt locked out of an enormous secret he was keeping, and yet she wasn't sure she had any rights of access to his world. *You made love with him once, which didn't exactly give you a license to pry, but he was like a man trapped. An aura of despair hung about him. And I care,* she thought.

She knocked on the door of the apartment. She heard a voice calling out. 'Coming, *coming*.' The door opened.

She smiled. 'Can I come in?'

'Do you have a warrant, Detective?'

'A warrant?'

'Just my feeble little joke. Enter.'

Eve stepped past Joshua Gold, who'd recently showered and was wrapped in a blue terry robe, his hair wet and glistening. 'I hope you're not here to ask me to be a model citizen again.'

Eve shook her head. 'Not this time.'

'And you haven't come to arrest me, or have you?'

'Not yet,' she said.

'That's a relief.'

She sat. *Make an excuse, get up, leave. This isn't necessary.*

But it was. She couldn't leave it alone.

Gold began to fuss with his plants in the window, using an eye-dropper to apply a pale-green liquid to the soil and leaves. 'What can I do for you?'

'It's a little delicate,' she said.

'Ah, now I'm *intrigued*.'

She watched him a second, wondering at his nervous energy, the way he fidgeted with the plants. Despite his initial attempt at levity she had the strong feeling he wasn't happy to see her again, didn't want her here in his apartment.

'The last time we spoke you said you'd seen Lieutenant Samsa . . .' She paused. It wasn't too late to back off.

'Let me hazard a guess. You don't want to believe your nice lieutenant goes slumming for his pleasures?' Gold asked. 'You hold him in very high regard.'

'As a matter of fact, I do.'

'It shows on your face, Detective.' Gold ran fingers through his damp hair. 'But he's only human, after all. As my mother always says, even the Pope needs to take a dump *now and then.*'

'You're sure you saw him?' she said.

'You want me to say I didn't, don't you? The great man must be *positively* untarnished.'

'I don't want you to lie, Joshua.'

'Okay. I didn't see him. It was a fable, Detective, from start to finish. Really. What difference does it make in the long run?'

Maybe Gold was right. If Greg had had a need to go on nocturnal prowls, checking the scene, fantasizing, did it really matter? She could understand it up to a point. But it was more than this. She was chasing something else, and at the same time she didn't want to get close enough to bring it into focus. *Let it be.*

'Why would you make it up?' she asked.

'Oh, total mischief.' He moved across the room, sprinkled food in the fish tank.

'I asked the lieutenant. He says you're mistaken.'

Gold expelled air in a flustered way. 'What do you want me to say?'

Eve had no direct answer to this question. She'd need to dig too deep to come up with one, and she wasn't prepared for that archaeology of the self. She got up, looked at the pictures on the wall, Joshua's neat signature on each one. 'Nice work,' she said. 'I like it.'

'It's an old hobby, but way too expensive for me. I quit a while ago. Are you through with your questions, Detective?'

'You still say you made it up about the lieutenant cruising?'

'Ask my friends. They'll tell you what a prankster I am.'
He isn't telling the truth, she thought. *He's fudging.*

701

Only she wasn't sure why. She glanced again at the photographs – young muscular men with artfully brooding expressions, a whole lot of shadows.

'I don't mean to kick you out, Detective, but I have somewhere to go very soon,' Gold said.

'Why do I get this odd feeling you're protecting him for some reason?'

'Why would I want to protect the lieutenant? I don't have any good reason. It was a *story*, that was all. Accept that.' He looked impatient now.

'I'm having a hard time with it, Joshua.'

'Don't you ever make things up, Detective? Just for the sheer hell of it? Because you want to sort of spice things up. You want to pour a pinch of real *fiery* chili powder into everyday humdrum. Maybe you just don't have a malicious streak the way I do.'

'You're playing with me, Joshua. I don't like that.'

'I have to dress. I have to go out. I wish you'd believe me, I really do. I've given it my best shot, and if you won't accept that it's not *my* problem. I'll walk you to the door.'

She heard the sound of a buzzer going off in another room, and her first thought was of some household appliance – a microwave, a tumble-dryer – signaling the end of its operation. The noise agitated Gold, who looked suddenly anxious, as if the buzzer meant something urgent to him.

'What's that?' she asked.

He was ushering her toward the door. 'It's only my alarm clock,' he said.

'Funny time to go off,' she said.

He had his hand placed in the small of her back, edging her in the direction of the door, pressuring her. He wanted her out quickly, even feverishly, because the buzzer was ringing, because he wanted to turn it off, he *had* to turn it off, and she knew no simple alarm clock could have this effect. *It was a timer*, she thought. *But not a clock. And whatever it was, he had to attend to it fast.*

'You're pushing me, Josh. I don't like being pushed.'

'Please. Just go.'

'Why don't you switch that thing off?'

'*Go*,' he said.

She swung round and faced him. The noise was coming from behind a door to the left. Gold, who looked stricken, flapped his hands in the manner of someone who doesn't know which way to turn.

'What's the big secret, Josh?' she asked, and she took a step toward the door.

'Wait,' and he tried to block her way.

'What the fuck are you hiding?' she asked.

'I'm not hiding *anything*.'

'You give a damn good impression of a guy who is,' she said, and she thrust a hand past him and grabbed the door handle. The buzzer kept going and going.

She twisted the handle, managed to reach beyond him and nudge the door with her foot, and it opened a crack.

'You lied to me, Josh.'

He shrugged and looked foolish, like an eavesdropper caught with his ear to a keyhole.

'Why don't you give me the guided tour,' she said.

37

BOYLE HIT THE FREEWAY AT NINETY MILES AN HOUR. HE HAD the windows *and* the air-conditioner blasting. The radio played a somber passage from Ravel's *Trio* for Piano, Violin and Cello, suggestive of a night funeral, slouched pallbearers shouldering a coffin under a full moon. It was Almond in the box, waxy and dead. *To cease upon the midnight with no pain.*

He wondered what she'd felt. If it was all over in a flash. Into the void immediately. He heard rats scamper in his skull. They were busy chewing things, building nests, breeding.

Who needs a boyfriend in the picture anyhow. He's bad news.

Braking only lightly, he left the freeway. The tires whined, rubber burning. He slowed when he reached the suburb, where it was all yield signs and intersections and kids on bikes half hidden under trees. He reached his destination, parked and got out the car in one fluid movement. He walked along the alley, came to the iron gate, opened it, wondered how much time had passed since he was last here. Sixty minutes max. He hoped he wasn't too late.

Sixty minutes was nothing when you were a kid with fire in your gonads. You could come and come again, maybe with a couple of cigarette interludes and some chit-chat between times.

Allow me to show you the downside of all this, asshole.

The rats were gnawing on timbers. *Chomp chomp*. The way to deal with them was to ignore them. They were figments anyhow, they were products of Samsa's dope. But that didn't go any way toward explaining why their small sharp teeth caused him flashes of pain in his head. Why he could smell their fur and their rancid breath and the small excited squeaks they made.

He looked through glass.

The pair on the floor were so caught up in their pursuit of the wild goose of gratification they didn't hear him. He stood and watched. He wondered how many times they'd fucked during the last hour.

He slid open a door and stood unnoticed.

What did he have to do to get some attention here? Introduce himself?

The girl opened her eyes and saw him, and with a look of surprise pushed the young man away from her. 'Who the hell are you?' she asked. 'Is this a robbery or something?'

Boyle said nothing. The rats had scurried away to some deeper level, and now there were steam valves opening in his head and hissing, a whole load of pressure. This was a real piece of chicanery going on here. This was dirty work.

The kid turned over and said, 'What the *fuck*?'

'What the fuck indeed,' Boyle said.

The kid snatched at his turquoise boxer shorts, which were lying at his feet. He got them straightened out and was drawing them up over his red erection when Boyle, stooping slightly, hearing the valves in his head release steam, punched him in the throat. Once, twice, a third time in quick succession. 'She's way.' *Punch*. 'Outta.' *Punch*. 'Your.' *Punch*. 'League.'

The kid moaned and the girl, covering her tits, yelled. 'What the fuck do you think you're *doing*?'

Boyle sideswiped her abruptly, a knuckle job. He felt her teeth against his bone. She flopped over, dazed, drooling blood. The kid was feeling his larynx with anxious fingers. 'Oh, man,' and his voice was just above a croak.

'I hate fucking turquoise,' Boyle said. 'If there's one color that goddam pisses me off it's turquoise.'

'Who are you?' the kid asked, froggy-voiced.

'I'm the fucking avenging angel,' Boyle said. 'I punish guys for their sordid deeds. I'm the one who tells you you're shit, you piece of scum.'

'You're insane, crazy fuck.'

Boyle pressed himself down on the guy, throttling him one-handed, driving his head into the floor. The sheer energy he felt. The unfettered strength to destroy. 'What's your name, asshole?'

'Nick.'

Boyle hammered him across the face with a solid fist. The kid's eye began to darken and swell almost immediately. 'Nick who?'

'Mancu . . . so. *Shit*. What's this all about?'

Boyle relaxed his grip a moment. 'This is about the company you keep, fuckhead.'

'What company?'

Boyle got up, walked a few paces away, seething, boiling, his heart like a yo-yo, then he turned round and kicked the kid in the mouth. He felt the lips yield to slackness, and the slackness give way to an open hollow. 'I've taken a fucking serious dislike to you.'

706

Wiping blood from his lip, Nick Mancuso said, 'What the fuck have I ever done to you? I've never even—'

'You don't have to do any one particular thing for me not to like you,' Boyle said. 'I flare up at stuff other people wouldn't even notice, hotshot.'

'Look, hey, please, leave us alone, go away. I don't know what you want. Here, take my watch. It's a Rolex.'

'Fuck your watch,' Boyle said. 'Did Daddy buy it for you, huh? Daddy lay out the bread for your goddam Rolex?'

'Yeah,' Mancuso said.

'Good old Daddy. May his name be blessed.' Boyle reached down, gripped one of the kid's nipples and twisted it viciously, then slapped his face back and forth.

'Hey – hey – *hey*,' Mancuso kept saying, blinking, trying to twist his head out of the way.

'And the car? Daddy buy the fucking car?'

'He helped.'

'I bet he did. Good for picking up babes, huh? A genuine pussy-wagon, huh? Chicks just want to jump in that car, right? It's a piece of shit, that's what it is. A piece of goddam flash German shit.' He was in freefall, hypersthenic, charged with the need to keep havoc going. He walked to the mantelpiece, where various sports trophies were lined up. He swiped his hand across them, and they tumbled to the floor and rolled away.

'*Why?*' Mancuso asked.

'You stay the fuck away from her,' Boyle said.

'Who?'

'Don't fuck with me, lover boy.'

Mancuso was looking at the prone girl, who was breathing badly. 'She's hurt.'

'That's the whole idea,' Boyle said. What else could he smash? What else could he just fucking destroy? He saw the fireside implements, horse-headed brass doodahs.

Monique had taken riding lessons – dressage, of course – every Saturday morning. One time, when she was eleven, she brought home a ribbon she'd won and Hugh hung it on the wall of his office. It was probably still hanging there, that goddam green ribbon, a souvenir of Monique's achievement. She had a horse called Mambo, a monster skewbald that had died in mysterious circumstances.

I poisoned its fucking food, Boyle thought. *You never even knew that, did you, Monique? You wept in the stable over the horse's big dead body. I can still hear your tears, you spoiled bitch. I can still see the truck from the abattoir coming to dispose of Mambo, the horse stiff, mouth gaping. I can remember feeling absolutely great. I remember the foul stench of the truck.*

He gripped the poker and hauled it out of the stand. He whacked it through the air, listening to the swish it made. Mancuso was starting to rise, hands held out in front of him, shaking his head as he watched the poker lash space.

'No,' he said.

Boyle stared at this spoiled-brat kid with his swollen eye and his mouth running blood. He heard the sirens of chaos, the whole choir of destruction singing in his head. 'You ever fuck her, Nick?'

'Who?'

'Darcy, you asshole.'

'Darcy?'

'You ever FUCK her, I asked.'

'No, I never did.'

'But you try.'

'Sure I try.'

'She doesn't let you.'

'Listen, why don't you put that poker down?'

'You tell her you love her?'

'Yeah, I tell her that. It's true.'

'Lying fuck.' Boyle whipped the poker just under Nick

Mancuso's nose. The kid stepped back fast. 'You tell her you love her because you figure that's the *numero uno* route to screwing her. But the thing is she's too smart for you. You're unworthy. You're some links down the great chain of life, Nick. She's floating on the pond like a lily, and you're down there in the dark-green slime with the fucking mosquito larvae. This blonde heap of shit is your level, just about.'

'What's Darcy got to do with you?'

'That's none of your goddam business. You just stay the hell out of her life,' Boyle said. He sliced the air with the brass poker. Mancuso stepped further back. The blonde, Mandy, raised her face and made a small choking sound of pain. She gazed at Mancuso, then at Boyle, as if she were trying to piece the events of her world together.

Don't bother, sweetheart, Boyle thought, and hit her across the skull with the poker. He hit her a second time smack on the forehead, and she fell back silent.

Mancuso, lowering his head like a young bullock, charged suddenly, roaring aloud as he came across the floor, and his skull struck Boyle in the chest. Boyle was thrown against the wall and lost his balance, sliding on one of the silver trophies on the floor, going down on his ass and striking out furiously with the poker, catching Nick Mancuso on the kneebone and feeling it snap under the force of brass. The kid crumpled and fell, hugging the knee to his chest and gasping with pain.

Boyle rose and stood over him. 'You stupid fucker,' he said.

He hit him time and again with the poker, working up a frenzy, a crescendo of rage, and then it wasn't just this kid he was beating to pulp, it was everybody who'd ever crossed him, everybody who'd interfered with his life, everybody and anybody who'd acted against him to his detriment: judges, lawyers, cops, social workers, professors, psychiatrists, counselors, Hugh – especially Hugh – and the world, the fucking world. Up and down and up and down, brass rising and falling, the kid's face mashed potato, welts rising on his body, and the choir singing full-throated in Boyle's ears, *He will awake no more, oh, never more*, and up and down, and on and on, the brass stick whacking cartilage and bone and ligament. *No refuge! No appeal!* Just metal hot in his hand and speed roaring through his system and *the abysses of the sky and the wild earth* and the kid bleeding and bleeding on the floor.

Breathless, elated, Boyle dropped the poker, which fell without any sound that he could hear.

38

SAMSA ENCOUNTERED THE REPORTERS AS SOON AS HE entered City Hall. Linda Kisminski from Channel 5, Vic Sebley from Channel 7, some print journalists, cameramen – jackals snapping around him.

'Is there any more info on this confession?'

'Can you name the guy?'

'Any chance of an arrest soon?'

Flustered, Samsa said he had no comment to make, it was too soon. Standard guff and the reporters wanted more. A flash popped, a video camera was pushed toward his face, Kisminski shoved a microphone in front of him, and Vic Sebley – sleek and bow-tied – was trying to get close. Samsa shoved his way past, but they came after him, hunting in a pack.

'Just tell us the name of the guy.'

'Is he guilty or is he not guilty? What's the feeling in the department?'

Samsa, crowded and hassled, repeated what he'd already told them.

Vic Sebley said, 'Come on, Greg, give us something we

can get our teeth into. Throw us a hunk of meat.'

'If you'll be good enough to excuse me.'

Linda Kisminski, persistent and fizzy as ever, followed him. 'Greg, be a sweetheart, give me *something* I can use? What's the skinny?'

'Jesus, Linda,' Samsa said. 'Later, later. Don't you guys ever listen?'

He made it to the top of the stairs that led down to the department offices. He descended without looking back, although he could hear the usual complaints the frustrated pack always made when they had to pull in their claws: 'It's like the Kremlin used to be around here at times. You can't squeeze a cent's worth of info out of anyone.'

He wondered how news of the confession had leaked anyhow, but it was fruitless to speculate. News always seeped out of the department. It had always been that way. The only surprise was that Ryan Pritt's name hadn't yet been revealed.

He went toward his office, pausing to tell Billy Fogue to have Pritt escorted to the interview room. He stood in front of the fan a few moments, opened the top button of his shirt, loosened his necktie, and thought about the journalists and how they snooped, digging away at the topsoil, scratching until they'd reached the place where the skeleton was interred. And then they exhumed it, they picked at the bones. They were all investigative reporters these days. They never left anything alone.

A scary prospect.

He was thinking about Darcy, wondering if he should call her and tell her there was no chance he'd be back before very late. But she'd have guessed that by now. He looked at his desk clock. Seven twenty-two. In the course of one long ruined day he'd depleted his bank account and stolen drugs from the evidence room, and in his hip pocket he carried a photograph that could destroy him. The other material from Boyle he'd already ditched, tearing it into tiny strips and flushing it down the toilet and watching it swirl away like the pieces of a jigsaw that had never been designed for assembly. And this last print, tightly folded in his pocket – he'd do the same thing with that.

The last print. If there was another one, if Boyle even so much as *tried* to put the bite on him again, he'd kill him. Regardless of consequence. You couldn't go on living with this palpitating menace. It was like existing in a freezing fog, waiting for an avalanche. But what would the death of Boyle accomplish? It wouldn't dissipate the fog. The avalanche, threatening and amorphous, would still be hanging in a precarious icy mass above him.

Still, the idea of emptying his gun into Lee Boyle's skull was tempting. He imagined the weapon bucking in his fist. But he wouldn't feel it, he'd be in that place where violence consumed everything.

Fogue put his head round the door. 'Pritt's ready.'

Samsa left his office and walked down the corridor to the interview room, where Ryan Pritt, smoking a cigarette, was seated at the table. A uniformed cop called Levine was also present, a young guy new to the department.

'Lieutenant,' Pritt said.

'Hello, Ryan,' Samsa said. He pulled up a chair and sat down.

'Checked out my story?' Pritt asked. He looked and sounded cheerful. He might have been asking an innocuous question: Seen any good movies lately?

'We're working on that, Ryan,' Samsa said. 'We'd like to look at your car. We have to check everything. You understand that.'

'Sure,' Pritt said.

'Where can we find the vehicle?'

'My car's in the garage at home, Lieutenant. The obvious place for it.' Pritt crushed out his cigarette.

'We need to run a few tests on it. Fingerprints and stuff.'

'You'd be wasting your time,' Pritt said.

Samsa glanced at Levine, who had an impassive face. *Of course we're wasting time*, Samsa thought. *We're going through this routine because it's necessary, not because it's useful, not because it has anything to do with truth. We're doing it for the benefit of Levine here. For Al Brodsky. For the department. Checking 'facts' that exist only inside your head, Ryan.*

Pritt said, 'See, I didn't use my own car to pick up the girl. I hear these stories about vice cops taking down license-plate numbers of cruisers for possible prosecution. I don't know if they're true, but it's crazy to run risks when you don't need to . . . I stole a car.'

Risks, Samsa thought. This from the guy who refused to wear a condom with a hooker. 'You *stole* a car?'

'Yeah. Well, borrowed is how I think of it. I do it every time I go down to that neighborhood.'

'You remember the make?'

'No, I don't. American, but I don't recall the brand.'

'Where did you steal it?'

'A street downtown. Primrose, I think . . .'

Samsa asked, 'Where did you leave it after?'

'Back where I found it.'

'You returned it to the same spot?'

'Why not? I couldn't just abandon it. It was bad enough stealing the thing in the first place.'

'Even in your panicky state of mind, you pulled yourself together enough to return the car to the same place?'

'I was thinking more clearly then. I was over the initial shock of what I'd done.'

Yeah, Samsa thought. *Naturally*. 'You remember *anything* about this car, Ryan? Color? How the interior looked? Anything like that?'

'Black leather seats, I think. Not genuine leather. Naugahyde. I think the car was dark brown.'

'A brown American car with a black interior.'

'Is that a problem?'

A brown car, black interior. A car with no unusual identifying features, no singularities. A car that couldn't be tracked down. A car that existed in Pritt's dream world, the same place where he'd killed a hooker and was overwhelmed by guilt.

'The thing is, Ryan, if we can't locate this auto, how can we be sure you picked up this girl? You see what I'm saying, don't you? The car, in all likelihood, would provide corroborative evidence. Without it ... I don't know.' Samsa heard an echo of Boyle's deep voice. *I'd grab this sucker's confession with both hands, man.*

'Try to remember anything you can about the car,' he said. This mockery. He had to *believe* in it. In his heart, in the fiber of himself.

'The fact I can't remember the goddam car doesn't affect my confession,' Pritt said, looking stubborn, jaw thrust out a little way. 'Look, I came in here of my own free will, I want to make a statement none of you guys seem prepared to take. I killed the goddam girl, Lieutenant. It's plain and simple. What more do you want?'

Samsa strolled around the room. This was being handed to him on a plate, for God's sake. Pritt knew enough basic details about the death of the girl to be convincing, and the car was way out there in the wild blue yonder. And the confession was a document that would bestow a kind of normality on his life. Just thinking this made him feel cowardly, shrinking inside himself, a husk of a person.

You could be pragmatic about it. You could tell yourself

that it made no sense for an experienced law-enforcement officer to trash his career and his usefulness on account of one misjudgement. It was a waste. You could go on and on, until you were inextricably lost in elaborate justifications.

But there was a bottom line. And it was silence. A big silence. You'd get your broken tooth fixed, the bruise would fade, you'd go on seeing Eve, maybe you'd even fall in love with her, who could say? But there would always be the big silence. There would always be that sense of balancing on the head of a pin, that fear of ultimate discovery. Even if he wrote down Pritt's confession himself he'd feel the dead girl's presence for the rest of his life.

He walked back to the table and stared at Pritt. 'Why the fuck are you doing this, Ryan?'

'If you don't want my confession, get me somebody that does. Get me that guy Brodsky.'

'You want to see your name in the papers, Pritt? Is that it? A little notoriety? A splash on the evening news? Or are you so fucked-up in your head you don't know what the hell you're doing? Tell me about all the little pills you pop. Have they seriously disrupted your reality?' He was aware of Levine just then, and wondered how the young cop felt to see his lieutenant lose his cool so easily.

'I don't need this,' Pritt said calmly. 'Maybe it's you should be taking the pills. What is it with you anyhow? You don't *want* me to be guilty?'

Samsa leaned across the table. *This is the place where you're all tangled up. Accept the confession. Don't accept it. Let Pritt walk out a free man. And then what reasons do you give to Brodsky and the department? What do you say? He was unconvincing, Al. I couldn't hold him.*

Why was that, Greg? Why was he unconvincing?
Because. I decided so. Call it instinct. A hunch, Al.

Pritt was standing now. 'Get me Brodsky,' he said.

'Let's just relax, Ryan, what do you say?'

'You're the one who's uptight, not me.'

'I shouted, okay, I didn't mean it,' Samsa said.

'I guess this is a high-pressure kind of job,' Pritt said. 'Things get you down. I know about pressures, believe me.'

Samsa's eyelids felt heavy. He was beginning to fade in and out. He said, 'What I want you to do is think really hard about all this, Ryan. Concentrate. See if you can remember any details about the car. Even the smallest thing could be useful. Meantime, I'll discuss the situation with Chief Brodsky. Then we'll see.'

See what? he wondered. It was just something to say, words you tossed out. He smiled at Pritt and walked to the door. 'Levine will take you back to your cell, Ryan. We'll talk again later.'

Samsa went out into the corridor. He walked a few yards, paused a moment to drink from a water fountain. Bending to the spout, he closed his eyes and imagined himself drinking from a mountain stream, the air around him chill and clear and his heart filled with the joy of being, and if he opened his eyes he'd see mountains, deep green valleys, a hawk circling freely and full-winged in the sky. But the water tasted of the chemicals the city treatment-plant pumped into it.

He splashed his face, let water spill down his shirt, then went back to his office. He'd phone Darcy now, check in on her. The good father. He reached for the phone and was halfway through punching the numbers when Al Brodsky appeared in the doorway.

Samsa put the handset back. Brodsky tossed a sheet of paper on the desk. Samsa picked up the sheet, which was pale-blue and flimsy, the kind used in the department for telephone messages. He stared at the handwriting and

717

somehow couldn't get beyond it to the message it contained, as if the meaning of the words were imprisoned within the letters.

'Life's a fucking bitch sometimes,' Brodsky said.

39

DARCY RODE THE BUS INTO THE CITY. SHE GOT OFF NEAR THE Greyhound station, a grubby neighborhood, full of drifters and panhandlers. She was wolf-whistled a couple of times, a few 'hey, babes'. Her black linen skirt was short and her white off-the-shoulder blouse revealed maybe a little too much. She thought her make-up made her look nineteen or twenty.

She crossed the street and walked a few blocks to a bar called Chang's. The sun was beginning to set, the sky hazy.

She knew absolutely nothing about him – what he did for a living, his background – yet here she was strolling toward a bar where she'd arranged to meet him. *You're out of your head.* It had seemed such a damn good idea at the time because Nick had been argumentative after school, getting on her nerves, nagging at her about the next step in their relationship, like it was a goddam ladder you climbed. Wasn't she ever going to 'come across', 'put out' – phrases she thought sexist and cheap, especially when they were delivered in a wheedling tone of voice designed to make her feel guilty for not fucking him.

'I'm a guy, I have needs, you don't seem to understand that, what are you, like this professional virgin?'

'Yeah, well I have needs too, Nick,' she'd said. 'And you're not exactly meeting them either. You think with your dick.'

'I love you, Darcy' – like that smoothed over all the cracks.

Then Nick had driven away in his small rasping car and the house had begun to feel like a tomb. There was no sign of her father, *as usual*, and she was bored, boxed in. And then she'd played piano for a time in a listless manner before she'd decided, *Oh, just do it, go ahead, pick up the telephone. Get out of this rut, this funk, this big empty house.*

Face it. There was something interesting about him. She couldn't say what exactly. He was an *adult*, and Nick – Nick was a big horny kid. This flattered her to some extent, sure. But it wasn't just flattery, because that alone wasn't enough to have brought her downtown to meet a stranger.

Sit with the clones. Conform. Be like everyone else.

Now *that* was the real turning point. He couldn't have known he'd thrown down a completely irresistible challenge when he'd said that. Until that moment she'd been quite prepared to step on the bus and ignore him, but he'd really stung her with those comments. And when he'd shoved his phone number into her hand she'd known there and then she'd call him.

Conform, she thought. *You just don't know me, whoever-you-are.*

She'd never been in a bar before, didn't have ID, wouldn't be served. The whole thing would be mortifying. She hesitated on the sidewalk.

Then he appeared in the doorway. 'Coming in or not?' he asked.

'I wasn't sure this was the right place,' she said.

'There's only one Chang's,' he said. He put a hand on her elbow, steered her inside the crowded bar, edged her through the throng to a table at the back of the big room. She was conscious of pink plaster flamingoes all over the place and the smell of his aftershave and the way his silk shirt shone.

'What would you like to drink?'

'Oh . . . rum and Coke?'

'*Uno momento*.' He went to the bar. She watched him force his way through. She barely had time to scan the room – which was filled with some business types, a few overdressed girls, groups of young men – before he came back carrying two drinks.

'Bacardi okay?'

'Sure. What's that you're drinking?' His glass contained a red-yellow liquid.

'A Suffering Bastard. Which translates into, you drink too many of these and you wake feeling embalmed. You look lovely by the way.'

The compliment embarrassed her. She wasn't going to say anything in response, though. Hadn't she read somewhere that it was a mark of maturity when you knew how to accept praise with graceful silence? She'd go with graceful silence.

'*A full-born beauty, new and exquisite,* quote unquote.'

'Shelley,' she said.

'I'm impressed.'

He pushed a pack of Camel Lights across the table. She took one, and he lit it for her with a Zippo. She wondered what would happen if somebody she knew walked in, a friend of her father's, say, or even her father himself. Oh Christ. She tasted her drink, made a face.

'Don't like it?' he asked.

'It's strong.' An unsophisticated response. She shouldn't

721

have said anything. 'It's good though.'

'Tell me about your family,' he said.

'There's only my father. My mother died a year ago.'

'That's too bad. How did she die?'

'She killed herself. You won't mind if I don't really want to talk about it?'

He looked genuinely sympathetic. 'What does your father do?'

She said, 'He's a cop.'

'A *cop*? Oh-oh. You mean I'm drinking with a policeman's daughter, who's obviously – whisper it – under the age limit for alcohol consumption? I'll be clapped in irons. Sent to the brig.'

'Only if he finds out, and I won't tell him.'

'I like secrets,' he said.

'What about you? What's your story?'

He drummed the top of the table with the palms of his hands. 'I'm a failed neurologist. So I took up spodomancy by way of compensation. You want to know what spodomancy is, don't you? Flick some cigarette ash in the ashtray.'

She did so, puzzled. He studied the ashes. 'You're going to have a long life and I see many babies. I also see a number of ocean voyages.'

'Really,' she said. 'What is it you do?'

'You don't buy the neurologist bit and you don't believe I can divine the future from the pattern of ashes?'

'Not a word.'

'You don't believe in myth and magic? Spells and incantations and casting the runes?'

'Do you?'

He shrugged and appeared to drift a moment. 'I believe everything in the world happens for a purpose,' and he leaned toward her in an earnest way she found a little unsettling, unexpected. Was he putting her on again? Or

722

was there some nugget of sincerity in what he was saying?

'Running into you, for example,' he said. 'I don't believe that was random.'

'You see that as part of what – like a design?'

'Everything's part of a design.'

'What kind?'

'That's the big question,' he said. 'I think everything fits together in some way. The trick is to fathom the pattern without a blueprint. Think of life as walking a high wire blindfolded.' He looked at her darkly and then laughed all of a sudden, and the veil of seriousness lifted. 'Okay. You prefer mundane truth? I taught college for a couple of years, gave up and went to Tibet in search of deep truths – which is what you do when you don't know what you're supposed to be doing. And then I came back here last year, and now I'm looking round for some business opportunities.'

It sounded plausible, but there was a light in his eyes that suggested a certain amount of bull, as if he wanted to project an image of himself that was part truth, part fabrication. 'What kind of business?' she asked.

'The only criterion is I make money. I like money. I make no excuses for liking it either.'

'You don't care how you get it.'

'So long as I stay on the good side of the law, he said to the cop's daughter.'

'Oh, forget I'm a cop's daughter,' she said. 'Were you born here?'

'San Francisco. I came east for a three-year gig at Rutgers teaching freshmen comp. Making freshman bozos construct simple sentences. Brain-dead kids with rich daddies. Who needs them?' He sounded bitter. She wondered why, if maybe he'd had a bad experience teaching. He said the word 'freshmen' as if it was an insect he'd found in his drink.

He pushed his glass toward her. 'See what you make of this cocktail.'

She tasted. It wasn't subtle. It burned in her chest like a blowtorch. 'What is *in* that stuff?'

'You don't want to know,' he said.

'Do your parents live out west?'

'Why don't you ask me my sign?'

'Your sign?'

'I'm only pointing out the drift in our conversation,' he said. 'All that background text and hubbub – who cares about it? Somewhere along the way of such chat your star sign inevitably comes up.'

She'd been making small talk, that was what he was saying. She felt annoyed with herself. This is the big world, Darcy, and you're not sure how to behave in it. He placed his hand over hers. The touch shocked her a little. She looked at his face and saw an expression of deep interest there, a probing, as if he wanted to get beyond superficialities as soon as he could. She slid her hand out from under his and helped herself to a second cigarette, which he lit for her. She never smoked except at parties. But she felt like smoking up a storm now.

'I don't even know your *name*,' she said. 'I can't believe I'm sitting in a bar drinking with a guy I don't know.'

'Vass. Lee Vass. Originally Russian. Vassinsky. Shortened somewhere along the way. Probably at Ellis Island. Maybe now you'll tell me your name.'

'Darcy,' she said.

'Darcy. I like it. It suggests stately homes, ivy on walls, butlers carrying trays, menials grooming horses. Oldie worldie.'

The alcohol was going to her head. She felt sober still, but a touch lopsided. And suddenly liberated. No Nick to bother her, no empty house to press down against her.

'You called me a clone,' she said. 'Which I regarded as an insult, Lee Vass.'

'That was a ploy. I knew all along you were a free spirit.'

She liked the sound of that. 'And I'm still puzzled why you phoned at three in the morning. And please don't deny it was you.'

'I didn't phone. I swear.'

'I *know* it was you.'

'*Ah happy Lycius – for she was a maid more beautiful than ever twisted braid.*'

'I don't know why you're hiding the fact,' she said. 'What's the mystery? You asked to talk with my father. Why?'

He crossed his heart. 'There's a mistake here. It wasn't me. What possible reason would I have for calling at – what time did you say? Three in the *morning*? Just drink up. We've got places to go.'

'Like where?'

'Here and there. Lee's tour of the city.'

She finished her drink and followed him out to the street, thinking maybe, just maybe, she was mistaken about that phone call. The last of the evening's sunlight came back off the rooftops with a soft glow, as if the world were filled suddenly with thousands of haloes. She saw pigeons in scattered leaden flight. He took her by the hand and began to run along the sidewalk, and she laughed as she tried to keep up with his pace.

'Where are we going, Lee?'

'You'll see.' He kept running faster, turning a corner into an alley.

'Are you always in such a hurry?'

'Always.'

He stopped alongside a white Ford and took the keys from his pocket.

'Where's the big blue thing with the fins you were driving before?'

'Gone and forgotten. Jump in.' He held the passenger door open for her, and just for a second she hesitated. She wasn't sure why, some tiny flicker of uneasiness, a sense of irresponsibility. Then she thought, *Screw it, I'm getting into this car. I'm doing what I like.* She stepped in and snapped her seat-belt buckle in place.

'Unbuckle it,' he said.

'Why?'

'It's just one more goddam restriction. Life's all petty rules and stupid little laws. Wear your seat belts. Don't smoke in public buildings. Fuck all that. You get tired of people telling you what to do.' He reached out and unclasped the buckle of her belt, and she felt the light pressure of his hand against her hip a moment, an intimacy that both disturbed and pleased her. She slumped back in her seat, stretched her legs, felt comfortable now.

He started the car and roared out of the alley. He drove with a furious recklessness, just making the lights before they changed to red, swerving once to avoid a bus disgorging passengers.

'You drive like a lunatic,' she said.

'Maybe because I am one,' and he glanced at her.

She said, 'I have nothing against lunatics.'

'Good. I'm a crazy bastard. You'll love me.'

No, she thought. *But I like you.*

He parked the car in a side street in a neighborhood she didn't know. Old crumbling tenements, a kind of broken-down cool about the place. He got out, walked round and opened her door. Tugging on her skirt, which had risen up her thighs, she slid out. She hoped she didn't appear clumsy. She noticed the way he looked at her legs. Not in a sneaky manner, but with open appreciation. He grasped her hand, helped her onto the sidewalk. Nick was never this courteous.

She didn't know where she was and she didn't know where she was going either, but it didn't matter, she had her hand in Lee's and he was leading her, and she didn't mind being led, being directed. It was his script she was following anyhow.

They walked a few yards before he drew her down a flight of steps to the basement of a building. She heard the lazy sound of a blues guitar being played somewhere, and then he was escorting her through a doorway into a badly lit room. It took her a few moments to get used to the gloom – candles on tables, a dull purple lamp on a small stage, where an old guy sat hunched over a guitar, black skin dyed blue by a trick of the light. The air was dense with smoke, and when you breathed it felt raw against the back of your throat. And it wasn't just tobacco. She detected reefer, rich and bittersweet.

Lee pulled out a chair from a table and she sat. He asked her if she wanted rum and Coke again, and she nodded, watching him disappear into the murk. She looked round, conscious now of other people at tables, faces glowing in the light from the candles that burned in red glass jars. It was the kind of place that might get raided at any moment: clandestine, somehow *exciting*. She listened to the guy on stage sing, *Black gal, black gal, don't lie to me. Tell me where did you sleep last night?* He had a voice like pebbles rattling inside a drum.

She saw Lee coming back through the haze. He sat, gave her the rum and Coke. He was drinking Heineken from a bottle. He placed his hand over hers and rubbed her skin with the tip of his thumb for a time. Then he leaned across the table and blew in her ear, and his breath tickled her. She laughed, pulled her head to one side, listened to the singer: *I slept in the pines where the sun*

727

never shines, And I shivered with cold, deadly cold.

She drank and felt the surge of alcohol to her brain. 'Are you trying to get me drunk?' she asked.

'Why would I do that?'

'Because. You might have devious motives.'

'Do you want me to have?'

She looked at him over the small red flame of the candle, and saw how the flickering light played in his eyes and created shifting shadows on his face and made the thin gold chain around his neck glitter. *Lee Vass, who is he really? Do you really want him to have devious motives? How are you supposed to act?* She drank more, felt loose, relaxed. She'd discarded the idea that her regular little world might intrude here – nobody she knew was going to see her in this place. She could be somebody other than the lieutenant's daughter for once. She could reinvent herself, drift into a pretend identity.

'I don't have a secret agenda,' he said. 'What you see is what you get.' He held the cellophane from his cigarette pack directly in the flame of a candle and it burned yellow with purple disturbances.

'And what is it I see?'

'People see different things in me,' he said. 'What you see is up to you.' He inclined his head and turned her hand over and kissed the palm. She'd never been kissed there before. It was a strange sensation, like a gentle electric current had been applied to a sensitive point. She closed her eyes. What was she getting into? She edged away from him, looked at him, saw how his face seemed to float on candlelight and his blue eyes reflected flame. *It's all going too fast*, she thought. *Slow down. Apply the brakes.*

'Your skin tastes nice,' he said.

'Nice. How?'

'Imagine if a starry sky had a flavor. It's like that.'

A starry sky. She laughed. He massaged her fingers slowly one by one.

She said, 'Lee, you're too old for me.'

'It's you that's too old for me,' he said. 'I'm very young inside.'

She felt his other hand on her knee beneath the table. '*Lee . . .*'

'I love your skin,' he said. 'I could develop an obsession about it. They'd have to whisk me off to some psychiatric clinic and experts would discuss my condition, which they'd call Vass's Syndrome. Men from Vienna would be hired on a consultancy basis. They'd make me lie down on couches and plumb the cesspool of my childhood.'

'Cesspool? That's a funny word to describe your childhood.'

He didn't appear to hear her. 'You know what they'd find? This crusted surface they'd have to shatter with jackhammers. Then, if they got through that, they'd reach murky water where they wouldn't be able to see a goddam thing. Just this rancid dank place with no rapid whirlpools spinning, and no mermaids, and no plant life.'

She didn't know quite what he was talking about, but somehow it didn't matter. She understood she was approaching a boundary she shouldn't cross, but she didn't want to quit. She was enjoying the way her perceptions were suddenly spilling one into another, as if her brain were undergoing some weirdo renovation. 'You know what I'd like?'

'I'm here only to serve,' he said.

'Grass. I'd like to smoke grass.'

'No problem,' he said. He got up from the table and disappeared somewhere. She finished her drink. She clapped when the singer ended his song and started another. *I ought to go home*, she thought.

Lee returned and handed her a thick joint, which he'd

already lit. He also had another rum and Coke for her.

'You think it's okay to smoke it here?' she asked.

'Consider this club a free-enterprise zone. Anything goes.'

She put the joint to her lips. It took only moments for her to feel the effect, and suddenly the music was rich with hidden revelations. Strong grass, mind-blowing in a dreamy way.

Lee leaned across the table and touched her hair. 'You okay?'

She passed the joint back. 'Oh, I'm fine, just fine.' *Scrambled Darcy.*

'Don't smoke too much of this,' he said. 'It's Thai, and I don't want you turning into a jellyfish because the night is still young. And miles to go et cetera.'

She raised a hand to look at her watch, then changed her mind. Time wasn't real. You couldn't touch it, you couldn't taste it. 'Tell me if I'm red-eyed,' she said. 'I don't want to go home all bloodshot.'

'Your eyes are beautiful and clear,' he said. 'You're not going home yet anyway. Hang loose.'

'I don't think I can get any looser,' and she laughed in the way dope makes you laugh. The whole world was a cheerful shambles.

'Drink up,' he said.

She finished her first drink and started on the second. Actually her third, if you counted the one she'd had at Chang's – but who's counting? The music was pounding inside her. Lee was still stroking her hair, but there was no urgency in the gesture, only a slow soft caressing. She felt joined to him in an easy way, his hand and her hair fused together.

'I am *stoned*,' she said. '*Really* stoned. I'm not going to freak, am I?'

'Would I let such a thing happen to you?' He had a

strand of her hair twisted around a finger. 'Finish your drink. Let's get out of here.'

'You don't ever sit still, do you?'

'I like to keep moving. Move move move. Mr Motion. That's me. Everything's a rush, everything's a blur.'

She drained her glass. She started to rise. Uh-oh, wobbly, legs like paper. She heard herself laugh at her own imbalance. Lee put an arm around her waist and led her toward the door.

'I like this place,' she said.

'You'll also like the next one.'

They were back on the street. It was dark and the street lamps had come on. They walked to his car and he opened the passenger door for her and helped her into the seat. She was dizzy a moment, but the feeling passed and she felt relaxed again, as if the air around her was warm water frothing in a jacuzzi. She reached for her seat belt – automatic pilot kicking in – and then she remembered she didn't need the goddam thing. Suddenly the whole idea of seat belts was *amazingly* silly.

She listened to the hum of the engine. She was aware of how light from the street lamps seemed to be threaded together in some way, as if the night was filled with electric linkages. Shiny beads.

Lee stopped the car in a backstreet where there were no lamps, and he flipped on the interior light.

'Pit stop, Darcy.' He had a plastic bag of white powder in his hand.

'Cocaine?'

He smiled. 'What else?'

'I've tried it before.'

'You want to try it again?'

'Sure.'

'You'll need this,' he said. He handed her a rolled-up twenty-dollar bill. He laid some of the powder on the console between them. She noticed how it twinkled here and there, like it contained fragments of crushed gems.

She angled her head downward, held the bill to her left nostril, sniffed up some of the powder, then repeated the action with the right. She felt it hit the back of her throat. She raised her head up quickly. Her nose stung inside. 'Woooee,' she said.

'Let's go,' and he drove out of the street, heading this time for the freeway entrance, and she wanted to ask where he was taking her, but she felt dislocated suddenly, as if her head was going in several directions at the same time, and all the lights of the freeway were unnaturally bright and her heartbeat was a little skippy. She wasn't sure she enjoyed this effect. It wasn't anything like the short-lived euphoria she'd had with cocaine before – this was different and harsh, almost menacing, like it was about to create dark unpredictable cracks in herself. This was flying with no sense of anyone in the cockpit.

She rolled down her window and the night air made her feel a little better. *Speeeeding* along and wondering if her emergency brake worked. She said, 'The coke I had last time was nothing like this. My pulses are *thumping*.'

'You probably had crap,' he said. 'This is *primo*.'

She felt the breeze in her hair. She dangled an arm from the window. She'd done too much too soon, that was it – booze, reefer *and* coke – and they were bombarding her senses like tracer-bullets, and now the suburbs alongside the freeway were fuzzy and so faraway they might have been constructs on a strange moon seen through a beveled telescope. Lee had one hand lying casually against her hip, his fingertips making small circular motions. And then he lowered his hand to where the hem of her skirt lay high on her leg, and he raised the skirt a little.

He rammed the car up a freeway ramp and she was swung to the side by the sudden swerving motion. He laughed as he screeched into a parking lot and brought the car to a dead stop. She looked through the windshield at a neon sign a hundred yards away that quivered in her vision.

'Uh,' she said. 'Is this what I think it is, Lee?'

'What do you think it is?' he asked.

The sign was red and discolored the sky above it. The Wayside Motor Lodge.

'One drink, Darcy.'

Before she could say anything, he was out of the car and holding open the passenger door for her, and she slid from her seat, feeling giddy. She was sweating and her hair was damp and yucky against her scalp.

'Lean on me if you need to,' he said. 'That's what I'm here for.'

40

SAMSA LOOKED THROUGH THE GLASS DOORS INTO THE BACK-yard. In the alley behind the house an ambulance spiked the dark with sharp turning lights, and a patrol car flashed red, white and blue. Cops in the yard searched the shrubbery under brilliant lamps that had been rigged up. He thought of the Purchase field. How could he not?

He had a hard time drawing his face away from the glass. He didn't want to look back at what lay in the room. He turned anyhow and saw Charlie Bird, a tall man whose head was a little too tiny. Bird reminded him, fittingly, of a stork, even in the manner he walked, delicately picking up his feet and avoiding anything that lay on the floor – in this case, trophies and silver cups that bore the name Mandy Robbins, and prizes for athletic achievements, swimming, track and field. The girl who'd won these trophies lay half naked near the fireplace. Her eyes were closed and the lids were like blood-red coins.

'This is savage,' Charlie Bird said. 'I never seen anything this bad before.'

Al Brodsky said, 'It's goddam brutal.'

Beyond a closed door directly behind the chief, be-wildered grief-struck people filled a corridor – relatives, neighbors, a priest who'd hurried to the scene and was out there whispering the only thing he could: platitudes. The shock of homicide. You never think it's coming to your house, touching your family.

Samsa shifted his eyes. He had an acid pain in his stomach.

Nick Mancuso lay close to the girl. His face was de-molished, hair thick with drying blood, bare upper body covered in deep incisions. He'd been beaten to death.

Charlie Bird said, 'We're looking for a guy hauling around some serious rage here. *Psychopathic* rage.'

Samsa turned his face from the two dead kids. His mind wandered to Darcy, and he wondered how he'd tell her about this. Murder was vile, but there was an added element here: betrayal. Nick had strayed.

Charlie Bird crouched near the fireplace. 'The poker's missing,' he said. 'These fireside sets always have a poker.'

'Could be your weapon,' Brodsky said.

Bird stood up and looked across the room at Samsa with a muted form of sullen hostility: *What the fuck are you doing here, this one is all mine, Pharaoh*. This was Bird's zone and Samsa, who felt like an interloper, gazed around, anywhere to take his eyes away from the sight on the floor. He saw the posters on the wall, mainly jock heroes, basketball superstars. He noticed a single bed in the corner and thought of the passion that must have flared up between Nick and Mandy, something so strong they couldn't even wait to make it as far as the bed.

'The girl's parents were gone all day,' Bird was saying. 'This is what they come home to.'

Brodsky said, 'Maybe there's a jealous boyfriend.'

'Who knows. Who knows anything these days,' Bird said. He looked inside the fireplace, reached up into the chimney and rummaged. He straightened his back. His hands were sooty. He was the kind of guy who didn't mind getting his hands dirty.

Samsa said, 'I don't know how I'm going to break this to Darcy.'

Charlie Bird looked puzzled. 'Who's Darcy?'

'My daughter,' Samsa said. 'She'd been seeing Nick Mancuso.'

'High-school romance?' Bird asked.

'Something like that.'

'I'll have to talk with her. Maybe she'd know if Mandy Robbins had a boyfriend somewhere. Maybe the guy walked in and found them screwing, lost control, went berserk big-time.'

'I'll talk to her for you,' Samsa said.

'She's your daughter.' Bird half kneeled alongside the dead boy, and stared at him as if he were about to give him a lecture on morality. 'So Nick was seeing Darcy and fooling around on the side. What kind of kid was he? Or do I have to ask?'

Samsa said, 'I only met him a couple of times. Seemed nice enough. Maybe trying too hard to please. Over-polite.'

Bird said, 'You wonder what's happening to the world.'

Samsa walked out into the hard sharp lights in the yard and watched men search the bushes silently. He took his cellular phone from his pocket and punched in his home number, but Darcy didn't answer. He let it ring a long time before he shut his unit off. If she wasn't at home, where was she? He tried to remember the names of her close friends. Ginny somebody. Maybe that's where she was.

Ginny who? Last name beginning with F?

Or maybe she was asleep and failed to hear the ringing.

Jesus Christ. How do you convey such horror to your own daughter? His bandaged hand pulsated.

736

Al Brodsky came and stood at his side. 'You talked to Pritt about that car?' he asked.

'He used a stolen vehicle. He can't remember the make. It's all very vague.'

'A stolen car. That's really helpful. What do you plan to do with him, Greg?'

'I'm waiting, see what Mcalister says.'

'You know, I'm beginning to feel like a juggler with too many hoops in the air,' Brodsky said. 'We've got thirty-seven unsolved homicides still active on the books. No, make that thirty-nine now. If Pritt's confession hangs together, it's one we can chalk off the list.'

Samsa thought how the numbers could pile up and defeat you. You could get crushed by the dead weight of statistics. All that grief out there in the city. All that badness. Sometimes the city seemed to hang over him like a big black nuclear cloud.

'You don't need me around here,' he said. 'Bird has it under control. I ought to see what Darcy has to say.'

'Good idea,' Brodsky said. He stepped a little nearer. 'You took your eye off the ball, Greg.'

'About Pritt's car, you mean?'

'Yeah. Maybe there's too much on your plate. Do you think that's it?'

'I'm tired. That's what I think.'

'You can't let yourself get tired on this job.'

'Is this a dressing-down, Al?'

'If it is, I'm soft-pedaling, believe me. Go home. Sleep. You look wasted.'

Samsa walked out into the alley where he'd parked his car. He drove in the direction of his house. He traveled a couple of blocks before he tried to call home again. Still no answer. *Where is she?* He couldn't remember the last name of her friend yet. Flynn? He chastized himself for knowing so little about Darcy's life.

I took my eye off more than one ball.

It was going to be okay. He'd see lights in the house, she'd be upstairs safe in her bed. He reached 1900 Devine and slid the car into the driveway. The house was in darkness. He got out and moved to the porch, fumbling for his door key. Okay, she didn't leave any lights on. Usually she did. This time she just forgot. That was the simple explanation. He unlocked the door, stepped inside, flipped on a light switch and breathed the still warm air of the hallway.

'Darcy,' he called out.

He climbed the stairs. He pushed open the door of her bedroom and turned on the light – no Darcy. He went through the house uselessly calling her name. There was clearly some very simple answer. There had to be. *What the hell was her friend's name?* He entered the living room, switched on a lamp, had the very strange feeling that the piano had been played recently and the vibration of a note still lingered at a sub-audible level. But that was nonsense, something shaped in the crucible of his growing panic.

He went to the table, where the address book lay, flicked the pages, F, F for Flagg, there it was. Ginny Flagg. He dialed the number and a sleepy-voiced woman answered.

He said, 'This is Gregory Samsa. Darcy's father? I hate to call at this hour. Is my daughter there?'

'I haven't seen her.'

'I'm trying to locate her.'

'Kids. They just don't think,' the woman said. 'They go AWOL without telling you. You have my sympathy.'

I don't want your sympathy. I want my daughter. 'You mind asking Ginny if she knows where Darcy is?'

'I'll try. She's probably sleeping.' The woman was gone a long time, and when she returned she said, 'No, Ginny doesn't know where she could be. I'm sorry.'

'What about other friends?' Samsa asked.

'You tried Lindy Prosecki's number?'

He couldn't remember ever having heard of Lindy Prosecki. 'I don't have it,' he said.

'Four zero nine, seven nine eight eight.'

Samsa scribbled this down, apologized again, then called the number he'd been given. He got an answering machine. 'We are not here to take your call . . .'

He hung up, walked into the kitchen, filled a glass with water and drank quickly. He saw his face reflected in the window, and for a moment was startled. He ripped off his bandage, looked at the dark cuts, and remembered Nick Mancuso. His own wounds were pitiful by comparison. He went to the bathroom, found some fresh bandage and wrapped it clumsily over the hand.

Darcy, where are you?

He went back into the living room. The trick was to relax. She'd have a good reason for not being here. He sat by the telephone, wondering who he could call next. He heard a sound on the porch, a footstep, and he thought, *Okay, here she is.*

Relieved, he went out into the hallway and opened the front door.

Eve was standing in the shadows. 'Is this a bad time to call?'

41

LEE BOYLE DREW THE CURTAINS. HE HEARD THE GIRL IN THE bathroom. He saw her bent over the washbasin, running cold water across her head and saying how very hot she felt. The inferno of crystal. She was in that clammy stage, sweating, too hyped after her last blast. He stepped into the bathroom and hung a towel around her neck.

'You'll be okay, just go with it,' he said.

She said nothing, kept her head under the faucet. He placed a hand flat against her spine, thinking what a delicate creature she was, how perfect the spinal column and unblemished the skin. Youth in all its intricate wonder.

She said, 'I shouldn't be here.'

He dried her face and hair with the towel, gently, gently. 'You're doing fine.'

'I shouldn't *be* here,' she said again. She gazed at her face in the mirror above the basin. 'I don't feel good.'

'Relax.' He led her out of the bathroom and made her lie down on the bed.

She shut her eyes. Her hair created a wet stain on the pillow.

He opened the little leather shaving-kit bag he'd brought up from the car. It contained his rig, cotton balls, a spoon, a nylon stocking, a tube of Preparation H for concealing tell-tale marks on the arm – and his gun, because he was carrying 15,000 bucks in his pocket, and maybe 3,000 dollars worth of crank, bounty worth protecting.

He placed the rig on the coffee table. The needle was brilliant steel. Shakily, he put a portion of finely chopped crystal in the spoon, added water from a glass, then tore a small chunk of cotton from one of the balls and dropped it in the spoon with the mixture. He tied the nylon stocking around his left arm – an intricacy he had down to an art – and flexed the arm. The big boost was coming. The fast shuttle to Ampsburg.

Darcy turned on her side and gazed at him. He pierced the cotton swab with the needle and filled the syringe, feeling the vein rigid in his arm, the tick-tick of glorious expectation, and always that annoying little voice somewhere at the back of his head – *Lee, lay off.*

She propped herself up on an elbow. Her face was white. 'I feel sick again. I think I want to throw up.' He watched her rise unsteadily from the bed. She slid against the door jamb, stumbled into the bathroom.

He pushed the needle into his vein, the galvanizing contact of steel and skin, a rapturous puncture, crank shooting through him like rocket fuel. He made up a second batch in the spoon and filled the syringe again.

Bless you, Samsa. For the money. The dope.

And your little girl.

You are my benefactor and I your confessor. The world is finely balanced.

He walked into the bathroom.

She was leaning over the basin. He stood behind her, massaged the back of her neck, then slid his hand down her spine to her waist. He pushed his body against hers. She lifted her head up from the basin. Her eyes were filled with water. She reached for a towel and buried her face in it. He shoved himself more forcefully against her. Her stomach was flat against the rim of the basin. In the mirror he saw his face loom behind hers.

She slipped the towel from her face and said, 'Lee, please . . .'

'We make an attractive couple,' he said.

'You're hurting me.'

She pushed against him, trying to turn and face him, but he kept her locked in place. She didn't say anything. She lowered her head and gazed bleakly into the porcelain.

He reached down, raised her skirt up, felt her shiver. 'You're not afraid of me, surely?' He rubbed her buttocks softly through the silky material of her panties. Oh yeah, firm young flesh. Nothing was more tasty than young meat. Old men everywhere should have daily access to this diet. She wasn't resisting and she wasn't encouraging either, she was just standing there with her back to him and her eyes directed into the basin, and this lack of participation bothered him. He tugged the panties down a little way, creating his own slow striptease gig, and thinking, *Move it, baby, move it. Respond.*

Samsa's child. Consider this, Lee, you've set loose the hounds of fucking *havoc* on this family: plundered Samsa's bank account, forced him to break the law he's sworn to uphold, degraded him – the man was on his *knees* goddamit – and now you have the daughter in a motel room, and she's so fucked-up she doesn't truly know where she is or what she's doing here, and that's the way you want it. Poor Samsa with a dead wife,

742

and this sweet little girl with no mother.

You are a mean sonofabitch. What are you?

He slid her panties down past her thighs, lowered himself on one knee and kissed her ass lightly and saw how goosebumps appeared on her skin. He pulled the underwear to her ankles, parted her legs, then he stood up and felt her tremble against him. He was trembling also, trying not to. He saw her face in the mirror again, her eyes shut and her angelic mouth halfway open, as if she meant to sing but couldn't remember the melody. I'll make you sing, little one. Lee H. Boyle will bring a song to the nightingale's throat.

And he plunged the needle in his left hand into her left arm, scoring a vein. She cried out, jerked her arm away, knocked the syringe out of his hand and it clattered into the sink. She said, 'Oh, Christ, no,' and she stared at her arm. The vein issued a drop of blood.

'That wouldn't have happened if you hadn't moved,' he said. 'You didn't get all of it. Goddamit.' He looked at the syringe in the sink. Saw milky liquid leak from the tip of the needle.

She tore a sheet of toilet paper from the roll on the wall and placed it over the blood. 'I didn't *ask*,' she said.

'It's good speed.'

'*Speed*,' she said.

'You've already been doing it up your nose. This way it just kicks in that little bit quicker.'

'Coke. You said it was coke.'

'Coke's for weenies who want a short lift. This is more long term, way more intense.'

She dabbed frantically at her arm with the tissue even though the vein had quit bleeding. He said, 'It's no big deal, for Christ's sake. It's not going to kill you.'

'What's going to happen to me?'

'The amount you've had? You'll feel energetic. As for sleep, forget it.'

He pulled her toward him, held her head against his chest, smelled her wet hair. She was fragile. She was lost in this world. *I'll show her the way. I'll take her places she's never been.*

She slumped a little in his arms. His head ached suddenly, a deep booming in his skull, suggestive of cannon fire. He picked her up, carried her into the bedroom and laid her on the bed. She was so light it felt like he was carrying nothing at all. She was Almond's weight.

He reached down and disentangled her panties from her ankles, let them fall to the floor. He slid her skirt up and she made an effort to force his hand away. Coy. He hated coy.

He didn't want this situation to turn sour. He had plans, cap P.

'Why did you come up here in the first place if you're going to be this unco-operative?' he asked. 'I said I'd get a room and you said that was fine with you. What was it? The booze talking? The dope? Or did you just like the idea of walking a precarious line, huh? Thought you were a big girl?'

Her eyes were wide and a little crazed. She didn't know speed, didn't know what to expect when it rushed through you. She turned her face to one side. 'I'm feeling sick. I want to leave, Lee.'

'Back to Daddy,' he said.

She started to rise, slid in a cumbersome way from the bed to the floor. He drew her up to her feet and shook her a couple of times with a vigor he couldn't keep in check. 'Back to fucking Daddy,' he said.

'I just want to go home, Lee. *Please.*'

'I just want to go home, Lee, please.' He pulled her face

744

toward him, cupped her chin in his hand and squeezed. 'Your daddy. The good lieutenant. You want to hear a nasty little truth about your daddy? He's *bad*. Your precious daddy killed a hooker. Picked her up, I don't doubt he fucked her, then killed her in a field.'

She tried to step back, but he held her face firmly, squashing her mouth. He had a strange experience, a little mind-shift, as if a crawlspace in his head had collapsed, and just for a moment he thought she looked more like Monique than Almond. Resemblances everywhere. Hadn't he sometimes thought that, from a certain angle and in a certain kind of muted light, Almond had faintly resembled his sister? Hadn't he found in that vague similarity some little nut of pleasure and glee? It was Monique he was sending to strange motel rooms. It was Monique walking the streets for him. Monique spreading her thighs for strangers in beds with gray sheets, or participating in seedy hurried couplings, or quick BJs in the back seats of cars. Then this thought dissipated, and he couldn't remember how accurate the memory was. Faces rushed at him – this one, that one, he couldn't keep them apart.

He shut his eyes and opened them again. This girl was Darcy Samsa, definitely. Chemical overspill. Warnings from Brain Central. Truant synapses rushing from class-rooms screaming.

'You're saying . . . What are you saying? My father killed somebody?'

'Yeah, and he's trying to keep it to himself, but *I* know. I know the whole fucking *story*. Oh, he's up shit creek, little Darcy. He's well and truly up shit creek.'

'My father would *never* kill anybody. You're out of your mind.'

'Ask him yourself. Hey, Daddy, you kill a girl called Cecily Suarez?'

'*Cecily Suarez?*'

'Go to the horse's mouth, babe.'

'I'll call him, I'll do it now.' She stretched an arm toward the phone.

'I don't think this is such a good time,' he said. He knocked the receiver out of her reach and it fell to the floor.

'You're a lying bastard,' she said.

He slapped her once, hard. She had to learn who was in control here. Her head snapped back. Blood leaked from her nostrils, and he was strangely moved by this sight. He grabbed a tissue from a box on the bedside table and applied it to her nose. She kept her eyes shut tight.

'Let's get one thing clear, babe. You're going nowhere unless I say so.'

She yanked herself free and made a movement toward the door, and he caught her before she'd gone three feet and tossed her down on the bed. He lay on top of her and she turned her face this way and that. *I have the power*, he thought. He kissed her, found her unyielding, forced the kiss on her, felt the wet warmth of her mouth. This is the way it's done, Darcy. I explore the contours of your body, all the secret cavities. I go where I like.

He gripped her arms, turned her over and tugged the skirt down her legs. He was hard, *hard*. She was speaking into the pillow – 'No no no' – and she was kicking her legs, thrashing around underneath him. She swiveled somehow, turning on her side, and he tried whispering in her ear, 'We'll go away. Your father won't find us in another city, you'll change your name. Life is going to be nice, I promise you. Just the two of us. We'll go to a place where music and moonlight and feeling are one.'

She clawed at his cheek, raked it. He could feel she'd drawn blood. Okay, he'd do this the hard way. He reached over to the coffee table, grabbed his bag and took out the gun. 'You see this?' He was feeling quirky hot flashes go through him like fireballs roaring down a tunnel.

She pressed herself against the headboard. How young she looked. How scared.

'Now. You are a microsecond away from oblivion. Try to get it through your head what we're here for. Okay?'

She smoothed hair from her face and looked up into his eyes, and he had it again, that flash of Monique. Get the fuck out my brain, Monique, go play with that lumbering bespectacled husband of yours, Austin I-am-a-big-time-money-maker Arganbright.

He was limp all of a sudden. Fucking Monique was still in his head, and he could see her wedding cake decorated with rainbow frosting. She liked goddam rainbows, considered them symbolic of something, he couldn't remember what. Some New Age guff.

This is the speed at work, buddy. This is years of self-destruction screeching back at you, and you are not silencing it.

The girl was sniffling.

He hated that sound. It reminded him of Monique weeping over her horse – *Oh, Daddy, bring him back to life, please*. Stamp your feet all you like, sister, the nag is plain fucking *dead*. Daddy can't do a Lazarus act for you. Hugh isn't Christ, despite what he might think.

He got up from the bed and walked up and down the room. A crack of pain shot across his scalp, and he was suddenly plunged back into that nocturnal world where people waited for him outside closed curtains. There were shadows in parking lots, men sitting in motionless cars, phones were tapped. Okay, you could blame the dope, but this *felt* real. He couldn't deflate this panicky feeling, this need to move.

He imagined Jimmy Plumm saying to Tom Bigshoes, *It*

might be interesting to know how Lee came into money. What scam does he have going? I want a cut of it. Break a few bones if you need to. He also imagined Samsa coming after him with a posse of his cop buddies and finding him with his daughter in a motel room. He could imagine even Rudy Vass turning against him in some foggy serpentine way.

And cops, there were always cops, black patrols of them, and he pictured them finding the poker he'd hidden in a place he considered altogether appropriate, *ironic even.* And though he'd wiped it clean, they probably had some kind of hypersensitive equipment that could pick up a fingerprint on Mars, for Chrissakes. All this was a marquee collapsing on him, tons of canvas, a hundred poles, miles of rope, the whole fucking business.

'We need to get out of here,' he said. 'We need to get the fuck out of this city and begin all over again.'

She stared at him. Wet eyes. 'I don't understand what you're saying,' she said.

'You don't have to understand. Nobody's asking you to understand. We move, that's all. Too many people know me around here. You see what I'm saying? People know me, I have all kinds of pressures coming down on me.'

He stuffed the gun in his bag and tossed the rig inside and all the rest of his stuff. *Lee Boyle is freaking,* he thought.

He grabbed her by the hand and stepped into the corridor, dragging her behind him. Halfway toward the elevators he experienced a razor-sharp pain at the back of his eyes, so fierce it sucked all the air out of him and dimmed the lights around him.

Is this it? Is this the legendary Seizureland, that theme park for dying speed-freaks? His heart was charged with explosives.

When the elevator arrived he hustled Darcy inside the mirrored cab, seeing multiplied reflections of his own pale image, sweat bright on his face, eyes feverish. As the elevator descended he had the thought that there were at least six Lee Boyles and Darcy Samsas riding down this shaft to God knows where.

42

SAMSA STARED OUT AT DARKNESS, HOPING HE'D SEE DARCY appear. But the street was silent and dreadful.

'When did you last see her?' Eve asked.

'This morning. No, yesterday morning. God, I'm losing track of time.'

He looked at Eve. She hadn't said why she'd turned up at the house. She seemed unusually reticent, as if she had some preoccupation beyond Darcy's troubling absence.

'You've tried her friends?' she asked.

'I called a couple of them. Nothing. The only thing I know for sure is that she isn't with Nick Mancuso.'

'I heard about that.'

'You also heard the circumstances.'

Eve nodded. 'Nick and this girl, yeah. If Darcy's already learned about that she can't possibly be handling it very well.'

He thought of Darcy out there on her own, perhaps wandering in a private blue haze. 'I phoned downtown,' he said. 'I gave the guys a description of her, but I don't know what she was wearing. I looked through her closet, but I can't tell what's missing.'

She sat on the stool at the piano, leaning forward a little and looking at the floor. She seemed downhearted. He walked across the room and touched her shoulder, and she edged almost imperceptibly away from him.

'Something bothering you?' he asked.

'Just Darcy.' She looked at her watch. 'Does she ever stay out this late?'

'Not without telling me she's spending the night with a friend or going to a party,' he said. He bent down, put his hand under her chin and lifted her face so he could see her eyes. 'There's something else on your mind.'

She got up from the stool and moved away from him. 'No,' she said. 'How's your hand?'

Changing the subject, he thought. Fine. Whatever was on her mind couldn't be forced out. She'd tell him when she was ready. 'It's okay. I bandaged it up again,' he said.

'You didn't do such a great job, did you? It's like something on a mummy.'

He made some passing reference to the logistical problems of bandaging your own hand, then he returned to the window, the silent street, the lamps that attracted a blizzard of moths.

'I can't stand this goddam waiting,' he said. 'Maybe I'll drive around, see if I run into her.'

'What if she comes back when you're gone?'

'I'll take my phone. I'll call the house every ten minutes or so.'

Eve said, 'You want company?'

He told her he'd welcome that. They went outside.

She said, 'Let's take my car.' Her mood was off-center, she'd retreated to a place he couldn't locate. He thought of Harriet suddenly, but Harriet's silences were

751

profoundly different, deep and mysterious. With Eve you knew something was simmering just below the surface.

She drove a couple of blocks and Samsa, thinking how uniform the neighborhood was, gazed out at trees and houses. Three a.m. and quiet, nothing moving on the streets. His mind was skipping like a flat stone thrown across water. Where to look? Where to begin? Down through the suburbs and into the city centre. And if she *had* gone there, why?

Here and there porch lights burned, some yellow, others orange. So many houses, windows, rooms. And all so goddam ordinary to look at. It was in one such ordinary house that Nick Mancuso and Mandy Robbins had been bludgeoned to death. Surfaces told you nothing.

'Is there any special direction you want me to take?' Eve asked.

'Just drive around,' he said. The pointlessness of this, scanning the night, hoping she'd materialize. He remembered stories of people who'd just vanished off the face of the earth. The department had scores of unsolved cases. Missing persons, people who'd fallen into mysterious cracks and were never seen again. And then he remembered how he and Darcy had mentioned the subject of runaways.

You'd never do that, would you?

Run away from home? Come on. I can't imagine the circumstances.

He beat the palm of his hand against his thigh. Why wasn't he receiving signals from that source people called paternal instinct? Why wasn't there some gut feeling to inform him he was worrying fruitlessly? Instead his mind was filled with shadows and his instincts were persistent little beeps of apprehension.

Eve said, 'She's a kid, and sometimes kids forget

about time. I used to worry my mother to death.'

'Darcy's usually good about these things,' he said.

'So this one time she forgot.'

He wondered why he wasn't convinced by that. 'Even when she cuts classes she doesn't hide it,' he said.

'She's open and honest,' Eve said.

'Yeah, she is.'

'But you don't *really* know that, do you? I mean, there's a sense in which we never know other people, isn't there? We go along thinking we do, then something happens right out of the blue, and all of a sudden your ideas of somebody else get changed around.'

'Why don't you just *say* what's bugging you, Eve?'

'Let's look for Darcy, okay? Let's concentrate on that.'

'But there's something.'

She stared ahead. 'Let's try and find your daughter, Greg.'

He fell silent. Okay, her barricades were up and this wasn't the time to storm the fortress. He looked out, saw a twenty-four-hour convenience market, bright and white. In the darkness of the vicinity it was like a big fluorescent spaceship, just landed.

They traveled in silence for a time through an assortment of neighborhoods that became progressively more mean, more shabby, the closer they got to the edge of downtown. He was trying to bring Darcy's face into sharp focus, wondering if there was any truth to the idea that if you could visualize a lost thing you could find it – but he supposed that only worked if you were the one who had misplaced it originally. Stupid thoughts, stoked by panic. His feelings were turning bad, his head was spinning. She's out there somewhere and I'm never going to find her again. I'll spend the rest of my life looking for a girl whose photograph is inside a missing persons folder that grows more and more musty with every year that passes. But you'd never forget. You'd look for ever. You'd imagine you caught a glimpse of her in a mall, a department store, a passing bus. Your life would be one of checking out reported sightings. You'd live on hope.

He took out his cellular phone and punched in his home number. No answer.

Eve asked, 'Where now?'

He had no directions to give. 'Anywhere,' he said.

'We might as well go downtown,' she said.

Somehow it didn't matter where she drove, the idea was to keep moving and looking. Downtown was a drab mausoleum at this hour. The streets were lifeless, save for a few cars and a couple of drunk pedestrians shuffling along unsteadily.

Eve turned off the main drag a few blocks before City Hall. She drove past the old Rialto Hotel, and Samsa glanced at the awning, the lights in the lobby.

Then she hung a left and they were moving into a neighborhood where he didn't want to go. He had the urge to tell her, No, not this way, but he didn't say so, he couldn't explain that this area was the last place on earth for him. But Eve was driving there anyhow, and suddenly there were ghostly girls and boys lingering on sidewalks, watching the car approach and probably thinking, *This might be a customer, some late-night score*. There were twenty or so, and they moved toward the curb, desperate to do business, gesticulating, calling out. Eve slowed the car a little, and he wondered why.

Hands reached out from the sidewalk, signs were made. A girl in short tight spangled pants swiveled her pelvis and laughed, another flashed a breast, cupping it in her hand and thrusting it forward as if she had a thirsty infant to feed. A slinky boy in a leather jacket and tight jeans clutched his crotch. Samsa noticed he had platinum-dyed hair.

'We're not going to find Darcy in this place,' he said.

'Oh, you never know what you're going to find down here,' Eve said.

He didn't like that cutting little note in her voice. He remembered what Joshua Gold had told her: *He saw you cruising, Greg.* Did she believe Gold? Had something happened to make her imagine Gold was telling the truth? He dismissed the questions. He didn't have space in his mind for anything but Darcy, finding Darcy, turning this goddam city upside down if he had to.

Eve was moving the car slowly along the edge of the sidewalk. Somebody on the curb reached out and touched the window on Eve's right, leaving a smear of what looked to Samsa like Vaseline – he couldn't tell – a greasy streak of something or other. He wished she'd give the goddam car some gas and get out of here. What was she playing at, idling along like this?

He said, 'Let's blow this place.'

'You want a change of scene? Okay, you got it. I'll give you a change of scene.' She accelerated away from the sidewalk. She drove without saying anything, taking corners fast, making her tires screech and leave echoes between buildings. She drove like this for several blocks, manic, like she didn't give a damn.

'For God's sake, slow down,' he said.

'You want slow? I can do slow.' She had the car crawling now, fifteen miles an hour.

'What the hell is your *problem*, Eve?'

'I don't have a problem, Greg.'

'Pardon me for thinking otherwise,' he said. 'Ever since you showed up on my doorstep you've been wound like a goddam clock.'

She pulled the car over and laid her face for a moment against the wheel. He touched the back of her neck, even though he understood it involved a risk because he had the feeling she didn't want to be touched. She stared through the windshield at the dead street ahead. She didn't look at him.

'I'm fine, Greg. I'm perfectly okay.'

'No, you're not.' He wanted a cigarette suddenly. He hadn't smoked in years and now he wanted to light a cigarette he didn't have. Craving nicotine. He didn't know what to do with his hands. He punched his home number into his phone and, as before, received no answer.

He tapped in a second number and heard Duff's voice. 'Anything happening? Anybody seen my daughter?'

'Not so far,' Duff said.

'Call me at once if you hear anything.' Samsa cut the connection. He turned to Eve. 'Look, if you don't feel like driving, I'll do it.'

'I don't mind,' she said.

They passed the Greyhound station where a bus from a faraway city was disgorging weary passengers. The light from the terminal building was muted, dreary. A few taxi-cabs idled outside the station. Two uniformed cops were standing close to the doorway, nervy and vigilant. This area was a hang-out for small-time drug dealers, and sometimes there were occasional disputes that turned violent. It was also a place where runaways disembarked. He found himself imagining Cecily Suarez stepping off a bus right here, in a city that was strange to her, a place chosen at random because she didn't have enough money to get any further away from home. He wished to God she'd had a few more dollars to spare.

'Say something, Eve. Explain this ... this mood. Please.'

'I have my highs and lows, Greg. I have my expectations and my disappointments, like everyone else.'

'So you're disappointed with something. That's a start.'

'Sometimes I just hear things crashing in my head. Does that make sense to you?'

'Explain some more,' he said.

'You were the most honest man I knew.'

'But something's happened to make you think otherwise,' he said, and he could feel it coming, rumbling in the distance as it rolled toward him, a runaway train unstoppable and gathering speed. He looked down at his hands flattened against his legs. The bandage was coming undone. He hadn't bound it properly, he'd left loose ends. He'd left loose ends all over the place. *Eve knows. Somehow she knows.*

She said, 'I don't have a clue what I believe any more.'

He heard his phone buzzing. He snatched it out of his pocket and held it to his ear. *It has to be Duff*, he thought. Darcy's been picked up by a patrol car and she's safe.

'Hey, Lieutenant, *sir*.'

No, he thought.

'*She seemed at once some penanced lady elf, Some demon's mistress, or the demon's self.*'

'Why the fuck are you calling me?'

'*I took compassion on her, bade her steep her hair in weird syrups*, Lieutenant, *sir*.'

'Talk sense, for Christ's sake.'

'I'm talking good sense, and you're too moronic to know. *Tell me only where my nymph has fled.*'

Samsa said, 'Darcy. You're talking about Darcy.'

'Oh, you're one bright sonofabitch, Gregory J. You want to know where your nymph has fled, don't you? Huh?'

'If you touch her, if you fucking harm her—'

'*She began to sing, happy in beauty, life and love and everything.*'

'Where the fuck are you?'

757

'I don't know for sure. But I see a sign that says, *All hope abandon ye who enter here.* Now where do you suppose that might be?'

The line was dead and the phone sticky in his unsteady hand.

43

SHE SAT IN THE CAR AND WATCHED HIM STEP INSIDE A PAY-phone adjacent to a darkened gas station. She thought, *Take a chance and run*, but he was only ten yards away with the gun in his hand, and even though he held it loosely at his side, he could easily aim and fire if she made a wrong move. She curled up in the passenger seat. He came back and got in behind the wheel. He slid the key into the ignition. His movements were weird, spazzy, like he had no control over his muscles. His face was sweaty, as if he'd come from a steam bath.

'I just spoke to your daddy,' he said.

'What did you say to him?'

'I had this overwhelming urge to toss a little *gasolina* on his bonfire. Now Daddy's worried sick. He's gnawing on his fingertips. He's all chewed up.'

She stared at the road ahead. She imagined her father's state of mind. 'You told him I was with you?'

'I pointed him in that general direction,' he said.

'He'll come after you. You know that.'

He laughed. '"A man, to be greatly good, must imagine

759

intensely and comprehensively. He must put himself in the place of another. The pains and pleasures of his species must become his own."'

What was he talking about? The dope in her system wasn't helping her think clearly. She was alert, but she had druggy distortions in her head, and thoughts slipped like fish through nets. Only one emotion kept coming back to her with leaden consistency: dread. Where was he taking her? What did he plan to do with her? He'd rambled on about driving her to another city and starting some kind of new life – *together*, for Christ's sake.

Like how? Lovers? Did he imagine that?

He pulled the car over. She recognized the neighborhood. The dark swath of greenery on her left was Ludlow Park, about five miles from her home. She watched him shove more speed up his nose, spilling a bunch of it in the process. His nostrils and his upper lip were white and sparkling, and dope had fallen into his lap, but he didn't notice. He was totaled.

'I could have been greatly good,' he said. 'You know what held me back? Because people are all so fucking *unworthy*. So totally immoral. Like your daddy. You know how much money he paid me?'

'I don't believe he gave you any money,' she said.

'Check it out. Fifteen K give or take.' He tugged bills from his pockets and tossed them flamboyantly in the air, a downpour of fifties and hundreds floating and falling inside the car.

'And where do you think all the dope came from, huh? He stole it for me. Because I know his big secret, nightingale.' He drew a hand across his brow.

'You're dreaming,' she said. 'All this stuff about him killing that girl. You made it up. I know my father. I know what he's capable of and what he's not.'

He didn't seem to hear her. 'I'm always dreaming. Around the next corner, somewhere over the big fucking rainbow, is the place where my dreams will come true. Who needs reality? Reality's a pisser, a downer. You, now. You're out of a dream. *I arise from dreams of thee*, you know what I'm saying? Never knock dreams, babe. They are the *stuff* of life.'

He slid his hand up her leg, touched her thigh. She thought, *I can distance myself from his damp hot touch, squeeze it out of my mind*, but then she was jolted back into the motel bedroom and the fear she'd felt when he'd produced the gun and she knew he could do anything to her he pleased. She could still feel the sting of his slap like a thorn embedded in her cheek.

What am I going to say if I get through this nightmare? I went out with this guy willingly to a motel room? I halfway imagined I wanted him to make love to me, then it all spun out of control? Was it like that? She couldn't remember with certainty. All she could bring back to mind was the memory of wanting to do something *risky*. Something different. Picking up a challenge. *Darcy comes of age, daringly.*

Stupidly.

A couple of hundred-dollar bills lay in her lap, caught in the creases of her skirt. She felt Lee's hand motionless and moist as a basking crab on her skin. Sometimes he emitted a tiny gasp, which might have been a sound of pain, she wasn't sure. He was forever dabbing his shirt-sleeve against his face, so that sometimes the wheel was unattended and the car veered to the edge of the side-walk, and she wanted to reach out to take control, but she was afraid of his reactions. He was erratic, careless, volatile.

She was unaware of the cop car behind until it flashed its rooflights and its siren whined once. Lee looked in the rear-view mirror and said, 'Say absolutely nothing. I'll do the talking. You got that?'

She twisted her head. She was blinded by the way the spinning lights fragmented the dark. She saw somebody get out of the cruiser and come towards the car in brisk strides. *Rescue me*.

The cop inclined his face and Lee rolled down the window.

'Problem, officer?' he asked.

'Please step out of the car,' the cop said.

Darcy looked at the cop's face. She'd met a few cops through her father, but this one was new to her. *Scream*, she thought – but Lee had the gun stuck in the pocket of the door and he could reach it in a second. And he'd use it. She had no doubt about that. She wondered how she might get a message to this cop. What pantomime move she might make. What sign.

'Give me one good reason why I should step out of the car.'

'Because I'm telling you.'

'Because *you're* telling me? I have every goddam right to know *why* you want me to get out of the fucking car. Or did we vote some Fascist government into power when my back was turned? Huh?'

'Get out. Just do as I say.'

Lee drew his hand across his mouth. 'What is your problem, man?'

'Don't make this any harder than it is,' the cop said. He was very young. He'd cultivated a tiny mustache to give himself a dimension of authority. But there was stress in his eyes, maybe the fear of confrontation.

'I'm asking what rights you have,' Lee said. 'Isn't that simple enough for you?'

'A car that fits the description of this one was reported stolen,' the cop said, and he laid a hand on the door handle, drew the door slightly open. 'Get your ass out. *Now*. Where I can see you.'

Darcy heard herself say, 'Wait—'

The cop seemed to notice her for the first time, and, alerted by an instinct of danger, probably baffled by the sight of so much cash lying around, reached for the gun on his hip and dragged it out, but he was cumbersome and inexperienced, and he hadn't made the right moves. Lee shoved the door open violently, and it rammed the young policeman in the gut, and then Lee had the gun in his hand and was firing it – once, twice, Darcy's head reverberated – and the cop staggered back like a man whose legs had turned to flawed glass under him. He fell down in the grassy verge of the street and lay still, and Darcy couldn't get the scream out of her throat.

She was aware of motion, the stolen car traveling at speed, Lee saying, *Oh lift me from the grass, I die, I faint, I fail*, and laughing vigorously.

'You shot him,' she said.

'Yeah I shot him. So?'

'You *killed* him.' She had a wild teeter-totter feeling in her stomach. She could see the cop falling even now, and the dread she'd been feeling deepened. She'd never seen a man shot before. She didn't know what to do with the image of the cop, where to put it, how to stick it into a compartment where she wouldn't keep seeing it.

Lee said, 'Maybe he's dead, maybe he's not. The thing is, it doesn't matter, it doesn't belong inside my equation. Do you know what I'm saying? He was in the wrong goddam place at the wrong goddam time. Some people have a knack for that. Some people just don't see the fucking boundaries. They want to get inside your life and eat away at your plans like maggots. They want to keep you squashed and down.'

He might have been speaking in a language of lost

763

tongues. She didn't understand what he was talking about. He was driving through neighborhoods she didn't recognize, heading for a destination only he knew. Then he stopped the car, and sat back with his eyes shut and a pained frown on his face and he groaned. 'Oh *shit,* this is bad, this is really downright kick-ass *baaad.*' He put a hand flat to the side of his skull. 'It's like some fucking monstrous kid who's been given a set of drums for Christmas, and the little cocksucker won't stop beating on them.' He was sweating so profusely he might have been ice melting. His eyelids fluttered. 'Somebody take his fucking drums away.'

She thought, *I could run now while he's like this.* But, as if he'd read her mind, he pressed the electronic door lock in the key. She heard all the doors of the car click shut.

He said, 'You stay with me. Don't fuck with me like that cop back there.'

'I'll stay,' she said.

'Yeah, you'll stay. Damn right.' He groaned, inclined his face, pressed his fingertips firmly into his scalp. 'Because I need you.' And he began rambling about sea blooms and the sapless foliage of the ocean, losing it completely. Sometimes he punctuated his words with a small laugh, which wasn't exactly a joyful sound, but sad in some way.

Then he appeared to gain control of himself. She couldn't decide which was more dangerous: these times of composure or the flights he took into lunacy. He turned his face and smiled at her in a woozy way. 'We'll look back at all this one day from a long distance, and we'll laugh,' he said.

'Laugh at what, Lee? You're not even going to get me out of this city. My father will have cops everywhere looking for me.'

'Your father the whore-killer,' he said. 'Your father,

764

big-time guardian of morality. This is right, this is wrong. Don't do this, don't do that. Who the fuck does he think he is? Your father couldn't handle traffic duty, for Christ's sake. Your father couldn't even write a goddam parking ticket. He's through. He's all washed up. Maybe he'll find a job as a security guard working the night shift at some piss-ant factory. If he's lucky.'

'Stop,' she said. 'Just *stop*.'

'Your daddy's so much shit. He's like something came down a sewage pipe. He's waste. He's human crap that happens to carry a badge. The truth upset you, huh? Is that it? Hey, face it, people don't ever come up to expectations. You think the sun shines out their ass, but that's only because you're wearing gold-tinted lenses. You see what you want to see. You blind yourself.'

She wasn't going to listen. She didn't have to hear this. The man Lee was talking about wasn't anybody she knew, certainly not her father.

He turned the key in the ignition.

'Where are we going?' she asked.

'Sightseeing,' was all he said.

44

SAMSA HEARD HIS FOOTSTEPS CLATTER ON THE MARBLE floor, and the strange hush of the vast interior of City Hall, unlit except for a few pale lamps in the lobby. High black spaces hung above him, and the central stairway terminated in midair as if it were unfinished. Eve, hurrying after him, might have been nothing more substantial than an elongated shadow he cast. He rushed in the direction of the department offices, taking the stairs rapidly. He needed help if he was going to find Darcy.

Duff was leaning against the corner of his desk with a phone in his hand. There was motion in the rooms behind Duff: the night cops doing paperwork at their desks, a handcuffed guy with a sky-blue bandanna knotted on his head being booked. The air smelled of stewed coffee and the afterburn of the absent Fogue's cheroots. Stephen Rebb, yawning, wandered into view.

This is the high noon of my panic, Samsa thought.

Duff put his phone down as soon as he saw Samsa. 'I was just trying to call you, Lieutenant. I don't know if this relates to your daughter, but we have an officer down—'

'Who?'

'Kid called Ron Askew.'

Samsa didn't know the name. 'How bad?'

'He took two slugs, one in the stomach, the other in the shoulder. He's on his way to County. He's conscious, but kind of in and out.'

'Come to the point, Duff.' Samsa tried to check his impatience, but he was beyond etiquette.

'Askew stopped a car reportedly stolen. A white Ford Taurus. The driver shot him. Askew says there was a girl in the car. Short hair, brown, brown-to-black. Askew says she resembled the description we issued of Darcy. The driver was a blond guy of about thirty, who acted like he was stoned out of his skull.'

'Boyle,' Samsa said.

'Boyle? *Lee* Boyle?' Rebb asked. 'Your kid might be riding around with *Lee* Boyle?'

'I don't think there's any *might* involved, Rebb. Don't ask me how it happened, but it did. That's all I know.'

'Like a kidnap thing?' Rebb asked.

'I don't know if it's a kidnap thing. I don't know what it is.'

Samsa looked at Eve's concerned face, then at Duff and Rebb, and beyond them to the cops in the other rooms, some of whom had become aware of the lieutenant's presence and were listening.

'Where did this happen?' he asked.

'Stafford, where it intersects Dolores Drive,' Duff said.

Dolores Drive. He knew where it was located. He knew where it led.

He headed at once for the stairs. Eve followed him up. He crossed the lobby, stepped out into the street. It was empty, but it was an emptiness that assaulted him, coming at him in brutal waves of silence. He had the feeling the city was one he'd never visited in this lifetime, and yet it was familiar in the unsettling way of dreamscapes.

He got inside Eve's car, closed the door. She sat behind the wheel.

'Boyle didn't actually *say* she was with him, did he?' Eve asked.

You want to know where your nymph has fled, don't you? Huh? It didn't take a whole lot of literary analysis to understand he was talking about Darcy. 'She's with him all right. I don't have any doubts about that, Eve. What really worries the hell out of me right now is his record of violence.'

Samsa stopped dead on the last word of his sentence, remembering what Rebb had said about a girl called Nancy, how Boyle had beaten her so badly she'd ended up in hospital. And he imagined Boyle threatening Darcy, hurting her. He tried to excise that thought.

'What do you imagine happened?' Eve asked. 'He went to your house, lured Darcy away on some pretext?'

'He's smooth when he wants to be,' Samsa said. 'I can see where he might be impressive, if you're a fifteen-year-old girl. Maybe Darcy went along with him willingly. I don't know.' He recalled something from Boyle's rap-sheet. *Sex with a minor.* He had an image of Boyle and Darcy locked together, Boyle fucking her. It took some effort to eject this picture from his mind, but somewhere at the back of his head it continued to unwind, like a video cassette playing in the next room.

Eve said, 'He could have used force.'

'He could have.' Samsa tried to picture Boyle calling at the house, grabbing Darcy, hustling her off inside a car. But she'd have yelled, drawn attention to the situation, and the Petersons next door, neighborhood eagles who missed nothing, would have heard her and called the cops.

'We'll look in the general neighborhood of Dolores Drive to start with,' she said.

'Fine,' he said. Where else? It was all they had to go on. He pictured Dolores Drive, darkness on either side of it. Why that direction? Why there into the quicksands of his own life?

Eve drove quickly. Samsa, dry-mouthed and tense beyond his experience, pondered the destruction Boyle had wreaked on his life. It was like surveying driftwood on a lonesome stretch of beach. He stared ahead, tried to concentrate only on his daughter. But there was an unfinished conversation with Eve, and even if he would have preferred to avoid it, he drew a deep breath and said, 'You were saying something before about my honesty, I remember. You were talking about your disappointment. I guess you want to pick up the threads of that?'

'It can wait.'

'I don't want it to wait,' he said.

'This isn't the time, Greg.'

'Make it the time,' he said. 'I can't take your moods any more, Eve.'

'Okay. That's what you want.' She removed something from her pocket and flashed it in front of him.

He didn't want to see whatever she was holding.

She shoved it toward him, and he squinted at it, then closed his eyes, searching his mind for some tiny corner where he might be safe. But all he could see was his daughter's face, and all he could hear was Lee Boyle's voice: *All hope abandon ye who enter here.*

45

DARCY SHUT HER EYES AND PRESSED HER KNUCKLES INTO HER lids, seeing bright visual flashes, and thinking they had a name, *phosphenes*, something like that, and if she just concentrated on unusual words she'd be fine, she wouldn't need to listen to what Lee was saying.

But his words filtered through anyhow. 'The way I see it, they'll love you. They'll wait in long lines for you, babe. I imagine you in a wine-colored velvet skirt, not too short, and maybe a pricey lace blouse. No see-through crap. Something with class. And we'll stay away from the streets, because it's a snake-pit down there. It's going to be hotels, good hotels. I don't want you out there with the goddam riff-raff. You're better than that.'

She peered at him through slatted fingers. His face was white and glistening. The gun lay in his lap. The leather bag with the dope sat on the console. Much of the dope was spilled. Money was strewn inside the car. Everything was chaos and displacement.

'This is a fresh beginning. Gleaming spires in the distance. Lee is moving up in the world. Lee will have a kidskin Filofax and a state-of-the-fucking-art cellular phone and a car that has taste written all over it.'

She saw this future he was talking about. He couldn't possibly be serious. But he was. He was animated and purposeful and his voice was resolute, and he was chopping the air in karate fashion with one hand to emphasize everything he was saying.

'You think—? You're *crazy*,' she said.

'I have been told that on more than one occasion, nightingale. Always by wrong-headed people lacking perception. People who cut me down, took pot-shots at me. The trees are thick with snipers. My head's always in somebody's cross-sights. Not this time, because Lee has had *enough*. You understand what I'm saying? Lee takes no more shit.'

She was traveling through another person's nightmare, the strands of somebody else's reality – or in Lee's case no reality at all, but some kind of deformed relationship he had with the world.

Phosphorite.

Just keep the words coming, Darcy. Just fill your head with words.

He said, 'I'm not saying it's going to be easy at first. I realize that. You'll probably hate yourself, you'll definitely hate *me*, but we'll get round that. The trick is, you don't think about what you're doing, you just numb yourself. After a while it comes naturally to you. It's just a job you do.'

It comes naturally. Going to hotel rooms to fuck strangers. She pictured herself taking her clothes off, fat men pawing her, slobbering over her, screwing her, she thought of dirt under fingernails and sweat and bad breath.

'And if any of the customers step out of line – hey, I'm there to see you're protected. I'll look after you all the way. And we won't work it too hard, we'll do it nice and easy.'

Yes, Lee. Whatever you say, Lee. She looked from the window and wondered about her father, where he was, why he wasn't looking for her, why she didn't hear the wail of sirens. She saw houses float past, and then abruptly there was darkness and the lit streets were left somewhere behind and the car was traveling through a black wormhole in the texture of space.

Phosphate.

But the words weren't working. She couldn't play this game any longer. She couldn't hide from her predicament. She looked at the oil-black landscape on either side of the road, which was narrow and unmarked, and she realized where she was, and that the city was slipping away behind her, her father receding, the notion of safety diminishing.

'You're a natural,' he was saying. 'The way you walk. From the hips, you know what I mean? With a little pelvic thrust that says, Hey, guys, consider it a privilege just to *breathe* the same air as me. And that mouth of yours – people will think you stole it from an angel. We'll need to color the hair, I figure. Red? No, I don't think red. One of those offbeat colors – purple? A streak of gold? Not too much, though, because we don't want you looking tacky. When you strut inside a room I want men going fucking wild with desire. I want them drooling because a goddess has condescended to visit.'

He was expelling his words like tiny torpedoes of air. She was looking into the darkness, thinking, thinking, fearful, seeing the headlights gleam on the blacktop. Humor him. Go along with him. Crossing him now was dangerous. *Think.* Nobody's going to help you out of this. You're on your own.

She said, 'It all sounds terrific, Lee.'

'It *is* terrific, no two ways about it,' he said. 'First time

I saw you, I thought, She's the one, she's my girl,' and he reached out to touch the back of her hand. 'Or maybe it was when I heard your voice. What the hell. It doesn't matter, does it?'

She couldn't stand the feel of his skin. She was aware of blackness zooming past. Do something. But what? The only thing that came to mind was risky and dangerous, but she was beyond thinking of any consequences, all she wanted was to disrupt a sequence of events that in Boyle's mind was inevitable. Becoming a whore. His.

Just do it.

She hesitated a moment and then thought, *Go for it, now or never*, and made a grab for the wheel, thinking she could make the car swerve, maybe crash it, derail everything somehow. But it was a hapless effort, doomed from the start because Boyle anticipated her. He was too quick, he struck her wrist with the hard edge of his hand, and she pulled her arm back to her side.

He braked, turned to her with a fierce look. 'What the *fuck* do you think you're trying to do? You could have killed us both, for Christ's sake. Did you imagine you could somehow get away? Huh? Some crazy notion of freedom entered that little head of yours?' He smiled suddenly. 'Oh, you are precious, nightingale. Totally precious. Devious and sly. You've got the instincts of a whore. See, you're halfway there already. Just don't *ever* think about fucking with me again. Any time a similar stunt pops into your head, take my advice and strangle it at birth.'

He laughed in a discordant fashion, and turned off the blacktop at a place where the incline into the field was gradual and easy, and then he was driving through long stalks of grass that slowed the progress of the car, and straight ahead was a big tree made white by the glossy glare of the headlights.

'Now the sightseeing,' he said. 'And after that we move move move, *all hastening onward*, and no more fucking *games*. One more off-the-wall prank and you're a dead little girl and Daddy's going to have to arrange a funeral. Think about that, nightingale.'

46

SAMSA LET THE PRINT SLIP OUT OF HIS HAND. IT FELL DOWN the side of his seat and he didn't reach to retrieve it, didn't want to touch it.

'They've been blackmailing you,' Eve said. 'Gold and Lee Boyle.'

'*Gold?* I didn't know Gold was involved.' Gold and Boyle conspiring in the fissures of the city: Gold taking the furtive picture, Boyle exploiting it.

'I can just *about* understand you picking up that girl. Just about. And I can see how your reputation would be compromised seriously after the accident. And maybe I'm being naïve and idealistic, but what really blows me out the water is the fact you didn't tell the truth from the beginning, because in the long run it's easier—'

'*Easier?* When you're faced with the dead body of a young girl you don't always make the right choices, Eve. All that training you get to stay composed in the face of pressure, it's nothing, it goes haywire. You create a lie and suddenly everything's built around it, and you can't see a way out because you can't go back and undo it—'

'By covering it up, you *compounded* it, for Christ's sake. You got yourself tangled up in this whole diabolic mess, going through the motions of an investigation you knew was a total fiction. And now Darcy's out there . . .'

He laid his cheek against the window of the car. What did he feel anyway? A release? Or a darker guilt? It didn't matter now.

She said, 'I thought seriously about never mentioning this to you and just choking it down and going on as if I'd never learned about it in the first place. But I can't live like that, Greg. I'd see you every day. There would be this effort at pretense, and I wouldn't know how to carry that off.'

'You'll go to Brodsky,' he said.

'That's not up to me,' she replied.

She had an expression he'd never seen before on her face – pinched and sorrowful, and her green eyes were a shade darker. There were right ways to do things, and wrong ways, and she knew the difference. *And you, Samsa, in the most terrible overheated moment of your life, you forgot.*

Eve said, 'I'll ask for a transfer if it comes down to that. I'll make up some excuse: I need a change of scenery, I'm tired of homicide, whatever. But I won't tell him what I know, Greg. It's up to you to straighten it out.'

He looked at the street ahead. The city was dead space in which his daughter was lost. He half imagined she'd suddenly materialize in the darkness unharmed, she'd come strolling along the sidewalk, that Boyle's phone call was just a cruel hoax.

'I had you up on a pedestal,' Eve said.

'Where I didn't belong.'

'More naïvety, I guess. That was my mistake.'

'We all make them,' he said.

'I thought . . . well, maybe we had the germ of something. Stupid me. *Naïve* me.'

'And now it's changed. What happened between us is just something hit by a fucking truck and bleeding at the side of the road. Is that how you see it?'

'I should have left it alone,' she said. 'I shouldn't have gone back to see Gold, I shouldn't have looked inside his goddam darkroom. The timer on his developer was buzzing and I keep hearing it—'

'You did what you had to,' he said.

'And what good has that done?'

'You can sleep nights,' he said.

'I'm not so sure. How much has this cost you so far?'

He told her.

She said, 'You gave him twenty-five thousand dollars. You stole State's evidence and *handed* it over to him. And now he's got your daughter. This guy has it in for you in a big way.'

I killed his girl, Samsa thought. *He thinks I still owe him. And the last installment of the debt is Darcy.*

'You forgot one simple truth,' she said. 'Blackmailers always come back, Greg. Always.'

'I didn't forget it,' he said.

'You hoped he'd just *evaporate*?'

'I don't know what I hoped. Maybe he'd just see the well was dry and take a hike. I don't *know*.'

She drove for a few moments in silence. 'Gold is terrified. He'll testify against Boyle in the matter of extortion. He wants very badly to be law-abiding. Basically he doesn't want to be a piece of gay white ass in a prison.'

Samsa wasn't interested in what Gold would or wouldn't do. 'There's only one thing on my mind right now. Everything else can keep.' He looked at her, searched her face for some tiny glimmer of sympathy, but found none.

She said, 'I keep wondering what you would have done if I hadn't gone back to see Gold. Would you have kept up this masquerade? God, I want to believe you'd have come to your senses, because basically I always considered you a decent man, Greg. I'll never *really* know now, will I?'

'Then we're in the same boat,' he said. He touched her hand and she permitted the contact a moment before she drew away.

The car was beginning to rise up through narrow streets in the direction of Dolores Drive. He glanced back and saw the city spread out below in spidery interstices of light the color of jaundiced flesh.

Dolores Drive. It was a narrow blacktop that sliced through the badlands where everything in his life had gone wrong. He thought of the great dark unkempt mass of the Purchase property that lay on either side of Dolores.

And he wondered why Lee Boyle had taken Darcy into that vicinity.

Dear God.

If Boyle had taken Darcy anywhere close to the Purchase property, he could have only one reason for doing so.

Samsa could think of no other.

Boyle was redressing the balance of things as he perceived them. Squaring the accounts. The debt paid in full.

We're even now, Samsa.

He leaned forward in his seat, staring ahead, seeing nothing, listening to his own roaring pulses. The field filled his head. Damp grass, a branch cracking and falling, wheels spinning, metal crunching against wood.

'Pull over,' he said.

'Pull over? Why?'

'Just do it, Eve.'

'I don't see the reason for—'

778

'Pull over, I said. Here.'

'Okay, *Lieutenant*,' she said. 'Whatever you say.'

She braked, looked at him in a puzzled way.

'I'll drive,' he said. 'Change places with me.'

She shrugged, stepped out of the car reluctantly and slammed the door.

He slid his body behind the wheel, saw Eve walk round the hood to the passenger side. He waited until she was reaching for the handle of the door and then slammed his foot on the gas and drove forward. In the rear-view mirror he saw her standing in the middle of the street, a diminishing figure with one arm raised in a gesture – of what? Anger? Bewilderment?

It didn't matter what she felt. He was the one who'd constructed this nightmare. He was the one who'd have to go into the depths of his own creation. Nobody else. It was beyond police business now, outside the law, it lay in that uncertain territory where no book of procedure dictated the rules.

He was alone.

47

THE FORD STAMMERED TO A HALT ABOUT FIFTY YARDS FROM the tree. Boyle cursed, turned the key, heard the engine hack. He twisted the key again, then again, nothing. Out of gas, okay, that wasn't going to be a problem. He wouldn't allow it to become one. It was a minor inconvenience. Don't blow it up into something enormous.

'What are you going to do now, Lee?' she asked. She looked into his blue eyes by what scant moonlight there was, and they were cold, like icicles hammered all the way into his skull.

'I'll steal another goddam car,' he said. 'There's a whole suburb over there filled with them,' and he pointed into the distance, where dim streetlamps were visible way beyond the foliage. Then he swung round and kicked a front tire of the Ford in a petulant way and said, 'The fucking fuel gauge is probably faulty.'

He stopped himself. Waste of energy kicking rubber. He'd forgotten why he'd driven down here in the first place, then it came back to him, and he gripped Darcy by the wrist and walked to the tree. 'The guided tour,' he said. 'This is the spot where your daddy crashed his car. You can see the gouge.'

She found herself staring at the tree. She didn't want to look. Didn't want to listen to him.

'Touch it. Try to picture Daddy smacking into this. Imagine a little girl dead.'

'No—'

'Just do what I fucking *say*, for Christ's sake.' He seized her hand and forced it against the trunk, and she didn't have the strength to resist.

She encountered a jagged indentation with her fingertips. Something moved in the crevice – an ant, a spider. She drew back, alarmed. She watched Lee stick his fingers into the gash. Ants, scores of them, criss-crossed his hand. He imagined them working their way into his flesh, tunneling into his veins. He thought of himself as a building occupied by busy black tenants always making demands. He brushed them off.

He walked around the tree. A large branch lay some feet away. 'This probably came off when he whacked into the trunk.' He stared into the distance and had the strange feeling that just beyond the range of his vision a hooded figure lingered in the bushes, one crooked finger beckoning from the fold of a long sleeve, a voice saying, *Step right this way, Lee. I'll take you to a place nobody ever comes back from.*

'Your daddy dumped her like a piece of trash. Just walked off the scene. Free as a bird. You think I'm making this up?'

She shook her head. *I don't know what you're making up and what you're not*, she thought. *All I know is you scare me to death. All I know is I want to be a million miles away from you, a galaxy away.*

He grabbed her arm again and pushed her forcefully back in the direction of the car. He began to rummage inside the car, gathering money together and stuffing it in his pockets, rescuing his dope, some of which lay spilled on the floor and the console. Working quickly. Gotta move. Get out of here. Time is an eagle.

She watched him move around in a frantic way. He raised to his nose a little pile of speed balanced on the back of one hand and sniffed deeply. How could he keep doing that stuff on and on?

He finished collecting his money and then –

– wowee, here it comes, the rush, the familiar big jolt. He had the feeling that his skeletal structure was changing, as if pins had been implanted to hold his bones together, knobs of steel, little screws. As if he'd undergone surgery, his skin peeled back, men in surgical masks screwing bolts into his exposed skeleton. His skull had been reassembled too, the cracks fused together with thin metallic stitches, but they weren't holding, they were beginning to come undone, and with each pop there was a tiny hand-grenade burst. When he stood upright from his bending position, he heard the pins creaking inside him and his skull splitting open.

He shivered and rubbed his hands together briskly, thinking how even the bones of his fingers felt odd, like they were steel inserts under his skin. He licked his dry lips. Numb, tasted of stone. 'Now it's time for some grand theft auto. Then we're history, kid. We are truly *history*.'

And he bent down, groped around in the dark below the exposed roots of the tree, then rose with something in his fist. He looked at the girl and said, 'Can I trust you?'

She nodded her head slowly. She couldn't see what he had in his hand. He concealed it, tucking it in his waistband, his shirt hanging over it.

'Can I? *Can I?*' He grabbed a sleeve of her blouse, pulled her close to his body and listened to the heavy way she breathed and felt how her heart thudded. *This is the power.*

'Yes,' she whispered.

'Yes what?'

'Yes. You can trust me.'

He gripped her hand, twisted her fingers back until she made a low moaning sound. 'Again,' he said.

'You can trust me, Lee. I *swear . . .*'

He released her and thought, *Not for a moment, nightingale.*

48

HE DROVE AT HIGH SPEED THROUGH STOP AND YIELD SIGNS, saw the dull moon rush behind clouds. He parked at the edge of the blacktop and scanned the expanse of the field. The property was a motionless sea that had sucked all light out of the sky.

He scrambled down the slope.

He wanted moon. He wanted light.

I want Darcy back.

At the bottom of the slope he found himself ankle-deep in the puddle where the girl had died.

He'd hoped never to return to this place. Yet here he was.

His shoes squelched. He walked through the grass, saw the Ford when he was about thirty yards from it. The door on the driver's side hung open and the interior light burned a muted yellow-brown. He approached quietly, carefully.

No Boyle. No evidence of Darcy.

He saw some dazzling little swirls of white dust on the console: spilled speed. A key dangled from the ignition.

He looked at the instrument panel, saw the red glow of the battery and oil-pressure lights, and the fuel gauge, which registered a bright red E.

Boyle had run out of gas.

Samsa backed away from the car. He touched the gun holstered at the base of his spine. Reassurance. He circled the big black tree slowly, approached the fallen branch, half imagining he'd stumble across his daughter's body. His breath was like a dense gas in his throat, and he had the shivery feeling of trespassing on somebody's grave. Boyle wants to close the circle, wants a reckoning, and so he brings Darcy to this specific place in this wilderness because he has a demented notion about the poetry of justice, and it has to be as neat and exact as a fucking couplet, two girls dead in the same godforsaken field.

Samsa stepped quietly round the fallen branch. The silence was huge and overwhelming. The sullen secretive hour before dawn. Everything sleeps.

Please don't let anything happen to her.

If it's not too late already.

Head inclined, he listened for a sigh, a twig breaking, the whisper of clothing against stalks of grass. Anything. But the dark was still and mute and unforgiving. He stared at the lights of Chackstone. They were fuzzy and faraway.

There was a brief shifting of cloud and a sparse milky light spilled across the landscape, but it lasted only long enough to glaze the tree where the Chrysler had come to a battered halt, then was drawn back behind cloud cover.

Samsa moved away from the tree. The dark was crowded with apprehensions, flutters of awful anxiety. In some places the grass grew knee-high and parted grudgingly when he forced his way through. He had the odd feeling he was somehow seeking another version of himself in this wild meadow, a spectral Samsa who'd taken a wrong turning. He wanted to catch this phantom and warn him. Do it differently, make another decision.

He paused, tried to empty his mind of extraneous stuff. *Nothing else matters here except Darcy.* Concentrate on her. But suddenly he couldn't picture her face clearly, couldn't bring her to mind. He experienced a thrum of alarm. She was fading away, disappearing. He quickened his pace now, pressured by the sudden fear that Boyle may have killed Darcy and concealed her in an obscure corner of this field, and then entered the subdivision in search of a car to steal. Maybe he was already long gone. Maybe he'd never be found. Maybe he'd vanish into a remote part of the continent, another name, an assumed identity . . .

Or just maybe Darcy was still alive, and Boyle had other plans for her that Samsa couldn't begin to guess. Consider that. Yes. Why not. This slender thread of hope propelled him, and he started to run. The lights of the subdivision burned a little brighter beyond the trees and the cedar fence. The grass impeded him and he had to force himself, *push* himself. The bandage around his hand had unraveled almost entirely and flapped as he moved. The trees at the edge of the property were a hundred yards away, and he could see orange street lamps beyond, the tops of red-shingled rooftops, chimney pots. He was going as fast as he could now, conscious of the wet sound his shoes made and the creaking of blades.

'You make way too much noise, *amigo*.'

Samsa stopped dead. He hadn't seen Boyle emerge from the trees. He'd been too focused on the lamps, the fence, finding Darcy. Boyle's shirt hung outside his pants and he had a gun held firmly in his hand.

'Where is she?' Samsa asked.

'Paternal instincts,' Boyle said. 'I wonder what they feel like.'

'Where is she, Boyle?'

'Marriage and babies don't come into my general equation. Maybe when I'm old and wasted and drooling in front of a fire on some fucking freezing wintry day, and my pants are damp with piss, I'll wish I had a daughter that came to visit. You think that's likely, Samsa?'

'Where the fuck is Darcy?'

'Darcy, Darcy,' Boyle said. 'You should have taken better care of her, Samsa. You don't seem to do too well when it comes to little girls in general, do you?'

Samsa's urge was to rush Boyle, shatter his face, blow after blow after blow. Destruction. But Boyle had that gun in his hand.

'That dope has done a fearful number on me, Samsa. What was in it? My heart has been doing loops. It's like there's this dangerous little stunt pilot in my goddam chest. And *he's* on speed as well—'

'One more time, Boyle. *Where's my daughter?*'

Boyle came nearer. He placed a hand on Samsa's shoulder. '*Whither fled Lamia?*'

Samsa said, 'Spare me the goddam quotes,' and moved slightly, but Boyle's hand remained on his shoulder.

'You know they're looking for me,' Boyle said. 'Everybody's looking for me: you, your cop buddies, Jimmy Plumm, two goons despatched by a guy called Crassman. Fuck only knows who else. I am being *hounded.*'

Samsa thought, *He's gone, scattered.* Tiny white flecks of spit adhered to the corners of Boyle's lips. He was moving his jawbone from side to side as if it were locked too tight. He looked unhealthy, affected by a general air of extreme edginess, and there was a touch of desperation in his dry voice. The hand on Samsa's shoulder fluttered and trembled. He considered the gun in his holster, weighed his options, which were seriously limited by the pistol in

Boyle's fist. And Boyle, primed like a detonating device, had to be handled with enormous care.

'You could always give up,' Samsa said.

'As in surrender?'

'You could give me the gun.'

Boyle tightened his fingers on Samsa's shoulder. 'It's not like I don't appreciate the offer, sport. The thing is, it doesn't fit my future plans.'

'You don't have a future.'

'Oh you're wrong, you are so *very* wrong. Me and Darcy have all kinds of plans. She's such a willing girl, Greg.'

Samsa struggled to keep the tone of his voice calm. 'What does that mean exactly?'

Boyle brought his face very close to Samsa's and winked. Samsa saw the lid lower over an eye that was slightly bloodshot, and then open again. The gesture was furtive and obscene, insinuating that a sexual transaction had taken place between Darcy and Lee Boyle. Bad pictures rushed into Samsa's head, and he tried to shove them aside, but they created a disturbing kaleidoscope of images, flesh superimposed on flesh. His daughter in this creep's bed. That intimate locking of parts. He labored to hang on to whatever control he had of himself, because it would be fruitless to enrage the man, and kamikaze to strike out at him.

Boyle said, 'The circular nature of things is downright fucking astonishing at times. You took my girl away from me. Now I've taken yours. There's a power in nature, a balance. I feel it at this very moment. I'm standing here and I can feel the whole field hum under my feet, and I'm overawed by this dynamo, Gregory. I am flooded with notions of a lovely symmetry. You feel it, too?'

He's tuned to other dimensions, Samsa thought. Mad

rooms where he can't be reached. 'I'm not blessed with your insights,' he said.

Boyle dropped his hand finally from Samsa's shoulder and stared out across the meadow as if he'd heard something move in the black grass. His eyes probed the dark and he frowned. 'They're out there. They're coming toward me. You hear them? Listen. Listen real hard. Tell me you don't hear people out there in the grass.'

'Sure. I hear them.'

'Don't patronize me, Greg.'

'I said I *hear* them. People moving. Voices whispering. Yeah. I hear them.' Samsa had the odd feeling of standing on the threshold of Boyle's speed-afflicted fucked-up world, a place of derangements and bizarre anomalies, where silences were translated into sounds, light into dark, life into death. He watched Boyle wipe the back of his hand with his arm, and just for a moment what he felt wasn't loathing but some mutant form of pity, a sensation that came up out of nowhere and surprised him. *He isn't worth it. This is a weakness in yourself, a chamber of misplaced charity in your heart. Boyle shot a young cop, blackmailed you, ruined you, stole your daughter. He isn't worth pity.*

Boyle said, 'This fucking stunt pilot insists on flying his little plane again,' and he laid a hand upon his chest, and worked his jaw from side to side again, like a man who has just had gum-stiffening oral surgery. He inclined his head toward the center of the field, his expression that of somebody listening very hard to hear through reams of static and interference.

'Your best bet is to give me the gun,' Samsa said, 'and tell me where Darcy is.'

'Assuming she's anywhere,' Boyle said. 'You bandy the present tense around too freely, Lieutenant.'

'What the hell are you trying to say?'

Boyle smiled a little thinly. 'Am I getting past and present all mixed up, huh? What do you think?'

Assuming she's anywhere, Samsa thought. Boyle was fueling his dread. His worst fear was one he didn't want to confront – that Boyle's realities had collided, and in one of them Darcy was dead, in another she was still alive, and he didn't know which to believe. He was unsteady on his feet for a moment. He felt heat rush to his head and heard himself say, 'They're getting closer, Boyle. I'm catching all kinds of sounds now. You haven't got a chance in hell.' And he thought how easy it was to believe that the grass concealed figures fanning out in all directions, how easy to enter into Boyle's whacked perceptions.

Boyle said, 'Shut up, let me think. I can't think with you droning on. Jesus Christ.'

'Listen,' Samsa said. 'Somebody just said your name. Did you catch that? "There's Lee Boyle."'

'Shut the fuck up.' Boyle raised a hand and, open-palmed, smacked Samsa across the side of the face.

A whining went through Samsa's ears like a chill wind. He wouldn't listen to it, he'd ignore it. He'd keep jerking Boyle's chain, pushing him, niggling him. Screw the risk. 'Didn't you hear it, Lee? They'll shoot you. They don't give a damn about you. But I can promise you safety. I won't let them kill you, Lee. You have my word.'

'I don't need the word of some fucking hypocrite cop. I'm still in charge of my destiny. I am *this* close to pulling the trigger, sport.'

'Before you reach a decision about shooting me, just tell me where Darcy is.'

'And put your mind at rest?'

'You're running out of time,' and Samsa glanced back, seeing a half-assed moon pock the grass. 'Did you hear that, Lee? The distinct sound of somebody chambering cartridges. *Click click click*. One cartridge, two, three.'

Boyle stared into the reaches of darkness. 'Yeah, I heard.'

'They're not far away, Lee.'

Boyle said, 'I hear them, I fucking *hear* them. Don't keep reminding me.'

'Thirty, forty yards tops—'

'I said don't keep *reminding* me.' Boyle raised a hand and swung it against the side of Samsa's neck, a chopping blow Samsa had no time to avoid. He felt the thud of Boyle's fist, and for a second he was dizzy and listed to one side. But he wasn't going down. He was determined to keep his balance, pain be damned.

Lee Boyle pointed his gun toward the field – the big dark silence he'd populated with figments. Then he directed the weapon at Samsa, but there was a look of uncertainty on his face. His attention, already fractured by chemicals, was divided between what he believed lay out there in darkness, and Samsa.

Samsa said, 'Shoot me, *sport*, and you're a dead man. Because my colleagues hidden out there are wired for instant response. Besides, they've taken a very serious dislike to you.'

Boyle, the sweat on his white face silvered by the moon, turned his head this way and that like an animal perplexed by an array of dangerous scents.

'Hand me the gun, Lee. Do yourself a favor.'

Boyle pointed the pistol at Samsa, then swiveled it once again toward the wilderness, then back at Samsa.

'This is something of a *bind* for you, Lee,' Samsa said, and thought, *Where is Darcy?* The question lodged in his head like a conundrum he couldn't solve, didn't even want to entertain.

Boyle pressed his hand flat upon his chest, and his face contorted as if he'd swallowed something sour, and his mouth opened slackly. 'Shit, this is *hurting* again. And I'm

791

oozing pints of sweat. Did you spike that dope, Samsa? Did you say to yourself, I'll poison this ice before I give it to him? Just a few drops of something toxic, not enough so he'd notice immediately? More a cumulative effect, huh?'

'You need treatment, Lee. You need your stomach pumped—'

'You poisoned me, didn't you? You put bad shit into the speed.'

Samsa said, 'Maybe it was bad to begin with. And you're OD'ing.'

Boyle grimaced, pushed the gun into the side of Samsa's neck. 'You motherfucker. You stepped on the dope with *poison*.'

Samsa felt the discomfort of steel pressed against the muscles in his neck. Stress. Cold fear.

'What is it, Samsa? Arsenic? Is that what you used? Weedkiller? Something like that?'

'You've lost it, Lee,' Samsa said. 'You've really lost it.'

Boyle prodded the gun harder into Samsa's neck. 'So have you, *amigo*. Welcome to the chump's club.' And he laughed for no reason Samsa could tell, a dry back-of-the-throat laugh that sounded like sand being shifted around.

Boyle took a few steps back and lowered the gun from Samsa's neck. He doubled over, clutching his chest. 'This goddam pain is *crucifying* me. I can't breathe.'

'Let me get you to a hospital.'

'Stay away, don't come near me.'

'Give me the gun—'

Boyle fired the weapon wildly. A flash, a roar. The shot split the air and the dark was suddenly filled with movement: crows cawing as they flapped across the field. Boyle went down on one knee, head inclined forward. He was breathing in a labored manner, and his shirt was soaked black with perspiration. Samsa again thought of reaching

792

for his own holstered weapon, but Boyle was still holding the gun aimed generally in his direction.

'I won't miss next time,' Boyle said.

Samsa, deafened by the gunfire, said, 'They'll move in now, Lee. You know that, don't you? I can hear them coming. Listen.'

Lee Boyle raised his face toward the field. His eyes had the glazed look of a man in serious pain. 'Yeah, I hear them, Samsa.'

It was a moment of inattention on Boyle's part, a tiny window of chance, and Samsa understood he had to take it, because it might never open again. He moved quickly, crossing the space between himself and Boyle. Boyle turned his head, saw Samsa rush him, brought up his gun. Samsa launched a foot, clipped the pistol, watched it fly from Boyle's hand, then reached back to draw his own gun. But Boyle reacted with unexpected haste. He lunged at Samsa's legs, caught them, caused Samsa to lose his balance and fall into the grass. And then Boyle was on top of him even as he pulled something out of his waistband, something that had been concealed by his overhanging shirt, and he whacked it down toward Samsa, who twisted his face away at the last possible second, hearing a *whish* of air, seeing the pale orange-tinted implement in Boyle's hand. Boyle raised it again, and Samsa, trapped by Boyle's surprising strength, kicked and shoved to get out from under the man. But he was locked in place and couldn't reach his weapon, and the implement, a hard metal rod, was coming down again, and this time it struck his scalp and he felt a searing sensation and his field of vision was dark around the edges. Boyle struck him again. Samsa felt the metal split the skin of his cheek and thought, *He's killing me*.

He caught Boyle's arm, struggled to keep it from coming down another time, pushed with all the force he could collect, muscles straining. He looked into Boyle's eyes, listened to the strange angry whimpering Boyle made, and he felt a rage equivalent to Boyle's, and realized he was imprisoned with Boyle in the same raw airless space, beyond any considerations except survival.

'Your little girl fucks like a well-oiled machine, Samsa.'

Boyle's broken whisper was accompanied by a small stressed smile. Samsa shifted his hand from Boyle's arm, caught the man's lower lip and yanked it downward with his fingers. Then he tried to raise his bandaged hand and force it into Boyle's eyes, but the hand was as useful as a damaged paw, and Boyle pulled his face back beyond reach.

'Your little girl's a whore. She blew me, had me doing fucking cartwheels of joy. Almond suck *your* cock, Lieutenant?'

A whore. Samsa felt a choking sensation. Weakening, strength seeping out of him, the lights between the trees dimming. He needed to make one great effort to get out from under Boyle. Where was Boyle finding his energy? Speed, what else, the same speed that devastated him also galvanized him.

Boyle raised the tool yet again, and suddenly Samsa realized what it was, saw the horse-head glimmer faintly.

He felt the poker smack against his forehead and felt a pain too severe to quantify. He imagined this same implement raining down from Boyle's hand and Nick Mancuso trying to crawl out of range, begging for mercy where there was none to be had, plodding on hands and knees as Boyle lashed him time and again in a rage that was beyond rage, a murderous fury. *And this is going to happen to me. I am going to die in this place, never knowing what has happened to Darcy.*

He couldn't feel his face. He knew it had to be shattered. He caught Boyle's hand, twisted it, hoped if he could bend the hand back the poker would be released and fall away, and all the time Boyle was whispering, 'A well-oiled machine, a slut, she gives head like there's no tomorrow,' and Samsa said, 'You lying bastard,' and then quit listening. Boyle's words were so much empty air, and Boyle's weight was squeezing the life out of him. He had the feeling he was being forced into the ground and sooner or later the earth would just open up and he'd be gone, and all at once he was drifting toward a realm of incongruously placid thoughts, such as a man drowning was said to experience, a sweet torpor, a dreamy descent.

Boyle said, '*Au revoir*, sport.'

No, not yet, not like *this*. Samsa concentrated with intense purpose, fighting not only Boyle, but also the strange soporific sense that possessed him, and he forced the heel of his hand under Boyle's chin and *thrust* with all the strength he could muster. Push, push, the situation finely balanced, his diminishing strength pitted against Boyle. He felt Boyle's head go back an inch or so, and he kept shoving, because if he didn't he knew he'd slip back down inside that enticing lethargy and that would be the end. His lungs were constricted and blood ran into his eyes, but he couldn't quit now, wouldn't quit. He had to keep forcing Boyle back.

'Dear sweet Christ,' Boyle said.

And Samsa felt Boyle yield and slump a little, and he gazed into the man's face and saw something abruptly shift and change there, saw eyelids flutter. The architecture of his face appeared to implode. The mouth was wrenched to one side, and Boyle was rolling away from him, turning over in the grass and gasping. Samsa, barely able to rise, got to his knees. A voice in his head told him, *Go for your gun*, but his movements were slow motion, and even when he had the weapon in his hand he was halfway certain he was dreaming. He crawled toward Boyle, who lay flat on his back with his arms at his sides and the poker held limply in one hand.

'This what I'd call ... acute gridlock on Cardiac Boulevard.' Boyle's voice was choked and distant, like a man speaking through a tightly bound gag.

Samsa, drenched in blood, bent over Boyle.

'Last rites?' Boyle asked.

'Go fuck yourself,' Samsa said. 'Where's Darcy?'

Lee Boyle clutched his chest. His skin was the color of wet paper. 'It's a little too late for Darcy.'

'What the fuck does too late mean?'

'She got lippy, *amigo*. I had to ...'

'You had to *what*?'

'Kind of quiet her down.'

'Quiet her down? What have you done with her, you fucker? What are you saying?' And Samsa thought, *What small strand remains of your better instincts tells you to do something. This man is dying, call an ambulance, something.* But he didn't give a damn, he was beyond all the niceties of civilized response. Way beyond. Further than ever in his life. 'You killed her? Is that what you're telling me? You killed Darcy?'

Boyle blinked, gazed at Samsa. '*Our Adonais has drunk poison.*'

'You're a piece of shit, Boyle. Unspeakable shit.' Samsa heard the sound of a tide in his brain. He imagined Darcy was crying out to him. She was being swept away on these waters, drawn out into darkness, and he couldn't reach her, and her voice was fading.

Boyle had a small sunken half-smile. '*I am borne darkly, fearfully, afar. Samsa.*'

Samsa drew himself up on his knees, looked down at Lee Boyle and raised his gun. Boyle lifted a hand, tugged Samsa's sleeve, held it. The gesture was beyond Samsa's interpretation – a plea for mercy? A request to hurry the inevitable?

Samsa felt an immense despondency that deepened when he fired the first shot into Boyle's stomach and watched the body kick. He fired the second shot into Boyle's neck, the third into his skull. And then he emptied the gun blindly into Boyle before he dropped it in the grass, rose and stumbled away into the trees, swaying from side to side as he went, thinking of going through the cedar fence, some vague notion of making a phone call, although he wasn't sure to whom. He was conscious of the moon flying free in the sky and a rash of stars shining weakly beyond. He walked between the trees, concentrating on the lights that appeared to recede the closer he came, as if everything in the world was being sucked away from him, until eventually there would be nothing. And Darcy was lost to him, the way Harriet had been lost, and any chance with Eve, too. His whole life was an accretion of losses.

He kept moving. Overhanging branches caught his face, but he didn't feel them. The world was all illusion. He wondered if this was what dying felt like, if the pressure inside his skull was more than the brain could withstand, if there was cerebral damage, and too much blood lost. He slipped, inclined his body against a tree for support, and drew air into his mouth. He was going back inside the dream again.

Dreaming of his daughter now.

He imagined he saw her sitting with her back to a tree, her face tilted to one side, her mouth bound with strips of a white ectoplasmic material, her hands tethered behind her by more of the same binding. He dreamed he went toward her, slid down onto his knees, placed his hands on either side of her face and looked into her eyes. Her upper body was naked. He heard her utter a strange little sound.

And then he was no longer sure of anything. He was adrift at that strange juncture where reality and illusion conflicted.

The same place where Lee Boyle had lived much of his life.

'Darcy,' he said.

Then it was dark, very dark. And Samsa, faintly conscious of the whirring spinning lights of police cars beyond the fence, was disintegrating.

49

PALE GREEN GHOSTS CAME AND WENT. A PERIOD OF DRIFT.
Samsa was X-rayed and brain-scanned and shot with
painkillers. He had no true sense of time and the dope
made him feel disembodied during his waking moments.
And yet something kept sneaking into his mind with a
certain urgent clarity, something he knew he was
supposed to do, *obliged* to do.

He had a room to himself, a narrow hospital bed, a
window shaded by a yellow blind. The walls were light
blue. He felt connected to his environment only in a tan-
gential way. Through his pain, which the morphine could
only dim, he had recurring images, some of them involving Lee Boyle, but there was an unreality to most of them,
as if Boyle were a person he'd invented on the worst day
of his life.

Once he dreamed of Harriet in a bathtub of rose-
colored water, and saw wet curls of her razor-chopped
hair float on the surface like dark wasted flowers. He saw
Boyle standing over the bathtub, saying, 'She's never
coming back, sport,' and dipping his hand into the

discolored water, parting Harriet's pink-tinted legs, smiling.

Samsa woke, remembering a fact he'd forgotten: Harriet had shaved her pubic hair too. Then sliced her veins.

Nightmares. Pictures shimmered.

He was thirsty. On the bedside table somebody had left a glass of water, which he managed to sip through an angled straw, but the effort drained him and the water tasted stale.

A physician came to check on him, a young man – too young, surely, to have graduated medical school – with a thick mass of dark hair and Coke-bottle glasses. He spoke of a hairline fracture in the forehead, serious lacerations to the cheek and scalp, like somebody reciting a threnody. Samsa listened to this list of his injuries, but couldn't relate them to himself. The physician talked about treatment, painkillers, bedrest. He said he believed time was the best healer, finally. Stitches in the scalp and cheek would dissolve eventually, obviously leaving scars, but they'd fade. The bone in the forehead would knit back.

'All in all, the prognosis is good, Mr Samsa. It might have been much worse. Your daughter's waiting to see you. Keep it down to a few minutes, okay?' The physician left.

Darcy came into the room. She was dressed in blue jeans and black T-shirt and sneakers. She drew a chair up to the bed and held his hand. She was uncomfortable, her movements awkward.

'You look . . .' she said.

'I look what?'

She didn't answer.

Samsa thought, *It's been a bad time, I'm not supposed to look great.* Darcy's hand was cold. He remembered the obscenities Boyle had whispered, and he wondered.

She began to cry quietly, reached for a tissue on the table and held it to her face. 'I swore this wouldn't happen,' she said.

He squeezed her hand. She crumpled the tissue and looked at the window and appeared annoyed with herself. 'I keep thinking about Nick . . .'

'We'll get beyond that. Somehow we'll get through all that.' Samsa reached for his water, spilled some slicks down his chest. His hand, he noticed, had been newly bandaged.

'Will we?' she said. She gazed at him. Her brown eyes seemed wary. He thought, *They're not the eyes of a fifteen-year-old girl any longer. The child is gone.*

'It seems to me there's a whole lot to get through,' she said. 'Maybe too much.'

Samsa floated just a moment, a little morphine shift. 'Whatever it is, whatever it takes, we'll do it.'

'How?' She bent forward, laid her head on the bed. Samsa stroked her hair and felt an awesome sadness. He had no answer to her question. He might have uttered words like fortitude or courage, or platitudes about how life goes on and you pick up the pieces. But these would have been porous noises lacking substance. His own actions had allowed Boyle to vandalize their lives, and the destruction had to be mended. He didn't know what it would take. What adhesive. How long.

Darcy raised her face. Tears crossed her cheeks and gathered at the edges of her lips. He'd never been able to bear the sight of his daughter crying, and it was even worse now. This sad girl with the pretty face broke his heart. He thought about the accumulation of neglect. The way time dwindled and every day was one day less left to you. And you never really noticed because you imagined an unlimited future, some form of immortality. Wrong.

'How?' she asked again.

'When I get out of here we'll go away somewhere,' he said. 'Let's do that.'

She reached for another tissue and blew her nose. 'I *encouraged* him, for Christ's sake. He *attracted* me.'

For a moment Samsa didn't know if she was referring to Nick or to Boyle, then he realized. 'How were you supposed to know what he was really like,' he said. He heard his voice catch at the back of his throat. There was a fade taking place inside him, the yellow blind shedding sunlight, Darcy's face going in and out.

She flicked hair from her forehead. She walked to the window and pulled back the blind. He wished he could go to her, soothe the hurt and bewilderment she carried. As a kid she'd come to him, never to Harriet – bruises, cuts, scrapes – and he'd always magicked them away.

But this was something else. This would take more than pretend.

She walked back to the bed. 'He said,' and she paused. 'He said something about this young girl. Something about you killing her.'

'And you want to know if it's true?'

'Is it?'

Samsa was aware of an intersection here. One way carried him in the direction he'd been traveling lately, back into lies. The other was different and unexplored.

'He was blackmailing me. But I didn't kill anyone.'

'Tell me about it. I want to know.'

'When I'm more alert I'll explain.'

'So he lied, that's what you're saying?'

'He had his own brand of truth,' Samsa said.

'But he lied, didn't he?'

Samsa remembered: *Your little girl's a whore. She blew me, had me doing fucking cartwheels of joy.* Boyle's delusions. 'Yes. He lied.'

She lifted his hand and held it to her lips. 'They'll throw me out of here if I don't go now.'

'Will you manage at home?'

'Haven't I always,' she said.

'If there's anything, I'm sure you can phone Eve,' he said.

'She hasn't called, you know. I can't figure it. I thought she'd be asking for health bulletins every half-hour.' Darcy stepped away from the bed and opened the door. 'Al Brodsky wants to talk to me about what happened. I'll come back tonight.'

He watched the door close and wondered about Eve, why she hadn't telephoned, why she hadn't paid a visit. She'd changed towards him. But he wanted to see her regardless. He wanted her presence, even if there was nothing left to build on between them.

He lay for a time with his eyes turned to the blind. Then, through his exhaustion and pain, he remembered what it was he needed to do. He raised himself on one elbow, picked up the phone, punched in the department's number and asked to be connected to Ed Duff.

Darcy goes down the corridor, passing orderlies, nurses. Thinking of her father's broken face. Stitches, swelling. Thinking how he must hurt. Thinking of Nick beaten to death with the poker. Thinking of her father being lifted onto a stretcher. Brodsky, who'd appeared out of nowhere, had supervised the bearers. 'Easy now. Don't rush him. Easy easy. He's precious cargo.'

Thinks of Lee. She doesn't want to.

He rips off her blouse and tears it into shreds.

He ties her hands behind her back with the strips.

This comes back to her, the way it has kept coming back since it happened. Before dawn. Twelve hours ago, more.

He's forgotten all about stealing a car. It's slipped his mind, what's left of his mind. He doesn't care any more. He's reached an extreme of himself.

He says, 'Let's see what you're made of.'

He holds it in the palm of his hand. 'Let's see if you can get me going.'

And then he pauses and listens to somebody trampling through grass.

'Not a sound out of you, understand?'

He stuffs her mouth with ragged strips of her ruined blouse.

'I'll be back,' he says.

And later, a long time later it seems, there's gunfire. And then her father is coming toward her.

Not Lee. He's never coming back again.

Except in her dreams.

Al Brodsky arrived at five minutes past seven. He pulled a chair up to the side of the bed. 'How's the patient doing, Greg?'

'I've had better days,' Samsa said. He'd been dozing fitfully, dreaming of Darcy, though he couldn't remember anything specific.

Brodsky placed a brown-paper bag on the bedside table. 'Grapes. Seedless, so you don't have to keep spitting.'

'Thanks,' Samsa said. He was hoarse.

Brodsky said, 'Nice room.'

Samsa waited for the question he knew Al had come to ask. But Brodsky appeared hesitant, as if he were unsure of Samsa's state of mind and how morphine might have affected it.

'I had a chat with Darcy,' he said. 'I get the strong feeling she's not telling me everything. The situation she was in, the stuff Boyle put her through, the boyfriend killed . . . it's only natural she'd keep some of it to herself, because she hasn't had time to put the pieces together in any coherent way. I'll talk with her some more tomorrow. But you know what I think? She's gonna need counseling down the line, Greg.'

Samsa's face was stiff and ached. 'You may be right, Al.'

Brodsky drummed his fingertips on his knees. 'According to Zane's report, you fired six shots into Boyle.'

'I don't remember how many exactly,' Samsa said.

Brodsky reached out, plucked one of the grapes and popped it in his mouth. He chewed a moment, then spat out a seed into the palm of his hand. '*Goddam*. They were marked seedless in the supermarket. I can't believe that.'

He looked back at Samsa. 'The thing is, some hotshot investigator in Internal Affairs is going to ask why you had to shoot him six times. It's the kind of thing I'd understand myself. The guy's trying to kill you, you defend yourself. And you're not thinking right, you don't know what he's done with your daughter, you're desperate, out of control.'

Samsa said, 'Is this important, Al?'

'Not to me, but some of those guys don't like cops firing guns needlessly. They're gonna ask you if it was necessary to use that much ammunition. *I* know it's bullshit. *You* know it's bullshit. But it's the kind of bone they love to chew on. The worst expression in their whole vocabulary is *excessive*, applied to a cop who's used a gun.'

Samsa was light-headed, drifting again, when what he really needed was focus and clarity for a few more minutes.

Brodsky said, 'All I'm saying is, expect to be questioned. Be prepared.'

'You're beating around the bush, Al. You didn't come here to talk about how many times I fired my gun.'

Brodsky paused. 'No, you're right.'

Samsa shifted his head on the pillows. His forehead throbbed, but he didn't want to ring the nurse for a painkiller just yet.

Brodsky said, 'You phoned Ed Duff earlier. You ordered Pritt's release.'

'Yeah, I did.'

'So naturally I'm very curious. We have a guy panting to confess, and you want him sent home? We haven't even had the psychiatric report yet.'

Samsa experienced a moment of tension, and then he thought, *There's only one way to go. There are no options. There had never been any, not really.* 'Pritt didn't kill the girl, Al.'

'How can you be so sure of that?' Brodsky asked.

Samsa told him.

He told him without halting. He heard his own voice echo in his head. It was easy, so damn easy, he'd expected it to be wrenching and difficult. He felt the lifting of an iron burden. An amazing calm settled inside him. Brodsky looked down at the floor as he listened. Halfway through Samsa's narrative, the chief got up and walked round the room in an agitated way, then returned to the bed.

Samsa finished. He was conscious of his systems beginning to shut down.

Al Brodsky stared at him. 'Why the fuck didn't you come to me in the beginning,' he said.

'What would you have done if I had?'

Brodsky said, 'That's not the question any more, Greg. The question is, what am I going to do now?'

'There's nothing you can do,' Samsa said.

Brodsky looked pensive. 'Let me run something past you. We free Pritt, okay. We make some cursory inquiries into the girl's death, under my direction. They don't lead anywhere, of course, then it begins to fade away, the

806

newspapers and the TV lose interest because it's stale, it's yesterday's news, then we quietly shut the book and Cecily Suarez goes into the unsolved bin. Who's ever going to ask, Greg? Who's ever going to start poking round?'

'We bury it,' Samsa said.

'Exactly that.' Brodsky sat on the edge of the bed. 'Look, you've got a lot of time under your belt in the department. Why waste it all on account of one mishap?'

Mishap, Samsa thought. A mishap was when you stubbed your toe in the shower. Slipped on a wax floor. 'You'd do that for me.'

'You're a good cop, Greg. A good friend.'

'You understand what you're suggesting?'

'Fully.'

Samsa leaned back and shut his eyes. Back behind his desk in two or three weeks, however long it took him to mend. Working cases. Living among the city's dead. The brutality. The savagery.

'We never talk about this again,' Brodsky said. 'Subject closed. This conversation never happened.'

It was tempting. Samsa opened his eyes. 'I don't think so,' he said.

'Say again?'

'It's over, Al. I've got a bad taste in my mouth, and I don't think it's associated with the drugs they've been shooting into me. It's all over.'

'Look, maybe you're too doped out to get this, Greg. I'm offering you an escape route. I'm going out on a fucking limb for you —'

'And I've said I'm grateful. But this is the end of the line.'

Al Brodsky got up from the bed and frowned. 'You're talking like a crazy man.'

'I don't think so,' Samsa said.

'Tell you what. You sleep on it. See how you feel in the morning. A new day, a clear head. Things'll look different.' He patted his pockets as if he were checking on something, then stepped toward the door. 'I'll see you tomorrow, Greg.'

Samsa didn't answer. Alone, he rang the bell for the nurse. He thought of twenty-one years dissolving all around him. A dead past. He still had Darcy to deal with, his story to tell all over again. He wondered how she'd react.

He was asleep before the nurse arrived.

And he didn't wake when Darcy came and sat alongside him for fifteen minutes and gazed at his face. Before she left she placed three oranges and a Snickers bar on the table.

Samsa woke in bright daylight. He was aware of somebody standing in silhouette at the window.

'I brought you flowers.'

He raised his face from his pillows. From the corner of his eye he noticed carnations in a vase on the table. And oranges and a candy bar from somewhere.

'Don't look at me unless you want to be frightened,' he said.

'I already looked. You don't scare me.'

She turned and approached the bed.

He said, 'I didn't think you'd come.'

'Darcy phoned me. Did she tell you? She needs somebody to talk to.'

'She can talk to me,' Samsa said.

'I guess it's another woman she wants right now, Greg. She's hurting.'

'I know she is.'

'I mean *hurting*. And she's lonely.'

'With any luck I'll be out of here in a few days—'

'She doesn't want to be on her own, Greg. So I took the liberty of asking her to stay at my place. At least until you're home again. She's lost and confused at the moment, and if I can help her I will.'

Samsa wanted to hold her hand. He wanted her to come close enough so he could reach out and touch her. He smelled her scent. He was reminded of her bedroom, the robe sliding from her body, that sweet giddy time.

'You don't mind having her as a room-mate?' he asked.

'I get lonely sometimes too.'

'What about...' The leaden density of unfinished questions. He wasn't sure he wanted an answer.

She said, 'You and me? Is that what you want to know? I haven't thought about it.'

'Will you?'

'Where do you pick up the threads? Where do you start again? I don't know.'

'You go back to the beginning,' he said.

'What did we have anyway? One night, Greg. That's all.'

'Does it have to stop at one night?'

She sat on the chair by the bed and looked at him. 'You're not a pretty sight, are you?'

'Was I ever?' He gazed at her. 'Has Pritt been released?'

'I hear Brodsky wants to hold him.'

'I ordered his release,' Samsa said.

'Did you? When?'

'Last night. I think it was last night. I'm not keeping up with time all that well.'

She sat very still. 'Did you say why you wanted him freed?'

'I explained it all to Brodsky.'

'All?'

Samsa nodded.

'How did he react?' she asked.

Samsa was remembering Al Brodsky's visit. The past can be disregarded. The job is still yours. This conversation never took place. There was another level of reality, Samsa thought, where Brodsky operated, a place where deals were struck and never recorded, and exchanges that took place never actually happened. A world of convenience. Lies of omission.

I've been in that world, he thought. *Where the currency is concealment.*

I know exactly what I'm going to do.

He reached for the telephone and pressed the numbers that would connect him directly to Al Brodsky. He was aware of Eve watching him. The sun caught and fired her red hair. She looked wary, defensive, as if she didn't want to give any of her trust until she was certain. And perhaps not even then.

Brodsky came on the line. 'Greg,' he said.

'I've slept on it, Al.'

'And?'

'That conversation we never had,' Samsa said.

'What conversation?' Brodsky laughed.

'Send Pritt home, Al.'

'Let me ask you one question, Greg.'

'Go ahead.'

'You know the consequences for you?'

'Just send him home.'

'You're on your own now,' Brodsky said. 'You know that, don't you?'

'Yeah. I know that.'

Brodsky said, 'Questions will be asked about Cecily Suarez, and I'm obliged to answer them. Because if you don't want the deal I offered, consider it withdrawn as of now. It saves me the hassle of playing around with the truth. And if they crucify you in public, don't expect to hear a squeak out of me on your behalf. If your name's